THE CR

and Ot.

The Crystal Egg

and Other Stories

———— ◆ ————

H. G. WELLS

with an Introduction and Endnotes by

CEDRIC WATTS

WORDSWORTH CLASSICS

For my husband
ANTHONY JOHN RANSON
with love from your wife, the publisher.
Eternally grateful for your unconditional love.

Readers who are interested in other titles from
Wordsworth Editions are invited to visit our website at
www.wordsworth-editions.com

First published in 2017 by Wordsworth Editions Limited
8B East Street, Ware, Hertfordshire SG12 9HJ

ISBN 978 1 84022 739 0

Text © Wordsworth Editions Limited, 2017
Introduction and Endnotes © Cedric Watts, 2017

Wordsworth® is a registered trademark of
Wordsworth Editions Limited

Wordsworth Editions
is the company founded in 1987 by
MICHAEL TRAYLER

All rights reserved. This publication may not be
reproduced, stored in a retrieval system or
transmitted, in any form or by any means, electronic,
mechanical, photocopying, recording or otherwise,
without the prior permission of the publishers.

Typeset in Great Britain by Antony Gray
Printed and bound by Clays Ltd, St Ives plc

CONTENTS

GENERAL INTRODUCTION   vii

BIOGRAPHY OF THE AUTHOR   vii

INTRODUCTION   x

FURTHER READING   xxix

The Crystal Egg   1

The Cone   17

The Country of the Blind   27

The Man Who Could Work Miracles   49

A Story of the Stone Age   65

The Star   113

The Red Room   123

In the Abyss   131

The Plattner Story   145

The New Accelerator   163

A Slip under the Microscope   175

The Stolen Bacillus   191

The Remarkable Case of Davidson's Eyes   197

The Lord of the Dynamos   207

The Grisly Folk   215

The Door in the Wall   227

The Diamond Maker   243

Under the Knife   251

The Sea-Raiders   263

The Purple Pileus   273

The Truth about Pyecraft   283

Jimmy Goggles the God   293

The Flowering of the Strange Orchid   305

The Argonauts of the Air   313

Miss Winchelsea's Heart   325

A Vision of Judgement   341

The Land Ironclads   347

The Flying Man   367

In the Avu Observatory   373

The Triumphs of a Taxidermist   379

A Deal in Ostriches   383

Through a Window   387

The Temptation of Harringay   395

The Beautiful Suit   401

ENDNOTES   405

GENERAL INTRODUCTION

Wordsworth Classics are inexpensive editions designed to appeal to the general reader and students. We commissioned teachers and specialists to write wide ranging, jargon-free Introductions and to provide Notes that would assist the understanding of our readers rather than interpret the stories for them. In the same spirit, because the pleasures of reading are inseparable from the surprises, secrets and revelations that all narratives contain, we strongly advise you to enjoy these tales before turning to the Introduction.

KEITH CARABINE
General Adviser
Rutherford College,
University of Kent at Canterbury

BIOGRAPHY OF THE AUTHOR

Herbert George Wells, known as 'Bertie' or 'H. G.', was born on 21 September 1866 in Atlas House, on the High Street of what was then the Kentish market town of Bromley. His father Joseph, a former gardener, kept a shop and played professional cricket; after his father broke his leg when Wells was ten, Wells's mother Sarah returned to domestic service at the country house Uppark, near Midhurst, in Sussex.

Wells's elder brothers had both been apprenticed to drapers, a trade that Sarah Wells considered to be highly respectable. Wells was apprenticed to drapers in Windsor and Southsea but was much keener to continue to be educated, and he persuaded his mother to let him become a pupil-teacher at Midhurst Grammar School. Wells's exam results at Midhurst were so strong that he won a scholarship aimed at increasing the number of science teachers in Britain at the Normal School (now Imperial College London), under 'Darwin's bulldog', the biologist T. H. Huxley. Wells drew extensively on his experiences as a student for his 1900 novel *Love and Mr Lewisham*. Ill-fed, poor and increasingly discontented by both the quality of the teaching he received and the social organisation of the world, Wells became more and more interested in politics and in imaginative literature, especially Plato, Blake and Carlyle. He also began writing, providing articles and a time-travel story, 'The Chronic Argonauts', for the college magazine the *Science Schools Journal*.

Wells failed his final exams and found work as a teacher in Wales. After being fouled in a rugby game, he suffered severe kidney damage, and for much of the 1890s Wells feared he would die prematurely. Returning to London and completing his degree, he worked as a correspondence tutor and in 1893 wrote his first books *Honours Physiography* and *A Textbook of Biology*. His writing branched out into literary journalism and popular scientific writing, and in 1895 alone Wells published four further books: *Select Conversations with an Uncle*, *The Wonderful Visit*, *The Stolen Bacillus and Other Incidents* and his masterpiece, *The Time Machine*. This first 'scientific romance' was swiftly followed by *The Island of Doctor Moreau* (1896), *The Invisible Man* (1897) and *The War of the Worlds* (1898). None has ever been out of print since; Wells was swiftly hailed as a man of genius by his contemporaries. Both sociable and irascible, Wells became friends, and fell out, with other writers such as George Gissing, Joseph Conrad, Stephen Crane, George Bernard Shaw, Arnold Bennett, Ford Madox Ford, and Henry James, whom Wells would later cruelly lampoon in his 1915 novel *Boon*, the climax of a long disagreement between the two writers about the purpose and nature of the novel.

Wells never wanted to be limited to writing scientific romances, and during this period he also wrote realistic prose fiction set in a recognisable real world, whose disorganisation and unfairness these novels sought to diagnose: *The Wheels of Chance* (1896), *Kipps* (1905), *Tono-Bungay*, *Ann Veronica* (both 1909) and *The History of Mr Polly* (1910). Wells's early-twentieth-century science fiction, such as *The Food of the Gods* (1905) and *In the Days of the Comet* (1906), increasingly showed a vision of the world as Wells would want to order it. His political and utopian writing from *Anticipations of the Reactions of Mechanical and Scientific Progress upon Human Life and Thought* (1901) and *A Modern Utopia* (1905) also demonstrated Wells's commitment to creating a utopian government, a World State that would ensure that mankind would never go to war.

Following the First World War, Wells's passion for this project intensified, and he embarked on an ambitious collaborative project to write the first history of the world, hoping that if future generations were better educated, then rivalries between nations would be unnecessary, and world government would follow. *The Outline of History* (1919) was Wells's best-selling book in his own lifetime, selling millions of copies internationally, and was followed by the school version *A Short History of the World* (1922) and by equivalents for science, *The Science of Life* (1930), and social science, *The Work, Wealth and Happiness of Mankind* (1931). At its height, Wells's fame was as much as a thinker and public intellectual as a novelist. He met or corresponded with the greatest figures of the first half of the twentieth century: Winston Churchill, Lenin and Stalin, Theodore and Franklin Roosevelt, Albert Einstein and Sigmund Freud. His later novels from *The New Machiavelli* (1911) onward tend to be more overtly engaged with Wells's 'Open Conspiracy' to convert his readership to his own political point of view, often at a cost to these books' literary merit and subsequent afterlife.

Wells had married his cousin Isabel in 1891, but the couple proved incompatible and he left her for his pupil Amy Catherine Robbins whom he rechristened 'Jane'. In spite of Wells's many infidelities, which Jane seemed prepared to tolerate, the couple were happily married until Jane's death from cancer in 1928; and they had two sons, Gip and Frank. An affair with the writer Amber Reeves produced a daughter, Anna Jane, and Wells's long affair with novelist Rebecca West saw the birth of a further son, Anthony West. Wells also enjoyed liaisons with, amongst others, Dorothy Richardson, Elizabeth von Arnim, Margaret Sanger and, following Jane's death, Odette Keun and Moura Budberg.

Wells's writing was prophetic in both senses of the term: as exhorting humankind to mend its ways, and in foreseeing the future. His writing imagined before they existed the aeroplane, the tank, space travel, the atomic bomb and the internet. In later life, the emphasis of his political writing turned more towards the rights of the individual, and his 1940 book *The Rights of Man: Or, What Are We Fighting For?* is a key text in the history of human rights.

Wells often despaired thof at his warnings ever being sufficiently heeded, declaring that his epitaph should be: 'God *damn* you, you fools – I told you so.' None the less, the influence of his hundred and fifty books and pamphlets of science fiction, novels, politics, utopia, history, biography and autobiography has been enormous throughout the twentieth century and beyond.

SIMON J. JAMES
Professor of English Literature at Durham University
and author of *Maps of Utopia: H. G. Wells,
Modernity and the End of Culture*

INTRODUCTION

If you *don't* know Wells's short stories, you're in for a treat. If you think you *do* know them, you may have some surprises.

This volume contains a generous selection of the tales of H. G. Wells, who was astonishingly productive. They demonstrate his immense imaginative energy, and some of his most original thinking is to be found in them. They illustrate his range, for he knew a great deal about many subjects, as one would expect of the eventual author of *An Outline of History* and *A Short History of the World.* The very number of the endnotes to this volume testifies to his encyclopaedic mind,[1] and the diverse modes adopted in the tales display his fecund creativity. Some of the stories are slight; some are very substantial. Repeatedly, it is the imaginative plenitude that is so impressive.

In this Introduction, I first show the congenial circumstances which facilitated Wells's output of short fiction. Secondly, I discuss some of his antecedents, for Wells learnt by imitating or surpassing earlier writers. Thirdly, I show his anticipations of future events. Fourthly, I suggest ways in which he influenced subsequent writers. And, finally, I offer a summing-up.

1

Most of the tales in this volume were written in the period 1890 to 1910, a golden age for British short-story writers.

In Great Britain, the electorate of a soaring population had been increased by the Reform Bills of 1832 and, particularly, of 1867, and governments came to see the merits of 'civilising' the electorate by means of educational reform. The Education Act of 1870, for example, established locally elected school boards which could compel the attendance of children aged from five to thirteen (inclusive, fees being waived for poor parents) and which were empowered to build new schools maintained in part by local rates, while existing Church schools received increased grants. During the subsequent twenty years, a huge school-building programme proceeded. Publishing houses multiplied to supply the needs of an increasing readership; a diversity of magazines flourished. Technological advances reduced the production-cost of

1 'The fuller the terminology the finer the mind,' says Dr Raven in Wells's *The Shape of Things to Come*, Hutchinson, London, 1936, p. 323.

magazines, and advertising on the printed page burgeoned. Periodicals which gave hospitality to short pieces of fiction multiplied.

H. G. Wells said that his own prolific period as a writer of tales began when C. L. Hind, editor of the *Pall Mall Budget*, urged him to contribute some to that journal:

> I found that, taking almost anything as a starting-point and letting my thoughts play about it, there would presently come out of the darkness, in a manner quite inexplicable, some absurd or vivid little incident more or less relevant to that initial nucleus. Little men in canoes upon sunlit oceans would come floating out of nothingness, incubating the eggs of prehistoric monsters unawares; violent conflicts would break out amidst the flower-beds of suburban gardens; I would discover I was peering into remote and mysterious worlds ruled by an order logical indeed but other than our common sanity.[2]

Wells himself emphasises that the 1890s were a particularly propitious period for short-story writers. 'Short stories broke out everywhere'; and magazines taking them, he said, included the *Fortnightly Review*, *Longman's Magazine*, the *Yellow Book*, the *National Observer* and the *New Review*. To his selection we may add (of course) the *Pall Mall Budget*, then the *Queen*, *Black and White*, the *Strand*, the *Graphic*, the *Illustrated London News*, the *Idler*, the *Butterfly*, the *Unicorn*, *Phil May's Annual*, the *Weekly Sun Literary Supplement*, the *New Budget* and the *St James's Gazette*: all these published tales by Wells. Noted contributors cited by Wells included Rudyard Kipling, J. M. Barrie, Frank Harris, R. L. Stevenson, Max Beerbohm, Henry James, George Gissing, Stephen Crane, Joseph Conrad, Jerome K. Jerome, George Moore, Grant Allen, George Egerton, W. W. Jacobs, E. Nesbit and Kenneth Graham; some formidable rivals appear in that list.

Such writers found that it was possible to be paid four or five times for the same piece of work. A tale might appear in a British magazine and in an American magazine; syndication might distribute it more widely; it could then be collected into a book of items, which might sell in Britain, in the USA and on the Continent (for example, in the volumes published by Baron Tauchnitz). International copyright agreements had taken place: in particular, the Chace Act of 1891 ensured that British authors would receive royalties when their works were published in the USA. In 1897, some magazines were paying fees of £40

---

2 H. G. Wells, Introduction to *'The Country of the Blind' and Other Stories*, Nelson, London, no date given, p. iv.

to £50 for a tale, at a time when the average earnings of an adult male in England approximated £56 per year. In 1901, Wells told Arnold Bennett that the *Strand* paid him £125 for a story. Literary agents (notably A. P. Watt, W. M. Colles and J. B. Pinker) appeared, to help publicise and market the writers' products. Indeed, Pinker's generosity and foresight kept Joseph Conrad solvent for many years, until the time when Conrad at last became profitable. Henry James was delighted by Pinker's help. As agent for Wells, Pinker was energetic in supplying publicity to the leading weekly journals, and was astute, as when, for example, he persuaded Wells to undertake a tour of the USA to publicise his new writings.

Not only were the eighteen-nineties good for such writers from a commercial point of view; there was also a warmly receptive audience for those tales. Many periodicals reviewed literary works, and those reviews were often far more lengthy and detailed than would be possible fifty years later. Wells claimed: 'People talked about them [the tales] tremendously, compared them, and ranked them. That was the thing that mattered.'[3] Furthermore, literary cross-fertilisation was another marked feature of the period. For example, in his depiction of talking animals in 'A Story of the Stone Age' (1897), Wells has clearly been influenced by the tales of Kipling, notably those gathered in *The Jungle Book* (1894) and *The Second Jungle Book* (1895); and both collections featured stories which had previously appeared in magazines.

Though Wells found the sheer quantity of critical discussion encouraging, some of that critical talk was unintelligent: as when certain commentators claimed that the short story was a form as definable as the sonnet, or tried to distinguish between the true short story and the mere anecdote. Wells, however, declares:

> The short story is a fiction that may be read in something under an hour, and so that it is moving and delightful, it does not matter whether it is as 'trivial' as a Japanese print of insects seen closely between grass stems, or as spacious as the prospect of the plain of Italy from Monte Mottarone. It does not matter whether it is human or inhuman, or whether it leaves you thinking deeply or radiantly but superficially pleased . . . It may be horrible or pathetic or funny or beautiful or profoundly illuminating . . . [4]

---

3 Introduction to *'The Country of the Blind' and Other Stories, op. cit.*, p. vi.
4 Introduction to *'The Country of the Blind' and Other Stories, op. cit.*, p. viii.

The only essential is 'that it should take from fifteen to fifty minutes to read aloud'.

Even that criterion, which seems loose enough, is not sufficiently loose to accommodate some of his own shorter works. For example, as we shall see, 'A Story of the Stone Age' is long enough to be termed 'a novella' (a short novel) rather than 'a tale'; but, as 'a tale' is what Wells termed it, this collection receives it gladly.

2

Wells learnt by imitating and surpassing other writers. I've suggested a debt to Kipling in the matter of the talking animals. Kipling was also a master of the grimly macabre, and we may recall Kipling's 'The Strange Ride of Morrowbie Jukes', in which a man finds himself hideously trapped, as we read Wells's 'The Country of the Blind'.

Another instance: Edgar Allan Poe's 'Fall of the House of Usher', a classic Gothic tale of the maçabre and the supernatural, is clearly echoed in Wells's 'The Red Room'. This story is Wells's contribution to a familiar sub-genre of Gothic fiction, the tale of the haunted (or supposedly haunted) room. We learn that in the past, in this red room of the ancient castle, a cruel old earl decided to terrify his young wife, a countess, with the result that she died. Perhaps the earl's act of cruelty explains why the house is termed 'this house of sin'. The narrator's apparent innovation is to suggest that the room in question is haunted not by any ghost but by the sheer spirit of *fear itself*, a 'Power of Darkness' which terminates any source of light. We may then recall that Poe's Roderick Usher had thought that he would lose 'life and reason' in some struggle 'with the grim phantom, FEAR'.[5]

An unexpected antecedent for Wells is Hans Christian Andersen, but Andersen's tales of folk-lore and sentimental fantasy are evidently part of the hinterland of 'The Beautiful Suit', a strange short piece. It is a lyrical allegory: the act of rebellion by the 'little man' is, for him, liberating, transformative and ecstatic, though, from an external viewpoint, he is deranged and self-destructive. What is streaming silver to him is duckweed to an outsider. The agent of his death is a moth that brushes his lips. As Wells knew, the Greek word *psyche* means 'moth', 'butterfly' and 'soul'. The moth and butterfly both have legendary associations with death and with the departure of the soul from the

5 Edgar Allan Poe, 'The Fall of the House of Usher', in *The Complete Tales and Poems of Edgar Allan Poe*, Penguin, London, 1982, p. 235.

body. John Keats's 'Ode to Melancholy' says, 'Nor let the beetle, nor the death-moth be / Your mournful Psyche', meaning: 'Don't let the death-watch beetle or the death's-head moth be symbols of your soul, thus rendered mournful.' Thomas Hardy's *The Return of the Native* associates the moth with fatal love. In Holman Hunt's painting 'The Hireling Shepherd', the shepherd ominously holds a death's-head moth as he woos his young woman: a reminder that death haunts even Arcadia: '*et in Arcadia ego*'.[6] In Wells's tale 'The Moth' (not included in this collection), the ghost of Professor Pawkins apparently takes the form of a new genus of moth to torment his rival, Hapley the entomologist. And in 'The Beautiful Suit' the 'great dim moth' is the agent of a death which is both ecstatic and base. The once-joyous rebel is found with a broken neck, his beautiful clothes now bloody, foul and stained. It recalls the ambiguity of the death at the end of 'The Door in the Wall'. There, Lionel Wallace may have accidentally fallen into the deep excavation near the underground station; or he may at last have escaped into a more beautiful world: the 'enchanted garden' which is vividly evoked in surrealistic imagery of statues, marble-edged flower-borders, gentle spotted panthers and a welcoming girl.

Of course, several of the items here display Wells's mastery of science fiction. Indeed, as we read 'The Crystal Egg', 'The Star', 'The Plattner Story' and 'In the Abyss', we soon understand why Brian Aldiss termed Wells 'the Prospero of all the brave new worlds of the mind, and the Shakespeare of science fiction'.[7] Like Shakespeare, Wells learnt from others, established his own distinctive range, and was repeatedly imitated. If Jules Verne comes to mind as an obvious antecedent, Wells vehemently – indeed, too vehemently – opposed the notion. He claimed that Verne 'dealt always with actual possibilities of invention and discovery', whereas Wells offers 'fantasies; . . . they aim indeed only at the same amount of conviction as one gets in a good gripping dream'.[8]

6 '*Et in Arcadia ego*' is one of the titles of a painting (1637–8) by Nicolas Poussin. It depicts shepherds contemplating a tomb bearing that inscription, meaning 'Even in Arcadia am I', the 'I' being Death, Arcadia being the idyllic region of pastoral song and poetry. (An alternative translation makes the 'I' a fellow-shepherd.)

7 Brian Aldiss, *Billion Year Spree*, Weidenfeld & Nicolson, London, 1973, p. 132.

8 Wells, quoted in *H. G. Wells's Literary Criticism*, ed. Patrick Parrinder and Robert M. Philmus, Harvester Press, Brighton / Barnes & Noble, Totowa, NJ, 1980, pp. 241, 242.

But sometimes Verne, too, could achieve the dreamlike or nightmarish. The nightmarish is exemplified when Axel, in *Voyage au centre de la terre* (*Journey to the Centre of the Earth*, 1864) finds himself utterly lost in the labyrinthine passages deep below the earth's surface. The dreamlike is exemplified when, in the same novel, the explorers are restored to the earth's surface by means of a volcanic eruption which leaves them unharmed. But certainly Wells had a quicker, more versatile and cornucopian imagination.

Wells claims as his precursors *The Golden Ass* of Apuleius, the *True Histories* of Lucian, Jonathan Swift's *Gulliver's Travels*, Adalbert von Chamisso's *Peter Schlemihl's Miraculous Story* and Mary Shelley's *Frankenstein*.[9] Like Swift, Wells used fantasy to comment critically on matters of politics and religion. The novel *The Island of Doctor Moreau* assails Christianity (and vivisection); *The Time Machine* projects into the future Victorian class-divisions, so that the descendants of the working class treat the descendants of the upper class and the bourgeoisie as a food-supply; and the second law of thermodynamics, the law of entropy, mocks all human endeavours. In the tales in our collection, 'The Star' postulates a global disaster caused by a planet which passes too close to the earth: the narrator stresses human vulnerability and the fragility of our ecosystem. At least, we are told, after the devastation there grew 'a new brotherhood' among men; and 'Martian astronomers' think the earth was fortunate to sustain relatively little damage. The narrator comments: 'Which only shows how small the vastest of human catastrophes may seem, at a distance of a few million miles.' This device of the sudden perspectival shift (which in varying degrees also terminates 'A Story of the Stone Age', 'Under the Knife' and 'The Land Ironclads') was magnified by William Golding, a student of Wells's writings, in the endings of *Lord of the Flies* and *Pincher Martin*. But Wells had learnt from Swift.

Prompted by the development of the telescope and the microscope, and by Rochester's mockery of 'that vain *Animal*, who is so proud of being rational', Jonathan Swift, in *Gulliver's Travels*, depicted human beings variously as tiny, as gigantic, and as monkey-like, thereby inviting us to assess their true stature and merit. Wells employs some of Swift's shifts in perspective, chronological and spatial, to subvert any sense of the security and durability of civilisation. Sometimes, in his tales, he postulates humans who are being watched by observers on a distant planet or in another dimension, as in 'The Star', 'The Crystal

9 *Ibid.*, p. 240.

Egg' and 'The Plattner Story'. Elsewhere, he tells how the incursion of humans into a remote realm is treated there as a religious event (so that thereby he satirises religion as the misreading of the natural), as in 'In the Abyss' and 'Jimmy Goggles the God'. 'Under the Knife' offers a vision of a 'huge, shadowy Hand, upon which the whole Universe of Matter lay like an unconsidered speck of dust'. In 'A Vision of Judgement', the wicked man and the saint alike are shamed by the 'pitiless and cynical exposition' of the Recording Angel. This item, however, is not science fantasy but a fantastic vision, a theological fable postulating the humiliating notion that if there is an omnipotent God, he is not constrained by any moral notions that we may presume to attribute to him. There, God's final message to humanity is 'Try again': which was indeed the gist of Wells's message in the numerous didactic works in which he admonished mankind.

Wells said that the writer of science fiction should help the reader 'to *domesticate* the impossible hypothesis':

> As soon as the magic trick has been done[,] the whole business of the fantasy writer is to keep everything real and human. Touches of prosaic detail are imperative . . . [10]

In 'The Flowering of the Strange Orchid', the notion of a man-eating orchid is made passably plausible by the fact that the victim, Winter-Wedderburn, is 'a shy, lonely, rather ineffectual man', who complains, 'Nothing ever does happen to me.' After his narrow escape, he is at last granted the 'glory' of having achieved an adventure. In the case of 'The Man Who Could Work Miracles', the preposterous premise is vindicated by the comedy resulting from the character and environment of the bewildered miracle-worker, in this tale which dares to assure the reader that she or he was indeed killed but, having been restored to life while losing recollection, is unaware of the fact. Science fiction? Some scientific lore about the earth's speed of travel is employed, but, predominantly, the tale is a fantasy incorporating some farcical social satire. Elsewhere, Wells offers black-comic fantasy with a scientific pretext. 'Jimmy Goggles the God' comes into this category; so does 'The Stolen Bacillus'.

Some of these tales are relatively realistic and sociological. 'A Slip under the Microscope' is one example, recalling Wells's time as a penurious student at the Normal School of Science in Kensington. It

10   *H. G. Wells's Literary Criticism*, op. cit., p. 241.

was dramatised for radio by George Orwell.[11] Another example is 'Miss Winchelsea's Heart', about which more will be said later. In both tales, sad irony invests the central character's endeavours.

3

Wells the prophet is amply represented in this volume. We know that Wells foresaw atomic warfare (and the land thereafter polluted by radio-activity), rows of wind-vanes amid the English countryside, motorways, and a London of skyscrapers; he predicted aerial combat, the destruction of cities by bombing, and a United Nations Organisation.[12] In this volume, there are depictions of a flight by aeroplane, an escape by parachute, an attack by tanks, and a descent into the ocean's depths in a bathysphere: all pre-dating the practical historic use of these devices. He shrewdly envisages sea-creatures that seek and attack humans. He even anticipates the psychedelic era.

The tale 'The Purple Pileus', first published in 1896, presages that psychedelic culture of the 1960s. A 'pileus' is the cap of a mushroom-type fungus, and the tale, a satiric account of lower-middle-class life, tells how the marriage and career of Mr Coombes were transformed for the better by his consumption of 'magic mushrooms' which he had expected to be lethally poisonous. The theme is a familiar one in Wells's imagination: the successful revolt of a little man against hostile circum-stances. Wells himself, once a draper's assistant, had triumphantly

11   Orwell's dramatised version of 'A Slip under the Microscope', retaining
     Wells's title, was broadcast on the BBC's Eastern Service on 6 October
     1943. The full script is given in *The Complete Works of George Orwell*,
     Volume 15, Secker & Warburg, London, 1998, pp. 256–65.
12   In *The World Set Free* (1914), Wells foresaw atomic warfare which destroys
     cities and leaves the land polluted by radio-activity. *When the Sleeper Wakes*
     culminates in a battle by aircraft over London. In 'A Story of the Days
     to Come', English hills are dominated by rows of wind-vanes generating
     electrical current; motorways have fast lanes for vehicles travelling at 200
     miles per hour; and London is a city of tower-blocks. Repeatedly, Wells
     envisaged what might be termed a United Nations Organisation with
     power to rule the nations of the earth: he particularly liked the idea of a
     'Samurai' class of enlightened people, who, like the Guardians in Plato's
     Republic, would be the benign rulers of the new world. (In *A Modern Utopia*,
     one of the legislators is W. E. Henley, editor of the *New Review* and poet
     of 'Invictus'.)

revolted against his situation.[13] It's a theme of *The History of Mr Polly*. In the tale, the quiet man embarks on a farcically transformative rampage. The generally positive tenor of the narrative is marred by an element of misogyny, but Wells deftly evokes the atmosphere and circumstances of the shabby household and its incursionary guests.

Wells's anticipations are prominent in 'The Flying Man' and 'The Argonauts of the Air'. In the former tale, dated 1899, a lieutenant escapes from ambush by improvising a parachute. The story thus anticipates by more than twenty years the first military use of the parachute in actuality: that was in World War I, when artillery observers, coming under fire, sometimes had to jump from tethered observation balloons. Again, 'The Argonauts of the Air', though first published in 1895, looks astutely ahead. This tale was prompted by the aeronautical experiments of Hiram S. Maxim in Baldwyn Park at Bexley: he used a tethered flying machine. In the tale, the experiment ends in disaster, but the narrator remarks that 'the easy dreaming of a literary man' encompasses 'the flying-machine that will start off some fine day, . . . all loaded up with bombshells and guns'. And this was eight years before the Wright brothers' first successful flights, and sixteen years before aircraft were used in warfare, by Italians against the Turks in Tripoli in 1911. The climax of Wells's novel *When the Sleeper Wakes* (1899, subsequently entitled *The Sleeper Awakes*) is a battle between monoplanes over London; and *The World Set Free* (1914) describes cities destroyed by bombing.

Another remarkable anticipation is provided by 'The Land Ironclads' (1903). In this tale, a war in which entrenched defences are widespread is transformed by the arrival of tanks (the 'land ironclads' of the title). These have the capacity to cross the trenches and direct machine-gun fire at the defenders. (Admittedly, Wells envisages wheels fitted with flexible 'feet', rather than the caterpillar tracks eventually adopted.) Tanks were first used in warfare in World War I, when British tanks were deployed on 15 September 1916 at the Battle of the Somme. Although some of the tanks broke down, others progressed successfully, crossing trenches and crushing barbed wire. If more people had learnt the lesson of Wells's tale, tanks might have been deployed sooner and

13 In 'My Auto-Obituary', Wells says: 'The most interesting thing about Wells was his refusal to accept the social inferiority to which he seemed to have been born.' See *H. G. Wells: Interviews and Recollections*, ed. J. R. Hammond, Macmillan, London and Basingstoke, 1980, p. 117.

on a larger scale by the British and French, and that Great War of 1914–19[14] might have come to a speedier conclusion.

'In the Abyss' (1896) is also shrewdly predictive. In the tale, Elstead has invented a submersible machine. It is spherical, about nine feet in diameter, and built of steel and lead, with windows of extremely thick glass, so as to withstand the immense pressures it will encounter. In the late 1920s, a *cylindrical* submersible device was planned by the American inventor William Beebe, but fortunately Otis Barton, an engineer, persuaded him that only a spherical design would be strong enough. Eventually, from 1930 onwards, their spherical bathysphere, 4.75 feet in diameter, made of one-inch-thick cast steel and with windows of fused quartz, accomplished repeated descents, permitting (as Wells had predicted) the observation of numerous hitherto unknown species of sea-creature. Of course, those real explorers of the depths did not encounter the humanoid creatures who, in the story, worship the beings who descend from on high: but Wells is taking the opportunity to make again the anti-theological point that humanoid creatures mistake an unusual incursion for divine intervention. When writing 'In the Abyss', Wells may have been prompted by reports from HMS *Challenger*, a vessel which between 1872 and 1888 carried out surveys of the oceans' depths, collecting samples by dredges; but, in a flight of the intelligent imagination, he has envisaged a deep-sea sphere remarkably similar to the one which was employed more than thirty-five years later.

'The Sea-Raiders' tells how, on the English south coast, human beings were assailed by specimens of *Haploteuthis ferox*: a ferocious member of that cephalopod family which includes the octopus, squid and cuttlefish. Wells lends authenticity to his tale by citing an actual report of the discovery of relics of a big cephalopod. The report, by the Prince of Monaco, entitled 'Notes sur un cachalot', was published in the *Bulletin du Muséum d'histoire naturelle*, 1895, number 8, pp. 305–10; and an early part of Wells's narrative makes detailed use of that article. Of course, a battle with some kind of sea-monster was, in literature, familiar material: Beowulf had battled with Grendel, who came from a watery lair. In Victor Hugo's *Les Travailleurs de la mer* (*Toilers of the Sea*, 1866), Gilliatt wrestles with a huge octopus; and in Jules Verne's *Vingt mille lieues sous les mers* (*Twenty Thousand Leagues under the Sea*, 1870), men battle with gigantic cuttlefish. Wells is superbly adept at evoking

14   The Armistice of 1918 was, of course, only a truce. The Great War (later called 'World War I') ended with the signing of the Treaty of Versailles on 28 June 1919.

the terror and the horrific carnage exacted by the alien shoal. His tale ends with the hope that the vile creatures have 'returned for good to the sunless depths of the middle seas'. In recent times, however, documentary films have shown people being attacked by squid; and gigantic squid certainly exist, for, on 1 March 2015, one specimen *fifty feet long* was washed up on a beach at Punakaiki in New Zealand.[15]

4

Wells also anticipated future *literary* developments. The lengthiest item in this collection is 'A Story of the Stone Age', which originally was published in three parts between May and August 1897 in the *Idler* magazine. Whether Wells looked into the distant future or the remote past, the same process was often at work: the process whereby he built on scientific knowledge, but used a powerful imagination to animate the envisaged world. This particular tale is a reminder of the ways in which Wells fascinated and provoked later writers, for here he repeatedly brings to mind what is probably the finest work of the Nobel-Prize-winning author William Golding. We encounter a similar precursory effect when we read 'The Grisly Folk' (first published as 'The Grisly Folk and Their War with Men' in *Storyteller Magazine*, April 1921).

The most brilliant novel about the remote past and prehistoric man is undoubtedly Golding's *The Inheritors* (1955). Golding makes clear a debt to Wells, for, in the epigraph, he quotes Wells's *The Outline of History*. But he also owed much to 'The Grisly Folk'. There, Wells describes the lethal rivalry between the 'grisly' (bristly) people, the Neanderthalers, and our ancestors, *Homo sapiens*. Eventually our clever ancestors triumph over their cannibalistic assailants. Golding transvalued the situation. In his account, the Neanderthalers are relatively benign; our ancestors are the fallen beings, cannibalistic and crafty. (A central image is that of 'the fall', a waterfall which is mnemonic of the Fall of Man.) Wells had said: 'But the grisly folk we cannot begin to understand . . . As well might we try to dream and feel as a gorilla dreams and feels.' Golding rises exuberantly to this challenge, making us empathise keenly with the struggling victims, the Neanderthalers.

Golding appears to owe a further debt to 'A Story of the Stone Age'. Both *The Inheritors* and 'A Story of the Stone Age' are set in a region

---

15 See, for instance, the 'YouTube' items, 'Giant Squid Attack', 'Diver Mauled in Squid Attack' and 'Giant Squid Found'.

which corresponds geographically to modern south-east England; both deal with ruthless striving within a tribe of 'new people', the young watching jealously the old; both show all-too-familiar emotions at work within our remote ancestors, and exploit the paradox that we experience growing empathy with people ostensibly so primitive compared with ourselves; and both show important steps towards civilisation being made by the more intelligent beings. In Golding, Fa, the intelligent Neanderthal female, discovers the principle of agriculture; in Wells, Ugh, the primitive man, discovers how to make a stone axe from a pebble and a stick, thereby gaining both a tool and a weapon, and he becomes the first horse-rider. Both narratives centre on a loving couple, their love tested by violence, fear and loss. The wise old woman who guards the fire in Golding's novel has some resemblances to the shrewd old woman who becomes leader of the tribe in Wells's tale, but Golding, whose imagination worked antithetically, seeking to reverse prejudices of the past, has made his old woman a benevolent contrast to Wells's witch-like being. Of course, Wells's rich narrative includes several of those chase-sequences which always elicited his stirring fervency, and Golding displays intensive emulation.

Golding, subtly anti-racist and anti-imperialist, greatly expands the use of defamiliarisation and 'delayed decoding' which are such natural features of Wells's tale.[16] As Wells is describing humans and animals who lack our intelligence, reality is often rendered unfamiliar, and we, the readers, often find that our 'decoding' of the evidence is therefore delayed. In the following passage from Wells's story, a bear does not realise that two humans ('drab animals'), on a ledge above him, are trying to kill him by dropping a rock:

> He yawned again. There was a tap overhead, and a big mass of chalk flew out from the cliff face, dropped a yard in front of his nose, and starred into a dozen unequal fragments. It startled him extremely.
>
> When he had recovered a little from his shock, he went and sniffed curiously at the representative pieces of the fallen projectile. They had a distinctive flavour, oddly reminiscent of the two drab animals of the ledge. He sat up and pawed the larger lump, and walked round it several times, trying to find a man about it somewhere . . .

16 'Delayed decoding' (a term coined by Ian Watt) occurs when a writer imposes a delay between the presentation of puzzling material and its decipherment. This technique may defamiliarise or 'make strange' the event described. See Ian Watt's *Conrad in the Nineteenth Century*, Chatto & Windus, London, 1980, pp. 176-9.

And here is Golding's account, in *The Inheritors*, of the time when the uncomprehending Lok, a Neanderthal man, has a poisoned arrow shot at him by one of the New Men:

> The man turned sideways in the bushes and looked at Lok along his shoulder. A stick rose upright and there was a lump of bone in the middle ... The stick began to grow shorter at both ends. Then it shot out to full length again.
>
> The dead tree by Lok's ear acquired a voice.
>
> 'Clop!'
>
> His ears twitched and he turned to the tree. By his face there had grown a twig: a twig that smelt of other, and of goose, and of the bitter berries that Lok's stomach told him he must not eat. This twig had a white bone at the end. There were hooks in the bone and sticky brown stuff hung in the crooks. His nose examined this stuff and did not like it.[17]

In each case, a keen sense of smell yields vital information which is not sufficiently comprehended: a lethal threat remains.

The relationship between these texts of Wells's and Golding's *The Inheritors* is thus mimetic, congruent and adversarial. It is mimetic, when we perceive that some elements of Golding's fiction derive from Wells's. It is congruent, when both writers appear to share the same outlook, as when both seek to 'make these bones live', bringing the distant past to vivid life. And it is adversarial, when the later writer attempts to challenge and oppose the reading of history made by the earlier.

When we read Wells's tale 'The Remarkable Case of Davidson's Eyes' (1895), we find another possible example of 'mimetic' influence. In this case, Golding's *Pincher Martin* appears to have derived some hallucinatory features from the Wellsian story. Davidson intensely perceives a distant location, but his immediate location, holding his body, increasingly impinges on his perception: the outcome is salutary. Golding's Pincher intensely perceives a location which seems to be preserving him, but his perception is increasingly disrupted by unwelcome reminders of his actual situation: his willed dream of survival is eventually destroyed by the incursion of reality. It is another 'adversarial' reading.

By crafty touches of detail, Wells has given vividness to Davidson's hallucinatory experience: as when, for example, in the sea he encounters 'some glowing phosphorescent forms that were shaken and writhed as

---

17 William Golding: *The Inheritors* (1955), Faber & Faber, London, 1963, p. 106.

the fish bit at them': half-eaten corpses, we realise. Golding's novel surpasses Wells's short tale in vividness, but repeatedly brings it to mind. For example, when Pincher Martin shouts at the 'black lightning' which assails him, we recall how Davidson, in a thunderstorm, 'lay and shouted at the silent flashes'. And finally Golding grants clear acknowledgement to Wells's tale; for the last word in the novel *Pincher Martin* is given to a naval officer who, quite wrongly, assures an enquirer that Martin could not have suffered; and that officer is called *Davidson*. Incidentally, Wells's story may in turn owe a literary debt: it recalls Rudyard Kipling's 'The Finest Story in the World' (1891), in which the main character is divided between two existences, living in the mundane present but having powerful recollections of a prior sea-going life.

Unexpectedly, another great writer anticipated in the pages of this selection is E. M. Forster. Forster studied Wells's writings, and one outcome was 'The Machine Stops' (1909), Forster's acclaimed science-fiction story about the end of organised civilisation. The tale, explained Forster, was 'a reaction to one of the earlier heavens of H. G. Wells': probably *A Modern Utopia* (1905).[18] Remarkably, Wells's story 'Miss Winchelsea's Heart' (1898) reads like a prelude to Forster's novel *A Room with a View* (1908). In both cases, the authors, with mildly satiric humour, depict a group of young Englishwomen who travel to Italy. In the tale, they visit Florence before proceeding to Rome; in the novel, the main setting abroad is Rome. The Baedeker guide-book features in both. The unreliable Miss Lavish, in the novel, confiscates Lucy's Baedeker (the *Handbook to Northern Italy*), saying that Baedeker 'does but touch the surface'; but the sensible Mr Emerson approves of it, and Lucy finds loss of it a nuisance. Typically, in the tale, Miss Winchelsea (who does not wish to appear 'touristy') covers her Baedeker in grey 'to hide its glaring red', but later finds that while others 'fumbled helplessly with Baedeker', she is happy to be guided by a pleasant young man – who will prove, to her dismay, to bear the surname 'Snooks'. And in both cases, English snobbery, insularity and inhibitions are gently mocked. The English people take to Italy their prejudices but also a capacity to learn, albeit slowly. In Wells's tale, the possible love-relationship of Miss Winchelsea and Mr Snooks is blighted because of her snobbish recoil from his vulgar-seeming surname. Her priggishness is a source of comedy for the reader but of tragedy for her; and we recognise the sad irony that since her own surname is a place-name, she might have

18 Forster's Introduction to his *Collected Short Stories* (1947), Penguin, Harmondsworth, 1954, p. 6.

surmised that his was a contraction of 'Sevenoaks'. In Forster's novel, Lucy, after plausible confusion, manages to rise above conventionality and snobbery to recognise and fulfil her love for George Emerson. It seems as if Forster's novel, in passing, offers a positive riposte to the tale.

Wells provides another precursory model: 'Through a Window' anticipates fictional works featuring a hero who is bed-ridden or crippled and is therefore peculiarly handicapped when confronted with a threat. Suspense hinges on how he will be able to save himself. Examples of this sub-genre are the tale 'It Had to be Murder' (1942) by Carney Woolrich, the basis of the famous Alfred Hitchcock film *Rear Window* (1954), starring James Stewart. (Woolrich was said to be influenced by Wells's tale.) Another instance is the Stephen King thriller, *Misery* (1987), which was admirably filmed in 1990, earning the 'Best Actress' Oscar for Kathy Bates, who played the crippled hero's assailant. *Misery* subsequently became a stage play and a musical. 'Through a Window' also anticipates those works in which, at the dramatic finale, a malefactor belatedly displays again potentially lethal aggression: suddenly the person who seemed to be no longer a threat returns violently. The film *Fatal Attraction*, 1987, well illustrated this protracted peril.

Another instance of Wells's versatility is 'A Deal in Ostriches', a tale which would have delighted O. Henry (William Sydney Porter), for, like O. Henry's stories at their most characteristic, this one has a 'twist in the tail', an ending which casts a retrospective transforming light on all that has gone before. Again, as in an O. Henry story, the narrative seems to show intimate knowledge of the ways of tricksters and 'confidence men'.

6

In his great works of the 1890s, particularly *The Time Machine* and *The Island of Doctor Moreau*, Wells was involved with literary Modernism. He was then on friendly terms with Henry James and Joseph Conrad, who responded enthusiastically to his early writings; and *The Time Machine* has certainly left its mark on Conrad's masterpiece, *Heart of Darkness*. In both works we perceive the ironic use of doubly oblique narration; both works ask radical and daunting questions about the direction and destiny of civilisation; both combine realism with symbolism; and both employ the literary device of covert plotting. Conrad's novella may owe some details to Wells: the ichthyosaurus is mentioned in Wells's tale and in Marlow's reflections; and Marlow likens his journey into darkest Africa to a journey in time: 'Going up that river was like travelling back to the earliest beginnings of the world.'[19] In both works, the returned traveller tells his admonitory story to a partly-sceptical audience. Incidentally, the novel *The Inheritors* (1901, the same title as that later used by Golding), by Conrad and F. M. Hueffer (Ford Madox Ford), seems to have been prompted partly by the discussion of the 'fourth dimension' in *The Time Machine*: their science-fiction fantasy and political *roman à clef* (novel alluding to real people) tells how ruthless 'Fourth Dimensionists' invade the earth.

As he became more preoccupied by plans for improving humanity, Wells became fiercely critical of James and Conrad (notably in his satiric medley, *Boon*, 1915), and ceased to be involved in Modernism. Nevertheless, he became an inspiration to two writers who have often been termed Postmodernists, Vladimir Nabokov (1899–1977) and Jorge Luis Borges (1899–1986).

Modernism occasionally mimicked madness; Postmodernism sometimes embraced it. Given the immense diversity of writings deemed 'Modernist', Postmodernism could be seen both as a continuation of Modernist experimentation and as a reaction against some features of Modernism. Deriving from Pyrrho of Elis (the pioneering sceptic, *c.*360–*c.*270BC), Postmodernism was characterised by extreme, systematic and paradoxical scepticism. For instance, its metanarrative was the denial that metanarratives exist (so that the grand narratives of theologians or politicians are false), and it even sought to deny the existence of truth (in which case, the denial could not be true).[20] One characteristic of literary Postmodernism was metafiction, which foregrounded the role of author and reader in inventing and receiving the fiction. (In Nabokov's *Pnin*, the author personally intervenes, breaching traditional literary decorum, to save his protagonist from death.) Another is intertextuality, which often in practice meant that the work invoked numerous other works. In Nabokov's *Pale Fire* (its title drawn from Shakespeare's *Timon of Athens*), the novel takes the form of an edited poem, itself amply allusive, with copious notes, many of which contain false allusions.

In 1914, Nabokov was present when Wells and his translator were guests of Nabokov's father in St Petersburg. (That translator, Zinaida Vengerova, embarrassingly informed Wells, 'You know, *my* favourite

19 Joseph Conrad, *Heart of Darkness and Other Tales*, edited by Cedric Watts, Oxford University Press, Oxford, 2002, p. 136.

20 Jacques Derrida, for instance, advocated 'a world of signs without fault, without truth, and without origin': *Writing and Difference*, translated by Alan Bass, Routledge & Kegan Paul, London, 1981, p. 292.

work of yours is *The Lost World*.') Nabokov later referred to Wells thus: 'H. G. Wells, a great artist . . . His sociological cogitations can be ignored, of course, but his romances and fantasies are superb.' Of the tales, he particularly praised 'The Country of the Blind'.[21] This is a tale with a richly allegoric potential, and it may ultimately derive from Plato's famous image, in *The Republic*, of the cave-dwellers who assume wrongly that their shadow-land is the real world. Wells's blind people are so accustomed to blindness that they regard it as normality; and, as for the sighted man's claims, these they regard as a kind of madness to be cured by blinding. The theme of 'the sighted man among the blind' was congenial to Nabokov, an exile from Tsarist Russia who feared that too many Americans were looking admiringly at the Soviet tyranny. In *Bend Sinister*, the decency of Krug, the protagonist, is unavailing against the predominant crassness, vulgarity and cruelty of the totalitarian state in which he is trapped. H. G. Wells, of course, liked to depict, in his tales, a closely-observed mundane world which is suddenly challenged by the incursion of the fantastic. Nabokov, in his distinctive way, relishes that form of juxtaposition. In *Lolita*, the America of middle-class suburbs, motels and roadside diners is meticulously evoked, but the grotesque Clare Quilty brings the fantastic to the narrative; and, in *Pale Fire*, while John Shade, the poet, is eminently humane and reasonable, his editor, Charles Kinbote, is lethally obsessed by the fantasy of Zembla. Finally, as Alexander M. Luxemburg has pointed out, Wells's novel *Apropos of Dolores* (1938) appears to be a source of Nabokov's *Lolita*: for instance, in both works the story by the protagonist, a killer, 'is mockingly presented as the hearings of a case in court'.[22] In *Ada*, Nabokov (as if in emulation of Wells's imaginary other-worlds) created the surrealistic realm, Antiterra.

The eminent Argentinian author, Jorge Luis Borges, praised Wells in his essay 'The First Wells' (1942). He said:

> Of the vast and diversified library he left us, nothing has pleased me more than his narration of some atrocious miracles: *The Time Machine*, *The Island of Doctor Moreau*, *The Plattner Story*, *The First Men*

---

21 Vladimir Nabokov, interviewed for *The Paris Review*, 41, Summer–Fall 1967 (see www.theparisreview.org/interviews/4310/the-art-of-fiction-no-40-vladimir-nabokov).

22 Alexander M. Luxemburg: 'The Mystery of Vladimir Nabokov's Sources: Some New Ideas on *Lolita*'s Intertextual Links', in *Connotations: A Journal for Critical Debate*, 14: 1–3 (2004/2005), pp. 119–34; also to be found at www.connotations.uni-tuebingen.de/luxemburgD1413.htm.

in the Moon. They are the first books I read; perhaps they will be the last. I think they will be incorporated, like the fables of Theseus or Ahasuerus, into the general memory of the species and even transcend the fame of their creator or the extinction of the language in which they were written. [23]

In particular, Borges acknowledged Wells's 'The Crystal Egg' as the source of his own 'The Aleph' and 'The Zahir'.[24] The crystal egg permits a vision of a different planet, evidently Mars, and its inhabitants; and those inhabitants, by means of such crystal eggs, are observing our planet. The owner of the egg watches the watchers. Borges expands the idea to infinity. His protagonist (called Borges) visits the cellar where a neighbour keeps the 'Aleph'. Although it is a small sphere, only two or three centimetres in diameter, the man who looks into it sees in a short time an infinity of objects: 'I saw the earth in the Aleph and in the earth the Aleph once more and the earth in the Aleph.' But (typically of Borges) this Aleiph may be a false one, the true Aleph being that mentioned by Captain Burton in the nineteenth century as located in a column in Cairo.

In Wells's tale, the owner of the crystal egg became obsessed by it and is unwilling to part with it. The 'Zahir' of Borges's tale is a particular coin which (according to various authorities) gradually dominates the person who beholds it. Eventually, says the narrator,

> Others will dream that I am mad, and I shall dream of the Zahir. And when everybody on earth thinks of the Zahir day and night, which will be a dream and which a reality, the earth or the Zahir? [25]

To that question, one ruthless answer has already been given by Wells. He says: 'Nothing remains interesting when anything may happen.'[26] For all Borges's scintillating erudition, his obsessive conceptual games can sometimes descend into pedantic whimsy. Wells's diversity contains a substantial ballast of empirical realism, and is the better for it.

23   Jorge Luis Borges, 'The First Wells', in *Other Inquisitions, 1937–1962*, translated by Ruth L. C. Simms (1964), Souvenir Press, London, 1973, p. 88.

24   Epílogo (Epilogue) to *El Aleph*, Emecé, Buenos Aires, 1971, p. 182.

25   'The Zahir', in Jorge Luis Borges, *A Personal Anthology*, Cape, London, 1968, p. 137.

26   *H. G. Wells's Literary Criticism*, op. cit., p. 241.

5

Emphasising Wells's variety, I deliberately chose to end the selection with that odd item, 'The Beautiful Suit', to which I return. By the author of the macabre horror-story 'The Cone', 'The Beautiful Suit' is contrastingly lyrical and is narrowly saved from sentimentality by paradox. The apotheosis of the suit entails the spoliation of the suit. The celebration is a destruction. The rebellion is outwardly a failure but inwardly a success. Wells employs remarkable descriptive power to make credible that fantastic triumph:

> . . . moonshine was tangled in the hedges and stretched in phantom cobwebs from spray to spray. Every flower was gleaming white or crimson black, and the air was a-quiver with the thridding of small crickets and nightingales singing unseen in the depths of the trees.

Here is Wells the lyricist, wresting language towards paradoxes for his purpose: 'crimson black'; 'a-quiver with the thridding of small crickets'. Within Wells, the professed foe of aestheticism, there lurked a repressed poet; but sometimes, that poet breaks through the repression: as here in the little man's rebellious journey; or when, in 'Under the Knife', 'the whole headlong rush of stellar universe closed in . . . like a veil of light that is gathered together'; or when the boy in 'The Door in the Wall' passes into the strange garden where spotted panthers tamely roam. This selection of tales reveals an H. G. Wells whose full imaginative range has yet to gain the ample appreciation it deserves.

In his comments on his own fictional writings, particularly when contrasting his endeavours with those of Joseph Conrad and Henry James, Wells tended to sell himself short. In his powers of poetic expressiveness, the author of these tales and of *The Time Machine* has more in common with Conrad than he later indicated; and we are also reminded that in the 1890s, when so many of these stories were written, Wells was mixing with reformers, scientists, visionaries and *aesthetes*; and they nourished aspects of himself.

Wells was an educator, a historian, a reformer and a politician. This selection of stories reminds us that he was also one of the most entertaining, versatile and thought-provoking literary artists of his era. He was a man of formidable creative energy, as a result of which his tales can stir fruitful turbulence in the imaginations of readers today. Read this selection, and you'll be amply entertained and surprisingly instructed.

CEDRIC WATTS

FURTHER READING

(The order is chronological.)

Geoffrey H. Wells, *The Works of H. G. Wells, 1887–1925: A Bibliography, Dictionary and Subject Index*, Routledge, London / H. W. Wilson, New York, 1926

H. G. Wells, *An Experiment in Autobiography: Discoveries and Conclusions of a Very Ordinary Brain (since 1866)*, 2 vols, Victor Gollancz and the Cresset Press, London, 1934

George Orwell, 'Wells, Hitler and the World State' (1941), in *The Complete Works of George Orwell*, Volume 12: *A Patriot After All: 1940–1941*, edited by Peter Davison, Secker & Warburg, London, 1998

Vincent Brome, *H. G. Wells: A Biography*, Longmans, Green, London, 1951

Bernard Bergonzi, *The Early H. G. Wells: A Study of the Scientific Romances*, Manchester University Press, Manchester, 1961

Mark R. Hillegas, *The Future as Nightmare: H. G. Wells and the Anti-Utopians*, Oxford University Press, Oxford, 1967

Samuel Hynes, *The Edwardian Turn of Mind*, Princeton University Press, Princeton, NJ, 1968

Patrick Parrinder, *H. G. Wells*, Oliver & Boyd, London, 1970

Patrick Parrinder (ed.), *H. G. Wells: The Critical Heritage* (1972), Routledge, London, 1997

Brian Aldiss, *Billion Year Spree*, Weidenfeld & Nicolson, London, 1973

Norman and Jeanne MacKenzie, *The Time Traveller: The Life of H. G. Wells*, Weidenfeld & Nicolson, London, 1973

Bernard Bergonzi (ed.), *H. G. Wells: A Collection of Critical Essays*, Prentice-Hall, Englewood Cliffs, NJ, 1976

J. R. Hammond, *Herbert George Wells: An Annotated Bibliography of His Works*, Garland, New York and London, 1977

J. R. Hammond, *An H. G. Wells Companion: A Guide to the Novels, Romances and Short Stories*, Macmillan, London and Basingstoke, 1979

Roslynn D. Haynes, *H. G. Wells: Discoverer of the Future: The Influence of Science on His Thought*, Macmillan, London and Basingstoke, 1980

J. R. Hammond (ed.), *H. G. Wells: Interviews and Recollections*, Macmillan, London and Basingstoke, 1980

John Huntington, *The Logic of Fantasy: H. G. Wells and Science Fiction*, Columbia University Press, New York, 1982

Peter Kemp, *H. G. Wells and the Culminating Ape* (1982), Macmillan, London and Basingstoke/St Martin's Press, New York, 1996

Anthony West, *H. G. Wells: Aspects of a Life* (1984), Hutchinson, London, 2007

John Batchelor, *H. G. Wells*, Cambridge University Press, Cambridge, 1985

David C. Smith, *H. G. Wells: Desperately Mortal: A Biography*, Yale University Press, New Haven and London, 1986

Krishan Kumar, *Utopia and Anti-Utopia in Modern Times*, Blackwell, Oxford, 1987

Linda R. Anderson, *Bennett, Wells and Conrad: Narrative in Transition*, Macmillan, London and Basingstoke, 1988

Patrick Parrinder and Christopher Rolfe (ed.), *H. G. Wells Under Revision*, Associated University Presses, London, 1990

Brian Murray, *H. G. Wells*, Continuum, New York, 1990

John Carey, *The Intellectuals and the Masses: Pride and Prejudice among the Literary Intelligentsia, 1880–1939*, Faber & Faber, London, 1992

Michael Foot, *H. G. – The History of Mr Wells*, Doubleday, London and New York, 1995

Patrick Parrinder, *Shadows of the Future: H. G. Wells, Science Fiction and Prophecy*, Liverpool University Press, Liverpool, 1995

John Hammond, *H. G. Wells*, Longman, Harlow and London, 2001

P. J. Waller, *Writers, Readers and Reputations: Literary Life in Britain, 1870–1918*, Oxford University Press, Oxford, 2006

Steven McLean (ed.), *H. G. Wells: Interdisciplinary Essays*, Cambridge Scholars Publishing, Newcastle, 2008

Steven McLean, *The Early Fiction of H. G. Wells: Fantasies of Science*, Palgrave Macmillan, Basingstoke, 2009

David Lodge, *A Man of Parts* (2011), Vintage, London, 2012

Simon J. James, *Maps of Utopia: H. G. Wells, Modernity, and the End of Culture*, Oxford University Press, Oxford, 2012

Linda Dryden, *Joseph Conrad and H. G. Wells: The Fin-de-Siècle Literary Scene*, Palgrave Macmillan, Basingstoke, 2015

The Crystal Egg[1]

There was, until a year ago, a little and very grimy-looking shop near Seven Dials[2] over which, in weather-worn yellow lettering, the name of C. CAVE, NATURALIST AND DEALER IN ANTIQUITIES, was inscribed. The contents of its window were curiously variegated. They comprised some elephant tusks and an imperfect set of chessmen, beads and weapons, a box of eyes, two skulls of tigers and one human, several moth-eaten stuffed monkeys (one holding a lamp), an old-fashioned cabinet, a fly-blown ostrich egg or so, some fishing-tackle, and an extraordinarily dirty, empty glass fish-tank. There was also, at the moment the story begins, a mass of crystal, worked into the shape of an egg and brilliantly polished. And at that two people, who stood outside the window, were looking, one of them a tall, thin clergyman, the other a black-bearded young man of dusky complexion and unobtrusive costume. The dusky young man spoke with eager gesticulation, and seemed anxious for his companion to purchase the article.

While they were there, Mr Cave came into his shop, his beard still wagging with the bread and butter of his tea. When he saw these men and the object of their regard, his countenance fell. He glanced guiltily over his shoulder, and softly shut the door. He was a little old man, with pale face and peculiar watery blue eyes; his hair was a dirty grey, and he wore a shabby blue frock-coat, an ancient silk hat and carpet slippers very much down at heel. He remained watching the two men as they talked. The clergyman went deep into his trouser pocket, examined a handful of money, and showed his teeth in an agreeable smile. Mr Cave seemed still more depressed when they came into the shop.

The clergyman, without any ceremony, asked the price of the crystal egg. Mr Cave glanced nervously towards the door leading into the parlour, and said five pounds.[3] The clergyman protested that the price was high, to his companion as well as to Mr Cave – it was, indeed, very much more than Mr Cave had intended to ask when he had stocked the article – and an attempt at bargaining ensued. Mr Cave stepped to the shop-door, and held it open. 'Five pounds is my price,' he said, as though he wished to save himself the trouble of unprofitable discussion. As he did so, the upper portion of a woman's face appeared above the blind in the glass upper panel of the door leading into the parlour, and stared curiously at the two customers. 'Five pounds is my price,' said Mr Cave, with a quiver in his voice.

The swarthy young man had so far remained a spectator, watching Cave keenly. Now he spoke. 'Give him five pounds,' he said. The clergyman glanced at him to see if he were in earnest, and, when he looked at Mr Cave again, he saw that the latter's face was white. 'It's a lot of money,' said the clergyman, and diving into his pocket, began counting his resources. He had little more than thirty shillings,[4] and he appealed to his companion, with whom he seemed to be on terms of considerable intimacy. This gave Mr Cave an opportunity of collecting his thoughts, and he began to explain in an agitated manner that the crystal was not, as a matter of fact, entirely free for sale. His two customers were naturally surprised at this, and enquired why he had not thought of that before he began to bargain. Mr Cave became confused, but he stuck to his story, that the crystal was not in the market that afternoon, that a probable purchaser of it had already appeared. The two, treating this as an attempt to raise the price still further, made as if they would leave the shop. But at this point the parlour door opened, and the owner of the dark fringe and the little eyes appeared.

She was a coarse-featured, corpulent woman, younger and very much larger than Mr Cave; she walked heavily, and her face was flushed. 'That crystal is for sale,' she said. 'And five pounds is a good enough price for it. I can't think what you're about Cave, not to take the gentleman's offer!'

Mr Cave, greatly perturbed by the irruption, looked angrily at her over the rims of his spectacles, and without excessive assurance, asserted his right to manage his business in his own way. An altercation began. The two customers watched the scene with interest and some amusement, occasionally assisting Mrs Cave with suggestions. Mr Cave, hard driven, persisted in a confused and impossible story of an enquiry for the crystal that morning, and his agitation became painful. But he stuck to his point with extraordinary persistence. It was the young Oriental who ended this curious controversy. He proposed that they should call again in the course of two days – so as to give the alleged enquirer a fair chance. 'And then we must insist,' said the clergyman. 'Five pounds.' Mrs Cave took it on herself to apologise for her husband, explaining that he was sometimes 'a little odd', and as the two customers left, the couple prepared for a free discussion of the incident in all its bearings.

Mrs Cave talked to her husband with singular directness. The poor little man, quivering with emotion, muddled himself between his stories, maintaining on the one hand that he had another customer in view, and on the other asserting that the crystal was honestly worth ten guineas.[5] 'Why did you ask five pounds?' said his wife. 'Do let me manage my business my own way!' said Mr Cave.

Mr Cave had living with him a stepdaughter and a stepson, and at supper that night the transaction was rediscussed. None of them had a high opinion of Mr Cave's business methods, and this action seemed a culminating folly.

'It's my opinion he's refused that crystal before,' said the stepson, a loose-limbed lout of eighteen.

'But *Five Pounds*!' said the stepdaughter, an argumentative young woman of six-and-twenty.

Mr Cave's answers were wretched; he could only mumble weak assertions that he knew his own business best. They drove him from his half-eaten supper into the shop, to close it for the night, his ears aflame and tears of vexation behind his spectacles. 'Why had he left the crystal in the window so long? The folly of it!' That was the trouble closest in his mind. For a time he could see no way of evading sale.

After supper his stepdaughter and stepson smartened themselves up and went out and his wife retired upstairs to reflect upon the business aspects of the crystal, over a little sugar and lemon and so forth in hot water. Mr Cave went into the shop, and stayed there until late, ostensibly to make ornamental rockeries for goldfish cases but really for a private purpose that will be better explained later. The next day Mrs Cave found that the crystal had been removed from the window, and was lying behind some second-hand books on angling. She replaced it in a conspicuous position. But she did not argue further about it, as a nervous headache disinclined her from debate. Mr Cave was always disinclined. The day passed disagreeably. Mr Cave was, if anything, more absent-minded than usual, and uncommonly irritable withal. In the afternoon, when his wife was taking her customary sleep, he removed the crystal from the window again.

The next day Mr Cave had to deliver a consignment of dogfish at one of the hospital schools, where they were needed for dissection. In his absence Mrs Cave's mind reverted to the topic of the crystal, and the methods of expenditure suitable to a windfall of five pounds. She had already devised some very agreeable expedients, among others a dress of green silk for herself and a trip to Richmond, when a jangling of the front-door bell summoned her into the shop. The customer was an examination coach who came to complain of the non-delivery of certain frogs asked for the previous day. Mrs Cave did not approve of this particular branch of Mr Cave's business, and the gentleman, who had called in a somewhat aggressive mood, retired after a brief exchange of words – entirely civil so far as he was concerned. Mrs Cave's eye then naturally turned to the window; for the sight of the crystal was an assurance of the five pounds and of her dreams. What was her surprise to find it gone!

She went to the place behind the locker on the counter, where she had discovered it the day before. It was not there; and she immediately began an eager search about the shop.

When Mr Cave returned from his business with the dogfish, about a quarter to two in the afternoon, he found the shop in some confusion, and his wife extremely exasperated and on her knees behind the counter, routing among his taxidermic material. Her face came up hot and angry over the counter, as the jangling bell announced his return, and she forthwith accused him of 'hiding it'.

'Hid *what*?' asked Mr Cave.

'The crystal!'

At that Mr Cave, apparently much surprised, rushed to the window. 'Isn't it here?' he said. 'Great heavens! What has become of it?'

Just then, Mr Cave's stepson re-entered the shop from the inner room – he had come home a minute or so before Mr Cave – and he was blaspheming freely. He was apprenticed to a second-hand furniture dealer down the road, but he had his meals at home, and he was naturally annoyed to find no dinner ready.

But when he heard of the loss of the crystal, he forgot his meal, and his anger was diverted from his mother to his stepfather. Their first idea, of course, was that he had hidden it. But Mr Cave stoutly denied all knowledge of its fate – freely offering his bedabbled affidavit[6] in the matter – and at last was worked up to the point of accusing first his wife and then his stepson of having taken it with a view to a private sale. So began an exceedingly acrimonious and emotional discussion, which ended for Mrs Cave in a peculiar nervous condition midway between hysterics and amuck,[7] and caused the stepson to be half an hour late at the furniture establishment in the afternoon. Mr Cave took refuge from his wife's emotions in the shop.

In the evening the matter was resumed, with less passion and in a judicial spirit, under the presidency of the stepdaughter. The supper passed unhappily and culminated in a painful scene. Mr Cave gave way at last to extreme exasperation, and went out banging the front door violently. The rest of the family, having discussed him with the freedom his absence warranted, hunted the house from garret to cellar, hoping to light upon the crystal.

The next day the two customers called again. They were received by Mrs Cave almost in tears. It transpired that no one *could* imagine all that she had stood from Cave at various times in her married pilgrimage ... She also gave a garbled account of the disappearance. The clergyman and the Oriental laughed silently at one another, and said it was very extraordinary. As Mrs Cave seemed disposed to give them the complete history of her life they made to leave the shop. Thereupon Mrs Cave, still clinging to hope, asked for the clergyman's address, so that, if she could get anything out of Cave, she might communicate it. The address was duly given, but apparently was afterwards mislaid. Mrs Cave can remember nothing about it.

In the evening of that day, the Caves seem to have exhausted their emotions, and Mr Cave, who had been out in the afternoon, supped in a gloomy isolation that contrasted pleasantly with the impassioned controversy of the previous days. For some time matters were very badly strained in the Cave household, but neither crystal nor customer reappeared.

Now, without mincing the matter, we must admit that Mr Cave was a liar. He knew perfectly well where the crystal was. It was in the rooms of Mr Jacoby Wace, Assistant Demonstrator at St Catherine's Hospital, Westbourne Street. It stood on the sideboard partially covered by a black velvet cloth, and beside a decanter of American whiskey. It is from Mr Wace, indeed, that the particulars upon which this narrative is based were derived. Cave had taken off the thing to the hospital hidden in the dogfish sack, and there had pressed the young investigator to keep it for him. Mr Wace was a little dubious at first. His relationship to Cave was peculiar. He had a taste for singular characters, and he had more than once invited the old man to smoke and drink in his rooms, and to unfold his rather amusing views of life in general and of his wife in particular. Mr Wace had encountered Mrs Cave too, on occasions when Mr Cave was not at home to attend to him. He knew the constant interference to which Cave was subjected, and having weighed the story judicially, he decided to give the crystal a refuge. Mr Cave promised to explain the reasons for his remarkable affection for the crystal more fully on a later occasion, but he spoke distinctly of seeing visions therein. He called on Mr Wace the same evening.

He told a complicated story. The crystal he said had come into his possession with other oddments at the forced sale of another curiosity dealer's effects, and not knowing what its value might be, he had ticketed it at ten shillings. It had hung upon his hands at that price for some months, and he was thinking of 'reducing the figure', when he made a singular discovery.

At that time his health was very bad – and it must be borne in mind that throughout all this experience his physical condition was one of ebb – and he was in considerable distress by reason of the negligence, the positive ill-treatment even, he received from his wife and step-children. His wife was vain, extravagant, unfeeling and had a growing taste for private drinking; his stepdaughter was mean and over-reaching; and his stepson had conceived a violent dislike for him, and lost no chance of showing it. The requirements of his business pressed heavily upon him, and Mr Wace does not think that he was altogether free from occasional intemperance. He had begun life in a comfortable position and he was a man of fair education, but he suffered, for weeks at a stretch, from melancholia and insomnia. Afraid to disturb his family, he would slip quietly from his wife's side, when his thoughts became intolerable, and wander about the house. And about three o'clock one morning, late in August, chance directed him into the shop.

The dirty little place was impenetrably black except in one spot, where he perceived an unusual glow of light. Approaching this, he discovered it to be the crystal egg, which was standing on the corner of the counter towards the window. A thin ray smote through a crack in the shutters, impinged upon the object, and seemed as it were to fill its entire interior.

It occurred to Mr Cave that this was not in accordance with the laws of optics as he had known them in his younger days. He could understand the rays being refracted by the crystal and coming to a focus in its interior, but this diffusion jarred with his physical conceptions. He approached the crystal nearly, peering into it and round it, with a transient revival of the scientific curiosity that in his youth had determined his choice of a calling. He was surprised to find the light not steady, but writhing within the substance of the egg, as though that object was a hollow sphere of some luminous vapour. In moving about to get different points of view, he suddenly found that he had come between it and the ray, and that the crystal none the less remained luminous. Greatly astonished, he lifted it out of the light ray and carried it to the darkest part of the shop. It remained bright for some four or five minutes, when it slowly faded and went out. He placed it in the thin streak of daylight, and its luminousness was almost immediately restored.

So far, at least, Mr Wace was able to verify the remarkable story of Mr Cave. He had himself repeatedly held this crystal in a ray of light (which had to be of a less diameter than one millimetre). And in a perfect darkness, such as could be produced by velvet wrapping, the crystal did undoubtedly appear very faintly phosphorescent. It would seem, however, that the luminousness was of some exceptional sort, and not equally visible to all eyes; for Mr Harbinger – whose name will be familiar to the scientific reader in connection with the Pasteur Institute[8] – was quite unable to see any light whatever. And Mr Wace's own capacity for its appreciation was out of comparison inferior to that of Mr Cave's. Even with Mr Cave the power varied very considerably: his vision was most vivid during states of extreme weakness and fatigue.

Now, from the outset, this light in the crystal exercised a curious fascination upon Mr Cave. And it says more for his loneliness of soul than a volume of pathetic writing could do that he told no human being of his curious observations. He seems to have been living in such an atmosphere of petty spite that to admit the existence of a pleasure would have been to risk the loss of it. He found that as the dawn advanced, and the amount of diffused light increased, the crystal became to all appearance non-luminous. And for some time he was unable to see anything in it except at night-time in dark corners of the shop.

But the use of an old velvet cloth, which he used as a background for a collection of minerals, occurred to him, and by doubling this, and putting it over his head and hands, he was able to get a sight of the luminous movement within the crystal even in the daytime. He was very cautious lest he should be thus discovered by his wife, and he practised this occupation only in the afternoons, while she was asleep upstairs, and then circumspectly in a hollow under the counter. And one day, turning the crystal about in his hands, he saw something. It came and went like a flash, but it gave him the impression that the object had for a moment opened to him the view of a wide and spacious and strange country; and turning it about, he did, just as the light faded, see the same vision again.

Now, it would be tedious and unnecessary to state all the phases of Mr Cave's discovery from this point. Suffice that the effect was this: the crystal, being peered into at an angle of about 137 degrees from the direction of the illuminating ray, gave a clear and consistent picture of a wide and peculiar countryside. It was not dreamlike at all: it produced a definite impression of reality, and the better the light the more real and solid it seemed. It was a moving picture: that is to say, certain objects moved in it, but slowly in an orderly manner like real things, and according as the direction of the lighting and vision changed, the picture changed also. It must, indeed, have been like looking through an oval glass at a view, and turning the glass about to get at different aspects.

Mr Cave's statements, Mr Wace assures me, were extremely circumstantial, and entirely free from any of that emotional quality that taints hallucinatory impressions. But it must be remembered that all the efforts of Mr Wace to see any similar clarity in the faint opalescence of the crystal were wholly unsuccessful, try as he would. The difference in intensity of the impressions received by the two men was very great, and it is quite conceivable that what was a view to Mr Cave was a mere blurred nebulosity to Mr Wace.

The view, as Mr Cave described it, was invariably of an extensive plain, and he seemed always to be looking at it from a considerable height, as if from a tower or a mast. To the east and to the west the plain was bounded at a remote distance by vast reddish cliffs, which reminded him of those he had seen in some picture; but what the picture was Mr Wace was unable to ascertain. These cliffs passed north and south – he could tell the points of the compass by the stars that were visible of a night – receding in an almost illimitable perspective and fading into the mists of the distance before they met. He was nearer the eastern set of cliffs, on the occasion of his first vision; the sun was rising over them, and black against the sunlight and pale against their shadow appeared a multitude of soaring forms that Mr Cave regarded as birds. A vast range of buildings spread below him; he seemed to be looking down upon them; and as they approached the blurred and refracted edge of the picture, they became indistinct. There were also trees curious in shape, and in colouring, a deep mossy green and an exquisite grey, beside a wide and shining canal.[9] And something great and brilliantly coloured flew across the picture. But the first time Mr Cave saw these pictures he saw only in flashes, his hands shook, his head moved, the vision came and went, and grew foggy and indistinct. And at first he had the greatest difficulty in finding the picture again once the direction of it was lost.

His next clear vision, which came about a week after the first, the interval having yielded nothing but tantalising glimpses and some useful experience, showed him the view down the length of the valley. The view was different, but he had a curious persuasion, which his subsequent observations abundantly confirmed, that he was regarding this strange world from exactly the same spot, although he was looking in a different direction. The long façade of the great building, whose roof he had looked down upon before, was now receding in perspective. He recognised the roof. In the front of the façade was a terrace of massive proportions and extraordinary length, and down the middle of the terrace, at certain intervals, stood huge but very graceful masts, bearing small shiny objects which reflected the setting sun. The import of these small objects did not occur to Mr Cave until some time after, as he was describing the scene to Mr Wace. The terrace overhung a thicket of the most luxuriant and graceful vegetation, and beyond this was a wide grassy lawn on which certain broad creatures, in form like beetles but enormously larger, reposed. Beyond this again was a richly decorated causeway of pinkish stone; and beyond that, and lined with dense red weeds,[10] and passing up the valley exactly parallel with the distant cliffs, was a broad and mirror-like expanse of water. The air seemed full of squadrons of great birds, manoeuvring in stately curves; and across the river was a multitude of splendid buildings, richly coloured and glittering with metallic tracery and facets, among a forest of moss-like and lichenous trees. And suddenly something flapped repeatedly across the vision, like the fluttering of a jewelled fan or the beating of a wing, and a face, or rather the upper part of a face with very large eyes, came as it were close to his own and as if on the other side of the crystal. Mr Cave was so startled and so impressed by the absolute reality of these eyes, that he drew his head back from the crystal to look behind it. He had become so absorbed in watching that he was quite surprised to find himself in the cool darkness of his little shop, with its familiar odour of methyl,[11] mustiness and decay. And as he blinked about him, the glowing crystal faded, and went out.

Such were the first general impressions of Mr Cave. The story is curiously direct and circumstantial. From the outset, when the valley first flashed momentarily on his senses, his imagination was strangely affected, and, as he began to appreciate the details of the scene he saw, his wonder rose to the point of a passion. He went about his business listless and distraught, thinking only of the time when he should be able to return to his watching. And then a few weeks after his first sight of the valley came the two customers, the stress and excitement of their offer, and the narrow escape of the crystal from sale, as I have already told.

Now, while the thing was Mr Cave's secret, it remained a mere wonder, a thing to creep to covertly and peep at, as a child might peep upon a forbidden garden. But Mr Wace has, for a young scientific investigator, a particularly lucid and consecutive habit of mind. Directly the crystal and its story came to him, and he had satisfied himself, by seeing the phosphorescence with his own eyes, that there really was a certain evidence for Mr Cave's statements, he proceeded to develop the matter systematically. Mr Cave was only too eager to come and feast his eyes on this wonderland he saw, and he came every night from half-past eight until half-past ten, and sometimes, in Mr Wace's absence, during the day. On Sunday afternoons, also he came. From the outset Mr Wace made copious notes, and it was due to his scientific method that the relation between the direction from which the initiating ray entered the crystal and the orientation of the picture were proved. And, by covering the crystal in a box perforated only with a small aperture to admit the exciting ray, and by substituting black holland for his buff blinds, he greatly improved the conditions of the observations; so that in a little while they were able to survey the valley in any direction they desired.

So, having cleared the way, we may give a brief account of this visionary world within the crystal. The things were in all cases seen by Mr Cave, and the method of working was invariably for him to watch the crystal and report what he saw, while Mr Wace (who as a science student had learnt the trick of writing in the dark) wrote a brief note of his report. When the crystal faded, it was put into its box in the proper position and the electric light turned on. Mr Wace asked questions, and suggested observations to clear up difficult points. Nothing, indeed, could have been less visionary and more matter-of-fact.

The attention of Mr Cave had been speedily directed to the birdlike creatures he had seen so abundantly present in each of his earlier visions. His first impression was soon corrected, and he considered for a time that they might represent a diurnal species of bat. Then he thought, grotesquely enough, that they might be cherubs. Their heads were round, and curiously human, and it was the eyes of one of them that had so startled him on his second observation. They had broad, silvery wings, not feathered, but glistening almost as brilliantly as new-killed fish and with the same subtle play of colour, and these wings were not built on the plan of a bird-wing or bat, Mr Wace learned, but supported by curved ribs radiating from the body. (A sort of butterfly wing with curved ribs seems best to express their appearance.) The body was small, but fitted with two bunches of prehensile organs, like long tentacles, immediately under the mouth. Incredible as it appeared to Mr Wace, the persuasion at last became irresistible, that it was these creatures which owned the great quasi-human buildings and the magnificent garden that made the broad valley so splendid. And Mr Cave perceived that the buildings, with other peculiarities, had no doors, but that the great circular windows, which opened freely, gave the creatures egress and entrance. They would alight upon their tentacles, fold their wings to a smallness almost rodlike, and hop into the interior. But among them was a multitude of smaller-winged creatures, like great dragonflies and moths and flying beetles, and across the greensward brilliantly coloured gigantic ground-beetles crawled lazily to and fro. Moreover, on the causeways and terraces, large-headed creatures similar to the greater winged flies, but wingless, were visible, hopping busily upon their hand-like tangle of tentacles.

Allusion has already been made to the glittering objects upon masts that stood upon the terrace of the nearer building. It dawned upon Mr Cave, after regarding one of these masts very fixedly on one particularly vivid day, that the glittering object there was a crystal exactly like that into which he peered. And a still more careful scrutiny convinced him that each one in a vista of nearly twenty carried a similar object.

Occasionally one of the large flying creatures would flutter up to one, and folding its wings and coiling a number of its tentacles about the mast, would regard the crystal fixedly for a space – sometimes for as long as fifteen minutes. And a series of observations, made at the suggestion of Mr Wace, convinced both watchers that, so far as this visionary world was concerned, the crystal into which they peered actually stood at the summit of the end-most mast on the terrace, and that on one occasion at least one of these inhabitants of this other world had looked into Mr Cave's face while he was making these observations.

So much for the essential facts of this very singular story. Unless we dismiss it all as the ingenious fabrication of Mr Wace, we have to believe one of two things: either that Mr Cave's crystal was in two worlds at once, and that, while it was carried about in one, it remained stationary in the other, which seems altogether absurd; or else that it had some peculiar relation of sympathy with another and exactly similar crystal in this other world, so that what was seen in the interior of the one in this world was, under suitable conditions, visible to an observer in the corresponding crystal in the other world; and vice versa. At present, indeed, we do not know of any way in which two crystals could so come *en rapport*,[12] but nowadays we know enough to understand that the thing is not altogether impossible. This view of the crystals as *en rapport* was the supposition that occurred to Mr Wace, and to me at least it seems extremely plausible . . .

And where was this other world? On this, also, the alert intelligence of Mr Wace speedily threw light. After sunset, the sky darkened rapidly – there was a very brief twilight interval indeed – and the stars shone out. They were recognisably the same as those we see, arranged in the same constellations. Mr Cave recognised the Bear, the Pleiades,

Aldebaran and Sirius: so that the other world must be somewhere in the solar system, and, at the utmost, only a few hundreds of millions of miles from our own. Following up this clue, Mr Wace learned that the midnight sky was a darker blue even than our midwinter sky, and that the sun seemed a little smaller. *And there were two small moons!* [13] – 'like our moon but smaller, and quite differently marked' – one of which moved so rapidly that its motion was clearly visible as one regarded it. These moons were never high in the sky, but vanished as they rose; that is, every time they revolved they were eclipsed because they were so near their primary planet. And all this answers quite completely although, Mr Cave did not know it, to what must be the condition of things on Mars.

Indeed, it seems an exceedingly plausible conclusion that peering into this crystal Mr Cave did actually see the planet Mars and its inhabitants. And, if that was the case, then the evening star that shone so brilliantly in the sky of that distant vision was neither more nor less than our own familiar earth.

For a time the Martians – if they were Martians – do not seem to have known of Mr Cave's inspection. Once or twice one would come to peer, and go away very shortly to some other mast, as though the vision was unsatisfactory. During this time Mr Cave was able to watch the proceedings of these winged people without being disturbed by their attentions, and although his report is necessarily vague and fragmentary, it is nevertheless very suggestive. Imagine the impression of humanity a Martian observer would get who, after a difficult process of preparation and with considerable fatigue to the eyes, was able to peer at London from the steeple of St Martin's Church[14] for stretches, at longest, of four minutes at a time. Mr Cave was unable to ascertain if the winged Martians were the same as the Martians who hopped about the causeways and terraces, and if the latter could put on wings at will. He several times saw certain clumsy bipeds, dimly suggestive of apes, white and partially translucent, feeding among certain of the lichenous trees, and once some of these fled before one of the hopping, round-headed Martians. The latter caught one in its tentacles, and then the picture faded suddenly and left Mr Cave most tantalisingly in the dark. On another occasion a vast thing, that Mr Cave thought at first was some gigantic insect, appeared advancing along the causeway beside the canal with extraordinary rapidity. As this drew nearer Mr Cave perceived that it was a mechanism of shining metals and of extraordinary complexity. And then, when he looked again, it had passed out of sight.

After a time Mr Wace aspired to attract the attention of the Martians, and the next time that the strange eyes of one of them appeared close to the crystal Mr Cave cried out and sprang away, and they immediately turned on the light and began to gesticulate in a manner suggestive of signalling. But when at last Mr Cave examined the crystal again the Martian had departed.

Thus far these observations had progressed in early November, and then Mr Cave, feeling that the suspicions of his family about the crystal were allayed, began to take it to and fro with him in order that, as occasion arose in the daytime or night, he might comfort himself with what was fast becoming the most real thing in his existence.

In December, Mr Wace's work in connection with a forthcoming examination became heavy, the sittings were reluctantly suspended for a week, and for ten or eleven days – he is not quite sure which – he saw nothing of Cave. He then grew anxious to resume these investigations, and the stress of his seasonal labours being abated, he went down to Seven Dials. At the corner he noticed a shutter before a bird fancier's window, and then another at a cobbler's. Mr Cave's shop was closed.

He rapped and the door was opened by the stepson in black. He at once called Mrs Cave, who was, Mr Wace could not but observe, in cheap but ample widow's weeds of the most imposing pattern. Without any very great surprise Mr Wace learnt that Cave was dead and already buried. She was in tears, and her voice was a little thick. She had just returned from Highgate. Her mind seemed occupied with her own prospects and the honourable details of the obsequies, but Mr Wace was at last able to learn the particulars of Cave's death. He had been found dead in his shop in the early morning, the day after his last visit to Mr Wace, and the crystal had been clasped in his stone-cold hands. His face was smiling, said Mrs Cave, and the velvet cloth from the minerals lay on the floor at his feet. He must have been dead five or six hours when he was found.

This came as a great shock to Wace, and he began to reproach himself bitterly for having neglected the plain symptoms of the old man's ill-health. But his chief thought was of the crystal. He approached that topic in a gingerly manner, because he knew Mrs Cave's peculiarities. He was dumbfounded to learn that it was sold.

Mrs Cave's first impulse, directly Cave's body had been taken upstairs, had been to write to the mad clergyman who had offered five pounds for the crystal, informing him of its recovery; but after a violent hunt in which her daughter joined her, they were convinced of the loss of his address. As they were without the means required to mourn and bury Cave in the elaborate style the dignity of an old Seven Dials inhabitant demands, they had appealed to a friendly fellow-tradesman in Great Portland Street. He had very kindly taken over a portion of the stock at a valuation. The valuation was his own and the crystal egg was included in one of the lots. Mr Wace, after a few suitable consolatory observations, a little off-handedly proffered perhaps, hurried at once to Great Portland Street. But there he learned that the crystal egg had already been sold to a tall, dark man in grey. And there the material facts in this curious and, to me at least, very suggestive story come abruptly to an end. The Great Portland Street dealer did not know who the tall dark man in grey was, nor had he observed him with sufficient attention to describe him minutely. He did not even know which way this person had gone after leaving the shop. For a time Mr Wace remained in the shop, trying the dealer's patience with hopeless questions, venting his own exasperation. And, at last, realising abruptly that the whole thing had passed out of his hands, had vanished like a vision of the night, he returned to his own rooms, a little astonished to find the notes he had made still tangible and visible upon his untidy table.

His annoyance and disappointment were naturally very great. He made a second call (equally ineffectual) upon the Great Portland Street dealer, and he resorted to advertisements in such periodicals as were likely to come into the hands of a bric-à-brac collector. He also wrote letters to the *Daily Chronicle* and *Nature*,[15] but both those periodicals, suspecting a hoax, asked him to reconsider his action before they printed, and he was advised that such a strange story, unfortunately so bare of supporting evidence, might imperil his reputation as an investigator. Moreover, the calls of his proper work were urgent. So that after a month or so, save for an occasional reminder to certain dealers, he had reluctantly to abandon the quest for the crystal egg, and from that day to this it remains undiscovered. Occasionally however, he tells me, and I can quite believe him, he has bursts of zeal, in which he abandons his more urgent occupation and resumes the search.

Whether or not it will remain lost for ever, with the material and origin of it, are things equally speculative at the present time. If the present purchaser is a collector, one would have expected the enquiries of Mr Wace to have reached him through the dealers. He has been able to discover Mr Cave's clergyman and 'Oriental' – no other than the Revd James Parker and the young Prince of Bosso-Kuni in Java. I am obliged to them for certain particulars. The object of the prince was simply curiosity – and extravagance. He was so eager to buy because Cave was so oddly reluctant to sell. It is just as possible that the buyer in the second instance was simply a casual purchaser and not a collector at all, and the crystal egg, for all I know, may at the present moment be within a mile of me, decorating a drawing-room or serving as a paperweight – its remarkable functions all unknown. Indeed, it is partly with the idea of such a possibility that I have thrown this narrative into a form that will give it a chance of being read by the ordinary consumer of fiction.

My own ideas in the matter are practically identical with those of Mr Wace. I believe the crystal on the mast in Mars and the crystal egg of Mr Cave's to be in some physical, but at present quite inexplicable, way *en rapport*, and we both believe further that the terrestrial crystal must have been – possibly at some remote date – sent hither from that planet, in order to give the Martians a near view of our affairs. Possibly the fellows to the crystals on the other masts are also on our globe. No theory of hallucination suffices for the facts.

The Cone[16]

The night was hot and overcast, the sky red, rimmed with the lingering sunset of midsummer. They sat at the open window, trying to fancy the air was fresher there. The trees and shrubs of the garden stood stiff and dark; beyond in the roadway a gas-lamp burnt, bright orange against the hazy blue of the evening. Farther were the three lights of the railway signal against the lowering sky. The man and woman spoke to one another in low tones.

'He does not suspect?' said the man, a little nervously.

'Not he,' she said peevishly, as though that too irritated her. 'He thinks of nothing but the works and the prices of fuel. He has no imagination, no poetry.'

'None of these men of iron have,' he said sententiously. 'They have no hearts.'

'He has not,' she said. She turned her discontented face towards the window. The distant sound of a roaring and rushing drew nearer and grew in volume; the house quivered; one heard the metallic rattle of the tender. As the train passed, there was a glare of light above the cutting and a driving tumult of smoke; one, two, three, four, five, six, seven, eight black oblongs – eight trucks – passed across the dim grey of the embankment, and were suddenly extinguished one by one in the throat of the tunnel, which, with the last, seemed to swallow down train, smoke and sound in one abrupt gulp.

'This country was all fresh and beautiful once,' he said; 'and now – it is Gehenna.[17] Down that way – nothing but pot-banks and chimneys belching fire and dust into the face of heaven . . . But what does it matter? An end comes, an end to all this cruelty . . . *Tomorrow*.' He spoke the last word in a whisper.

'*Tomorrow*,' she said, speaking in a whisper too, and still staring out of the window.

'Dear!' he said, putting his hand on hers.

She turned with a start, and their eyes searched one another's. Hers softened to his gaze. 'My dear one!' she said, and then: 'It seems so strange – that you should have come into my life like this – to open – ' She paused.

'To open?' he said.

'All this wonderful world – ' she hesitated, and spoke still more softly – 'this world of *love* to me.'

Then suddenly the door clicked and closed. They turned their heads, and he started violently back. In the shadow of the room stood a great shadowy figure – silent. They saw the face dimly in the half-light, with unexpressive dark patches under the penthouse brows.[18] Every muscle in Raut's body suddenly became tense. When could the door have opened? What had he heard? Had he heard all? What had he seen? A tumult of questions.

The newcomer's voice came at last, after a pause that seemed interminable. 'Well?' he said.

'I was afraid I had missed you, Horrocks,' said the man at the window, gripping the window-ledge with his hand. His voice was unsteady.

The clumsy figure of Horrocks came forward out of the shadow. He made no answer to Raut's remark. For a moment he stood above them.

The woman's heart was cold within her. 'I told Mr Raut it was just possible you might come back,' she said, in a voice that never quivered.

Horrocks, still silent, sat down abruptly in the chair by her little work-table. His big hands were clenched; one saw now the fire of his eyes under the shadow of his brows. He was trying to get his breath. His eyes went from the woman he had trusted to the friend he had trusted, and then back to the woman.

By this time and for the moment all three half understood one another. Yet none dared say a word to ease the pent-up things that choked them.

It was the husband's voice that broke the silence at last.

'You wanted to see me?' he said to Raut.

Raut started as he spoke. 'I came to see you,' he said, resolved to lie to the last.

'Yes,' said Horrocks.

'You promised,' said Raut, 'to show me some fine effects of moonlight and smoke.'

'I promised to show you some fine effects of moonlight and smoke,' repeated Horrocks in a colourless voice.

'And I thought I might catch you tonight before you went down to the works,' proceeded Raut, 'and come with you.'

There was another pause. Did the man mean to take the thing coolly? Did he after all know? How long had he been in the room? Yet even at the moment when they heard the door, their attitudes . . . Horrocks glanced at the profile of the woman, shadowy pallid in the half-light. Then he glanced at Raut, and seemed to recover himself suddenly. 'Of course,' he said, 'I promised to show you the works under their proper dramatic conditions. It's odd how I could have forgotten.'

'If I am troubling you – ' began Raut.

Horrocks started again. A new light had suddenly come into the sultry gloom of his eyes. 'Not in the least,' he said.

'Have you been telling Mr Raut of all these contrasts of flame and shadow you think so splendid?' said the woman, turning now to her husband for the first time, her confidence creeping back again, her voice just one half-note too high. 'That dreadful theory of yours that machinery is beautiful, and everything else in the world ugly. I thought he would not spare you, Mr Raut. It's his great theory, his one discovery in art.'

'I am slow to make discoveries,' said Horrocks grimly, damping her suddenly. 'But what I discover . . . ' He stopped.

'Well?' she said.

'Nothing;' and suddenly he rose to his feet.

'I promised to show you the works,' he said to Raut, and put his big, clumsy hand on his friend's shoulder. 'And you are ready to go?'

'Quite,' said Raut, and stood up also.

There was another pause. Each of them peered through the indistinctness of the dusk at the other two. Horrocks's hand still rested on Raut's shoulder. Raut half fancied still that the incident was trivial after all. But Mrs Horrocks knew her husband better, knew that grim quiet in his voice, and the confusion in her mind took a vague shape of physical evil. 'Very well,' said Horrocks, and dropping his hand, turned towards the door.

'My hat?' Raut looked round in the half-light.

'That's my workbasket,' said Mrs Horrocks, with a gust of hysterical laughter. Their hands came together on the back of the chair. 'Here it is!' he said. She had an impulse to warn him in an undertone, but she could not frame a word. 'Don't go!' and 'Beware of him!' struggled in her mind, and the swift moment passed.

'Got it?' said Horrocks, standing with the door half open.

Raut stepped towards him. 'Better say goodbye to Mrs Horrocks,' said the ironmaster, even more grimly quiet in his tone than before.

Raut started and turned. 'Good-evening, Mrs Horrocks,' he said, and their hands touched.

Horrocks held the door open with a ceremonial politeness unusual in him towards men. Raut went out, and then, after a wordless look at her, her husband followed. She stood motionless while Raut's light footfall and her husband's heavy tread, like bass and treble, passed down the passage together. The front door slammed heavily. She went to the window, moving slowly, and stood watching – leaning forward. The two men appeared for a moment at the gateway in the road, passed under the street-lamp, and were hidden by the black masses of the shrubbery. The lamplight fell for a moment on their faces, showing only unmeaning pale patches, telling nothing of what she still feared, and doubted, and craved vainly to know. Then she sank down into a crouching attitude in the big armchair, her eyes wide open and staring out at the red lights from the furnaces that flickered in the sky. An hour after she was still there, her attitude scarcely changed.

The oppressive stillness of the evening weighed heavily upon Raut. They went side by side down the road in silence, and in silence turned into the cinder-made byway that presently opened out the prospect of the valley.

A blue haze, half dust, half mist, touched the long valley with mystery. Beyond were Hanley and Etruria,[19] grey and dark masses, outlined thinly by the rare golden dots of the street-lamps, and here and there a gaslit window, or the yellow glare of some late-working factory or crowded public-house. Out of the masses, clear and slender against the evening sky, rose a multitude of tall chimneys, many of them reeking,[20] a few smokeless during a season of 'play'. Here and there a pallid patch and ghostly stunted beehive shapes showed the position of a pot-bank, or a wheel, black and sharp against the hot lower sky, marked some colliery where they raised the iridescent coal of the place. Nearer at hand was the broad stretch of railway, and half-invisible trains shunted – a steady puffing and rumbling, with every now and then a ringing concussion and a rhythmic series of impacts, and a passage of intermittent puffs of white steam across the farther view. And to the left, between the railway and the dark mass of the low hill beyond, dominating the whole view, colossal, inky-black, and crowned with smoke and fitful flames, stood the great cylinders of the Jeddah Company Blast Furnaces, the central edifices of the big ironworks of which Horrocks was the manager. They stood heavy and threatening, full of an incessant turmoil of flames and seething molten iron, and about the feet of them rattled the rolling-mills, and the steam-hammer beat heavily and splashed the white iron sparks hither and thither. Even as they looked, a truckful of fuel was shot into one of the giants, and the red flames gleamed out, and a confusion of smoke and black dust came boiling upwards towards the sky.

'Certainly you get some fine effects of colour with your furnaces,' said Raut, breaking a silence that had become apprehensive.

Horrocks grunted. He stood with his hands in his pockets, frowning down at the dim steaming railway and the busy ironworks beyond, frowning as if he were thinking out some knotty problem.

Raut glanced at him and away again. 'At present your moonlight effect is hardly ripe,' he continued, looking upward. 'The moon is still smothered by the vestiges of daylight.'

Horrocks stared at him with the expression of a man who has suddenly awakened. 'Vestiges of daylight . . . ? Of course, of course.' He too looked up at the moon, pale still in the midsummer sky. 'Come along,' he said suddenly, and gripping Raut's arm in his hand, made a move towards the path that dropped from them to the railway.

Raut hung back. Their eyes met and saw a thousand things in a moment that their lips came near to say. Horrocks's hand tightened and then relaxed. He let go, and before Raut was aware of it, they were arm in arm, and walking, one unwillingly enough, down the path.

'You see the fine effect of the railway signals towards Burslem,'[21] said Horrocks, suddenly breaking into loquacity, striding fast, and tightening the grip of his elbow the while. 'Little green lights and red and white lights, all against the haze. You have an eye for effect, Raut. It's a fine effect. And look at those furnaces of mine, how they rise upon us as we come down the hill. That to the right is my pet – seventy feet of him. I packed him myself, and he's boiled away cheerfully with iron in his guts for five long years. I've a particular fancy for *him*. That line of red there – a lovely bit of warm orange you'd call it, Raut – that's the puddlers'[22] furnaces, and there, in the hot light, three black figures – did you see the white splash of the steam-hammer then – ? That's the rolling mills. Come along! Clang, clatter, how it goes rattling across the floor! Sheet tin, Raut – amazing stuff. Glass mirrors are not in it when that stuff comes from the mill. And squelch – ! There goes the hammer again. Come along!'

He had to stop talking to catch at his breath. His arm twisted into Raut's with benumbing tightness. He had come striding down the black path towards the railway as though he was possessed.

Raut had not spoken a word, had simply hung back against Horrocks's pull with all his strength.

'I say,' he said now, laughing nervously, but with an undernote of snarl in his voice, 'why on earth are you nipping my arm off, Horrocks, and dragging me along like this?'

At length Horrocks released him. His manner changed again. 'Nipping your arm off?' he said. 'Sorry. But it's you taught me the trick of walking in that friendly way.'

'You haven't learnt the refinements of it yet then,' said Raut, laughing artificially again. 'By Jove! I'm black and blue.' Horrocks offered no apology. They stood now near the bottom of the hill, close to the fence that bordered the railway. The ironworks had grown larger and spread out with their approach. They looked up to the blast furnaces now instead of down; the further view of Etruria and Hanley had dropped out of sight with their descent. Before them, by the stile, rose a notice-board, bearing still dimly visible the words BEWARE OF THE TRAINS, half hidden by splashes of coaly mud.

'Fine effects,' said Horrocks, waving his arm. 'Here comes a train. The puffs of smoke, the orange glare, the round eye of light in front of it, the melodious rattle. Fine effects! But these furnaces of mine used to be finer, before we shoved cones in their throats, and saved the gas.'

'How?' said Raut. 'Cones?'

'Cones, my man, cones. I'll show you one nearer. The flames used to flare out of the open throats, great – what is it – ? Pillars of cloud by day, red and black smoke, and pillars of fire by night.[23] Now we run it off in pipes, and burn it to heat the blast, and the top is shut by a cone. You'll be interested in that cone.'

'But every now and then,' said Raut, 'you get a burst of fire and smoke up there.'

'The cone's not fixed, it's hung by a chain from a lever, and balanced by an equipoise. You shall see it nearer. Else of course, there'd be no way of getting fuel into the thing. Every now and then the cone dips, and out comes the flare.'

'I see,' said Raut. He looked over his shoulder. 'The moon gets brighter,' he said.

'Come along,' said Horrocks abruptly, gripping his shoulder again, and moving him suddenly towards the railway crossing. And then came one of those swift incidents, vivid, but so rapid that they leave one doubtful and reeling. Halfway across, Horrocks's hand suddenly clenched upon him like a vice, and swung him backward and through a half-turn, so that he looked up the line. And there a chain of lamp-lit carriage-windows telescoped swiftly as it came towards them, and the red and yellow lights of an engine grew larger and larger, rushing down upon them. As he grasped what this meant, he turned his face to Horrocks, and pushed with all his strength against the arm that held him back between the rails. The struggle did not last a moment. Just as certain as it was that Horrocks held him there, so certain was it that he had been violently lugged out of danger.

'Out of the way,' said Horrocks, with a gasp, as the train came rattling by, and they stood panting by the gate into the ironworks.

'I did not see it coming,' said Raut, still, even in spite of his own apprehensions, trying to keep up an appearance of ordinary intercourse.

Horrocks answered with a grunt. 'The cone,' he said, and then, as one who recovers himself, 'I thought you did not hear.'

'I didn't,' said Raut.

'I wouldn't have had you run over then for the world,' said Horrocks.

'For a moment I lost my nerve,' said Raut.

Horrocks stood for half a minute, then turned abruptly towards the ironworks again. 'See how fine these great mounds of mine, these clinker-heaps, look in the night! That truck yonder, up above there! Up it goes, and out-tilts the slag. See the palpitating red stuff go sliding down the slope. As we get nearer, the heap rises up and cuts the blast furnaces. See the quiver up above the big one. Not that way! This way, between the heaps. That goes to the puddling furnaces, but I want to show you the canal first.' He came and took Raut by the elbow, and so they went along side by side. Raut answered Horrocks vaguely. What, he asked himself, had really happened on the line? Was he deluding himself with his own fancies, or had Horrocks actually held him back in the way of the train? Had he just been within an ace of being murdered?

Suppose this slouching, scowling monster *did* know anything? For a minute or two then Raut was really afraid for his life, but the mood passed as he reasoned with himself. After all, Horrocks might have heard nothing. At any rate, he had pulled him out of the way in time. His odd manner might be due to the mere vague jealousy he had shown once before. He was talking now of the ash-heaps and the canal. 'Eigh?' said Horrocks.

'What?' said Raut. 'Rather! The haze in the moonlight. Fine!'

'Our canal,' said Horrocks, stopping suddenly. 'Our canal by moon-light and firelight is an immense effect. You've never seen it? Fancy that! You've spent too many of your evenings philandering up in New-castle there. I tell you, for real florid effects – But you shall see. Boiling water . . .'

As they came out of the labyrinth of clinker-heaps and mounds of coal and ore, the noises of the rolling-mill sprang upon them suddenly, loud, near and distinct. Three shadowy workmen went by and touched their caps to Horrocks. Their faces were vague in the darkness. Raut felt a futile impulse to address them, but before he could frame his words they passed into the shadows. Horrocks pointed to the canal close before them now: a weird-looking place it seemed, in the blood-red reflections of the furnaces. The hot water that cooled the tuyères [24] came into it, some fifty yards up – a tumultuous, almost boiling effluent, and the steam rose up from the water in silent white wisps and streaks, wrapping damply about them, an incessant succession of ghosts coming up from the black and red eddies, a white uprising that made the head swim. The shining black tower of the larger blast-furnace rose overhead out of the mist, and its tumultuous riot filled their ears. Raut kept away from the edge of the water, and watched Horrocks.

'Here it is red,' said Horrocks, 'blood-red vapour as red and hot as sin; but yonder there, where the moonlight falls on it and it drives across the clinker-heaps, it is as white as death.'

Raut turned his head for a moment, and then came back hastily to his watch on Horrocks. 'Come along to the rolling-mills,' said Horrocks. The threatening hold was not so evident this time, and Raut felt a little reassured. But all the same, what on earth did Horrocks mean about 'white as death' and 'red as sin'? Coincidence, perhaps?

They went and stood behind the puddlers for a little while, and then through the rolling-mills, where amidst an incessant din the deliberate steam-hammer beat the juice out of the succulent iron, and black, half-naked Titans rushed the plastic bars, like hot sealing-wax, between the wheels. 'Come on,' said Horrocks in Raut's ear, and they went and peeped through the little glass hole behind the tuyères, and saw the tumbled fire writhing in the pit of the blast-furnace. It left one eye blinded for a while. Then, with green and blue patches dancing across the dark, they went to the lift by which the trucks of ore and fuel and lime were raised to the top of the big cylinder.

And out upon the narrow rail that overhung the furnace, Raut's doubts came upon him again. Was it wise to be here? If Horrocks did know – everything! Do what he would, he could not resist a violent trembling. Right under foot was a sheer depth of seventy feet. It was a dangerous place. They pushed by a truck of fuel to get to the railing that crowned the place. The reek of the furnace, a sulphurous vapour streaked with pungent bitterness, seemed to make the distant hillside of Hanley quiver. The moon was riding out now from among a drift of clouds, halfway up the sky above the undulating wooded outlines of Newcastle.[25] The steaming canal ran away from below them under an indistinct bridge, and vanished into the dim haze of the flat fields towards Burslem.

'That's the cone I've been telling you of,' shouted Horrocks; 'and, below that, sixty feet of fire and molten metal, with the air of the blast frothing through it like gas in soda-water.'

Raut gripped the handrail tightly, and stared down at the cone. The heat was intense. The boiling of the iron and the tumult of the blast made a thunderous accompaniment to Horrocks's voice. But the thing had to be gone through now. Perhaps, after all . . .

'In the middle,' bawled Horrocks, 'temperature near a thousand degrees. If *you* were dropped into it . . . flash into flame like a pinch of gunpowder in a candle. Put your hand out and feel the heat of his breath. Why, even up here I've seen the rainwater boiling off the trucks. And that cone there. It's a damned sight too hot for roasting cakes. The top side of it's three hundred degrees.'

'Three hundred degrees!' said Raut.

'Three hundred centigrade, mind!' said Horrocks. 'It will boil the blood out of you in no time.'

'Eigh?' said Raut, and turned.

'Boil the blood out of you in . . . No, you don't!'

'Let me go!' screamed Raut. 'Let go my arm!'

With one hand he clutched at the handrail, then with both. For a moment the two men stood swaying. Then suddenly, with a violent jerk, Horrocks had twisted him from his hold. He clutched at Horrocks and missed, his foot went back into empty air; in mid-air he twisted himself, and then cheek and shoulder and knee struck the hot cone together.

He clutched the chain by which the cone hung, and the thing sank an infinitesimal amount as he struck it. A circle of glowing red appeared about him, and a tongue of flame, released from the chaos within, flickered up towards him. An intense pain assailed him at the knees, and he could smell the singeing of his hands. He raised himself to his feet, and tried to climb up the chain, and then something struck his head. Black and shining with the moonlight, the throat of the furnace rose about him.

Horrocks, he saw, stood above him by one of the trucks of fuel on the rail. The gesticulating figure was bright and white in the moonlight, and shouting, 'Fizzle, you fool! Fizzle, you hunter of women! You hot-blooded hound! Boil! Boil! Boil!'

Suddenly he caught up a handful of coal out of the truck, and flung it deliberately, lump after lump, at Raut.

'Horrocks!' cried Raut. 'Horrocks!'

He clung crying to the chain, pulling himself up from the burning of the cone. Each missile Horrocks flung hit him. His clothes charred and glowed, and as he struggled the cone dropped, and a rush of hot suffocating gas whooped out and burned round him in a swift breath of flame.

His human likeness departed from him. When the momentary red had passed, Horrocks saw a charred, blackened figure, its head streaked with blood, still clutching and fumbling with the chain, and writhing in agony – a cindery animal, an inhuman, monstrous creature that began a sobbing intermittent shriek.

Abruptly, at the sight, the ironmaster's anger passed. A deadly sickness came upon him. The heavy odour of burning flesh came drifting up to his nostrils. His sanity returned to him.

'God have mercy upon me!' he cried. 'O God! What have I done?'

He knew the thing below him, save that it still moved and felt, was already a dead man – that the blood of the poor wretch must be boiling in his veins. An intense realisation of that agony came to his mind, and overcame every other feeling. For a moment he stood irresolute, and then, turning to the truck, he hastily tilted its contents upon the struggling thing that had once been a man. The mass fell with a thud, and went radiating over the cone. With the thud the shriek ended, and a boiling confusion of smoke, dust, and flame came rushing up towards him. As it passed, he saw the cone clear again.

Then he staggered back, and stood trembling, clinging to the rail with both hands. His lips moved, but no words came to them.

Down below was the sound of voices and running steps. The clangour of rolling in the shed ceased abruptly.

The Country of the Blind[26]

Three hundred miles and more from Chimborazo, one hundred from the snows of Cotopaxi,[27] in the wildest wastes of Ecuador's Andes, there lies that mysterious mountain valley, cut off from all the world of men, the Country of the Blind. Long years ago that valley lay so far open to the world that men might come at last through frightful gorges and over an icy pass into its equable meadows, and thither indeed men came, a family or so of Peruvian half-breeds fleeing from the lust and tyranny of an evil Spanish ruler. Then came the stupendous outbreak of Mindobamba,[28] when it was night in Quito for seventeen days, and the water was boiling at Yaguachi and all the fish floating dying even as far as Guayaquil;[29] everywhere along the Pacific slopes there were landslips and swift thawings and sudden floods, and one whole side of the old Arauca[30] crest slipped and came down in thunder, and cut off the Country of the Blind for ever from the exploring feet of men. But one of these early settlers had chanced to be on the hither side of the gorges when the world had so terribly shaken itself, and he perforce had to forget his wife and his child and all the friends and possessions he had left up there, and start life over again in the lower world. He started it again but ill, blindness overtook him, and he died of punishment in the mines; but the story he told begot a legend that lingers along the length of the Cordilleras[31] of the Andes to this day.

He told of his reason for venturing back from that fastness, into which he had first been carried lashed to a llama, beside a vast bale of gear, when he was a child. The valley, he said, had in it all that the heart of man could desire – sweet water, pasture, an even climate, slopes of rich brown soil with tangles of a shrub that bore an excellent fruit, and on one side great hanging forests of pine that held the avalanches high. Far overhead, on three sides, vast cliffs of grey-green rock were capped by cliffs of ice; but the glacier stream came not to them, but flowed away by the farther slopes, and only now and then huge ice masses fell on the valley side. In this valley it neither rained nor snowed, but the abundant springs gave a rich green pasture, that irrigation would spread over all the valley space. The settlers did well indeed there. Their beasts did well and multiplied, and but one thing marred their happiness. Yet it was enough to mar it greatly. A strange disease had come upon them and had made all the children born to them there – and indeed, several older children also – blind. It was to seek some charm or antidote against this plague of blindness that he had with fatigue and danger and difficulty returned down the gorge. In those days, in such cases, men did not think of germs and infections, but of sins, and it seemed to him that the reason for this affliction must lie in the negligence of these priestless immigrants to set up a shrine so soon as they entered the valley. He wanted a shrine – a handsome, cheap, effectual shrine – to be erected in the valley; he wanted relics and suchlike potent things of faith, blessed objects and mysterious medals and prayers. In his wallet he had a bar of native silver for which he would not account; he insisted there was none in the valley with something of the insistence of an inexpert liar. They had all clubbed their money and ornaments together, having little need for such treasure up there, he said, to buy them holy help against their ill. I figure this dim-eyed young mountaineer, sunburnt, gaunt and anxious, hat brim clutched feverishly, a man all unused to the ways of the lower world, telling this story to some keen-eyed, attentive priest before the great convulsion; I can picture him presently seeking to return with pious and infallible remedies against that trouble, and the infinite dismay with which he must have faced the tumbled vastness where the gorge had once come out. But the rest of his story of mischances is lost to me, save that I know of his evil death after several years. Poor stray from that remoteness! The stream that had once made the gorge now bursts from the mouth of a rocky cave, and the legend his poor, ill-told story set going developed into the legend of a race of blind men somewhere 'over there' one may still hear today.

And amidst the little population of that now isolated and forgotten valley the disease ran its course. The old became groping, the young saw but dimly, and the children that were born to them never saw at all. But life was very easy in that snow-rimmed basin, lost to all the world, with neither thorns nor briers, with no evil insects nor any beasts save the gentle breed of llamas they had lugged and thrust and followed up the beds of the shrunken rivers in the gorges up which they had come. The seeing had become purblind so gradually that they scarcely noticed their loss. They guided the sightless youngsters hither and thither until they knew the whole valley marvellously, and when at last sight died out among them the race lived on. They had even time to adapt themselves to the blind control of fire, which they made carefully in stoves of stone. They were a simple strain of people at the first, unlettered, only slightly touched with the Spanish civilisation, but with something of a tradition of the arts of old Peru[32] and of its lost philosophy. Generation followed generation. They forgot many things; they devised many things. Their tradition of the greater world they came from became mythical in colour and uncertain. In all things save sight they were strong and able, and presently chance sent one who had an original mind and who could talk and persuade among them, and then afterwards another. These two passed, leaving their effects, and the little community grew in numbers and in understanding, and met and settled social and economic problems that arose. Generation followed generation. Generation followed generation. There came a time when a child was born who was fifteen generations from that ancestor who went out of the valley with a bar of silver to seek God's aid, and who never returned. Thereabout it chanced that a man came into this community from the outer world. And this is the story of that man.

He was a mountaineer from the country near Quito, a man who had been down to the sea and had seen the world, a reader of books in an original way, an acute and enterprising man, and he was taken on by a party of Englishmen who had come out to Ecuador to climb mountains, to replace one of their three Swiss guides who had fallen ill. He climbed here and he climbed there, and then came the attempt on Parascotopetl, the Matterhorn of the Andes,[33] in which he was lost to the outer world. The story of that accident has been written a dozen times. Pointer's narrative is the best. He tells how the little party worked their difficult and almost vertical way up to the very foot of the last and greatest precipice, and how they built a night shelter amidst the snow upon a little shelf of rock, and, with a touch of real dramatic power, how presently they found Nunez had gone from them. They shouted, and there was no reply; shouted and whistled, and for the rest of that night they slept no more.

As the morning broke they saw the traces of his fall. It seems impossible he could have uttered a sound. He had slipped eastward towards the unknown side of the mountain; far below he had struck a steep slope of snow, and ploughed his way down it in the midst of a snow avalanche. His track went straight to the edge of a frightful precipice, and beyond that everything was hidden. Far, far below, and hazy with distance, they could see trees rising out of a narrow, shut-in valley – the lost Country of the Blind. But they did not know it was the lost Country of the Blind, nor distinguish it in any way from any other narrow streak of upland valley. Unnerved by this disaster, they abandoned their attempt in the afternoon, and Pointer was called away to the war before he could make another attack. To this day

Parascotopetl lifts an unconquered crest, and Pointer's shelter crumbles unvisited amidst the snows.

And the man who fell survived.

At the end of the slope he fell a thousand feet, and came down in the midst of a cloud of snow upon a snow slope even steeper than the one above. Down this he was whirled, stunned and insensible, but without a bone broken in his body; and then at last came to gentler slopes, and at last rolled out and lay still, buried amidst a softening heap of the white masses that had accompanied and saved him. He came to himself with a dim fancy that he was ill in bed; then realised his position with a mountaineer's intelligence and worked himself loose and, after a rest or so, out until he saw the stars. He rested flat upon his chest for a space, wondering where he was and what had happened to him. He explored his limbs, and discovered that several of his buttons were gone and his coat turned over his head. His knife had gone from his pocket and his hat was lost, though he had tied it under his chin. He recalled that he had been looking for loose stones to raise his piece of the shelter wall. His ice-axe had disappeared.

He decided he must have fallen, and looked up to see, exaggerated by the ghastly light of the rising moon, the tremendous flight he had taken. For a while he lay, gazing blankly at the vast, pale cliff towering above, rising moment by moment out of a subsiding tide of darkness. Its phantasmal, mysterious beauty held him for a space, and then he was seized with a paroxysm of sobbing laughter . . .

After a great interval of time he became aware that he was near the lower edge of the snow. Below, down what was now a moonlit and practicable slope, he saw the dark and broken appearance of rock-strewn turf. He struggled to his feet, aching in every joint and limb, got down painfully from the heaped loose snow about him, went downward until he was on the turf, and there dropped rather than lay beside a boulder, drank deep from the flask in his inner pocket, and instantly fell asleep . . .

He was awakened by the singing of birds in the trees far below.

He sat up and perceived he was on a little alp at the foot of a vast precipice that sloped only a little in the gully down which he and his snow had come. Over against him another wall of rock reared itself against the sky. The gorge between these precipices ran east and west and was full of the morning sunlight, which lit to the westward the mass of fallen mountain that closed the descending gorge. Below him it seemed there was a precipice equally steep, but behind the snow in the gully he found a sort of chimney-cleft dripping with snow-water, down which a desperate man might venture. He found it easier than it seemed, and came at last to another desolate alp, and then after a rock climb of no particular difficulty, to a steep slope of trees. He took his bearings and turned his face up the gorge, for he saw it opened out above upon green meadows, among which he now glimpsed quite distinctly a cluster of stone huts of unfamiliar fashion. At times his progress was like clambering along the face of a wall, and after a time the rising sun ceased to strike along the gorge, the voices of the singing birds died away, and the air grew cold and dark about him. But the distant valley with its houses was all the brighter for that. He came presently to talus,[34] and among the rocks he noted – for he was an observant man – an unfamiliar fern that seemed to clutch out of the crevices with intense green hands. He picked a frond or so and gnawed its stalk, and found it helpful.

About midday he came at last out of the throat of the gorge into the plain and the sunlight. He was stiff and weary; he sat down in the shadow of a rock, filled up his flask with water from a spring and drank it down, then remained for a time resting before he went on to the houses.

They were very strange to his eyes, and indeed the whole aspect of that valley became, as he regarded it, queerer and more unfamiliar. The greater part of its surface was lush green meadow, starred with many beautiful flowers, irrigated with extraordinary care, and bearing evidence of systematic cropping piece by piece. High up and ringing the valley about was a wall, and what appeared to be a circumferential water-channel, from which the little trickles of water that fed the meadow plants came, and on the higher slopes above this flocks of llamas cropped the scanty herbage. Sheds, apparently shelters or feeding-places for the llamas, stood against the boundary wall here and there. The irrigation streams ran together into a main channel down the centre of the valley, and this was enclosed on either side by a wall breast high. This gave a singularly urban quality to this secluded place, a quality that was greatly enhanced by the fact that a number of paths paved with black and white stones, and each with a curious little kerb at the side, ran hither and thither in an orderly manner. The houses of the central village were quite unlike the casual and higgledy-piggledy agglomeration of the mountain villages he knew; they stood in a continuous row on either side of a central street of astonishing clean-ness; here and there their parti-coloured façade was pierced by a door, but not a solitary window broke their even frontage. They were parti-coloured with extraordinary irregularity, smeared with a sort of plaster that was sometimes grey, sometimes drab, sometimes slate-coloured or dark brown; and it was the sight of this wild plastering first brought the word 'blind' into the thoughts of the explorer. 'The good man who did that,' he thought, 'must have been as blind as a bat.'

He descended a steep place, and so came to the wall and channel that ran about the valley, near where the latter spouted out its surplus contents into the deeps of the gorge in a thin and wavering thread of cascade. He could now see a number of men and women resting on piled heaps of grass, as if taking a siesta, in the remoter part of the meadow, and nearer the village a number of recumbent children, and then nearer at hand three men carrying pails on yokes along a little path that ran from the encircling wall towards the houses. These latter were clad in garments of llama cloth and boots and belts of leather, and they wore caps of cloth with back and ear flaps. They followed one another in single file, walking slowly and yawning as they walked, like men who have been up all night. There was something so reassuringly prosperous and respectable in their bearing that after a moment's hesitation Nunez stood forward as conspicuously as possible upon his rock and gave vent to a mighty shout that echoed round the valley.

The three men stopped, and moved their heads as though they were looking about them. They turned their faces this way and that, and Nunez gesticulated with freedom. But they did not appear to see him for all his gestures, and after a time, directing themselves towards the mountains far away to the right, they shouted as if in answer. Nunez bawled again, and then once more, and as he gestured ineffectually the word 'blind' came up to the top of his thoughts. 'The fools must be blind,' he said.

When at last, after much shouting and wrath, Nunez crossed the stream by a little bridge, came through a gate in the wall, and approached them, he was sure that they were blind. He was sure that this was the Country of the Blind of which the legends told. Conviction had sprung upon him, and a sense of great and rather enviable adventure. The three stood side by side, not looking at him, but with their ears directed towards him, judging him by his unfamiliar steps. They stood close together like men a little afraid, and he could see their eyelids closed and sunken, as though the very balls beneath had shrunk away. There was an expression near awe on their faces.

'A man,' one said, in hardly recognisable Spanish – 'A man it is – a man or a spirit – coming down from the rocks.'

But Nunez advanced with the confident steps of a youth who enters upon life. All the old stories of the lost valley and the Country of the

Blind had come back to his mind, and through his thoughts ran this old proverb, as if it were a refrain –

> In the Country of the Blind the One-Eyed Man is King.
> In the Country of the Blind the One-Eyed Man is King.[35]

And very civilly he gave them greeting. He talked to them and used his eyes.

'Where does he come from, brother Pedro?' asked one.

'Down out of the rocks.'

'Over the mountains I come,' said Nunez, 'out of the country beyond there – where men can see. From near Bogota,[36] where there are a hundred thousand people, and where the city passes out of sight.'

'Sight?' muttered Pedro. 'Sight?'

'He comes,' said the second blind man, 'out of the rocks.'

The cloth of their coats, Nunez saw, was curiously fashioned, each with a different sort of stitching.

They startled him by a simultaneous movement towards him, each with a hand outstretched. He stepped back from the advance of these spread fingers.

'Come hither,' said the third blind man, following his motion and clutching him neatly.

And they held Nunez and felt him over, saying no word further until they had done so.

'Carefully,' he cried, with a finger in his eye, and found they thought that organ, with its fluttering lids, a queer thing in him. They went over it again.

'A strange creature, Correa,' said the one called Pedro. 'Feel the coarseness of his hair. Like a llama's hair.'

'Rough he is as the rocks that begot him,' said Correa, investigating Nunez's unshaven chin with a soft and slightly moist hand. 'Perhaps he will grow finer.'

Nunez struggled a little under their examination, but they gripped him firm.

'Carefully,' he said again.

'He speaks,' said the third man. 'Certainly he is a man.'

'Ugh!' said Pedro, at the roughness of his coat.

'And you have come into the world?' asked Pedro.

'*Out* of the world. Over mountains and glaciers; right over above there, halfway to the sun. Out of the great, big world that goes down, twelve days' journey, to the sea.'

They scarcely seemed to heed him. 'Our fathers have told us men may be made by the forces of nature,' said Correa. 'It is the warmth of things, and moisture, and rottenness – rottenness.'

'Let us lead him to the elders,' said Pedro.

'Shout first,' said Correa, 'lest the children be afraid. This is a marvellous occasion.'

So they shouted, and Pedro went first and took Nunez by the hand to lead him to the houses.

He drew his hand away. 'I can see,' he said.

'See?' said Correa.

'Yes; see,' said Nunez, turning towards him, and stumbled against Pedro's pail.

'His senses are still imperfect,' said the third blind man. 'He stumbles, and talks unmeaning words. Lead him by the hand.'

'As you will,' said Nunez, and was led along laughing.

It seemed they knew nothing of sight.

Well, all in good time he would teach them.

He heard people shouting, and saw a number of figures gathering together in the middle roadway of the village.

He found it taxed his nerve and patience more than he had anticipated, that first encounter with the population of the Country of the Blind. The place seemed larger as he drew near to it, and the smeared plasterings queerer, and a crowd of children and men and women (the women and girls he was pleased to note had, some of them, quite sweet faces, for all that their eyes were shut and sunken) came about him, holding on to him, touching him with soft, sensitive hands, smelling at him, and listening at every word he spoke. Some of the maidens and children, however, kept aloof as if afraid, and indeed his voice seemed coarse and rude beside their softer notes. They mobbed him. His three guides kept close to him with an effect of proprietorship, and said again and again, 'A wild man out of the rocks.'

'Bogota,' he said. 'Bogota. Over the mountain crests.'

'A wild man – using wild words,' said Pedro. 'Did you hear that – Bogota? His mind has hardly formed yet. He has only the beginnings of speech.'

A little boy nipped his hand. 'Bogota!' he said mockingly.

'Aye! A city to your village. I come from the great world – where men have eyes and see.'

'His name's Bogota,' they said.

'He stumbled,' said Correa, 'stumbled twice as we came hither.'

'Bring him in to the elders.'

And they thrust him suddenly through a doorway into a room as black as pitch, save at the end there faintly glowed a fire. The crowd closed in behind him and shut out all but the faintest glimmer of day, and before he could arrest himself he had fallen headlong over the feet of a seated man. His arm, out-flung, struck the face of someone else as he went down; he felt the soft impact of features and heard a cry of anger, and for a moment he struggled against a number of hands that clutched him. It was a one-sided fight. An inkling of the situation came to him and he lay quiet.

'I fell down,' he said; 'I couldn't see in this pitchy darkness.'

There was a pause as if the unseen persons about him tried to understand his words. Then the voice of Correa said: 'He is but newly formed. He stumbles as he walks and mingles words that mean nothing with his speech.'

Others also said things about him that he heard or understood imperfectly.

'May I sit up?' he asked, in a pause. 'I will not struggle against you again.'

They consulted and let him rise.

The voice of an older man began to question him, and Nunez found himself trying to explain the great world out of which he had fallen, and the sky and mountains and suchlike marvels, to these elders who sat in darkness in the Country of the Blind. And they would believe and understand nothing whatever that he told them, a thing quite outside his expectation. They would not even understand many of his words. For fourteen generations these people had been blind and cut off from all the seeing world; the names for all the things of sight had faded and changed; the story of the outer world was faded and changed to a child's story; and they had ceased to concern themselves with anything beyond the rocky slopes above their circling wall. Blind men of genius had arisen among them and questioned the shreds of belief and tradition they had brought with them from their seeing days, and had dismissed all these things as idle fancies and replaced them with new and saner explanations. Much of their imagination had shrivelled with their eyes, and they had made for themselves new imaginations with their ever more sensitive ears and fingertips. Slowly Nunez realised this: that his expectation of wonder and reverence at his origin and his gifts was not to be borne out; and after his poor attempt to explain sight to them had been set aside as the confused version of a new-made being describing the marvels of his incoherent sensations, he subsided, a little dashed, into listening to their instruction. And the eldest of the blind men explained to him life and philosophy and religion, how that the world (meaning their valley) had been first an empty hollow in the rocks, and then had come first inanimate things without the gift of touch, and llamas and a few other creatures that had little sense, and then men, and at last angels, whom one could hear singing and making fluttering sounds, but whom no one could touch at all, which puzzled Nunez greatly until he thought of the birds.

He went on to tell Nunez how here time had been divided into the warm and the cold, which are the blind equivalents of day and night, and how it was good to sleep in the warm and work during the cold, so that now, but for his advent, the whole town of the blind would have been asleep. He said Nunez must have been specially created to learn and serve the wisdom they had acquired, and that for all his mental incoherency and stumbling behaviour he must have courage and do his best to learn, and at that all the people in the doorway murmured encouragingly. He said the night – for the blind call their day night – was now far gone, and it behooved everyone to go back to sleep. He asked Nunez if he knew how to sleep, and Nunez said he did, but that before sleep he wanted food.

They brought him food – llama's milk in a bowl and rough salted bread – and led him into a lonely place to eat out of their hearing, and afterwards to slumber until the chill of the mountain evening roused them to begin their day again. But Nunez slumbered not at all.

Instead, he sat up in the place where they had left him, resting his limbs and turning the unanticipated circumstances of his arrival over and over in his mind.

Every now and then he laughed, sometimes with amusement and sometimes with indignation.

'Unformed mind!' he said. 'Got no senses yet! They little know they've been insulting their heaven-sent king and master. I see I must bring them to reason. Let me think – Let me think.'

He was still thinking when the sun set.

Nunez had an eye for all beautiful things, and it seemed to him that the glow upon the snowfields and glaciers that rose about the valley on every side was the most beautiful thing he had ever seen. His eyes went from that inaccessible glory to the village and irrigated fields, fast sinking into the twilight, and suddenly a wave of emotion took him, and he thanked God from the bottom of his heart that the power of sight had been given him.

He heard a voice calling to him from out of the village.

'Ya ho there, Bogota! Come hither!'

At that he stood up, smiling. He would show these people once and for all what sight would do for a man. They would seek him, but not find him.

'You move not, Bogota,' said the voice.

He laughed noiselessly and made two stealthy steps aside from the path.

'Trample not on the grass, Bogota; that is not allowed.'

Nunez had scarcely heard the sound he made himself. He stopped, amazed.

The owner of the voice came running up the piebald path towards him.

He stepped back into the pathway. 'Here I am,' he said.

'Why did you not come when I called you?' said the blind man. 'Must you be led like a child? Cannot you hear the path as you walk?'

Nunez laughed. 'I can see it,' he said.

'There is no such word as *see*,' said the blind man, after a pause. 'Cease this folly and follow the sound of my feet.'

Nunez followed, a little annoyed.

'My time will come,' he said.

'You'll learn,' the blind man answered. 'There is much to learn in the world.'

'Has no one told you, "In the Country of the Blind the One-Eyed Man is King"?'

'What is blind?' asked the blind man, carelessly, over his shoulder.

Four days passed and the fifth found the King of the Blind still *incognito*, a clumsy and useless stranger among his subjects.

It was, he found, much more difficult to proclaim himself than he had supposed, and in the meantime, while he meditated his *coup d'état*,[37] he did what he was told and learnt the manners and customs of the Country of the Blind. He found working and going about at night a particularly irksome thing, and he decided that that should be the first thing he would change.

They led a simple, laborious life, these people, with all the elements of virtue and happiness as these things can be understood by men. They toiled, but not oppressively; they had food and clothing sufficient for their needs; they had days and seasons of rest; they made much of music and singing, and there was love among them and little children.

It was marvellous with what confidence and precision they went about their ordered world. Everything, you see, had been made to fit their needs; each of the radiating paths of the valley area had a constant angle to the others, and was distinguished by a special notch upon its kerbing;

all obstacles and irregularities of path or meadow had long since been cleared away; all their methods and procedure arose naturally from their special needs. Their senses had become marvellously acute; they could hear and judge the slightest gesture of a man a dozen paces away – could hear the very beating of his heart. Intonation had long replaced expression with them, and touches gesture, and their work with hoe and spade and fork was as free and confident as garden work can be. Their sense of smell was extraordinarily fine; they could distinguish individual differences as readily as a dog can, and they went about the tending of llamas, who lived among the rocks above and came to the wall for food and shelter, with ease and confidence. It was only when at last Nunez sought to assert himself that he found how easy and confident their movements could be.

He rebelled only after he had tried persuasion.

He tried at first on several occasions to tell them of sight. 'Look you here, you people,' he said. 'There are things you do not understand in me.'

Once or twice one or two of them attended to him; they sat with faces downcast and ears turned intelligently towards him, and he did his best to tell them what it was to see. Among his hearers was a girl, with eyelids less red and sunken than the others, so that one could almost fancy she was hiding eyes, whom especially he hoped to persuade. He spoke of the beauties of sight, of watching the mountains, of the sky and the sunrise, and they heard him with amused incredulity that presently became condemnatory. They told him there were indeed no mountains at all, but that the end of the rocks where the llamas grazed was indeed the end of the world; thence sprang a cavernous roof of the universe, from which the dew and the avalanches fell; and when he maintained stoutly the world had neither end nor roof such as they supposed, they said his thoughts were wicked. So far as he could describe sky and clouds and stars to them it seemed to them a hideous void, a terrible blankness in the place of the smooth roof to things in which they believed – it was an article of faith with them that the cavern roof was exquisitely smooth to the touch. He saw that in some manner he shocked them, and gave up that aspect of the matter altogether, and tried to show them the practical value of sight. One morning, he saw Pedro in the path called Seventeen and coming towards the central houses, but still too far off for hearing or scent, and he told them as much. 'In a little while,' he prophesied, 'Pedro will be here.' An old man remarked that Pedro had no business on path Seventeen, and then, as if in confirmation, that individual as he drew near turned and went transversely into path Ten, and so back with nimble paces towards the outer wall. They mocked Nunez when Pedro did not arrive, and afterwards, when he asked Pedro questions to clear his character, Pedro denied and out-faced him, and was afterwards hostile to him.

Then he induced them to let him go a long way up the sloping meadows towards the wall with one complaisant individual, and to him he promised to describe all that happened among the houses. He noted certain goings and comings, but the things that really seemed to signify to these people happened inside or behind the windowless houses – the only things they took note of to test him by – and of those he could see or tell nothing; and it was after the failure of this attempt, and the ridicule they could not repress, that he resorted to force. He thought of seizing a spade and suddenly smiting one or two of them to earth, and so in fair combat showing the advantage of eyes. He went so far with that resolution as to seize his spade, and then he discovered a new thing about himself, and that was that it was impossible for him to hit a blind man in cold blood.

He hesitated, and found them all aware that he had snatched up the spade. They stood all alert, with their heads on one side, and bent ears towards him for what he would do next.

'Put that spade down,' said one, and he felt a sort of helpless horror. He came near obedience.

Then he had thrust one backwards against a house wall, and fled past him and out of the village.

He went athwart one of their meadows, leaving a track of trampled grass behind his feet, and presently sat down by the side of one of their ways. He felt something of the buoyancy that comes to all men in the beginning of a fight, but more perplexity. He began to realise that you cannot even fight happily with creatures who stand upon a different mental basis to yourself. Far away he saw a number of men carrying spades and sticks come out of the street of houses and advance in a spreading line along the several paths towards him. They advanced slowly, speaking frequently to one another, and ever and again the whole cordon would halt and sniff the air and listen.

The first time they did this Nunez laughed. But afterwards he did not laugh.

One struck his trail in the meadow grass and came stooping and feeling his way along it.

For five minutes he watched the slow extension of the cordon, and then his vague disposition to do something forthwith became frantic. He stood up, went a pace or so towards the circumferential wall, turned and went back a little way. There they all stood in a crescent, still and listening.

He also stood still, gripping his spade very tightly in both hands. Should he charge them?

The pulse in his ears ran into the rhythm of 'In the Country of the Blind the One-Eyed Man is King.'

Should he charge them?

He looked back at the high and unclimbable wall behind – unclimbable because of its smooth plastering, but withal pierced with many little doors – and at the approaching line of seekers. Behind these others were now coming out of the street of houses.

Should he charge them?

'Bogota!' called one. 'Bogota! Where are you?'

He gripped his spade still tighter and advanced down the meadows towards the place of habitations, and directly he moved they converged upon him. 'I'll hit them if they touch me,' he swore; 'by heaven, I will. I'll hit.' He called aloud, 'Look here, I'm going to do what I like in this valley! Do you hear? I'm going to do what I like and go where I like.'

They were moving in upon him quickly, groping, yet moving rapidly. It was like playing blind man's buff with everyone blindfolded except one. 'Get hold of him!' cried one. He found himself in the arc of a loose curve of pursuers. He felt suddenly he must be active and resolute.

'You don't understand,' he cried, in a voice that was meant to be great and resolute but which broke. 'You are blind and I can see. Leave me alone!'

'Bogota! Put down that spade and come off the grass!'

The last order, grotesque in its urban familiarity, produced a gust of anger. 'I'll hurt you,' he said, sobbing with emotion. 'By heaven, I'll hurt you! Leave me alone!'

He began to run, not knowing clearly where to run. He ran from the nearest blind man, because it was a horror to hit him. He stopped, and then made a dash to escape from their closing ranks. He made for where a gap was wide, and the men on either side, with a quick perception of the approach of his paces, rushed in on one another. He sprang forward, and then saw he must be caught, and *swish*! The spade had struck. He felt the soft thud of hand and arm, and the man was down with a yell of pain, and he was through.

Through! And then he was close to the street of houses again, and blind men, whirling spades and stakes, were running with a reasoned swiftness hither and thither.

He heard steps behind him just in time, and found a tall man rushing forward and swiping at the sound of him. He lost his nerve, hurled his spade a yard wide of this antagonist, and whirled about and fled, fairly yelling as he dodged another.

He was panic-stricken. He ran furiously to and fro, dodging when there was no need to dodge, and in his anxiety to see on every side of him at once, stumbling. For a moment he was down and they heard his fall. Far away in the circumferential wall a little doorway looked like heaven, and he set off in a wild rush for it. He did not even look round at his pursuers until it was gained, and then he stumbled across the bridge, clambered a little way among the rocks, to the surprise and dismay of a young llama, who went leaping out of sight, and lay down sobbing for breath.

And so his *coup d'état* came to an end.

He stayed outside the wall of the Valley of the Blind for two nights and days without food or shelter, and meditated upon the unexpected. During these meditations he repeated very frequently and always with a profounder note of derision the exploded proverb: 'In the Country of the Blind the One-Eyed Man is King.' He thought chiefly of ways of fighting and conquering these people, and it grew clear that for him no practicable way was possible. He had no weapons, and now it would be hard to get one.

The canker of civilisation had got to him even in Bogota, and he could not find it in himself to go down and assassinate a blind man. Of course, if he did that, he might then dictate terms on the threat of assassinating them all. But – sooner or later he must sleep . . . !

He tried also to find food among the pine trees, to be comfortable under pine boughs while the frost fell at night, and – with less confidence – to catch a llama by artifice in order to try to kill it – perhaps by hammering it with a stone – and so finally, perhaps, to eat some of it. But the llamas had a doubt of him and regarded him with distrustful brown eyes and spat when he drew near. Fear came on him the second day and fits of shivering. Finally he crawled down to the wall of the Country of the Blind and tried to make his terms. He crawled along by the stream, shouting, until two blind men came out to the gate and talked to him.

'I was mad,' he said. 'But I was only newly made.'

They said that was better.

He told them he was wiser now, and repented of all he had done.

Then he wept without intention, for he was very weak and ill now, and they took that as a favourable sign.

They asked him if he still thought he could '*see*'.

'No,' he said. 'That was folly. The word means nothing – less than nothing!'

They asked him what was overhead.

'About ten times ten the height of a man there is a roof above the world – of rock – and very, very smooth . . . ' He burst again into hysterical tears. 'Before you ask me any more, give me some food or I shall die!'

He expected dire punishments, but these blind people were capable of toleration. They regarded his rebellion as but one more proof of his general idiocy and inferiority, and after they had whipped him they appointed him to do the simplest and heaviest work they had for anyone to do, and he, seeing no other way of living, did submissively what he was told.

He was ill for some days and they nursed him kindly. That refined his submission. But they insisted on his lying in the dark, and that was a great misery. And blind philosophers came and talked to him of the wicked levity of his mind, and reproved him so impressively for his doubts about the lid of rock that covered their cosmic casserole that he almost doubted whether indeed he was not the victim of hallucination in not seeing it overhead.

So Nunez became a citizen of the Country of the Blind, and these people ceased to be a generalised people and became individualities to him, and familiar to him, while the world beyond the mountains became more and more remote and unreal. There was Yacob, his master, a kindly man when not annoyed; there was Pedro, Yacob's nephew; and there was Medina-saroté, who was the youngest daughter of Yacob. She was little esteemed in the world of the blind, because she had a clear-cut face and lacked that satisfying, glossy smoothness that is the blind man's ideal of feminine beauty, but Nunez thought her beautiful at first, and presently the most beautiful thing in the whole creation. Her closed eyelids were not sunken and red after the common way of the valley, but lay as though they might open again at any moment; and she had long eyelashes, which were considered a grave disfigurement. And her voice was weak and did not satisfy the acute hearing of the valley swains. So that she had no lover.

There came a time when Nunez thought that, could he win her, he would be resigned to live in the valley for all the rest of his days.

He watched her; he sought opportunities of doing her little services and presently he found that she observed him. Once at a rest-day gathering they sat side by side in the dim starlight, and the music was sweet. His hand came upon hers and he dared to clasp it. Then very tenderly she returned his pressure. And one day, as they were at their meal in the darkness, he felt her hand very softly seeking him, and as it chanced the fire leapt then, and he saw the tenderness of her face.

He sought to speak to her.

He went to her one day when she was sitting in the summer moon-light spinning. The light made her a thing of silver and mystery. He sat down at her feet and told her he loved her, and told her how beautiful she seemed to him. He had a lover's voice, he spoke with a tender reverence that came near to awe, and she had never before been touched by adoration. She made him no definite answer, but it was clear his words pleased her.

After that he talked to her whenever he could take an opportunity. The valley became the world for him, and the world beyond the mountains where men lived by day seemed no more than a fairy tale he would someday pour into her ears. Very tentatively and timidly he spoke to her of sight.

Sight seemed to her the most poetical of fancies, and she listened to his description of the stars and the mountains and her own sweet white-lit beauty as though it was a guilty indulgence. She did not believe, she could only half understand, but she was mysteriously delighted, and it seemed to him that she completely understood.

His love lost its awe and took courage. Presently he was for demanding her of Yacob and the elders in marriage, but she became fearful and delayed. And it was one of her elder sisters who first told Yacob that Medina-saroté and Nunez were in love.

There was from the first very great opposition to the marriage of Nunez and Medina-saroté; not so much because they valued her as because they held him as a being apart, an idiot, incompetent thing below the permissible level of a man. Her sisters opposed it bitterly as bringing discredit on them all; and old Yacob, though he had formed a sort of liking for his clumsy, obedient serf, shook his head and said the thing could not be. The young men were all angry at the idea of corrupting the race, and one went so far as to revile and strike Nunez. He struck back. Then for the first time he found an advantage in seeing, even by twilight, and after that fight was over no one was disposed to raise a hand against him. But they still found his marriage impossible.

Old Yacob had a tenderness for his last little daughter, and was grieved to have her weep upon his shoulder.

'You see, my dear, he's an idiot. He has delusions; he can't do any-thing right.'

'I know,' wept Medina-saroté. 'But he's better than he was. He's getting better. And he's strong, dear father, and kind – stronger and kinder than any other man in the world. And he loves me – and, father, I love him.'

Old Yacob was greatly distressed to find her inconsolable, and besides – what made it more distressing – he liked Nunez for many things. So he went and sat in the windowless council-chamber with the other elders and noted the trend of the talk, and said, at the proper time, 'He's better than he was. Very likely, someday, we shall find him as sane as ourselves.'

Then afterwards one of the elders, who thought deeply, had an idea. He was a great doctor among these people, their medicine-man, and he had a very philosophical and inventive mind, and the idea of curing Nunez of his peculiarities appealed to him. One day when Yacob was present he returned to the topic of Nunez. 'I have examined Nunez,' he said, 'and the case is clearer to me. I think very probably he might be cured.'

'This is what I have always hoped,' said old Yacob.

'His brain is affected,' said the blind doctor.

The elders murmured assent.

'Now, *what* affects it?'

'Ah!' said old Yacob.

'*This*,' said the doctor, answering his own question. 'Those queer things that are called the eyes, and which exist to make an agreeable depression in the face, are diseased, in the case of Nunez, in such a way as to affect his brain. They are greatly distended, he has eyelashes, and his eyelids move, and consequently his brain is in a state of constant irritation and distraction.'

'Yes?' said old Yacob. 'Yes?'

'And I think I may say with reasonable certainty that, in order to cure him completely, all that we need to do is a simple and easy surgical operation – namely, to remove these irritant bodies.'

'And then he will be sane?'

'Then he will be perfectly sane, and a quite admirable citizen.'

'Thank heaven for science!' said old Yacob, and went forth at once to tell Nunez of his happy hopes.

But Nunez's manner of receiving the good news struck him as being cold and disappointing.

'One might think,' he said, 'from the tone you take that you did not care for my daughter.'

It was Medina-saroté who persuaded Nunez to face the blind surgeons.

'You do not want me,' he said, 'to lose my gift of sight?'

She shook her head.

'My world is sight.'

Her head drooped lower.

'There are the beautiful things, the beautiful little things – the flowers, the lichens amidst the rocks, the light and softness on a piece of fur, the far sky with its drifting dawn of clouds, the sunsets and the stars. And there is *you*. For you alone it is good to have sight, to see your sweet, serene face, your kindly lips, your dear, beautiful hands folded together . . . It is these eyes of mine you won, these eyes that hold me to you, that these idiots seek. Instead, I must touch you, hear you, and never see you again. I must come under that roof of rock and stone and darkness, that horrible roof under which your imaginations stoop . . . No; you would not have me do that?'

A disagreeable doubt had arisen in him. He stopped and left the thing a question.

'I wish,' she said, 'sometimes – ' She paused.

'Yes?' he said, a little apprehensively.

'I wish sometimes – you would not talk like that.'

'Like what?'

'I know it's pretty – it's your imagination. I love it, but now – '

He felt cold. '*Now?*' he said, faintly.

She sat quite still.

'You mean – you think – I should be better, better perhaps – '

He was realising things very swiftly. He felt anger, indeed, anger at the dull course of fate, but also sympathy for her lack of understanding – a sympathy near akin to pity.

'*Dear*,' he said, and he could see by her whiteness how tensely her spirit pressed against the things she could not say. He put his arms about her, he kissed her ear, and they sat for a time in silence.

'If I were to consent to this?' he said at last, in a voice that was very gentle.

She flung her arms about him, weeping wildly. 'Oh, if you would,' she sobbed, 'if only you would!'

For a week before the operation that was to raise him from his servitude and inferiority to the level of a blind citizen, Nunez knew nothing of sleep, and all through the warm, sunlit hours, while the others slumbered happily, he sat brooding or wandered aimlessly, trying to bring his mind to bear on his dilemma. He had given his answer, he had given his consent, and still he was not sure. And at last work-time was over, the sun rose in splendour over the golden crests, and his last day of vision began for him. He had a few minutes with Medina-saroté before she went apart to sleep.

'Tomorrow,' he said, 'I shall see no more.'

'Dear heart!' she answered, and pressed his hands with all her strength.

'They will hurt you but little,' she said; 'and you are going through this pain – you are going through it, dear lover, for me . . . Dear, if a woman's heart and life can do it, I will repay you. My dearest one, my dearest with the tender voice, I will repay.'

He was drenched in pity for himself and her.

He held her in his arms, and pressed his lips to hers and looked on her sweet face for the last time. 'Goodbye!' he whispered to that dear sight, 'Goodbye!'

And then in silence he turned away from her.

She could hear his slow retreating footsteps, and something in the rhythm of them threw her into a passion of weeping.

He walked away.

He had fully meant to go to a lonely place, where the meadows were beautiful with white narcissus, and there remain until the hour of his sacrifice should come, but as he walked he lifted up his eyes and saw the morning, the morning like an angel in golden armour, marching down the steeps . . .

It seemed to him that, before this splendour, he and this blind world in the valley and his love and all were no more than a pit of sin.

He did not turn aside as he had meant to do, but went on and passed through the wall of the circumference and out upon the rocks, and his eyes were always upon the sunlit ice and snow.

He saw their infinite beauty, and his imagination soared over them to the things beyond he was now to resign for ever.

He thought of that great free world that he was parted from, the world that was his own, and he had a vision of those farther slopes, distance beyond distance, with Bogota, a place of multitudinous stirring beauty, a glory by day, a luminous mystery by night, a place of palaces and fountains and statues and white houses, lying beautifully in the middle distance. He thought how for a day or so one might come down through passes drawing ever nearer and nearer to its busy streets and ways. He thought of the river journey, day by day, from great Bogota to the still vaster world beyond, through towns and villages, forest and desert places, the rushing river day by day, until its banks receded, and the big steamers came splashing by and one had reached the sea – the limitless sea, with its thousand islands, its thousands of islands, and its ships seen dimly far away in their incessant journeyings round and about that greater world. And there, unpent by mountains, one saw the sky – the sky, not such a disc as one saw it here, but an arch of immeasurable blue, a deep of deeps in which the circling stars were floating . . .

His eyes scrutinised the great curtain of the mountains with a keener enquiry.

For example; if one went so, up that gully and to that chimney there, then one might come out high among those stunted pines that ran round in a sort of shelf and rose still higher and higher as it passed above the gorge. And then? That talus might be managed. Thence perhaps a climb might be found to take him up to the precipice that came below the snow; and if that chimney failed, then another farther to the east might serve his purpose better. And then? Then one would be out upon the amber-lit snow there, and halfway up to the crest of those beautiful desolations. And suppose one had good fortune!

He glanced back at the village, then turned right round and regarded it with folded arms.

He thought of Medina-saroté, and she had become small and remote.

He turned again towards the mountain wall down which the day had come to him.

Then very circumspectly he began his climb.

When sunset came he was no longer climbing, but he was far and high. He had been higher, but he was still very high. His clothes were torn, his limbs were blood-stained, he was bruised in many places, but he lay as if he were at his ease, and there was a smile on his face.

From where he rested the valley seemed as if it were in a pit and nearly a mile below. Already it was dim with haze and shadow, though the mountain summits around him were things of light and fire, and the little details of the rocks near at hand were drenched with light and beauty, a vein of green mineral piercing the grey, a flash of small crystal here and there, a minute, minutely beautiful orange lichen close beside his face. There were deep, mysterious shadows in the gorge, blue deepening into purple, and purple into a luminous darkness, and over-head was the illimitable vastness of the sky. But he heeded these things no longer, but lay quite still there, smiling as if he were content now merely to have escaped from the Valley of the Blind, in which he had thought to be King.

The glow of the sunset passed, and the night came, and still he lay peacefully contented under the cold clear stars.

The Man Who Could Work Miracles

A Pantoum in Prose[38]

It is doubtful whether the gift was innate. For my own part, I think it
came to him suddenly. Indeed, until he was thirty he was a sceptic, and
did not believe in miraculous powers. And here, since it is the most
convenient place, I must mention that he was a little man, and had eyes
of a hot brown, very erect red hair, a moustache with ends that he twisted
up, and freckles. His name was George McWhirter Fotheringay – not
the sort of name by any means to lead to any expectation of miracles –
and he was clerk at Gomshott's. He was greatly addicted to assertive
argument. It was while he was asserting the impossibility of miracles that
he had his first intimation of his extraordinary powers. This particular
argument was being held in the bar of the Long Dragon, and Toddy
Beamish was conducting the opposition by a monotonous but effective,
'So *you* say,' that drove Mr Fotheringay to the very limit of his patience.

There were present, besides these two, a very dusty cyclist, landlord
Cox, and Miss Maybridge, the perfectly respectable and rather portly
barmaid of the Dragon. Miss Maybridge was standing with her back to
Mr Fotheringay, washing glasses; the others were watching him, more
or less amused by the present ineffectiveness of the assertive method.
Goaded by the Torres Vedras tactics[39] of Mr Beamish, Mr Fotheringay
determined to make an unusual rhetorical effort. 'Looky here, Mr
Beamish,' said Mr Fotheringay. 'Let us clearly understand what a miracle
is. It's something contrariwise to the course of nature, done by power of
Will, something what couldn't happen without being specially willed.'

'So *you* say,' said Mr Beamish, repulsing him.

Mr Fotheringay appealed to the cyclist, who had hitherto been a
silent auditor, and received his assent – given with a hesitating cough
and a glance at Mr Beamish. The landlord would express no opinion,
and Mr Fotheringay, returning to Mr Beamish, received the unexpected
concession of a qualified assent to his definition of a miracle.

'For instance,' said Mr Fotheringay, greatly encouraged. 'Here would
be a miracle. That lamp, in the natural course of nature, couldn't burn
like that upsy-down, could it, Beamish?'

'*You* say it couldn't,' said Beamish.

'And you?' said Fotheringay. 'You don't mean to say – eh?'

'No,' said Beamish reluctantly. 'No, it couldn't.'

'Very well,' said Mr Fotheringay. 'Then here comes someone, as it might be me, along here, and stands as it might be here, and says to that lamp, as I might do, collecting all my will – "Turn upsy-down without breaking, and go on burning steady," and – Hello!'

It was enough to make anyone say "Hello!" The impossible, the incredible, was visible to them all. The lamp hung inverted in the air, burning quietly with its flame pointing down. It was as solid, as indisputable as ever a lamp was, the prosaic common lamp of the Long Dragon bar.

Mr Fotheringay stood with an extended forefinger and the knitted brows of one anticipating a catastrophic smash. The cyclist, who was sitting next the lamp, ducked and jumped across the bar. Everybody jumped, more or less. Miss Maybridge turned and screamed. For nearly three seconds the lamp remained still. A faint cry of mental distress came from Mr Fotheringay. 'I can't keep it up,' he said, 'any longer.' He staggered back, and the inverted lamp suddenly flared, fell against the corner of the bar, bounced aside, smashed upon the floor, and went out.

It was lucky it had a metal receiver, or the whole place would have been in a blaze. Mr Cox was the first to speak, and his remark, shorn of needless excrescences, was to the effect that Fotheringay was a fool. Fotheringay was beyond disputing even so fundamental a proposition as that! He was astonished beyond measure at the thing that had occurred. The subsequent conversation threw absolutely no light on the matter so far as Fotheringay was concerned; the general opinion not only followed Mr Cox very closely but very vehemently. Everyone accused Fotheringay of a silly trick, and presented him, to himself, as a foolish destroyer of comfort and security. His mind was in a tornado of perplexity, he was himself inclined to agree with them, and he made a remarkably ineffectual opposition to the proposal of his departure.

He went home flushed and heated, coat-collar crumpled, eyes smarting and ears red. He watched each of the ten street lamps nervously as he passed them. It was only when he found himself alone in his little bedroom in Church Row that he was able to grapple seriously with his memories of the occurrence, and ask, 'What on earth happened?'

He had removed his coat and boots, and was sitting on the bed with his hands in his pockets repeating the text of his defence for the seventeenth time, '*I* didn't want the confounded thing to upset,' when it occurred to him that at the precise moment he had said the commanding words he had inadvertently willed the thing he said, and that when he had seen the lamp in the air he had felt it depended on him to maintain it there without being clear how this was to be done. He had not a particularly complex mind, or he might have stuck for a time at that 'inadvertently willed', embracing, as it does, the abstrusest problems of voluntary action; but as it was, the idea came to him with a quite acceptable haziness. And from that, following, as I must admit, no clear logical path, he came to the test of experiment.

He pointed resolutely to his candle and collected his mind, though he felt he did a foolish thing. 'Be raised up,' he said. But in a second that feeling vanished. The candle was raised, hung in the air one giddy moment, and as Mr Fotheringay gasped, fell with a smash on his toilet-table, leaving him in darkness save for the expiring glow of its wick.

For a time Mr Fotheringay sat in the darkness, perfectly still. 'It did happen, after all,' he said. 'And 'ow I'm to explain it I *don't* know.' He sighed heavily, and began feeling in his pockets for a match. He could find none, and he rose and groped about the toilet-table. 'I wish I had a match,' he said. He resorted to his coat, and there was none there, and then it dawned upon him that miracles were possible even with matches. He extended a hand and scowled at it in the dark. 'Let there be a match in that hand,' he said. He felt some light object fall across his palm, and his fingers closed upon a match.

After several ineffectual attempts to light this, he discovered it was a safety-match.[40] He threw it down, and then it occurred to him that he might have willed it lit. He did, and perceived it burning in the midst of his toilet-table mat. He caught it up hastily, and it went out. His perception of possibilities enlarged, and he felt for and replaced the candle in its candlestick. 'Here! *You* be lit,' said Mr Fotheringay, and forthwith the candle was flaring, and he saw a little black hole in the toilet-cover, with a wisp of smoke rising from it. For a time he stared from this to the little flame and back, and then looked up and met his own gaze in the looking glass. By this help he communed with himself in silence for a time.

'How about miracles now?' said Mr Fotheringay at last, addressing his reflection.

The subsequent meditations of Mr Fotheringay were of a severe but confused description. So far, he could see it was a case of pure willing with him. The nature of his experiences so far disinclined him for any further experiments, at least until he had reconsidered them. But he lifted a sheet of paper, and turned a glass of water pink and then green, and he created a snail, which he miraculously annihilated, and got himself a miraculous new toothbrush. Somewhere in the small hours he had reached the fact that his will-power must be of a particularly rare and pungent quality, a fact of which he had certainly had inklings before, but no certain assurance. The scare and perplexity of his first discovery was now qualified by pride in this evidence of singularity and by vague intimations of advantage. He became aware that the church clock was striking one, and as it did not occur to him that his daily duties at Gomshott's might be miraculously dispensed with, he resumed undressing, in order to get to bed without further delay. As he struggled to get his shirt over his head, he was struck with a brilliant idea. 'Let me be in bed,' he said, and found himself so. 'Undressed,' he stipulated; and finding the sheets cold, added hastily, 'and in my nightshirt – no, in a nice soft woollen nightshirt. Ah!' he said with immense enjoyment. 'And now let me be comfortably asleep . . . '

He awoke at his usual hour and was pensive all through breakfast-time, wondering whether his overnight experience might not have been a particularly vivid dream. At length his mind turned again to cautious experiments. For instance, he had three eggs for breakfast; two his landlady had supplied, good but shoppy, and one was a delicious fresh goose-egg, laid, cooked and served by his extraordinary will. He hurried off to Gomshott's in a state of profound but carefully concealed excitement, and only remembered the shell of the third egg when his landlady spoke of it that night. All day he could do no work because of this astonishingly new self-knowledge, but this caused him no inconvenience, because he made up for it miraculously in his last ten minutes.

As the day wore on his state of mind passed from wonder to elation, albeit the circumstances of his dismissal from the Long Dragon were still disagreeable to recall, and a garbled account of the matter that had reached his colleagues led to some badinage. It was evident he must be careful how he lifted frangible articles, but in other ways his gift promised more and more as he turned it over in his mind. He intended among other things to increase his personal property by unostentatious acts of creation. He called into existence a pair of very splendid diamond studs, and hastily annihilated them again as young Gomshott came across the counting-house to his desk. He was afraid young Gomshott might wonder how he had come by them. He saw quite clearly the gift required caution and watchfulness in its exercise, but so far as he could judge the difficulties attending its mastery would be no greater than those he had already faced in the study of cycling. It was that analogy, perhaps, quite as much as the feeling that he would be unwelcome in the Long Dragon, that drove him out after supper into the lane beyond the gasworks to rehearse a few miracles in private.

There was possibly a certain want of originality in his attempts, for apart from his will-power Mr Fotheringay was not a very exceptional man. The miracle of Moses' rod[41] came to his mind, but the night was dark and unfavourable to the proper control of large miraculous snakes. Then he recollected the story of *Tannhäuser* that he had read on the back of the Philharmonic programme.[42] That seemed to him singularly attractive and harmless. He stuck his walking-stick – a very nice Poona-Penang lawyer[43] – into the turf that edged the footpath, and commanded the dry wood to blossom. The air was immediately full of the scent of roses, and by means of a match he saw for himself that this beautiful miracle was indeed accomplished. His satisfaction was ended by advancing footsteps. Afraid of a premature discovery of his powers, he addressed the blossoming stick hastily: 'Go back.' What he meant was 'Change back;' but of course he was confused. The stick receded at a considerable velocity, and incontinently came a cry of anger and a bad word from the approaching person. 'Who are you throwing brambles at, you fool?' cried a voice. 'That got me on the shin.'

'I'm sorry, old chap,' said Mr Fotheringay, and then realising the awkward nature of the explanation, caught nervously at his moustache. He saw Winch, one of the three Immering constables, advancing.

'What d'yer mean by it?' asked the constable. 'Hello! It's you, is it? The gent that broke the lamp at the Long Dragon!'

'I don't mean anything by it,' said Mr Fotheringay. 'Nothing at all.'

'What d'yer do it for then?'

'Oh, bother!' said Mr Fotheringay.

'Bother indeed! D'yer know that stick hurt? What d'yer do it for, eh?'

For the moment Mr Fotheringay could not think what he had done it for. His silence seemed to irritate Mr Winch. 'You been assaulting the police, young man, this time. That's what *you* done.'

'Look here, Mr Winch,' said Mr Fotheringay, annoyed and confused, 'I'm very sorry. The fact is – '

'Well?'

He could think of no way but the truth. 'I was working a miracle.' He tried to speak in an offhand way, but try as he would he couldn't.

'Working a – ! 'Ere, don't you talk rot. Working a miracle, indeed! Miracle! Well, that's downright funny! Why, you's the chap that don't believe in miracles . . . Fact is, this is another of your silly conjuring tricks – that's what this is. Now, I tell you – '

But Mr Fotheringay never heard what Mr Winch was going to tell him. He realised he had given himself away, flung his valuable secret to all the winds of heaven. A violent gust of irritation swept him to action.

He turned on the constable swiftly and fiercely. 'Here,' he said, 'I've had enough of this, I have! I'll show you a silly conjuring trick, I will! Go to Hades![44] Go, now!'

He was alone!

Mr Fotheringay performed no more miracles that night nor did he trouble to see what had become of his flowering stick. He returned to the town, scared and very quiet, and went to his bedroom. 'Lord!' he said, 'it's a powerful gift – an extremely powerful gift. I didn't hardly mean as much as that. Not really . . . I wonder what Hades is like!'

He sat on the bed taking off his boots. Struck by a happy thought, he transferred the constable to San Francisco, and without any more interference with normal causation went soberly to bed. In the night he dreamt of the anger of Winch.

The next day Mr Fotheringay heard two interesting items of news. Someone had planted a most beautiful climbing rose against the elder Mr Gomshott's private house in the Lullaborough Road, and the river as far as Rawling's Mill was to be dragged for Constable Winch.

Mr Fotheringay was abstracted and thoughtful all that day, and performed no miracles except certain provisions for Winch, and the miracle of completing his day's work with punctual perfection in spite of all the bee-swarm of thoughts that hummed through his mind. And the extraordinary abstraction and meekness of his manner was remarked by several people, and made a matter for jesting. For the most part he was thinking of Winch.

On Sunday evening he went to chapel and, oddly enough, Mr Maydig, who took a certain interest in occult matters, preached about 'things that are not lawful'. Mr Fotheringay was not a regular chapel goer, but the system of assertive scepticism, to which I have already alluded, was now very much shaken. The tenor of the sermon threw an entirely new light on these novel gifts, and he suddenly decided to consult Mr Maydig immediately after the service. So soon as that was determined, he found himself wondering why he had not done so before.

Mr Maydig, a lean, excitable man with quite remarkably long wrists and neck, was gratified at a request for a private conversation from a young man whose carelessness in religious matters was a subject for general remark in the town. After a few necessary delays, he conducted him to the study of the Manse, which was contiguous to the chapel, seated him comfortably, and standing in front of a cheerful fire – his legs threw a Rhodian arch[45] of shadow on the opposite wall – requested Mr Fotheringay to state his business.

At first Mr Fotheringay was a little abashed, and found some difficulty in opening the matter. 'You will scarcely believe me, Mr Maydig, I am afraid – ' and so forth for some time. He tried a question at last, and asked Mr Maydig his opinion of miracles.

Mr Maydig was still saying 'Well' in an extremely judicial tone, when Mr Fotheringay interrupted again: 'You don't believe, I suppose, that some common sort of person – like myself, for instance – as it might be sitting here now, might have some sort of twist inside him that made him able to do things by his will.'

'It's possible,' said Mr Maydig. 'Something of the sort, perhaps, is possible.'

'If I might make free with something here, I think I might show you by a sort of experiment,' said Mr Fotheringay. 'Now, take that tobacco-jar on the table, for instance. What I want to know is whether what I am going to do with it is a miracle or not. Just half a minute, Mr Maydig, please.'

He knitted his brows, pointed to the tobacco-jar and said: 'Be a bowl of violets.'

The tobacco-jar did as it was ordered.

Mr Maydig started violently at the change, and stood looking from the thaumaturgist[46] to the bowl of flowers. He said nothing. Presently he ventured to lean over the table and smell the violets; they were fresh-picked and very fine ones. Then he stared at Mr Fotheringay again.

'How did you do that?' he asked.

Mr Fotheringay pulled his moustache. 'Just told it – and there you are. Is that a miracle, or is it black art, or what is it? And what do you think's the matter with me? That's what I want to ask.'

'It's a most extraordinary occurrence.'

'And this day last week I knew no more that I could do things like that than you did. It came quite sudden. It's something odd about my will, I suppose, and that's as far as I can see.'

'Is *that* – the only thing? Could you do other things besides that?'

'Lord, yes!' said Mr Fotheringay. 'Just anything.' He thought, and suddenly recalled a conjuring entertainment he had seen. 'Here!' He pointed. 'Change into a bowl of fish – no, not that – change into a glass bowl full of water with goldfish swimming in it. That's better! You see that, Mr Maydig?'

'It's astonishing. It's incredible. You are either a most extraordinary . . . But no – '

'I could change it into anything,' said Mr Fotheringay. 'Just anything. Here! Be a pigeon, will you?'

In another moment a blue pigeon was fluttering round the room and making Mr Maydig duck every time it came near him. 'Stop there, will you,' said Mr Fotheringay; and the pigeon hung motionless in the air. 'I could change it back to a bowl of flowers,' he said, and after replacing the pigeon on the table worked that miracle. 'I expect you will want your pipe in a bit,' he said, and restored the tobacco-jar.

Mr Maydig had followed all these later changes in a sort of ejaculatory silence. He stared at Mr Fotheringay and, in a very gingerly manner, picked up the tobacco-jar, examined it, replaced it on the table. 'Well!' was the only expression of his feelings.

'Now, after that it's easier to explain what I came about,' said Mr Fotheringay; and proceeded to a lengthy and involved narrative of his strange experiences, beginning with the affair of the lamp in the Long Dragon and complicated by persistent allusions to Winch. As he went on, the transient pride Mr Maydig's consternation had caused passed away; he became the very ordinary Mr Fotheringay of everyday inter-course again. Mr Maydig listened intently, the tobacco-jar in his hand, and his bearing changed also with the course of the narrative. Presently, while Mr Fotheringay was dealing with the miracle of the third egg, the minister interrupted with a fluttering extended hand –

'It is possible,' he said. 'It is credible. It is amazing, of course, but it reconciles a number of amazing difficulties. The power to work miracles is a gift – a peculiar quality like genius or second sight – hitherto it has come very rarely and to exceptional people. But in this case . . . I have always wondered at the miracles of Mahomet, and at Yogis' miracles, and the miracles of Madame Blavatsky.[47] But, of course! Yes, it is simply a gift! It carries out so beautifully the arguments of that great thinker – ' Mr Maydig's voice sank – 'his Grace the Duke of Argyll.[48] Here we plumb some profounder law – deeper than the ordinary laws of nature. Yes – yes. Go on. Go on!'

Mr Fotheringay proceeded to tell of his misadventure with Winch, and Mr Maydig, no longer overawed or scared, began to jerk his limbs about and interject astonishment. 'It's this what troubled me most,' proceeded Mr Fotheringay; 'it's this I'm most mijitly [49] in want of advice for; of course he's in San Francisco – wherever San Francisco may be – but of course it's awkward for both of us, as you'll see, Mr Maydig. I don't see how he can understand what has happened, and I dare say he's scared and exasperated something tremendous, and trying to get at me. I dare say he keeps on starting off to come here. I send him back, by a miracle, every few hours, when I think of it. And, of course, that's a thing he won't be able to understand, and it's bound to annoy him; and, of course, if he takes a ticket every time it will cost him a lot of money. I done the best I could for him, but of course it's difficult for him to put himself in my place. I thought afterwards that his clothes might have got scorched, you know – if Hades is all it's supposed to be [50] – before I shifted him. In that case I suppose they'd have locked him up in San Francisco. Of course, I willed a new suit of clothes on him directly I thought of it. But, you see, I'm already in a deuce of a tangle – '

Mr Maydig looked serious. 'I see you are in a tangle. Yes, it's a difficult position. How you are to end it . . . ' He became diffuse and inconclusive.

'However, we'll leave Winch for a little and discuss the larger question. I don't think this is a case of the black art or anything of the sort. I don't think there is any taint of criminality about it at all, Mr Fotheringay – none whatever, unless you are suppressing material facts. No, it's miracles – pure miracles – miracles, if I may say so, of the very highest class.'

He began to pace the hearthrug and gesticulate, while Mr Fotheringay sat with his arm on the table and his head on his arm, looking worried. 'I don't see how I'm to manage about Winch,' he said.

'A gift of working miracles – apparently a very powerful gift,' said Mr Maydig, 'will find a way about Winch – never fear. My dear sir, you are a most important man – a man of the most astonishing possibilities. As evidence, for example! And in other ways, the things you may do . . . '

'Yes, *I've* thought of a thing or two,' said Mr Fotheringay. 'But – some of the things came a bit twisty. You saw that fish at first? Wrong sort of bowl and wrong sort of fish. And I thought I'd ask someone.'

'A proper course,' said Mr Maydig, 'a very proper course – altogether the proper course.' He stopped and looked at Mr Fotheringay. 'It's practically an unlimited gift. Let us test your powers, for instance. If they really *are* . . . If they really are all they seem to be.'

And so, incredible as it may seem, in the study of the little house behind the Congregational Chapel, on the evening of Sunday, 10 November 1896, Mr Fotheringay, egged on and inspired by Mr Maydig, began to work miracles. The reader's attention is specially and definitely called to the date. He will object, probably has already objected, that certain points in this story are improbable, that if any things of the sort already described had indeed occurred, they would have been in all the papers a year ago. The details immediately following he will find particularly hard to accept, because among other things they involve the conclusion that he or she, the reader in question, must have been killed in a violent and unprecedented manner more than a year ago. Now a miracle is nothing if not improbable, and as a matter of fact the reader *was* killed in a violent and unprecedented manner a year ago. In the subsequent course of this story, that will become perfectly clear and credible, as every right-minded and reasonable reader will admit. But this is not the place for the end of the story, being but little beyond the hither side of the middle. And at first the miracles worked by Mr Fotheringay were timid little miracles – little things with the cups and parlour fitments, as feeble as the miracles of Theosophists, but, feeble as they were, they were received with awe by his collaborator. He would have preferred to settle the Winch business out of hand, but Mr Maydig would not let him. But after they had worked a dozen of these domestic trivialities, their sense of power grew, their imagination began to show signs of stimulation, and their ambition enlarged. Their first larger enterprise was due to hunger and the negligence of Mrs Minchin, Mr Maydig's housekeeper. The meal to which the minister conducted Mr Fotheringay was certainly ill-laid and uninviting as refreshment for two industrious miracle-workers; but they were seated, and Mr Maydig was descanting in sorrow rather than in anger upon his housekeeper's shortcomings, before it occurred to Mr Fotheringay that an opportunity lay before him. 'Don't you think, Mr Maydig,' he said, 'if it isn't a liberty, I – '

'My dear Mr Fotheringay! Of course! No – I didn't think.'

Mr Fotheringay waved his hand. 'What shall we have?' he said, in a large, inclusive spirit, and at Mr Maydig's order, revised the supper very thoroughly. 'As for me,' he said, eyeing Mr Maydig's selection, 'I am always particularly fond of a tankard of stout and a nice Welsh rarebit, and I'll order that. I ain't much given to Burgundy,' and forthwith stout and Welsh rarebit promptly appeared at his command. They sat long at their supper, talking like equals, as Mr Fotheringay presently perceived, with a glow of surprise and gratification, of all the miracles they would presently do. 'And by the by, Mr Maydig,' said Mr Fotheringay, 'I might perhaps be able to help you – in a domestic way.'

'Don't quite follow,' said Mr Maydig pouring out a glass of miraculous old Burgundy.

Mr Fotheringay helped himself to a second Welsh rarebit out of vacancy, and took a mouthful. 'I was thinking,' he said, 'I might be able (*chum, chum*) to work (*chum, chum*) a miracle with Mrs Minchin (*chum, chum*) – make her a better woman.'

Mr Maydig put down the glass and looked doubtful. 'She's – she strongly objects to interference, you know, Mr Fotheringay. And – as a matter of fact – it's well past eleven and she's probably in bed and asleep. Do you think, on the whole – '

Mr Fotheringay considered these objections. 'I don't see that it shouldn't be done in her sleep.'

For a time Mr Maydig opposed the idea, and then he yielded. Mr Fotheringay issued his orders, and a little less at their ease perhaps, the two gentlemen proceeded with their repast. Mr Maydig was enlarging on the changes he might expect in his housekeeper next day, with an optimism that seemed even to Mr Fotheringay's super senses a little forced and hectic, when a series of confused noises from upstairs began. Their eyes exchanged interrogations, and Mr Maydig left the room hastily. Mr Fotheringay heard him calling up to his housekeeper and then his footsteps going softly up to her.

In a minute or so the minister returned, his step light, his face radiant. 'Wonderful!' he said, 'and touching! Most touching!'

He began pacing the hearthrug. 'A repentance – a most touching repentance – through the crack of the door. Poor woman! A most wonderful change! She had got up. She must have got up at once. She had got up out of her sleep to smash a private bottle of brandy in her box. And to confess it too! . . . But this gives us – it opens – a most amazing vista of possibilities. If we can work this miraculous change in *her* . . . '

'The thing's unlimited seemingly,' said Mr Fotheringay. 'And about Mr Winch – '

'Altogether unlimited.' And from the hearthrug Mr Maydig, waving the Winch difficulty aside, unfolded a series of wonderful proposals – proposals he invented as he went along.

Now what those proposals were does not concern the essentials of this story. Suffice it that they were designed in a spirit of infinite benevolence, the sort of benevolence that used to be called post-prandial.[51] Suffice it too, that the problem of Winch remained unsolved. Nor is it necessary to describe how far that series got to its fulfilment. There were astonishing changes. The small hours found Mr Maydig and Mr Fotheringay careering across the chilly market-square under the still moon in a sort of ecstasy of thaumaturgy, Mr Maydig all flap and gesture, Mr Fotheringay short and bristling, and no longer abashed at his greatness. They had reformed every drunkard in the parliamentary division and changed all the beer and alcohol to water (Mr Maydig had overruled Mr Fotheringay on this point); they had, further, greatly improved the railway communication of the place, drained Flinder's swamp, improved the soil of One Tree Hill and cured the vicar's wart. And they were going to see what could be done with the injured pier at South Bridge. 'The place,' gasped Mr Maydig, 'won't be the same place tomorrow. How surprised and thankful everyone will be!' And just at that moment the church clock struck three.

'I say,' said Mr Fotheringay, 'that's three o'clock! I must be getting back. I've got to be at business by eight. And besides, Mrs Wimms – '

'We're only beginning,' said Mr Maydig, full of the sweetness of unlimited power. 'We're only beginning. Think of all the good we're doing. When people wake – '

'But – ' said Mr Fotheringay.

Mr Maydig gripped his arm suddenly. His eyes were bright and wild. 'My dear chap,' he said, 'there's no hurry. Look' – he pointed to the moon at the zenith – 'Joshua!'[52]

'Joshua?' said Mr Fotheringay.

'Joshua,' said Mr Maydig. 'Why not? Stop it.'

Mr Fotheringay looked at the moon.

'That's a bit tall,' he said after a pause.

'Why not?' said Mr Maydig. 'Of course it doesn't stop. You stop the rotation of the earth, you know. Time stops. It isn't as if we were doing harm.'

'H'm!' said Mr Fotheringay. 'Well.' He sighed. 'I'll try. Here – '

He buttoned up his jacket and addressed himself to the habitable globe, with as good an assumption of confidence as lay in his power. 'Jest stop rotating, will you,' said Mr Fotheringay.

Incontinently he was flying head over heels through the air at the rate of dozens of miles a minute. In spite of the innumerable circles he was describing per second, he thought; for thought is wonderful – sometimes as sluggish as flowing pitch, sometimes as instantaneous as light. He thought in a second, and willed, 'Let me come down safe and sound. Whatever else happens, let me down safe and sound.'

He willed it only just in time, for his clothes, heated by his rapid flight through the air, were already beginning to singe. He came down with a forcible but by no means injurious bump in what appeared to be a mound of fresh-turned earth. A large mass of metal and masonry, extraordinarily like the clock-tower in the middle of the market-square, hit the earth near him, ricochetted over him, and flew into stonework, bricks and masonry, like a bursting bomb. A hurtling cow hit one of the larger blocks and smashed like an egg. There was a crash that made all the most violent crashes of his past life seem like the sound of falling dust, and this was followed by a descending series of lesser crashes. A vast wind roared throughout earth and heaven, so that he could scarcely lift his head to look. For a while he was too breathless and astonished even to see where he was or what had happened. And his first movement was to feel his head and reassure himself that his streaming hair was still his own.

'Lord!' gasped Mr Fotheringay, scarce able to speak for the gale, 'I've had a squeak! What's gone wrong? Storms and thunder. And only a minute ago a fine night. It's Maydig set me on to this sort of thing. *What* a wind! If I go on fooling in this way, I'm bound to have a thundering accident . . . !

'Where's Maydig?

'What a confounded mess everything's in!'

He looked about him so far as his flapping jacket would permit. The appearance of things was really extremely strange. 'The sky's all right anyhow,' said Mr Fotheringay. 'And that's about all that is all right. And even there it looks like a terrific gale coming up. But there's the moon overhead, just as it was just now. Bright as midday. But as for the rest – Where's the village? Where's – where's anything? And what on earth set this wind a-blowing? I didn't order no wind.'

Mr Fotheringay struggled to get to his feet in vain, and after one failure, remained on all fours, holding on. He surveyed the moonlit world to leeward, with the tails of his jacket streaming over his head. 'There's something seriously wrong,' said Mr Fotheringay. 'And what it is – goodness knows.'

Far and wide nothing was visible in the white glare through the haze of dust that drove before a screaming gale but tumbled masses of earth and heaps of inchoate ruins, no trees, no houses, no familiar shapes, only a wilderness of disorder vanishing at last into the darkness beneath the whirling columns and streamers, the lightnings and thunderings of a swiftly rising storm. Near him in the livid glare was something that might once have been an elm tree, a smashed mass of splinters, shivered from boughs to base, and further a twisted mass of iron girders – only too evidently the viaduct – rose out of the piled confusion.

You see, when Mr Fotheringay had arrested the rotation of the solid globe, he had made no stipulation concerning the trifling movables upon its surface. And the earth spins so fast that the surface at its equator is travelling at rather more than a thousand miles an hour, and in these latitudes at more than half that pace. So that the village, and Mr Maydig, and Mr Fotheringay, and everybody and everything had been jerked violently forward at about nine miles per second[53] – that is to say, much more violently than if they had been fired out of a cannon. And every human being, every living creature, every house and every tree – all the world as we know it – had been so jerked and smashed and utterly destroyed. That was all.

These things Mr Fotheringay did not, of course, fully appreciate. But he perceived that his miracle had miscarried, and with that a great disgust of miracles came upon him. He was in darkness now, for the clouds had swept together and blotted out his momentary glimpse of the moon, and the air was full of fitful struggling tortured wraiths of hail. A great roaring of wind and waters filled earth and sky, and, peering under his hand through the dust and sleet to windward, he saw by the play of the lightnings a vast wall of water pouring towards him.

'Maydig!' screamed Mr Fotheringay's feeble voice amid the elemental uproar. 'Here! – Maydig!

'Stop!' cried Mr Fotheringay to the advancing water. 'Oh, for goodness' sake, stop!

'Just a moment,' said Mr Fotheringay to the lightnings and thunder. 'Stop jest a moment while I collect my thoughts . . . And now what shall I do?' he said. 'What *shall* I do? Lord! I wish Maydig was about.

'I know,' said Mr Fotheringay. 'And for goodness' sake let's have it right *this* time.'

He remained on all fours, leaning against the wind, very intent to have everything right.

'Ah!' he said. 'Let nothing what I'm going to order happen until I say "Off!" Lord! I wish I'd thought of that before!'

He lifted his little voice against the whirlwind, shouting louder and louder in the vain desire to hear himself speak. 'Now then! – Here goes! Mind about that what I said just now. In the first place, when all I've got to say is done, let me lose my miraculous power, let my will become just like anybody else's will, and all these dangerous miracles be stopped. I don't like them. I'd rather, I didn't work 'em. Ever so much. That's the first thing. And the second is – let me be back just before the miracles began; let everything be just as it was before that blessed lamp turned up. It's a big job, but it's the last. Have you got it? No more miracles, everything as it was – me back in the Long Dragon just before I drank my half-pint. That's it! Yes.'

He dug his fingers into the mould, closed his eyes, and said 'Off!'

Everything became perfectly still. He perceived that he was standing erect.

'So *you* say,' said a voice.

He opened his eyes. He was in the bar of the Long Dragon, arguing about miracles with Toddy Beamish. He had a vague sense of some great thing forgotten that instantaneously passed. You see, except for the loss of his miraculous powers, everything was back as it had been; his mind and memory therefore were now just as they had been at the time when this story began. So that he knew absolutely nothing of all that is told here, knows nothing of all that is told here to this day. And among other things, of course, he still did not believe in miracles.

'I tell you that miracles, properly speaking, can't possibly happen,' he said, 'whatever you like to hold. And I'm prepared to prove it up to the hilt.'

'That's what *you* think,' said Toddy Beamish, and, 'Prove it if you can.'

'Looky here, Mr Beamish,' said Mr Fotheringay. 'Let us clearly understand what a miracle is. It's something contrariwise to the course of nature done by power of Will . . . '

A Story of the Stone Age [54]

1. UGH-LOMI AND UYA

This story is of a time beyond the memory of man, before the beginning
of history, a time when one might have walked dry-shod from France
(as we call it now) to England, and when a broad and sluggish Thames
flowed through its marshes to meet its father Rhine, flowing through a
wide and level country that is under water in these latter days and which
we know by the name of the North Sea. In that remote age, the valley
which runs along the foot of the Downs did not exist, and the south of
Surrey was a range of hills, fir-clad on the middle slopes, and snow-
capped the better part of the year. The cores of its summits still remain
as Leith Hill, and Pitch Hill, and Hindhead. [55] On the lower slopes of
the range below the grassy spaces where the wild horses grazed were
forests of yew and sweet-chestnut and elm, and the thickets and dark
places hid the grizzly bear and the hyaena, and the grey apes clambered
through the branches. And still lower amidst the woodland and marsh
and open grass along the Wey [56] did this little drama play itself out to
the end that I have to tell. Fifty thousand years ago [57] it was, fifty
thousand years – if the estimates of the geologists are correct.

And in those days the springtime was as joyful as it is now, and sent
the blood coursing in just the same fashion. The afternoon sky was blue
with piled white clouds sailing through it, and the south-west wind
came like a soft caress. The new-come swallows drove to and fro. The
reaches of the river were spangled with white ranunculus, the marshy
places were starred with lady's-smock [58] and lit with marshmallow
wherever the regiments of the sedges lowered their swords, and
the northward-moving hippopotami, shiny black monsters, sporting
clumsily, came floundering and blundering through it all, rejoicing
dimly and possessed with one clear idea, to splash the river muddy.

Up the river and well in sight of the hippopotami, a number of little
buff-coloured animals dabbled in the water. There was no fear, no rivalry
and no enmity between them and the hippopotami. As the great bulks
came crashing through the reeds and smashed the mirror of the water
into silvery splashes, these little creatures shouted and gesticulated with
glee. It was the surest sign of high spring. 'Boloo!' they cried. 'Baayah.

Boloo!' They were the children of the men folk, the smoke of whose encampment rose from the knoll at the river's bend. Wild-eyed youngsters they were, with matted hair and little broad-nosed impish faces, covered (as some children are covered even nowadays) with a delicate down of hair. They were narrow in the loins and long in the arms. And their ears had no lobes, and had little pointed tips, a thing that still, in rare instances, survives. Stark-naked vivid little gypsies, as active as monkeys and as full of chatter, though a little wanting in words.

Their elders were hidden from the wallowing hippopotami by the crest of the knoll. The human squatting-place was a trampled area among the dead brown fronds of Royal Fern,[59] through which the crosiers of this year's growth were unrolling to tie light and warmth. The fire was a smouldering heap of char,[60] light grey and black, replenished by the old women from time to time with brown leaves. Most of the men were asleep – they slept sitting with their foreheads on their knees. They had killed that morning a good quarry, enough for all, a deer that had been wounded in a rutting fight; so that there had been no quarrelling among them, and some of the women were still gnawing the bones that lay scattered about. Others were making a heap of leaves and sticks to feed Brother Fire when the darkness came again, that he might grow strong and tall therewith, and guard them against the beasts. And two were piling flints that they brought, an armful at a time, from the bend of the river where the children were at play.

None of these buff-skinned savages were clothed, but some wore about their hips rude girdles of adder-skin or crackling undressed hide, from which depended little bags, not made, but torn from the paws of beasts, and carrying the rudely-dressed flints that were men's chief weapons and tools. And one woman, the mate of Uya the Cunning Man, wore a wonderful necklace of perforated fossils – that others had worn before her. Beside some of the sleeping men lay the big antlers of the elk, with the tines[61] chipped to sharp edges, and long sticks, hacked at the ends with flints into sharp points. There was little else save these things and the smouldering fire to mark these human beings off from the wild animals that ranged the country. But Uya the Cunning did not sleep, but sat with a bone in his hand and scraped busily thereon with a flint, a thing no animal would do. He was the oldest man in the tribe, beetle-browed, prognathous,[62] lank-armed; he had a beard and his cheeks were hairy, and his chest and arms were black with thick hair. And by virtue both of his strength and cunning he was master of the tribe, and his share was always the most and the best.

Eudena had hidden herself among the alders, because she was afraid of Uya. She was still a girl, and her eyes were bright and her smile pleasant to see. He had given her a piece of the liver, a man's piece, and a wonderful treat for a girl to get; but as she took it the other woman with the necklace had looked at her, an evil glance, and Ugh-lomi had made a noise in his throat. At that, Uya had looked at him long and steadfastly, and Ugh-lomi's face had fallen. And then Uya had looked at her. She was frightened and she had stolen away, while the feeding was still going on and Uya was busy with the marrow of a bone. Afterwards he had wandered about as if looking for her. And now she crouched among the alders, wondering mightily what Uya might be doing with the flint and the bone. And Ugh-lomi was not to be seen.

Presently a squirrel came leaping through the alders, and she lay so quiet the little man was within six feet of her before he saw her. Whereupon he dashed up a stem in a hurry and began to chatter and scold her.[63] 'What are you doing here,' he asked, 'away from the other men beasts?' 'Peace,' said Eudena, but he only chattered more, and then she began to break off the little black cones to throw at him. He dodged and defied her, and she grew excited and rose up to throw better, and then she saw Uya coming down the knoll. He had seen the movement of her pale arm amidst the thicket – he was very keen-eyed.

At that she forgot the squirrel and set off through the alders and reeds as fast as she could go. She did not care where she went so long as she escaped Uya. She splashed nearly knee-deep through a swampy place, and saw in front of her a slope of ferns – growing more slender and greener as they passed up out of the light into the shade of the young chestnut trees. She was soon amidst the trees – she was very fleet of foot, and she ran on and on, until the forest was old and the trees great, and the vines about their stems where the light came were thick as young trees, and the ropes of ivy stout and tight. On she went, and she doubled and doubled again, and then at last lay down amidst some ferns in a hollow place near a thicket, and listened with her heart beating in her ears.

She heard footsteps presently rustling among the dead leaves, far off, and they died away and everything was still again, except the scandalising[64] of the midges – for the evening was drawing on – and the incessant whisper of the leaves. She laughed silently to think the cunning Uya should go by her. She was not frightened. Sometimes, playing with the other girls and lads, she had fled into the wood, though never so far as this. It was pleasant to be hidden and alone.

She lay a long time there, glad of her escape, and then she sat up listening.

It was a rapid pattering growing louder and coming towards her, and in a little while she could hear grunting noises and the snapping of twigs. It was a drove of lean grisly wild swine. She turned about her, for a boar is an ill fellow to pass too closely, on account of the sideway slash of his tusks, and she made off slantingly through the trees. But the patter came nearer, they were not feeding as they wandered, but going fast – or else they would not overtake her – and she caught the limb of a tree, swung on to it, and ran up the stem with something of the agility of a monkey.

Down below the sharp bristling backs of the swine were already passing when she looked down. And she knew the short, sharp grunts they made meant fear. What were they afraid of? A man? They were in a great hurry for just a man.

And then, so suddenly it made her grip on the branch tighten involuntarily, a fawn started[65] in the brake and rushed after the swine. Something else went by, low and grey, with a long body; she did not know what it was, indeed she saw it only momentarily through the interstices of the young leaves; and then there came a pause.

She remained stiff and expectant, rigid almost as though she was a part of the tree she clung to, peering down.

Then far away among the trees, clear for a moment, then hidden, then visible knee-deep in ferns, then gone again, ran a man. She knew it was young Ugh-lomi by the fair colour of his hair, and there was red upon his face. Somehow his frantic flight and that scarlet mark made her feel sick. And then nearer, running heavily and breathing hard, came another man also running. At first she could not see, and then she saw, foreshortened and clear to her, Uya, running with great strides and his eyes staring. He was not going after Ugh-lomi. His face was white. It was Uya – *afraid*! He passed, and was still well within hearing, when something else, something large and with grizzled fur, swinging along with soft swift strides, came rushing in pursuit of him.

Eudena suddenly became rigid, ceased to breathe, her clutch convulsive and her eyes starting.

She had never seen the thing before, she did not even see him clearly now, but she knew at once it was the Terror of the Woodshade. His name was a legend, the children would frighten one another, frighten even themselves with his name and run screaming to the squatting-place. No man had ever killed any of his kind. Even the mighty mammoth feared his anger. It was the grizzly bear, the lord of world as the world went then.

As he ran he made a continuous growling rumble. 'Men in my very lair! Fighting and blood. At the very mouth of my lair. Men, men, men. Fighting and blood.' For he was the lord of the wood and of the caves.

Long after he had passed she remained a girl of stone, staring down through the branches. All her power of action had gone from her. She gripped by instinct with hands and knees and feet. It was some time before she could think, and then only one thing was clear in her mind, that the Terror was between her and the tribe – that it would be impossible to descend.

Presently when her fear was a little abated she clambered into a more comfortable position, where a great branch forked. The trees rose about her, so that she could see nothing of Brother Fire, who is black by day. Birds began to stir about her, and things that had gone into hiding for fear of her movements crept out . . .

After a time the blue overhead deepened, and the taller branches flamed out at the touch of the sunset. High overhead the rooks, who were wiser than men, went cawing home to their squatting-places among the elms. Looking down, things were clearer and darker. Eudena thought of going back to the squatting-place; she let herself down some way, and then the fear of the Terror of the Woodshade came again. While she hesitated a rabbit squealed dismally, and she dared not descend farther.

The shadows gathered, and the deeps of the forest began stirring. Eudena went up the tree again to be nearer the light. Down below the shadows came out of their hiding-places and walked abroad. Overhead the blue deepened. A dreadful stillness came, and then the leaves began whispering.

Eudena shivered and thought of Brother Fire.

The shadows now were gathering in the trees, they sat on the branches and watched her. Branches and leaves were turned to ominous, quiet black shapes that would spring on her if she stirred. Then the white owl, flitting silently, came ghostly through the shades. Darker grew the world and darker, until the leaves and twigs against the sky were black, and the ground was hidden.

She remained there all night, an age-long vigil, straining her ears for the things that went on below in the darkness, and keeping motionless lest some stealthy beast should discover her. Man in those days was never alone in the dark, save for such rare accidents as this. Age after age he had learnt the lesson of its terror – a lesson we poor children of his have nowadays painfully to unlearn. Eudena, though in age a woman, was in heart like a little child. She kept as still, poor little animal, as a hare before it is started.

The stars gathered and watched her – her one grain of comfort. In one bright one she fancied there was something like Ugh-lomi. Then she fancied it *was* Ugh-lomi. And near him, red and duller, was Uya, and as the night passed Ugh-lomi fled before him up the sky.

She tried to see Brother Fire, who guarded the squatting-place from beasts, but he was not in sight. And far away she heard the mammoths trumpeting as they went down to the drinking-place, and once some huge bulk with heavy paces hurried along, making a noise like a calf, but what it was she could not see. But she thought from the voice it was Yaaa the rhinoceros, who stabs with his nose, goes always alone, and rages without cause.

At last the little stars began to hide, and then the larger ones. It was like all the animals vanishing before the Terror. The sun was coming, lord of the sky, as the grizzly was lord of the forest. Eudena wondered what would happen if one star stayed behind. And then the sky paled to the dawn.

When the daylight came the fear of lurking things passed, and she could descend. She was stiff, but not so stiff as you would have been, dear young lady (by virtue of your upbringing),[66] and as she had not been trained to eat at least once in three hours, but instead had often fasted three days, she did not feel uncomfortably hungry. She crept down the tree very cautiously, and went her way stealthily through the wood, and not a squirrel sprang or deer started, but the terror of the grizzly bear froze her marrow.

Her desire was now to find her people again. Her dread of Uya the Cunning was consumed by a greater dread of loneliness. But she had lost her direction. She had run heedlessly overnight, and she could not tell whether the squatting-place was sunward or where it lay. Ever and again she stopped and listened, and at last, very far away, she heard a measured chinking. It was so faint even in the morning stillness that she could tell it must be far away. But she knew the sound was that of a man sharpening a flint.

Presently the trees began to thin out, and then came a regiment of nettles barring the way. She turned aside, and then she came to a fallen tree that she knew, with a noise of bees about it. And so presently she was in sight of the knoll, very far off, and the river under it, and the children and the hippopotami just as they had been yesterday, and the thin spire of smoke swaying in the morning breeze. Far away by the river was the cluster of alders where she had hidden. And at the sight of that the fear of Uya returned, and she crept into a thicket of bracken, out of which a rabbit scuttled, and lay awhile to watch the squatting-place.

The men were mostly out of sight, saving Wau, the flint-chopper; and at that she felt safer. They were away hunting food, no doubt. Some of the women, too, were down in the stream, stooping intent, seeking mussels, crayfish, and water-snails, and at the sight of their occupation Eudena felt hungry. She rose, and ran through the fern, designing to join them. As she went she heard a voice among the bracken calling softly. She stopped. Then suddenly she heard a rustle behind her and, turning, saw Ugh-lomi rising out of the fern. There were streaks of brown blood and dirt on his face, and his eyes were fierce, and the white stone of Uya, the white Fire Stone, that none but Uya dared to touch, was in his hand. In a stride he was beside her and gripped her arm. He swung her about, and thrust her before him towards the woods. 'Uya,' he said, and waved his arms about. She heard a cry, looked back, and saw all the women standing up, and two wading out of the stream. Then came a nearer howling, and the old woman with the beard, who watched the fire on the knoll, was waving her arms, and Wau, the man who had been chipping the flint, was getting to his feet. The little children too, were hurrying and shouting.

'Come!' said Ugh-lomi, and dragged her by the arm.

She still did not understand.

'Uya has called the death-word,' said Ugh-lomi, and she glanced back again at the screaming curve of figures, and dimly understood.

Wau and all the women and children were coming towards them, a scattered array of buff shockheaded figures, howling, leaping and crying. Over the knoll two youths hurried. Down among the ferns to the right came a man, heading them off from the wood. Ugh-lomi dropped her arm, and the two began running side by side, leaping the bracken and stepping clear and wide. Eudena, knowing her fleetness and the fleetness of Ugh-lomi, laughed aloud at the unequal chase. They were an exceptionally straight-limbed couple for those days.

They soon cleared the open, and drew near the wood of chestnut trees again – neither afraid now because neither was alone. They slackened their pace, already not excessive. And suddenly Eudena cried and swerved aside, pointing, and looking up through the tree-stems. Ugh-lomi saw the feet and legs of men running towards him. Eudena was already running off at a tangent. And as he turned to follow her they heard the voice of Uya coming through the trees, and roaring out his rage at them.

Then terror came in their hearts, not the terror that numbs, but the terror that makes one silent and swift. They were cut off now on two sides. They were in a sort of corner of pursuit. On the right hand, and

near by them, came the men swift and heavy, with bearded Uya, antler
in hand, leading them; and on the left, scattered as one scatters corn,
yellow dashes among the fern and grass, ran Wau and the women; and
even the little children from the shallow had joined the chase. The two
parties converged upon them. Off they went, with Eudena ahead.

They knew there was no mercy for them. There was no hunting so
sweet to these ancient men as the hunting of men. Once the fierce
passion of the chase was lit, the feeble beginnings of humanity in them
were thrown to the winds. And Uya in the night had marked Ugh-lomi
with the death-word. Ugh-lomi was the day's quarry.

They ran straight – it was their only chance – taking whatever ground
came in the way – a spread of stinging nettles, an open glade, a clump of
grass out of which a hyaena fled snarling. Then woods again, long
stretches of shady leaf-mould and moss under the green trunks. Then a
stiff slope, tree-clad, and long vistas of trees, a glade, a succulent green
area of black mud, a wide open space again, and then a clump of
lacerating brambles, with beast tracks through it. Behind them the chase
trailed out and scattered, with Uya ever at their heels. Eudena kept the
first place, running light and with her breath easy, for Ugh-lomi carried
the Fire Stone in his hand.

It told on his pace – not at first, but after a time. His footsteps behind
her suddenly grew remote. Glancing over her shoulder as they crossed
another open space, Eudena saw that Ugh-lomi was many yards behind
her, and Uya close upon him, with antler already raised in the air to
strike him down. Wau and the others were but just emerging from the
shadow of the woods.

Seeing Ugh-lomi in peril, Eudena ran sideways, looking back, and
threw up her arms and cried aloud, just as the antler flew. And young
Ugh-lomi, expecting this and understanding her cry, ducked his head,
so that the missile merely struck his scalp lightly, making but a trivial
wound, and flew over him. He turned forthwith, the quartzite Fire
Stone in both hands, and hurled it straight at Uya's body as he ran loose
from the throw. Uya shouted, but could not dodge it. It took him under
the ribs, heavy and flat, and he reeled and went down without a cry.
Ugh-lomi caught up the antler – one tine of it was tipped with his own
blood – and came running on again with a red trickle just coming out of
his hair.

Uya rolled over twice, and lay a moment before he got up, and then
he did not run fast. The colour of his face was changed. Wau overtook
him, and then others, and he coughed and laboured in his breath. But
he kept on.

At last the two fugitives gained the bank of the river, where the stream ran deep and narrow, and they still had fifty yards in hand of Wau, the foremost pursuer, the man who made the smiting stones. He carried one, a large flint, the shape of an oyster and double the size, chipped to a chisel edge, in either hand.

They sprang down the steep bank into the stream, rushed through the water, swam the deep current in two or three strokes, and came out wading again, dripping and refreshed, to clamber up the farther bank. It was undermined, and with willows growing thickly therefrom, so that it needed clambering. And while Eudena was still among the silvery branches and Ugh-lomi still in the water – for the antler had encumbered him – Wau came up against the sky on the opposite bank, and the smiting stone, thrown cunningly, took the side of Eudena's knee. She struggled to the top and fell.

They heard the pursuers shout to one another, and Ugh-lomi, climbing to her and moving jerkily to mar Wau's aim, felt the second smiting stone graze his ear, and heard the water splashing below him.

Then it was Ugh-lomi, the stripling, proved himself to have come to man's estate. For running on, he found Eudena fallen behind, limping, and at that he turned, and crying savagely and with a face terrible with sudden wrath and trickling blood, ran swiftly past her back to the bank, whirling the antler round his head. And Eudena kept on, running stoutly still, though she must needs limp at every step, and the pain was already sharp.

And now Wau, rising over the edge and clutching the straight willow branches, saw Ugh-lomi towering over him, gigantic against the blue; saw his whole body swing round, the grip of his hands upon the antler. The edge of the antler came sweeping through the air, and he saw no more. The water under the osiers whirled and eddied and went crimson six feet down the stream. Uya following, stopped knee-high across the stream, and the man who was swimming turned about.

The other men who trailed after – they were none of them very mighty men (for Uya was more cunning than strong, brooking no sturdy rivals) – slackened momentarily at the sight of Ugh-lomi standing there above the willows, bloody and terrible, between them and the halting girl, with the huge antler waving in his hand. It seemed as though he had gone into the water a youth, and come out of it a man full grown.

He knew what there was behind him. A broad stretch of grass, and then a thicket, and in that Eudena could hide. That was clear in his mind, though his thinking powers were too feeble to see what should happen thereafter. Uya stood knee-deep, undecided and unarmed. His heavy mouth hung open, showing his canine teeth, and he panted heavily. His side was flushed and bruised under the hair. The other man beside him carried a sharpened stick. The rest of the hunters came up one by one to the top of the bank, hairy, long-armed men clutching flints and sticks. Two ran off along the bank downstream, and then clambered down to the water, where Wau had come to the surface struggling weakly. They gibbered at him without any sane attempt to help, and presently he went under again. Two others threatened Ugh-lomi from the bank.

He answered back, shouts, vague insults, gestures. Then Uya, who had been standing hesitating, roared with rage, and whirling his fists came plunging through the water. His followers came splashing after him.

Ugh-lomi glanced over his shoulder and found Eudena already vanished into the thicket. He would perhaps have waited for Uya, but Uya preferred to spar in the water below him until the others were beside him. Human tactics in those days, in all serious fighting, were the tactics of the pack. Prey that turned at bay they gathered around and rushed. Ugh-lomi felt the rush coming, and hurling the antler at Uya, turned about and fled.

When he halted to look back from the shadow of the thicket, he found only three of his pursuers had followed him across the river, and they were going back again. Uya, with a bleeding mouth, was on the farther side of the stream again, but lower down, and he held his hand to his side. The others were in the river dragging something to shore. For a time at least the chase was intermitted.

Ugh-lomi stood watching for a space, and snarled at the sight of Uya. Then he turned and plunged into the thicket.

In a minute, Eudena came hastening to join him, and they went on hand in hand. He dimly perceived the pain she suffered from the cut and bruised knee, and chose the easier ways. But they went on all that day, mile after mile, through wood and thicket, until at last they came to the chalkland, open grass with rare woods of beech, and the birch growing near water, and they saw the Wealden mountains[67] nearer, and groups of horses grazing together. They went circumspectly, keeping always near thicket and cover, for this was a strange region – even its ways were strange. Steadily the ground rose, until the chestnut forests spread wide and blue below them, and the Thames marshes shone silvery, high and far. They saw no men, for in those days men were still only just come into this part of the world, and were moving but slowly along the riverways. Towards evening they came on the river again, but now it ran in a gorge, between high cliffs of white chalk that sometimes overhung it. Down the cliffs was a scrub of birches and there were many birds there. And high up the cliff was a little shelf by a tree, whereon they clambered to pass the night.

They had had scarcely any food; it was not the time of year for berries, and they had no time to go aside to snare or waylay. They tramped in a hungry weary silence, gnawing at twigs and leaves. But over the surface of the cliffs were a multitude of snails, and in a bush were the freshly laid eggs of a little bird, and then Ugh-lomi threw at and killed a squirrel in a beech tree, so that at last they fed well. Ugh-lomi watched during the night, his chin on his knees; and he heard young foxes crying hard by, and the noise of mammoths down the gorge, and the hyenas yelling and laughing far away. It was chilly, but they dared not light a fire. Whenever he dozed, his spirit went abroad, and straightway met with the spirit of Uya, and they fought. And always Ugh-lomi was paralysed so that he could not smite nor run, and then he would awake suddenly. Eudena too, dreamt evil things of Uya, so that they both awoke with the fear of him in their hearts, and by the light of the dawn they saw a woolly rhinoceros go blundering down the valley.

During the day they caressed one another and were glad of the sunshine, and Eudena's leg was so stiff she sat on the ledge all day. Ugh-lomi found great flints sticking out of the cliff face, greater than any he had seen, and he dragged some to the ledge and began chipping, so as to be armed against Uya when he came again. And at one he laughed heartily, and Eudena laughed, and they threw it about in derision. It had a hole in it. They stuck their fingers through it, it was very funny indeed. Then they peeped at one another through it. Afterwards, Ugh-lomi got himself a stick, and thrusting by chance at this foolish flint, the stick went in and stuck there. He had rammed it in too tightly to withdraw it. That was still stranger – scarcely funny, terrible almost, and for a time Ugh-lomi did not greatly care to touch the thing. It was as if the flint had bit and held with its teeth. But then he got familiar with the odd combination. He swung it about, and perceived dimly that the stick with the heavy stone on the end struck a better blow than anything he knew. He went to and fro swinging it, and striking with it; but later he tired of it and threw it aside. In the afternoon he went up over the brow of the white cliff, and lay watching by a rabbit-warren until the rabbits came out to play. There were no men thereabouts, and the rabbits were heedless. He threw a smiting stone he had made and got a kill.

That night they made a fire from flint sparks and bracken fronds, and talked and caressed by it. And in their sleep Uya's spirit came again, and suddenly, while Ugh-lomi was trying to fight vainly, the foolish flint on the stick came into his hand, and he struck Uya with it, and behold! It killed him. But afterwards came other dreams of Uya – for spirits take a lot of killing, and he had to be killed again. Then after that the stone would not keep on the stick. He awoke tired and rather gloomy, and was sulky all the forenoon, in spite of Eudena's kindliness, and instead of hunting he sat chipping a sharp edge to the singular flint, and looking strangely at her. Then he bound the perforated flint on to the stick with strips of rabbit. And afterwards he walked up and down the ledge, striking with it, and muttering to himself, and thinking of Uya. It felt very fine and heavy in the hand.

Several days, more than there was any counting in those days, five days, it may be, or six, did Ugh-lomi and Eudena stay on that shelf in the gorge of the river, and they lost all fear of men, and their fire burnt redly of a night. And they were very merry together; there was food every day, sweet water, and no enemies. Eudena's knee was well in a couple of days, for those ancient savages had quick-healing flesh. Indeed, they were very happy.

On one of those days, although it has little to do with this story, Ugh-lomi dropped a chunk of flint on the cliff. He saw it fall, and go bounding across the river bank into the river, and after laughing and thinking it over a little he tried another. This smashed a bush of hazel in the most interesting way. They spent all the morning dropping stones from the ledge and in the afternoon they discovered this new and interesting pastime was also possible from the cliff brow. The next day they had forgotten this delight. Or at least, it seemed they had forgotten.

But Uya came in dreams to spoil the paradise. Three nights he came fighting Ugh-lomi. In the morning after these dreams Ugh-lomi would walk up and down, threatening him and swinging the axe, and at last came the night after Ugh-lomi brained the otter, and they had feasted. Uya went too far. Ugh-lomi awoke, scowling under his heavy brows, and he took his axe, and extending his hand towards Eudena he bade her wait for him upon the ledge. Then he clambered down the white declivity, glanced up once from the foot of it and flourished his axe, and without looking back again went striding along the river bank until the overhanging cliff at the bend hid him.

Two days and nights did Eudena sit alone by the fire on the ledge waiting, and in the night the beasts howled over the cliffs and down the valley, and on the cliff over against her the hunched hyenas prowled black against the sky. But no evil thing came near her save fear. Once, far away, she heard the roaring of a lion, following the horses as they came northward over the grasslands with the spring. All that time she waited – the waiting that is pain.

And the third day Ugh-lomi came back, up the river. The plumes of a raven were in his hair. The axe was red-stained, and had long dark hairs upon it, and he carried the necklace that had marked the favourite of Uya in his hand. He walked in the soft places, giving no heed to his trail. Save a raw cut below his jaw there was not a wound upon him. 'Uya!' cried Ugh-lomi exultant, and Eudena saw it was well. He put the necklace on Eudena, and they ate and drank together. And after eating he began to rehearse the whole story from the beginning, when Uya had cast his eyes on Eudena, and Uya and Ugh-lomi, fighting in the forest, had been chased by the bear, eking out his scanty words with abundant pantomime, springing to his feet and whirling the stone axe round when it came to the fighting. The last fight was a mighty one, stamping and shouting, and once a blow at the fire that sent a torrent of sparks up into the night. And Eudena sat red in the light of the fire, gloating on him, her face flushed and her eyes shining, and the necklace Uya had made about her neck. It was a splendid time, and the stars that look down on us looked down on her, our ancestor – who has been dead now these fifty thousand years.

2 THE CAVE BEAR

In the days when Eudena and Ugh-lomi fled from the people of Uya towards the fir-clad mountains of the Weald, across the forests of sweet-chestnut and the grass-clad chalkland, and hid themselves at last in the gorge of the river between the chalk cliffs, men were few and their squatting-places far between. The nearest men to them were those of the tribe, a full day's journey down the river, and up the mountains there were none. Man was indeed a newcomer to this part of the world in that ancient time, coming slowly along the rivers, generation after generation, from one squatting-place to another, from the south-westward. And the animals that held the land, the hippopotami and rhinoceros of the river valleys, the horses of the grass plains, the deer and swine of the woods, the grey apes in the branches, the cattle of the uplands, feared him but little – let alone the mammoths in the mountains and the elephants that came through the land in the summertime out of the south. For why should they fear him, when the rough, chipped flints that he had not learnt to haft[68] and which he threw but ill and the poor spear of sharpened wood were all his weapons against hoof and horn, tooth and claw?

Andoo, the huge cave bear, who lived in the cave up the gorge, had never even seen a man in all his wise and respectable life, until midway through one night, as he was prowling down the gorge along the cliff edge, he saw the glare of Eudena's fire upon the ledge, and Eudena red and shining, and Ugh-lomi, with a gigantic shadow, mocking him upon the white cliff, going to and fro, shaking his mane of hair and waving the axe of stone – the first axe of stone – while he chanted of the killing of Uya. The cave bear was far up the gorge, and he saw the thing slanting-ways and far off. He was so surprised he stood quite still upon the edge, sniffing the novel odour of burning bracken, and wondering whether the dawn was coming up in the wrong place.

He was the lord of the rocks and caves, was the cave bear, as his slighter brother, the grizzly, was lord of the thick woods below, and as the dappled lion – the lion of those days was dappled – was lord of the thorn-thickets, reed-beds and open plains. He was the greatest of all meat-eaters; he knew no fear, none preyed on him, and none gave him battle; only the rhinoceros was beyond his strength. Even the mammoth shunned his country. This invasion perplexed him. He noticed these new beasts were shaped like monkeys, and sparsely hairy like young pigs. 'Monkey and young pig,' said the cave bear. 'It might not be so bad. But that red thing that jumps, and the black thing jumping with it yonder! Never in my life have I seen such things before.'

He came slowly along the brow of the cliff towards them, stopping thrice to sniff and peer, and the reek of the fire grew stronger. A couple of hyenas also were so intent upon the thing below that Andoo, coming soft and easy, was close upon them before they knew of him or he of them. They started guiltily and went lurching off. Coming round in a wheel, a hundred yards off, they began yelling and calling him names for the start they had had. 'Ya-ha!' they cried. 'Who can't grub his own burrow? Who eats roots like a pig . . . ? Ya-ha!' For even in those days the hyaena's manners were just as offensive as they are now.

'Who answers the hyaena?' growled Andoo, peering through the midnight dimness at them, and then going to look at the cliff edge.

There was Ugh-lomi still telling his story, and the fire getting low, and the scent of the burning hot and strong.

Andoo stood on the edge of the chalk cliff for some time, shifting his vast weight from foot to foot, and swaying his head to and fro, with his mouth open, his ears erect and twitching, and the nostrils of his big black muzzle sniffing. He was very curious, was the cave bear, more curious than any of the bears that live now, and the flickering fire and the incomprehensible movements of the man, let alone the intrusion into his indisputable province, stirred him with a sense of strange new happenings. He had been after red-deer fawn that night, for the cave bear was a miscellaneous hunter, but this quite turned him from that enterprise.

'Ya-ha!' yelled the hyenas behind. 'Ya-ha-ha!'

Peering through the starlight, Andoo saw there were now three or four going to and fro against the grey hillside. 'They will hang about me now all the night until I kill,' said Andoo. 'Filth of the world!' And mainly to annoy them, he resolved to watch the red flicker in the gorge until the dawn came to drive the hyaena scum home. And after a time they vanished, and he heard their voices, like a party of Cockney bean-feasters,[69] away in the beech-woods. Then they came slinking near again. Andoo yawned and went on along the cliff, and they followed. Then he stopped and went back.

It was a splendid night, beset with shining constellations, the same stars, but not the same constellations we know, for since those days all the stars have had time to move into new places. Far away across the open space beyond where the heavy-shouldered, lean-bodied hyenas blundered and howled, was a beech-wood, and the mountain slopes rose beyond, a dim mystery, until their snow-capped summits came out white and cold and clear, touched by the first rays of the yet unseen moon. It was a vast silence, save when the yell of the hyenas flung a vanishing discordance across its peace, or when from down the hills the trumpeting of the new-come elephants came faintly on the faint breeze. And below now, the red flicker had dwindled and was steady, and shone a deeper red, and Ugh-lomi had finished his story and was preparing to sleep, and Eudena sat and listened to the strange voices of unknown beasts, and watched the dark eastern sky growing deeply luminous at the advent of the moon. Down below, the river talked to itself, and things unseen went to and fro.

After a time the bear went away, but in an hour he was back again. Then, as if struck by a thought, he turned, and went up the gorge . . .

The night passed, and Ugh-lomi slept on. The waning moon rose and lit the gaunt white cliff overhead with a light that was pale and vague. The gorge remained in a deeper shadow, and seemed all the darker. Then by imperceptible degrees the day came stealing in the wake of the moonlight. Eudena's eyes wandered to the cliff brow overhead once, and then again. Each time the line was sharp and clear against the sky, and yet she had a dim perception of something lurking there. The red of the fire grew deeper and deeper, grey scales spread upon it, its vertical column of smoke became more and more visible, and up and down the gorge things that had been unseen grew clear in a colourless illumination. She may have dozed.

Suddenly she started up from her squatting position, erect and alert, scrutinising the cliff up and down.

She made the faintest sound, and Ugh-lomi too, light sleeping like an animal, was instantly awake. He caught up his axe and came noiselessly to her side.

The light was still dim, the world now all in black and dark grey, and one sickly star still lingered overhead. The ledge they were on was a little grassy space, six feet wide perhaps, and twenty feet long, sloping outwardly, and with a handful of St John's wort[70] growing near the edge. Below it, the soft white rock fell away in a steep slope of nearly fifty feet to the thick bush of hazel that fringed the river. Down the river this slope increased, until some way off a thin grass held its own right up to the crest of the cliff. Overhead, forty or fifty feet of rock bulged into the great masses characteristic of chalk, but at the end of the ledge a gully, a precipitous groove of discoloured chalk, slashed the face of the cliff, and gave a footing to a scrubby growth, by which Eudena and Ugh-lomi went up and down.

They stood as noiseless as startled deer, with every sense expectant. For a minute they heard nothing, and then came a faint rattling of dust down the gully, and the creaking of twigs.

Ugh-lomi gripped his axe, and went to the edge of the ledge, for the bulge of the chalk overhead had hidden the upper part of the gully. And forthwith, with a sudden contraction of the heart, he saw the cave bear halfway down from the brow, and making a gingerly backward step with his flat hind-foot. His hindquarters were towards Ugh-lomi, and he clawed at the rocks and bushes so that he seemed flattened against the cliff. He looked none the less for that. From his shining snout to his stumpy tail he was a lion and a half, the length of two tall men. He looked over his shoulder, and his huge mouth was open with the exertion of holding up his great carcase, and his tongue lay out . . .

He got his footing, and came down slowly, a yard nearer.

'Bear,' said Ugh-lomi, looking round with his face white.

But Eudena, with terror in her eyes, was pointing down the cliff.

Ugh-lomi's mouth fell open. For down below, with her big forefeet against the rock, stood another big brown-grey bulk – the she-bear. She was not so big as Andoo, but she was big enough for all that.

Then suddenly Ugh-lomi gave a cry, and catching up a handful of the litter of ferns that lay scattered on the ledge, he thrust it into the pallid ash of the fire. 'Brother Fire!' he cried, 'Brother Fire!' And Eudena, starting into activity, did likewise. 'Brother Fire! Help, help! Brother Fire!'

Brother Fire was still red in his heart, but he turned to grey as they scattered him. 'Brother Fire!' They screamed. But he whispered and passed, and there was nothing but ashes. Then Ugh-lomi danced with anger and struck the ashes with his fist. But Eudena began to hammer the firestone against a flint. And the eyes of each were turning ever and again towards the gully by which Andoo was climbing down. Brother Fire!

Suddenly the huge furry hindquarters of the bear came into view, beneath the bulge of the chalk that had hidden him. He was still clambering gingerly down the nearly vertical surface. His head was yet out of sight, but they could hear him talking to himself. 'Pig and monkey,' said the cave bear. 'It ought to be good.'

Eudena struck a spark and blew at it; it twinkled brighter and then – went out. At that she cast down flint and firestone and began wringing her hands. Her face was wet with tears. Then she sprang to her feet and scrambled a dozen feet up the cliff above the ledge. How she hung on even for a moment I do not know, for the chalk was vertical and without grip for a monkey. In a couple of seconds she had slid back to the ledge again with bleeding hands.

Ugh-lomi was making frantic rushes about the ledge – now he would go to the edge, now to the gully. He did not know what to do, he could not think. The she-bear looked smaller than her mate – much. If they rushed down on her together, *one* might live. 'Ugh?' said the cave bear, and Ugh-lomi turned again and saw his little eyes peering under the bulge of the chalk.

Eudena, cowering at the end of the ledge, began to scream like a gripped rabbit.

At that a sort of madness came upon Ugh-lomi. With a mighty cry, he caught up his axe and began to clamber up the gully to the bear. He uttered neither word nor cry. The monster gave a grunt of surprise. In a moment Ugh-lomi was clinging to a bush right underneath the bear, and in another he was hanging to its back half buried in fur, with one fist clutched in the hair under its jaw. The bear was too astonished at this fantastic attack to do more than cling passive. And then the axe, the first of all axes, rang on its skull.

The bear's head twisted from side to side, and he began a petulant scolding growl. The axe bit within an inch of the left eye, and the hot blood blinded that side. At that the brute roared with surprise and anger, and his teeth gnashed six inches from Ugh-lomi's face. Then the axe, clubbed close, came down heavily on the corner of the jaw.

The next blow blinded the right side and called forth a roar, this time of pain. Eudena saw the huge flat feet slipping and sliding, and suddenly the bear gave a clumsy leap sideways, as if for the ledge. Then everything vanished, and the hazels smashed, and a roar of pain and a tumult of shouts and growls came up from far below.

Eudena screamed and ran to the edge and peered over. For a moment, man and bears were a heap together, Ugh-lomi uppermost; and then he had sprung clear and was scaling the gully again, with the bears rolling and striking at one another among the hazels. But he had left his axe below, and three knob-ended streaks of carmine were shooting down his thigh. 'Up!' he cried, and in a moment Eudena was preceding him to the top of the cliff.

In half a minute they were at the crest, their hearts pumping noisily, with Andoo and his wife far and safe below them. Andoo was sitting on his haunches, both paws at work, trying with quick exasperated movements to wipe the blindness out of his eyes, and the she-bear stood on all-fours a little way off, ruffled in appearance and growling angrily. Ugh-lomi flung himself flat on the grass, and lay panting and bleeding with his face on his arms.

For a second Eudena regarded the bears, then she came and sat beside him, looking at him . . .

Presently she put forth her hand timidly and touched him, and made the guttural sound that was his name. He turned over and raised himself on his arm. His face was pale, like the face of one who is afraid. He looked at her steadfastly for a moment, and then suddenly he laughed. 'Waugh!' he said exultantly.

'Waugh!' said she – a simple but expressive conversation.

Then Ugh-lomi came and knelt beside her, and on hands and knees peered over the brow and examined the gorge. His breath was steady now, and the blood on his leg had ceased to flow, though the scratches the she-bear had made were open and wide. He squatted up and sat staring at the footmarks of the great bear as they came to the gully – they were as wide as his head and twice as long. Then he jumped up and went along the cliff face until the ledge was visible. Here he sat down for some time thinking, while Eudena watched him.

At last Ugh-lomi rose, as one whose mind is made up. He returned towards the gully, Eudena keeping close by him, and together they clambered to the ledge. They took the firestone and a flint, and then

Ugh-lomi went down to the foot of the cliff very cautiously, and found his axe. They returned to the cliff now as quietly as they could, and turning their faces resolutely upstream set off at a brisk walk. The ledge was a home no longer with such callers in the neighbourhood. Ugh-lomi carried the axe and Eudena the firestone. So simple was a Palaeolithic removal.

They went upstream, although it might lead to the very lair of the cave bear, because there was no other way to go. Down the stream was the tribe, and had not Ugh-lomi killed Uya and Wau? By the stream they had to keep – because of drinking.

So they marched through beech trees, with the gorge deepening until the river flowed, a frothing rapid, five hundred feet below them. And of all the changeful things in this world of change, the courses of rivers, in deep valleys change least. It was the river Wey, the river we know today, and they marched over the very spots where nowadays stand little Guildford and Godalming – the first human beings to come into the land. Once a grey ape chattered and vanished, and all along the cliff edge, vast and even, ran the spoor of the great cave bear.

And then the spoor of the bear fell away from the cliff, showing, Ugh-lomi thought, that he came from some place to the left, and keeping to the cliff's edge, they presently came to an end. They found themselves looking down on a great semicircular space caused by the collapse of the cliff. It had smashed right across the gorge, banking the upstream water back in a pool which overflowed in a rapid. The slip had happened long ago. It was grassed over, but the face of the cliffs that stood about the semicircle was still almost fresh-looking and white as on the day when the rock must have broken and slid down. Starkly exposed and black under the foot of these cliffs were the mouths of several caves. And as they stood there, looking at the space, and disinclined to skirt it, because they thought the bears' lair lay somewhere on the left in the direction they must needs take, they saw suddenly first one bear and then two coming up the grass slope to the right and going across the amphitheatre towards the caves. Andoo was first, and he dropped a little on his forefoot, and his mien was despondent, and the she-bear came shuffling behind.

Eudena and Ugh-lomi stepped quite noiselessly back from the cliff until they could just see the bears over the verge. Then Ugh-lomi stopped. Eudena pulled his arm, but he turned with a forbidding gesture, and her hand dropped. Ugh-lomi stood watching the bears, with his axe in his hand, until they had vanished into the cave. He growled softly, and shook the axe at the she-bear's receding quarters.

Then to Eudena's terror, instead of creeping off with her, he lay flat down and crawled forward into such a position that he could just see the cave. It was bears – and he did it as calmly as if it had been rabbits he was watching!

He lay still, like a barked log, sun-dappled, in the shadow of the trees. He was thinking. And Eudena had learnt, even when a little girl, that when Ugh-lomi became still like that, jaw-bone on fist, novel things presently began to happen.

It was an hour before the thinking was over; it was noon when the two little savages had found their way to the cliff brow that overhung the bears' cave. And all the long afternoon they fought desperately with a great boulder of chalk; trundling it, with nothing but their unaided sturdy muscles, from the gully where it had hung like a loose tooth, towards the cliff top. It was full two yards about, it stood as high as Eudena's waist, it was obtuse-angled and toothed with flints. And when the sun set it was poised, three inches from the edge, above the cave of the great cave bear.

In the cave, conversation languished during the afternoon. The she-bear snoozed sulkily in her corner – for she was fond of pig and monkey – and Andoo was busy licking the side of his paw and smearing his face to cool the smart and inflammation of his wounds. Afterwards he went and sat just within the mouth of the cave, blinking out at the afternoon sun with his uninjured eye, and thinking.

'I never was so startled in my life,' he said at last. 'They are the most extraordinary beasts. Attacking *me*!'

'I don't like them,' said the she-bear, out of the darkness behind.

'A feebler sort of beast I *never* saw. I can't think what the world is coming to. Scraggy, weedy legs . . . Wonder how they keep warm in winter?'

'Very likely they don't,' said the she-bear.

'I suppose it's a sort of monkey gone wrong.'

'It's a change,' said the she-bear.

A pause.

'The advantage he had was merely accidental,' said Andoo. 'These things *will* happen at times.'

'I can't understand why you let go,' said the she-bear.

That matter had been discussed before, and settled. So Andoo, being a bear of experience, remained silent for a space. Then he resumed upon a different aspect of the matter. 'He has a sort of claw – a long claw that he seemed to have first on one paw and then on the other. Just one claw. They're very odd things. The bright thing, too, they seemed to have – like that glare that comes in the sky in daytime – only it jumps about – it's really worth seeing. It's a thing with a root, too – like grass when it is windy.'

'Does it bite?' asked the she-bear. 'If it bites it can't be a plant.'

'No – I don't know,' said Andoo. 'But it's curious, anyhow.'

'I wonder if they *are* good eating?' said the she-bear.

'They look it,' said Andoo, with appetite – for the cave bear, like the polar bear, was an incurable carnivore – no roots or honey for *him*.

The two bears fell into a meditation for a space. Then Andoo resumed his simple attentions to his eye. The sunlight up the green slope before the cave mouth grew warmer in tone and warmer, until it was a ruddy amber.

'Curious sort of thing – day,' said the cave bear. 'Lot too much of it, I think. Quite unsuitable for hunting. Dazzles me always. I can't smell nearly so well by day.'

The she-bear did not answer, but there came a measured crunching sound out of the darkness. She had turned up a bone. Andoo yawned. 'Well,' he said. He strolled to the cave mouth and stood with his head projecting, surveying the amphitheatre. He found he had to turn his head completely round to see objects on his right-hand side. No doubt that eye would be all right tomorrow.

He yawned again. There was a tap overhead, and a big mass of chalk flew out from the cliff face, dropped a yard in front of his nose, and starred into a dozen unequal fragments. It startled him extremely.

When he had recovered a little from his shock, he went and sniffed curiously at the representative pieces of the fallen projectile. They had a distinctive flavour, oddly reminiscent of the two drab animals of the ledge. He sat up and pawed the larger lump, and walked round it several times trying to find a man about it somewhere . . .

When night had come he went off down the river gorge to see if he could cut off either of the ledge's occupants. The ledge was empty, there were no signs of the red thing, but as he was rather hungry he did not loiter long that night, but pushed on to pick up a red-deer fawn. He forgot about the drab animals. He found a fawn, but the doe was close by and made an ugly fight for her young. Andoo had to leave the fawn, but as her blood was up she stuck to the attack, and at last he got in a blow of his paw at her nose, and so got hold of her. More meat but less delicacy, and the she-bear, following, had her share. The next afternoon, curiously enough, the very fellow of the first white rock fell, and smashed precisely according to precedent.

The aim of the third, that fell the night after, however, was better. It hit Andoo's unspeculative skull with a crack that echoed up the cliff, and the white fragments went dancing to all the points of the compass. The she-bear coming after him and sniffing curiously at him, found him lying in an odd sort of attitude, with his head wet and all out of shape. She was a young she-bear, and inexperienced, and having sniffed about him for some time and licked him a little, and so forth, she decided to leave him until the odd mood had passed, and went on her hunting alone.

She looked up the fawn of the red doe they had killed two nights ago, and found it. But it was lonely hunting without Andoo, and she returned caveward before dawn. The sky was grey and overcast, the trees up the gorge were black and unfamiliar, and into her ursine mind came a dim sense of strange and dreary happenings. She lifted up her voice and called Andoo by name. The sides of the gorge re-echoed her call.

As she approached the caves she saw in the half light, and heard, a couple of jackals scuttle off, and immediately after a hyena howled, and a dozen clumsy bulks went lumbering up the slope, and stopped and yelled derision. 'Lord of the rocks and caves – ya-ha!' came down the wind. The dismal feeling in the she-bear's mind became suddenly acute. She shuffled across the amphitheatre.

'Ya-ha!' said the hyenas, retreating. 'Ya-ha!'

The cave bear was not lying quite in the same attitude, because the hyenas had been busy, and in one place his ribs showed white. Dotted over the turf about him lay the smashed fragments of the three great lumps of chalk. And the air was full of the scent of death.

The she-bear stopped dead. Even now, that the great and wonderful Andoo was killed was beyond her believing. Then she heard far overhead a sound, a queer sound, a little like the shout of a hyena but fuller and lower in pitch. She looked up, with her little dawn-blinded eyes, seeing little, her nostrils quivering. And there, on the cliff edge, far above her against the bright pink of dawn, were two little shaggy round dark things, the heads of Eudena and Ugh-lomi, as they shouted derision at her. But though she could not see them very distinctly she could hear, and dimly she began to apprehend. A novel feeling as of imminent strange evils came into her heart.

She began to examine the smashed fragments of chalk that lay about Andoo. For a space she stood still, looking about her and making a low continuous sound that was almost a moan. Then she went back incredulously to Andoo to make one last effort to rouse him.

3 THE FIRST HORSEMAN

In the days before Ugh-lomi killed the great cave bear there was little trouble between the horses and men. Indeed they lived apart – the men in the river swamps and thickets, the horses on the wide grassy uplands between the chestnuts and the pines. Sometimes a pony would come straying into the clogging marshes to make a flint-hacked meal, and sometimes the tribe would find one, the kill of a lion, and drive off the jackals, and feast heartily while the sun was high. These horses of the old time were clumsy at the fetlock and dun-coloured, with a rough tail and big head. They came every springtime north-westward into the country, after the swallows and before the hippopotami, as the grass on the wide downland stretches grew long. They came only in small bodies thus far, each herd, a stallion and two or three mares and a foal or so, having its own stretch of country, and they went again when the chestnut trees were yellow and the wolves came down the Wealden mountains.

It was their custom to graze right out in the open, going into cover only in the heat of the day. They avoided the long stretches of thorn and beechwood, preferring an isolated group of trees, void of ambuscade, so that it was hard to come upon them. They were never fighters; their heels and teeth were for one another, but in the clear country, once they were started, no living thing came near them, though perhaps the elephant might have done so, had he felt the need. And in those days man seemed a harmless thing enough. No whisper of prophetic intelligence told the species of the terrible slavery that was to come, of the whip and spur and bearing-rein, the clumsy load and the slippery street, the insufficient food and the knacker's yard, that was to replace the wide grassland and the freedom of the earth.

Down in the Wey marshes Ugh-lomi and Eudena had never seen the horses closely, but now they saw them every day as the two of them raided out from their lair on the ledge in the gorge, raiding together in search of food. They had returned to the ledge after the killing of Andoo; for of the she-bear they were not afraid. The she-bear had become afraid of them, and when she winded[71] them she went aside. The two went together everywhere; for since they had left the tribe Eudena was not so much Ugh-lomi's woman as his mate; she learnt to hunt even – as much that is, as any woman could. She was indeed a marvellous woman. He would lie for hours watching a beast, or planning catches in that shock head of his, and she would stay beside him, with her bright eyes upon him, offering no irritating suggestions – as still as any man. A wonderful woman!

At the top of the cliff was an open grassy lawn and then beechwoods, and going through the beechwoods one came to the edge of the rolling grassy expanse, and in sight of the horses. Here, on the edge of the wood and bracken, were the rabbit-burrows, and here among the fronds Eudena and Ugh-lomi would lie with their throwing-stones ready, until the little people came out to nibble and play in the sunset. And while Eudena would sit, a silent figure of watchfulness, regarding the burrows, Ugh-lomi's eyes were ever away across the greensward at those wonderful grazing strangers.

In a dim way he appreciated their grace and their supple nimbleness. As the sun declined in the evening-time, and the heat of the day passed, they would become active, would start chasing one another, neighing, dodging, shaking their manes, coming round in great curves, sometimes so close that the pounding of the turf sounded like hurried thunder. It looked so fine that Ugh-lomi wanted to join in badly. And sometimes one would roll over on the turf, kicking four hoofs heavenward, which seemed formidable and was certainly much less alluring.

Dim imaginings ran through Ugh-lomi's mind as he watched – by virtue of which two rabbits lived the longer. And sleeping, his brains were clearer and bolder – for that was the way in those days. He came near the horses, he dreamt, and fought, smiting-stone against hoof, but then the horses changed to men or, at least, to men with horses' heads, and he awoke in a cold sweat of terror.

Yet the next day in the morning, as the horses were grazing, one of the mares whinnied, and they saw Ugh-lomi coming up the wind. They all stopped their eating and watched him. Ugh-lomi was not coming towards them, but strolling obliquely across the open, looking at anything in the world but horses. He had stuck three fern-fronds into the mat of his hair, giving him a remarkable appearance, and he walked very slowly. 'What's up now?' said the Master Horse, who was capable, but inexperienced.

'It looks more like the first half of an animal than anything else in the world,' he said. 'Forelegs and no hind.'

'It's only one of those pink monkey things,' said the Eldest Mare. 'They're a sort of river monkey. They're quite common on the plains.'

Ugh-lomi continued his oblique advance. The Eldest Mare was struck with the want of motive in his proceedings.

'Fool!' said the Eldest Mare, in a quick conclusive way she had.

She resumed her grazing. The Master Horse and the Second Mare followed suit.

'Look! He's nearer,' said the Foal with a stripe.

One of the younger foals made uneasy movements. Ugh-lomi squatted down and sat regarding the horses fixedly. In a little while he was satisfied that they meant neither flight nor hostilities. He began to consider his next procedure. He did not feel anxious to kill, but he had his axe with him, and the spirit of sport was upon him. How would one kill one of these creatures – ? These great beautiful creatures!

Eudena, watching him with a fearful admiration from the cover of the bracken, saw him presently go on all fours, and so proceed again. But the horses preferred him a biped to a quadruped, and the Master Horse threw up his head and gave the word to move. Ugh-lomi thought they were off for good, but after a minute's gallop they came round in a wide curve, and stood winding [72] him. Then, as a rise in the ground hid him, they tailed out, the Master Horse leading, and approached him spirally.

He was as ignorant of the possibilities of a horse as they were of his. And at this stage it would seem he funked. He knew this kind of stalking would make red deer or buffalo charge, if it was persisted in. At any rate Eudena saw him jump up and come walking towards her with the fern plumes held in his hand.

She stood up, and he grinned to show that the whole thing was an immense lark, and that what he had done was just what he had planned to do from the very beginning. So that incident ended. But he was very thoughtful all that day.

The next day this foolish drab creature with the leonine mane, instead of going about the grazing or hunting he was made for, was prowling round the horses again. The Eldest Mare was all for silent contempt. 'I suppose he wants to learn something from us,' she said, and, '*Let* him.' The next day he was at it again. The Master Horse decided he meant absolutely nothing. But as a matter of fact, Ugh-lomi, the first of men to feel that curious spell of the horse that binds us even to this day, meant a great deal. He admired them unreservedly. There was a rudiment of the snob in him, I am afraid, and he wanted to be near these beautifully-curved animals. Then here were vague conceptions of a kill. If only they would let him come near them! But they drew the line, he found, at fifty yards. If he came nearer than that they moved off – with dignity. I suppose it was the way he had blinded Andoo that made him think of leaping on the back of one of them. But though Eudena after a time came out in the open too, and they did some unobtrusive stalking, things stopped there.

Then one memorable day a new idea came to Ugh-lomi. The horse looks down and level, but he does not look up. No animals look up – they have too much common-sense. It was only that fantastic creature, man, could waste his wits skyward. Ugh-lomi made no philosophical deductions, but he perceived the thing was so. So he spent a weary day in a beech that stood in the open, while Eudena stalked. Usually the horses went into the shade in the heat of the afternoon, but that day the sky was overcast, and they would not, in spite of Eudena's solicitude.

It was two days after that that Ugh-lomi had his desire. The day was blazing hot, and the multiplying flies asserted themselves. The horses stopped grazing before midday, and came into the shadow below him, and stood in couples nose to tail, flapping.

The Master Horse, by virtue of his heels, came closest to the tree. And suddenly there was a rustle and a creak, a *thud* . . . Then a sharp chipped flint bit him on the cheek. The Master Horse stumbled, came on one knee, rose to his feet, and was off like the wind. The air was full of the whirl of limbs, the prance of hoofs, and snorts of alarm. Ugh-lomi was pitched a foot in the air, came down again, up again, his stomach was hit violently, and then his knees got a grip of something between them. He found himself clutching with knees, feet and hands, careering violently with extraordinary oscillation through the air – his axe gone heaven knows whither. 'Hold tight,' said Mother Instinct, and he did.

He was aware of a lot of coarse hair in his face, some of it between his teeth, and of green turf streaming past in front of his eyes. He saw the shoulder of the Master Horse, vast and sleek, with the muscles flowing swiftly under the skin. He perceived that his arms were round the neck, and that the violent jerkings he experienced had a sort of rhythm.

Then he was in the midst of a wild rush of tree-stems, and then there were fronds of bracken about, and then more open turf. Then a stream of pebbles rushing past, little pebbles flying sideways athwart the stream from the blow of the swift hoofs. Ugh-lomi began to feel frightfully sick and giddy, but he was not the stuff to leave go simply because he was uncomfortable.

He dared not leave his grip, but he tried to make himself more comfortable. He released his hug on the neck, gripping the mane instead. He slipped his knees forward, and pushing back, came into a sitting position where the quarters broaden.

It was nervous work, but he managed it, and at last he was fairly seated astride, breathless indeed, and uncertain, but with that frightful pounding of his body at any rate relieved.

Slowly the fragments of Ugh-lomi's mind got into order again. The pace seemed to him terrific, but a kind of exultation was beginning to oust his first frantic terror. The air rushed by, sweet and wonderful, the rhythm of the hoofs changed and broke up and returned into itself again. They were on turf now, a wide glade – the beech trees a hundred yards away on either side, and a succulent band of green, starred with pink blossom and shot with silver water here and there, meandered down the middle. Far off was a glimpse of blue valley – far away. The exultation grew. It was man's first taste of pace.

Then came a wide space dappled with flying fallow deer scattering this way and that, and then a couple of jackals, mistaking Ugh-lomi for a lion, came hurrying after him. And when they saw it was not a lion they still came on out of curiosity. On galloped the horse, with his one idea of escape, and after him the jackals, with pricked ears and quickly-barked remarks. 'Which kills which?' said the first jackal. 'It's the horse being killed,' said the second. They gave the howl of following, and the horse answered to it as a horse answers nowadays to the spur.

On they rushed, a little tornado through the quiet day, putting up startled birds, sending a dozen unexpected things darting to cover, raising a myriad of indignant dung-flies, smashing little blossoms, flowering complacently, back into their parental turf. Trees again, and then splash, splash across a torrent; then a hare shot out of a tuft of grass under the very hoofs of the Master Horse, and the jackals left them incontinently. So presently they broke into the open again, a wide expanse of turfy hillside – the very fellow of the grassy downs that fall northward nowadays from the Epsom Stand.[73]

The first hot bolt of the Master Horse was long since over. He was falling into a measured trot, and Ugh-lomi, albeit bruised exceedingly and quite uncertain of the future, was in a state of glorious enjoyment. And now came a new development. The pace broke again, the Master Horse came round on a short curve, and stopped dead . . .

Ugh-lomi became alert. He wished he had a flint, but the throwing flint he had carried in a thong about his waist was – like the axe – heaven knows where. The Master Horse turned his head, and Ugh-lomi became aware of an eye and teeth. He whipped his leg into a position of security, and hit at the cheek with his fist. Then the head went down somewhere out of existence apparently, and the back he was sitting on flew up into a dome. Ugh-lomi became a thing of instinct again – strictly prehensile; he held by knees and feet, and his head seemed sliding towards the turf. His fingers were twisted into the shock of mane, and the rough hair of the horse saved him. The gradient he was on lowered again, and then – 'Whup!' said Ugh-lomi astonished, and the slant was the other way up.

But Ugh-lomi was a thousand generations nearer the primordial than man: no monkey could have held on better. And the lion had been training the horse for countless generations against the tactics of rolling and rearing back. But he kicked like a master, and buck-jumped rather neatly. In five minutes Ugh-lomi lived a lifetime. If he came off, the horse would kill him, he felt assured.

Then the Master Horse decided to stick to his old tactics again, and suddenly went off at a gallop. He headed down the slope, taking the steep places at a rush, swerving neither to the right nor to the left, and, as they rode down, the wide expanse of valley sank out of sight behind the approaching skirmishers of oak and hawthorn. They skirted a sudden hollow with the pool of a spring, rank weeds and silver bushes. The ground grew softer and the grass taller, and on the right-hand side and the left came scattered bushes of May – still splashed with belated blossom. Presently the bushes thickened until they lashed the passing rider, and little flashes and gouts of blood came out on horse and man. Then the way opened again.

And then came a wonderful adventure. A sudden squeal of unreasonable anger rose amidst the bushes, the squeal of some creature bitterly wronged. And crashing after them appeared a big, grey-blue shape. It was Yaaa, the big-horned rhinoceros, in one of those fits of fury of his, charging full tilt, after the manner of his kind. He had been startled at his feeding, and someone, it did not matter who, was to be ripped and trampled therefore. He was bearing down on them from the left, with his wicked little eye red, and his great horn down, and his tail like a jury-mast[74] behind him. For a minute Ugh-lomi was minded to slip off and dodge, and then behold! The staccato of the hoofs grew swifter, and the rhinoceros and his stumpy hurrying little legs seemed to slide out at the back corner of Ugh-lomi's eye. In two minutes they were through the bushes of May, and out in the open, going fast. For a space he could hear the ponderous paces in pursuit receding behind him, and then it was just as if Yaaa had not lost his temper, as if Yaaa had never existed.

The pace never faltered, on they rode and on.

Ugh-lomi was now all exultation. To exult in those days was to insult. 'Ya-ha! Big nose,' he said, trying to crane back and see some remote speck of a pursuer. 'Why don't you carry your smiting-stone in your fist?' he ended, with a frantic whoop.

But that whoop was unfortunate, for coming close to the ear of the horse, and being quite unexpected, it startled the stallion extremely. He shied violently. Ugh-lomi suddenly found himself uncomfortable again. He was hanging on to the horse, he found, by one arm and one knee.

The rest of the ride was honourable but unpleasant. The view was chiefly of blue sky, and that was combined with the most unpleasant physical sensations. Finally a bush of thorn lashed him and he let go.

He hit the ground with his cheek and shoulder, and then, after a complicated and extraordinarily rapid movement, hit it again with the end of his backbone. He saw splashes and sparks of light and colour. The ground seemed bouncing about just like the horse had done. Then he found he was sitting on turf, six yards beyond the bush. In front of him was a space of grass, growing greener and greener, and a number of human beings in the distance, and the horse was going round at a smart gallop quite a long way off to the right.

The human beings were on the opposite side of the river, some still in the water, but they were all running away as hard as they could go. The advent of a monster that took to pieces was not the sort of novelty they cared for. For quite a minute Ugh-lomi sat regarding them in a purely spectacular spirit. The bend of the river, the knoll among the reeds and royal ferns, the thin streams of smoke going up to heaven, were all perfectly familiar to him. It was the squatting-place of the Sons of Uya, of Uya from whom he had fled with Eudena and whom he had waylaid in the chestnut woods and killed with the First Axe.

He rose to his feet, still dazed from his fall, and as he did so the scattering fugitives turned and regarded him. Some pointed to the receding horse and chattered. He walked slowly towards them, staring. He forgot the horse, he forgot his own bruises, in the growing interest of this encounter. There were fewer of them than there had been – he supposed the others must have hidden – the heap of fern for the night fire was not so high. By the flint heaps should have sat Wau – but then he remembered he had killed Wau. Suddenly brought back to this familiar scene, the gorge and the bears and Eudena seemed things remote, things dreamt of.

He stopped at the bank and stood regarding the tribe. His mathematical abilities were of the slightest, but it was certain there were fewer. The men might be away, but there were fewer women and children. He gave the shout of homecoming. His quarrel had been with Uya and Wau – not with the others. 'Children of Uya!' he cried. They answered with his name, a little fearfully because of the strange way he had come.

For a space they spoke together. Then an old woman lifted a shrill voice and answered him. 'Our Lord is a Lion.'

Ugh-lomi did not understand that saying. They answered him again, several together, 'Uya comes again. He comes as a lion. Our Lord is a

Lion. He comes at night. He slays whom he will. But none other may slay us, Ugh-lomi. None other may slay us.'

Still Ugh-lomi did not understand.

'Our Lord is a Lion. He speaks no more to men.'

Ugh-lomi stood regarding them. He had had dreams – he knew that though he had killed Uya, Uya still existed. And now they told him Uya was a lion.

The shrivelled old woman, the mistress of the fire-minders, suddenly turned and spoke softly to those next to her. She was a very old woman indeed; she had been the first of Uya's wives, and he had let her live beyond the age to which it is seemly a woman should live. She had been cunning from the first, cunning to please Uya and to get food. And now she was great in counsel. She spoke softly, and Ugh-lomi watched her shrivelled form across the river with a curious distaste. Then she called aloud, 'Come over to us, Ugh-lomi.'

A girl suddenly lifted up her voice. 'Come over to us, Ugh-lomi,' she said. And they all began crying, 'Come over to us, Ugh-lomi.'

It was strange how their manner changed after the old woman called.

He stood quite still watching them all. It was pleasant to be called, and the girl who had called first was a pretty one. But she made him think of Eudena.

'Come over to us, Ugh-lomi,' they cried, and the voice of the shrivelled old woman rose above them all. At the sound of her voice his hesitation returned.

He stood on the river bank – Ugh-lomi, Ugh the Thinker – with his thoughts slowly taking shape. Presently one and then another paused to see what he would do. He was minded to go back, he was minded not to. Suddenly his fear or his caution got the upper hand. Without answering them he turned, and walked back towards the distant thorn trees, the way he had come. Forthwith, the whole tribe started crying to him again very eagerly. He hesitated and turned, then he went on, then he turned again, and then once again, regarding them with troubled eyes as they called. The last time he took two paces back, before his fear stopped him. They saw him stop once more, and suddenly shake his head and vanish among the hawthorn trees.

Then all the women and children lifted up their voices together, and called to him in one last vain effort.

Far down the river the reeds were stirring in the breeze, where, convenient for his new sort of feeding, the old lion, who had taken to man-eating, had made his lair.

The old woman turned her face that way, and pointed to the hawthorn thickets. 'Uya,' she screamed, 'there goes thine enemy! There goes thine enemy, Uya! Why do you devour us nightly? We have tried to snare him! There goes thine enemy, Uya!'

But the lion who preyed upon the tribe was taking his siesta. The cry went unheard. That day he had dined on one of the plumper girls, and his mood was a comfortable placidity. He really did not understand that he was Uya or that Ugh-lomi was his enemy.

So it was that Ugh-lomi rode the horse, and heard first of Uya the lion, who had taken the place of Uya the Master, and was eating up the tribe. And as he hurried back to the gorge, his mind was no longer full of the horse, but of the thought that Uya was still alive, to slay or be slain. Over and over again he saw the shrunken band of women and children crying that Uya was a lion. Uya was a lion!

And presently, fearing the twilight might come upon him, Ugh-lomi began running.

4. UYA THE LION

The old lion was in luck. The tribe had a certain pride in their ruler, but that was all the satisfaction they got out of it. He came the very night that Ugh-lomi killed Uya the Cunning, and so it was they named him Uya. It was the old woman, the fire-minder, who first named him Uya. A shower had lowered the fires to a glow, and made the night dark. And as they conversed together, and peered at one another in the darkness, and wondered fearfully what Uya would do to them in their dreams now that he was dead, they heard the mounting reverberations of the lion's roar close at hand. Then everything was still.

They held their breath, so that almost the only sounds were the patter of the rain and the hiss of the raindrops in the ashes. And then, after an interminable time, a crash, and a shriek of fear, and a growling. They sprang to their feet, shouting, screaming, running this way and that, but brands would not burn, and in a minute the victim was being dragged away through the ferns. It was Irk, the brother of Wau.

So the lion came.

The ferns were still wet from the rain the next night, and he came and took Click with the red hair. That sufficed for two nights. And then in the dark between the moons he came three nights, night after night, and that though they had good fires. He was an old lion with stumpy teeth, but very silent and very cool; he knew of fires before; these were not the first of mankind that had ministered to his old age. The third night he came between the outer fire and the inner, and he leapt the flint heap, and pulled down Irm the son of Irk, who had seemed like to be the leader. That was a dreadful night, because they lit great flares of fern and ran screaming, and the lion missed his hold of Irm. By the glare of the fire they saw Irm struggle up, and run a little way towards them, and then the lion in two bounds had him down again. That was the last of Irm.

So fear came, and all the delight of spring passed out of their lives. Already there were five gone out of the tribe, and four nights added three more to the number. Food-seeking became spiritless, none knew who might go next, and all day the women toiled, even the favourite women, gathering litter and sticks for the night fires. And the hunters hunted ill: in the warm springtime hunger came again as though it was still winter. The tribe might have moved, had they had a leader, but they had no leader, and none knew where to go that the lion could not follow them. So the old lion waxed fat and thanked heaven for the race of men. Two of the children and a youth died while the moon was still new, and then it was the shrivelled old fire-minder first bethought herself in a dream of Eudena and Ugh-lomi, and of the way Uya had been slain. She had lived in fear of Uya all her days, and now she lived in fear of the lion. That Ugh-lomi could kill Uya for good – Ugh-lomi whom she had seen born – was impossible. It was Uya still seeking his enemy!

And then came the strange return of Ugh-lomi, a wonderful animal seen galloping far across the river, that suddenly changed into two animals, a horse and a man. Following this portent, the vision of Ugh-lomi on the farther bank of the river . . . Yes, it was all plain to her. Uya was punishing them because they had not hunted down Ugh-lomi and Eudena.

The men came straggling back to the chances of the night while the sun was still golden in the sky. They were received with the story of Ugh-lomi. She went across the river with them and showed them his spoor hesitating on the farther bank. Siss the Tracker knew the feet for Ugh-lomi's. 'Uya needs Ugh-lomi,' cried the old woman, standing on the left of the bend, a gesticulating figure of flaring bronze in the sunset. Her cries were strange sounds, flitting to and fro on the borderland of speech, but this was the sense they carried: 'The lion needs Eudena. He comes night after night seeking Eudena and Ugh-lomi. When he cannot find Eudena and Ugh-lomi, he grows angry and he kills. Hunt Eudena and Ugh-lomi, Eudena whom he pursued and Ugh-lomi for whom he gave the death-word! Hunt Eudena and Ugh-lomi!'

She turned to the distant reed-bed, as sometimes she had turned to

Uya in his life. 'Is it not so, my lord?' she cried. And as if in answer, the tall reeds bowed before a breath of wind.

Far into the twilight the sound of hacking was heard from the squatting-places. It was the men sharpening their ashen spears against the hunting of the morrow. And in the night, early, before the moon rose, the lion came and took the girl of Siss the Tracker.

In the morning before the sun had risen, Siss the Tracker, and the lad Wau-hau, who now chipped flints, and One Eye, and Bo, and Snail-eater, the two red-haired men, and Cat's-skin and Snake, all the men that were left alive of the Sons of Uya, taking their ash spears and their smiting-stones, and with throwing stones in the beast-paw bags, started forth upon the trail of Ugh-lomi through the hawthorn thickets where Yaaa the Rhinoceros and his brothers were feeding, and up the bare downland towards the beechwoods.

That night the fires burnt high and fierce, as the waxing moon set, and the lion left the crouching women and children in peace.

And the next day, while the sun was still high, the hunters returned – all save One Eye, who lay dead with a smashed skull at the foot of the ledge. (When Ugh-lomi came back that evening from stalking the horses, he found the vultures already busy over him.) And with them the hunters brought Eudena, bruised and wounded, but alive. That had been the strange order of the shrivelled old woman, that she was to be brought alive – 'She is no kill for us. She is for Uya the Lion.' Her hands were tied with thongs, as though she had been a man, and she came weary and drooping – her hair over her eyes and matted with blood. They walked about her, and ever and again Snail-eater, whose name she had given him, would laugh and strike her with his ashen spear. And after he had struck her with his spear, he would look over his shoulder like one who had done an over-bold deed. The others, too, looked over their shoulders ever and again, and all were in a hurry save Eudena. When the old woman saw them coming, she cried aloud with joy.

They made Eudena cross the river with her hands tied, although the current was strong, and when she slipped the old woman screamed, first with joy and then for fear she might be drowned. And when they had dragged Eudena to shore, she could not stand for a time, albeit they beat her sore. So they let her sit with her feet touching the water, and her eyes staring before her, and her face set, whatever they might do or say. All the tribe came down to the squatting-place, even curly little Haha, who as yet could scarcely toddle, and stood staring at Eudena and the old woman, as now we should stare at some strange wounded beast and its captor.

The old woman tore off the necklace of Uya that was about Eudena's neck, and put it on herself – she had been the first to wear it. Then she tore at Eudena's hair, and took a spear from Siss and beat her with all her might. And when she had vented the warmth of her heart on the girl she looked closely into her face. Eudena's eyes were closed and her features were set, and she lay so still that for a moment the old woman feared she was dead – until her nostrils quivered. At that the old woman slapped her face and laughed and gave the spear to Siss again, and went a little way off from her and began to talk and jeer at her after her manner.

The old woman had more words than any in the tribe. And her talk was a terrible thing to hear. Sometimes she screamed and moaned incoherently, and sometimes the shape of her guttural cries was the mere phantom of thoughts. But she conveyed to Eudena, nevertheless, much of the things that were yet to come, of the lion and of the torment he would do her. 'And Ugh-lomi! Ha, ha! Ugh-lomi was slain?'

And suddenly Eudena's eyes opened and she sat up again, and her look met the old woman's fair and level. 'No,' she said slowly, like one trying to remember, 'I did not see my Ugh-lomi slain. I did not see my Ugh-lomi slain.'

'Tell her,' cried the old woman. 'Tell her – he that killed him. Tell her how Ugh-lomi was slain.'

She looked, and all the women and children there looked, from man to man.

None answered her. They stood shamefaced.

'Tell her,' said the old woman. The men looked at one another.

Eudena's face suddenly lit.

'Tell her,' she said. 'Tell her, mighty men! Tell her the killing of Ugh-lomi.'

The old woman rose and struck her sharply across her mouth.

'We could not find Ugh-lomi,' said Siss the Tracker, slowly. 'Who hunts two, kills none.'

Then Eudena's heart leapt, but she kept her face hard. It was well, for the old woman looked at her sharply, with murder in her eyes.

Then the old woman turned her tongue upon the men because they had feared to go on after Ugh-lomi. She dreaded no one now Uya was slain. She scolded them as one scolds children. And they scowled at her, and began to accuse one another. Until suddenly Siss the Tracker raised his voice and bade her hold her peace.

And so when the sun was setting they took Eudena and went – though their hearts sank within them – along the trail the old lion had made in the reeds. All the men went together. At one place was a group of alders, and here they hastily bound Eudena where the lion might find her when he came abroad in the twilight, and having done so they hurried back until they were near the squatting-place. Then they stopped. Siss stopped first and looked back again at the alders. They could see her head even from the squatting-place, a little black shock under the limb of the larger tree. That was as well.

All the women and children stood watching upon the crest of the mound. And the old woman stood and screamed for the lion to take her whom he sought, and counselled him on the torments he might do her.

Eudena was very weary now, stunned by beatings and fatigue and sorrow, and only the fear of the thing that was still to come upheld her. The sun was broad and blood-red between the stems of the distant chestnuts, and the west was all on fire; the evening breeze had died to a warm tranquillity. The air was full of midge swarms, the fish in the river hard by would leap at times, and now and again a cockchafer would drone through the air. Out of the corner of her eye Eudena could see a part of the squatting-knoll, and little figures standing and staring at her. And – a very little sound but very clear – she could hear the beating of the firestone. Dark and near to her and very still was the reed-fringed thicket of the lair.

Presently the firestone ceased. She looked for the sun and found he had gone, and overhead and growing brighter was the waxing moon. She looked towards the thicket of the lair, seeking shapes in the reeds, and then suddenly she began to wriggle and wriggle, weeping and calling upon Ugh-lomi.

But Ugh-lomi was far away. When they saw her head moving with her struggles, they shouted together on the knoll, and then she desisted and was still. And then came the bats, and the star that was like Ugh-lomi crept out of its blue hiding-place in the west. She called to it, but softly, because she feared the lion. And all through the coming of the twilight the thicket was still.

So the dark crept upon Eudena, and the moon grew bright, and the shadows of things that had fled up the hillside and vanished with the evening came back to them short and black, And the dark shapes in the thicket of reeds and alders where the lion lay gathered, and a faint stir began there. But nothing came out therefrom all through the gathering of the darkness.

She looked at the squatting-place and saw the fires glowing smoky-red, and the men and women going to and fro. The other way, over the river, a white mist was rising. Then far away came the whimpering of young foxes and the yell of a hyena.

There were long gaps of aching waiting. After a long time some animal splashed in the water, and seemed to cross the river at the ford beyond the lair, but what animal it was she could not see. From the distant drinking-pools she could hear the sound of splashing, and the noise of elephants – so still was the night.

The earth was now a colourless arrangement of white reflections and impenetrable shadows, under the blue sky. The silvery moon was already spotted with the filigree crests of the chestnut woods, and over the shadowy eastward hills the stars were multiplying. The knoll fires were bright red now, and black figures stood waiting against them. They were waiting for a scream . . . Surely it would be soon.

The night suddenly seemed full of movement. She held her breath. Things were passing – one, two, three – subtly sneaking shadows . . . Jackals.

Then a long waiting again.

Then, asserting itself as real at once over all the sounds her mind had imagined, came a stir in the thicket, then a vigorous movement. There was a snap. The reeds crashed heavily, once, twice, thrice, and then everything was still save a measured swishing. She heard a low tremulous growl, and then everything was still again. The stillness lengthened – would it never end? She held her breath; she bit her lips to stop screaming. Then something scuttled through the undergrowth. Her scream was involuntary. She did not hear the answering yell from the mound.

Immediately the thicket woke up to vigorous movement again. She saw the grass stems waving in the light of the setting moon, the alders swaying. She struggled violently – her last struggle. But nothing came towards her. A dozen monsters seemed rushing about in that little place for a couple of minutes, and then again came silence. The moon sank behind the distant chestnuts and the night was dark.

Then an odd sound, a sobbing panting, that grew faster and fainter. Yet another silence, and then dim sounds and the grunting of some animal.

Everything was still again. Far away eastwards an elephant trumpeted, and from the woods came a snarling and yelping that died away.

In the long interval the moon shone out again, between the stems of the trees on the ridge, sending two great bars of light and a bar of darkness across the reedy waste. Then came a steady rustling, a splash, and the reeds swayed wider and wider apart. And at last they broke open, cleft from root to crest . . . The end had come.

She looked to see the thing that had come out of the reeds. For a moment it seemed certainly the great head and jaw she expected, and then it dwindled and changed. It was a dark low thing that remained silent, but it was not the lion. It became still – everything became still. She peered. It was like some gigantic frog, two limbs and a slanting body. Its head moved about searching the shadows . . .

A rustle, and it moved clumsily, with a sort of hopping. And as it moved it gave a low groan.

The blood rushing through her veins was suddenly joy. '*Ugh-lomi!*' she whispered.

The thing stopped. '*Eudena*,' he answered softly, with pain in his voice and peering into the alders.

He moved again, and came out of the shadow beyond the reeds into the moonlight. All his body was covered with dark smears. She saw he was dragging his legs, and that he gripped his axe, the first axe, in one hand. In another moment he had struggled into the position of all fours, and had staggered over to her. 'The lion,' he said in a strange mingling of exultation and anguish. 'Wau – ! I have slain a lion. With my own hand. Even as I slew the great bear.' He moved to emphasise his words, and suddenly broke off with a faint cry. For a space he did not move.

'Let me free,' whispered Eudena . . .

He answered her no words but pulled himself up from his crawling attitude by means of the alder stem, and hacked at her thongs with the sharp edge of his axe. She heard him sob at each blow. He cut away the thongs about her chest and arms, and then his hand dropped. His chest struck against her shoulder and he slipped down beside her and lay still.

But the rest of her release was easy. Very hastily she freed herself. She made one step from the tree, and her head was spinning, Her last conscious movement was towards him. She reeled, and suddenly fell headlong beside him. Her hand fell upon his thigh. It was soft and wet, and gave way under her pressure; he cried out at her touch, and writhed and lay still again.

Presently a dark doglike shape came very softly through the reeds. This stopped dead and stood sniffing, hesitated, and at last turned and slunk back into the shadows.

Long was the time they remained there motionless, with the light of the setting moon shining on their limbs. Very slowly, as slowly as the setting of the moon, did the shadow of the reeds towards the mound flow over them. Presently their legs were hidden, and Ugh-lomi was but a bust of silver. The shadow crept to his neck, crept over his face, and so at last the darkness of the night swallowed them up.

The shadow became full of instinctive stirrings. There was a patter of feet, and a faint snarling – the sound of a blow.

There was little sleep that night for the women and children at the squatting-place until they heard Eudena scream. But the men were weary and sat dozing. When Eudena screamed they felt assured of their safety, and hurried to get the nearest places to the fire. The old woman laughed at the scream, and laughed again because Si, the little sister of Eudena, whimpered. Directly the dawn came, they were all alert and looking towards the alders. They could see that Eudena had been taken. They could not help feeling glad to think that Uya was appeased. But across the minds of the men the thought of Ugh-lomi fell like a shadow. They could understand revenge, for the world was old in revenge, but they did not think of rescue. Suddenly a hyena fled out of the thicket, and came galloping across the reed space. His muzzle and paws were dark-stained. At that sight all the men shouted and clutched at throwing-stones and ran towards him, for no animal is so pitiful a coward as the hyena by day. All men hated the hyena because he preyed on children, and would come and bite when one was sleeping on the edge of the squatting-place. And Cat's-skin, throwing fair and straight, hit the brute shrewdly on the flank, whereat the whole tribe yelled with delight.

At the noise they made there came a flapping of wings from the lair of the lion, and three white-headed vultures rose slowly and circled and came to rest amidst the branches of an alder, overlooking the lair. 'Our lord is abroad,' said the old woman, pointing. 'The vultures have their share of Eudena.' For a space they remained there, and then first one and then another dropped back into the thicket.

Then over the eastern woods, and touching the whole world to life and colour, poured, with the exaltation of a trumpet blast, the light of the rising sun. At the sight of him the children shouted together, and clapped their hands and began to race off towards the water. Only little Si lagged behind and looked wonderingly at the alders where she had seen the head of Eudena at nightfall.

But Uya, the old lion, was not abroad but at home, and he lay very still, and a little on one side. He was not in his lair, but some way from it in a place of trampled grass. Under one eye was a minor wound, the feeble bite of the first axe. But all the ground beneath his chest was ruddy brown with a vivid streak, and in his chest was a little hole that had been made by Ugh-lomi's stabbing-spear. Along his side and at his neck the vultures had marked their claims. For so Ugh-lomi had slain him, lying stricken under his paw and thrusting haphazard at his chest. He had driven the spear in with all his strength and stabbed the giant to the heart. So it was the reign of the lion, of the second incarnation of Uya the Master, came to an end.

From the knoll the bustle of preparation grew, the hacking of spears and throwing-stones. None spoke the name of Ugh-lomi for fear that it might bring him. The men were going to keep together, close together, in the hunting for a day or so. And their hunting was to be Ugh-lomi, lest instead he should come a-hunting them.

But Ugh-lomi was lying very still and silent, outside the lion's lair, and Eudena squatted beside him, with the ash spear, all smeared with lion's blood, gripped in her hand.

5 THE FIGHT IN THE LION'S THICKET

Ugh-lomi lay still, his back against an alder, and his thigh was a red mass terrible to see. No civilised man could have lived who had been so sorely wounded, but Eudena got him thorns to close his wounds, and squatted beside him day and night, smiting the flies from him with a fan of reeds by day, and in the night threatening the hyenas who came too near with the first axe in her hand; and in a little while he began to heal. It was high summer, and there was no rain. Little food they had during the first two days his wounds were open. In the low place where they hid were no roots nor little beasts, and the stream, with its water-snails and fish, was in the open, a hundred yards away. She could not go abroad by day for fear of the tribe, her brothers and sisters, nor by night for fear of the beasts, both on his account and hers. So they shared the lion with the vultures. But there was a trickle of water near by, and Eudena brought him plenty in her hands.

Where Ugh-lomi lay was well hidden from the tribe by a thicket of alders, and all fenced about with bulrushes and tall reeds. The dead lion he had killed lay near his old lair on a place of trampled reeds fifty yards away, in sight through the reed-stems, and the vultures fought each other for the choicest pieces and kept the jackals off him. Very soon a cloud of flies that looked like bees hung over him, and Ugh-lomi could hear their humming. And when Ugh-lomi's flesh was already healing – and it was not many days before that began – only a few bones of the lion remained scattered and shining white.

For the most part Ugh-lomi sat still during the day, looking before him at nothing, sometimes he would mutter of the horses and bears and lions, and sometimes he would beat the ground with the first axe and say the names of the tribe – he seemed to have no fear of bringing the tribe – for hours together. But chiefly he slept, dreaming little because of his loss of blood and the slightness of his food. During the short summer night both kept awake. All the while the darkness lasted things moved about them, things they never saw by day. For some nights the hyenas did not come, and then one moonless night near a dozen came and fought for what was left of the lion. The night was a tumult of growling, and Ugh-lomi and Eudena could hear the bones snap in their teeth. But they knew the hyena dare not attack any creature alive and awake, and so they were not greatly afraid.

Of a daytime Eudena would go along the narrow path the old lion had made in the reeds until she was beyond the bend, and then she would creep into the thicket and watch the tribe. She would lie close by the alders, where they had bound her to offer her up to the lion, and thence she could see them on the knoll by the fire, little and clear, as she had seen them that night. But she told Ugh-lomi little of what she saw, because she feared to bring them by their names. For so they believed in those days – that naming called.

She saw the men prepare stabbing-spears and throwing-stones on the morning after Ugh-lomi had slain the lion, and go out to hunt him, leaving the women and children on the knoll. Little they knew how near he was as they tracked off in single file towards the hills, with Siss the Tracker leading them. And she watched the women and children, after the men had gone, gathering fern-fronds and twigs for the night fire, and the boys and girls running and playing together. But the very old woman made her feel afraid. After a long space towards noon, when most of the others were down at the stream by the bend, she came and stood on the hither side of the knoll, a gnarled brown figure, and gesticulated so that Eudena could scarce believe she was not seen. Eudena lay like a hare in its form, with shining eyes fixed on the bent witch away there, and presently she dimly understood it was the lion the old woman was worshipping – the lion Ugh-lomi had slain.

And the next day the hunters came back weary, carrying a fawn, and Eudena watched the feast enviously. And then came a strange thing. She saw – distinctly she heard – the old woman shrieking and gesticulating and pointing towards her. She was afraid, and crept like a snake out of sight again. But presently curiosity overcame her and she was back at her spying-place, and as she peered her heart stopped, for there were all the men, with their weapons in their hands, walking together towards her from the knoll.

She dared not move lest her movement should be seen, but she pressed herself close to the ground. The sun was low and the golden light was in the faces of the men. She saw they carried a piece of rich red meat thrust through by an ashen stake. Presently they stopped. 'Go on!' screamed the old woman. Cat's-skin grumbled, and they came on, searching the thicket with sun-dazzled eyes. 'Here!' said Siss. And they took the ashen stake with the meat upon it and thrust it into the ground. 'Uya!' cried Siss, 'Behold thy portion. And Ugh-lomi we have slain. Of a truth we have slain Ugh-lomi. This day we slew Ugh-lomi, and tomorrow we will bring his body to you.' And the others repeated the words.

They looked at each other and behind them, and partly turned and began going back. At first they walked half turned to the thicket, then facing the mound they walked faster, looking over their shoulders, then faster; soon they ran, it was a race at last, until they were near the knoll. Then Siss who was hindmost was first to slacken his pace.

The sunset passed and the twilight came, the fire glowed red against the hazy blue of the distant chestnut trees, and the voices over the mound were merry. Eudena lay scarcely stirring, looking from the mound to the meat and then to the mound. She was hungry, but she was afraid. At last she crept back to Ugh-lomi.

He looked round at the little rustle of her approach. His face was in shadow. 'Have you got me some food?' he said.

She said she could find nothing, but that she would seek further, and went back along the lion's path until she could see the mound again, but she could not bring herself to take the meat; she had the brute's instinct of a snare. She felt very miserable.

She crept back at last towards Ugh-lomi and heard him stirring and moaning. She turned back to the mound again; then she saw something in the darkness near the stake, and peering distinguished a jackal. In a flash she was brave and angry; she sprang up, cried out, and ran towards the offering. She stumbled and fell, and heard the growling of the jackal going off.

When she arose only the ashen stake lay on the ground, the meat was gone. So she went back, to fast through the night with Ugh-lomi; and Ugh-lomi was angry with her, because she had no food for him; but she told him nothing of the things she had seen.

Two days passed and they were near starving when the tribe slew a horse. Then came the same ceremony, and a haunch was left on the ashen stake; but this time Eudena did not hesitate.

By acting and words she made Ugh-lomi understand, but he ate most of the food before he understood; and then he grew merry with his food. 'I am Uya,' he said; 'I am the Lion. I am the Great Cave Bear, I who was only Ugh-lomi. I am Wau the Cunning. It is well that they should feed me, for presently I will kill them all.'

Then Eudena's heart was light, and she laughed with him; and afterwards she ate what he had left of the horseflesh with gladness.

After that it was he had a dream, and the next day he made Eudena bring him the lion's teeth and claws – so much of them as she could find – and hack him a club of alder, and he put the teeth and claws very cunningly into the wood so that the points were outward. Very long it took him, and he blunted two of the teeth hammering them in, and was very angry and threw the thing away; but afterwards he dragged himself to where he had thrown it and finished it – a club of a new sort set with teeth. That day there was more meat for them both, an offering to the lion from the tribe.

It was one day – more than a hand's fingers of days, more than anyone has skill to count – after Ugh-lomi had made the club, that Eudena (while he was asleep) was lying in the thicket watching the squatting-place. There had been no meat for three days. And the old woman came and worshipped after her manner. Now while she worshipped, Eudena's little sister Si and another, the child of the first girl Siss had loved, came over the knoll and stood regarding her skinny figure, and presently they began to mock her. Eudena found this entertaining, but suddenly the old woman turned on them quickly and saw them. For a moment she stood and they stood motionless, and then with a shriek of rage she rushed towards them, and all three disappeared over the crest of the knoll.

Presently the children reappeared among the ferns over the shoulder of the hill. Little Si ran first, for she was an active girl, and the other child ran squealing with the old woman close upon her. And over the knoll came Siss with a bone in his hand, and Bo and Cat's-skin obsequiously behind him, each holding a piece of food, and they laughed aloud and shouted to see the old woman so angry. And with a shriek the child was caught and the old woman set to work slapping her and the child was screaming, and it was very good after-dinner fun for them. Little Si ran on a little way and stopped at last between fear and curiosity.

And suddenly came the mother of the child, with hair streaming, panting, and with a stone in her hand, and the old woman turned about like a wild cat. She was the equal of any woman, was the old chief of the fire-minders, in spite of her years; but before she could do anything Siss shouted to her and the clamour rose loud. Other shock heads came into sight. It seemed the whole tribe was at home and feasting. But the old woman dared not go on wreaking herself on the child Siss befriended. Nevertheless it was a fine row.

Everyone made noises and called names, even little Si. Abruptly the old woman let go of the child she had caught and made a swift run at Si, who had no friends; and Si, realising her danger when it was almost upon her, with a faint cry of terror made off headlong, not heeding whither she ran, straight to the lair of the lion. She swerved aside into the reeds presently, not realising whither she went.

But the old woman was a wonderful old woman, as active as she was spiteful, and she caught Si by the streaming hair within thirty yards of Eudena. All the tribe now was running down the knoll and shouting, ready to see the fun.

Then something stirred in Eudena and, thinking all of little Si and nothing of her fear, she sprang up from her ambush and ran swiftly forward. The old woman did not see her, for she was busy beating little Si's face with her hand, beating with all her heart, and suddenly something hard and heavy struck her cheek. She went reeling, and saw Eudena with flaming eyes and cheeks between her and little Si. She shrieked with astonishment and terror, and little Si, not understanding, set off towards the gaping tribe. They were quite close now, for the sight of Eudena had driven their fading fear of the lion out of their heads.

In a moment Eudena had turned from the cowering old woman and overtaken Si. 'Si!' she cried, 'Si!' She caught the child up in her arms as she stopped, pressed the nail-lined face to hers, and turned about to run towards her lair, the lair of the old lion. The old woman stood waist-high in the reeds, and screamed foul things and inarticulate rage, but did not dare to intercept her; and at the bend of the path Eudena looked back and saw all the men of the tribe crying to one another and Siss coming at a trot along the lion's trail.

She ran straight along the narrow way through the reeds to the shady place where Ugh-lomi sat with his healing thigh, just awakened by the shouting and rubbing his eyes. She came to him, a woman, with little Si in her arms. Her heart throbbed in her throat. 'Ugh-lomi!' she cried, 'Ugh-lomi, the tribe comes!'

Ugh-lomi sat staring in stupid astonishment at her and Si.

She pointed with Si in one arm. She sought among her feeble store of words to explain. She could hear the men calling. Apparently they had stopped outside. She put down Si and caught up the new club with the lion's teeth, and put it into Ugh-lomi's hand, and ran three yards and picked up the first axe.

'Ah!' said Ugh-lomi, waving the new club, and suddenly he perceived the occasion and, rolling over, began to struggle to his feet.

He stood, but clumsily. He supported himself by one hand against the tree, and just touched the ground gingerly with the toe of his wounded leg. In the other hand he gripped the new club. He looked at his healing thigh; and suddenly the reeds began whispering, and ceased and whispered again, and coming cautiously along the track among the reeds, bending down and holding his fire-hardened stabbing-stick of ash in his hand, appeared Siss. He stopped dead, and his eyes met Ugh-lomi's.

Ugh-lomi forgot he had a wounded leg. He stood firmly on both feet. Something trickled. He glanced down and saw a little gout of blood had oozed out along the edge of the healing wound. He rubbed his hand there to give him the grip of his club, and fixed his eyes again on Siss.

'Wau!' he cried, and sprang forward, and Siss, still stooping and watchful, drove his stabbing-stick up very quickly in an ugly thrust. It ripped Ugh-lomi's guarding arm and the club came down in a counter that Siss was never to understand. He fell, as an ox falls to the poleaxe, at Ugh-lomi's feet.

To Bo it seemed the strangest thing. He had a comforting sense of tall reeds on either side, and an impregnable rampart, Siss, between him and any danger. Snail-eater was close behind and there was no danger there. He was prepared to shove behind and send Siss to death or victory. That was his place as second man. He saw the blunt of the spear Siss carried leap away from him, and suddenly a dull whack and the broad back fell away forward, and he looked Ugh-lomi in the face over his prostrate leader. It felt to Bo as if his heart had fallen down a well. He had a throwing-stone in one hand and an ashen stabbing-stick in the other. He did not live to the end of his momentary hesitation which to use.

Snail-eater was a readier man, and besides Bo did not fall forward as Siss had done, but gave at his knees and hips, crumpling up with the toothed club upon his head. Snail-eater drove his spear forward, swift and straight, and took Ugh-lomi in the muscle of the shoulder, and then he drove him hard with the smiting-stone in his other, shouting out as he did so. The new club swished ineffectually through the reeds. Eudena saw Ugh-lomi come staggering back from the narrow path into the open space, tripping over Siss and with a foot of ashen stake sticking out of him over his arm, and then Snail-eater, whose name she had given him, had his final injury from her, as his exultant face came out of the reeds after his spear. For she swung the first axe swift and high, and hit him fair and square on the temple; and down he went on Siss at prostrate Ugh-lomi's feet.

But before Ugh-lomi could get to his feet, the two red-haired men were tumbling out of the reeds, spears and smiting-stones ready, and Snake hard behind them. One she struck on the neck, but not to fell him, and he blundered aside and spoilt his brother's blow at Ugh-lomi's head. In a moment Ugh-lomi dropped his club and had his assailant by the waist, and had pitched him sideways sprawling. He snatched at his club again and recovered it. The man Eudena had hit stabbed at her with his spear as he stumbled from her blow, and involuntarily she gave ground to avoid him. He hesitated between her and Ugh-lomi, half turned, gave a vague cry at finding Ugh-lomi so near, and in a moment Ugh-lomi had him by the throat, and the club had its third victim. As he went down Ugh-lomi shouted – no words, but an exultant cry.

The other red-haired man was six feet from her with his back to her, and a darker red streaking his head. He was struggling to his feet. She had an irrational impulse to stop his rising. She flung the axe at him, missed, saw his face in profile, and he had swerved beyond little Si, and was running through the reeds. She had a transitory vision of Snake standing in the throat of the path, half turned away from her, and then she saw his back. She saw the club whirling through the air, and the shock head of Ugh-lomi, with blood in his hair and blood upon his shoulder, vanishing below the reeds in pursuit. Then she heard Snake scream like a woman.

She ran past Si to where the handle of the axe stuck out of a clump of fern, and turning, found herself panting and alone with three motionless bodies. The air was full of shouts and screams. For a space she was sick and giddy, and then it came into her head that Ugh-lomi was being killed along the reed-path, and with an inarticulate cry she leapt over the body of Bo and hurried after him. Snake's feet lay across the path, and his head was among the reeds. She followed the path until it bent round and opened out by the alders, and thence she saw all that was left of the tribe in the open, scattering like dead leaves before a gale, and going back over the knoll. Ugh-lomi was hard upon Cat's-skin.

But Cat's-skin was fleet of foot and got away, and so did young Wau-Hau when Ugh-lomi turned upon him, and Ugh-lomi pursued Wau-Hau far beyond the knoll before he desisted. He had the rage of battle on him now, and the wood thrust through his shoulder stung him like a spur. When she saw he was in no danger she stopped running and stood panting, watching the distant active figures run up and vanish one by one over the knoll. In a little time she was alone again. Everything had happened very swiftly. The smoke of Brother Fire rose straight and steady from the squatting-place, just as it had done ten minutes ago, when the old woman had stood yonder worshipping the lion.

And after a long time, as it seemed, Ugh-lomi reappeared over the knoll, and came back to Eudena, triumphant and breathing heavily. She stood, her hair about her eyes and hot-faced, with the blood-stained axe in her hand, at the place where the tribe had offered her as a sacrifice to the lion. 'Wau!' cried Ugh-lomi at the sight of her, his face alight with the fellowship of battle, and he waved his new club, red now and hairy; and at the sight of his glowing face her tense pose relaxed somewhat, and she stood weeping and rejoicing.

Ugh-lomi had a queer unaccountable pang at the sight of her tears; but he only shouted, 'Wau!' the louder and shook the axe east and west. He called to her to follow him and turned back, striding, with the club swinging in his hand, towards the squatting-place, as if he had never left the tribe; and she stopped weeping and followed as a woman should.

So Ugh-lomi and Eudena came back to the squatting-place from which they had fled many days before from the face of Uya; and by the squatting-place lay a deer half eaten, just as there had been before Ugh-lomi was man or Eudena woman. So Ugh-lomi sat down to eat, and Eudena beside him like a man, and the rest of the tribe watched them from safe hiding-places. And after a time one of the elder girls came back timorously, carrying little Si in her arms, and Eudena called to them by name, and offered them food. But the elder girl was afraid and would not come, though Si struggled to come to Eudena. Afterwards, when Ugh-lomi had eaten, he sat dozing, and at last he slept, and slowly the others came out of the hiding-places and drew near. And when Ugh-lomi woke, save that there were no men to be seen, it seemed as though he had never left the tribe.

Now there is a thing strange but true: that all through this fight Ugh-lomi forgot that he was lame, and was not lame, and after he had rested behold! he was a lame man; and he remained a lame man to the end of his days.

Cat's-skin and the second red-haired man and Wau-Hau, who chipped flints cunningly, as his father had done before him, fled from the face of Ugh-lomi, and none knew where they hid. But two days after they came and squatted among the bracken under the chestnuts a good way off from the knoll and watched. Ugh-lomi's rage had gone, he moved to go against them and did not, and at sundown they went away. That day too, they found the old woman among the ferns, where Ugh-lomi had blundered upon her when he had pursued Wau-Hau. She was dead and more ugly than ever, but whole. The jackals and vultures had tried her and left her – she was ever a wonderful old woman.

The next day the three men came again and squatted nearer, and Wau-Hau had two rabbits to hold up, and the red-haired man a wood-pigeon, and Ugh-Lomi stood before their women and mocked them.

The next day they sat again nearer – without stones or sticks, and with the same offerings, and Cat's-skin had a trout. It was rare men caught fish in those days but Cat's-skin would stand silently in the water for hours and catch them with his hand. And the fourth day Ugh-lomi suffered these three to come to the squatting-place in peace, with the food they had with them. Ugh-lomi ate the trout. Thereafter for many moons Ugh-lomi was master, and had his will in peace. And in the fullness of time he was killed and eaten even as Uya had been slain.

The Star[75]

It was on the first day of the new year that the announcement was made, almost simultaneously from three observatories, that the motion of the planet Neptune, the outermost of all the planets that wheel about the sun, had become very erratic. Ogilvy[76] had already called attention to a suspected retardation in its velocity in December. Such a piece of news was scarcely calculated to interest a world the greater portion of whose inhabitants were unaware of the existence of the planet Neptune, nor outside the astronomical profession did the subsequent discovery of a faint remote speck of light in the region of the perturbed planet cause any very great excitement. Scientific people, however, found the intelligence[77] remarkable enough, even before it became known that the new body was rapidly growing larger and brighter, that its motion was quite different from the orderly progress of the planets, and that the deflection of Neptune and its satellite was becoming now of an unprecedented kind.

Few people without a training in science can realise the huge isolation of the solar system. The sun with its specks of planets, its dust of planetoids, and its impalpable comets, swims in a vacant immensity that almost defeats the imagination. Beyond the orbit of Neptune there is space, vacant so far as human observation has penetrated, without warmth or light or sound, blank emptiness, for twenty million times a million miles. That is the smallest estimate of the distance to be traversed before the very nearest of the stars is attained. And saving a few comets more unsubstantial than the thinnest flame, no matter had ever to human knowledge crossed this gulf of space, until early in the twentieth century this strange wanderer appeared. A vast mass of matter it was, bulky, heavy, rushing without warning out of the black mystery of the sky into the radiance of the sun. By the second day it was clearly visible to any decent instrument, as a speck with a barely sensible diameter, in the constellation Leo near Regulus. In a little while an opera glass could attain it.

On the third day of the new year the newspaper readers of two hemispheres were made aware for the first time of the real importance of this unusual apparition in the heavens. A PLANETARY COLLISION, one London paper headed the news, and proclaimed Duchaine's opinion that this strange new planet would probably collide with Neptune. The leader writers enlarged upon the topic; so that in most of the capitals of the world, on January 3rd, there was an expectation, however vague, of some imminent phenomenon in the sky; and as the night followed the sunset round the globe, thousands of men turned their eyes skyward to see – the old familiar stars just as they had always been . . .

Until it was dawn in London and Pollux setting and the stars overhead grown pale. The winter's dawn it was, a sickly filtering accumulation of daylight, and the light of gas and candles shone yellow in the windows to show where people were astir. But the yawning policeman saw the thing, the busy crowds in the markets stopped agape, workmen going to their work betimes, milkmen, the drivers of news-carts, dissipation going home jaded and pale, homeless wanderers, sentinels on their beats, and, in the country, labourers trudging afield, poachers slinking home; all over the dusky quickening country it could be seen – and out at sea by seamen watching for the day – a great white star, come suddenly into the westward sky!

Brighter it was than any star in our skies; brighter than the evening star at its brightest. It still glowed out white and large, no mere twinkling spot of light, but a small round clear shining disc, an hour after the day had come. And where science has not reached, men stared and feared, telling one another of the wars and pestilences that are foreshadowed by these fiery signs in the heavens. Sturdy Boers, dusky Hottentots,[78] Gold Coast negroes, Frenchmen, Spaniards, Portuguese, stood in the warmth of the sunrise watching the setting of this strange new star.

And in a hundred observatories there had been suppressed excitement, rising almost to shouting pitch, as the two remote bodies had rushed together; and a hurrying to and fro, to gather photographic apparatus and spectroscope,[79] and this appliance and that, to record this novel astonishing sight, the destruction of a world. For it was a world, a sister planet of our earth, far greater than our earth indeed, that had so suddenly flashed into flaming death. Neptune it was had been struck, fairly and squarely, by the strange planet from outer space and the heat of the concussion had incontinently turned two solid globes into one vast mass of incandescence. Round the world that day, two hours before the dawn, went the pallid great white star, fading only as it sank westward and the sun mounted above it. Everywhere men marvelled at it, but of all those who saw it none could have marvelled more than those sailors, habitual watchers of the stars, who far away at sea had heard nothing of its advent and saw it now rise like a pigmy moon and climb zenithward and hang overhead and sink westward with the passing of the night.

And when next it rose over Europe, everywhere were crowds

of watchers on hilly slopes, on house-roofs, in open spaces, staring eastward for the rising of the great new star. It rose with a white glow in front of it, like the glare of a white fire, and those who had seen it come into existence the night before cried out at the sight of it. 'It is larger,' they cried. 'It is brighter!' And indeed the moon, a quarter full and sinking in the west, was in its apparent size beyond comparison, but scarcely in all its breadth had it as much brightness now as the little circle of the strange new star.

'It is brighter!' cried the people clustering in the streets. But in the dim observatories the watchers held their breath and peered at one another. '*It is nearer*,' they said. '*Nearer!*'

And voice after voice repeated, 'It is nearer,' and the clicking telegraph took that up, and it trembled along telephone wires, and in a thousand cities grimy compositors fingered the type. 'It is nearer.' Men writing in offices, struck with a strange realisation, flung down their pens; men talking in a thousand places suddenly came upon a grotesque possibility in those words, 'It is nearer.' It hurried along wakening streets, it was shouted down the frost-stilled ways of quiet villages; men who had read these things from the throbbing tape[80] stood in yellow-lit doorways shouting the news to the passers-by. 'It is nearer.' Pretty women, flushed and glittering, heard the news told jestingly between the dances, and feigned an intelligent interest they did not feel. 'Nearer! Indeed. How curious! How very, very clever people must be to find out things like that!'

Lonely tramps faring through the wintry night murmured those words to comfort themselves – looking skyward. 'It has need to be nearer, for the night's as cold as charity. Don't seem much warmth from it, if it is nearer, all the same.'

'What is a new star to me?' cried the weeping woman kneeling beside her dead.

The schoolboy, rising early for his examination work, puzzled it out for himself – with the great white star shining broad and bright through the frost-flowers[81] of his window. 'Centrifugal, centripetal,' he said, with his chin on his fist. 'Stop a planet in its flight, rob it of its centrifugal force, what then? Centripetal has it, and down it falls into the sun! And this – ! Do *we* come in the way? I wonder – '

The light of that day went the way of its brethren, and with the later watches of the frosty darkness rose the strange star again. And it was now so bright that the waxing moon seemed but a pale yellow ghost of itself, hanging huge in the sunset. In a South African city a great man had married, and the streets were alight to welcome his return with his bride. 'Even the skies have illuminated,' said the flatterer. Under Capricorn, two negro lovers, daring the wild beasts and evil spirits for love of one another, crouched together in a cane brake where the fireflies hovered. 'That is our star,' they whispered, and felt strangely comforted by the sweet brilliance of its light.

The master mathematician sat in his private room and pushed the papers from him. His calculations were already finished. In a small white phial there still remained a little of the drug that had kept him awake and active for four long nights. Each day, serene, explicit, patient as ever, he had given his lecture to his students, and then had come back at once to this momentous calculation. His face was grave, a little drawn and hectic from his drugged activity. For some time he seemed lost in thought. Then he went to the window, and the blind went up with a click. Halfway up the sky, over the clustering roofs, chimneys and steeples of the city, hung the star.

He looked at it as one might look into the eyes of a brave enemy. 'You may kill me,' he said after a silence. 'But I can hold you – and all the universe for that matter – in the grip of this little brain. I would not change. Even now.'[82]

He looked at the little phial. 'There will be no need of sleep again,' he said. The next day at noon, punctual to the minute, he entered his lecture theatre, put his hat on the end of the table as his habit was, and carefully selected a large piece of chalk. It was a joke among his students that he could not lecture without that piece of chalk to fumble in his fingers, and once he had been stricken to impotence by their hiding his supply. He came and looked under his grey eyebrows at the rising tiers of young fresh faces, and spoke with his accustomed studied common- ness of phrasing. 'Circumstances have arisen – circumstances beyond my control,' he said and paused, 'which will debar me from completing the course I had designed. It would seem, gentlemen, if I may put the thing clearly and briefly, that – Man has lived in vain.'

The students glanced at one another. Had they heard aright? Mad? Raised eyebrows and grinning lips there were, but one or two faces remained intent upon his calm grey-fringed face. 'It will be interesting,' he was saying, 'to devote this morning to an exposition, so far as I can make it clear to you, of the calculations that have led me to this conclusion. Let us assume – '

He turned towards the blackboard, meditating a diagram in the way that was usual to him. 'What was that about "lived in vain"?' whispered one student to another. 'Listen,' said the other, nodding towards the lecturer.

And presently they began to understand.

That night the star rose later, for its proper eastward motion had carried it some way across Leo towards Virgo, and its brightness was so great that the sky became a luminous blue as it rose, and every star was hidden in its turn, save only Jupiter near the zenith, Capella, Aldebaran, Sirius and the pointers of the Bear.[83] It was very white and beautiful. In many parts of the world that night a pallid halo encircled it about. It was perceptibly larger; in the clear refractive sky of the tropics it seemed as if it were nearly a quarter the size of the moon. The frost was still on the ground in England, but the world was as brightly lit as if it were midsummer moonlight. One could see to read quite ordinary print by that cold clear light, and in the cities the lamps burnt yellow and wan.

And everywhere the world was awake that night, and throughout Christendom a sombre murmur hung in the keen air over the country-side like the belling of bees[84] in the heather, and this murmurous tumult grew to a clangour in the cities. It was the tolling of the bells in a million belfry towers and steeples, summoning the people to sleep no more, to sin no more, but to gather in their churches and pray. And overhead, growing larger and brighter as the earth rolled on its way and the night passed, rose the dazzling star.

And the streets and houses were alight in all the cities, the shipyards glared, and whatever roads led to high country were lit and crowded all night long. And in all the seas about the civilised lands, ships with throbbing engines, and ships with bellying[85] sails, crowded with men and living creatures, were standing out to ocean and the north. For already the warning of the master mathematician had been telegraphed all over the world, and translated into a hundred tongues. The new planet and Neptune, locked in a fiery embrace, were whirling headlong, ever faster and faster, towards the sun. Already every second this blazing mass flew a hundred miles, and every second its terrific velocity increased. As it flew now, indeed, it must pass a hundred million miles wide of the earth and scarcely affect it. But near its destined path, as yet only slightly perturbed, spun the mighty planet Jupiter and his moons, sweeping splendid round the sun. Every moment now the attraction between the fiery star and the greatest of the planets grew stronger. And the result of that attraction? Inevitably Jupiter would be deflected from its orbit into an elliptical path, and the burning star, swung by his attraction wide of its sunward rush, would 'describe a curved path' and perhaps collide with, and certainly pass very close to, our earth.

'Earthquakes, volcanic outbreaks, cyclones, sea waves, floods, and a steady rise in temperature to I know not what limit – ' so prophesied the master mathematician.

And overhead, to carry out his words, lonely and cold and livid, blazed the star of the coming doom.

To many who stared at it that night until their eyes ached, it seemed that it was visibly approaching. And that night, too, the weather changed, and the frost that had gripped all Central Europe and France and England softened towards a thaw.

But you must not imagine because I have spoken of people praying through the night and people going aboard ships and people fleeing toward mountainous country that the whole world was already in a terror because of the star. As a matter of fact, use and wont still ruled the world, and save for the talk of idle moments and the splendour of the night, nine human beings out of ten were still busy at their common occupations. In all the cities, the shops, save one here and there, opened and closed at their proper hours, the doctor and the undertaker plied their trades, the workers gathered in the factories, soldiers drilled, scholars studied, lovers sought one another, thieves lurked and fled, politicians planned their schemes. The presses of the newspapers roared through the night, and many a priest of this church and that would not open his holy building to further what he considered a foolish panic. The newspapers insisted on the lesson of the year 1000 – for then, too, people had anticipated the end.[86] The star was no star – mere gas – a comet; and were it a star it could not possibly strike the earth. There was no precedent for such a thing. Common sense was sturdy everywhere, scornful, jesting, a little inclined to persecute the obdurate fearful. That night, at seven-fifteen by Greenwich time,[87] the star would be at its nearest to Jupiter. Then the world would see the turn things would take. The master mathematician's grim warnings were treated by many as so much mere elaborate self-advertisement. Common sense at last, a little heated by argument, signified its unalterable convictions by going to bed. So, too, barbarism and savagery, already tired of the novelty, went about their nightly business, and save for a howling dog here and there, the beast world left the star unheeded.

And yet, when at last the watchers in the European states saw the star rise, an hour later it is true, but no larger than it had been the night before, there were still plenty awake to laugh at the master mathematician – to take the danger as if it had passed.

But hereafter the laughter ceased. The star grew – it grew with a terrible steadiness hour after hour, a little larger each hour, a little nearer the midnight zenith, and brighter and brighter, until it had turned night into a second day. Had it come straight to the earth instead of in a curved path, had it lost no velocity to Jupiter, it must have leapt the intervening gulf in a day, but as it was it took five days altogether to come by our planet. The next night it had become a third the size of the moon before it set to English eyes, and the thaw was assured. It rose over America near the size of the moon, but blinding white to look at, and hot; and a breath of hot wind blew now with its rising and gathering strength, and in Virginia, and Brazil, and down the St Lawrence valley, it shone intermittently through a driving reek[88] of thunderclouds, flickering violet lightning, and hail unprecedented. In Manitoba was a thaw and devastating floods. And upon all the mountains of the earth the snow and ice began to melt that night, and all the rivers coming out of high country flowed thick and turbid, and soon – in their upper reaches – with swirling trees and the bodies of beasts and men. They rose steadily, steadily in the ghostly brilliance, and came trickling over their banks at last, behind the fleeing population of their valleys.

And along the coast of Argentina and up the South Atlantic the tides were higher than they had ever been in the memory of man, and the storms drove the waters in many cases scores of miles inland, drowning whole cities. And so great grew the heat during the night that the rising of the sun was like the coming of a shadow. The earthquakes began and grew until all down America from the Arctic Circle to Cape Horn, hillsides were sliding, fissures were opening, and houses and walls crumbling to destruction. The whole side of Cotopaxi[89] slipped out in one vast convulsion, and a tumult of lava poured out so high and broad and swift and liquid that in one day it reached the sea.

So the star, with the wan moon in its wake, marched across the Pacific, trailed the thunderstorms like the hem of a robe, and the growing tidal wave that toiled behind it, frothing and eager, poured over island and island and swept them clear of men. Until that wave came at last – in a blinding light and with the breath of a furnace, swift and terrible it came – a wall of water, fifty feet high, roaring hungrily, upon the long coasts of Asia, and swept inland across the plains of China. For a space the star, hotter now and larger and brighter than the sun in its strength, showed with pitiless brilliance the wide and populous country: towns and villages with their pagodas and trees, roads, wide cultivated fields, millions of sleepless people staring in helpless terror at the incandescent sky; and then, low and growing, came the murmur of the flood. And thus it was with millions of men that night – a flight no-whither, with limbs heavy with heat and breath fierce and scant, and the flood like a wall swift and white behind. And then death.

China was lit glowing white, but over Japan and Java and all the islands of Eastern Asia the great star was a ball of dull red fire because of the steam and smoke and ashes the volcanoes were spouting forth to salute its coming. Above was the lava, hot gases and ash, and below the seething floods, and the whole earth swayed and rumbled with the earthquake shocks. Soon the immemorial snows of Tibet and the Himalayas were melting and pouring down by ten million deepening converging channels upon the plains of Burma and Hindustan.[90] The tangled summits of the Indian jungles were aflame in a thousand places, and below the hurrying waters around the stems were dark objects that still struggled feebly and reflected the blood-red tongues of fire. And in a rudderless confusion a multitude of men and women fled down the broad riverways to that one last hope of men – the open sea.

Larger grew the star, and larger, hotter and brighter with a terrible swiftness now. The tropical ocean had lost its phosphorescence, and the whirling steam rose in ghostly wreaths from the black waves that plunged incessantly, speckled with storm-tossed ships.

And then came a wonder. It seemed to those who in Europe watched for the rising of the star that the world must have ceased its rotation. In a thousand open spaces of downland and upland the people who had fled thither from the floods and the falling houses and sliding slopes of hill watched for that rising in vain. Hour followed hour through a terrible suspense, and the star rose not. Once again men set their eyes upon the old constellations they had counted lost to them for ever. In England it was hot and clear overhead, though the ground quivered perpetually, but in the tropics, Sirius and Capella and Aldebaran showed through a veil of steam. And when at last the great star rose near ten hours late, the sun rose close upon it, and in the centre of its white heart was a disc of black.

Over Asia it was the star had begun to fall behind the movement of the sky, and then suddenly, as it hung over India, its light had been veiled. All the plain of India from the mouth of the Indus to the mouths of the Ganges was a shallow waste of shining water that night, out of which rose temples and palaces, mounds and hills, black with people. Every minaret was a clustering mass of people, who fell one by one into the turbid waters, as heat and terror overcame them. The whole land seemed a-wailing, and suddenly there swept a shadow across that furnace of despair, and a breath of cold wind, and a gathering of clouds, out of the cooling air. Men looking up, near blinded, at the star, saw that a black disc was creeping across the light. It was the moon, coming between the star and the earth. And even as men cried to God at this respite, out of the East with a strange inexplicable swiftness sprang the sun. And then star, sun and moon rushed together across the heavens.

So it was that presently, to the European watchers, star and sun rose close upon each other, drove headlong for a space and then slower, and at last came to rest, star and sun merged into one glare of flame at the zenith of the sky. The moon no longer eclipsed the star but was lost to sight in the brilliance of the sky. And though those who were still alive regarded it for the most part with that dull stupidity that hunger, fatigue, heat and despair engender, there were still men who could perceive the meaning of these signs. Star and earth had been at their nearest, had swung about one another, and the star had passed. Already it was receding, swifter and swifter, in the last stage of its headlong journey downward into the sun.

And then the clouds gathered, blotting out the vision of the sky, the thunder and lightning wove a garment round the world; all over the earth was such a downpour of rain as men had never before seen, and where the volcanoes flared red against the cloud canopy there descended torrents of mud. Everywhere the waters were pouring off the land, leaving mud-silted ruins, and the earth littered like a storm-worn beach with all that had floated and the dead bodies of the men and brutes, its children. For days the water streamed off the land, sweeping away soil and trees and houses in the way, and piling huge dykes and scooping out titanic [91] gullies over the countryside. Those were the days of darkness that followed the star and the heat. All through them, and for many weeks and months, the earthquakes continued.

But the star had passed, and men, hunger-driven and gathering courage only slowly, might creep back to their ruined cities, buried granaries and sodden fields. Such few ships as had escaped the storms of that time came stunned and shattered and sounding their way cautiously through the new marks and shoals of once familiar ports. And as the storms subsided men perceived that everywhere the days were hotter than of yore, and the sun larger, and the moon, shrunk to a third of its former size, took now fourscore days between its new and next new moon.

But of the new brotherhood that grew presently among men, of the saving of laws and books and machines, of the strange change that had come over Iceland and Greenland and the shores of Baffin's Bay, [92] so that the sailors coming there presently found them green and gracious, and could scarce believe their eyes, this story does not tell. Nor of the movement of mankind, now that the earth was hotter, northward and southward towards the poles of the earth. It concerns itself only with the coming and the passing of the Star.

The Martian astronomers – for there are astronomers on Mars, although they are very different beings from men – were naturally profoundly interested by these things. They saw them from their own standpoint, of course.

Considering the mass and temperature of the missile that was flung through our solar system into the sun [one wrote], it is astonishing what a little damage the Earth, which it missed so narrowly, has sustained. All the familiar continental markings and the masses of the seas remain intact, and indeed the only difference seems to be a shrinkage of the white discoloration (supposed to be frozen water) round either pole.

Which only shows how small the vastest of human catastrophes may seem from a distance of a few million miles.

The Red Room

'I can assure you,' said I, 'that it will take a very tangible ghost to frighten me.' And I stood up before the fire with my glass in my hand.

'It is your own choosing,' said the man with the withered arm, and glanced at me askance.

'Eight-and-twenty years,' said I, 'I have lived, and never a ghost have I seen as yet.'

The old woman sat staring hard into the fire, her pale eyes wide open. 'Ay,' she broke in; 'and eight-and-twenty years you have lived and never seen the likes of this house, I reckon. There's a many things to see, when one's still but eight-and-twenty.' She swayed her head slowly from side to side. 'A many things to see and sorrow for.'

I half suspected the old people were trying to enhance the spiritual terrors of their house by their droning insistence. I put down my empty glass on the table and looked about the room, and caught a glimpse of myself, abbreviated and broadened to an impossible sturdiness, in the queer old mirror at the end of the room. 'Well,' I said, 'if I see anything tonight, I shall be so much the wiser. For I come to the business with an open mind.'

'It's your own choosing,' said the man with the withered arm, once more.

I heard the sound of a stick and a shambling step on the flags in the passage outside, and the door creaked on its hinges as a second old man entered, more bent, more wrinkled, more aged even than the first. He supported himself by a single crutch, his eyes were covered by a shade, and his lower lip, half averted, hung pale and pink from his decaying yellow teeth. He made straight for an armchair on the opposite side of the table, sat down clumsily, and began to cough. The man with the withered arm gave this newcomer a short glance of positive dislike; the old woman took no notice of his arrival, but remained with her eyes fixed steadily on the fire.

'I said – it's your own choosing,' said the man with the withered arm, when the coughing had ceased for a while.

'It's my own choosing,' I answered.

The man with the shade became aware of my presence for the first time, and threw his head back for a moment and sideways, to see me. I caught a momentary glimpse of his eyes, small and bright and inflamed. Then he began to cough and splutter again.

'Why don't you drink?' said the man with the withered arm, pushing the beer towards him. The man with the shade poured out a glassful with a shaky arm that splashed half as much again on the deal table. A monstrous shadow of him crouched upon the wall and mocked his action as he poured and drank. I must confess I had scarce expected these grotesque custodians. There is to my mind something inhuman in senility, something crouching and atavistic; the human qualities seem to drop from old people insensibly day by day. The three of them made me feel uncomfortable, with their gaunt silences, their bent carriage, their evident unfriendliness to me and to one another.

'If,' said I, 'you will show me to this haunted room of yours, I shall make myself comfortable there.'

The old man with the cough jerked his head back so suddenly that it startled me, and shot another glance of his red eyes at me from under the shade; but no one answered me. I waited a minute, glancing from one to the other.

'If,' I said a little louder, 'if you will show me to this haunted room of yours, I shall relieve you from the task of entertaining me.'

'There's a candle on the slab outside the door,' said the man with the withered arm, looking at my feet as he addressed me. 'But if you go to the red room tonight – '

('This night of all nights!' said the old woman.)

' – you go alone.'

'Very well,' I answered. 'And which way do I go?'

'You go along the passage for a bit,' said he, 'until you come to a door, and through that is a spiral staircase, and halfway up that is a landing and another door, covered with baize. Go through that and down the long corridor to the end, and the red room is on your left up the steps.'

'Have I got that right?' I said, and repeated his directions. He corrected me in one particular.

'And are you really going?' said the man with the shade, looking at me again for the third time, with that queer, unnatural tilting of the face.

('This night of all nights!' said the old woman.)

'It is what I came for,' I said, and moved towards the door. As I did so, the old man with the shade rose and staggered round the table, so as to be closer to the others and to the fire. At the door I turned and looked at them, and saw they were all close together, dark against the firelight, staring at me over their shoulders, with an intent expression on their ancient faces.

'Good-night,' I said, setting the door open.

'It's your own choosing,' said the man with the withered arm.

I left the door wide open until the candle was well alight, and then I shut them in and walked down the chilly, echoing passage.

I must confess that the oddness of these three old pensioners in whose charge her ladyship had left the castle, and the deep-toned, old-fashioned furniture of the housekeeper's room in which they fore-gathered, affected me in spite of my efforts to keep myself at a matter-of-fact phase. They seemed to belong to another age, an older age, an age when things spiritual were different from this of ours, less certain; an age when omens and witches were credible, and ghosts beyond denying. Their very existence was spectral; the cut of their clothing, fashions born in dead brains. The ornaments and conveniences of the room about them were ghostly – the thoughts of vanished men, which still haunted, rather than participated in the world of today. But with an effort I sent such thoughts to the right-about.[94] The long, draughty subterranean passage was chilly and dusty, and my candle flared and made the shadows cower and quiver. The echoes rang up and down the spiral staircase, and a shadow came sweeping up after me, and one fled before me into the darkness overhead. I came to the landing and stopped there for a moment, listening to a rustling that I fancied I heard; then, satisfied of the absolute silence, I pushed open the baize-covered door and stood in the corridor.

The effect was scarcely what I expected, for the moonlight, coming in by the great window on the grand staircase, picked out everything in vivid black shadow or silvery illumination. Everything was in its place: the house might have been deserted on the yesterday instead of eighteen months ago. There were candles in the sockets of the sconces,[95] and whatever dust had gathered on the carpets or upon the polished flooring was distributed so evenly as to be invisible in the moonlight. I was about to advance, and stopped abruptly. A bronze group stood upon the landing, hidden from me by the corner of the wall, but its shadow fell with marvellous distinctness upon the white panelling, and gave me the impression of someone crouching to waylay me. I stood rigid for half a minute perhaps. Then, with my hand in the pocket that held my revolver, I advanced, only to discover a Ganymede and Eagle[96] glistening in the moonlight. That incident for at time restored my nerve, and a porcelain Chinaman on a buhl table, whose head rocked silently as I passed him, scarcely startled me.[97]

The door to the red room and the steps up to it were in a shadowy corner. I moved my candle from side to side, in order to see clearly the nature of the recess in which I stood before opening the door. Here it was, thought I, that my predecessor was found, and the memory of that story gave me a sudden twinge of apprehension. I glanced over my shoulder at the Ganymede in the moonlight, and opened the door of the red room rather hastily, with my face half turned to the pallid silence of the landing.

I entered, closed the door behind me at once, turned the key I found in the lock within, and stood with the candle held aloft, surveying the scene of my vigil, the great red room of Lorraine Castle, in which the young duke had died. Or rather, in which he had begun his dying, for he had opened the door and fallen headlong down the steps I had just ascended. That had been the end of his vigil, of his gallant attempt to conquer the ghostly tradition of the place; and never, I thought, had apoplexy better served the ends of superstition. And there were other and older stories that clung to the room, back to the half-credible beginning of it all, the tale of a timid wife and the tragic end that came to her husband's jest of frightening her. And looking around that large shadowy room, with its shadowy window bays, its recesses and alcoves, one could well understand the legends that had sprouted in its black corners, its germinating darkness. My candle was a little tongue of flame in its vastness that failed to pierce the opposite end of the room, and left an ocean of mystery and suggestion beyond its island of light.

I resolved to make a systematic examination of the place at once, and dispel the fanciful suggestions of its obscurity before they obtained a hold upon me. After satisfying myself of the fastening of the door, I began to walk about the room, peering round each article of furniture, tucking up the valances[98] of the bed, and opening its curtains wide. I pulled up the blinds and examined the fastenings of the several windows before closing the shutters, leant forward and looked up the blackness of the wide chimney and tapped the dark oak panelling for any secret opening. There were two big mirrors in the room, each with a pair of sconces bearing candles, and on the mantelshelf, too, were more candles in china candlesticks. All these I lit one after the other. The fire was laid – an unexpected consideration from the old housekeeper – and I lit it, to keep down any disposition to shiver, and when it was burning well, I stood round with my back to it and regarded the room again. I had pulled up a chintz-covered armchair and a table to form a kind of barricade before me, and on this lay my revolver ready to hand. My precise examination had done me good, but I still found the remoter darkness of the place, and its perfect stillness, too stimulating for the imagination. The echoing of the stir and crackling of the fire was no sort of comfort to me. The shadow in the alcove at the end in particular had that undefinable quality of a presence, that odd suggestion of a lurking, living thing that comes so easily in silence and solitude. At last, to reassure myself, I walked with a candle into it, and satisfied myself that there was nothing tangible there. I stood that candle upon the floor of the alcove, and left it in that position.

By this time I was in a state of considerable nervous tension, although to my reason there was no adequate cause for the condition. My mind, however, was perfectly clear. I postulated quite unreservedly that nothing supernatural could happen, and to pass the time I began to string some rhymes together, Ingoldsby fashion,[99] of the original legend of the place. A few I spoke aloud, but the echoes were not pleasant. For the same reason I also abandoned, after a time, a conversation with myself upon the impossibility of ghosts and haunting. My mind reverted to the three old and distorted people downstairs, and I tried to keep it upon that topic. The sombre reds and blacks of the room troubled me; even with seven candles the place was merely dim. The one in the alcove flared in a draught, and the fire-flickering kept the shadows and penumbra[100] perpetually shifting and stirring. Casting about for a remedy, I recalled the candles I had seen in the passage, and, with a slight effort, walked out into the moonlight, carrying a candle and leaving the door open, and presently returned with as many as ten. These I put in various knick-knacks of china with which the room was sparsely adorned, lit and placed them where the shadows had lain deepest, some on the floor, some in the window recesses, until at last my seventeen candles were so arranged that not an inch of the room but had the direct light of at least one of them. It occurred to me that when the ghost came, I could warn him not to trip over them. The room was now quite brightly illuminated. There was something very cheery and reassuring in these little streaming flames, and snuffing them[101] gave me an occupation, and afforded a helpful sense of the passage of time.

Even with that, however, the brooding expectation of the vigil weighed heavily upon me. It was after midnight that the candle in the alcove suddenly went out, and the black shadow sprang back to its place. I did not see the candle go out; I simply turned and saw that the darkness was there, as one might start and see the unexpected presence of a stranger. 'By Jove!' said I aloud, 'that draught's a strong one!' and, taking the matches from the table, I walked across the room in a leisurely manner to relight the corner again. My first match would not strike, and as I succeeded with the second, something seemed to blink on the wall before me. I turned my head involuntarily, and saw that the two candles on the little table by the fireplace were extinguished. I rose at once to my feet.

'Odd!' I said. 'Did I do that myself in a flash of absent-mindedness?'

I walked back and relit one, and as I did so, I saw the candle in the right sconce of one of the mirrors wink and go right out, and almost immediately its companion followed it. There was no mistake about it. The flame vanished, as if the wick had been suddenly nipped between a finger and thumb, leaving the wick neither glowing nor smoking, but black. While I stood gaping, the candle at the foot of the bed went out, and the shadows seemed to take another step towards me.

'This won't do!' said I, and first one and then another candle on the mantelshelf followed. 'What's up?' I cried, with a queer high note getting into my voice somehow. At that the candle on the wardrobe went out, and the one I had relit in the alcove followed.

'Steady on!' I said. 'These candles are wanted,' speaking with a half-hysterical facetiousness, and scratching away at a match, all the while, for the mantel candlesticks. My hands trembled so much that twice I missed the rough paper of the matchbox. As the mantel emerged from darkness again, two candles in the remoter end of the window were eclipsed. But with the same match I also relit the larger mirror candles, and those on the floor near the doorway, so that for the moment I seemed to gain on the extinctions. But then in a volley[102] there vanished four lights at once in different corners of the room, and I struck another match in quivering haste, and stood hesitating whither to take it.

As I stood undecided, an invisible hand seemed to sweep out the two candles on the table. With a cry of terror, I dashed at the alcove, then into the corner and then into the window, relighting three, as two more vanished by the fireplace; then, perceiving a better way, I dropped the matches on the iron-bound deed-box in the corner, and caught up the bedroom candlestick. With this I avoided the delay of striking matches; but for all that the steady process of extinction went on, and the shadows I feared and fought against returned, and crept in upon me, first a step gained on this side of me and then on that. It was like a ragged storm-cloud sweeping out the stars. Now and then one returned for a minute, and was lost again. I was now almost frantic with the horror of the coming darkness, and my self-possession deserted me. I leaped panting and dishevelled from candle to candle in a vain struggle against that remorseless advance.

I bruised myself on the thigh against the table, I sent a chair headlong, I stumbled and fell and whisked the cloth from the table in my fall. My candle rolled away from me, and I snatched another as I rose. Abruptly this was blown out as I swung it off the table by the wind of my sudden movement, and immediately the two remaining candles followed. But there was light still in the room, a red light that stayed off the shadows from me. The fire! Of course, I could still thrust my candle between the bars and relight it!

I turned to where the flames were still dancing between the glowing coals and splashing red reflections upon the furniture, made two steps towards the grate, and incontinently the flames dwindled and vanished, the glow vanished, the reflections rushed together and vanished, and as I thrust the candle between the bars, darkness closed upon me like the shutting of an eye, wrapped about me in a stifling embrace, sealed my vision and crushed the last vestiges of reason from my brain. The candle fell from my hand. I flung out my arms in a vain effort to thrust that ponderous blackness away from me, and, lifting up my voice, screamed with all my might – once, twice, thrice. Then I think I must have staggered to my feet. I know I thought suddenly of the moonlit corridor and, with my head bowed and my arms over my face, made a run for the door.

But I had forgotten the exact position of the door, and struck myself heavily against the corner of the bed. I staggered back, turned, and was either struck or struck myself against some other bulky furniture. I have a vague memory of battering myself thus, to and fro in the darkness, of a cramped struggle, and of my own wild crying as I darted to and fro, of a heavy blow at last upon my forehead, a horrible sensation of falling that lasted an age, of my last frantic effort to keep my footing, and then I remember no more.

I opened my eyes in daylight. My head was roughly bandaged, and the man with the withered arm was watching my face. I looked about me, trying to remember what had happened, and for a space I could not recollect. I turned to the corner, and saw the old woman, no longer abstracted, pouring out some drops of medicine from a little blue phial into a glass. 'Where am I?' I asked; 'I seem to remember you, and yet I cannot remember who you are.'

They told me then, and I heard of the haunted red room as one who hears a tale. 'We found you at dawn,' said he, 'and there was blood on your forehead and lips.'

It was very slowly I recovered my memory of my experience. 'You believe now,' said the old man, 'that the room is haunted?' He spoke no longer as one who greets an intruder, but as one who grieves for a broken friend.

'Yes,' said I; 'the room is haunted.'

'And you have seen it. And we, who have lived here all our lives, have never set eyes upon it. Because we have never dared . . . Tell us, is it truly the old earl who – '

'No,' said I; 'it is not.'

'I told you so,' said the old lady, with the glass in her hand. 'It is his poor young countess who was frightened – '

'It is not,' I said. 'There is neither ghost of earl nor ghost of countess in that room, there is no ghost there at all; but worse, far worse – '

'Well?' they said.

'The worst of all the things that haunt poor mortal man,' said I; 'and that is, in all its nakedness – *Fear*![103] Fear that will not have light nor sound, that will not bear with reason, that deafens and darkens and overwhelms. It followed me through the corridor, it fought against me in the room – '

I stopped abruptly. There was an interval of silence. My hand went up to my bandages.

Then the man with the shade sighed and spoke. 'That is it,' said he. 'I knew that was it. A Power of Darkness. To put such a curse upon a woman! It lurks there always. You can feel it even in the daytime, even of a bright summer's day, in the hangings, in the curtains, keeping behind you however you face about. In the dusk it creeps along the corridor and follows you, so that you dare not turn. There is Fear in that room of hers – black Fear,[104] and there will be – so long as this house of sin endures.'

In the Abyss[105]

The lieutenant stood in front of the steel sphere and gnawed a piece of pine splinter. 'What do you think of it, Steevens?'[106] he said.

'It's an idea,' said Steevens, in the tone of one who keeps an open mind.

'I believe it will smash – flat,' said the lieutenant.

'He seems to have calculated it all out pretty well,' said Steevens, still impartial.

'But think of the pressure,' said the lieutenant. 'At the surface of the water it's fourteen pounds to the inch, thirty feet down it's double that; sixty, treble; ninety, four times; nine hundred, forty times; five thousand, three hundred – that's a mile – it's two hundred and forty times fourteen pounds; that's – let's see – thirty hundredweight – a ton and a half, Steevens; *a ton and a half* to the square inch. And the ocean where he's going is five miles deep. That's seven and a half – '

'Sounds a lot,' said Steevens, 'but it's jolly thick steel.'

The lieutenant made no answer, but resumed his pine splinter. The object of their conversation was a huge ball of steel, having an exterior diameter of perhaps nine feet. It looked like the shot for some titanic piece of artillery. It was elaborately nested in a monstrous scaffolding built into the framework of the vessel, and the gigantic spars that were presently to sling it overboard gave the stern of the ship an appearance that had raised the curiosity of every decent sailor who had sighted it, from the Pool of London[107] to the Tropic of Capricorn. In two places, one above the other, the steel gave place to a couple of circular windows of enormously thick glass, and one of these, set in a steel frame of great solidity, was now partially unscrewed. Both the men had seen the interior of this globe for the first time that morning. It was elaborately padded with air cushions, with little studs sunk between bulging pillows to work the simple mechanism of the affair. Everything was elaborately padded, even the Myers apparatus[108] which was to absorb carbonic acid and replace the oxygen inspired by its tenant, when he had crept in by the glass manhole and had been screwed in. It was so elaborately padded that a man might have been fired from a gun in it with perfect safety.[109] And it had need to be, for presently a man was to crawl in through that glass manhole, to be screwed up tightly, and to be flung overboard, and to sink down – down – down, for five miles, even as the lieutenant said. It had taken the strongest hold of his imagination; it made him a bore at mess; and he found Steevens, the new arrival aboard, a godsend to talk to about it, over and over again.

'It's my opinion,' said the lieutenant, 'that that glass will simply bend in and bulge and smash under pressure of that sort. Daubrée[110] has made rocks run like water under big pressure – and you mark my words – '

'If the glass did break in,' said Steevens, 'what then?'

'The water would shoot in like a jet of iron. Have you ever felt a straight jet of high pressure water? It would hit as hard as a bullet. It would simply smash him and flatten him. It would tear down his throat, and into his lungs; it would blow in his ears – '

'What a detailed imagination you have!' protested Steevens, who saw things vividly.

'It's a simple statement of the inevitable,' said the lieutenant.

'And the globe?'

'Would just give out a few little bubbles, and it would settle down comfortably against the Day of Judgement, among the oozes and the bottom clay – with poor Elstead spread over his own smashed cushions like butter over bread.'

He repeated this sentence as though he liked it very much. 'Like butter over bread,' he said.

'Having a look at the jigger?'[111] said a voice, and Elstead stood behind them, spick and span in white, with a cigarette between his teeth and his eyes smiling out of the shadow of his ample hat-brim. 'What's that about bread and butter, Weybridge? Grumbling as usual about the insufficient pay of naval officers? It won't be more than a day now before I start. We are to get the slings ready today. This clean sky and gentle swell is just the kind of thing for swinging off a dozen tons of lead and iron, isn't it?'

'It won't affect you much,' said Weybridge.

'No. Seventy or eighty feet down – and I shall be there in a dozen seconds – there's not a particle moving, though the wind shriek itself hoarse up above, and the water lift halfway to the clouds. No. Down there – ' He moved to the side of the ship and the other two followed him. All three leant forward on their elbows and stared down into the yellow-green water.

'*Peace*,' said Elstead, finishing his thought aloud.

'Are you dead certain that clockwork will act?' asked Weybridge presently.

'It has worked thirty-five times,' said Elstead. 'It's bound to work.'

'But if it doesn't?'

'Why shouldn't it?'

'I wouldn't go down in that confounded thing,' said Weybridge, 'for twenty thousand pounds.'

'Cheerful chap you are,' said Elstead, and spat sociably at a bubble below.

'I don't understand yet how you mean to work the thing,' said Steevens.

'In the first place, I'm screwed into the sphere,' said Elstead, 'and when I've turned the electric light off and on three times to show I'm cheerful, I'm swung out over the stern by that crane, with all those big lead sinkers slung below me. The top lead weight has a roller carrying a hundred fathoms of strong cord rolled up, and that's all that joins the sinkers to the sphere, except the slings that will be cut when the affair is dropped. We use cord rather than wire rope because it's easier to cut and more buoyant – necessary points, as you will see.

'Through each of these lead weights you notice there is a hole, and an iron rod will be run through that and will project six feet on the lower side. If that rod is rammed up from below, it knocks up a lever and sets the clockwork in motion at the side of the cylinder on which the cord winds.

'Very well. The whole affair is lowered gently into the water, and the slings are cut. The sphere floats – with the air in it, it's lighter than water – but the lead weights go down straight and the cord runs out. When the cord is all paid out, the sphere will go down too, pulled down by the cord.'

'But why the cord?' asked Steevens. 'Why not fasten the weights directly to the sphere?'

'Because of the smash down below. The whole affair will go rushing down, mile after mile, at a headlong pace at last. It would be knocked to pieces on the bottom if it wasn't for that cord. But the weights will hit the bottom, and directly they do, the buoyancy of the sphere will come into play. It will go on sinking slower and slower; come to stop at last, and then begin to float upward again.

'That's where the clockwork comes in. Directly the weights smash against the sea bottom, the rod will be knocked through and will kick up the clockwork, and the cord will be rewound on the reel. I shall be lugged down to the sea bottom. There I shall stay for half an hour, with the electric light on, looking about me. Then the clockwork will release a spring knife, the cord will be cut, and up I shall rush again, like a soda-water bubble. The cord itself will help the flotation.'

'And if you should chance to hit a ship?' said Weybridge.

'I should come up at such a pace, I should go clean through it,' said Elstead, 'like a cannon ball. You needn't worry about that.'

'And suppose some nimble crustacean should wriggle into your clock-work –'

'It would be a pressing sort of invitation for me to stop,' said Elstead, turning his back on the water and staring at the sphere.

They had swung Elstead overboard by eleven o'clock. The day was serenely bright and calm, with the horizon lost in haze. The electric glare in the little upper compartment beamed cheerfully three times. Then they let him down slowly to the surface of the water, and a sailor in the stern chains[112] hung ready to cut the tackle that held the lead weights and the sphere together. The globe, which had looked so large on deck, looked the smallest thing conceivable under the stern of the ship. It rolled a little, and its two dark windows, which floated uppermost, seemed like eyes turned up in round wonderment at the people who crowded the rail. A voice wondered how Elstead liked the rolling. 'Are you ready?' sang out the commander. 'Ay, ay, sir!' 'Then let her go!'

The rope of the tackle tightened against the blade and was cut, and an eddy rolled over the globe in a grotesquely helpless fashion. Some-one waved a handkerchief, someone else tried an ineffectual cheer, a middy[113] was counting slowly, 'Eight, nine, ten!' Another roll, then with a jerk and a splash the thing righted itself.

It seemed to be stationary for a moment, to grow rapidly smaller, and then the water closed over it, and it became visible, enlarged by refraction and dimmer, below the surface. Before one could count to three it had disappeared. There was a flicker of white light far down in the water that diminished to a speck and vanished. Then there was nothing but a depth of water going down into blackness, through which a shark was swimming.

Then suddenly the screw of the cruiser began to rotate, the water was crickled, the shark disappeared in a wrinkled confusion, and a torrent of foam rushed across the crystalline clearness that had swallowed up Elstead. 'What's the idea?' said one A.B.[114] to another.

'We're going to lay off about a couple of miles, for fear he should hit us when he comes up,' said his mate.

The ship steamed slowly to her new position. Aboard her almost everyone who was unoccupied remained watching the breathing swell into which the sphere had sunk. For the next half-hour it is doubtful if a word was spoken that did not bear directly or indirectly on Elstead.

The December sun was now high in the sky, and the heat very considerable.

'He'll be cold enough down there,' said Weybridge. 'They say that below a certain depth sea water's always just about freezing.'

'Where'll he come up?' asked Steevens. 'I've lost my bearings.'

'That's the spot,' said the commander, who prided himself on his omniscience. He extended a precise finger south-eastward. 'And this, I reckon, is pretty nearly the moment,' he said. 'He's been thirty-five minutes.'

'How long does it take to reach the bottom of the ocean?' asked Steevens.

'For a depth of five miles, and reckoning – as we did – an acceleration of two feet per second, both ways, it takes just about three-quarters of a minute.'

'Then he's overdue,' said Weybridge.

'Pretty nearly,' said the commander. 'I suppose it takes a few minutes for that cord of his to wind in.'

'I forgot that,' said Weybridge, evidently relieved.

And then began the suspense. A minute slowly dragged itself out, and no sphere shot out of the water. Another followed, and nothing broke the low oily swell. The sailors explained to one another that little point about the winding-in of the cord. The rigging was dotted with expectant faces. 'Come up, Elstead!' called one hairy-chested salt impatiently, and the others caught it up, and shouted as though they were waiting for the curtain of a theatre to rise.

The commander glanced irritably at them.

'Of course, if the acceleration's less than two,' he said, 'he'll be all the longer. We aren't absolutely certain that was the proper figure. I'm no slavish believer in calculations.'

Steevens agreed concisely. No one on the quarter-deck spoke for a couple of minutes. Then Steevens's watchcase clicked.

When, twenty-one minutes after, the sun reached the zenith, they were still waiting for the globe to reappear, and not a man aboard had dared to whisper that hope was dead. It was Weybridge who first gave expression to that realisation. He spoke while the sound of eight bells[115] still hung in the air. 'I always distrusted that window,' he said quite suddenly to Steevens.

'Good God!' said Steevens; 'you don't think – ?'

'Well!' said Weybridge, and left the rest to his imagination.

'I'm no great believer in calculations myself,' said the commander dubiously, 'so that I'm not altogether hopeless yet.' And at midnight the gunboat was steaming slowly in a spiral round the spot where the globe had sunk, and the white beam of the electric light fled and halted and swept discontentedly onward again over the waste of phosphorescent waters under the little stars.

'If his window hasn't burst and smashed him,' said Weybridge, 'then it's a cursed sight worse, for his clockwork has gone wrong, and he's alive now, five miles under our feet, down there in the cold and dark, anchored in that little bubble of his, where never a ray of light has shone or a human being lived since the waters were gathered together.[116] He's there without food, feeling hungry and thirsty and scared, wondering whether he'll starve or stifle. Which will it be? The Myers apparatus is running out, I suppose. How long do they last?

'Good heavens!' he exclaimed; 'what little things we are! What daring little devils! Down there, miles and miles of water – all water, and all this empty water about us and this sky. Gulfs!' He threw his hands out, and as he did so, a little white streak swept noiselessly up the sky, travelled more slowly, stopped and became a motionless dot, as though a new star had fallen up into the sky. Then it went sliding back again and lost itself amidst the reflections of the stars and the white haze of the sea's phosphorescence.

At the sight he stopped, arms extended and mouth open. He shut his mouth, opened it again, and waved his arms with an impatient gesture. Then he turned, shouted, 'Elstead ahoy!' to the first watch, and went at a run to Lindley and the searchlight. 'I saw him,' he said. 'Starboard there! His light's on, and he's just shot out of the water. Bring the light round. We ought to see him drifting when he lifts on the swell.'

But they never picked up the explorer until dawn. Then they almost ran him down. The crane was swung out and a boat's crew hooked the chain to the sphere. When they had shipped the sphere, they unscrewed the manhole and peered into the darkness of the interior (for the electric light chamber was intended to illuminate the water about the sphere and was shut off entirely from its general cavity).

The air was very hot within the cavity, and the india rubber at the lip of the manhole was soft. There was no answer to their eager questions and no sound of movement within. Elstead seemed to be lying motionless, crumpled in the bottom of the globe. The ship's doctor crawled in and lifted him out to the men outside. For a moment or so they did not know whether Elstead was alive or dead. His face, in the yellow light of the ship's lamps, glistened with perspiration. They carried him down to his own cabin.

He was not dead, they found, but in a state of absolute nervous collapse, and besides, cruelly bruised. For some days he had to lie perfectly still. It was a week before he could tell his experiences.

Almost his first words were that he was going down again. The sphere would have to be altered, he said, in order to allow him to throw off the cord if need be, and that was all. He had had the most marvellous experience. 'You thought I should find nothing but ooze,' he said. 'You laughed at my explorations, and I've discovered a new world!' He told his story in disconnected fragments, and chiefly from the wrong end, so that it is impossible to retell it in his words. But what follows is the narrative of his experience.

It began atrociously, he said. Before the cord ran out, the thing kept rolling over. He felt like a frog in a football. He could see nothing but the crane and the sky overhead, with an occasional glimpse of people on the ship's rail. He couldn't tell a bit which way the thing would roll next. Suddenly he would find his feet going up, and try to step, and over he went rolling, head over heels, and just anyhow, on the padding. Any other shape would have been more comfortable, but no other shape was to be relied upon under the huge pressure of the nethermost abyss.

Suddenly the swaying ceased; the globe righted, and when he had picked himself up, he saw the water all about him greeny-blue, with an attenuated light filtering down from above, and a shoal of little floating things went rushing up past him, as it seemed to him, towards the light. And even as he looked, it grew darker and darker, until the water above was as dark as the midnight sky, albeit of greener shade, and the water below black. And little transparent things in the water developed a faint glint of luminosity, and shot past him in faint greenish streaks.

And the feeling of falling! It was just like the start of a lift, he said, only it kept on. One has to imagine what that means, that keeping on. It was then of all times that Elstead repented of his adventure. He saw the chances against him in an altogether new light. He thought of the big cuttlefish people knew to exist in the middle waters, the kind of things they find half-digested in whales at times or floating dead and rotten and half-eaten by fish. Suppose one caught hold and wouldn't let go. And had the clockwork really been sufficiently tested? But whether he wanted to go on or go back mattered not the slightest now.

In fifty seconds everything was as black as night outside, except where the beam from his light struck through the waters and picked out every now and then some fish or scrap of sinking matter. They flashed by too fast for him to see what they were. Once he thinks he passed a shark. And then the sphere began to get hot by friction against the water. They had underestimated this, it seems.

The first thing he noticed was that he was perspiring, and then he heard a hissing growing louder under his feet, and saw a lot of little bubbles – very little bubbles they were – rushing upward like a fan through the water outside. Steam! He felt the window, and it was hot. He turned on the minute glow-lamp that lit his own cavity, looked at the padded watch by the studs, and saw he had been travelling now for two minutes. It came into his head that the window would crack through the conflict of temperatures, for he knew the bottom water is very near freezing.

Then suddenly the floor of the sphere seemed to press against his feet, the rush of bubbles outside grew slower and slower, and the hissing diminished. The sphere rolled a little. The window had not cracked, nothing had given, and he knew that the dangers of sinking, at any rate, were over.

In another minute or so he would be on the floor of the abyss. He thought, he said, of Steevens and Weybridge and the rest of them five miles overhead, higher to him than the highest clouds that ever floated over land are to us, steaming slowly and staring down and wondering what had happened to him.

He peered out of the window. There were no more bubbles now, and the hissing had stopped. Outside there was a heavy blackness – as black as black velvet – except where the electric light pierced the empty water and showed the colour of it – a yellow-green. Then three things like shapes of fire swam into sight, following each other through the water. Whether they were little and near or big and far off he could not tell.

Each was outlined in a bluish light almost as bright as the lights of a fishing smack, a light which seemed to be smoking greatly, and all along the sides of them were specks of this, like the lighter port-holes of a ship. Their phosphorescence seemed to go out as they came into the radiance of his lamp, and he saw then that they were little fish of some strange sort, with huge heads, vast eyes and dwindling bodies and tails. Their eyes were turned towards him, and he judged they were following him down. He supposed they were attracted by his glare.

Presently others of the same sort joined them. As he went on down, he noticed that the water became of a pallid colour, and that little specks twinkled in his ray like motes in a sunbeam. This was probably due to the clouds of ooze and mud that the impact of his leaden sinkers had disturbed.

By the time he was drawn down to the lead weights he was in a dense fog of white that his electric light failed altogether to pierce for more than a few yards, and many minutes elapsed before the hanging sheets of sediment subsided to any extent. Then, lit by his light and by the transient phosphorescence of a distant shoal of fishes, he was able to see under the huge blackness of the super-incumbent water an undulating expanse of greyish-white ooze, broken here and there by tangled thickets of a growth of sea lilies, waving hungry tentacles in the air.

Farther away were the graceful, translucent outlines of a group of gigantic sponges. About this floor there were scattered a number of bristling flattish tufts of rich purple and black, which he decided must be some sort of sea-urchin, and small, large-eyed or blind things, having a curious resemblance some to woodlice and others to lobsters, crawled sluggishly across the track of the light and vanished into the obscurity again, leaving furrowed trails behind them.

Then suddenly the hovering swarm of little fishes veered about and came towards him as a flight of starlings might do. They passed over him like a phosphorescent snow, and then he saw behind them some larger creature advancing towards the sphere.

At first he could see it only dimly, a faintly moving figure remotely suggestive of a walking man, and then it came into the spray of light that the lamp shot out. As the glare struck it, it shut its eyes, dazzled. He stared in rigid astonishment.

It was a strange vertebrated animal. Its dark purple head was dimly suggestive of a chameleon, but it had such a high forehead and such a braincase as no reptile ever displayed before; the vertical pitch of its face gave it a most extraordinary resemblance to a human being.

Two large and protruding eyes projected from sockets in chameleon fashion, and it had a broad reptilian mouth with horny lips beneath its little nostrils. In the position of the ears were two huge gill-covers, and out of these floated a branching tree of coralline filaments, almost like the treelike gills that very young rays and sharks possess.

But the humanity of the face was not the most extraordinary thing about the creature. It was a biped; its almost globular body was poised on a tripod of two froglike legs and a long thick tail, and its fore limbs, which grotesquely caricatured the human hand, much as a frog's do, carried a long shaft of bone, tipped with copper. The colour of the creature was variegated: its head, hands and legs were purple, but its skin, which hung loosely upon it, even as clothes might do, was a phosphorescent grey. And it stood there blinded by the light.

At last this unknown creature of the abyss blinked its eyes open, and shading them with its disengaged hand, opened its mouth and gave vent to a shouting noise, articulate almost as speech might be, that penetrated even the steel case and padded jacket of the sphere. How a shouting may be accomplished without lungs Elstead does not profess to explain. It then moved sideways out of the glare into the mystery of shadow that bordered it on either side, and Elstead felt rather than saw that it was coming towards him. Fancying the light had attracted it, he turned the switch that cut off the current. In another moment something soft dabbed upon the steel, and the globe swayed.

Then the shouting was repeated, and it seemed to him that a distant echo answered it. The dabbing recurred, and the whole globe swayed and ground against the spindle over which the wire was rolled. He stood in the blackness and peered out into the everlasting night of the abyss. And presently he saw, very faint and remote, other phosphorescent quasi-human forms hurrying towards him.

Hardly knowing what he did, he felt about in his swaying prison for the stud of the exterior electric light, and came by accident against his own small glow-lamp in its padded recess. The sphere twisted, and then threw him down; he heard shouts like shouts of surprise, and when he rose to his feet, he saw two pairs of stalked eyes peering into the lower window and reflecting his light.

In another moment hands were dabbing vigorously at his steel casing, and there was a sound, horrible enough in his position, of the metal protection of the clockwork being vigorously hammered. That indeed sent his heart into his mouth, for if these strange creatures succeeded in stopping that, his release would never occur. Scarcely had he thought as much when he felt the sphere sway violently, and the floor of it press hard against his feet. He turned off the small glow-lamp that lit the interior, and sent the ray of the large light in the separate compartment out into the water. The sea-floor and the manlike creatures had disappeared, and a couple of fish chasing each other dropped suddenly by the window.

He thought at once that these strange denizens of the deep sea had broken the rope and that he had escaped. He drove up faster and faster, and then stopped with a jerk that sent him flying against the padded roof of his prison. For half a minute perhaps, he was too astonished to think.

Then he felt that the sphere was spinning slowly, and rocking, and it seemed to him that it was also being drawn through the water. By crouching close to the window, he managed to make his weight effective and roll that part of the sphere downward, but he could see nothing save the pale ray of his light striking down ineffectively into the darkness. It occurred to him that he would see more if he turned the lamp off, and allowed his eyes to grow accustomed to the profound obscurity.

In this he was wise. After some minutes the velvety blackness became a translucent blackness, and then, far away, and as faint as the zodiacal light of an English summer evening, he saw shapes moving below. He judged these creatures had detached his cable, and were towing him along the sea bottom.

And then he saw something faint and remote across the undulations of the submarine plain, a broad horizon of pale luminosity that extended this way and that way as far as the range of his little window permitted him to see. To this he was being towed, as a balloon might be towed by men out of the open country into a town. He approached it very slowly, and very slowly the dim irradiation was gathered together into more definite shapes.

It was nearly five o'clock before he came over this luminous area, and by that time he could make out an arrangement suggestive of streets and houses grouped about a vast roofless erection that was grotesquely suggestive of a ruined abbey. It was spread out like a map below him. The houses were all roofless enclosures of walls, and their substance, being as he afterwards saw of phosphorescent bones, gave the place an appearance as if it were built of drowned moonshine.

Among the inner caves of the place waving trees of crinoid[117] stretched their tentacles, and tall, slender, glassy sponges shot like shining minarets and lilies of filmy light out of the general glow of the city. In the open spaces of the place he could see a stirring movement as of crowds of people, but he was too many fathoms above them to distinguish the individuals in those crowds.

Then slowly they pulled him down, and as they did so, the details of the place crept slowly upon his apprehension. He saw that the courses of the cloudy buildings were marked out with beaded lines of round objects, and then he perceived that at several points below him, in broad open spaces, were forms like the encrusted shapes of ships.

Slowly and surely he was drawn down, and the forms below him became brighter, clearer, more distinct. He was being pulled down, he perceived, towards the large building in the centre of the town, and he could catch a glimpse ever and again of the multitudinous forms that were lugging at his cord. He was astonished to see that the rigging of one of the ships, which formed such a prominent feature of the place, was crowded with a host of gesticulating figures regarding him, and then the walls of the great building rose about him silently, and hid the city from his eyes.

And such walls they were, of waterlogged wood, and twisted wire-rope, and iron spars, and copper, and the bones and skulls of dead men.

The skulls ran in zigzag lines and spirals and fantastic curves over the building; and in and out of their eye-sockets, and over the whole surface of the place, lurked and played a multitude of silvery little fishes.

Suddenly his ears were filled with a low shouting and a noise like the violent blowing of horns, and this gave place to a fantastic chant. Down the sphere sank, past the huge pointed windows, through which he saw vaguely a great number of these strange, ghostlike people regarding him, and at last he came to rest, as it seemed, on a kind of altar that stood in the centre of the place.

And now he was at such a level that he could see these strange people of the abyss plainly once more. To his astonishment, he perceived that they were prostrating themselves before him, all save one, dressed as it seemed in a robe of placoid scales[118] and crowned with a luminous diadem, who stood with his reptilian mouth opening and shutting, as though he led the chanting of the worshippers.

A curious impulse made Elstead turn on his small glow-lamp again, so that he became visible to these creatures of the abyss, albeit the glare made them disappear forthwith into night. At this sudden sight of him, the chanting gave place to a tumult of exultant shouts; and Elstead, being anxious to watch them, turned his light off again, and vanished from before their eyes. But for a time he was too blind to make out what they were doing, and when at last he could distinguish them, they were kneeling again. And thus they continued worshipping him, without rest or intermission, for a space of three hours.

Most circumstantial was Elstead's account of this astounding city and its people, these people of perpetual night, who have never seen sun or moon or stars, green vegetation, nor any living, air-breathing creatures, who know nothing of fire, nor any light but the phosphorescent light of living things.

Startling as is his story, it is yet more startling to find that scientific men, of such eminence as Adams[119] and Jenkins, find nothing incredible in it. They tell me they see no reason why intelligent, water-breathing, vertebrated creatures, inured to a low temperature and enormous pressure, and of such a heavy structure that neither alive nor dead would they float, might not live upon the bottom of the deep sea, quite unsuspected by us, descendants like ourselves of the great Theriomorpha of the New Red Sandstone Age.[120]

We should be known to them, however, as strange, meteoric creatures, wont to fall catastrophically dead out of the mysterious blackness of their watery sky. And not only we ourselves, but our ships, our metals, our appliances, would come raining down out of the night. Sometimes sinking things would smite down and crush them, as if it were the judgement of some unseen power above, and sometimes would come things of utmost rarity or utility, or shapes of inspiring suggestion. One can understand, perhaps, something of their behaviour at the descent of a living man if one thinks what a barbaric people might do, to whom an enhaloed, shining creature came suddenly out of the sky.

At one time or another Elstead probably told the officers of the *Ptarmigan*[121] every detail of his strange twelve hours in the abyss. That he also intended to write them down is certain, but he never did, and so unhappily we have to piece together the discrepant fragments of his story from the reminiscences of Commander Simmons, Weybridge, Steevens, Lindley, and the others.

We see the thing darkly in fragmentary glimpses – the huge ghostly building, the bowing, chanting people, with their dark chameleon-like heads and faintly luminous clothing, and Elstead, with his light turned on again, vainly trying to convey to their minds that the cord by which the sphere was held was to be severed. Minute after minute slipped away, and Elstead, looking at his watch, was horrified to find that he had oxygen only for four hours more. But the chant in his honour kept on as remorselessly as if it was the marching song of his approaching death.

The manner of his release he does not understand, but to judge by the end of cord that hung from the sphere, it had been cut through by rubbing against the edge of the altar. Abruptly the sphere rolled over, and he swept up, out of their world, as an ethereal creature clothed in a vacuum would sweep through our own atmosphere back to its native ether again. He must have torn out of their sight as a hydrogen bubble hastens upwards from our air. A strange ascension it must have seemed to them.

The sphere rushed up with even greater velocity than, when weighted with the lead sinkers, it had rushed down. It became exceedingly hot. It drove up with the windows uppermost, and he remembers the torrent of bubbles frothing against the glass. Every moment he expected this to fly. Then suddenly something like a huge wheel seemed to be released in his head, the padded compartment began spinning about him, and he fainted. His next recollection was of his cabin, and of the doctor's voice.

But that is the substance of the extraordinary story that Elstead related in fragments to the officers of the *Ptarmigan*. He promised to write it all down at a later date. His mind was chiefly occupied with the improvement of his apparatus, which was effected at Rio.

It remains only to tell that on February 2, 1896, he made his second descent into the ocean abyss, with the improvements his first experience suggested. What happened we shall probably never knew. He never returned.[122] The *Ptarmigan* beat about over the point of his submersion, seeking him in vain for thirteen days. Then she returned to Rio, and the news was telegraphed to his friends. So the matter remains for the present. But it is hardly probable that no further attempt will be made to verify his strange story of these hitherto unsuspected cities of the deep sea.

The Plattner Story[123]

Whether the story of Gottfried Plattner is to be credited or not, is a pretty question in the value of evidence. On the one hand, we have seven witnesses – to be perfectly exact, we have six and a half pairs of eyes, and one undeniable fact; and on the other we have – what is it – ? Prejudice, common sense, the inertia of opinion. Never were there seven more honest-seeming witnesses; never was there a more undeniable fact than the inversion of Gottfried Plattner's anatomical structure, and – never was there a more preposterous story than the one they have to tell! The most preposterous part of the story is the worthy Gottfried's contribution (for I count him as one of the seven). Heaven forbid that I should be led into giving countenance to superstition by a passion for impartiality, and so come to share the fate of Eusapia's patrons![124] Frankly, I believe there is something crooked about this business of Gottfried Plattner; but what that crooked factor is, I will admit as frankly, I do not know. I have been surprised at the credit accorded to the story in the most unexpected and authoritative quarters. The fairest way to the reader, however, will be for me to tell it without further comment.

Gottfried Plattner is, in spite of his name, a freeborn Englishman. His father was an Alsatian[125] who came to England in the sixties, married a respectable English girl of unexceptionable antecedents, and died, after a wholesome and uneventful life (devoted, I understand, chiefly to the laying of parquet flooring), in 1887. Gottfried's age is seven-and-twenty. He is, by virtue of his heritage of three languages, modern languages master in a small private school in the South of England. To the casual observer he is singularly like any other modern languages master in any other small private school. His costume is neither very costly nor very fashionable, but on the other hand it is not markedly cheap or shabby; his complexion, like his height and his bearing, is inconspicuous. You would notice perhaps that, like the majority of people, his face was not absolutely symmetrical, his right eye a little larger than the left, and his jaw a trifle heavier on the right side. If you, as an ordinary careless person, were to bare his chest and feel his heart beating, you would probably find it quite like the heart of anyone else. But here you and the trained observer would part company. If you found his heart quite ordinary, the trained observer would find it quite otherwise. And once the thing was pointed out to you, you too would perceive the peculiarity easily enough. It is that Gottfried's heart beats on the right side of his body.

Now, that is not the only singularity of Gottfried's structure, although it is the only one that would appeal to the untrained mind. Careful sounding of Gottfried's internal arrangements, by a well-known surgeon, seems to point to the fact that all the other unsymmetrical parts of his body are similarly misplaced. The right lobe of his liver is on the left side, the left on his right; while his lungs, too, are similarly contraposed. What is still more singular, unless Gottfried is a consummate actor, we must believe that his right hand has recently become his left. Since the occurrences we are about to consider (as impartially as possible), he has found the utmost difficulty in writing, except from right to left across the paper with his left hand. He cannot throw with his right hand, he is perplexed at meal times between knife and fork, and his ideas of the rule of the road – he is a cyclist[126] – are still a dangerous confusion. And there is not a scrap of evidence to show that before these occurrences Gottfried was at all left-handed. There is yet another wonderful fact in this preposterous business. Gottfried produces three photographs of himself. You have him at the age of five or six, thrusting fat legs at you from under a plaid frock, and scowling. In that photograph his left eye is a little larger than his right, and his jaw is a trifle heavier on the left side. This is the reverse of his present living conditions. The photograph of Gottfried at fourteen seems to contradict these facts, but that is because it is one of those cheap 'Gem' photographs[127] that were then in vogue, taken direct upon metal, and therefore reversing things just as a looking-glass would. A third photograph represents him at one-and-twenty and confirms the record of the others. There seems here evidence of the strongest confirmatory character that Gottfried has exchanged his left side for his right. Yet how a human being can be so changed, short of a fantastic and pointless miracle, it is exceedingly hard to suggest.

In one way, of course, these facts might be explicable on the sup-position that Plattner has undertaken an elaborate mystification, on the strength of his heart's displacement. Photographs may be fudged, and left-handedness imitated. But the character of the man does not lend itself to any such theory. He is quiet, practical, unobtrusive and thoroughly sane, from the Nordau[128] standpoint. He likes beer, and smokes moderately, takes walking exercise daily, and has a healthily high estimate of the value of his teaching. He has a good but untrained tenor voice, and takes a pleasure in singing airs of a popular and cheerful character. He is fond, but not morbidly fond, of reading – chiefly fiction pervaded with a vaguely pious optimism – sleeps well, and rarely dreams. He is in fact, the very last person to evolve a fantastic fable. Indeed, so far from forcing this story upon the world, he has been singularly reticent on the matter. He meets enquirers with a certain engaging – bashfulness is almost the word, that disarms the most suspicious. He seems genuinely ashamed that anything so unusual has occurred to him.

It is to be regretted that Plattner's aversion to the idea of post-mortem dissection may postpone, perhaps for ever, the positive proof that his entire body has had its left and right sides transposed. Upon that fact mainly the credibility of his story hangs. There is no way of taking a man and moving him about *in space*, as ordinary people understand space, that will result in our changing his sides. Whatever you do, his right is still his right, his left his left. You can do that with a perfectly thin and flat thing, of course. If you were to cut a figure out of paper, any figure with a right and left side, you could change its sides simply by lifting it up and turning it over. But with a solid it is different. Mathematical theorists tell us that the only way in which the right and left sides of a solid body can be changed is by taking that body clean out of space as we know it – taking it out of ordinary existence, that is, and turning it somewhere outside space. This is a little abstruse, no doubt, but anyone with any knowledge of mathematical theory will assure the reader of its truth. To put the thing in technical language, the curious inversion of Plattner's right and left sides is proof that he has moved out of our space into what is called the Fourth Dimension,[129] and that he has then returned again to our world. Unless we choose to consider ourselves the victims of an elaborate and motiveless fabrication, we are almost bound to believe that this has occurred.

So much for the tangible facts. We come now to the account of the phenomena that attended his temporary disappearance from the world. It appears that in the Sussexville Proprietary School, Plattner not only discharged the duties of modern languages master, but also taught chemistry, commercial geography, bookkeeping, shorthand, drawing, and any other additional subject to which the changing fancies of the boys' parents might direct attention. He knew little or nothing of these various subjects, but in secondary as distinguished from Board or elementary schools,[130] knowledge in the teacher is, very properly, by no means so necessary as high moral character and gentlemanly tone. In chemistry he was particularly deficient, knowing, he says, nothing beyond the Three Gases[131] (whatever the three gases may be). As, however, his pupils began by knowing nothing, and derived all their information from him, this caused him (or anyone) but little inconvenience for several terms. Then a little boy named Whibble joined the school, who had been educated (it seems) by some mischievous relative into an enquiring habit of mind. This little boy followed Plattner's lessons with marked and sustained interest, and, in order to exhibit his zeal for the subject, brought at various times substances for Plattner to analyse. Plattner, flattered by this evidence of his power of awakening interest, and trusting to the boy's ignorance, analysed these, and even made general statements as to their composition. Indeed he was so far stimulated by his pupil as to obtain a work upon analytical chemistry and study it during his supervision of the evening's preparation. He was surprised to find chemistry quite an interesting subject.

So far the story is absolutely commonplace. But now the greenish powder comes upon the scene. The source of that greenish powder seems, unfortunately, lost. Master Whibble tells a tortuous story of finding it done up in a packet in a disused limekiln near the Downs. It would have been an excellent thing for Plattner, and possibly for Master Whibble's family, if a match could have been applied to that powder there and then. The young gentleman certainly did not bring it to school in a packet, but in a common eight-ounce graduated medicine bottle, plugged with masticated newspaper. He gave it to Plattner at the end of the afternoon school. Four boys had been detained after school prayers in order to complete some neglected tasks, and Plattner was supervising these in the small classroom in which the chemical teaching was conducted. The appliances for the practical teaching of chemistry in the Sussexville Proprietary School, as in most small schools in this country, are characterised by a severe simplicity. They are kept in a small cupboard standing in a recess, and having about the same capacity as a common travelling trunk. Plattner, being bored with his passive superintendence, seems to have welcomed the intervention of Whibble with his green powder as an agreeable diversion, and unlocking this cupboard, proceeded at once with his analytical experiments. Whibble sat, luckily for himself, at a safe distance, regarding him. The four malefactors, feigning a profound absorption in their work, watched him furtively with the keenest interest. For even within the limits of the Three Gases, Plattner's practical chemistry was, I understand, temerarious.[132]

They are practically unanimous in their account of Plattner's proceedings. He poured a little of the green powder into a test-tube, and tried the substance with water, hydrochloric acid, nitric acid and sulphuric acid in succession. Getting no result, he emptied out a little heap – nearly half the bottleful, in fact – upon a slate and tried a match. He held the medicine bottle in his left hand. The stuff began to smoke and melt, and then – exploded with deafening violence and a blinding flash.

The five boys, seeing the flash and being prepared for catastrophes, ducked below their desks, and were none of them seriously hurt. The window was blown out into the playground, and the blackboard on its easel was upset. The slate was smashed to atoms. Some plaster fell from the ceiling. No other damage was done to the school edifice or appliances, and the boys at first, seeing nothing of Plattner, fancied he was knocked down and lying out of their sight below the desks. They jumped out of their places to go to his assistance, and were amazed to find the space empty. Being still confused by the sudden violence of the report, they hurried to the open door, under the impression that he must have been hurt, and have rushed out of the room. But Carson, the foremost, nearly collided in the doorway with the principal, Mr Lidgett.

Mr Lidgett is a corpulent, excitable man with one eye. The boys describe him as stumbling into the room mouthing some of those tempered expletives irritable schoolmasters accustom themselves to use – lest worse befall. 'Wretched mumchancer!'[133] he said. 'Where's Mr Plattner?' The boys are agreed on the very words. ('Wobbler', 'snivelling puppy' and 'mumchancer' are, it seems, among the ordinary small change of Mr Lidgett's scholastic commerce.)

Where's Mr Plattner? That was a question that was to be repeated many times in the next few days. It really seemed as though that frantic hyperbole 'blown to atoms' had for once realised itself. There was not a visible particle of Plattner to be seen; not a drop of blood nor a stitch of clothing to be found. Apparently he had been blown clean out of existence and left not a wrack behind.[134] Not so much as would cover a sixpenny piece, to quote a proverbial[135] expression! The evidence of his absolute disappearance, as a consequence of that explosion, is indubitable.

It is not necessary to enlarge here upon the commotion excited in the Sussexville Proprietary School, and in Sussexville and elsewhere, by this event. It is quite possible, indeed, that some of the readers of these pages may recall hearing of some remote and dying version of that excitement during the last summer holidays. Lidgett, it would seem, did everything in his power to suppress and minimise the story. He instituted a penalty of twenty-five lines for any mention of Plattner's name among the boys, and stated in the schoolroom that he was clearly aware of his assistant's whereabouts. He was afraid, he explains, that the possibility of an explosion happening, in spite of the elaborate precautions taken to minimise the practical teaching of chemistry, might injure the reputation of the school; and so might any mysterious quality in Plattner's departure. Indeed, he did everything in his power to make the occurrence seem as ordinary as possible. In particular, he cross-examined the five eyewitnesses of the occurrence so searchingly that they began to doubt the plain evidence of their senses. But in spite of these efforts, the tale, in a magnified and distorted state, made a nine days' wonder in the district, and several parents withdrew their sons on colourable[136] pretexts. Not the least remarkable point in the matter is the fact that a large number of people in the neighbourhood dreamed singularly vivid dreams of Plattner during the period of excitement before his return, and that these dreams had a curious uniformity. In almost all of them Plattner was seen, sometimes singly, sometimes in company, wandering about through a coruscating iridescence.[137] In all cases his face was pale and distressed, and in some he gesticulated towards the dreamer. One or two of the boys, evidently under the influence of nightmare, fancied that Plattner approached them with remarkable swiftness, and seemed to look closely into their very eyes. Others fled with Plattner from the pursuit of vague and extraordinary creatures of a globular shape. But all these fancies were forgotten in enquiries and speculations when, on the Wednesday next but one after the Monday of the explosion, Plattner returned.

The circumstances of his return were as singular as those of his departure. So far as Mr Lidgett's somewhat choleric outline can be filled in from Plattner's hesitating statements, it would appear that on Wednesday evening, towards the hour of sunset, the former gentleman, having dismissed evening preparation, was engaged in his garden, picking and eating strawberries, a fruit of which he is inordinately fond. It is a large old-fashioned garden, secured from observation, fortunately, by a high and ivy-covered red-brick wall. Just as he was stooping over a particularly prolific plant, there was a flash in the air and a heavy thud, and before he could look round, some heavy body struck him violently from behind. He was pitched forward, crushing the strawberries he held in his hand, and with such force that his silk hat – Mr Lidgett adheres to the older ideas of scholastic costume – was driven violently down upon his forehead, and almost over one eye. This heavy missile, which slid over him sideways and collapsed into a sitting posture among the strawberry plants, proved to be our long-lost Mr Gottfried Plattner, in an extremely dishevelled condition. He was collarless and hatless, his linen was dirty, and there was blood upon his hands. Mr Lidgett was so indignant and surprised that he remained on all-fours, with his hat jammed down on his eye, while he expostulated vehemently with Plattner for his disrespectful and unaccountable conduct.

This scarcely idyllic scene completes what I may call the exterior version of the Plattner story – its exoteric aspect.[138] It is quite unnecessary to enter here into all the details of his dismissal by Mr Lidgett. Such details, with the full names and dates and references, will be found in the larger report of these occurrences that was laid before the Society for the Investigation of Abnormal Phenomena.[139] The singular transposition of Plattner's right and left sides was scarcely observed for the first day or so, and then first in connection with his disposition to write from right to left across the blackboard. He concealed rather than ostended[140] this curious confirmatory circumstance, as he considered it would unfavourably affect his prospects in a new situation. The displacement of his heart was discovered some months after, when he was having a tooth extracted under anaesthetic. He then, very unwillingly, allowed a cursory surgical examination to be made of himself, with a view to a brief account in the *Journal of Anatomy*.[141] That exhausts the statement of the material facts; and we may now go on to consider Plattner's account of the matter.

But first let us clearly differentiate between the preceding portion of this story and what is to follow. All I have told thus far is established by such evidence as even a criminal lawyer would approve. Every one of the witnesses is still alive; the reader, if he have the leisure, may hunt the lads out tomorrow, or even brave the terrors of the redoubtable Lidgett, and cross-examine and trap and test to his heart's content; Gottfried Plattner himself, and his twisted heart and his three photographs are producible. It may be taken as proved that he did disappear for nine days as the consequence of an explosion; that he returned almost as violently, under circumstances in their nature annoying to Mr Lidgett, whatever the details of those circumstances may be; and that he returned inverted, just as a reflection returns from a mirror. From the last fact, as I have already stated, it follows almost inevitably that Plattner, during those nine days, must have been in some state of existence altogether out of space. The evidence to these statements is, indeed, far stronger than that upon which most murderers are hanged. But for his own particular account of where he had been, with its confused explanations and well-nigh self-contradictory details, we have only Mr Gottfried Plattner's word. I do not wish to discredit that, but I must point out – what so many writers upon obscure psychic phenomena fail to do – that we are passing here from the practically undeniable to that kind of matter which any reasonable man is entitled to believe or reject as he thinks proper. The previous statements render it plausible; its discordance with common experience tilts it towards the incredible. I would prefer not to sway the beam of the reader's judgement either way, but simply to tell the story as Plattner told it me. He gave me his narrative, I may state, at my house in Chislehurst,[142] and so soon as he had left me that evening, I went into my study and wrote down everything as I remembered it. Subsequently he was good enough to read over a typewritten copy, so that its substantial correctness is undeniable.

He states that at the moment of the explosion he distinctly thought he was killed. He felt lifted off his feet and driven forcibly backwards. It is a curious fact for psychologists that he thought clearly during his backward flight, and wondered whether he should hit the chemistry cupboard or the blackboard easel. His heels struck ground, and he staggered and fell heavily into a sitting position on something soft and firm. For a moment the concussion stunned him. He became aware at once of a vivid scent of singed hair, and he seemed to hear the voice of Lidgett asking for him. You will understand that for a time his mind was greatly confused.

At first he was distinctly under the impression that he was still in the classroom. He perceived quite distinctly the surprise of the boys and the entry of Mr Lidgett. He is quite positive upon that score. He did not hear their remarks; but that he ascribed to the deafening effect of the experiment. Things about him seemed curiously dark and faint, but his mind explained that on the obvious but mistaken idea that the explosion had engendered a huge volume of dark smoke.

Through the dimness the figures of Lidgett and the boys moved, as faint and silent as ghosts. Plattner's face still tingled with the stinging heat of the flash. He was, he says, 'all muddled'. His first definite thoughts seem to have been of his personal safety. He thought he was perhaps blinded and deafened. He felt his limbs and face in a gingerly manner. Then his perceptions grew clearer, and he was astonished to miss the old familiar desks and other schoolroom furniture about him. Only dim, uncertain, grey shapes stood in the place of these. Then came a thing that made him shout aloud, and awoke his stunned faculties to instant activity. *Two of the boys, gesticulating, walked one after the other clean through him!* Neither manifested the slightest consciousness of his presence. It is difficult to imagine the sensation he felt. They came against him, he says, with no more force than a wisp of mist.

Plattner's first thought after that was that he was dead. Having been brought up with thoroughly sound views in these matters, however, he was a little surprised to find his body still about him. His second conclusion was that he was not dead, but that the others were: that the explosion had destroyed the Sussexville Proprietary School and every soul in it except himself. But that, too, was scarcely satisfactory. He was thrown back upon astonished observation.

Everything about him was extraordinarily dark: at first it seemed to have an altogether ebony blackness. Overhead was a black firmament. The only touch of light in the scene was a faint greenish glow at the edge of the sky in one direction, which threw into prominence a horizon of undulating black hills. This, I say, was his impression at first. As his eye grew accustomed to the darkness, he began to distinguish a faint quality of differentiating greenish colour in the circumambient night. Against this background the furniture and occupants of the classroom, it seems, stood out like phosphorescent spectres, faint and impalpable. He extended his hand, and thrust it without an effort through the wall of the room by the fireplace.

He describes himself as making a strenuous effort to attract attention. He shouted to Lidgett, and tried to seize the boys as they went to and fro. He only desisted from these attempts when Mrs Lidgett, whom he (as an assistant master) naturally disliked, entered the room. He says the sensation of being in the world, and yet not a part of it, was an extraordinarily disagreeable one. He compared his feelings, not inaptly, to those of a cat watching a mouse through a window. Whenever he made a motion to communicate with the dim, familiar world about him, he found an invisible, incomprehensible barrier preventing inter-course. He then turned his attention to his solid environment. He found the medicine bottle still unbroken in his hand, with the remainder of the green powder therein. He put this in his pocket, and began to feel about him. Apparently, he was sitting on a boulder of rock covered with a velvety moss. The dark country about him he was unable to see, the faint, misty picture of the schoolroom blotting it out, but he had a feeling (due perhaps to a cold wind) that he was near the crest of a hill, and that a steep valley fell away beneath his feet. The green glow along the edge of the sky seemed to be growing in extent and intensity. He stood up, rubbing his eyes.

It would seem that he made a few steps, going steeply downhill, and then stumbled, nearly fell, and sat down again upon a jagged mass of rock to watch the dawn. He became aware that the world about him was absolutely silent. It was as still as it was dark, and though there was a cold wind blowing up the hill-face, the rustle of grass and the soughing of the boughs that should have accompanied it were absent.

He could hear, therefore, if he could not see, that the hillside upon which he stood was rocky and desolate. The green grew brighter every moment, and as it did so, a faint, transparent, blood-red mingled with, but did not mitigate, the blackness of the sky overhead and the rocky desolations about him. Having regard to what follows, I am inclined to think that that redness may have been an optical effect due to contrast. Something black fluttered momentarily against the livid yellow-green of the lower sky, and then the thin and penetrating voice of a bell rose out of the black gulf below him. An oppressive expectation grew with the growing light.

It is probable that an hour or more elapsed while he sat there, the strange green light growing brighter every moment, and spreading slowly, in flamboyant fingers, upward towards the zenith. As it grew, the spectral vision of *our* world became relatively or absolutely fainter. Probably both, for the time must have been about that of our earthly sunset. So far as his vision of our world went, Plattner, by his few steps downhill, had passed through the floor of the classroom, and was now, it seemed, sitting in midair in the larger schoolroom downstairs. He saw the boarders distinctly, but much more faintly than he had seen Lidgett. They were preparing their evening tasks, and he noticed with interest that several were cheating with their Euclid riders[143] by means of a crib, a compilation whose existence he had hitherto never suspected. As the time passed, they faded steadily, as steadily as the light of the green dawn increased.

Looking down into the valley, he saw that the light had crept far down its rocky sides, and that the profound blackness of the abyss was now broken by a minute green glow, like the light of a glow-worm. And almost immediately the limb of a huge heavenly body of blazing green rose over the basaltic undulations of the distant hills, and the monstrous hill-masses about him came out gaunt and desolate, in green light and deep, ruddy black shadows. He became aware of a vast number of ball-shaped objects drifting as thistledown drifts over the high ground. There were none of these nearer to him than the opposite side of the gorge. The bell below twanged quicker and quicker, with something like impatient insistence, and several lights moved hither and thither. The boys at work at their desks were now almost imperceptibly faint.

This extinction of our world, when the green sun of this other universe rose, is a curious point upon which Plattner insists. During the Other-World night, it is difficult to move about, on account of the vividness with which the things of this world are visible. It becomes a riddle to explain why, if this is the case, we in this world catch no glimpse of the Other-World. It is due, perhaps, to the comparatively vivid illumination of this world of ours. Plattner describes the midday of the Other-World, at its brightest, as not being nearly so bright as this world at full moon, while its night is profoundly black. Consequently, the amount of light, even in an ordinary dark room, is sufficient to render the things of the Other-World invisible, on the same principle that faint phosphorescence is only visible in the profoundest darkness. I have tried, since he told me his story, to see something of the Other-World by sitting for a long space in a photographer's dark room at night. I have certainly seen indistinctly the form of greenish slopes and rocks, but only, I must admit, very indistinctly indeed. The reader may possibly be more successful. Plattner tells me that since his return he has dreamt and seen and recognised places in the Other-World, but this is probably due to his memory of these scenes. It seems quite possible that people with unusually keen eyesight may occasionally catch a glimpse of this strange Other-World about us.

However, this is a digression. As the green sun rose, a long street of black buildings became perceptible, though only darkly and indistinctly, in the gorge, and after some hesitation, Plattner began to clamber down the precipitous descent towards them. The descent was long and exceedingly tedious, being so not only by the extraordinary steepness, but also by reason of the looseness of the boulders with which the whole face of the hill was strewn. The noise of his descent – now and then his heels struck fire from the rocks – seemed now the only sound in the universe, for the beating of the bell had ceased. As he drew nearer, he perceived that the various edifices had a singular resemblance to tombs and mausoleums and monuments, saving only that they were all uniformly black instead of being white, as most sepulchres are. And then he saw, crowding out of the largest building, very much as people disperse from church, a number of pallid, rounded, pale-green figures. These dispersed in several directions about the broad street of the place, some going through side alleys and reappearing upon the steepness of the hill, others entering some of the small black buildings which lined the way.

At the sight of these things drifting up towards him, Plattner stopped, staring. They were not walking – they were, indeed, limbless – and they had the appearance of human heads beneath which a tadpole-like body[144] swung. He was too astonished at their strangeness, too full indeed of strangeness, to be seriously alarmed by them. They drove towards him, in front of the chill wind that was blowing uphill, much as soap-bubbles drive before a draught. And, as he looked at the nearest of those approaching, he saw it was indeed a human head, albeit with singularly large eyes, and wearing such an expression of distress and anguish as he had never seen before upon mortal countenance. He was surprised to find that it did not turn to regard him, but seemed to be watching and following some unseen moving thing. For a moment he was puzzled, and then it occurred to him that this creature was watching with its enormous eyes something that was happening in the world he had just left. Nearer it came, and nearer, and he was too astonished to cry out. It made a very faint fretting sound as it came close to him. Then it struck his face with a gentle pat – its touch was very cold – and drove past him, and upward towards the crest of the hill.

An extraordinary conviction flashed across Plattner's mind that this head had a strong likeness to Lidgett. Then he turned his attention to the other heads that were now swarming thickly up the hillside. None made the slightest sign of recognition. One or two, indeed, came close to his head and almost followed the example of the first, but he dodged convulsively out of the way. Upon most of them he saw the same expression of unavailing regret he had seen upon the first, and heard the same faint sounds of wretchedness from them. One or two wept, and one rolling swiftly uphill wore an expression of diabolical rage. But others were cold, and several had a look of gratified interest in their eyes. One, at least, was almost in an ecstasy of happiness. Plattner does not remember that he recognised any more likenesses in those he saw at this time.

For several hours, perhaps, Plattner watched these strange things dispersing themselves over the hills, and not till long after they had ceased to issue from the clustering black buildings in the gorge did he resume his downward climb. The darkness about him increased so much that he had difficulty in stepping true. Overhead the sky was now a bright, pale green. He felt neither hunger nor thirst. Later, when he did, he found a chilly stream running down the centre of the gorge, and the rare moss upon the boulders, when he tried it at last in desperation, was good to eat.

He groped about among the tombs that ran down the gorge, seeking vaguely for some clue to these inexplicable things. After a long time he came to the entrance of the big mausoleum-like building from which the heads had issued. In this he found a group of green lights burning upon a kind of basaltic altar, and a bell-rope from a belfry overhead hanging down into the centre of the place. Round the wall ran a lettering of fire in a character unknown to him. While he was still wondering at the purport of these things, he heard the receding tramp of heavy feet echoing far down the street. He ran out into the darkness again, but he could see nothing. He had a mind to pull the bell-rope, and finally decided to follow the footsteps. But, although he ran far, he never overtook them; and his shouting was of no avail. The gorge seemed to extend an interminable distance. It was as dark as earthly starlight throughout its length, while the ghastly green day lay along the upper edge of its precipices. There were none of the heads, now, below. They were all, it seemed, busily occupied along the upper slopes. Looking up, he saw them drifting hither and thither, some hovering stationary, some flying swiftly through the air. It reminded him, he said, of 'big snowflakes'; only these were black and pale green.

In pursuing the firm, undeviating footsteps that he never overtook, in groping into new regions of this endless devil's dyke,[145] in clambering up and down the pitiless heights, in wandering about the summits, and in watching the drifting faces, Plattner states that he spent the better part of seven or eight days. He did not keep count, he says. Though once or twice he found eyes watching him, he had word with no living soul. He slept among the rocks on the hillside. In the gorge things earthly were invisible, because from the earthly standpoint, it was far underground. On the altitudes, so soon as the earthly day began, the world became visible to him. He found himself sometimes stumbling over the dark green rocks, or arresting himself on a precipitous brink, while all about him the green branches of the Sussexville lanes were swaying; or again, he seemed to be walking through the Sussexville streets, or watching unseen the private business of some household. And then it was he discovered that to almost every human being in our world there pertained some of these drifting heads: that everyone in the world is watched intermittently by these helpless disembodiments.

What are they – these Watchers of the Living? Plattner never learned. But two, that presently found and followed him, were like his childhood's memory of his father and mother. Now and then other faces turned their eyes upon him: eyes like those of dead people who had swayed him, or injured him, or helped him in his youth and manhood. Whenever they looked at him, Plattner was overcome with a strange sense of responsibility. To his mother he ventured to speak; but she made no answer. She looked sadly, steadfastly and tenderly – a little reproachfully, too, it seemed – into his eyes.

He simply tells this story; he does not endeavour to explain. We are left to surmise who these Watchers of the Living may be, or, if they are indeed the Dead, why they should so closely and passionately watch a world they have left for ever. It may be – indeed to my mind it seems just – that, when our life has closed, when evil or good is no longer a choice for us, we may still have to witness the working out of the train of consequences we have laid. If human souls continue after death, then surely human interests continue after death. But that is merely my own guess at the meaning of the things seen. Plattner offers no interpretation, for none was given him. It is well the reader should understand this clearly. Day after day, with his head reeling, he wandered about this green-lit world outside the world, weary and, towards the end, weak and hungry. By day – by our earthly day, that is – the ghostly vision of the old familiar scenery of Sussexville, all about him, irked and worried him. He could not see where to put his feet, and ever and again with a chilly touch one of these Watching Souls would come against his face. And after dark the multitude of these Watchers about him, and their intent distress, confused his mind beyond describing. A great longing to return to the earthly life that was so near and yet so remote consumed him. The unearthliness of things about him produced a positively painful mental distress. He was worried beyond describing by his own particular followers. He would shout at them to desist from staring at him, scold at them, hurry away from them. They were always mute and intent. Run as he might over the uneven ground, they followed his destinies.

On the ninth day, towards evening, Plattner heard the invisible footsteps approaching, far away down the gorge. He was then wandering over the broad crest of the same hill upon which he had fallen on his entry into this strange Other-World of his. He turned to hurry down into the gorge, feeling his way hastily, and was arrested by the sight of the thing that was happening in a room in a back street near the school. Both of the people in the room he knew by sight. The windows were open, the blinds up, and the setting sun shone clearly into it, so that it came out quite brightly at first, a vivid oblong of room, lying like a magic-lantern picture upon the black landscape and the livid green dawn. In addition to the sunlight, a candle had just been lit in the room.

On the bed lay a lank man, his ghastly white face terrible upon the tumbled pillow. His clenched hands were raised above his head. A little table beside the bed carried a few medicine bottles, some toast and water, and an empty glass. Every now and then the lank man's lips fell apart to indicate a word he could not articulate. But the woman did not notice that he wanted anything, because she was busy turning out papers from an old-fashioned bureau in the opposite corner of the room. At first the picture was very vivid indeed, but as the green dawn behind it grew brighter and brighter, so it became fainter and more and more transparent.

As the echoing footsteps paced nearer and nearer, those footsteps that sound so loud in that Other-World and come so silently in this, Plattner perceived about him a great multitude of dim faces gathering together out of the darkness and watching the two people in the room. Never before had he seen so many of the Watchers of the Living. A multitude had eyes only for the sufferer in the room; another multitude, in infinite anguish, watched the woman as she hunted with greedy eyes for something she could not find. They crowded about Plattner, they came across his sight and buffeted his face, the noise of their unavailing regrets was all about him. He saw clearly only now and then. At other times the picture quivered dimly, through the veil of green reflections upon their movements. In the room it must have been very still, and Plattner says the candle flame streamed up into a perfectly vertical line of smoke, but in his ears each footfall and its echoes beat like a clap of thunder. And the faces! Two more particularly, near the woman's: one a woman's also, white and clear-featured, a face which might have once been cold and hard, but which was now softened by the touch of a wisdom strange to earth; the other might have been the woman's father. Both were evidently absorbed in the contemplation of some act of hateful meanness, so it seemed, which they could no longer guard against and prevent. Behind were others, teachers, it may be, who had taught ill, friends whose influence had failed. And over the man, too – a multitude, but none that seemed to be parents or teachers. Faces that might once have been coarse, now purged to strength by sorrow. And in the forefront one face, a girlish one, neither angry nor remorseful, but merely patient and weary, and, as it seemed to Plattner, waiting for relief. His powers of description fail him at the memory of this multitude of ghastly countenances. They gathered on the stroke of the bell. He saw them all in the space of a second. It would seem that he was so worked on by his excitement that, quite involuntarily, his restless fingers took the bottle of green powder out of his pocket and held it before him. But he does not remember that.

Abruptly the footsteps ceased. He waited for the next, and there was silence, and then suddenly, cutting through the unexpected stillness like a keen, thin blade, came the first stroke of the bell. At that the multitudinous faces swayed to and fro and a louder crying began all about him. The woman did not hear; she was burning something now in the candle flame. At the second stroke everything grew dim, and a breath of wind, icy cold, blew through the host of watchers. They swirled about him like an eddy of dead leaves in the spring, and at the third stroke something was extended through them to the bed. You have heard of a beam of light. This was like a beam of darkness, and looking again at it, Plattner saw that it was a shadowy arm and hand.

The green sun was now topping the black desolations of the horizon, and the vision of the room was very faint. Plattner could see that the white of the bed struggled, and was convulsed; and that the woman looked round over her shoulder at it, startled.

The cloud of watchers lifted high like a puff of green dust before the wind and swept swiftly downward towards the temple in the gorge. Then suddenly Plattner understood the meaning of the shadowy black arm that stretched across his shoulder and clutched its prey. He did not dare turn his head to see the Shadow behind the arm. With a violent effort, and covering his eyes, he set himself to run, made perhaps twenty strides, then slipped on a boulder and fell. He fell forward on his hands; and the bottle smashed and exploded as he touched the ground.

In another moment he found himself, stunned and bleeding, sitting face to face with Lidgett in the old walled garden behind the school.

There the story of Plattner's experiences ends. I have resisted, I believe successfully, the natural disposition of a writer of fiction to dress up incidents of this sort. I have told the thing as far as possible in the order in which Plattner told it to me. I have carefully avoided any attempt at style, effect or construction. It would have been easy, for instance, to have worked the scene of the deathbed into a kind of plot in which Plattner might have been involved. But, quite apart from the objectionableness of falsifying a most extraordinary true story, any such trite devices would spoil, to my mind, the peculiar effect of this dark world, with its livid green illumination and its drifting Watchers of the Living, which, unseen and unapproachable to us, is yet lying all about us.

It remains to add that a death did actually occur in Vincent Terrace, just beyond the school garden, and so far as can be proved, at the moment of Plattner's return. Deceased was a rate-collector and insurance agent. His widow, who was much younger than himself, married last month a Mr Whymper, a veterinary surgeon of Allbeeding.[146] As the portion of this story given here has in various forms circulated orally in Sussexville, she has consented to my use of her name, on condition that I make it distinctly known that she emphatically contradicts every detail of Plattner's account of her husband's last moments. She burnt no will, she says, although Plattner never accused her of doing so; her husband made but one will, and that just after their marriage. Certainly, from a man who had never seen it, Plattner's account of the furniture of the room was curiously accurate.

One other thing, even at the risk of an irksome repetition, I must insist upon, lest I seem to favour the credulous, superstitious view. Plattner's absence from the world for nine days is, I think, proved. But that does not prove his story. It is quite conceivable that even outside space hallucinations may be possible. That, at least, the reader must bear distinctly in mind.

The New Accelerator[147]

Certainly, if ever a man found a guinea when he was looking for a pin it is my good friend Professor Gibberne. I have heard before of investigators overshooting the mark, but never quite to the extent that he has done. He has really, this time at any rate, without any touch of exaggeration in the phrase, found something to revolutionise human life. And that when he was simply seeking an all-round nervous stimulant to bring languid people up to the stresses of these pushful days. I have tasted the stuff now several times, and I cannot do better than describe the effect the thing had on me. That there are astonishing experiences in store for all in search of new sensations will become apparent enough.

Professor Gibberne, as many people know, is my neighbour in Folkestone.[148] Unless my memory plays me a trick, his portrait at various ages has already appeared in *The Strand Magazine*[149] – I think late in 1899; but I am unable to look it up because I have lent that volume to someone who has never sent it back. The reader may, perhaps, recall the high forehead and the singularly long black eyebrows that give such a Mephistophelian[150] touch to his face. He occupies one of those pleasant little detached houses in the mixed style that make the western end of the Upper Sandgate Road[151] so interesting. His is the one with the Flemish gables and the Moorish portico, and it is in the little room with the mullioned bay window that he works when he is down here, and in which of an evening we have so often smoked and talked together. He is a mighty jester, but besides, he likes to talk to me about his work; he is one of those men who find a help and stimulus in talking, and so I have been able to follow the conception of the New Accelerator right up from a very early stage. Of course, the greater portion of his experimental work is not done in Folkestone, but in Gower Street, in the fine new laboratory next to the hospital[152] that he has been the first to use.

As everyone knows, or at least as all intelligent people know, the special department in which Gibberne has gained so great and deserved a reputation among physiologists is that of the action of drugs upon the nervous system. Upon soporifics, sedatives and anaesthetics he is, I am told, unequalled. He is also a chemist of considerable eminence, and I suppose in the subtle and complex jungle of riddles that centres about the ganglion cell and the axis fibre[153] there are little cleared places of his making, little glades of illumination, that, until he sees fit to publish his results, are still inaccessible to every other living man. And in the last few years he has been particularly assiduous upon this question of nervous stimulants, and already, before the discovery of the New Accelerator, very successful with them. Medical science has to thank him for at least three distinct and absolutely safe invigorators of unrivalled value to practising men. In cases of exhaustion, the preparation known as Gibberne's B Syrup[154] has, I suppose, saved more lives already than any lifeboat round the coast.

'But none of these little things begin to satisfy me yet,' he told me nearly a year ago. 'Either they increase the central energy without affecting the nerves or they simply increase the available energy by lowering the nervous conductivity; and all of them are unequal and local in their operation. One wakes up the heart and viscera and leaves the brain stupefied, one gets at the brain champagne fashion and does nothing good for the solar plexus,[155] and what I want – and what, if it's an earthly possibility, I mean to have – is a stimulant that stimulates all round, that wakes you up for a time from the crown of your head to the tip of your great toe, and makes you go two – or even three to everybody else's one. Eh? That's the thing I'm after.'

'It would tire a man,' I said.

'Not a doubt of it. And you'd eat double or treble – and all that. But just think what the thing would mean. Imagine yourself with a little phial like this' – he held up a little bottle of green glass and marked his points with it – 'and in this precious phial is the power to think twice as fast, move twice as quickly, do twice as much work in a given time as you could otherwise do.'

'But is such a thing possible?'

'I believe so. If it isn't, I've wasted my time for a year. These various preparations of the hypophosphites,[156] for example, seem to show that something of the sort . . . Even if it was only one and a half times as fast it would do.'

'It *would* do,' I said.

'If you were a statesman in a corner, for example, time rushing up against you, something urgent to be done, eh?'

'He could dose his private secretary,' I said.

'And gain – double time. And think if *you*, for example, wanted to finish a book.'

'Usually,' I said, 'I wish I'd never begun 'em.'

'Or a doctor, driven to death, wants to sit down and think out a case. Or a barrister – or a man cramming for an examination.'

'Worth a guinea a drop,'[157] said I, 'and more – to men like that.'

'And in a duel, again,' said Gibberne, 'where it all depends on your quickness in pulling the trigger.'

'Or in fencing,' I echoed.

'You see,' said Gibberne, 'if I get it as an all-round thing it will really do you no harm at all – except perhaps to an infinitesimal degree it brings you nearer old age. You will just have lived twice to other people's once – '

'I suppose,' I meditated, 'in a duel – it would be fair?'

'That's a question for the seconds,' said Gibberne.

I harked back further. 'And you really think such a thing *is* possible?' I said.

'As possible,' said Gibberne, and glanced at something that went throbbing by the window, 'as a motor-bus. As a matter of fact – '

He paused and smiled at me deeply, and tapped slowly on the edge of his desk with the green phial. 'I think I know the stuff . . . Already I've got something coming.' The nervous smile upon his face betrayed the gravity of his revelation. He rarely talked of his actual experimental work unless things were very near the end. 'And it may be, it may be – I shouldn't be surprised – it may even do the thing at a greater rate than twice.'

'It will be rather a big thing,' I hazarded.

'It will be, I think, rather a big thing.'

But I don't think he quite knew what a big thing it was to be, for all that.

I remember we had several talks about the stuff after that. 'The New Accelerator' he called it, and his tone about it grew more confident on each occasion. Sometimes he talked nervously of unexpected physiological results its use might have, and then he would get a little unhappy; at others he was frankly mercenary, and we debated long and anxiously how the preparation might be turned to commercial account. 'It's a good thing,' said Gibberne, 'a tremendous thing. I know I'm giving the world something, and I think it only reasonable we should expect the world to pay. The dignity of science is all very well, but I think somehow I must have the monopoly of the stuff for, say ten years. I don't see why all the fun in life should go to the dealers in ham.'

My own interest in the coming drug certainly did not wane in the time. I have always had a queer little twist towards metaphysics in my mind. I have always been given to paradoxes about space and time, and it seemed to me that Gibberne was really preparing no less than the absolute acceleration of life. Suppose a man repeatedly dosed with such a preparation: he would live an active and record life indeed, but he would be an adult at eleven, middle-aged at twenty-five, and by thirty well on the road to senile decay. It seemed to me that so far Gibberne was only going to do for anyone who took his drug exactly what nature has done for the Jews and Orientals,[158] who are men in their teens and aged by fifty, and quicker in thought and act than we are all the time. The marvel of drugs has always been great to my mind: you can madden a man, calm a man, make him incredibly strong and alert or a helpless log, quicken this passion and allay that, all by means of drugs; and here was a new miracle to be added to this strange armoury of phials the doctors use! But Gibberne was far too eager upon his technical points to enter very keenly into my aspect of the question.

It was the 7th or 8th of August when he told me the distillation that would decide his failure or success for a time was going forward as we talked, and it was on the 10th that he told me the thing was done and the New Accelerator a tangible reality in the world. I met him as I was going up the Sandgate Hill towards Folkestone – I think I was going to get my hair cut, and he came hurrying down to meet me – I suppose he was coming to my house to tell me at once of his success. I remember that his eyes were unusually bright and his face flushed, and I noted even then the swift alacrity of his step.

'It's done,' he cried, and gripped my hand, speaking very fast; 'it's more than done. Come up to my house and see.'

'Really?'

'Really!' he shouted. 'Incredibly! Come up and see.'

'And it does – twice?

'It does more, much more. It scares me. Come up and see the stuff. Taste it! Try it! It's the most amazing stuff on earth.' He gripped my arm and, walking at such a pace that he forced me into a trot, went shouting with me up the hill. A whole charabancful of people turned and stared at us in unison after the manner of people in charabancs. It was one of those hot, clear days that Folkestone sees so much of, every colour incredibly bright and every outline hard. There was a breeze, of course, but not so much breeze as sufficed under these conditions to keep me cool and dry. I panted for mercy.

'I'm not walking fast, am I?' cried Gibberne, and slackened his pace to a quick march.

'You've been taking some of this stuff,' I puffed.

'No,' he said. 'At the utmost a drop of water that stood in a beaker from which I had washed out the last traces of the stuff. I took some last night, you know. But that is ancient history, now.'

'And it goes twice?' I said, nearing his doorway in a grateful perspiration.

'It goes a thousand times, many thousand times!' cried Gibberne, with a dramatic gesture, flinging open his Early English carved-oak gate.

'Phew!' said I, and followed him to the door.

'I don't know how many times it goes,' he said, with his latch-key in his hand.

'And you – '

'It throws all sorts of light on nervous physiology, it kicks the theory of vision into a perfectly new shape . . . ! Heaven knows how many thousand times. We'll try all that after – The thing is to try the stuff now.'

'Try the stuff?' I said, as we went along the passage.

'Rather,' said Gibberne, turning on me in his study. 'There it is in that little green phial there! Unless you happen to be afraid?'

I am a careful man by nature, and only theoretically adventurous. I *was* afraid. But on the other hand, there is pride.

'Well,' I haggled. 'You say you've tried it?'

'I've tried it,' he said, 'and I don't look hurt by it, do I? I don't even look livery and I *feel* – '

I sat down. 'Give me the potion,' I said. 'If the worst comes to the worst it will save having my hair cut, and that I think is one of the most hateful duties of a civilised man. How do you take the mixture?'

'With water,' said Gibberne, whacking down a carafe.

He stood up in front of his desk and regarded me in my easy chair; his manner was suddenly affected by a touch of the Harley Street specialist.[159]

'It's rum stuff, you know,' he said.

I made a gesture with my hand.

'I must warn you in the first place as soon as you've got it down to shut your eyes, and open them very cautiously in a minute or so's time. One still sees. The sense of vision is a question of length of vibration, and not of multitude of impacts; but there's a kind of shock to the retina, a nasty giddy confusion just at the time, if the eyes are open. Keep 'em shut.'

'Shut,' I said. 'Good!'

'And the next thing is, keep still. Don't begin to whack about. You may fetch something a nasty rap if you do. Remember you will be going several thousand times faster than you ever did before, heart, lungs, muscles, brain – everything – and you will hit hard without knowing it. You won't know it, you know. You'll feel just as you do now. Only everything in the world will seem to be going ever so many thousand times slower than it ever went before. That's what makes it so deuced queer.'

'Lor',' I said. 'And you mean – '

'You'll see,' said he, and took up a little measure. He glanced at the material on his desk. 'Glasses,' he said, 'water. All here. Mustn't take too much for the first attempt.'

The little phial glucked out its precious contents.

'Don't forget what I told you,' he said, turning the contents of the measure into a glass in the manner of an Italian waiter measuring whisky. 'Sit with the eyes tightly shut and in absolute stillness for two minutes,' he said. 'Then you will hear me speak.'

He added an inch or so of water to the little dose in each glass.

'By the by,' he said, 'don't put your glass down. Keep it in your hand and rest your hand on your knee. Yes – so. And now – '

He raised his glass.

'The New Accelerator,' I said.

'The New Accelerator,' he answered, and we touched glasses and drank, and instantly I closed my eyes.

You know that blank non-existence into which one drops when one has taken 'gas'.[160] For an indefinite interval it was like that. Then I heard Gibberne telling me to wake up, and I stirred and opened my eyes. There he stood as he had been standing, glass still in hand. It was empty, that was all the difference.

'Well?' said I.

'Nothing out of the way?'

'Nothing. A slight feeling of exhilaration, perhaps. Nothing more.'

'Sounds?'

'Things are still,' I said. 'By Jove! Yes! They *are* still. Except the sort of faint pat, patter, like rain falling on different things. What is it?'

'Analysed sounds,' I think he said, but I am not sure. He glanced at the window. 'Have you ever seen a curtain before a window fixed in that way before?'

I followed his eyes, and there was the end of the curtain, frozen as it were, corner high, in the act of flapping briskly in the breeze.

'No,' said I; 'that's odd.'

'And here,' he said, and opened the hand that held the glass. Naturally I winced, expecting the glass to smash. But so far from smashing it did not even seem to stir; it hung in midair – motionless.

'Roughly speaking,' said Gibberne, 'an object in these latitudes falls sixteen feet in the first second. This glass is falling sixteen feet in a second now. Only you see, it hasn't been falling yet for the hundredth part of a second. That gives you some idea of the pace of my Accelerator.' And he waved his hand round and round, over and under the slowly sinking glass. Finally, he took it by the bottom, pulled it down, and placed it very carefully on the table. 'Eh?' he said to me, and laughed.

'That seems all right,' I said, and began very gingerly to raise myself from my chair. I felt perfectly well, very light and comfortable, and quite confident in my mind. I was going fast all over. My heart, for example, was beating a thousand times a second, but that caused me no discomfort at all. I looked out of the window. An immovable cyclist, head down and with a frozen puff of dust behind his driving-wheel, scorched to overtake a galloping charabanc[161] that did not stir. I gaped in amazement at this incredible spectacle. 'Gibberne,' I cried, 'how long will this confounded stuff last?'

'Heaven knows!' he answered. 'Last time I took it I went to bed and slept it off. I tell you, I was frightened. It must have lasted some minutes, I think – it seemed like hours. But after a bit it slows down rather suddenly, I believe.'

I was proud to observe that I did not feel frightened – I suppose because there were two of us. 'Why shouldn't we go out?' I asked.

'Why not?'

'They'll see us.'

'Not they. Goodness, no! Why, we shall be going a thousand times faster than the quickest conjuring trick that was ever done. Come along! Which way shall we go? Window, or door?'

And out by the window we went.

Assuredly of all the strange experiences that I have ever had, or imagined, or read of other people having or imagining, that little raid I made with Gibberne on the Folkestone Leas,[162] under the influence of the New Accelerator, was the strangest and maddest of all. We went out by his gate into the road, and there we made a minute examination of the statuesque passing traffic. The tops of the wheels and some of the legs of the horses of this charabanc, the end of the whiplash and the lower jaw of the conductor – who was just beginning to yawn – were perceptibly in motion, but all the rest of the lumbering conveyance seemed still. And quite noiseless except for a faint rattling that came from one man's throat! And as parts of this frozen edifice there were a driver, you know, and a conductor, and eleven people! The effect as we walked about the thing began by being madly queer, and ended by being – disagreeable. There they were, people like ourselves and yet not like ourselves, frozen in careless attitudes, caught in mid-gesture. A girl and a man smiled at one another, a leering smile that threatened to last for evermore; a woman in a floppy capelline[163] rested her arm on the rail and stared at Gibberne's house with the unwinking stare of eternity; a man stroked his moustache like a figure of wax, and another stretched a tiresome stiff hand with extended fingers towards his loosened hat. We stared at them, we laughed at them, we made faces at them, and then a sort of disgust of them came upon us, and we turned away and walked round in front of the cyclist towards the Leas.

'Goodness!' cried Gibberne, suddenly; 'Look there!'

He pointed, and there at the tip of his finger and sliding down the air with wings flapping slowly and at the speed of an exceptionally languid snail – was a bee.

And so we came out upon the Leas. There the thing seemed madder than ever. The band was playing in the upper stand, though all the sound it made for us was a low-pitched, wheezy rattle, a sort of prolonged last sigh that passed at times into a sound like the slow, muffled ticking of some monstrous clock. Frozen people stood erect, strange, silent, self-conscious-looking dummies hung unstably in mid-stride, promenading upon the grass. I passed close to a little poodle dog suspended in the act of leaping, and watched the slow movement of his legs as he sank to earth. 'Lord, look here!' cried Gibberne, and we halted for a moment before a magnificent person in white faint-striped flannels, white shoes and a Panama hat,[164] who turned back to wink at two gaily dressed ladies he had passed. A wink, studied with such leisurely deliberation as we could afford, is an unattractive thing. It loses any quality of alert gaiety, and one remarks that the winking eye does not completely close, that under its drooping lid appears the lower edge of an eyeball and a little line of white. 'Heaven give me memory,' said I, 'and I will never wink again.'

'Or smile,' said Gibberne, with his eye on the lady's answering teeth.

'It's infernally hot somehow,' said I. 'Let's go slower.'

'Oh, come along!' said Gibberne.

We picked our way among the Bath-chairs[165] in the path. Many of the people sitting in the chairs seemed almost natural in their passive poses, but the contorted scarlet of the bandsmen was not a restful thing to see. A purple-faced little gentleman was frozen in the midst of a violent struggle to refold his newspaper against the wind; there were many evidences that all these people in their sluggish way were exposed to a considerable breeze, a breeze that had no existence so far as our sensations went. We came out and walked a little way from the crowd, and turned and regarded it. To see all that multitude changed to a picture, smitten rigid, as it were, into the semblance of realistic wax, was impossibly wonderful. It was absurd, of course; but it filled me with an irrational, an exultant sense of superior advantage. Consider the wonder of it! All that I had said, and thought, and done since the stuff had begun to work in my veins had happened, so far as those people, so far as the world in general went, in the twinkling of an eye.

'The New Accelerator – ' I began, but Gibberne interrupted me.

'There's that infernal old woman!' he said.

'What old woman?'

'Lives next door to me,' said Gibberne. 'Has a lapdog that yaps. Gods! The temptation is strong!'

There is something very boyish and impulsive about Gibberne at times. Before I could expostulate with him he had dashed forward, snatched the unfortunate animal out of visible existence, and was running violently with it towards the cliff of the Leas. It was most extraordinary. The little brute, you know, didn't bark or wriggle or make the slightest sign of vitality. It kept quite stiffly in an attitude of somnolent repose, and Gibberne held it by the neck. It was like running about with a dog of wood. 'Gibberne,' I cried, 'put it down!' Then I said something else. 'If you run like that, Gibberne,' I cried, 'you'll set your clothes on fire. Your linen trousers are going brown as it is!'

He clapped his hand on his thigh and stood hesitating on the verge. 'Gibberne,' I cried, coming up, 'put it down. This heat is too much! It's our running so! Two or three miles a second! Friction of the air!'

'What?' he said, glancing at the dog.

'Friction of the air,' I shouted. 'Friction of the air. Going too fast. Like meteorites and things. Too hot. And, Gibberne! Gibberne! I'm all over pricking and a sort of perspiration. You can see people stirring slightly. I believe the stuff's working off! Put that dog down.'

'Eh?' he said.

'It's working off,' I repeated. 'We're too hot and the stuff's working off! I'm wet through.'

He stared at me. Then at the band, the wheezy rattle of whose performance was certainly going faster. Then with a tremendous sweep of the arm he hurled the dog away from him and it went spinning upwards, still inanimate, and hung at last over the grouped parasols of a knot of chattering people. Gibberne was gripping my elbow. 'By Jove!' he cried. 'I believe it is! A sort of hot pricking and – yes. That man's moving his pocket-handkerchief! Perceptibly. We must get out of this, sharp.'

But we could not get out of it sharply enough. Luckily, perhaps! For we might have run, and if we had run we should, I believe, have burst into flames. Almost certainly we should have burst into flames! You know we had neither of us thought of that . . . But before we could even begin to run the action of the drug had ceased. It was the business of a minute fraction of a second. The effect of the New Accelerator passed like the drawing of a curtain, vanished in the movement of a hand. I heard Gibberne's voice in infinite alarm. 'Sit down,' he said, and flop, down upon the turf at the edge of the Leas I sat – scorching as I sat. There is a patch of burnt grass there still where I sat down. The whole stagnation seemed to wake up as I did so: the disarticulated vibration of the band rushed together into a blast of music, the promenaders put their feet down and walked their ways, the papers and flags began flapping, smiles passed into words, the winker finished his wink and went on his way complacently, and all the seated people moved and spoke.

The whole world had come alive again, was going as fast as we were, or rather we were going no faster than the rest of the world. It was like slowing down as one comes into a railway station. Everything seemed to spin round for a second or two, I had the most transient feeling of nausea, and that was all. And the little dog which had seemed to hang for a moment when the force of Gibberne's arm was expended fell with a swift acceleration clean through a lady's parasol!

That was the saving of us. Unless it was for one corpulent old gentleman in a Bath-chair, who certainly did start at the sight of us and afterwards regarded us at intervals with a darkly suspicious eye, and finally, I believe, said something to his nurse about us, I doubt if a solitary person remarked our sudden appearance among them. Plop! We must have appeared abruptly. We ceased to smoulder almost at once, though the turf beneath me was uncomfortably hot. The attention of everyone – including even the Amusements' Association Band, which on this occasion, for the only time in its history, got out of tune – was arrested by the amazing fact, and the still more amazing yapping and uproar caused by the fact, that a respectable, over-fed lapdog sleeping quietly to the east of the bandstand should suddenly fall through the parasol of a lady to the west – in a slightly singed condition due to the extreme velocity of its movements through the air. In these absurd days,[166] too, when we are all trying to be as psychic and silly and superstitious as possible! People got up and trod on other people, chairs were overturned, the Leas policeman ran. How the matter settled itself

I do not know – we were much too anxious to disentangle ourselves from the affair and get out of range of the eye of the old gentleman in the Bath-chair to make minute enquiries. As soon as we were sufficiently cool and sufficiently recovered from our giddiness and nausea and confusion of mind to do so, we stood up and, skirting the crowd, directed our steps back along the road below the Metropole[167] towards Gibberne's house. But amidst the din I heard very distinctly the gentleman who had been sitting beside the lady of the ruptured sunshade using quite unjustifiable threats and language to one of those chair-attendants who have 'Inspector' written on their caps. 'If you didn't throw the dog,' he said, 'who *did*?'

The sudden return of movement and familiar noises, and our natural anxiety about ourselves (our clothes were still dreadfully hot, and the fronts of the thighs of Gibberne's white trousers were scorched a drabbish brown), prevented the minute observations I should have liked to make on all these things. Indeed, I really made no observations of any scientific value on that return. The bee, of course, had gone. I looked for that cyclist, but he was already out of sight as we came into the Upper Sandgate Road or hidden from us by traffic; the charabanc, however, with its people now all alive and stirring, was clattering along at a spanking pace almost abreast of the nearer church.

We noted, however, that the window-sill on which we had stepped in getting out of the house was slightly singed, and that the impressions of our feet on the gravel of the path were unusually deep.

So it was I had my first experience of the New Accelerator. Practically we had been running about and saying and doing all sorts of things in the space of a second or so of time. We had lived half an hour while the band had played perhaps two bars. But the effect it had upon us was that the whole world had stopped for our convenient inspection. Considering all things, and particularly considering our rashness in venturing out of the house, the experience might certainly have been much more disagreeable than it was. It showed, no doubt, that Gibberne has still much to learn before his preparation is a manageable convenience, but its practicability it certainly demonstrated beyond all cavil.

Since that adventure he has been steadily bringing its use under control, and I have several times, and without the slightest bad result, taken measured doses under his direction; though I must confess I have not yet ventured abroad again while under its influence. I may mention, for example, that this story has been written at one sitting and without interruption, except for the nibbling of some chocolate, by its means. I began at 6.25, and my watch is now very nearly at the minute past the half-hour. The convenience of securing a long, uninterrupted spell of work in the midst of a day full of engagements cannot be exaggerated. Gibberne is now working at the quantitative handling of his preparation, with especial reference to its distinctive effects upon different types of constitution. He then hopes to find a Retarder with which to dilute its present rather excessive potency. The Retarder will, of course, have the reverse effect to the Accelerator; used alone it should enable the patient to spread a few seconds over many hours of ordinary time, and so to maintain an apathetic inaction, a glacierlike absence of alacrity, amidst the most animated or irritating surroundings. The two things together must necessarily work an entire revolution in civilised existence. It is the beginning of our escape from that Time Garment of which Carlyle speaks.[168] While this Accelerator will enable us to concentrate ourselves with tremendous impact upon any moment or occasion that demands our utmost sense and vigour, the Retarder will enable us to pass in passive tranquillity through infinite hardship and tedium. Perhaps I am a little optimistic about the Retarder, which has indeed still to be discovered, but about the Accelerator there is no possible sort of doubt whatever. Its appearance upon the market in a convenient, controllable and assimilable form is a matter of the next few months. It will be obtainable at all chemists and druggists, in small green bottles, at a high but, considering its extraordinary qualities, by no means excessive price. Gibberne's Nervous Accelerator it will be called, and he hopes to be able to supply it in three strengths: one in 200, one in 900, and one in 2000, distinguished by yellow, pink and white labels respectively.

No doubt its use renders a great number of very extraordinary things possible; for, of course, the most remarkable and, possibly, even criminal proceedings may be effected with impunity by thus dodging, as it were, into the interstices of time. Like all potent preparations it will be liable to abuse. We have, however, discussed this aspect of the question very thoroughly, and we have decided that this is purely a matter of medical jurisprudence and altogether outside our province. We shall manufacture and sell the Accelerator, and as for the consequences – we shall see.

A Slip under the Microscope[169]

Outside the laboratory windows was a watery-grey fog, and within a close warmth and the yellow light of the green-shaded gas lamps that stood two to each table down its narrow length. On each table stood a couple of glass jars containing the mangled vestiges of the crayfish, mussels, frogs and guinea-pigs upon which the students had been working, and down the side of the room, facing the windows, were shelves bearing bleached dissections in spirits, surmounted by a row of beautifully executed anatomical drawings in whitewood frames and overhanging a row of cubical lockers. All the doors of the laboratory were panelled with blackboard, and on these were the half-erased diagrams of the previous day's work. The laboratory was empty, save for the demonstrator, who sat near the preparation-room door, and silent, save for a low, continuous murmur and the clicking of the rocker microtome[170] at which he was working. But scattered about the room were traces of numerous students: handbags, polished boxes of instruments, in one place a large drawing covered by newspaper, and in another a prettily bound copy of *News from Nowhere*,[171] a book oddly at variance with its surroundings. These things had been put down hastily as the students had arrived and hurried at once to secure their seats in the adjacent lecture theatre. Deadened by the closed door, the measured accents of the professor sounded as a featureless muttering.

Presently, faint through the closed windows came the sound of the Oratory clock[172] striking the hour of eleven. The clicking of the microtome ceased, and the demonstrator looked at his watch, rose, thrust his hands into his pockets, and walked slowly down the laboratory towards the lecture-theatre door. He stood listening for a moment, and then his eye fell on the little volume by William Morris. He picked it up, glanced at the title, smiled, opened it, looked at the name on the flyleaf, ran the leaves through with his hand, and put it down. Almost immediately the even murmur of the lecturer ceased, there was a sudden burst of pencils rattling on the desks in the lecture theatre, a stirring, a scraping of feet and a number of voices speaking together. Then a firm footfall approached the door, which began to open, and stood ajar, as some indistinctly heard question arrested the newcomer.

The demonstrator turned, walked slowly back past the microtome, and left the laboratory by the preparation-room door. As he did so, first one and then several students carrying notebooks entered the laboratory from the lecture theatre and distributed themselves among the little tables, or stood in a group about the doorway. They were an exceptionally heterogeneous assembly, for while Oxford and Cambridge still recoil from the blushing prospect of mixed classes, the College of Science anticipated America[173] in the matter years ago – mixed socially, too, for the prestige of the college is high, and its scholarships,[174] free of any age limit, dredge deeper even than do those of the Scotch universities. The class numbered one-and-twenty, but some remained in the theatre questioning the professor, copying the blackboard diagrams before they were washed off, or examining the special specimens he had produced to illustrate the day's teaching. Of the nine who had come into the laboratory three were girls, one of whom, a little fair woman, wearing spectacles and dressed in greyish-green, was peering out of the window at the fog, while the other two, both wholesome-looking, plain-faced schoolgirls, unrolled and put on the brown holland[175] aprons they wore while dissecting. Of the men, two went down the laboratory to their places: one a pallid, dark-bearded man, who had once been a tailor; the other a pleasant-featured, ruddy young man of twenty, dressed in a well-fitting brown suit – young Wedderburn, the son of Wedderburn, the eye specialist. The others formed a little knot near the theatre door. One of these, a dwarfed, spectacled figure, with a hunchback, sat on a bentwood stool; two others, one a short, dark youngster and the other a flaxen-haired, reddish-complexioned young man, stood leaning side by side against the slate sink, while the fourth stood facing them, and maintained the larger share of the conversation.

This last person was named Hill. He was a sturdily built young fellow, of the same age as Wedderburn; he had a white face, dark grey eyes, hair of an indeterminate colour, and prominent, irregular features. He talked rather louder than was needful, and thrust his hands deeply into his pockets. His collar was frayed and blue with the starch of a careless laundress, his clothes were evidently ready-made, and there was a patch on the side of his boot near the toe. And as he talked or listened to the others, he glanced now and again towards the lecture-theatre door. They were discussing the depressing peroration of the lecture they had just heard, the last lecture it was in the introductory course in zoology. 'From ovum to ovum is the goal of the higher vertebrata,' the lecturer had said[176] in his melancholy tones, and so had neatly rounded off the sketch of comparative anatomy he had been developing. The spectacled hunchback had repeated it, with noisy appreciation, had tossed it towards the fair-haired student with an evident provocation, and had started one of these vague, rambling discussions on generalities, so unaccountably dear to the student mind all the world over.

'That is our goal, perhaps – I admit it, as far as science goes,' said the fair-haired student, rising to the challenge. 'But there are things above science.'

'Science,' said Hill confidently, 'is systematic knowledge. Ideas that don't come into the system – must anyhow – be loose ideas.' He was not quite sure whether that was a clever saying or a fatuity until his hearers took it seriously.

'The thing I cannot understand,' said the hunchback, at large, 'is whether Hill is a materialist or not.'·

'There is one thing above matter,' said Hill promptly, feeling he made a better point this time; aware, too, of someone in the doorway behind him and raising his voice a trifle for her benefit, 'and that is, the delusion that there is something above matter.'

'So we have your gospel at last,' said the fair student. 'It's all a delusion, is it? All our aspirations to lead something more than dogs' lives, all our work for anything beyond ourselves. But see how inconsistent you are. Your socialism, for instance. Why do you trouble about the interests of the race? Why do you concern yourself about the beggar in the gutter? Why are you bothering yourself to lend that book – ' he indicated William Morris by a movement of the head – 'to everyone in the lab?'

'Girl,' said the hunchback indistinctly, and glanced guiltily over his shoulder.

The girl in brown, with the brown eyes, had come into the laboratory, and stood on the other side of the table behind him, with her rolled-up apron in one hand, looking over her shoulder, listening to the discussion. She did not notice the hunchback, because she was glancing from Hill to his interlocutor. Hill's consciousness of her presence betrayed itself to her only in his studious ignorance of the fact; but she understood that, and it pleased her. 'I see no reason,' said he, 'why a man should live like a brute because he knows of nothing beyond matter, and does not expect to exist a hundred years hence.'

'Why shouldn't he?' said the fair-haired student.

'Why *should* he?' said Hill.

'What inducement has he?'

'That's the way with all you religious people. It's all a business of inducements. Cannot a man seek after righteousness for righteousness's sake?'

There was a pause. The fair man answered, with a kind of vocal padding, 'But – you see – inducement – when I said inducement . . . ' to gain time. And then the hunchback came to his rescue and inserted a question. He was a terrible person in the debating society with his questions, and they invariably took one form – a demand for a definition, 'What's your definition of righteousness?' said the hunchback at this stage.

Hill experienced a sudden loss of complacency at this question, but even as it was asked, relief came in the person of Brooks, the laboratory attendant, who entered by the preparation-room door, carrying a number of freshly killed guinea-pigs by their hind legs.

'This is the last batch of material this session,' said the youngster who had not previously spoken.

Brooks advanced up the laboratory, smacking down a couple of guinea-pigs at each table. The rest of the class, scenting the prey from afar, came crowding in by the lecture-theatre door, and the discussion perished abruptly as the students who were not already in their places hurried to them to secure the choice of a specimen. There was a noise of keys rattling on split rings as lockers were opened and dissecting instruments taken out. Hill was already standing by his table, and his box of scalpels was sticking out of his pocket. The girl in brown came a step towards him, and leaning over his table, said softly, 'Did you see that I returned your book, Mr Hill?'

During the whole scene she and the book had been vividly present in his consciousness; but he made a clumsy pretence of looking at the book and seeing it for the first time. 'Oh, yes,' he said, taking it up. 'I see. Did you like it?'

'I want to ask you some questions about it – sometime.'

'Certainly,' said Hill. 'I shall be glad.' He stopped awkwardly. 'You liked it?' he said.

'It's a wonderful book. Only some things I don't understand.'

Then suddenly the laboratory was hushed by a curious braying noise. It was the demonstrator. He was at the blackboard ready to begin the day's instruction, and it was his custom to demand silence by a sound midway between the 'Er' of common intercourse and the blast of a trumpet. The girl in brown slipped back to her place: it was immediately in front of Hill's, and Hill, forgetting her forthwith, took a notebook out of the drawer of his table, turned over its leaves hastily, drew a stumpy pencil from his pocket, and prepared to make a copious note of the coming demonstration. For demonstrations and lectures are the sacred text of the college students. Books, saving only the professor's own, you may – it is even expedient to – ignore.

Hill was the son of a Landport[177] cobbler, and had been hooked by a chance blue paper[178] the authorities had thrown out to the Landport Technical College. He kept himself in London on his allowance of a guinea a week,[179] and found that, with proper care, this also covered his clothing allowance, an occasional waterproof collar, that is; and ink and needles and cotton, and suchlike necessaries for a man about town. This was his first year and his first session, but the brown old man in Landport had already got himself detested in many public-houses by boasting of his son, 'the Professor'. Hill was a vigorous youngster, with a serene contempt for the clergy of all denominations, and a fine ambition to reconstruct the world. He regarded his scholarship as a brilliant opportunity. He had begun to read at seven, and had read steadily whatever came in his way, good or bad, since then. His worldly experience had been limited to the island of Portsea,[180] and acquired chiefly in the wholesale boot factory in which he had worked by day, after passing the seventh standard[181] of the Board school. He had a considerable gift for speech, as the College Debating Society, which met amidst the crushing machines and mine models in the metallurgical theatre downstairs, already recognised – recognised by a violent battering of desks whenever he rose. And he was just at that fine emotional age when life opens at the end of a narrow pass like a broad valley at one's feet, full of the promise of wonderful discoveries and tremendous achievements. And his own limitations, save that he knew that he knew neither Latin nor French, were all unknown to him.

At first his interest had been divided pretty equally between his biological work at the college and social and theological theorising, an employment which he took in deadly earnest. Of a night, when the big museum library was not open, he would sit on the bed of his room in Chelsea with his coat and a muffler on, and write out the lecture notes and revise his dissection memoranda until Thorpe called him out by a whistle – the landlady objected to open the door to attic visitors – and then the two would go prowling about the shadowy, shiny, gas-lit streets, talking, very much in the fashion of the sample just given, of the God Idea, and Righteousness, and Carlyle,[182] and the Reorganisation of Society. And in the midst of it all Hill, arguing not only for Thorpe, but for the casual passer-by, would lose the thread of his argument glancing at some pretty painted face that looked meaningly at him as he passed.

Science and Righteousness! But once or twice lately there had been signs that a third interest was creeping into his life, and he had found his attention wandering from the fate of the mesoblastic somites[183] or the probable meaning of the blastopore,[184] to the thought of the girl with the brown eyes who sat at the table before him.

She was a paying student; she descended inconceivable social altitudes to speak to him. At the thought of the education she must have had, and the accomplishments she must possess, the soul of Hill became abject within him. She had spoken to him first over a difficulty about the alisphenoid[185] of a rabbit's skull, and he had found that, in biology at least, he had no reason for self-abasement. And from that, after the manner of young people starting from any starting-point, they got to generalities, and while Hill attacked her upon the question of socialism – some instinct told him to spare her a direct assault upon her religion – she was gathering resolution to undertake what she told herself was his aesthetic education. She was a year or two older than he, though the thought never occurred to him. The loan of *News from Nowhere* was the beginning of a series of cross loans. Upon some absurd first principle of his, Hill had never 'wasted time' upon poetry, and it seemed an appalling deficiency to her. One day in the lunch hour, when she chanced upon him alone in the little museum where the skeletons were arranged, shamefully eating the bun that constituted his midday meal, she retreated, and returned to lend him, with a slightly furtive air, a volume of Browning.[186] He stood sideways towards her and took the book rather clumsily, because he was holding the bun in the other hand. And in the retrospect his voice lacked the cheerful clearness he could have wished.

That occurred after the examination in comparative anatomy, on the day before the college turned out its students and was carefully locked up by the officials for the Christmas holidays. The excitement of cramming for the first trial of strength had for a little while dominated Hill, to the exclusion of his other interests. In the forecasts of the result in which everyone indulged he was surprised to find that no one regarded him as a possible competitor for the Harvey Commemoration Medal,[187] of which this and the two subsequent examinations disposed. It was about this time that Wedderburn, who so far had lived inconspicuously on the uttermost margin of Hill's perceptions, began to take on the appearance of an obstacle. By a mutual agreement, the nocturnal prowlings with Thorpe ceased for the three weeks before the examination, and his landlady pointed out that she really could not supply so much lamp oil at the price. He walked to and fro the college with little slips of mnemonics in his hand, lists of crayfish appendages, rabbits' skull-bones and vertebrate nerves, for example, and became a positive nuisance to foot passengers in the opposite direction.

But by a natural reaction, Poetry and the girl with the brown eyes ruled the Christmas holiday. The pending results of the examination became such a secondary consideration that Hill marvelled at his father's excitement. Even had he wished it, there was no comparative anatomy to read in Landport, and he was too poor to buy books, but the stock of poets in the library was extensive, and Hill's attack was magnificently sustained. He saturated himself with the fluent numbers of Longfellow and Tennyson, and fortified himself with Shakespeare; found a kindred soul in Pope, and a master in Shelley, and heard and fled the siren voices of Eliza Cook and Mrs Hemans.[188] But he read no more Browning, because he hoped for the loan of other volumes from Miss Haysman when he returned to London.

He walked from his lodgings to the college with that volume of Browning in his shiny black bag, and his mind teeming with the finest general propositions about poetry. Indeed, he framed first this little speech and then that with which to grace the return. The morning was an exceptionally pleasant one for London; there was a clear, hard frost and undeniable blue in the sky, a thin haze softened every outline, and warm shafts of sunlight struck between the house blocks and turned the sunny side of the street to amber and gold. In the hall of the college he pulled off his glove and signed his name with fingers so stiff with cold that the characteristic dash under the signature he cultivated became a quivering line. He imagined Miss Haysman about him everywhere. He turned at the staircase, and there, below, he saw a crowd struggling at the foot of the noticeboard. This, possibly, was the biology list. He forgot Browning and Miss Haysman for the moment, and joined the scrimmage. And at last, with his cheek flattened against the sleeve of the man on the step above him, he read the list:

CLASS 1

H. J. SOMERS WEDDERBURN

WILLIAM HILL

and thereafter followed a second class that is outside our present sympathies. It was characteristic that he did not trouble to look for Thorpe on the physics list, but backed out of the struggle at once, and in a curious emotional state between pride over common second-class humanity and acute disappointment at Wedderburn's success, went on his way upstairs. At the top, as he was hanging up his coat in the passage, the zoological demonstrator, a young man from Oxford, who secretly regarded him as a blatant 'mugger'[189] of the very worst type, offered his heartiest congratulations.

At the laboratory door Hill stopped for a second to get his breath, and then entered. He looked straight up the laboratory and saw all five girl students grouped in their places, and Wedderburn, the once retiring Wedderburn, leaning rather gracefully against the window, playing with the blind tassel and talking, apparently, to the five of them. Now, Hill could talk bravely enough and even overbearingly to one girl, and he could have made a speech to a roomful of girls, but this business of standing at ease and appreciating, fencing, and returning quick remarks round a group was, he knew, altogether beyond him. Coming up the staircase his feelings for Wedderburn had been generous, a certain admiration perhaps, a willingness to shake his hand conspicuously and heartily as one who had fought but the first round. But before Christmas Wedderburn had never gone up to that end of the room to talk. In a flash Hill's mist of vague excitement condensed abruptly to a vivid dislike of Wedderburn. Possibly his expression changed. As he came up to his place, Wedderburn nodded carelessly to him, and the others glanced round. Miss Haysman looked at him and away again, the faintest touch of her eyes. 'I can't agree with you, Mr Wedderburn,' she said.

'I must congratulate you on your first-class, Mr Hill,' said the spectacled girl in green, turning round and beaming at him.

'It's nothing,' said Hill, staring at Wedderburn and Miss Haysman talking together, and eager to hear what they talked about.

'We poor folks in the second class don't think so,' said the girl in spectacles.

What was it Wedderburn was saying? Something about William Morris! Hill did not answer the girl in spectacles, and the smile died out of his face. He could not hear, and failed to see how he could 'cut in'. Confound Wedderburn! He sat down, opened his bag, hesitated whether to return the volume of Browning forthwith, in the sight of all, and instead drew out his new notebooks for the short course in elementary botany that was now beginning, and which would terminate in February. As he did so, a fat, heavy man, with a white face and pale grey eyes – Bindon, the professor of botany, who came up from Kew[190] for January and February – came in by the lecture-theatre door, and passed, rubbing his hands together and smiling, in silent affability down the laboratory.

*

In the subsequent six weeks Hill experienced some very rapid and curiously complex emotional developments. For the most part he had Wedderburn in focus – a fact that Miss Haysman never suspected. She told Hill (for in the comparative privacy of the museum she talked a good deal to him of socialism and Browning and general propositions) that she had met Wedderburn at the house of some people she knew, and 'he's inherited his cleverness; for his father, you know, is the great eye specialist'.

'My father is a cobbler,' said Hill, quite irrelevantly, and perceived the want of dignity even as he said it. But the gleam of jealousy did not offend her. She conceived herself the fundamental source of it. He suffered bitterly from a sense of Wedderburn's unfairness, and a realisation of his own handicap. Here was this Wedderburn who had picked up a prominent man for a father, and instead of his losing so many marks on the score of that advantage, it was counted to him for righteousness![191] And while Hill had to introduce himself and talk to Miss Haysman clumsily over mangled guinea-pigs in the laboratory, this Wedderburn in some backstairs way, had access to her social altitudes, and could converse in a polished argot that Hill understood, perhaps, but felt incapable of speaking. Not, of course, that he wanted to. Then it seemed to Hill that for Wedderburn to come there day after day with cuffs unfrayed, neatly tailored, precisely barbered, quietly perfect, was in itself an ill-bred, sneering sort of proceeding. Moreover, it was a stealthy thing for Wedderburn to behave insignificantly for a space, to mock modesty, to lead Hill to fancy that he himself was beyond dispute the man of the year, and then suddenly to dart in front of him, and incontinently to swell up in this fashion. In addition to these things, Wedderburn displayed an increasing disposition to join in any conversational grouping that included Miss Haysman, and would venture, and indeed seek occasion, to pass opinions derogatory to socialism and atheism. He goaded Hill to incivilities by neat, shallow and exceedingly effective personal remarks about the socialist leaders, until Hill hated Bernard Shaw's graceful egotisms, William Morris's limited editions and luxurious wallpapers and Walter Crane's charmingly absurd ideal working men about as much as he hated Wedderburn.[192] The dissertations in the laboratory, that had been his glory in the previous term, became a danger and degenerated into inglorious tussles with Wedderburn, and Hill kept to them only out of an obscure perception that his honour was involved. In the debating society Hill knew quite clearly that, to a thunderous accompaniment of banged desks, he could have pulverised Wedderburn. Only Wedderburn never attended the debating society to be pulverised, because – nauseous affectation! – he 'dined late'.

You must not imagine that these things presented themselves in quite such a crude form to Hill's perception. Hill was a born generaliser. Wedderburn to him was not so much an individual obstacle as a type, the salient angle of a class. The economic theories that, after infinite ferment, had shaped themselves in Hill's mind, became abruptly concrete at the contact. The world became full of easy-mannered, graceful, gracefully dressed, conversationally dexterous, finally shallow Wedderburns – Bishops Wedderburn, Wedderburn MPs, Professors Wedderburn, Wedderburn landlords, all with finger-bowl shibboleths[193] and epigrammatic cities of refuge from a sturdy debater. And everyone ill-clothed or ill-dressed, from the cobbler to the cab-runner, was a man and a brother, a fellow-sufferer, to Hill's imagination. So that he became, as it were, a champion of the fallen and oppressed, albeit to outward seeming only a self-assertive, ill-mannered young man, and an unsuccessful champion at that. Again and again a skirmish over the afternoon tea that the girl students had inaugurated left Hill with flushed cheeks and a tattered temper, and the debating society noticed a new quality of sarcastic bitterness in his speeches.

You will understand now how it was necessary, if only in the interests of humanity, that Hill should demolish Wedderburn in the forthcoming examination and outshine him in the eyes of Miss Haysman; and you will perceive, too, how Miss Haysman fell into some common feminine misconceptions. The Hill-Wedderburn quarrel, for in his unostentatious way Wedderburn reciprocated Hill's ill-veiled rivalry, became a tribute to her indefinable charm; she was the Queen of Beauty in a tournament of scalpels and stumpy pencils. To her confidential friend's secret annoyance, it even troubled her conscience, for she was a good girl, and painfully aware, from Ruskin and contemporary fiction, how entirely men's activities are determined by women's attitudes.[194] And if Hill never by any chance mentioned the topic of love to her, she only credited him with the finer modesty for that omission.

So the time came on for the second examination, and Hill's increasing pallor confirmed the general rumour that he was working hard. In the Aerated Bread Shop[195] near South Kensington Station you would see him, breaking his bun and sipping his milk, with his eyes intent upon a paper of closely written notes. In his bedroom there were propositions about buds and stems round his looking-glass, a diagram to catch his eye, if soap should chance to spare it, above his washing basin. He missed several meetings of the debating society, but he found the chance encounters with Miss Haysman in the spacious ways of the adjacent art museum, or in the little museum at the top of the college, or in the college corridors, more frequent and very restful. In particular, they used to meet in a little gallery full of wrought-iron chests and gates, near the art library, and there Hill used to talk, under the gentle stimulus of her flattering attention, of Browning and his personal ambitions. A characteristic she found remarkable in him was his freedom from avarice. He contemplated quite calmly the prospect of living all his life on an income below a hundred pounds a year. But he was determined to be famous, to make, recognisably in his own proper person, the world a better place to live in. He took Bradlaugh and John Burns[196] for his leaders and models – poor, even impecunious, great men. But Miss Haysman thought that such lives were deficient on the aesthetic side, by which, though she did not know it, she meant good wallpaper and upholstery, pretty books, tasteful clothes, concerts, and meals nicely cooked and respectfully served.

At last came the day of the second examination, and the professor of botany, a fussy, conscientious man, rearranged all the tables in a long narrow laboratory to prevent copying, and put his demonstrator on a chair on a table (where he felt, he said, like a Hindu god) to see all the cheating, and stuck a notice outside the door, 'Door closed', for no earthly reason that any human being could discover. And all the morning from ten till one the quill of Wedderburn shrieked defiance at Hill's, and the quills of the others chased their leaders in a tireless pack; and so also it was in the afternoon. Wedderburn was a little quieter than usual, and Hill's face was hot all day, and his overcoat bulged with textbooks and notebooks against the last moment's revision. And the next day, in the morning and in the afternoon, was the practical examination, when sections had to be cut and slides identified. In the morning Hill was depressed because he knew he had cut a thick section, and in the afternoon came the mysterious slip.

It was just the kind of thing that the botanical professor was always doing. Like the income tax, it offered a premium to the cheat. It was a preparation under the microscope, a little glass slip, held in its place on the stage of the instrument by light steel clips, and the inscription set forth that the slip was not to be moved. Each student was to go in turn to it, sketch it, write in his book of answers what he considered it to be, and return to his place. Now, to move such a slip is a thing one can do by a chance movement of the finger and in a fraction of a second.

The professor's reason for decreeing that the slip should not be moved depended on the fact that the object he wanted identified was characteristic of a certain tree stem. In the position in which it was placed it was a difficult thing to recognise, but once the slip was moved so as to bring other parts of the preparation into view, its nature was obvious enough.

Hill came to this, flushed from a contest with staining re-agents, sat down on the little stool before the microscope, turned the mirror to get the best light, and then, out of sheer habit, shifted the slips. At once he remembered the prohibition, and with an almost continuous motion of his hands, moved it back, and sat paralysed with astonishment at his action.

Then slowly, he turned his head. The professor was out of the room; the demonstrator sat aloft on his impromptu rostrum, reading the *Q. Jour. Mi. Sci.*; the rest of the examinees were busy, and with their backs to him. Should he own up to the accident now? He knew quite clearly what the thing was. It was a lenticel,[197] a characteristic preparation from the elder tree. His eyes roved over his intent fellow-students and Wedderburn suddenly glanced over his shoulder at him with a queer expression in his eyes. The mental excitement that had kept Hill at an abnormal pitch of vigour these two days gave way to a curious nervous tension. His book of answers was beside him. He did not write down what the thing was, but with one eye at the microscope he began making a hasty sketch of it. His mind was full of this grotesque puzzle in ethics that had suddenly been sprung upon him. Should he identify it? Or should he leave this question unanswered? In that case Wedderburn would probably come out first in the second result. How could he tell now whether he might not have identified the thing without shifting it? It was possible that Wedderburn had failed to recognise it, of course. Suppose Wedderburn too had shifted the slide?

He looked up at the clock. There were fifteen minutes in which to make up his mind. He gathered up his book of answers and the coloured pencils he used in illustrating his replies and walked back to his seat.

He read through his manuscript, and then sat thinking and gnawing his knuckle. It would look queer now if he owned up. He *must* beat Wedderburn. He forgot the examples of those starry gentlemen, John Burns and Bradlaugh. Besides, he reflected, the glimpse of the rest of the slip he had had was, after all, quite accidental, forced upon him by chance, a kind of providential revelation rather than an unfair advantage. It was not nearly so dishonest to avail himself of that as it was of Broome, who believed in the efficacy of prayer, to pray daily for a first-class. 'Five minutes more,' said the demonstrator, folding up his paper and becoming observant. Hill watched the clock hands until two minutes remained; then he opened the book of answers and, with hot ears and an affectation of ease, gave his drawing of the lenticel its name.

When the second pass list appeared, the previous positions of Wedderburn and Hill were reversed, and the spectacled girl in green, who knew the demonstrator in private life (where he was practically human), said that in the result of the two examinations taken together Hill had the advantage of a mark – 167 to 166 out of a possible 200. Everyone admired Hill in a way, though the suspicion of 'mugging' clung to him. But Hill was to find congratulations and Miss Haysman's enhanced opinion of him, and even the decided decline in the crest of Wedderburn, tainted by an unhappy memory. He felt a remarkable access of energy at first, and the note of a democracy marching to triumph returned to his debating-society speeches; he worked at his comparative anatomy with tremendous zeal and effect, and he went on with his aesthetic education. But through it all, a vivid little picture was continually coming before his mind's eye – of a sneakish person manipulating a slide.

No human being had witnessed the act, and he was cocksure that no higher power existed to see it; but for all that it worried him. Memories are not dead things but alive; they dwindle in disuse, but they harden and develop in all sorts of queer ways if they are being continually fretted. Curiously enough, though at the time he perceived clearly that the shifting was accidental, as the days wore on his memory became confused about it, until at last he was not sure – although he assured himself that he *was* sure – whether the movement had been absolutely involuntary. Then it is possible that Hill's dietary was conducive to morbid conscientiousness: a breakfast frequently eaten in a hurry, a midday bun, and, at such hours after five as chanced to be convenient, such meat as his means determined, usually in a chop-house in a back street off the Brompton Road.[198] Occasionally he treated himself to threepenny or ninepenny classics,[199] and they usually represented a suppression of potatoes or chops. It is indisputable that outbreaks of self-abasement and emotional revival have a distinct relation to periods of scarcity. But apart from this influence on the feelings, there was in Hill a distinct aversion to falsity that the blasphemous Landport cobbler had inculcated by strap and tongue from his earliest years. Of one fact about professed atheists I am convinced: they may be – they usually are – fools, void of subtlety, revilers of holy institutions, brutal speakers, and mischievous knaves, but they lie with difficulty. If it were not so, if they had the faintest grasp of the idea of compromise, they would simply be liberal churchmen. And, moreover, this memory poisoned his regard for Miss Haysman. For she now so evidently preferred him to Wedder-burn that he felt sure he cared for her, and began reciprocating her attentions by timid marks of personal regard; at one time he even bought a bunch of violets, carried it about in his pocket, and produced it, with a stumbling explanation, withered and dead, in the gallery of old iron. It poisoned, too, the denunciation of capitalist dishonesty that had been one of his life's pleasures. And lastly, it poisoned his triumph in Wedderburn. Previously he had been Wedderburn's superior in his own eyes, and had raged simply at a want of recognition. Now he began to fret at the darker suspicion of positive inferiority. He fancied he found justifications for his position in Browning, but they vanished on analysis. At last – moved, curiously enough, by exactly the same motive forces that had resulted in his dishonesty – he went to Professor Bindon, and made a clean breast of the whole affair. As Hill was a paid student, Professor Bindon did not ask him to sit down, and he stood before the professor's desk as he made his confession.

'It's a curious story,' said Professor Bindon, slowly realising how the thing reflected on himself, and then letting his anger rise – 'a most remarkable story. I can't understand your doing it, and I can't under-stand this avowal. You're a type of student – Cambridge men would never dream – I suppose I ought to have thought – Why *did* you cheat?'

'I didn't cheat,' said Hill.

'But you have just been telling me you did.'

'I thought I explained –'

'Either you cheated or you did not cheat –'

'I said my motion was involuntary.'

'I am not a metaphysician, I am a servant of science – of fact. You were told not to move the slip. You did move the slip. If that is not cheating –'

'If I was a cheat,' said Hill, with the note of hysterics in his voice, 'should I come here and tell you?'

'Your repentance, of course, does you credit,' said Professor Bindon, 'but it does not alter the original facts.'

'No, sir,' said Hill, giving in in utter self-abasement.

'Even now you cause an enormous amount of trouble. The examin-ation list will have to be revised.'

'I suppose so, sir.'

'Suppose so? Of course it must be revised. And I don't see how I can conscientiously pass you.'

'Not pass me?' said Hill. 'Fail me?'

'It's the rule in all examinations. Or where should we be? What else did you expect? You don't want to shirk the consequences of your own acts?'

'I thought, perhaps – ' said Hill. And then, 'Fail me? I thought, as I told you, you would simply deduct the marks given for that slip.'

'Impossible!' said Bindon. 'Besides, it would still leave you above Wedderburn. Deduct only the marks! Preposterous! The Departmental Regulations distinctly say – '

'But it's my own admission, sir.'

'The Regulations say nothing whatever of the manner in which the matter comes to light. They simply provide – '

'It will ruin me. If I fail this examination, they won't renew my scholarship.'

'You should have thought of that before.'

'But, sir, consider all my circumstances – '

'I cannot consider anything. Professors in this college are machines. The Regulations will not even let us recommend our students for appointments. I am a machine, and you have worked me. I have to do – '

'It's very hard, sir.'

'Possibly it is.'

'If I am to be failed this examination, I might as well go home at once.'

'That is as you think proper.' Bindon's voice softened a little; he perceived he had been unjust, and provided he did not contradict himself, he was disposed to amelioration. 'As a private person,' he said, 'I think this confession of yours goes far to mitigate your offence. But you have set the machinery in motion, and now it must take its course. I – I am really sorry you gave way.'

A wave of emotion prevented Hill from answering. Suddenly, very vividly, he saw the heavily-lined face of the old Landport cobbler, his father. 'Good God! What a fool I have been!' he said hotly and abruptly.

'I hope,' said Bindon, 'that it will be a lesson to you.'

But, curiously enough, they were not thinking of quite the same indiscretion.

There was a pause.

'I would like a day to think, sir, and then I will let you know – about going home, I mean,' said Hill, moving towards the door.

The next day Hill's place was vacant. The spectacled girl in green was, as usual, first with the news. Wedderburn and Miss Haysman were talking of a performance of The Meistersingers[200] when she came up to them.

'Have you heard?' she said.

'Heard what?'

'There was cheating in the examination.'

'Cheating!' said Wedderburn, with his face suddenly hot.[201] 'How?'

'That slide – '

'Moved? Never!'

'It was. That slide that we weren't to move – '

'Nonsense!' said Wedderburn. 'Why! How could they find out? Who do they say – ?'

'It was Mr Hill.'

'*Hill!*'

'Mr Hill!'

'Not – surely not the immaculate Hill?' said Wedderburn, recovering.

'I don't believe it,' said Miss Haysman. 'How do you know?'

'I *didn't*,' said the girl in spectacles. 'But I know it now for a fact. Mr Hill went and confessed to Professor Bindon himself.'

'By Jove!' said Wedderburn. 'Hill of all people. But I am always inclined to distrust these philanthropists-on-principle – '

'Are you quite sure?' said Miss Haysman, with a catch in her breath.

'Quite. It's dreadful, isn't it? But, you know, what can you expect? His father is a cobbler.'

Then Miss Haysman astonished the girl in spectacles.

'I don't care. I will not believe it,' she said, flushing darkly under her warm-tinted skin. 'I will not believe it until he has told me so himself – face to face. I would scarcely believe it then,' and abruptly she turned her back on the girl in spectacles, and walked to her own place.

'It's true, all the same,' said the girl in spectacles, peering and smiling at Wedderburn.

But Wedderburn did not answer her. She was indeed one of those people who seemed destined to make unanswered remarks.

The Stolen Bacillus
202

'This again,' said the bacteriologist, slipping a glass slide under the microscope, 'is a preparation of the celebrated bacillus of cholera – the cholera germ.'

The pale-faced man peered down the microscope. He was evidently not accustomed to that kind of thing, and held a limp white hand over his disengaged eye. 'I see very little,' he said.

'Touch this screw,' said the bacteriologist; 'perhaps the microscope is out of focus for you. Eyes vary so much. Just the fraction of a turn this way or that.'

'Ah! Now I see,' said the visitor. 'Not so very much to see after all. Little streaks and shreds of pink. And yet those little particles, those mere atomies, might multiply and devastate a city! Wonderful!'

He stood up, and releasing the glass slip from the microscope, held it in his hand towards the window. 'Scarcely visible,' he said, scrutinising the preparation. He hesitated. 'Are these – alive? Are they dangerous now?'

'Those have been stained and killed,' said the bacteriologist. 'I wish, for my own part, we could kill and stain every one of them in the universe.'

'I suppose,' the pale man said with a slight smile, 'that you scarcely care to have such things about you in the living – in the active state?'

'On the contrary, we are obliged to,' said the bacteriologist. 'Here, for instance – ' He walked across the room and took up one of several sealed tubes. 'Here is the living thing. This is a cultivation of the actual living disease bacteria.' He hesitated. 'Bottled cholera, so to speak.'

A slight gleam of satisfaction appeared momentarily in the face of the pale man.

'It's a deadly thing to have in your possession,' he said, devouring the little tube with his eyes. The bacteriologist watched the morbid pleasure in his visitor's expression. This man, who had visited him that afternoon with a note of introduction from an old friend, interested him from the very contrast of their dispositions. The lank black hair and deep grey eyes, the haggard expression and nervous manner, the fitful yet keen interest of his visitor were a novel change from the phlegmatic deliberations of the ordinary scientific worker with whom the bacteriologist chiefly associated. It was perhaps natural, with a hearer evidently so impressionable to the lethal nature of his topic, to take the most effective aspect of the matter.

He held the tube in his hand thoughtfully. 'Yes, here is the pestilence imprisoned. Only break such a little tube as this into a supply of drinking-water, say to these minute particles of life that one must needs stain and examine with the highest powers of the microscope even to see, and that one can neither smell nor taste – say to them, 'Go forth, increase and multiply and replenish the cisterns,'[203] and death – mysterious, untraceable death, death swift and terrible, death full of pain and indignity – would be released upon this city, and go hither and thither seeking his victims. Here he would take the husband from the wife, here the child from its mother, here the statesman from his duty, and here the toiler from his trouble. He would follow the water-mains, creeping along streets, picking out and punishing a house here and a house there where they did not boil their drinking-water, creeping into the wells of the mineral-water makers, getting washed into salad, and lying dormant in ices. He would wait ready to be drunk in the horse-troughs, and by unwary children in the public fountains. He would soak into the soil, to reappear in springs and wells at a thousand unexpected places. Once start him at the water supply, and before we could ring him in, and catch him again, he would have decimated the metropolis.' He stopped abruptly. He had been told rhetoric was his weakness. 'But he is quite safe here, you know – quite safe.'

The pale-faced man nodded. His eyes shone. He cleared his throat. 'These Anarchist – rascals,' said he, 'are fools, blind fools – to use bombs[204] when this kind of thing is attainable. I think – '

A gentle rap, a mere light touch of the fingernails was heard at the door. The bacteriologist opened it. 'Just a minute, dear,' whispered his wife.

When he re-entered the laboratory his visitor was looking at his watch. 'I had no idea I had wasted an hour of your time,' he said. 'Twelve minutes to four. I ought to have left here by half-past three. But your things were really too interesting. No, positively, I cannot stop a moment longer. I have an engagement at four.'

He passed out of the room reiterating his thanks, and the bacteriologist accompanied him to the door, and then returned thoughtfully along the passage to his laboratory. He was musing on the ethnology of his visitor. Certainly the man was not a Teutonic type nor a common Latin one. 'A morbid product, anyhow, I am afraid,' said the bacteriologist to himself. 'How he gloated on those cultivations of disease-germs!' A disturbing thought struck him. He turned to the bench by the vapour-bath, and then very quickly to his writing-table. Then he felt hastily in his pockets, and then rushed to the door. 'I may have put it down on the hall table,' he said.

'Minnie!' he shouted hoarsely in the hall.

'Yes, dear,' came a remote voice.

'Had I anything in my hand when I spoke to you, dear, just now?'

Pause.

'Nothing, dear, because I remember – '

'Blue ruin!' cried the bacteriologist, and incontinently ran to the front door and down the steps of his house to the street.

Minnie, hearing the door slam violently, ran in alarm to the window. Down the street a slender man was getting into a cab. The bacteriologist, hatless, and in his carpet slippers, was running and gesticulating wildly towards this group. One slipper came off, but he did not wait for it. 'He has gone *mad*!' said Minnie. 'It's that horrid science of his,' and, opening the window, would have called after him. The slender man, suddenly glancing round, seemed struck with the same idea of mental disorder. He pointed hastily to the bacteriologist, said something to the cabman, the apron[205] of the cab slammed, the whip swished, the horse's feet clattered, and in a moment the cab, with bacteriologist hotly in pursuit, had receded up the vista of the roadway and disappeared round the corner.

Minnie remained straining out of the window for a minute. Then she drew her head back into the room again. She was dumbfounded. 'Of course he is eccentric,' she meditated. 'But running about London – in the height of the season, too – in his socks!' A happy thought struck her. She hastily put her bonnet on, seized his shoes, went into the hall, took down his hat and light overcoat from the pegs, emerged upon the doorstep, and hailed a cab that opportunely crawled by. 'Drive me up the road and round Havelock Crescent, and see if we can find a gentleman running about in a velveteen coat and no hat.'

'Velveteen coat, ma'am, and no 'at. Very good, ma'am.' And the cabman whipped up at once in the most matter-of-fact way, as if he drove to this address every day in his life.

Some few minutes later the little group of cabmen and loafers that collects round the cabmen's shelter at Haverstock Hill[206] were startled by the passing of a cab with a ginger-coloured screw of a horse,[207] driven furiously.

They were silent as it went by, and then as it receded – 'That's 'Arry 'Icks. Wot's *he* got?' said the stout gentleman known as 'old Tootles'.

'He's a-using his whip, he is, *to* rights,' said the ostler boy.[208]

'Hello!' said poor old Tommy Byles; 'here's another bloomin' loonatic. Blowed if there ain't.'

'It's old George,' said old Tootles, 'and he's drivin' a loonatic, as you say. Ain't he a-clawin' out of the keb? Wonder if he's after 'Arry 'Icks?'

The group round the cabmen's shelter became animated. Chorus: 'Go it, George!' 'It's a race.' 'You'll ketch 'em!' 'Whip up!'

'She's a goer, she is!' said the ostler boy.

'Strike me giddy!' cried old Tootles. 'Here! *I'm* a-goin' to begin in a minute. Here's another comin'. If all the kebs in Hampstead ain't gone mad this morning!'

'It's a fieldmale[209] this time,' said the ostler boy.

'She's a followin' *him*,' said old Tootles. 'Usually the other way about.'

'What's she got in her 'and?'

'Looks like a 'igh 'at.'

'What a bloomin' lark it is! Three to one on old George,' said the ostler boy. 'Next!'

Minnie went by in a perfect roar of applause. She did not like it but she felt that she was doing her duty, and whirled on down Haverstock Hill and Camden Town High Street[210] with her eyes ever intent on the animated back view of old George, who was driving her vagrant husband so incomprehensibly away from her.

The man in the foremost cab sat crouched in the corner, his arms tightly folded, and the little tube that contained such vast possibilities of destruction gripped in his hand. His mood was a singular mixture of fear and exultation. Chiefly he was afraid of being caught before he could accomplish his purpose, but behind this was a vaguer but larger fear of the awfulness of his crime. But his exultation far exceeded his fear. No Anarchist before him had ever approached this conception of his. Ravachol, Vaillant,[211] all those distinguished persons whose fame he had envied dwindled into insignificance beside him. He had only to make sure of the water supply, and break the little tube into a reservoir. How brilliantly he had planned it, forged the letter of introduction and got into the laboratory, and how brilliantly he had seized his opportunity! The world should hear of him at last. All those people who had sneered at him, neglected him, preferred other people to him, found his company undesirable, should consider him at last. Death, death, death! They had always treated him as a man of no importance. All the world had been in a conspiracy to keep him under. He would teach them yet, what it is to isolate a man. What was this familiar street? Great St Andrew's Street,[212] of course! How fared the chase? He craned out of the cab. The bacteriologist was scarcely fifty yards behind. That was bad. He would be caught and stopped yet. He felt in his pocket for money, and found half a sovereign. This he thrust up through the trap in the top of the cab into the man's face. 'More,' he shouted, 'if only we get away.'

The money was snatched out of his hand. 'Right you are,' said the cabman, and the trap slammed, and the lash lay along the glistening side of the horse. The cab swayed, and the Anarchist, half-standing under the trap, put the hand containing the little glass tube upon the apron to preserve his balance. He felt the brittle thing crack, and the broken half of it rang upon the floor of the cab. He fell back into the seat with a curse, and stared dismally at the two or three drops of moisture on the apron.

He shuddered.

'Well! I suppose I shall be the first. *Phew!* Anyhow, I shall be a Martyr. That's something. But it is a filthy death, nevertheless. I wonder if it hurts as much as they say.'

Presently a thought occurred to him – he groped between his feet. A little drop was still in the broken end of the tube, and he drank that to make sure. It was better to make sure. At any rate, he would not fail.

Then it dawned upon him that there was no further need to escape the bacteriologist. In Wellington Street[213] he told the cabman to stop, and got out. He slipped on the step, and his head felt queer. It was rapid stuff this cholera poison. He waved his cabman out of existence, so to speak, and stood on the pavement with his arms folded upon his breast awaiting the arrival of the bacteriologist. There was something tragic in his pose. The sense of imminent death gave him a certain dignity. He greeted his pursuer with a defiant laugh.

'Vive l'Anarchie![214] You are too late, my friend. I have drunk it. The cholera is abroad!'

The bacteriologist from his cab beamed curiously at him through his spectacles. 'You have drunk it! An Anarchist! I see now.' He was about to say something more, and then checked himself. A smile hung in the corner of his mouth. He opened the apron of his cab as if to descend, at which the Anarchist waved him a dramatic farewell and strode off towards Waterloo Bridge, carefully jostling his infected body against as many people as possible. The bacteriologist was so preoccupied with the vision of him that he scarcely manifested the slightest surprise at the appearance of Minnie upon the pavement with his hat and shoes and overcoat. 'Very good of you to bring my things,' he said, and remained lost in contemplation of the receding figure of the Anarchist.

'You had better get in,' he said, still staring. Minnie felt absolutely convinced now that he was mad, and directed the cabman home on her own responsibility. 'Put on my shoes? Certainly, dear,' said he, as the cab began to turn and hid the strutting black figure, now small in the distance, from his eyes. Then suddenly something grotesque struck him, and he laughed. Then he remarked, 'It is really very serious, though.

'You see, that man came to my house to see me, and he is an Anarchist. No – don't faint, or I cannot possibly tell you the rest. And I wanted to astonish him, not knowing he was an Anarchist, and took up a cultivation of that new species of bacterium I was telling you of, that infest, and I think cause, the blue patches upon various monkeys; and like a fool, I said it was Asiatic cholera. And he ran away with it to poison the water of London, and he certainly might have made things look blue for this civilised city. And now he has swallowed it. Of course, I cannot say what will happen, but you know it turned that kitten blue, and the three puppies – in patches, and the sparrow – bright blue. But the bother is, I shall have all the trouble and expense of preparing some more.

'Put on my coat on this hot day! Why? Because we might meet Mrs Jabber. My dear, Mrs Jabber is not a draught. But why should I wear a coat on a hot day because of Mrs – ? Oh! *very* well.'

The Remarkable Case of Davidson's Eyes[215]

The transitory mental aberration of Sidney Davidson, remarkable enough in itself, is still more remarkable if Wade's explanation is to be credited. It sets one dreaming of the oddest possibilities of inter-communication in the future, of spending an intercalary[216] five minutes on the other side of the world, or being watched in our most secret operations by unsuspected eyes. It happened that I was the immediate witness of Davidson's seizure, and so it falls naturally to me to put the story upon paper.

When I say that I was the immediate witness of his seizure, I mean that I was the first on the scene. The thing happened at the Harlow Technical College[217] just beyond the Highgate Archway.[218] He was alone in the larger laboratory when the thing happened. I was in the smaller room, where the balances are, writing up some notes. The thunderstorm had completely upset my work, of course. It was just after one of the louder peals that I thought I heard some glass smash in the other room. I stopped writing, and turned round to listen. For a moment I heard nothing; the hail was playing the devil's tattoo on the corrugated zinc of the roof. Then came another sound, a smash – no doubt of it this time. Something heavy had been knocked off the bench. I jumped up at once and went and opened the door leading into the big laboratory.

I was surprised to hear a queer sort of laugh, and saw Davidson standing unsteadily in the middle of the room, with a dazzled look on his face. My first impression was that he was drunk. He did not notice me. He was clawing out at something invisible a yard in front of his face. He put out his hand slowly, rather hesitatingly, and then clutched nothing. 'What's come to it?' he said. He held up his hands to his face, fingers spread out. 'Great Scott!' he said.[219] (The thing happened three or four years ago, when everyone swore by that personage.) Then he began raising his feet clumsily, as though he had expected to find them glued to the floor.

'Davidson!' cried I. 'What's the matter with you?' He turned round in my direction and looked about for me. He looked over me and at me and on either side of me, without the slightest sign of seeing me. 'Waves,' he said; 'and a remarkably neat schooner. I'd swear that was Bellows's voice. *Hello!*' he shouted suddenly at the top of his voice.

I thought he was up to some foolery. Then I saw littered about his feet the shattered remains of the best of our electrometers.[220] 'What's up, man?' said I. 'You've smashed the electrometer!'

'Bellows again!' said he. 'Friends left, if my hands are gone. Something about electrometers. Which way *are* you, Bellows?' He suddenly came staggering towards me. 'The damned stuff cuts like butter,' he said. He walked straight into the bench and recoiled. 'None so buttery, that!' he said, and stood swaying.

I felt scared. 'Davidson,' said I, 'what on earth's come over you?'

He looked round him in every direction. 'I could swear that was Bellows. Why don't you show yourself like a man, Bellows?'

It occurred to me that he must be suddenly struck blind. I walked round the table and laid my hand upon his arm. I never saw a man more startled in my life. He jumped away from me, and came round into an attitude of self-defence, his face fairly distorted with terror: 'Good God!' he cried. 'What was that?'

'It's I – Bellows. Confound it, Davidson!'

He jumped when I answered him and stared – how can I express it – ? Right through me. He began talking, not to me, but to himself. 'Here in broad daylight on a clear beach. Not a place to hide in.' He looked about him wildly. 'Here! I'm *off*.' He suddenly turned and ran headlong into the big electromagnet – so violently that, as we found afterwards, he bruised his shoulder and jawbone cruelly. At that he stepped back a pace, and cried out with almost a whimper, 'What, in heaven's name, has come over me?' He stood, blanched with terror and trembling violently, with his right arm clutching his left, where that had collided with the magnet.

By that time I was excited, and fairly scared. 'Davidson,' said I, 'don't be afraid.'

He was startled at my voice, but not so excessively as before. I repeated my words in as clear and firm a tone as I could assume.

'Bellows,' he said, 'is that you?'

'Can't you see it's me?'

He laughed. 'I can't even see it's myself. Where the devil are we?'

'Here,' said I, 'in the laboratory.'

'The laboratory!' he answered, in a puzzled tone, and put his hand to his forehead. 'I *was* in the laboratory – till that flash came, but I'm hanged if I'm there now. What ship is that?'

'There's no ship,' said I. 'Do be sensible, old chap.'

'No ship!' he repeated, and seemed to forget my denial forthwith. 'I suppose,' said he, slowly, 'we're both dead. But the rummy part is I feel just as though I still had a body. Don't get used to it all at once, I suppose. The old shop was struck by lightning, I suppose. Jolly quick thing, Bellows – eh?'

'Don't talk nonsense. You're very much alive. You are in the laboratory, blundering about. You've just smashed a new electrometer. I don't envy you when Boyce arrives.'

He stared away from me towards the diagrams of cryohydrates.[221] 'I must be deaf,' said he. 'They've fired a gun, for there goes the puff of smoke, and I never heard a sound.'

I put my hand on his arm again, and this time he was less alarmed. 'We seem to have a sort of invisible bodies,' said he. 'By Jove! There's a boat coming round the headland! It's very much like the old life after all – in a different climate.'

I shook his arm. 'Davidson,' I cried, 'wake up!'

It was just then that Boyce came in. So soon as he spoke Davidson exclaimed: 'Old Boyce! Dead too! What a lark!' I hastened to explain that Davidson was in a kind of somnambulistic trance. Boyce was interested at once. We both did all we could to rouse the fellow out of his extraordinary state. He answered our questions, and asked us some of his own, but his attention seemed distracted by his hallucination about a beach and a ship. He kept interpolating observations concerning some boat and the davits,[222] and sails filling with the wind. It made one feel queer, in the dusky laboratory, to hear him saying such things.

He was blind and helpless. We had to walk him down the passage, one at each elbow, to Boyce's private room, and while Boyce talked to him there, and humoured him about this ship idea, I went along the corridor and asked old Wade to come and look at him.

The voice of our Dean sobered him a little, but not very much. He asked where his hands were, and why he had to walk about up to his waist in the ground. Wade thought over him a long time – you know how he knits his brows – and then made him feel the couch, guiding his hands to it. 'That's a couch,' said Wade. 'The couch in the private room of Professor Boyce. Horsehair stuffing.'

Davidson felt about, and puzzled over it, and answered presently that he could feel it all right, but he couldn't see it.

'What *do* you see?' asked Wade. Davidson said he could see nothing but a lot of sand and broken-up shells. Wade gave him some other things to feel, telling him what they were, and watching him keenly.

'The ship is almost hull down,'[223] said Davidson, presently, apropos of nothing.

'Never mind the ship,' said Wade. 'Listen to me, Davidson. Do you know what hallucination means?'

'Rather,' said Davidson.

'Well, everything you see is hallucinatory.'

'Bishop Berkeley,' said Davidson.[224]

'Don't mistake me,' said Wade. 'You are alive, and in this room of Boyce's. But something has happened to your eyes. You cannot see; you can feel and hear, but not see. Do you follow me?'

'It seems to me that I see too much.' Davidson rubbed his knuckles into his eyes. 'Well?' he said.

'That's all. Don't let it perplex you. Bellows here and I will take you home in a cab.'

'Wait a bit.' Davidson thought. 'Help me to sit down,' said he, presently; 'and now – I'm sorry to trouble you – but will you tell me all that over again?'

Wade repeated it very patiently. Davidson shut his eyes, and pressed his hands upon his forehead. 'Yes,' said he. 'It's quite right. Now my eyes are shut I know you're right. That's you, Bellows, sitting by me on the couch. I'm in England again. And we're in the dark.'

Then he opened his eyes. 'And there,' said he, 'is the sun just rising, and the yards of the ship, and a tumbled sea, and a couple of birds flying. I never saw anything so real. And I'm sitting up to my neck in a bank of sand.'

He bent forward and covered his face with his hands. Then he opened his eyes again. 'Dark sea and sunrise! And yet I'm sitting on a sofa in old Boyce's room . . . ! God help me!'

That was the beginning. For three weeks this strange affection of Davidson's eyes continued unabated. It was far worse than being blind. He was absolutely helpless, and had to be fed like a newly hatched bird, and led about and undressed. If he attempted to move he fell over things or struck himself against walls or doors. After a day or so he got used to hearing our voices without seeing us, and willingly admitted he was at home, and that Wade was right in what he told him. My sister, to whom he was engaged, insisted on coming to see him, and would sit for hours every day while he talked about this beach of his. Holding her hand seemed to comfort him immensely. He explained that when we left the college and drove home – he lived in Hampstead Village – it appeared to him as if we drove right through a sandhill – it was perfectly black until he emerged again – and through rocks and trees and solid obstacles, and when he was taken to his own room it made him giddy and almost frantic with the fear of falling, because going upstairs seemed to lift him thirty or forty feet above the rocks of his imaginary island. He kept saying he should smash all the eggs. The end was that he had to be taken down into his father's consulting-room and laid upon a couch that stood there.

He described the island as being a bleak kind of place on the whole, with very little vegetation, except some peaty stuff, and a lot of bare rock. There were multitudes of penguins, and they made the rocks white and disagreeable to see. The sea was often rough, and once there was a thunderstorm, and he lay and shouted at the silent flashes. Once or twice seals pulled up on the beach, but only on the first two or three days. He said it was very funny the way in which the penguins used to waddle right through him, and how he seemed to lie among them without disturbing them.

I remember one odd thing, and that was when he wanted very badly to smoke. We put a pipe in his hands – he almost poked his eye out with it – and lit it. But he couldn't taste anything. I've since found it's the same with me – I don't know if it's the usual case – that I cannot enjoy tobacco at all unless I can see the smoke.

But the queerest part of his vision came when Wade sent him out in a Bath-chair to get fresh air. The Davidsons hired a chair, and got that deaf and obstinate dependent of theirs, Widgery, to attend to it. Widgery's ideas of healthy expeditions were peculiar. My sister, who had been to the Dogs' Home, met them in Camden Town, towards King's Cross,[225] Widgery trotting along complacently and Davidson, evidently most distressed, trying in his feeble, blind way to attract Widgery's attention.

He positively wept when my sister spoke to him. 'Oh, get me out of this horrible darkness!' he said, feeling for her hand. 'I must get out of it, or I shall die.' He was quite incapable of explaining what was the matter, but my sister decided he must go home, and presently, as they went up the hill towards Hampstead, the horror seemed to drop from him. He said it was good to see the stars again, though it was then about noon and a blazing day.

'It seemed,' he told me afterwards, 'as if I was being carried irresistibly towards the water. I was not very much alarmed at first. Of course, it was night there – a lovely night.'

'Of course?' I asked, for that struck me as odd.

'Of course,' said he. 'It's always night there when it is day here . . . Well, we went right into the water, which was calm and shining under the moonlight – just a broad swell that seemed to grow broader and flatter as I came down into it. The surface glistened just like a skin – it might have been empty space underneath for all I could tell to the contrary. Very slowly, for I rode slanting into it, the water crept up to my eyes. Then I went under, and the skin seemed to break and heal again about my eyes. The moon gave a jump up in the sky and grew green and dim, and fish, faintly glowing, came darting round me – and things that seemed made of luminous glass, and I passed through a tangle of seaweeds that shone with an oily lustre. And so I drove down into the sea, and the stars went out one by one, and the moon grew greener and darker, and the seaweed became a luminous purple-red. It was all very faint and mysterious, and everything seemed to quiver. And all the while I could hear the wheels of the Bath-chair creaking, and the footsteps of people going by, and a man in the distance selling the special *Pall Mall*.[226]

'I kept sinking down deeper and deeper into the water. It became inky black about me, not a ray from above came down into that darkness, and the phosphorescent things grew brighter and brighter. The snaky branches of the deeper weeds flickered like the flames of spirit-lamps; but after a time, there were no more weeds. The fishes came staring and gaping towards me, and into me and through me. I never imagined such fishes before. They had lines of fire along the sides of them as though they had been outlined with a luminous pencil. And there was a ghastly thing swimming backwards with a lot of twining arms. And then I saw, coming very slowly towards me through the gloom, a hazy mass of light that resolved itself as it drew nearer into multitudes of fishes, struggling and darting round something that drifted. I drove on straight towards it, and presently I saw in the midst of the tumult, and by the light of the fish, a bit of splintered spar looming over me, and a dark hull tilting over, and some glowing phosphorescent forms that were shaken and writhed as the fish bit at them. Then it was I began to try to attract Widgery's attention. A horror came upon me. Ugh! I should have driven right into those half-eaten – things, if your sister had not come! They had great holes in them, Bellows, and . . . Never mind. But it was ghastly!'

For three weeks Davidson remained in this singular state, seeing what at the time we imagined was an altogether phantasmal world, and stone blind to the world around him. Then, one Tuesday, when I called, I met old Davidson in the passage. 'He can see his thumb!' the old gentleman said, in a perfect transport. He was struggling into his over-coat. 'He can see his thumb, Bellows!' he said, with the tears in his eyes. 'The lad will be all right yet.'

I rushed in to Davidson. He was holding up a little book before his face, and looking at it and laughing in a weak kind of way.

'It's amazing,' said he. 'There's a kind of patch come there.' He pointed with his finger. 'I'm on the rocks as usual, and the penguins are staggering and flapping about as usual, and there's been a whale showing every now and then, but it's got too dark now to make him out. But put something *there*, and I see it – I do see it. It's very dim and broken in places, but I see it all the same, like a faint spectre of itself. I found it out this morning while they were dressing me. It's like a hole in this infernal phantom world. Just put your hand by mine. No – not there. Ah! Yes! I see it. The base of your thumb and a bit of cuff! It looks like the ghost of a bit of your hand sticking out of the darkening sky. Just by it there's a group of stars like a cross[227] coming out.'

From that time Davidson began to mend. His account of the change, like his account of the vision, was oddly convincing. Over patches of his field of vision the phantom world grew fainter, grew transparent, as it were, and through these translucent gaps he began to see dimly the real world about him. The patches grew in size and number, ran together and spread until only here and there were blind spots left upon his eyes. He was able to get up and steer himself about, feed himself once more, read, smoke, and behave like an ordinary citizen again. At first it was very confusing for him to have these two pictures overlapping each other like the changing views of a lantern,[228] but in a little while he began to distinguish the real from the illusory.

At first he was unfeignedly glad, and seemed only too anxious to complete his cure by taking exercise and tonics. But as that odd island of his began to fade away from him, he became queerly interested in it. He wanted particularly to go down into the deep sea again, and would spend half his time wandering about the low-lying parts of London, trying to find the waterlogged wreck he had seen drifting. The glare of real daylight very soon impressed him so vividly as to blot out everything of his shadowy world, but of a night time, in a darkened room, he could still see the white-splashed rocks of the island, and the clumsy penguins staggering to and fro. But even these grew fainter and fainter, and at last, soon after he married my sister, he saw them for the last time.

And now to tell of the queerest thing of all. About two years after his cure, I dined with the Davidsons, and after dinner a man named Atkins called in. He is a lieutenant in the Royal Navy, and a pleasant, talkative man. He was on friendly terms with my brother-in-law, and was soon on friendly terms with me. It came out that he was engaged to Davidson's cousin, and incidentally he took out a kind of pocket photograph case to show us a new rendering of his fiancée. 'And, by the by,' said he, 'here's the old *Fulmar*.'

Davidson looked at it casually. Then suddenly his face lit up. 'Good heavens!' said he. 'I could almost swear – '

'What?' said Atkins.

'That I had seen that ship before.'

'Don't see how you can have. She hasn't been out of the South Seas for six years, and before then – '

'But,' began Davidson, and then, 'Yes – that's the ship I dreamt of. I'm sure that's the ship I dreamt of. She was standing off an island that swarmed with penguins, and she fired a gun.'

'Good Lord!' said Atkins, who had never heard the particulars of the seizure. 'How the deuce could you dream that?'

And then, bit by bit, it came out that on the very day Davidson was seized, HMS *Fulmar* had actually been off a little rock to the south of Antipodes Island.[229] A boat had landed overnight to get penguins' eggs, had been delayed, and a thunderstorm drifting up, the boat's crew had waited until the morning before rejoining the ship. Atkins had been one of them, and he corroborated, word for word, the descriptions Davidson had given of the island and the boat. There is not the slightest doubt in any of our minds that Davidson has really seen the place. In some unaccountable way, while he moved hither and thither in London, his sight moved hither and thither, in a manner that corresponded, about this distant island. *How* is absolutely a mystery.

That completes the remarkable story of Davidson's eyes. It is perhaps the best authenticated case in existence of a real vision at a distance. Explanation, there is none forthcoming, except what Professor Wade has thrown out. But his explanation invokes the Fourth Dimension,[230] and a dissertation on theoretical kinds of space. To talk of there being 'a kink in space' seems mere nonsense to me; it may be because I am no mathematician. When I said that nothing would alter the fact that the place is eight thousand miles away, he answered that two points might be a yard away on a sheet of paper and yet be brought together by bending the paper round. The reader may grasp his argument, but I certainly do not. His idea seems to be that Davidson, stooping between the poles of the big electromagnet, had some extraordinary twist given to his retinal elements through the sudden change in the field of force due to the lightning.

He thinks, as a consequence of this, that it may be possible to live visually in one part of the world, while one lives bodily in another. He has even made some experiments in support of his views; but, so far, he has simply succeeded in blinding a few dogs. I believe that is the net result of his work, though I have not seen him for some weeks. Latterly,

I have been so busy with my work in connection with the Saint Pancras installation[231] that I have had little opportunity of calling to see him. But the whole of his theory seems fantastic to me. The facts concerning Davidson stand on an altogether different footing, and I can testify personally to the accuracy of every detail I have given.

The Lord of the Dynamos [232]

The chief attendant of the three dynamos that buzzed and rattled at Camberwell,[233] and kept the electric railway going, came out of Yorkshire, and his name was James Holroyd. He was a practical electrician, but fond of whisky, a heavy red-haired brute with irregular teeth. He doubted the existence of the Deity, but accepted Carnot's cycle,[234] and he had read Shakespeare and found him weak in chemistry. His helper came out of the mysterious East, and his name was Azuma-zi. But Holroyd called him Pooh-bah.[235] Holroyd liked a negro helper because he would stand kicking – a habit with Holroyd – and did not pry into the machinery and try to learn the ways of it. Certain odd possibilities of the negro mind brought into abrupt contact with the crown of our civilisation Holroyd never fully realised, though just at the end he got some inkling of them.

To define Azuma-zi was beyond ethnology. He was, perhaps, more negroid than anything else, though his hair was curly rather than frizzy, and his nose had a bridge. Moreover, his skin was brown rather than black, and the whites of his eyes were yellow. His broad cheek-bones and narrow chin gave his face something of the viperine V. His head, too, was broad behind and low and narrow at the forehead, as if his brain had been twisted round in the reverse way to a European's. He was short of stature and still shorter of English. In conversation, he made numerous odd noises of no known marketable value, and his infrequent words were carved and wrought into heraldic grotesqueness. Holroyd tried to elucidate his religious beliefs, and – especially after whisky – lectured to him against superstition and missionaries. Azuma-zi, however, shirked the discussion of his gods, even though he was kicked for it.

Azuma-zi had come, clad in white but insufficient raiment, out of the stokehole of the *Lord Clive*, from the Straits Settlements[236] and beyond, into London. He had heard even in his youth of the greatness and riches of London, where all the women are white and fair, and even the beggars in the streets are white, and he arrived, with newly-earned gold coins in his pocket, to worship at the shrine of civilisation. The day of his landing was a dismal one; the sky was dun, and a wind-worried drizzle filtered down to the greasy streets, but he plunged boldly into the delights of Shadwell,[237] and was presently cast up, shattered in health, civilised in costume, penniless and, except in matters of the direst necessity, practically a dumb animal, to toil for James Holroyd and to be bullied by him in the dynamo shed at Camberwell. And to James Holroyd bullying was a labour of love.

There were three dynamos with their engines at Camberwell. The two that had been there since the beginning were small machines; the larger one was new. The smaller machines made a reasonable noise; their straps hummed over the drums, every now and then the brushes buzzed and fizzled, and the air churned steadily, whoo! whoo! whoo! between their poles. One was loose in its foundations and kept the shed vibrating. But the big dynamo drowned these little noises altogether with the sustained drone of its iron core, which somehow set part of the ironwork humming. The place made the visitor's head reel with the throb, throb, throb of the engines, the rotation of the big wheels, the spinning ball-valves, the occasional spittings of the steam, and over all the deep, unceasing, surging note of the big dynamo. This last noise was from an engineering point of view a defect, but Azuma-zi accounted it unto the monster for mightiness and pride.

If it were possible we would have the noises of that shed always about the reader as he reads, we would tell all our story to such an accompaniment. It was a steady stream of din, from which the ear picked out first one thread and then another; there was the inter-mittent snorting, panting and seething of the steam-engines, the suck and thud of their pistons, the dull beat on the air as the spokes of the great driving wheels came round, a note the leather straps made as they ran tighter and looser and a fretful tumult from the dynamos; and over all, sometimes inaudible, as the ear tired of it, and then creeping back upon the senses again, was this trombone note of the big machine. The floor never felt steady and quiet beneath one's feet, but quivered and jarred. It was a confusing, unsteady place, and enough to send anyone's thoughts jerking into odd zigzags. And for three months, while the big strike of the engineers was in progress, Holroyd, who was a blackleg,[238] and Azuma-zi, who was a mere black, were never out of the stir and eddy of it, but slept and fed in the little wooden shanty between the shed and the gates.

Holroyd delivered a theological lecture on the text of his big machine soon after Azuma-zi came. He had to shout to be heard in the din. 'Look at that,' said Holroyd; 'where's your 'eathen idol to match 'im?' And Azuma-zi looked. For a moment Holroyd was inaudible, and then Azuma-zi heard: 'Kill a hundred men. Twelve per cent.[239] on the ordinary shares,' said Holroyd, 'and that's something like a Gord!'

Holroyd was proud of his big dynamo, and expatiated upon its size and power to Azuma-zi until heaven knows what odd currents of thought that and the incessant whirling and shindy set up within the curly black cranium. He would explain in the most graphic manner the dozen or so ways in which a man might be killed by it, and once he gave Azuma-zi a shock as a sample of its quality. After that, in the breathing times of his labour – it was heavy labour, being not only his own, but most of Holroyd's – Azuma-zi would sit and watch the big machine. Now and then the brushes would sparkle and spit blue flashes, at which Holroyd would swear, but all the rest was as smooth and rhythmic as breathing. The band ran shouting over the shaft, and ever behind one as one watched was the complacent thud of the piston. So it lived all day in this big airy shed, with him and Holroyd to wait upon it; not prisoned up and slaving to drive a ship as the other engines he knew – mere captive devils of the British Solomon[240] – had been, but a machine enthroned. Those two smaller dynamos Azuma-zi by force of contrast despised; the large one he privately christened the Lord of the Dynamos. They were fretful and irregular, but the big dynamo was steady. How great it was! How serene and easy in its working! Greater and calmer even than the Buddhas he had seen in Rangoon,[241] and yet not motionless, but living! The great black coils spun, spun, spun, the rings ran round under the brushes, and the deep note of its coil steadied the whole. It affected Azuma-zi queerly.

Azuma-zi was not fond of labour. He would sit about and watch the Lord of the Dynamos while Holroyd went away to persuade the yard porter to get whisky, although his proper place was not in the dynamo shed but behind the engines, and, moreover, if Holroyd caught him skulking he got hit for it with a rod of stout copper wire. He would go and stand close to the colossus and look up at the great leather band running overhead. There was a black patch on the band that came round, and it pleased him somehow among all the clatter to watch this return again and again. Odd thoughts spun with the whirl of it. Scientific people tell us that savages give souls to rocks and trees – and a machine is a thousand times more alive than a rock or a tree. And Azuma-zi was practically a savage still; the veneer of civilisation lay no deeper than his slop suit, his bruises and the coal grime on his face and hands. His father before him had worshipped a meteoric stone; kindred blood, it may be, had splashed the broad wheels of Juggernaut.[242]

He took every opportunity Holroyd gave him of touching and handling the great dynamo that was fascinating him. He polished and cleaned it until the metal parts were blinding in the sun. He felt a mysterious sense of service in doing this. He would go up to it and touch its spinning coils gently. The gods he had worshipped were all far away. The people in London hid their gods.

At last his dim feelings grew more distinct, and took shape in thoughts and at last in acts. When he came into the roaring shed one morning he salaamed to the Lord of the Dynamos, and then when Holroyd was away, he went and whispered to the thundering machine that he was its servant, and prayed it to have pity on him and save him from Holroyd. As he did so a rare gleam of light came in through the open archway of the throbbing machine-shed, and the Lord of the Dynamos, as he whirled and roared, was radiant with pale gold. Then Azuma-zi knew that his service was acceptable to his Lord. After that he did not feel so lonely as he had done, and he had indeed been very much alone in London. And even when his work-time was over, which was rare, he loitered about the shed.

The next time Holroyd maltreated him, Azuma-zi went presently to the Lord of the Dynamos and whispered, 'Thou seest, O my Lord!' and the angry whir of the machinery seemed to answer him. Thereafter it appeared to him that whenever Holroyd came into the shed a different note mingled with the sounds of the dynamo. 'My Lord bides his time,' said Azuma-zi to himself. 'The iniquity of the fool is not yet ripe.' And he waited and watched for the day of reckoning. One day there was evidence of short circuiting, and Holroyd, making an unwary examination – it was in the afternoon – got a rather severe shock. Azuma-zi from behind the engine saw him jump off and curse at the peccant coil.

'He is warned,' said Azuma-zi to himself. 'Surely my Lord is very patient.'

Holroyd had at first initiated his 'nigger' into such elementary conceptions of the dynamo's working as would enable him to take temporary charge of the shed in his absence. But when he noticed the manner in which Azuma-zi hung about the monster he became suspicious. He dimly perceived his assistant was 'up to something', and connecting him with the anointing of the coils with oil[243] that had rotted the varnish in one place, he issued an edict, shouted above the confusion of the machinery, 'Don't 'ee go nigh that big dynamo any more, Pooh-bah, or a'll take thy skin off!' Besides, if it pleased Azuma-zi to be near the big machine, it was plain sense and decency to keep him away from it.

Azuma-zi obeyed at the time, but later he was caught bowing before the Lord of the Dynamos. At which Holroyd twisted his arm and kicked him as he turned to go away. As Azuma-zi presently stood behind the engine and glared at the back of the hated Holroyd, the noises of the machinery took a new rhythm, and sounded like four words in his native tongue.

It is hard to say exactly what madness is. I fancy Azuma-zi was mad. The incessant din and whirl of the dynamo shed may have churned up his little store of knowledge and his big store of superstitious fancy, at last, into something akin to frenzy. At any rate, when the idea of making Holroyd a sacrifice to the Dynamo Fetich [244] was thus suggested to him, it filled him with a strange tumult of exultant emotion.

That night the two men and their black shadows were alone in the shed together. The shed was lit with one big arc-light that winked and flickered purple. The shadows lay black behind the dynamos, the ball governors [245] of the engines whirled from light to darkness, and their pistons beat loud and steady. The world outside seen through the open end of the shed seemed incredibly dim and remote. It seemed absolutely silent too, since the riot of the machinery drowned every external sound. Far away was the black fence of the yard with grey shadowy houses behind, and above was the deep blue sky and the pale little stars. Azuma-zi suddenly walked across the centre of the shed above which the leather bands were running, and went into the shadow by the big dynamo. Holroyd heard a click, and the spin of the armature changed.

'What are you dewin' with that switch?' he bawled in surprise. 'Han't I told you – '

Then he saw the set expression of Azuma-zi's eyes as the Asiatic came out of the shadow towards him.

In another moment the two men were grappling fiercely in front of the great dynamo.

'You coffee-headed fool!' gasped Holroyd, with a brown hand at his throat. 'Keep off those contact rings.' In another moment he was tripped and reeling back upon the Lord of the Dynamos. He instinctively loosened his grip upon his antagonist to save himself from the machine.

The messenger, sent in furious haste from the station to find out what had happened in the dynamo shed, met Azuma-zi at the porter's lodge by the gate. Azuma-zi tried to explain something, but the messenger could make nothing of the black's incoherent English, and hurried on to the shed. The machines were all noisily at work, and nothing seemed to be disarranged. There was, however, a queer smell of singed hair. Then he saw an odd-looking crumpled mass clinging to the front of the big dynamo, and, approaching, recognised the distorted remains of Holroyd.

The man stared and hesitated a moment. Then he saw the face, and shut his eyes convulsively. He turned on his heel before he opened them, so that he should not see Holroyd again, and went out of the shed to get advice and help.

When Azuma-zi saw Holroyd die in the grip of the Great Dynamo he had been a little scared about the consequences of his act. Yet he felt strangely elated, and knew that the favour of the Lord Dynamo was upon him. His plan was already settled when he met the man coming from the station, and the scientific manager who speedily arrived on the scene jumped at the obvious conclusion of suicide. This expert scarcely noticed Azuma-zi, except to ask a few questions. Did he see Holroyd kill himself? Azuma-zi explained that he had been out of sight at the engine furnace until he heard a difference in the noise from the dynamo. It was not a difficult examination, being untinctured by suspicion.

The distorted remains of Holroyd, which the electrician removed from the machine, were hastily covered by the porter with a coffee-stained tablecloth. Somebody, by a happy inspiration, fetched a medical man. The expert was chiefly anxious to get the machine at work again, for seven or eight trains had stopped midway in the stuffy tunnels of the electric railway. Azuma-zi, answering or misunderstanding the questions of the people who had by authority or impudence come into the shed, was presently sent back to the stokehole by the scientific manager. Of course, a crowd collected outside the gates of the yard – a crowd, for no known reason, always hovers for a day or two near the scene of a sudden death in London; two or three reporters percolated somehow into the engine shed, and one even got to Azuma-zi; but the scientific expert cleared them out again, being himself an amateur journalist.

Presently the body was carried away, and public interest departed with it. Azuma-zi remained very quietly at his furnace, seeing over and over again in the coals a figure that wriggled violently and became still. An hour after the murder to anyone coming into the shed it would have looked exactly as if nothing had ever happened there. Peeping presently from his engine-room the black saw the Lord Dynamo spin and whirl beside his little brothers, and the driving-wheels were beating round, and the steam in the pistons went thud, thud, exactly as it had been earlier in the evening. After all, from the mechanical point of view, it had been a most insignificant incident – the mere temporary deflection of a current. But now the slender form and slender shadow of the scientific manager replaced the sturdy outline of Holroyd travelling up and down the lane of light upon the vibrating floor under the straps between the engines and the dynamos.

'Have I not served my Lord?' said Azuma-zi inaudibly, from his shadow, and the note of the great dynamo rang out full and clear. As he looked at the big whirling mechanism, the strange fascination of it that had been a little in abeyance since Holroyd's death, resumed its sway.

Never had Azuma-zi seen a man killed so swiftly and pitilessly. The big humming machine had slain its victim without wavering for a second from its steady beating. It was indeed a mighty god.

The unconscious scientific manager stood with his back to him, scribbling on a piece of paper. His shadow lay at the foot of the monster.

'Was the Lord Dynamo still hungry? His servant was ready.'

Azuma-zi made a stealthy step forward; then stopped. The scientific manager suddenly ceased his writing, walked down the shed to the endmost of the dynamos, and began to examine the brushes.

Azuma-zi hesitated, and then slipped across noiselessly into the shadow by the switch. There he waited. Presently the manager's footsteps could be heard returning. He stopped in his old position, unconscious of the stoker crouching ten feet away from him. Then the big dynamo suddenly fizzled, and in another moment Azuma-zi had sprung out of the darkness upon him.

The scientific manager was gripped round the body and swung towards the big dynamo. Kicking with his knee and forcing his antagonist's head down with his hands, he loosened the grip on his waist and swung round away from the machine. Then the black grasped him again, putting a curly head against his chest, and they swayed and panted as it seemed for an age or so. Then the scientific manager was impelled to catch a black ear in his teeth and bite furiously. The black yelled hideously.

They rolled over on the floor, and the black, who had apparently slipped from the vice of the teeth or parted with some ear – the scientific manager wondered which at the time – tried to throttle him. The scientific manager was making some ineffectual attempts to claw something with his hands and to kick, when the welcome sound of quick footsteps sounded on the floor. The next moment Azuma-zi had left him and darted towards the big dynamo. There was a splutter amid the roar.

The officer of the company who had entered stood staring as Azuma-zi caught the naked terminals in his hands, gave one horrible convulsion, and then hung motionless from the machine, his face violently distorted.

'I'm jolly glad you came in when you did,' said the scientific manager, still sitting on the floor.

He looked at the still quivering figure.

'It's not a nice death to die, apparently – but it is quick.'

The official was still staring at the body. He was a man of slow apprehension.

There was a pause.

The scientific manager got up on his feet rather awkwardly. He ran his fingers along his collar thoughtfully, and moved his head to and fro several times.

'Poor Holroyd! I see now.' Then almost mechanically he went towards the switch in the shadow and turned the current into the railway circuit again. As he did so the singed body loosened its grip upon the machine and fell forward on its face. The core of the dynamo roared out loud and clear, and the armature beat the air.

So ended prematurely the worship of the Dynamo Deity, perhaps the most short-lived of all religions. Yet withal it could at least boast a Martyrdom and a Human Sacrifice.

The Grisly Folk[246]

'Can these bones live?'

Could anything be more dead, more mute and inexpressive to the inexpert eye than the ochreous fragments of bone and the fractured lumps of flint that constitute the first traces of something human in the world? We see them in the museum cases, sorted out in accordance with principles we do not understand, labelled with strange names. Chellean, Mousterian, Solutrian[247] and the like, taken mostly from the places Chelles, La Moustier, Solutre and so forth where the first specimens were found. Most of us stare through the glass at them, wonder vaguely for a moment at that half-savage, half-animal past of our race, and pass on. Primitive man, we say. Flint implements. The mammoth used to chase him. Few of us realise yet how much the subtle indefatigable cross-examination of the scientific worker has been extracting from the evidence of these rusty and obstinate witnesses during the last few years.

One of the most startling results of this recent work is the gradual realisation that great quantities of these flint implements and some of the earlier fragments of bone that used to be ascribed to humanity are the vestiges of creatures, very manlike in many respects, but not, strictly speaking, belonging to the human species. Scientific men call these vanished races man (*Homo*), just as they call lions and tigers cats (*Felis*), but there are the soundest reasons for believing that these earlier so-called men were not of our blood, not our ancestors, but a strange and vanished animal, like us, akin to us, but different from us, as the mammoth was like, and akin to, and yet different from, the elephant. Flint and bone implements are found in deposits of very considerable antiquity; some in our museums may be a million years old or more; but the traces of really human creatures, mentally and anatomically like ourselves, do not go back much earlier than twenty or thirty thousand years ago. True men appeared in Europe then, and we do not know whence they came. These other tool-using, fire-making animals, the things that were like men and yet were not men, passed away before the faces of the true men.

Scientific authorities already distinguish four species of these pseudo-men, and it is probable that we shall learn from time to time of other species. One strange breed made the implements called Chellean. These are chiefly sole-shaped blades of stone found in deposits of perhaps 300,000 or 400,000 years ago. Chellean implements are to be seen in any great museum. They are huge implements, *four or five times as big as those made by any known race of true men*, and they are not ill made. Certainly some creature with an intelligent brain made them. Big clumsy hands must have gripped and used these rocky chunks. But so far only one small fragment of a skeleton of this age has been found, a very massive chinless lower jawbone, with teeth rather *more* specialised than those of men today. We can only guess what strange foreshadowing of the human form once ate with that jaw, and struck at its enemies with those big but not unhandy flint blades. It may have been a tremendous fellow, probably much bigger in the body than a man. It may have been able to take bears by the scruff and the sabre-toothed lion by the throat. We do not know. We have just these great stone blades and that bit of a massive jaw and – the liberty to wonder.

Most fascinating riddle of all these riddles of the ages of ice and hardship before the coming of the true men is the riddle of the Mousterian men, because they were perhaps still living in the world when the true men came wandering into Europe. They lived much later than those unknown Chellean giants. They lived thirty or forty thousand years ago – a yesterday compared with the Chellean time. These Mousterians are also called Neandertalers.[248] Until quite recently it was supposed that they were true men like ourselves. But now we begin to realise that they were different, so different that it is impossible that they can be very close relations of ours.[249] They walked or shambled along with a peculiar slouch, they could not turn their heads up to the sky and their teeth were very different from those of true men. One oddity about them is that in one or two points they were less like apes than we are. The dog tooth, the third tooth from the middle, which is so big in the gorilla, and which in man is pointed and still quite distinct from the other teeth, is not distinct at all in the Neandertaler. He had a very even row of teeth, and his cheek teeth also were very unlike ours, and less like the apes' than ours. He had more face and less brow than true men, but that is not because he had a lesser brain; his brain was as big as a modern man's but it was different, bigger behind and smaller in front, so that probably he thought and behaved differently from us. Perhaps he had a better memory and less reasoning power than real men, or perhaps he had more nervous energy and less intelligence. He had no chin, and the way his jawbones come together below make it very doubtful if he could have used any such sounds in speech as we employ. Probably he did not talk at all. He could not hold a pin between his finger and thumb. The more we learn about this beast-man the stranger he becomes to us and the less like the Australoid savage[250] he was once supposed to be.

And as we realise the want of any close relationship between this ugly, strong, ungainly, manlike animal and mankind, the less likely it becomes that he had a naked skin and hair like ours and the more probable that he was different, and perhaps bristly or hairy in some queer inhuman fashion like the hairy elephant and the woolly rhinoceros who were his contemporaries. Like them he lived in a bleak land on the edge of the snows and glaciers that were even then receding northward. Hairy or grisly, with a big face like a mask, great brow ridges and no forehead, clutching an enormous flint, and running like a baboon with his head forward and not, like a man, with his head up, he must have been a fearsome creature for our forefathers to come upon.

Almost certainly they met, these grisly men and the true men. The true man must have come into the habitat of the Neandertaler, and the two must have met and fought. Someday we may come upon the evidences of this warfare.

Western Europe, which is the only part of the world that has yet been searched with any thoroughness for the remains of early men, was slowly growing warmer age by age; the glaciers that had once covered half the continent were receding, and wide stretches of summer pasture and thin woods of pine and birch were spreading slowly over the once icy land. South Europe then was like northern Labrador today. A few hardy beasts held out amidst the snows; the bears hibernated. With the spring grass and foliage came great herds of reindeer, wild horses, mammoth, elephant and rhinoceros, drifting northward from the slopes of the great warm valley that is now filled up with water – the Mediterranean Sea. It was in those days before the ocean waters broke into the Mediterranean that the swallows and a multitude of other birds acquired the habit of coming north, a habit that nowadays impels them to brave the passage of the perilous seas that flow over and hide the lost secrets of the ancient Mediterranean valleys. The grisly men rejoiced at the return of life, came out of the caves in which they had lurked during the winter, and took their toll of the beasts.

These grisly men must have been almost solitary creatures.

The winter food was too scanty for communities. A male may have gone with a female or so; perhaps they parted in the winter and came together in the summer; when his sons grew big enough to annoy him, the grisly man killed them or drove them off. If he killed them he may have eaten them. If they escaped him they may have returned to kill him. The grisly folk may have had long unreasoning memories and very set purposes.

The true men came into Europe, we know not whence, out of the South. When they appeared in Europe their hands were as clever as ours; they could draw pictures we still admire, they could paint and carve; the implements they made were smaller than the Mousterian ones, far smaller than the Chellean, but better made and more various. They wore no clothes worth speaking of, but they painted themselves and probably they talked. And they came in little bands. They were already more social than the Neandertaler; they had laws and self-restraints; their minds had travelled a long way along that path of adaptation and self-suppression which has led to the intricate mind of man today, with its concealed wishes, its confusions and laughter and fantasies and reveries and dreams. They were already held together, these men, and kept in order by the strange limitations of tabu.

They were still savages, very prone to violence and convulsive in their lusts and desires; but to the best of their poor ability they obeyed laws and customs already immemorably ancient, and they feared the penalties of wrongdoing. We can understand something of what was going on in their minds, those of us who can remember the fears, desires, fancies and superstitions of our childhood. Their moral struggles were ours – in cruder forms. They were our kind. But the grisly folk we cannot begin to understand. We cannot conceive in our different minds the strange ideas that chased one another through those queerly shaped brains. As well might we try to dream and feel as a gorilla dreams and feels.

We can understand how the true men drifted northward from the lost lands of the Mediterranean valley into the high Spanish valleys and the south and centre of France, and so on to what is now England – for there was no Channel then between England and France – and eastward to the Rhineland and over the broad wilderness which is now the North Sea, and the German plain. They would leave the snowy wilderness of the Alps, far higher then and covered with great glaciers, away on their right. These people drifted northward for the very good reason that their kind was multiplying and food diminishing. They would be oppressed by feuds and wars. They had no settled homes; they were accustomed to drift with the seasons; every now and then some band would be pushed by hunger and fear a little farther northward into the unknown.

We can imagine the appearance of a little group of these wanderers, our ancestors, coming over some grassy crest into these northern lands. The time would be late spring or early summer, and they would probably be following up some grazing beasts, a reindeer herd or horses.

By a score of different means our anthropologists have been able to reconstruct the particulars of the appearance and habits of these early pilgrim fathers of mankind.

They would not be a very numerous band, because if they were there would be no reason why they should have been driven northward out of their former roving grounds. Two or three older men of thirty or so, eight or ten women and girls with a few young children, a few lads between fourteen and twenty, might make up the whole community. They would be a brownish brown-eyed people with wavy dark hair; the fairness of the European and the straight blue-black hair of the Chinaman had still to be evolved in the world. The older men would probably lead the band, the women and children would keep apart from the youths and men, fenced off by complex and definite tabus from any close companionship. The leaders would be tracking the herd they were following. Tracking was then the supreme accomplishment of mankind. By signs and traces that would be invisible to any modern civilised eye, they would be reading the story of the previous day's trek of the herd of sturdy little horses ahead of them. They would be so expert that they would go on from one faint sign to another with as little delay as a dog who follows a scent.

The horses they were following were only a little way ahead – so the trackers read the signs – they were numerous and nothing had alarmed them. They were grazing and moving only very slowly. There were no traces of wild dog or other enemies to stampede them. Some elephants were also going north, and twice our human tribe had crossed the spoor of woolly rhinoceros roaming westward.

The tribe travelled light. They were mainly naked, but all of them were painted with white and black and red and yellow ochre. At this distance of time it is difficult to see whether they were tattooed. Probably they were not. The babies and small children were carried by the women on their backs in slings or bags made of animal skins, and perhaps some or all of them wore mantles and loin bands of skin and had pouches and belts of leather. The men had stone-pointed spears, and carried sharpened flints in their hands.

There was no Old Man who was lord and master and father of this particular crowd. Weeks ago the Old Man had been charged and trampled to a jelly by a great bull in the swamp far away. Then two of the girls had been waylaid and carried off by the young men of another larger tribe. It was because of these losses that this remnant was now seeking new hunting grounds.

The landscape that spread before the eyes of this little band as they crested the hill was a bleaker, more desolate and altogether unkempt version of the landscape of western Europe today. About them was a grassy down athwart which a peewit flew with its melancholy cry. Before them stretched a great valley ridged with transverse purple hills over which the April cloud-shadows chased one another. Pinewoods and black heather showed where these hills became sandy, and the valleys were full of brown brushwood, and down their undrained troughs ran a bright green band of peaty swamps and long pools of weedy water. In the valley thickets many beasts lurked unseen, and where the winding streams had cut into the soil there were cliffs and caves. Far away along the northern slopes of the ridge that were now revealed, the wild ponies were to be seen grazing.

At a sign from the two leaders the little straggle of menfolk halted, and a woman who had been chattering in subdued tones to a little girl became silent. The brothers surveyed the wide prospect earnestly.

'Ugh!' said one abruptly and pointed.

'Ugh!' cried his brother.

The eyes of the whole tribe swung round to the pointing finger.

The group became one rigid stare.

Every soul of them stood still, astonishment had turned them into a tense group of statuettes.

Far away down the slope with his body in profile and his head turned towards them, frozen by an equal amazement, stood a hunched grey figure, bigger but shorter than a man. He had been creeping up behind a fold in the ground to peer at the ponies; and suddenly he had turned his eyes and seen the tribe. His head projected like a baboon's. In his hand he carried what seemed to the menfolk a great rock.

For a little while this animal scrutiny held discoverers and discovered motionless. Then some of the women and children began to stir and line out to see the strange creature better. 'Man!' said an old crone of forty. '*Man!*' At the movement of the women the grisly man turned and ran clumsily for a score of yards or so towards a thicket of birch and budding thorn. Then he halted again for a moment to look at the newcomers, waved an arm strangely, and then dashed into cover.

The shadows of the thicket swallowed him up, and by hiding him seemed to make him enormous. It identified itself with him, and watched them with his eyes. Its tree stems became long silvery limbs, and a fallen trunk crouched and stared.

It was still early in the morning, and the leaders of the tribe had hoped to come up with the wild ponies as the day advanced and perhaps cut one off and drive it into difficulties among the bushes and swampy places below, and wound it and follow it up and kill it. Then they would have made a feast, and somewhere down in the valley they would have found water and dry bracken for litter and a fire before night. It had seemed a pleasant and hopeful morning to them until this moment. Now they were disconcerted. This grey figure was as if the sunny morning had suddenly made a horrible and inexplicable grimace.

The whole expedition stood gazing for a time, and then the two leaders exchanged a few words. Waugh, the elder, pointed. Click, his brother, nodded his head. They would go on, but instead of slanting down the slopes towards the thickets they would keep round the ridge.

'Come,' said Waugh, and the little band began to move again. But now it marched in silence. When presently a little boy began a question his mother silenced him by a threat. Everybody kept glancing at the thickets below.

Presently a girl cried out sharply and pointed. All started and stopped short.

There was the grisly thing again. It was running across an open space, running almost on all fours, in joltering leaps. It was hunchbacked and very big and low, a grey hairy wolf-like monster. At times its long arms nearly touched the ground. It was nearer than it had been before. It vanished amidst the bushes again. It seemed to throw itself down among some red dead bracken . . .

Waugh and Click took counsel.

A mile away was the head of the valley where the thickets had their beginning. Beyond stretched the woldy hills,[251] bare of cover. The horses were grazing up towards the sun, and away to the north the backs of a herd of woolly rhinoceros were now visible on a crest – just the ridges of their backs showing like a string of black beads.

If the tribe struck across those grassy spaces, then the lurking prowler would have either to stay behind or come into the open. If he came into the open the dozen youths and men of the tribe would know how to deal with him.

So they struck across the grass. The little band worked round to the head of the valley, and there the menfolk stayed at the crest while the women and children pushed on ahead across the open.

For a time the watchers remained motionless, and then Waugh was moved to gestures of defiance. Click was not to be outdone. There were shouts at the hidden watcher, and then one lad, who was something of a clown, after certain grimaces and unpleasant gestures, obliged with an excellent imitation of the grey thing's lumbering run. At that, scare gave place to hilarity.

In those days laughter was a social embrace. Men could laugh, but there was no laughter in the grisly pre-man who watched and wondered in the shadow. He marvelled. The men rolled about and guffawed and slapped their thighs and one another. Tears ran down their faces.

Never a sign came from the thickets.

'Yahah,' said the menfolk. 'Yahah! Bzzzz. Yahah! Yah!'

They forgot altogether how frightened they had been.

And when Waugh thought the women and children had gone on a sufficient distance, he gave the word for the men to follow them.

In some such fashion it was that men, our ancestors, had their first glimpse of the pre-men of the wilderness of western Europe.

The two breeds were soon to come to closer quarters.

The newcomers were pushing their way into the country of these grisly men. Presently came other glimpses of lurking semi-human shapes and grey forms that ran in the twilight. In the morning Click found long narrow footprints round the camp . . .

Then one day, one of the children, eating those little green thorn-buds that rustic English children speak of as bread and cheese, ventured too far from the others. There was a squeal and a scuffle and a thud, and something grey and hairy made off through the thickets carrying its victim, with Waugh and three of the younger men in hot pursuit. They chased the enemy into a dark gully, very much overgrown. This time it was not a solitary Neandertaler they had to deal with. Out of the bushes a big male came at them to cover the retreat of his mate, and hurled a rock that bowled over the youth it hit like a ninepin, so that thereafter he limped always. But Waugh with his throwing spear got the grey monster in the shoulder, and he halted snarling.

No further sound came from the stolen child.

The female showed herself for a moment up the gully, snarling, blood-stained and horrible, and the menfolk stood about afraid to continue their pursuit, and yet not caring to desist from it. One of them was already hobbling off with his hand to his knee.

How did that first fight go?

Perhaps it went against the men of our race. Perhaps the big Neandertaler male, his mane and beard bristling horribly, came down the gully with a thunderous roar, with a great rock in either hand. We do not know whether he threw those big discs of flint or whether he smote with them. Perhaps it was then that Waugh was killed in the act of running away. Perhaps it was bleak disaster then for the little tribe. Short of two of its members it presently made off over the hills as fast as it could go, keeping together for safety, and leaving the wounded youth far behind to limp along its tracks in lonely terror.

Let us suppose that he got back to the tribe at last – after nightmare hours.

Now that Waugh had gone, Click would become Old Man, and he made the tribe camp that night and build their fire on the high ridges among the heather far away from the thickets in which the grisly folk might be lurking.

The grisly folk thought we knew not how about the menfolk, and the men thought about the grisly folk in such ways as we can understand; they imagined how their enemies might act in this fashion or that, and schemed to circumvent them. It may have been Click who had the first dim idea of getting at the gorge in which the Neandertalers had their lair, from above. For, as we have said, the Neandertaler did not look up. Then the menfolk could roll a great rock upon him or pelt him with burning brands and set the dry bracken alight.

One likes to think of a victory for the human side. This Click we have conjured up had run in panic from the first onset of the grisly male, but as he brooded by the fire that night, he heard again in imagination the cry of the lost girl, and he was filled with rage. In his sleep, the grisly male came to him and Click fought in his dreams and started awake stiff with fury. There was a fascination for him in that gorge in which Waugh had been killed. He was compelled to go back and look again for the grisly beasts, to waylay them in their tracks, and watch them from an ambush. He perceived that the Neandertalers could not climb as easily as the menfolk could climb, nor hear so quickly, nor dodge with the same unexpectedness. These grisly men were to be dealt with as the bears were dealt with, the bears before whom you run and scatter, and then come at again from behind.

But one may doubt if the first human group to come into the grisly land was clever enough to solve the problems of the new warfare. Maybe they turned southward again to the gentler regions from which they had come, and were killed by or mingled with their own brethren again. Maybe they perished altogether in that new land of the grisly folk into which they had intruded. Yet the truth may be that they even held their own and increased. If they died there were others of their kind to follow them and achieve a better fate.

That was the beginning of a nightmare age for the little children of the human tribe. They knew they were watched.

Their steps were dogged. The legends of ogres and man-eating giants that haunt the childhood of the world may descend to us from those ancient days of fear. And for the Neandertalers it was the beginning of an incessant war that could end only in extermination.

The Neandertalers, albeit not so erect and tall as men, were the heavier, stronger creatures, but they were stupid, and they went alone or in twos and threes; the menfolk were swifter, quicker-witted, and more social – when they fought they fought in combination. They lined out and surrounded and pestered and pelted their antagonists from every side. They fought the men of that grisly race as dogs might fight a bear. They shouted to one another what each should do, and the Neandertaler had no speech; he did not understand. They moved too quickly for him and fought too cunningly.

Many and obstinate were the duels and battles these two sorts of men fought for this world in that bleak age of the windy steppes, thirty or forty thousand years ago.[252] The two races were intolerable to each other. They both wanted the caves and the banks by the rivers where the big flints were got. They fought over the dead mammoths that had been bogged in the marshes, and over the reindeer stags that had been killed in the rutting season. When a human tribe found signs of the grisly folk near their cave and squatting place, they had perforce to track them down and kill them; their own safety and the safety of their little ones was only to be secured by that killing. The Neandertalers thought the little children of men fair game and pleasant eating.

How long the grisly folk lived on in that chill world of pines and silver birch between the steppes and the glaciers, after the true menfolk came, we do not know. For ages they may have held out, growing more cunning and dangerous as they became rare. The true men hunted them down by their spoor and by their tracks, and watched for the smoke of their fires, and made food scarce for them.

Great Paladins[253] arose in that forgotten world, men who stood forth and smote the grey man-beast face to face and slew him. They made long spears of wood, hardened by fire at the tips; they raised shields of skin against his mighty blows. They struck at him with stones on cords, and slung them at him with slings. And it was not simply men who withstood the grisly beast but women. They stood over their children; they stood by their men against this eerie thing that was like and yet not like mankind. Unless the *savants* read all the signs awry, it was the women who were the makers of the larger tribes into which human families were already growing in those ancient times. It was the woman's subtle, love-guided wits which protected her sons from the fierce anger of the Old Man, and taught them to avoid his jealousy and wrath, and persuaded him to tolerate them and so have their help against the grisly enemy. It was woman, says Atkinson,[254] in the beginning of things human, who taught the primary tabus, that a son must go aside out of the way of his stepmother, and get himself a wife from another tribe, so as to keep the peace within the family. She came between the fratricides, and was the first peacemaker. Human societies in their beginnings were her work, done against the greater solitariness, the lonely fierceness of the adult male. Through her, men learnt the primary co-operation of sonship and brotherhood. The grisly folk had not learnt even the rudest elements of co-operation, and mankind had already spelt out the alphabet of a unity that may someday comprehend the whole earth. The menfolk kept together by the dozen and by the score. By ones and twos and threes therefore the grisly folk were beset and slain, until there were no more of them left in the world.

Generation after generation, age after age, that long struggle for existence went on between these men who were not quite men and the men, our ancestors, who came out of the south into western Europe. Thousands of fights and hunts, sudden murders and headlong escapes there were amidst the caves and thickets of that chill and windy world between the last age of glaciers and our own warmer time. Until at length the last poor grisly was brought to bay and faced the spears of his pursuers in anger and despair.

What leapings of the heart were there not throughout that long warfare! What moments of terror and triumph! What acts of devotion and desperate wonders of courage! And the strain of the victors was our strain; we are lineally identical with those sun-brown painted beings who ran and fought and helped one another, the blood in our veins glowed in those fights and chilled in those fears of the forgotten past. For it was forgotten. Except perhaps for some vague terrors in our dreaming life and for some lurking element of tradition in the legends and warnings of the nursery, it has gone altogether out of the memory of our race. But nothing is ever completely lost. Seventy or eighty years ago a few curious *savants*[255] began to suspect that there were hidden memories in certain big chipped flints and scraps of bone they found in ancient gravels. Much more recently others have begun to find hints of remote strange experiences in the dreams and odd kinks in modern minds.[256] By degrees these dry bones begin to live again.

This restoration of the past is one of the most astonishing adventures of the human mind. As humanity follows the gropings of scientific men among these ancient vestiges, it is like a man who turns over the yellow pages of some long-forgotten diary, some engagement book of his adolescence. His dead youth lives again. Once more the old excitements stir him, the old happiness returns. But the old passions that once burnt, only warm him now, and the old fears and distresses signify nothing.

A day may come when these recovered memories may grow as vivid as if we in our own persons had been there and shared the thrill and the fear of those primordial days; a day may come when the great beasts of the past will leap to life again in our imaginations, when we shall walk again in vanished scenes, stretch painted limbs we thought were dust, and feel again the sunshine of a million years ago.

The Door in the Wall²⁵⁷

One confidential evening, not three months ago, Lionel Wallace told me this story of the Door in the Wall. And at the time I thought that so far as he was concerned it was a true story.

He told it me with such a direct simplicity of conviction that I could not do otherwise than believe him. But in the morning, in my own flat, I woke to a different atmosphere, and as I lay in bed and recalled the things he had told me, stripped of the glamour of his earnest slow voice, denuded of the focused, shaded table light, the shadowy atmosphere that wrapped about us, and the pleasant bright things, the dessert and glasses and napery of the dinner we had shared, making them for the time a bright little world quite cut off from everyday realities, I saw it all as frankly incredible. 'He was mystifying!' I said, and then: 'How well he did it! . . . It isn't quite the thing I should have expected him, of all people, to do well.'

Afterwards, as I sat up in bed and sipped my morning tea, I found myself trying to account for the flavour of reality that perplexed me in his impossible reminiscences by supposing they did in some way suggest, present, convey – I hardly know which word to use – experiences it was otherwise impossible to tell.

Well, I don't resort to that explanation now. I have got over my intervening doubts. I believe now, as I believed at the moment of telling, that Wallace did to the very best of his ability strip the truth of his secret for me. But whether he himself saw or only thought he saw, whether he himself was the possessor of an inestimable privilege or the victim of a fantastic dream, I cannot pretend to guess. Even the facts of his death, which ended my doubts for ever, throw no light on that. That much the reader must judge for himself.

I forget now what chance comment or criticism of mine moved so reticent a man to confide in me. He was, I think, defending himself against an imputation of slackness and unreliability I had made in relation to a great public movement in which he had disappointed me. But he plunged suddenly. 'I have,' he said, 'a preoccupation –

'I know,' he went on, after a pause that he devoted to the study of his cigar ash, 'I have been negligent. The fact is – it isn't a case of ghosts or apparitions – but – it's an odd thing to tell of, Redmond – I am haunted.

I am haunted by something – that rather takes the light out of things, that fills me with longings . . . '

He paused, checked by that English shyness that so often overcomes us when we would speak of moving or grave or beautiful things. 'You were at St Athelstan's all through,' he said, and for a moment that seemed to me quite irrelevant. 'Well – ' and he paused. Then very haltingly at first, but afterwards more easily, he began to tell of the thing that was hidden in his life, the haunting memory of a beauty and a happiness that filled his heart with insatiable longings that made all the interests and spectacle of worldly life seem dull and tedious and vain to him.

Now that I have the clue to it, the thing seems written visibly in his face. I have a photograph in which that look of detachment has been caught and intensified. It reminds me of what a woman once said of him – a woman who had loved him greatly. 'Suddenly,' she said, 'the interest goes out of him. He forgets you. He doesn't care a rap for you – under his very nose . . . '

Yet the interest was not always out of him, and when he was holding his attention to a thing Wallace could contrive to be an extremely successful man. His career, indeed, is set with successes. He left me behind him long ago; he soared up over my head, and cut a figure in the world that I couldn't cut – anyhow. He was still a year short of forty, and they say now that he would have been in office and very probably in the new Cabinet if he had lived. At school he always beat me without effort – as it were by nature. We were at school together at St Athelstan's College in West Kensington for almost all our school-time. He came into the school as my co-equal, but he left far above me, in a blaze of scholarships and brilliant performance. Yet I think I made a fair average running. And it was at school I heard first of the 'Door in the Wall' that I was to hear of a second time only a month before his death.

To him at least the Door in the Wall was a real door leading through a real wall to immortal realities. Of that I am now quite assured.

And it came into his life early, when he was a little fellow between five and six. I remember how, as he sat making his confession to me with a slow gravity, he reasoned and reckoned the date of it. 'There was,' he said, 'a crimson Virginia creeper in it – all one bright uniform crimson in a clear amber sunshine against a white wall. That came into the impression somehow, though I don't clearly remember how, and there were horse-chestnut leaves upon the clean pavement outside the green door. They were blotched yellow and green, you know, not brown nor dirty, so that they must have been new fallen. I take it that means October. I look out for horse-chestnut leaves every year, and I ought to know.

'If I'm right in that, I was about five years and four months old.'

He was, he said, rather a precocious little boy – he learned to talk at an abnormally early age, and he was so sane and 'old-fashioned',[258] as people say, that he was permitted an amount of initiative that most children scarcely attain by seven or eight. His mother died when he was born, and he was under the less vigilant and authoritative care of a nursery governess. His father was a stern, preoccupied lawyer, who gave him little attention, and expected great things of him. For all his brightness he found life a little grey and dull, I think. And one day he wandered.

He could not recall the particular neglect that enabled him to get away, nor the course he took among the West Kensington roads. All that had faded among the incurable blurs of memory. But the white wall and the green door stood out quite distinctly.

As his memory of that remote childish experience ran, he did at the very first sight of that door experience a peculiar emotion, an attraction, a desire to get to the door and open it and walk in.

And at the same time he had the clearest conviction that either it was unwise or it was wrong of him – he could not tell which – to yield to this attraction. He insisted upon it as a curious thing that he knew from the very beginning – unless memory has played him the queerest trick – that the door was unfastened, and that he could go in as he chose.

I seem to see the figure of that little boy, drawn and repelled. And it was very clear in his mind, too, though why it should be so was never explained, that his father would be very angry if he went through that door.

Wallace described all these moments of hesitation to me with the utmost particularity. He went right past the door, and then with his hands in his pockets, and making an infantile attempt to whistle, strolled right along beyond the end of the wall. There he recalls a number of mean, dirty shops, and particularly that of a plumber and decorator, with a dusty disorder of earthenware pipes, sheet lead, ball taps, pattern books of wallpaper and tins of enamel. He stood pretending to examine these things, and *coveting*, passionately desiring, the green door.

Then he said, he had a gust of emotion. He made a run for it, lest hesitation should grip him again: he went plump with outstretched hand through the green door and let it slam behind him. And so, in a trice, he came into the garden that was to haunt all his life.

It was very difficult for Wallace to give me his full sense of that garden into which he came.

There was something in the very air of it that exhilarated, that gave one a sense of lightness and good happening and well-being; there was something in the sight of it that made all its colour clean and perfect and subtly luminous. In the instant of coming into it one was exquisitely glad – as only in rare moments, and when one is young and joyful, one can be glad in this world. And everything was beautiful there . . .

Wallace mused before he went on telling me. 'You see,' he said, with the doubtful inflection of a man who pauses at incredible things, 'there were two great panthers there . . . Yes, spotted panthers. And I was not afraid. There was a long wide path with marble-edged flower borders on either side, and these two huge velvety beasts were playing there with a ball. One looked up and came towards me, a little curious as it seemed. It came right up to me, rubbed its soft round ear very gently against the small hand I held out and purred. It was, I tell you, an enchanted garden. I know. And the size? Oh! it stretched far and wide, this way and that. I believe there were hills far away. Heaven knows where West Kensington had suddenly got to. And somehow it was just like coming home.

'You know, in the very moment the door swung to behind me, I forgot the road with its fallen chestnut leaves, its cabs and tradesmen's carts, I forgot the sort of gravitational pull back to the discipline and obedience of home, I forgot all hesitations and fear, forgot discretion, forgot all the intimate realities of this life. I became in a moment a very glad and wonder-happy little boy – in another world. It was a world with a different quality, a warmer, more penetrating and mellower light, with a faint clear gladness in its air and wisps of sun-touched cloud in the blueness of its sky. And before me ran this long wide path, invitingly, with weedless beds on either side, rich with untended flowers, and these two great panthers. I put my little hands fearlessly on their soft fur, and caressed their round ears and the sensitive corners under their ears, and played with them, and it was as though they welcomed me home. There was a keen sense of homecoming in my mind, and when presently a tall, fair girl appeared in the pathway and came to meet me, smiling, and said, 'Well?' to me, and lifted me, and kissed me, and put me down, and led me by the hand, there was no amazement, but only an impression of delightful rightness, of being reminded of happy things that had in some strange way been overlooked. There were broad steps, I remember, that came into view between spikes of delphinium, and up these we went to a great avenue between very old and shady dark trees.

All down this avenue, you know, between the red chapped stems, were marble seats of honour and statuary, and very tame and friendly white doves . . .

'And along this avenue my girl-friend led me, looking down – I recall the pleasant lines, the finely-modelled chin of her sweet kind face – asking me questions in a soft, agreeable voice, and telling me things, pleasant things I know, though what they were I was never able to recall . . . And presently a little Capuchin monkey, very clean, with a fur of ruddy brown and kindly hazel eyes, came down a tree to us and ran beside me, looking up at me and grinning, and presently leapt to my shoulder. So we went on our way in great happiness . . . '

He paused.

'Go on,' I said.

'I remember little things. We passed an old man musing among laurels, I remember, and a place gay with parakeets, and came through a broad shaded colonnade to a spacious cool palace, full of pleasant fountains, full of beautiful things, full of the quality and promise of heart's desire. And there were many things and many people, some that still seem to stand out clearly and some that are a little vague, but all these people were beautiful and kind. In some way – I don't know how – it was conveyed to me that they all were kind to me, glad to have me there, and filling me with gladness by their gestures, by the touch of their hands, by the welcome and love in their eyes. Yes – '

He mused for a while. 'Playmates I found there. That was very much to me, because I was a lonely little boy. They played delightful games in a grass-covered court where there was a sundial set about with flowers. And as one played one loved . . .

'But – it's odd – there's a gap in my memory. I don't remember the games we played. I never remembered. Afterwards as a child, I spent long hours trying, even with tears, to recall the form of that happiness. I wanted to play it all over again – in my nursery – by myself. No! All I remember is the happiness and two dear playfellows who were most with me . . . Then presently came a sombre dark woman, with a grave, pale face and dreamy eyes, a sombre woman wearing a soft long robe of pale purple, who carried a book, and beckoned and took me aside with her into a gallery above a hall – though my playmates were loth to have me go, and ceased their game and stood watching as I was carried away. 'Come back to us!' they cried. 'Come back to us soon!' I looked up at her face, but she heeded them not at all. Her face was very gentle and grave. She took me to a seat in the gallery, and I stood beside her, ready to look at her book as she opened it upon her knee. The pages fell open.

She pointed, and I looked, marvelling, for in the living pages of that book I saw myself; it was a story about myself, and in it were all the things that had happened to me since ever I was born . . .

'It was wonderful to me, because the pages of that book were not pictures, you understand, but realities.'

Wallace paused gravely – looked at me doubtfully.

'Go on,' I said. 'I understand.'

'They were realities – yes, they must have been; people moved and things came and went in them; my dear mother, whom I had near forgotten; then my father, stern and upright, the servants, the nursery, all the familiar things of home. Then the front door and the busy streets, with traffic to and fro. I looked and marvelled, and looked half doubtfully again into the woman's face and turned the pages over, skipping this and that, to see more of this book, and more, and so at last I came to myself hovering and hesitating outside the green door in the long white wall, and felt again the conflict and the fear.

' "And next?" I cried, and would have turned on, but the cool hand of the grave woman delayed me.

' "Next?" I insisted, and struggled gently with her hand, pulling up her fingers with all my childish strength, and as she yielded and the page came over she bent down upon me like a shadow and kissed my brow.

'But the page did not show the enchanted garden, nor the panthers, nor the girl who had led me by the hand, nor the playfellows who had been so loth to let me go. It showed a long grey street in West Kensington, on that chill hour of afternoon before the lamps are lit, and I was there, a wretched little figure, weeping aloud, for all that I could do to restrain myself, and I was weeping because I could not return to my dear playfellows who had called after me, "Come back to us! Come back to us soon!" I was there. This was no page in a book, but harsh reality; that enchanted place and the restraining hand of the grave mother at whose knee I stood had gone – whither had they gone?'

He halted again, and remained for a time, staring into the fire.

'Oh! The wretchedness of that return!' he murmured.

'Well?' I said after a minute or so.

'Poor little wretch I was! – Brought back to this grey world again! As I realised the fullness of what had happened to me, I gave way to quite ungovernable grief. And the shame and humiliation of that public weeping and my disgraceful homecoming remain with me still. I see again the benevolent-looking old gentleman in gold spectacles who stopped and spoke to me – prodding me first with his umbrella. "Poor little chap," said he; "and are you lost then? – " and me a London boy of five and more! And he must needs bring in a kindly young policeman and make a crowd of me, and so march me home. Sobbing, conspicuous and frightened, I came from the enchanted garden to the steps of my father's house.

'That is as well as I can remember my vision of that garden – the garden that haunts me still. Of course, I can convey nothing of that indescribable quality of translucent unreality, that *difference* from the common things of experience that hung about it all; but that – that is what happened. If it was a dream, I am sure it was a daytime and altogether extraordinary dream . . . H'm! – Naturally there followed a terrible questioning, by my aunt, my father, the nurse, the governess – everyone . . .

'I tried to tell them, and my father gave me my first thrashing for telling lies. When afterwards I tried to tell my aunt, she punished me again for my wicked persistence. Then, as I said, everyone was forbidden to listen to me, to hear a word about it. Even my fairy-tale books were taken away from me for a time – because I was too "imaginative". Eh? Yes, they did that! My father belonged to the old school . . . And my story was driven back upon myself. I whispered it to my pillow – my pillow that was often damp and salt to my whispering lips with childish tears. And I added always to my official and less fervent prayers this one heartfelt request: "Please God I may dream of the garden. Oh! Take me back to my garden! Take me back to my garden!"

'I dreamt often of the garden. I may have added to it, I may have changed it; I do not know . . . All this, you understand, is an attempt to reconstruct from fragmentary memories a very early experience. Between that and the other consecutive memories of my boyhood there is a gulf. A time came when it seemed impossible I should ever speak of that wonder glimpse again.'

I asked an obvious question.

'No,' he said. 'I don't remember that I ever attempted to find my way back to the garden in those early years. This seems odd to me now, but I think that very probably a closer watch was kept on my movements after this misadventure to prevent my going astray. No, it wasn't until you knew me that I tried for the garden again. And I believe there was a period – incredible as it seems now – when I forgot the garden altogether – when I was about eight or nine it may have been. Do you remember me as a kid at St Athelstan's?'

'Rather!'

'I didn't show any signs, did I, in those days of having a secret dream?'

He looked up with a sudden smile.

'Did you ever play North-West Passage[259] with me . . . ? No, of course, you didn't come my way!

'It was the sort of game,' he went on, 'that every imaginative child plays all day. The idea was the discovery of a North-West Passage to school. The way to school was plain enough; the game consisted in finding some way that wasn't plain, starting off ten minutes early in some almost hopeless direction, and working one's way round through unaccustomed streets to my goal. And one day I got entangled among some rather low-class streets on the other side of Campden Hill,[260] and I began to think that for once the game would be against me and that I should get to school late. I tried rather desperately a street that seemed a cul-de-sac, and found a passage at the end. I hurried through that with renewed hope. "I shall do it yet," I said, and passed a row of frowsy little shops that were inexplicably familiar to me, and behold! there was my long white wall and the green door that led to the enchanted garden!

'The thing whacked upon me suddenly. Then after all, that garden, that wonderful garden, wasn't a dream!'

He paused.

'I suppose my second experience with the green door marks the world of difference there is between the busy life of a schoolboy and the infinite leisure of a child. Anyhow this second time I didn't for a moment think of going in straight away. You see, for one thing my mind was full of the idea of getting to school in time – set on not breaking my record for punctuality. I must surely have felt *some* little desire at least to try the door – yes, I must have felt that . . . But I seem to remember the attraction of the door mainly as another obstacle to my overmastering determination to get to school. I was immediately interested by this discovery I had made, of course – I went on with my mind full of it – but I went on. It didn't check me. I ran past tugging out my watch, found I had ten minutes still to spare, and then I was going downhill into familiar surroundings. I got to school, breathless, it is true, and wet with perspiration, but in time. I can remember hanging up my coat and hat. Went right by it and left it behind me. Odd, eh?'

He looked at me thoughtfully. 'Of course, I didn't know then that it wouldn't always be there. Schoolboys have limited imaginations. I suppose I thought it was an awfully jolly thing to have it there, to know my way back to it, but there was the school tugging at me. I expect I was a good deal distraught and inattentive that morning, recalling what I could of the beautiful strange people I should presently see again. Oddly enough I had no doubt in my mind that they would be glad to see me . . . Yes, I must have thought of the garden that morning just as a jolly sort of place to which one might resort in the interludes of a strenuous scholastic career.

'I didn't go that day at all. The next day was a half-holiday, and that may have weighed with me. Perhaps, too, my state of inattention brought down impositions upon me and docked the margin of time necessary for the detour. I don't know. What I do know is that in the meantime the enchanted garden was so much upon my mind that I could not keep it to myself.

'I told – what was his name – ? A ferrety-looking youngster we used to call Squiff.'

'Young Hopkins,' said I.

'Hopkins it was. I did not like telling him. I had a feeling that in some way it was against the rules to tell him, but I did. He was walking part of the way home with me; he was talkative, and if we had not talked about the enchanted garden we should have talked of something else, and it was intolerable to me to think about any other subject. So I blabbed.

'Well, he told my secret. The next day in the play interval I found myself surrounded by half a dozen bigger boys, half teasing and wholly curious to hear more of the enchanted garden. There was that big Fawcett – you remember him? – and Carnaby and Morley Reynolds. You weren't there by any chance? No, I think I should have remembered if you were . . .

'A boy is a creature of odd feelings. I was, I really believe, in spite of my secret self-disgust, a little flattered to have the attention of these big fellows. I remember particularly a moment of pleasure caused by the praise of Crawshaw – you remember Crawshaw major,[261] the son of Crawshaw the composer? – who said it was the best lie he had ever heard. But at the same time there was a really painful undertow of shame at telling what I felt was indeed a sacred secret. That beast Fawcett made a joke about the girl in green – '

Wallace's voice sank with the keen memory of that shame. 'I pretended not to hear,' he said. 'Well, then Carnaby suddenly called me a young liar and disputed with me when I said the thing was true. I said I knew where to find the green door, could lead them all there in ten minutes. Carnaby became outrageously virtuous, and said I'd have to – and bear out my words or suffer. Did you ever have Carnaby twist your arm? Then perhaps you'll understand how it went with me. I swore my

story was true. There was nobody in the school then to save a chap
from Carnaby, though Crawshaw put in a word or so. Carnaby had
got his game. I grew excited and red-eared, and a little frightened, I
behaved altogether like a silly little chap, and the outcome of it all was
that instead of starting alone for my enchanted garden, I led the way
presently – cheeks flushed, ears hot, eyes smarting, and my soul one
burning misery and shame – for a party of six mocking, curious and
threatening schoolfellows.

'We never found the white wall and the green door . . . '

'You mean – ?'

'I mean I couldn't find it. I would have found it if I could.

'And afterwards when I could go alone I couldn't find it. I never
found it. I seem now to have been always looking for it through my
schoolboy days, but I've never come upon it – again.'

'Did the fellows – make it disagreeable?'

'Beastly . . . Carnaby held a council over me for wanton lying. I
remember how I sneaked home and upstairs to hide the marks of my
blubbering. But when I cried myself to sleep at last it wasn't for Carnaby,
but for the garden, for the beautiful afternoon I had hoped for, for the
sweet friendly women and the waiting playfellows and the game I had
hoped to learn again, that beautiful forgotten game . . .

'I believed firmly that if I had not told . . . I had bad times after that –
crying at night and wool-gathering by day. For two terms I slackened
and had bad reports. Do you remember? Of course you would! It was
you – your beating me in mathematics that brought me back to the
grind again.'

3

For a time my friend stared silently into the red heart of the fire. Then
he said: 'I never saw it again until I was seventeen.

'It leapt upon me for the third time – as I was driving to Paddington[262]
on my way to Oxford and a scholarship. I had just one momentary
glimpse. I was leaning over the apron[263] of my hansom smoking a
cigarette, and no doubt thinking myself no end of a man of the world,
and suddenly there was the door, the wall, the dear sense of unfor-
gettable and still attainable things.

'We clattered by – I too taken by surprise to stop my cab until we
were well past and round a corner. Then I had a queer moment, a
double and divergent movement of my will; I tapped the little door in

the roof of the cab, and brought my arm down to pull out my watch. "Yes, sir!" said the cabman, smartly. "Er – well – it's nothing," I cried. "*My* mistake! We haven't much time! Go on!" And he went on . . .

'I got my scholarship. And the night after I was told of that I sat over my fire in my little upper room, my study in my father's house, with his praise – his rare praise – and his sound counsels ringing in my ears, and I smoked my favourite pipe – the formidable bulldog of adolescence – and thought of that door in the long white wall. "If I had stopped," I thought, "I should have missed my scholarship, I should have missed Oxford – muddled all the fine career before me! I begin to see things better!" I fell musing deeply, but I did not doubt then this career of mine was a thing that merited sacrifice.

'Those dear friends and that clear atmosphere seemed very sweet to me, very fine, but remote. My grip was fixing now upon the world. I saw another door opening – the door of my career.'

He stared again into the fire. Its red lights picked out a stubborn strength in his face for just one flickering moment, and then it vanished again.

'Well', he said and sighed, 'I have served that career. I have done – much work, much hard work. But I have dreamt of the enchanted garden a thousand dreams, and seen its door, or at least glimpsed its door, four times since then. Yes – four times. For a while this world was so bright and interesting, seemed so full of meaning and opportunity, that the half-effaced charm of the garden was by comparison gentle and remote. Who wants to pat panthers on the way to dinner with pretty women and distinguished men? I came down to London from Oxford, a man of bold promise that I have done something to redeem. Something – and yet there have been disappointments . . .

'Twice I have been in love – I will not dwell on that – but once, as I went to someone who, I know, doubted whether I dared to come, I took a short cut at a venture through an unfrequented road near Earl's Court,[264] and so happened on a white wall and a familiar green door. "Odd!" said I to myself, "but I thought this place was on Campden Hill. It's the place I never could find somehow – like counting Stonehenge[265] – the place of that queer daydream of mine." And I went by it intent upon my purpose. It had no appeal to me that afternoon.

'I had just a moment's impulse to try the door, three steps aside were needed at the most – though I was sure enough in my heart that it would open to me – and then I thought that doing so might delay me on the way to that appointment in which I thought my honour was involved. Afterwards I was sorry for my punctuality – I might at least have peeped in I thought, and waved a hand to those panthers, but I knew enough by this time not to seek again belatedly that which is not found by seeking. Yes, that time made me very sorry . . .

'Years of hard work after that and never a sight of the door. It's only recently it has come back to me. With it there has come a sense as though some thin tarnish had spread itself over my world. I began to think of it as a sorrowful and bitter thing that I should never see that door again. Perhaps I was suffering a little from overwork – perhaps it was what I've heard spoken of as the feeling of forty. I don't know. But certainly the keen brightness that makes effort easy has gone out of things recently, and that just at a time – with all these new political developments – when I ought to be working. Odd, isn't it? But I do begin to find life toilsome, its rewards, as I come near them, cheap. I began a little while ago to want the garden quite badly. Yes – and I've seen it three times.'

'The garden?'

'No – The door! And I haven't gone in!'

He leaned over the table to me, with an enormous sorrow in his voice as he spoke. '*Thrice* I have had my chance – *thrice*! If ever that door offers itself to me again, I swore, I will go in out of this dust and heat, out of this dry glitter of vanity, out of these toilsome futilities. I will go and never return. This time I will stay . . . I swore it and when the time came – *I didn't go*.

'Three times in one year have I passed that door and failed to enter. Three times in the last year.'

'The first time was on the night of the snatch division[266] on the Tenants' Redemption Bill, on which the Government was saved by a majority of three. You remember? No one on our side – perhaps very few on the opposite side – expected the end that night. Then the debate collapsed like eggshells. I and Hotchkiss were dining with his cousin at Brentford; we were both unpaired,[267] and we were called up by telephone, and set off at once in his cousin's motor. We got in barely in time, and on the way we passed my wall and door – livid in the moonlight, blotched with hot yellow as the glare of our lamps lit it, but unmistakable. "My God!" cried I. "What?" said Hotchkiss. "Nothing!" I answered, and the moment passed.

' "I've made a great sacrifice," I told the whip as I got in. "They all have," he said, and hurried by.

'I do not see how I could have done otherwise then. And the next occasion was as I rushed to my father's bedside to bid that stern old man farewell. Then, too, the claims of life were imperative. But the third

time was different; it happened a week ago. It fills me with hot remorse
to recall it. I was with Gurker and Ralphs – it's no secret now, you know,
that I've had my talk with Gurker. We had been dining at Frobisher's,
and the talk had become intimate between us. The question of my place
in the reconstructed ministry lay always just over the boundary of the
discussion. Yes – yes. That's all settled. It needn't be talked about yet,
but there's no reason to keep a secret from you . . . Yes – Thanks!
Thanks! But let me tell you my story.

'Then, on that night things were very much in the air. My position
was a very delicate one. I was keenly anxious to get some definite word
from Gurker, but was hampered by Ralphs's presence. I was using the
best power of my brain to keep that light and careless talk not too
obviously directed to the point that concerned me. I had to. Ralphs's
behaviour since has more than justified my caution . . . Ralphs, I knew,
would leave us beyond the Kensington High Street, and then I could
surprise Gurker by a sudden frankness. One has sometimes to resort to
these little devices . . . And then it was that in the margin of my field of
vision I became aware once more of the white wall, the green door,
before us down the road.

'We passed it talking. I passed it. I can still see the shadow of Gurker's
marked profile, his opera hat tilted forward over his prominent nose,
the many folds of his neck wrap going before my shadow and Ralphs's
as we sauntered past.

'I passed within twenty inches of the door. "If I say good-night to
them, and go in," I asked myself, "what will happen?" And I was all a-
tingle for that word with Gurker.

'I could not answer that question in the tangle of my other problems.
"They will think me mad," I thought. "And suppose I vanish now! –
Amazing disappearance of a prominent politician!" That weighed with
me. A thousand inconceivably petty worldlinesses weighed with me in
that crisis.'

Then he turned on me with a sorrowful smile, and speaking slowly;
'Here I am!' he said.

'Here I am!' he repeated, 'and my chance has gone from me. Three
times in one year the door has been offered me – the door that goes into
peace, into delight, into a beauty beyond dreaming, a kindness no man
on earth can know. And I have rejected it, Redmond, and it has gone – '

'How do you know?'

'I know. I know. I am left now to work it out, to stick to the tasks that
held me so strongly when my moments came. You say, I have success –
this vulgar, tawdry, irksome, envied thing. I have it.' He had a walnut

in his big hand. 'If that was my success,' he said, and crushed it, and held it out for me to see.

'Let me tell you something, Redmond. This loss is destroying me. For two months, for ten weeks nearly now, I have done no work at all, except the most necessary and urgent duties. My soul is full of inappeasable regrets. At nights – when it is less likely I shall be recognised – I go out. I wander. Yes. I wonder what people would think of that if they knew. A Cabinet Minister, the responsible head of that most vital of all departments, wandering alone – grieving – sometimes near audibly lamenting – for a door, for a garden!'

4

I can see now his rather pallid face, and the unfamiliar sombre fire that had come into his eyes. I see him very vividly tonight. I sit recalling his words, his tones, and last evening's *Westminster Gazette* [268] still lies on my sofa, containing the notice of his death. At lunch today the club was busy with the riddle of his fate. We talked of nothing else.

They found his body very early yesterday morning in a deep excavation near East Kensington Station.[269] It is one of two shafts that have been made in connection with an extension of the railway southward. It is protected from the intrusion of the public by a hoarding upon the high road, in which a small doorway has been cut for the convenience of some of the workmen who live in that direction. The doorway was left unfastened through a misunderstanding between two gangers, and through it he made his way.

My mind is darkened with questions and riddles.

It would seem he walked all the way from the House that night – he has frequently walked home during the past Session – and so it is I figure his dark form coming along the late and empty streets, wrapped up, intent. And then did the pale electric lights near the station cheat the rough planking into a semblance of white? Did that fatal unfastened door awaken some memory?

Was there, after all, ever any green door in the wall at all?

I do not know. I have told his story as he told it to me. There are times when I believe that Wallace was no more than the victim of the coincidence between a rare but not unprecedented type of hallucination and a careless trap, but that indeed is not my profoundest belief. You may think me superstitious, if you will, and foolish; but, indeed, I am more than half convinced that he had, in truth, an abnormal gift, and a sense, something – I know not what – that in the guise of wall and door offered him an outlet, a secret and peculiar passage of escape into another and altogether more beautiful world. At any rate, you will say, it betrayed him in the end. But did it betray him? There you touch the inmost mystery of these dreamers, these men of vision and the imagination.

We see our world fair and common, the hoarding and the pit. By our daylight standard he walked out of security into darkness, danger and death. But did he see like that?

The Diamond Maker[270]

Some business had detained me in Chancery Lane[271] until nine in the evening, and thereafter, having some inkling of a headache, I was disinclined either for entertainment or further work. So much of the sky as the high cliffs of that narrow canon of traffic left visible spoke of a serene night, and I determined to make my way down to the Embankment, and rest my eyes and cool my head by watching the variegated lights upon the river. Beyond comparison the night is the best time for this place; a merciful darkness hides the dirt of the waters, and the lights of this transitional age, red, glaring orange, gas-yellow and electric white, are set in shadowy outlines of every possible shade between grey and deep purple. Through the arches of Waterloo Bridge a hundred points of light mark the sweep of the Embankment, and above its parapet rise the towers of Westminster,[272] warm grey against the starlight. The black river goes by with only a rare ripple breaking its silence and disturbing the reflections of the lights that swim upon its surface.

'A warm night,' said a voice at my side.

I turned my head, and saw the profile of a man who was leaning over the parapet beside me. It was a refined face, not unhandsome, though pinched and pale enough, and the coat collar turned up and pinned round the throat marked his status in life as sharply as a uniform. I felt I was committed to the price of a bed and breakfast if I answered him.

I looked at him curiously. Would he have anything to tell me worth the money, or was he the common incapable – incapable even of telling his own story? There was a quality of intelligence in his forehead and eyes and a certain tremulousness in his nether lip that decided me.

'Very warm,' said I; 'but not too warm for us here.'

'No,' he said, still looking across the water, 'it is pleasant enough here . . . just now.

'It is good,' he continued after a pause, 'to find anything so restful as this in London. After one has been fretting about business all day, about getting on, meeting obligations and parrying dangers, I do not know what one would do if it were not for such pacific corners.' He spoke with long pauses between the sentences. 'You must know a little of the irksome labour of the world or you would not be here. But I doubt if

you can be so brain-weary and footsore as I am . . . Bah! Sometimes I
doubt if the game is worth the candle. I feel inclined to throw the whole
thing over – name, wealth and position – and take to some modest
trade. But I know if I abandoned my ambition – hardly as she uses me –
I should have nothing but remorse left for the rest of my days.'

He became silent. I looked at him in astonishment. If ever I saw a
man hopelessly hard-up it was the man in front of me. He was ragged
and he was dirty, unshaven and unkempt; he looked as though he had
been left in a dustbin for a week. And he was talking to *me* of the
irksome worries of a large business. I almost laughed outright. Either
he was mad or playing a sorry jest on his own poverty.

'If high aims and high positions,' said I, 'have their drawbacks of hard
work and anxiety, they have their compensations. Influence, the power
of doing good, of assisting those weaker and poorer than ourselves; and
there is even a certain gratification in display.'

My banter under the circumstances was in very vile taste. I spoke on
the spur of the contrast of his appearance and speech. I was sorry even
while I was speaking.

He turned a haggard but very composed face upon me. Said he: 'I
forgot myself. Of course you would not understand.'

He measured me for a moment. 'No doubt it is very absurd. You
will not believe me even when I tell you, so that it is fairly safe to tell
you. And it will be a comfort to tell someone. I really have a big
business in hand, a very big business. But there are troubles just now.
The fact is . . . I make diamonds.'

'I suppose,' said I, 'you are out of work just at present?'

'I am sick of being disbelieved,' he said impatiently, and suddenly
unbuttoning his wretched coat he pulled out a little canvas bag that was
hanging by a cord round his neck. From this he produced a brown
pebble. 'I wonder if you know enough to know what that is?' He handed
it to me.

Now, a year or so ago, I had occupied my leisure in taking a London
science degree, so that I have a smattering of physics and mineralogy.
The thing was not unlike an uncut diamond of the darker sort, though
far too large, being almost as big as the top of my thumb. I took it, and
saw it had the form of a regular octahedron,[273] with the curved faces
peculiar to the most precious of minerals. I took out my penknife and
tried to scratch it – vainly. Leaning forward towards the gas-lamp, I
tried the thing on my watch-glass, and scored a white line across that,
with the greatest ease.

I looked at my interlocutor with rising curiosity. 'It certainly is rather like a diamond. But, if so, it is a Behemoth[274] of diamonds. Where did you get it?'

'I tell you I made it,' he said. 'Give it back to me.'

He replaced it hastily and buttoned his jacket. 'I will sell it to you for one hundred pounds,' he suddenly whispered eagerly. With that my suspicions returned. The thing might, after all, be merely a lump of that almost equally hard substance corundum,[275] with an accidental resemblance in shape to the diamond. Or if it was a diamond, how came he by it, and why should he offer it at a hundred pounds?

We looked into one another's eyes. He seemed eager, but honestly eager. At that moment I believed it was a diamond he was trying to sell. Yet I am a poor man, a hundred pounds would leave a visible gap in my fortunes and no sane man would buy a diamond by gaslight from a ragged tramp on his personal warranty only. Still, a diamond that size conjured up a vision of many thousands of pounds. Then, thought I, such a stone could scarcely exist without being mentioned in every book on gems, and again I called to mind the stories of contraband and light-fingered Kaffirs at the Cape.[276] I put the question of purchase on one side.

'How did you get it?' said I.

'I made it.'

I had heard something of Moissan,[277] but I knew his artificial diamonds were very small. I shook my head.

'You seem to know something of this kind of thing. I will tell you a little about myself. Perhaps then you may think better of the purchase.' He turned round with his back to the river, and put his hands in his pockets. He sighed. 'I know you will not believe me.

'Diamonds,' he began – and as he spoke his voice lost its faint flavour of the tramp and assumed something of the easy tone of an educated man – 'are to be made by throwing carbon out of combination in a suitable flux and under a suitable pressure; the carbon crystallises out, not as black-lead or charcoal-powder, but as small diamonds. So much has been known to chemists for years, but no one yet had hit upon exactly the right flux in which to melt up the carbon, or exactly the right pressure for the best results. Consequently the diamonds made by chemists are small and dark, and worthless as jewels. Now I, you know, have given up my life to this problem – given my life to it.'

'I began to work at the conditions of diamond making when I was seventeen, and now I am thirty-two. It seemed to me that it might take all the thought and energies of a man for ten years, or twenty years, but, even if it did, the game was still worth the candle. Suppose one to have at last just hit the right trick before the secret got out and diamonds became as common as coal, one might realise millions. Millions!'

He paused and looked for my sympathy. His eyes shone hungrily. 'To think,' said he, 'that I am on the verge of it all, and here!

'I had,' he proceeded, 'about a thousand pounds when I was twenty-one, and this, I thought, eked out by a little teaching, would keep my researches going. A year or two was spent in study, at Berlin chiefly, and then I continued on my own account. The trouble was the secrecy. You see, if once I had let out what I was doing, other men might have been spurred on by my belief in the practicability of the idea; and I do not pretend to be such a genius as to have been sure of coming in first, in the case of a race for the discovery. And, you see, it was important that if I really meant to make a pile, people should not know it was an artificial process and capable of turning out diamonds by the ton. So I had to work all alone. At first I had a little laboratory, but as my resources began to run out I had to conduct my experiments in a wretched unfurnished room in Kentish Town,[278] where I slept at last on a straw mattress on the floor among all my apparatus. The money simply flowed away. I grudged myself everything except scientific appliances. I tried to keep things going by a little teaching, but I am not a very good teacher, and I have no university degree, nor very much education except in chemistry, and I found I had to give a lot of time and labour for precious little money. But I got nearer and nearer the thing. Three years ago I settled the problem of the composition of the flux, and got near the pressure by putting this flux of mine and a certain carbon composition into a closed-up gun-barrel, filling up with water, sealing tightly, and heating.'

He paused.

'Rather risky,' said I.

'Yes. It burst, and smashed all my windows and a lot of my apparatus; but I got a kind of diamond powder nevertheless. Following out the problem of getting a big pressure upon the molten mixture from which the things were to crystallise, I hit upon some researches of Daubrée's at the Paris Laboratoire des Poudres et Salpêtres.[279] He exploded dynamite in a tightly screwed steel cylinder, too strong to burst, and I found he could crush rocks into a muck not unlike the South African bed in which diamonds are found. It was a tremendous strain on my resources, but I got a steel cylinder made for my purpose after his pattern. I put in all my stuff and my explosives, built up a fire in my furnace, put the whole concern in, and – went out for a walk.'

I could not help laughing at his matter-of-fact manner. 'Did you not think it would blow up the house? Were there other people in the place?'

'It was in the interest of science,' he said, ultimately. 'There was a costermonger family on the floor below, a begging-letter writer in the room behind mine, and two flower-women were upstairs. Perhaps it was a bit thoughtless. But possibly some of them were out.

'When I came back the thing was just where I had left it, among the white-hot coals. The explosive hadn't burst the case. And then I had a problem to face. You know time is an important element in crystallisation. If you hurry the process the crystals are small – it is only by prolonged standing that they grow to any size. I resolved to let this apparatus cool for two years, letting the temperature go down slowly during the time. And I was now quite out of money; and with a big fire and the rent of my room, as well as my hunger, to satisfy, I had scarcely a penny in the world.

'I can hardly tell you all the shifts I was put to while I was making the diamonds. I have sold newspapers, held horses, opened cab-doors. For many weeks I addressed envelopes. I had a place as assistant to a man who owned a barrow, and used to call down one side of the road while he called down the other.

'Once for a week I had absolutely nothing to do, and I begged. What a week that was! One day the fire was going out and I had eaten nothing all day, and a little chap taking his girl out gave me sixpence – to show-off. Thank heaven for vanity! How the fish-shops smelt! But I went and spent it all on coals, and had the furnace bright red again, and then – Well, hunger makes a fool of a man.

'At last, three weeks ago, I let the fire out. I took my cylinder and unscrewed it while it was still so hot that it punished my hands, and I scraped out the crumbling lava-like mass with a chisel, and hammered it into a powder upon an iron plate. And I found three big diamonds and five small ones. As I sat on the floor hammering, my door opened, and my neighbour, the begging-letter writer, came in. He was drunk – as he usually is. " 'Nerchist,"[280] said he. "You're drunk" said I. " 'Structive scoundrel," said he. "Go to your father," said I, meaning the Father of Lies.[281] "Never you mind," said he, and gave me a cunning wink, and hiccupped, and leaning up against the door, with his other eye against the doorpost, began to babble of how he had been prying in my room, and how he had gone to the police that morning, and how they had taken down everything he had to say – " 'siffiwas a ge'm" [282] said he. Then I suddenly realised I was in a hole. Either I should have to tell these police my little secret, and get the whole thing blown upon, or be lagged as an Anarchist. So I went up to my neighbour and took him by the collar, and rolled him about a bit, and then I gathered up my diamonds and cleared out. The evening newspapers called my den the Kentish-Town Bomb Factory. And now I cannot part with the things for love or money.

'If I go in to respectable jewellers they ask me to wait, and go and whisper to a clerk to fetch a policeman, and then I say I cannot wait. And I found out a receiver of stolen goods, and he simply stuck to the one I gave him and told me to prosecute if I wanted it back. I am going about now with several hundred thousand poundsworth of diamonds round my neck, and without either food or shelter. You are the first person I have taken into my confidence. But I like your face and I am hard-driven.'

He looked into my eyes.

'It would be madness,' said I, 'for me to buy a diamond under the circumstances. Besides, I do not carry hundreds of pounds about in my pocket. Yet I more than half believe your story. I will, if you like, do this: come to my office tomorrow . . . '

'You think I am a thief!' said he keenly. 'You will tell the police. I am not coming into a trap.'

'Somehow I am assured you are no thief. Here is my card. Take that, anyhow. You need not come to any appointment. Come when you will.'

He took the card, and an earnest of my goodwill.

'Think better of it and come,' said I.

He shook his head doubtfully. 'I will pay back your half-crown[283] with interest someday – such interest as will amaze you,' said he. 'Anyhow, you will keep the secret . . . ? Don't follow me.'

He crossed the road and went into the darkness towards the little steps under the archway leading into Essex Street,[284] and I let him go. And that was the last I ever saw of him.

Afterwards I had two letters from him asking me to send banknotes – not cheques – to certain addresses. I weighed the matter over and took what I conceived to be the wisest course. Once he called upon me when I was out. My urchin described him as a very thin, dirty and ragged man, with a dreadful cough. He left no message. That was the finish of him so far as my story goes. I wonder sometimes what has become of him. Was he an ingenious monomaniac, or a fraudulent dealer in pebbles, or has he really made diamonds as he asserted? The latter is just sufficiently credible to make me think at times that I have missed the most brilliant opportunity of my life. He may, of course, be dead, and his diamonds carelessly thrown aside – one, I repeat, was almost as big as my thumb. Or he may be still wandering about trying to sell the things. It is just possible he may yet emerge upon society, and, passing athwart my heavens in the serene altitude sacred to the wealthy and the well-advertised, reproach me silently for my want of enterprise. I sometimes think I might at least have risked five pounds.

Under the Knife[285]

'What if I die under it?' The thought recurred again and again, as I walked home from Haddon's. It was a purely personal question. I was spared the deep anxieties of a married man, and I knew there were few of my intimate friends but would find my death troublesome chiefly on account of their duty of regret. I was surprised indeed, and perhaps a little humiliated, as I turned the matter over, to think how few could possibly exceed the conventional requirement. Things came before me stripped of glamour, in a clear dry light, during that walk from Haddon's house over Primrose Hill.[286] There were the friends of my youth: I perceived now that our affection was a tradition, which we foregathered rather laboriously to maintain. There were the rivals and helpers of my later career: I suppose I had been cold-blooded or undemonstrative – one perhaps implies the other. It may be that even the capacity for friendship is a question of physique. There had been a time in my own life when I had grieved bitterly enough at the loss of a friend; but as I walked home that afternoon the emotional side of my imagination was dormant. I could not pity myself, nor feel sorry for my friends, nor conceive of them as grieving for me.

I was interested in this deadness of my emotional nature – no doubt a concomitant of my stagnating physiology; and my thoughts wandered off along the line it suggested. Once before, in my hot youth, I had suffered a sudden loss of blood, and had been within an ace of death. I remembered now that my affections as well as my passions had drained out of me, leaving scarce anything but a tranquil resignation, a dreg of self-pity.[287] It had been weeks before the old ambitions and tendernesses, and all the complex moral interplay of a man had reasserted themselves. It occurred to me that the real meaning of this numbness might be a gradual slipping away from the pleasure-pain guidance of the animal man. It has been proven, I take it, as thoroughly as anything can be proven in this world, that the higher emotions, the moral feelings, even the subtle unselfishness of love, are evolved from the elemental desires and fears of the simple animal:[288] they are the harness in which man's mental freedom goes. And it may be that as death overshadows us, as our possibility of acting diminishes, this complex growth of balanced impulse, propensity and aversion, whose interplay inspires our acts, goes with it. Leaving what?

I was suddenly brought back to reality by an imminent collision with the butcher-boy's tray. I found that I was crossing the bridge over the Regent's Park Canal, which runs parallel with that in the Zoological Gardens.[289] The boy in blue had been looking over his shoulder at a black barge advancing slowly, towed by a gaunt white horse. In the Gardens a nurse was leading three happy little children over the bridge. The trees were bright green; the spring hopefulness was still unstained by the dusts of summer; the sky in the water was bright and clear, but broken by long waves, by quivering bands of black, as the barge drove through. The breeze was stirring; but it did not stir me as the spring breeze used to do.

Was this dullness of feeling in itself an anticipation? It was curious that I could reason and follow out a network of suggestion as clearly as ever: so at least, it seemed to me. It was calmness rather than dullness that was coming upon me. Was there any ground for the belief in the presentiment of death? Did a man near to death begin instinctively to withdraw himself from the meshes of matter and sense, even before the cold hand was laid upon his? I felt strangely isolated – isolated without regret – from the life and existence about me. The children playing in the sun and gathering strength and experience for the business of life, the park-keeper gossiping with a nursemaid, the nursing mother, the young couple intent upon each other as they passed me, the trees by the wayside spreading new pleading leaves to the sunlight, the stir in their branches – I had been part of it all, but I had nearly done with it now.

Some way down the Broad Walk[290] I perceived that I was tired, and that my feet were heavy. It was hot that afternoon, and I turned aside and sat down on one of the green chairs that line the way. In a minute I had dozed into a dream, and the tide of my thoughts washed up a vision of the resurrection. I was still sitting in the chair, but I thought myself actually dead, withered, tattered, dried, one eye (I saw) pecked out by birds. 'Awake!' cried a voice; and incontinently the dust of the path and the mould under the grass became insurgent. I had never before thought of Regent's Park as a cemetery, but now, through the trees, stretching as far as eye could see, I beheld a flat plain of writhing graves and heeling tombstones. There seemed to be some trouble: the rising dead appeared to stifle as they struggled upward, they bled in their struggles, the red flesh was torn away from the white bones. 'Awake!' cried a voice; but I determined I would not rise to such horrors. 'Awake!' They would not let me alone. 'Wake up!' said an angry voice. A cockney angel! The man who sells the tickets was shaking me, demanding my penny.

I paid my penny, pocketed my ticket, yawned, stretched my legs, and feeling now rather less torpid, got up and walked on towards Langham Place. I speedily lost myself again in a shifting maze of thoughts about death. Going across Marylebone Road into that crescent[291] at the end of Langham Place, I had the narrowest escape from the shaft of a cab, and went on my way with a palpitating heart and a bruised shoulder. It struck me that it would have been curious if my meditations on my death on the morrow had led to my death that day.

But I will not weary you with more of my experiences that day and the next. I knew more and more certainly that I should die under the operation; at times I think I was inclined to pose to myself. At home I found everything prepared; my room cleared of needless objects and hung with white sheets; a nurse installed and already at loggerheads with my housekeeper. They wanted me to go to bed early, and after a little resistance I obeyed.

In the morning I was very indolent, and though I read my newspapers and the letters that came by the first post, I did not find them very interesting. There was a friendly note from Addison, my old school friend, calling my attention to two discrepancies and a printer's error in my new book, with one from Langridge venting some vexation over Minton.[292] The rest were business communications. I breakfasted in bed. The glow of pain at my side seemed more massive. I knew it was pain, and yet, if you can understand, I did not find it very painful. I had been awake and hot and thirsty in the night, but in the morning bed felt comfortable. In the night-time I had lain thinking of things that were past; in the morning I dozed over the question of immortality. Haddon came, punctual to the minute, with a neat black bag; and Mowbray soon followed. Their arrival stirred me up a little. I began to take a more personal interest in the proceedings. Haddon moved the little octagonal table close to the bedside, and, with his broad back to me, began taking things out of his bag. I heard the light click of steel upon steel. My imagination, I found, was not altogether stagnant. 'Will you hurt me much?' I said in an offhand tone.

'Not a bit,' Haddon answered over his shoulder. 'We shall chloroform you. Your heart's as sound as a bell.' And as he spoke, I had a whiff of the pungent sweetness of the anaesthetic.

They stretched me out, with a convenient exposure of my side, and, almost before I realised what was happening, the chloroform was being administered. It stings the nostrils, and there is a suffocating sensation at first. I knew I should die – that this was the end of consciousness for me. And suddenly I felt that I was not prepared for death: I had a vague sense of a duty overlooked – I knew not what. What was it I had not done? I could think of nothing more to do, nothing desirable left in life; and yet I had the strangest disinclination to death. And the physical sensation was painfully oppressive. Of course the doctors did not know they were going to kill me. Possibly I struggled. Then I fell motionless, and a great silence, a monstrous silence, and an impenetrable blackness came upon me.

There must have been an interval of absolute unconsciousness, seconds or minutes. Then with a chilly, unemotional clearness, I perceived that I was not yet dead. I was still in my body; but all the multitudinous sensations that come sweeping from it to make up the background of consciousness had gone, leaving me free of it all. No, not free of it all; for as yet something still held me to the poor stark flesh upon the bed – held me, yet not so closely that I did not feel myself external to it, independent of it, straining away from it. I do not think I saw, I do not think I heard; but I perceived all that was going on, and it was as if I both heard and saw. Haddon was bending over me, Mowbray behind me; the scalpel – it was a large scalpel – was cutting my flesh at the side under the flying ribs. It was interesting to see myself cut like cheese, without a pang, without even a qualm. The interest was much of a quality with that one might feel in a game of chess between strangers. Haddon's face was firm and his hand steady; but I was surprised to perceive (*how* I know not) that he was feeling the gravest doubt as to his own wisdom in the conduct of the operation.

Mowbray's thoughts too, I could see. He was thinking that Haddon's manner showed too much of the specialist. New suggestions came up like bubbles through a stream of frothing meditation, and burst one after another in the little bright spot of his consciousness. He could not help noticing and admiring Haddon's swift dexterity, in spite of his envious quality and his disposition to detract. I saw my liver exposed. I was puzzled at my own condition.[293] I did not feel that I was dead, but I was different in some way from my living self. The grey depression, that had weighed on me for a year or more and coloured all my thoughts, was gone. I perceived and thought without any emotional tint at all. I wondered if everyone perceived things in this way under chloroform, and forgot it again when he came out of it. It would be inconvenient to look into some heads, and not forget.

Although I did not think that I was dead, I still perceived quite clearly that I was soon to die. This brought me back to the consideration of

Haddon's proceedings. I looked into his mind, and saw that he was afraid of cutting a branch of the portal vein.[294] My attention was distracted from details by the curious changes going on in his mind. His consciousness was like the quivering little spot of light which is thrown by the mirror of a galvanometer.[295] His thoughts ran under it like a stream, some through the focus bright and distinct, some shadowy in the half-light of the edge. Just now the little glow was steady; but the least movement on Mowbray's part, the slightest sound from outside, even a faint difference in the slow movement of the living flesh he was cutting, set the light-spot shivering and spinning. A new sense-impression came rushing up through the flow of thoughts; and lo! The light-spot jerked away towards it, swifter than a frightened fish. It was wonderful to think that upon that unstable, fitful thing depended all the complex motions of the man; that for the next five minutes, therefore, my life hung upon its movements. And he was growing more and more nervous in his work. It was as if a little picture of a cut vein grew brighter, and struggled to oust from his brain another picture of a cut falling short of the mark. He was afraid: his dread of cutting too little was battling with his dread of cutting too far.

Then, suddenly, like an escape of water from under a lock-gate, a great uprush of horrible realisation set all his thoughts swirling, and simultaneously I perceived that the vein was cut. He started back with a hoarse exclamation, and I saw the brown-purple blood gather in a swift bead, and run trickling. He was horrified. He pitched the red-stained scalpel on to the octagonal table; and instantly both doctors flung themselves upon me, making hasty and ill-conceived efforts to remedy the disaster. 'Ice!' said Mowbray, gasping. But I knew that I was killed, though my body still clung to me.

I will not describe their belated endeavours to save me, though I perceived every detail. My perceptions were sharper and swifter than they had ever been in life; my thoughts rushed through my mind with incredible swiftness, but with perfect definition. I can only compare their crowded clarity to the effects of a reasonable dose of opium. In a moment it would all be over, and I should be free. I knew I was im-mortal, but what would happen I did not know. Should I drift off presently, like a puff of smoke from a gun, in some kind of half-material body, an attenuated version of my material self? Should I find myself suddenly among the innumerable hosts of the dead, and know the world about me for the phantasmagoria it had always seemed? Should I drift to some spiritualistic seance, and there make foolish, incomprehensible attempts to affect a purblind medium? It was a state of unemotional curiosity, of colourless expectation. And then I realised a growing stress upon me, a feeling as though some huge human magnet was drawing me upward out of my body. The stress grew and grew. I seemed an atom for which monstrous forces were fighting. For one brief, terrible moment sensation came back to me. That feeling of falling headlong which comes in nightmares, that feeling a thousand times intensified, that and a black horror swept across my thoughts in a torrent. Then the two doctors, the naked body with its cut side, the little room, swept away from under me and vanished as a speck of foam vanishes down an eddy.

I was in midair. Far below was the West End of London, receding rapidly – for I seemed to be flying swiftly upward – and, as it receded, passing westward like a panorama. I could see, through the faint haze of smoke, the innumerable roofs chimney-set, the narrow roadways, stippled with people and conveyances, the little specks of squares, and the church steeples like thorns sticking out of the fabric. But it spun away as the earth rotated on its axis, and in a few seconds (as it seemed) I was over the scattered clumps of town about Ealing,[296] the little Thames a thread of blue to the south, and the Chiltern Hills and the North Downs coming up like the rim of a basin, far away and faint with haze. Up I rushed. And at first I had not the faintest conception what this headlong rush upward could mean.

Every moment the circle of scenery beneath me grew wider and wider, and the details of town and field, of hill and valley, got more and more hazy and pale and indistinct, a luminous grey was mingled more and more with the blue of the hills and the green of the open meadows; and a little patch of cloud, low and far to the west, shone ever more dazzlingly white. Above, as the veil of atmosphere between myself and outer space grew thinner, the sky, which had been a fair springtime blue at first, grew deeper and richer in colour, passing steadily through the intervening shades, until presently it was as dark as the blue sky of midnight, and presently as black as the blackness of a frosty star-night, and at last as black as no blackness I had ever beheld. And first one star, and then many, and at last an innumerable host broke out upon the sky: more stars than anyone has ever seen from the face of the earth. For the blueness of the sky in the light of the sun and stars sifted and spread abroad blindingly: there is diffused light even in the darkest skies of winter, and we do not see the stars by day only because of the dazzling irradiation of the sun. But now I saw things – I know not how; assuredly with no mortal eyes – and that defect of bedazzlement blinded me no longer. The sun was incredibly strange and wonderful. The body of it was a disc of blinding white light: not yellowish, as it seems to those who live upon the earth, but livid white, all streaked with scarlet streaks and rimmed about with a fringe of writhing tongues of red fire. And shooting halfway across the heavens from either side of it and brighter than the Milky Way, were two pinions of silver-white, making it look more like those winged globes I have seen in Egyptian sculpture[297] than anything else I can remember upon earth. These I knew for the solar corona,[298] though I had never seen anything of it but a picture during the days of my earthly life.

When my attention came back to the earth again, I saw that it had fallen very far away from me. Field and town were long since indistinguishable, and all the varied hues of the country were merging into a uniform bright grey, broken only by the brilliant white of the clouds that lay scattered in flocculent[299] masses over Ireland and the west of England. For now I could see the outlines of the north of France and Ireland, and all this island of Britain, save where Scotland passed over the horizon to the north, or where the coast was blurred or obliterated by cloud. The sea was a dull grey, and darker than the land; and the whole panorama was rotating slowly towards the east.

All this had happened so swiftly that until I was some thousand miles or so from the earth I had no thought for myself. But now I perceived I had neither hands nor feet, neither parts nor organs, and that I felt neither alarm nor pain. All about me I perceived that the vacancy (for I had already left the air behind) was cold beyond the imagination of man; but it troubled me not. The sun's rays shot through the void, powerless to light or heat until they should strike on matter in their course. I saw things with a serene self-forgetfulness, even as if I were God. And down below there, rushing away from me – countless miles in a second – where a little dark spot on the grey marked the position of London, two doctors were struggling to restore life to the poor hacked and outworn shell I had abandoned. I felt then such release, such serenity as I can compare to no mortal delight I have ever known.

It was only after I had perceived all these things that the meaning of that headlong rush of the earth grew into comprehension. Yet it was so simple, so obvious, that I was amazed at my never anticipating the thing that was happening to me. I had suddenly been cut adrift from matter: all that was material of me was there upon earth, whirling away through space, held to the earth by gravitation, partaking of the earth's inertia, moving in its wreath of epicycles round the sun, and with the sun and the planets on their vast march through space. But the immaterial has no inertia, feels nothing of the pull of matter for matter: where it parts from its garment of flesh, there it remains (so far as space concerns it any longer) immovable in space. I was not leaving the earth: the earth was leaving *me*, and not only the earth but the whole solar system was streaming past. And about me in space, invisible to me, scattered in the wake of the earth upon its journey, there must be an innumerable multitude of souls, stripped like myself of the material, stripped like myself of the passions of the individual and the generous emotions of the gregarious brute, naked intelligences, things of newborn wonder and thought, marvelling at the strange release that had suddenly come on them!

As I receded faster and faster from the strange white sun in the black heavens, and from the broad and shining earth upon which my being had begun, I seemed to grow in some incredible manner vast: vast as regards this world I had left, vast as regards the moments and periods of a human life. Very soon I saw the full circle of the earth, slightly gibbous,[300] like the moon when she nears her full, but very large; and the silvery shape of America was now in the noonday blaze wherein (as it seemed) little England had been basking but a few minutes ago. At first the earth was large, and shone in the heavens, filling a great part of them; but every moment she grew smaller and more distant. As she shrank, the broad moon in its third quarter crept into view over the rim of her disc. I looked for the constellations. Only that part of Aries directly behind the sun and the Lion, which the earth covered, were hidden. I recognised the tortuous, tattered band of the Milky Way with Vega very bright between sun and earth; and Sirius and Orion shone splendid against the unfathomable blackness in the opposite quarter of the heavens. The Pole Star was overhead, and the Great Bear hung over the circle of the earth. And away beneath and beyond the shining corona of the sun were strange groupings of stars I had never seen in my life – notably a dagger-shaped group that I knew for the Southern Cross. All these were no larger than when they had shone on earth, but the little stars that one scarce sees shone now against the setting of black vacancy as brightly as the first-magnitudes had done, while the larger worlds were points of indescribable glory and colour. Aldebaran was a spot of blood-red fire, and Sirius condensed to one point the light of innumerable sapphires. And they shone steadily: they did not scintillate, they were calmly glorious. My impressions had an adamantine hardness and brightness: there was no blurring softness, no atmosphere, nothing but infinite darkness set with the myriads of these acute and brilliant points and specks of light. Presently, when I looked again, the little earth seemed no bigger than the sun, and it dwindled and turned as I looked, until in a second's space (as it seemed to me) it was halved; and so it went on swiftly dwindling. Far away in the opposite direction, a little pinkish pin's head of light, shining steadily, was the planet Mars. I swam motionless in vacancy, and, without a trace of terror or astonishment, watched the speck of cosmic dust we call the world fall away from me.

Presently it dawned upon me that my sense of duration had changed; that my mind was moving not faster but infinitely slower, that between each separate impression there was a period of many days. The moon spun once round the earth as I noted this; and I perceived clearly the motion of Mars in his orbit. Moreover, it appeared as if the time between thought and thought grew steadily greater, until at last a thousand years was but a moment in my perception.

At first the constellations had shone motionless against the black background of infinite space; but presently it seemed as though the group of stars about Hercules and the Scorpion was contracting, while Orion and Aldebaran and their neighbours were scattering apart. Flashing suddenly out of the darkness there came a flying multitude of particles of rock, glittering like dust-specks in a sunbeam, and encompassed in a faintly luminous cloud. They swirled all about me, and vanished again in a twinkling far behind. And then I saw that a bright spot of light, that shone a little to one side of my path, was growing very rapidly larger, and perceived that it was the planet Saturn rushing towards me. Larger and larger it grew, swallowing up the heavens behind it, and hiding every moment a fresh multitude of stars. I perceived its flattened, whirling body, its disc-like belt, and seven of its little satellites. It grew and grew, till it towered enormous; and then I plunged amid a streaming multitude of clashing stones and dancing dust-particles and gas-eddies, and saw for a moment the mighty triple belt like three concentric arches of moonlight above me, its shadow black on the boiling tumult below. These things happened in one-tenth of the time it takes to tell them. The planet went by like a flash of lightning; for a few seconds it blotted out the sun, and there and then became a mere black, dwindling, winged patch against the light. The earth, the mother mote of my being, I could no longer see.

So with a stately swiftness, in the profoundest silence, the solar system fell from me as it had been a garment, until the sun was a mere star amid the multitude of stars, with its eddy of planet-specks lost in the confused glittering of the remoter light. I was no longer a denizen of the solar system: I had come to the Outer Universe; I seemed to grasp and comprehend the whole world of matter. Ever more swiftly the stars closed in about the spot where Antares and Vega had vanished in a phosphorescent haze, until that part of the sky had the semblance of a whirling mass of nebulae, and ever before me yawned vaster gaps of vacant blackness, and the stars shone fewer and fewer. It seemed as if I moved towards a point between Orion's belt and sword; and the void about that region opened vaster and vaster every second, an incredible gulf of nothingness into which I was falling. Faster and ever faster the universe rushed by, a hurry of whirling motes at last, speeding silently into the void. Stars glowing brighter and brighter, with their circling planets catching the light in a ghostly fashion as I neared them, shone out and vanished again into inexistence; faint comets, clusters of meteorites, winking specks of matter, eddying light-points, whizzed past, some perhaps a hundred millions of miles or so from me at most, few nearer, travelling with unimaginable rapidity, shooting constellations, momentary darts of fire, through that black, enormous night. More than anything else it was like a dusty draught, sunbeam-lit. Broader and wider and deeper grew the starless space, the vacant Beyond, into which I was being drawn. At last a quarter of the heavens was black and blank, and the whole headlong rush of stellar universe closed in behind me like a veil of light that is gathered together. It drove away from me like a monstrous jack-o'-lantern[301] driven by the wind. I had come out into the wilderness of space. Ever the vacant blackness grew broader, until the hosts of the stars seemed only like a swarm of fiery specks hurrying away from me, inconceivably remote, and the darkness, the nothingness and emptiness, was about me on every side. Soon the little universe of matter, the cage of points in which I had begun to be, was dwindling, now to a whirling disc of luminous glittering and now to one minute disc of hazy light. In a little while it would shrink to a point, and at last would vanish altogether.

Suddenly feeling came back to me – feeling in the shape of overwhelming terror; such a dread of those dark vastitudes as no words can describe, a passionate resurgence of sympathy and social desire. Were there other souls, invisible to me as I to them, about me in the blackness? Or was I indeed, even as I felt, alone? Had I passed out of being into something that was neither being nor not-being? The covering of the body, the covering of matter, had been torn from me, and the hallucinations of companionship and security. Everything was black and silent. I had ceased to be. I was nothing. There was nothing, save only that infinitesimal dot of light that dwindled in the gulf. I strained myself to hear and see, and for a while there was naught but infinite silence, intolerable darkness, horror and despair.

Then I saw that about the spot of light into which the whole world of matter had shrunk there was a faint glow. And in a band on either side of that the darkness was not absolute. I watched it for ages, as it seemed to me, and through the long waiting the haze grew imperceptibly more distinct. And then about the band appeared an irregular cloud of the faintest, palest brown. I felt a passionate impatience; but the things grew brighter so slowly that they scarce seemed to change. What was unfolding itself? What was this strange reddish dawn in the interminable night of space?

The cloud's shape was grotesque. It seemed to be looped along its lower side into four projecting masses and above it ended in a straight line. What phantom was it? I felt assured I had seen that figure before; but I could not think what, nor where, nor when it was. Then the realisation rushed upon me. *It was a clenched Hand.* I was alone in space, alone with this huge, shadowy Hand, upon which the whole Universe of Matter lay like an unconsidered speck of dust. It seemed as though I watched it through vast periods of time. On the forefinger glittered a ring; and the universe from which I had come was but a spot of light upon the ring's curvature. And the thing that the hand gripped had the likeness of a black rod. Through a long eternity I watched this Hand, with the ring and the rod, marvelling and fearing and waiting helplessly on what might follow. It seemed as though nothing could follow: that I should watch for ever, seeing only the Hand and the thing it held, and understanding nothing of its import. Was the whole universe but a refracting speck upon some greater Being? Were our worlds but the atoms of another universe, and those again of another, and so on through an endless progression? And what was I? Was I indeed immaterial? A vague persuasion of a body gathering about me came into my suspense. The abysmal darkness about the Hand filled with impalpable suggestions, with uncertain, fluctuating shapes.

Came a sound, like the sound of a tolling bell: faint, as if infinitely far; muffled, as though heard through thick swathings of darkness: a deep, vibrating resonance, with vast gulfs of silence between each stroke. And the Hand appeared to tighten on the rod. And I saw far above the Hand, towards the apex of the darkness, a circle of dim phosphorescence, a ghostly sphere whence these sounds came throbbing; and at the last stroke the Hand vanished, for the hour had come, and I heard a noise of many waters. But the black rod remained as a great band across the sky. And then a voice, which seemed to run to the uttermost parts of space, spoke, saying, 'There will be no more pain.'[302]

At that an almost intolerable gladness and radiance rushed in upon me, and I saw the circle shining white and bright, and the rod black and shining, and many things else distinct and clear. And the circle was the face of the clock, and the rod the rail of my bed. Haddon was standing at the foot, against the rail, with a small pair of scissors on his fingers; and the hands of my clock on the mantel over his shoulder were clasped together over the hour of twelve. Mowbray was washing something in a basin at the octagonal table, and at my side I felt a subdued feeling that could scarce be spoken of as pain.

The operation had not killed me. And I perceived, suddenly, that the dull melancholy of half a year was lifted from my mind.

The Sea-Raiders[303]

Until the extraordinary affair at Sidmouth,[304] the peculiar species *Haploteuthis ferox*[305] was known to science only generically, on the strength of a half-digested tentacle obtained near the Azores,[306] and a decaying body, pecked by birds and nibbled by fish, found early in 1896 by Mr Jennings, near Land's End.[307]

In no department of zoological science, indeed, are we quite so much in the dark as with regard to the deep-sea cephalopods.[308] A mere accident, for instance, it was that led to the Prince of Monaco's discovery[309] of nearly a dozen new forms in the summer of 1895, a discovery in which the before-mentioned tentacle was included. It chanced that a cachalot was killed off Terceira[310] by some sperm whalers, and in its last struggles charged almost to the Prince's yacht, missed it, rolled under and died within twenty yards of his rudder. And in its agony it threw up a number of large objects, which the Prince, dimly perceiving they were strange and important, was by a happy expedient able to secure before they sank. He set his screws[311] in motion, and kept them circling in the vortices thus created until a boat could be lowered. And these specimens were whole cephalopods and fragments of cephalopods, some of gigantic proportions, and almost all of them unknown to science!

It would seem, indeed, that these large and agile creatures, living in the middle depths of the sea, must to a large extent for ever remain unknown to us, since under water they are too nimble for nets, and it is only by such rare, unlooked-for accidents that specimens can be obtained. In the case of *Haploteuthis ferox*, for instance, we are still altogether ignorant of its habitat, as ignorant as we are of the breeding-ground of the herring or the seaways of the salmon. And zoologists are altogether at a loss to account for its sudden appearance on our coast. Possibly it was the stress of a hunger migration that drove it hither out of the deep. But it will be, perhaps, better to avoid necessarily inconclusive discussion, and to proceed at once with our narrative.

The first human being to set eyes upon a living *Haploteuthis* – the first human being to survive, that is, for there can be little doubt now that the wave of bathing fatalities and boating accidents that travelled along

the coast of Cornwall and Devon in early May was due to this cause –
was a retired tea-dealer of the name of Fison, who was stopping at a
Sidmouth boarding-house. It was in the afternoon, and he was walking
along the cliff path between Sidmouth and Ladram Bay.[312] The cliffs
in this direction are very high, but down the red face of them in one
place a kind of ladder staircase has been made. He was near this when
his attention was attracted by what at first he thought to be a cluster of
birds struggling over a fragment of food that caught the sunlight and
glistened pinkish-white. The tide was right out, and this object was
not only far below him, but remote across a broad waste of rock reefs
covered with dark seaweed and interspersed with silvery shining tidal
pools. And he was, moreover, dazzled by the brightness of the farther
water.

In a minute, regarding this again, he perceived that his judgement
was in fault, for over this struggle circled a number of birds, jackdaws
and gulls for the most part, the latter gleaming blindingly when the
sunlight smote their wings, and they seemed minute in comparison
with it. And his curiosity was perhaps aroused all the more strongly
because of his first insufficient explanations.

As he had nothing better to do than amuse himself, he decided to
make this object, whatever it was, the goal of his afternoon walk, instead
of Ladram Bay, conceiving it might perhaps be a great fish of some sort,
stranded by some chance, and flapping about in its distress. And so he
hurried down the long steep ladder, stopping at intervals of thirty feet
or so to take breath and scan the mysterious movement.

At the foot of the cliff he was, of course, nearer his object than he had
been; but, on the other hand, it now came up against the incandescent
sky, beneath the sun, so as to seem dark and indistinct. Whatever was
pinkish of it was now hidden by a skerry[313] of weedy boulders. But he
perceived that it was made up of seven rounded bodies, distinct
or connected, and that the birds kept up a constant croaking and
screaming, but seemed afraid to approach it too closely.

Mr Fison, torn by curiosity, began picking his way across the wave-
worn rocks, and finding the wet seaweed that covered them thickly
rendered them extremely slippery, he stopped, removed his shoes and
socks, and rolled his trousers above his knees. His object was, of course,
merely to avoid stumbling into the rocky pools about him, and perhaps
he was rather glad, as all men are, of an excuse to resume, even for a
moment, the sensations of his boyhood. At any rate, it is to this, no
doubt, that he owes his life.

He approached his mark with all the assurance which the absolute security of this country against all forms of animal life gives its inhabitants. The round bodies moved to and fro, but it was only when he surmounted the skerry of boulders I have mentioned that he realised the horrible nature of the discovery. It came upon him with some suddenness.

The rounded bodies fell apart as he came into sight over the ridge, and displayed the pinkish object to be the partially devoured body of a human being, but whether of a man or woman he was unable to say. And the rounded bodies were new and ghastly-looking creatures, in shape somewhat resembling an octopus, with huge and very long and flexible tentacles, coiled copiously on the ground. The skin had a glistening texture, unpleasant to see, like shiny leather. The downward bend of the tentacle-surrounded mouth, the curious excrescence at the bend, the tentacles, and the large intelligent eyes, gave the creatures a grotesque suggestion of a face. They were the size of a fair-sized swine about the body, and the tentacles seemed to him to be many feet in length. There were, he thinks, seven or eight at least of the creatures. Twenty yards beyond them, amid the surf of the now returning tide, two others were emerging from the sea.

Their bodies lay flatly on the rocks, and their eyes regarded him with evil interest; but it does not appear that Mr Fison was afraid, or that he realised that he was in any danger. Possibly his confidence is to be ascribed to the limpness of their attitudes. But he was horrified, of course, and intensely excited and indignant, at such revolting creatures preying upon human flesh. He thought they had chanced upon a drowned body. He shouted to them, with the idea of driving them off, and, finding they did not budge, cast about him, picked up a big rounded lump of rock and flung it at one.

And then, slowly uncoiling their tentacles, they all began moving towards him – creeping at first deliberately, and making a soft purring sound to each other.

In a moment Mr Fison realised that he was in danger. He shouted again, threw both his boots, and started off, with a leap, forthwith. Twenty yards off he stopped and faced about, judging them slow, and behold! The tentacles of their leader were already pouring over the rocky ridge on which he had just been standing!

At that he shouted again, but this time not threatening but a cry of dismay, and began jumping, striding, slipping, wading across the uneven expanse between him and the beach. The tall red cliffs seemed suddenly at a vast distance, and he saw, as though they were creatures in another world, two minute workmen engaged in the repair of the ladder-way, and little suspecting the race for life that was beginning below them. At one time he could hear the creatures splashing in the pools not a dozen feet behind him, and once he slipped and almost fell.

They chased him to the very foot of the cliffs, and desisted only when he had been joined by the workmen at the foot of the ladder-way up the cliff. All three of the men pelted them with stones for a time, and then hurried to the cliff top and along the path towards Sidmouth, to secure assistance and a boat, and to rescue the desecrated body from the clutches of these abominable creatures.

2

And, as if he had not already been in sufficient peril that day, Mr Fison went with the boat to point out the exact spot of his adventure.

As the tide was down, it required a considerable detour to reach the spot, and when at last they came off the ladder-way, the mangled body had disappeared. The water was now running in, submerging first one slab of slimy rock and then another, and the four men in the boat – the workmen, that is, the boatman, and Mr Fison – now turned their attention from the bearings offshore to the water beneath the keel.

At first they could see little below them save a dark jungle of laminaria[314] with an occasional darting fish. Their minds were set on adventure, and they expressed their disappointment freely. But presently they saw one of the monsters swimming through the water seaward, with a curious rolling motion that suggested to Mr Fison the spiring[315] roll of a captive balloon. Almost immediately after, the waving streamers of laminaria were extraordinarily perturbed, parted for a moment, and three of these beasts became darkly visible, struggling for what was probably some fragment of the drowned man. In a moment the copious olive-green ribbons had poured again over this writhing group.

At that all four men, greatly excited, began beating the water with oars and shouting, and immediately they saw a tumultuous movement among the weeds. They desisted to see more clearly, and as soon as the water was smooth, they saw, as it seemed to them, the whole sea bottom among the weeds set with eyes.

'Ugly swine!' cried one of the men. 'Why, there's dozens!'

And forthwith the things began to rise through the water about them. Mr Fison has since described to the writer this startling eruption out of the waving laminaria meadows. To him it seemed to occupy a considerable time, but it is probable that really it was an affair of a few seconds only. For a time nothing but eyes, and then he speaks of tentacles streaming out and parting the weed fronds this way and that. Then these things grew larger, until at last the bottom was hidden by their intercoiling forms, and the tips of tentacles rose darkly here and there into the air above the swell of the waters.

One came up boldly to the side of the boat, and clinging to this with three of its sucker-set tentacles, threw four others over the gunwale, as if with an intention either of oversetting the boat or of clambering into it. Mr Fison at once caught up the boathook, and jabbing furiously at the soft tentacles, forced it to desist. He was struck in the back and almost pitched overboard by the boatman, who was using his oar to resist a similar attack on the other side of the boat. But the tentacles on either side at once relaxed their hold, slid out of sight, and splashed into the water.

'We'd better get out of this,' said Mr Fison, who was trembling violently. He went to the tiller, while the boatman and one of the workmen seated themselves and began rowing. The other workman stood up in the fore part of the boat with the boathook, ready to strike any more tentacles that might appear. Nothing else seems to have been said. Mr Fison had expressed the common feeling beyond amendment. In a hushed, scared mood, with faces white and drawn, they set about escaping from the position into which they had so recklessly blundered.

But the oars had scarcely dropped into the water before dark, tapering, serpentine ropes had bound them and were about the rudder; and creeping up the sides of the boat with a looping motion came the suckers again. The men gripped their oars and pulled, but it was like trying to move a boat in a floating raft of weeds. 'Help here!' cried the boatman, and Mr Fison and the second workman rushed to help lug at the oar.

Then the man with the boathook – his name was Ewan, or Ewen – sprang up with a curse and began striking downward over the side, as far as he could reach, at the bank of tentacles that now clustered along the boat's bottom. And, at the same time, the two rowers stood up to get a better purchase for the recovery of their oars. The boatman handed his to Mr Fison, who lugged desperately, and, meanwhile, the boatman opened a big clasp-knife, and, leaning over the side of the boat, began hacking at the spiralling arms upon the oar shaft.

Mr Fison, staggering with the quivering rocking of the boat, his teeth set, his breath coming short, and the veins starting on his hands as he pulled at his oar, suddenly cast his eyes seaward. And there, not fifty yards off, across the long rollers of the incoming tide, was a large boat standing in towards them, with three women and a little child in it. A boatman was rowing, and a little man in a pink-ribboned straw hat and whites stood in the stern hailing them. For a moment, of course, Mr Fison thought of help, and then he thought of the child. He abandoned his oar forthwith, threw up his arms in a frantic gesture, and screamed to the party in the boat to keep away 'for God's sake!' It says much for the modesty and courage of Mr Fison that he does not seem to be aware that there was any quality of heroism in his action at this juncture. The oar he had abandoned was at once drawn under, and presently reappeared floating about twenty yards away.

At the same moment Mr Fison felt the boat under him lurch violently, and a hoarse scream, a prolonged cry of terror from Hill, the boatman, caused him to forget the party of excursionists altogether. He turned, and saw Hill crouching by the forward rowlock, his face convulsed with terror, and his right arm over the side and drawn tightly down. He gave now a succession of short, sharp cries, 'Oh! Oh! Oh! – Oh!' Mr Fison believes that he must have been hacking at the tentacles below the water-line and have been grasped by them, but of course, it is quite impossible to say now certainly what had happened. The boat was heeling over, so that the gunwale was within ten inches of the water, and both Ewan and the other labourer were striking down into the water, with oar and boathook, on either side of Hill's arm. Mr Fison instinctively placed himself to counterpoise them.

Then Hill, who was a burly, powerful man, made a strenuous effort, and rose almost to a standing position. He lifted his arm, indeed, clean out of the water. Hanging to it was a complicated tangle of brown ropes, and the eyes of one of the brutes that had hold of him, glaring straight and resolute, showed momentarily above the surface. The boat heeled more and more, and the green-brown water came pouring in a cascade over the side. Then Hill slipped and fell with his ribs across the side, and his arm and the mass of tentacles about it splashed back into the water. He rolled over; his boot kicked Mr Fison's knee as that gentleman rushed forward to seize him, but in another moment fresh tentacles had whipped about his waist and neck, and, after a brief, convulsive struggle, in which the boat was nearly capsized, Hill was lugged overboard. The boat righted with a violent jerk that all but sent Mr Fison over the other side and hid the struggle in the water from his eyes.

He stood staggering to recover his balance for a moment, and as he did so he became aware that the struggle and the inflowing tide had carried them close upon the weedy rocks again. Not four yards off a table of rock still rose in rhythmic movements above the in-wash of the tide. In a moment Mr Fison seized the oar from Ewan, gave one vigorous stroke, then dropping it, ran to the bows and leapt. He felt his feet slide over the rock, and by a frantic effort, leapt again towards a further mass. He stumbled over this, came to his knees, and rose again.

'Look out!' cried someone, and a large drab body struck him. He was knocked flat into a tidal pool by one of the workmen, and as he went down he heard smothered, choking cries that he believed at the time came from Hill. Then he found himself marvelling at the shrillness and variety of Hill's voice. Someone jumped over him, and a curving rush of foamy water poured over him, and passed. He scrambled to his feet dripping, and, without looking seaward, ran as fast as his terror would let him shoreward. Before him, over the flat space of scattered rocks, stumbled the two workmen – one a dozen yards in front of the other.

He looked over his shoulder at last, and seeing that he was not pursued, faced about. He was astonished. From the moment of the rising of the cephalopods out of the water he had been acting too swiftly fully to comprehend his actions. Now it seemed to him as if he had suddenly jumped out of an evil dream.

For there were the sky, cloudless and blazing with the afternoon sun, the sea weltering under its pitiless brightness, the soft creamy foam of the breaking water, and the low, long, dark ridges of rock. The righted boat floated, rising and falling gently on the swell about a dozen yards from shore. Hill and the monsters, all the stress and tumult of that fierce fight for life, had vanished as though they had never been.

Mr Fison's heart was beating violently; he was throbbing to the fingertips, and his breath came deep.

There was something missing. For some seconds he could not think clearly enough what this might be. Sun, sky, sea, rocks – what was it? Then he remembered the boatload of excursionists. It had vanished. He wondered whether he had imagined it. He turned, and saw the two workmen standing side by side under the projecting masses of the tall pink cliffs. He hesitated whether he should make one last attempt to save the man Hill. His physical excitement seemed to desert him suddenly and leave him aimless and helpless. He turned shoreward, stumbling and wading towards his two companions.

He looked back again, and there were now two boats floating, and the one farthest out at sea pitched clumsily, bottom upward.

So it was *Haploteuthis ferox* made its appearance upon the Devonshire coast. So far, this has been its most serious aggression. Mr Fison's account, taken together with the wave of boating and bathing casualties to which I have already alluded, and the absence of fish from the Cornish coasts that year, points clearly to a shoal of these voracious deep-sea monsters prowling slowly along the sub-tidal coastline. Hunger migration has, I know, been suggested as the force that drove them hither; but, for my own part, I prefer to believe the alternative theory of Hemsley. Hemsley holds that a pack or shoal of these creatures may have become enamoured of human flesh by the accident of a foundered ship sinking among them, and have wandered in search of it out of their accustomed zone; first waylaying and following ships, and so coming to our shores in the wake of the Atlantic traffic. But to discuss Hemsley's cogent and admirably-stated arguments would be out of place here.

It would seem that the appetites of the shoal were satisfied by the catch of eleven people – for, so far as can be ascertained, there were ten people in the second boat, and certainly these creatures gave no further signs of their presence off Sidmouth that day. The coast between Seaton and Budleigh Salterton was patrolled all that evening and night by four Preventive Service boats,[316] the men in which were armed with harpoons and cutlasses, and as the evening advanced, a number of more or less similarly equipped expeditions, organised by private individuals, joined them. Mr Fison took no part in any of these expeditions.

About midnight excited hails were heard from a boat about a couple of miles out at sea to the south-east of Sidmouth, and a lantern was seen waving in a strange manner to and fro and up and down. The nearer boats at once hurried towards the alarm. The venturesome occupants of the boat, a seaman, a curate and two schoolboys, had actually seen the monsters passing under their boat. The creatures, it seems, like most deep-sea organisms, were phosphorescent, and they had been floating, five fathoms deep or so, like creatures of moonshine through the blackness of the water, their tentacles retracted and as if asleep, rolling over and over, and moving slowly in a wedgelike formation towards the south-east.

These people told their story in gesticulated fragments, as first one boat drew alongside and then another. At last there was a little fleet of eight or nine boats collected together, and from them a tumult, like the chatter of a marketplace, rose into the stillness of the night. There was little or no disposition to pursue the shoal, the people had neither weapons nor experience for such a dubious chase, and presently – even with a certain relief, it may be – the boats turned shoreward.

And now to tell what is perhaps the most astonishing fact in this whole astonishing raid. We have not the slightest knowledge of the subsequent movements of the shoal, although the whole south-west coast was now alert for it. But it may, perhaps, be significant that a cachalot was stranded off Sark[317] on June 3. Two weeks and three days after this Sidmouth affair, a living *Haploteuthis* came ashore on Calais sands. It was alive, because several witnesses saw its tentacles moving in a convulsive way. But it is probable that it was dying. A gentleman named Pouchet obtained a rifle and shot it.

That was the last appearance of a living *Haploteuthis*. No others were seen on the French coast. On the 15th of June a dead carcass, almost complete, was washed ashore near Torquay, and a few days later a boat from the Marine Biological Station, engaged in dredging off Plymouth, picked up a rotting specimen, slashed deeply with a cutlass wound. How the former had come by its death it is impossible to say. And on the last day of June, Mr Egbert Caine, an artist, bathing near Newlyn, threw up his arms, shrieked, and was drawn under. A friend bathing with him made no attempt to save him, but swam at once for the shore. This is the last fact to tell of this extraordinary raid from the deeper sea. Whether it is really the last of these horrible creatures it is, as yet, premature to say. But it is believed, and certainly it is to be hoped, that they have returned now, and returned for good, to the sunless depths of the middle seas, out of which they had so strangely and so mysteriously arisen.

The Purple Pileus[318]

Mr Coombes was sick of life. He walked away from his unhappy home, and, sick not only of his own existence but of everybody else's, turned aside down Gaswork Lane to avoid the town, and, crossing the wooden bridge that goes over the canal to Starling's Cottages, was presently alone in the damp pine woods and out of sight and sound of human habitation. He would stand it no longer. He repeated aloud with blasphemies unusual to him that he would stand it no longer.

He was a pale-faced little man, with dark eyes and a fine and very black moustache. He had a very stiff, upright collar, slightly frayed, that gave him an illusory double chin, and his overcoat (albeit shabby) was trimmed with astrachan.[319] His gloves were a bright brown with black stripes over the knuckles and split at the finger ends. His appearance, his wife had said once in the dear, dead days beyond recall – before he married her, that is – was military. But now she called him – it seems a dreadful thing to tell of between husband and wife, but she called him 'a little grub'. It wasn't the only thing she had called him, either.

The row had arisen about that beastly Jennie again. Jennie was his wife's friend, and, by no invitation of Mr Coombes, she came in every blessed Sunday to dinner, and made a shindy all the afternoon. She was a big, noisy girl, with a taste for loud colours and a strident laugh; and this Sunday she had outdone all her previous intrusions by bringing in a fellow with her, a chap as showy as herself. And Mr Coombes, in a starchy, clean collar and his Sunday frock-coat, had sat dumb and wrathful at his own table, while his wife and her guests talked foolishly and undesirably, and laughed aloud. Well, he stood that, and after dinner (which, 'as usual', was late) what must Miss Jennie do but go to the piano and play banjo tunes,[320] for all the world as if it were a weekday! Flesh and blood could not endure such goings on. They would hear next door, they would hear in the road, it was a public announcement of their disrepute. He had to speak.

He had felt himself go pale, and a kind of rigour had affected his respiration as he delivered himself. He had been sitting on one of the chairs by the window – the new guest had taken possession of the armchair. He turned his head. 'Sun Day!' he said over the collar, in the voice of one who warns. 'Sun Day!' What people call a 'nasty' tone, it was.

Jennie had kept on playing, but his wife, who was looking through some music that was piled on the top of the piano, had stared at him. 'What's wrong now?' she said; 'Can't people enjoy themselves?'

'I don't mind rational 'njoyment, at all,' said little Coombes, 'but I ain't a-going to have weekday tunes playing on a Sunday in this house.'

'What's wrong with my playing now?' said Jennie, stopping and twirling round on the music-stool with a monstrous rustle of flounces.

Coombes saw it was going to be a row, and opened too vigorously, as is common with your timid, nervous men all the world over. 'Steady on with that music-stool!' said he; 'It ain't made for 'eavy-weights.'

'Never you mind about weights,' said Jennie, incensed. 'What was you saying behind my back about my playing?'

'Surely you don't 'old with not having a bit of music on a Sunday, Mr Coombes?' said the new guest, leaning back in the armchair, blowing a cloud of cigarette smoke and smiling in a kind of pitying way. And simultaneously his wife said something to Jennie about, 'Never mind 'im. You go on, Jinny.'

'I do,' said Mr Coombes, addressing the new guest.

'May I arst why?' said the new guest, evidently enjoying both his cigarette and the prospect of an argument. He was, by the by, a lank young man, very stylishly dressed in bright drab,[321] with a white cravat and a pearl and silver pin. It had been better taste to come in a black coat, Mr Coombes thought.

'Because,' began Mr Coombes, 'it don't suit me. I'm a businessman. I 'ave to study my connection. Rational 'njoyment – '

'His connection!' said Mrs Coombes scornfully. 'That's what he's always a-saying. We got to do this, and we got to do that – '

'If you don't mean to study my connection,' said Mr Coombes, 'what did you marry me for?'

'I wonder,' said Jennie, and turned back to the piano.

'I never saw such a man as you,' said Mrs Coombes. 'You've altered all round since we were married. Before – '

Then Jennie began at the tum, tum, tum again.

'Look here!' said Mr Coombes, driven at last to revolt, standing up and raising his voice. 'I tell you I won't have that.' The frock-coat heaved with his indignation.

'No vi'lence, now,' said the long young man in drab, sitting up.

'Who the juice[322] are you?' said Mr Coombes fiercely.

Whereupon they all began talking at once. The new guest said he was

Jennie's 'intended', and meant to protect her, and Mr Coombes said he was welcome to do so anywhere but in his (Mr Coombes's) house; and Mrs Coombes said he ought to be ashamed of insulting his guests, and (as I have already mentioned) that he was getting a regular little grub; and the end was that Mr Coombes ordered his visitors out of the house, and they wouldn't go, and so he said he would go himself. With his face burning and tears of excitement in his eyes, he went into the passage, and as he struggled with his overcoat – his frock-coat sleeves got con-certinaed up his arm – and gave a brush at his silk hat, Jennie began again at the piano, and strummed him insultingly out of the house. Tum, tum, tum. He slammed the shop door so that the house quivered. That, briefly, was the immediate making of his mood. You will perhaps begin to understand his disgust with existence.

As he walked along the muddy path under the firs – it was late October, and the ditches and heaps of fir needles were gorgeous with clumps of fungi – he recapitulated the melancholy history of his marriage. It was brief and commonplace enough. He now perceived with sufficient clearness that his wife had married him out of a natural curiosity and in order to escape from her worrying, laborious and uncertain life in the workroom; and, like the majority of her class, she was far too stupid to realise that it was her duty to cooperate with him in his business. She was greedy of enjoyment, loquacious and socially-minded, and evidently disappointed to find the restraints of poverty still hanging about her. His worries exasperated her, and the slightest attempt to control her proceedings resulted in a charge of 'grumbling'. Why couldn't he be nice – as he used to be? And Coombes was such a harmless little man, too, nourished mentally on *Self-Help*,[323] and with a meagre ambition of self-denial and competition that was to end in a 'sufficiency'. Then Jennie came in as a female Mephistopheles,[324] a gabbling chronicle of 'fellers', and was always wanting his wife to go to theatres, and 'all that'. And in addition were aunts of his wife, and cousins (male and female) to eat up capital, insult him personally, upset business arrangements, annoy good customers, and generally blight his life. It was not the first occasion by many that Mr Coombes had fled his home in wrath and indignation and something like fear, vowing furiously and even aloud that he wouldn't stand it, and so frothing away his energy along the line of least resistance. But never before had he been quite so sick of life as on this particular Sunday afternoon. The Sunday dinner may have had its share in his despair – and the greyness of the sky. Perhaps too, he was beginning to realise his unendurable frustration as a businessman as the consequence of his marriage.

Presently bankruptcy, and after that . . . Perhaps she might have reason to repent when it was too late. And destiny, as I have already intimated, had planted the path through the wood with evil-smelling fungi, thickly and variously planted it, not only on the right side but on the left.

A small shopman is in such a melancholy position if his wife turns out a disloyal partner. His capital is all tied up in his business, and to leave her means to join the unemployed in some strange part of the earth. The luxuries of divorce are beyond him altogether.[325] So that the good old tradition of marriage for better or worse holds inexorably for him, and things work up to tragic culminations. Bricklayers kick their wives to death, and dukes betray theirs; but it is among the small clerks and shopkeepers nowadays that it comes most often to a cutting of throats. Under the circumstances it is not so very remarkable – and you must take it as charitably as you can – that the mind of Mr Coombes ran for a while on some such glorious close to his disappointed hopes, and that he thought of razors, pistols, breadknives and touching letters to the coroner denouncing his enemies by name, and praying piously for forgiveness. After a time his fierceness gave way to melancholia. He had been married in this very overcoat, in his first and only frock-coat that was buttoned up beneath it. He began to recall their courting along this very walk, his years of penurious saving to get capital, and the bright hopefulness of his marrying days. For it all to work out like this! Was there no sympathetic ruler anywhere in the world? He reverted to death as a topic.

He thought of the canal he had just crossed, and doubted whether he shouldn't stand with his head out, even in the middle, and it was while drowning was in his mind that the purple pileus caught his eye. He looked at it mechanically for a moment, and stopped and stooped towards it to pick it up, under the impression that it was some such small leather object as a purse. Then he saw that it was the purple top of a fungus, a peculiarly poisonous-looking purple: slimy, shiny and emitting a sour odour. He hesitated with his hand an inch or so from it, and the thought of poison crossed his mind. With that he picked the thing, and stood up again with it in his hand.

The odour was certainly strong – acrid, but by no means disgusting. He broke off a piece, and the fresh surface was a creamy white that changed like magic in the space of ten seconds to a yellowish-green colour. It was even an inviting-looking change. He broke off two other pieces to see it repeated. They were wonderful things these fungi, thought Mr Coombes, and all of them the deadliest poisons, as his father had often told him. Deadly poisons!

There is no time like the present for a rash resolve. Why not here and now? thought Mr Coombes. He tasted a little piece, a very little piece indeed – a mere crumb. It was so pungent that he almost spat it out again, then merely hot and full-flavoured. A kind of German mustard with a touch of horseradish and – well, mushroom. He swallowed it in the excitement of the moment. Did he like it or did he not? His mind was curiously careless. He would try another bit. It really wasn't bad – it was good. He forgot his troubles in the interest of the immediate moment. Playing with death it was. He took another bite, and then deliberately finished a mouthful. A curious tingling sensation began in his fingertips and toes. His pulse began to move faster. The blood in his ears sounded like a mill-race. 'Try bi' more,' said Mr Coombes. He turned and looked about him, and found his feet unsteady. He saw, and struggled towards, a little patch of purple a dozen yards away. 'Jol' goo' stuff,' said Mr Coombes. 'E – lomore ye'.'[326] He pitched forward and fell on his face, his hands outstretched towards the cluster of pilei. But he did not eat any more of them. He forgot forthwith.

He rolled over and sat up with a look of astonishment on his face. His carefully brushed silk hat had rolled away towards the ditch. He pressed his hand to his brow. Something had happened, but he could not rightly determine what it was. Anyhow, he was no longer dull – he felt bright, cheerful.[327] And his throat was afire. He laughed in the sudden gaiety of his heart. Had he been dull? He did not know; but at any rate he would be dull no longer. He got up and stood unsteadily, regarding the universe with an agreeable smile. He began to remember. He could not remember very well, because of a steam roundabout that was beginning in his head. And he knew he had been disagreeable at home, just because they wanted to be happy. They were quite right; life should be as gay as possible. He would go home and make it up, and reassure them. And why not take some of this delightful toadstool with him, for them to eat? A hatful, no less. Some of those red ones with white spots as well, and a few yellow.[328] He had been a dull dog, an enemy to merriment; he would make up for it. It would be gay to turn his coat-sleeves inside out, and stick some yellow gorse into his waistcoat pockets. Then home – singing – for a jolly evening.

After the departure of Mr Coombes, Jennie discontinued playing, and turned round on the music-stool again. 'What a fuss about nothing!' said Jennie.

'You see, Mr Clarence, what I've got to put up with,' said Mrs Coombes.

'He is a bit hasty,' said Mr Clarence judicially.

'He ain't got the slightest sense of our position,' said Mrs Coombes; 'that's what I complain of. He cares for nothing but his old shop; and if I have a bit of company, or buy anything to keep myself decent, or get any little thing I want out of the housekeeping money, there's disagreeables. "Economy", he says; "struggle for life", and all that. He lies awake of nights about it, worrying how he can screw me out of a shilling.[329] He wanted us to eat Dorset butter[330] once. If once I was to give in to him – there!'

'Of course,' said Jennie.

'If a man values a woman,' said Mr Clarence, lounging back in the armchair, 'he must be prepared to make sacrifices for her. For my own part,' said Mr Clarence, with his eye on Jennie, 'I shouldn't think of marrying till I was in a position to do the thing in style. It's downright selfishness. A man ought to go through the rough-and-tumble by himself, and not drag her – '

'I don't agree altogether with that,' said Jennie. 'I don't see why a man shouldn't have a woman's help, provided he doesn't treat her meanly, you know. It's meanness – '

'You wouldn't believe,' said Mrs Coombes. 'But I was a fool to 'ave 'im. I might 'ave known. If it 'adn't been for my father, we shouldn't 'ave 'ad not a carriage to our wedding.'

'Lord! He didn't stick out at that?' said Mr Clarence, quite shocked.

'Said he wanted the money for his stock, or some such rubbish. Why, he wouldn't have a woman in to help me once a week if it wasn't for my standing out plucky. And the fusses he makes about money – comes to me, well, pretty near crying, with sheets of paper and figgers. "If only we can tide over this year," he says, "the business is bound to go." "If only we can tide over this year," I says; "then it'll be, if only we can tide over next year. I know you," I says. "And you don't catch me screwing myself lean and ugly. Why didn't you marry a slavey?" I says, "if you wanted one – instead of a respectable girl," I says.'

So Mrs Coombes. But we will not follow this unedifying conversation further. Suffice it that Mr Coombes was very satisfactorily disposed of, and they had a snug little time round the fire. Then Mrs Coombes went to get the tea, and Jennie sat coquettishly on the arm of Mr Clarence's chair until the tea-things clattered outside. 'What was that I heard?' asked Mrs Coombes playfully, as she entered, and there was badinage about kissing. They were just sitting down to the little circular table when the first intimation of Mr Coombes's return was heard.

This was a fumbling at the latch of the front door.

' 'Ere's my lord,' said Mrs Coombes. 'Went out like a lion and comes back like a lamb, I'll lay.'[331]

Something fell over in the shop: a chair, it sounded like. Then there was a sound as of some complicated step exercise in the passage. Then the door opened and Coombes appeared. But it was Coombes trans-figured. The immaculate collar had been torn carelessly from his throat. His carefully-brushed silk hat, half-full of a crush of fungi, was under one arm; his coat was inside out, and his waistcoat adorned with bunches of yellow-blossomed furze. These little eccentricities of Sunday costume, however, were quite overshadowed by the change in his face; it was livid white, his eyes were unnaturally large and bright, and his pale blue lips were drawn back in a cheerless grin. 'Merry!' he said. He had stopped dancing to open the door. 'Rational 'njoyment. Dance.' He made three fantastic steps into the room, and stood bowing.

'Jim!' shrieked Mrs Coombes, and Mr Clarence sat petrified, with a dropping lower jaw.

'Tea,' said Mr Coombes. 'Jol' thing, tea. Tose-stools, too. Brosher.'[332]

'He's drunk,' said Jennie in a weak voice. Never before had she seen this intense pallor in a drunken man, or such shining, dilated eyes.

Mr Coombes held out a handful of scarlet agaric to Mr Clarence. 'Jo' stuff,' said he; 'ta' some.'

At that moment he was genial. Then at the sight of their startled faces he changed, with the swift transition of insanity, into overbearing fury. And it seemed as if he had suddenly recalled the quarrel of his departure. In such a huge voice as Mrs Coombes had never heard before, he shouted, 'My house. I'm master 'ere. Eat what I give yer!' He bawled this, as it seemed, without an effort, without a violent gesture, standing there as motionless as one who whispers, holding out a handful of fungus.

Clarence approved himself a coward. He could not meet the mad fury in Coombes's eyes; he rose to his feet, pushing back his chair, and turned, stooping. At that Coombes rushed at him. Jennie saw her opportunity and, with the ghost of a shriek, made for the door. Mrs Coombes followed her. Clarence tried to dodge. Over went the tea-table with a smash as Coombes clutched him by the collar and tried to thrust the fungus into his mouth. Clarence was content to leave his collar behind him, and shot out into the passage with red patches of fly agaric still adherent to his face. 'Shut 'im in!' cried Mrs Coombes, and would have closed the door, but her supports deserted her; Jennie saw the shop door open, and vanished thereby, locking it behind her, while Clarence went on hastily into the kitchen. Mr Coombes came heavily against the door, and Mrs Coombes, finding the key was inside, fled upstairs and locked herself in the spare bedroom.

So the new convert to *joie de vivre*[333] emerged upon the passage, his decorations a little scattered, but that respectable hatful of fungi still under his arm. He hesitated at the three ways, and decided on the kitchen. Whereupon Clarence, who was fumbling with the key, gave up the attempt to imprison his host, and fled into the scullery, only to be captured before he could open the door into the yard. Mr Clarence is singularly reticent of the details of what occurred. It seems that Mr Coombes's transitory irritation had vanished again, and he was once more a genial playfellow. And as there were knives and meat choppers about, Clarence very generously resolved to humour him and so avoid anything tragic. It is beyond dispute that Mr Coombes played with Mr Clarence to his heart's content; they could not have been more playful and familiar if they had known each other for years. He insisted gaily on Clarence trying the fungi and, after a friendly tussle, was smitten with remorse at the mess he was making of his guest's face. It also appears that Clarence was dragged under the sink and his face scrubbed with the blacking brush – he being still resolved to humour the lunatic at any cost – and that finally, in a somewhat dishevelled, chipped and discoloured condition, he was assisted to his coat and shown out by the back door, the shopway being barred by Jennie. Mr Coombes's wandering thoughts then turned to Jennie. Jennie had been unable to unfasten the shop door, but she shot the bolts against Mr Coombes's latchkey, and remained in possession of the shop for the rest of the evening.

It would appear that Mr Coombes then returned to the kitchen, still in pursuit of gaiety, and, albeit a strict Good Templar,[334] drank (or spilt down the front of the first and only frock-coat) no less than five bottles of the stout Mrs Coombes insisted upon having for her health's sake. He made cheerful noises by breaking off the necks of the bottles with several of his wife's wedding-present dinner-plates, and during the earlier part of this great drunk he sang divers merry ballads. He cut his finger rather badly with one of the bottles – the only bloodshed in this story – and, what with that and the systematic convulsion of his inexperienced physiology by the liquorice brand of Mrs Coombes's stout, it may be the evil of the fungus poison was somehow allayed. But we prefer to draw a veil over the concluding incidents of this Sunday afternoon. They ended in the coal cellar, in a deep and healing sleep.

*

An interval of five years elapsed. Again it was a Sunday afternoon in October, and again Mr Coombes walked through the pine wood beyond the canal. He was still the same dark-eyed, black-moustached little man that he was at the outset of the story, but his double chin was now scarcely so illusory as it had been. His overcoat was new, with a velvet lapel, and a stylish collar with turn-down corners, free of any coarse starchiness, had replaced the original all-round article. His hat was glossy, his gloves newish – though one finger had split and been carefully mended. And a casual observer would have noticed about him a certain rectitude of bearing, a certain erectness of head that marks the man who thinks well of himself. He was a master now, with three assistants. Beside him walked a larger sunburnt parody of himself, his brother Tom, just back from Australia. They were recapitulating their early struggles, and Mr Coombes had just been making a financial statement.

'It's a very nice little business, Jim,' said brother Tom. 'In these days of competition you're jolly lucky to have worked it up so. And you're jolly lucky, too, to have a wife who's willing to help like yours does.'

'Between ourselves,' said Mr Coombes, 'it wasn't always so. It wasn't always like this. To begin with, the missus was a bit giddy. Girls are funny creatures.'

'Dear me!'

'Yes. You'd hardly think it, but she was downright extravagant, and always having slaps at me. I was a bit too easy and loving, and all that, and she thought the whole blessed show was run for her. Turned the 'ouse into a regular caravanserai,[335] always having her relations and girls from business in, and their chaps. Comic songs a' Sunday, it was getting to, and driving trade away. And she was making eyes at the chaps, too! I tell you, Tom, the place wasn't my own.'

'Shouldn't 'a' thought it.'

'It was so. Well – I reasoned with her. I said, "I ain't a duke, to keep a wife like a pet animal. I married you for 'elp and company." I said, "You got to 'elp and pull the business through." She wouldn't 'ear of it. "Very well," I says; "I'm a mild man till I'm roused," I says, "and it's getting to that." But she wouldn't 'ear of no warnings.'

'Well?'

'It's the way with women. She didn't think I 'ad it in me to be roused. Women of her sort (between ourselves, Tom) don't respect a man until they're a bit afraid of him. So I just broke out to show her. In comes a girl named Jennie, that used to work with her, and her chap. We 'ad a bit of a row, and I came out 'ere – it was just such another day as this – and I thought it all out. Then I went back and pitched into them.'

'You did?'

'I did. I was mad, I can tell you. I wasn't going to 'it 'er if I could 'elp it, so I went back and licked into this chap, just to show 'er what I could do. 'E was a big chap, too. Well, I chucked him, and smashed things about, and gave 'er a scaring, and she ran up and locked 'erself into the spare room.'

'Well?'

'That's all. I says to 'er the next morning, 'Now you know,' I says, 'what I'm like when I'm roused.' And I didn't have to say anything more.'

'And you've been happy ever after, eh?'

'So to speak. There's nothing like putting your foot down with them. If it 'adn't been for that afternoon I should 'a' been tramping the roads now, and she'd 'a' been grumbling at me, and all her family grumbling for bringing her to poverty – I know their little ways. But we're all right now. And it's a very decent little business, as you say.'

They proceeded on their way meditatively.

'Women are funny creatures,' said brother Tom.

'They want a firm hand,' said Coombes.

'What a lot of these funguses there are about here!' remarked brother Tom presently. 'I can't see what use they are in the world.'

Mr Coombes looked. 'I dessay they're sent for some wise purpose,' said Mr Coombes.

And that was as much thanks as the purple pileus ever got for maddening this absurd little man to the pitch of decisive action, and so altering the whole course of his life.

The Truth about Pyecraft [336]

He sits not a dozen yards away. If I glance over my shoulder I can see him. And if I catch his eye – and usually I catch his eye – it meets me with an expression –

It is mainly an imploring look – and yet with suspicion in it.

Confound his suspicion! If I wanted to tell on him I should have told long ago. I don't tell and I don't tell, and he ought to feel at his ease. As if anything so gross and fat as he could feel at ease! Who would believe me if I did tell?

Poor old Pyecraft! Great, uneasy jelly of substance! The fattest club-man in London.

He sits at one of the little club tables in the huge bay by the fire, stuffing. What is he stuffing? I glance judiciously and catch him biting at a round of hot buttered teacake, with his eyes on me. Confound him! – With his eyes on me!

That settles it, Pyecraft! Since you *will* be abject, since you *will* behave as though I was not a man of honour, here, right under your embedded eyes, I write the thing down – the plain truth about Pyecraft. The man I helped, the man I shielded, and who has requited me by making my club unendurable, absolutely unendurable, with his liquid appeal, with the perpetual 'don't tell' of his looks.

And, besides, why does he keep on eternally eating?

Well, here goes for the truth, the whole truth, and nothing but the truth! [337]

Pyecraft . . . I made the acquaintance of Pyecraft in this very smoking-room. I was a young, nervous new member, and he saw it. I was sitting all alone, wishing I knew more of the members, and suddenly he came, a great rolling front of chins and abdomina, towards me; and grunted and sat down in a chair close by me and wheezed for a space, and scraped for a space with a match and lit a cigar, and then addressed me. I forget what he said – something about the matches not lighting properly, and after-wards as he talked he kept stopping the waiters one by one as they went by, and telling them about the matches in that thin, fluty voice he has. But, anyhow, it was in some such way we began our talking.

He talked about various things and came round to games. And thence to my figure and complexion. 'You ought to be a good cricketer,' he said.[338] I suppose I am slender, slender to what some people would call lean, and I suppose I am rather dark, still – I am not ashamed of having a Hindu great-grandmother, but for all that, I don't want casual strangers to see through me at a glance to *her*. So that I was set against Pyecraft from the beginning.

But he only talked about me in order to get to himself.

'I expect,' he said, 'you take no more exercise than I do, and probably you eat no less.' (Like all excessively obese people he fancied he ate nothing.) 'Yet' – and he smiled an oblique smile – 'we differ.'

And then he began to talk about his fatness and his fatness; all he did for his fatness and all he was going to do for his fatness; what people had advised him to do for his fatness and what he had heard of people doing for fatness similar to his. '*A priori*,'[339] he said, 'one would think a question of nutrition could be answered by dietary and a question of assimilation by drugs.' It was stifling. It was dumpling talk. It made me feel swelled to hear him.

One stands that sort of thing once in a way at a club, but a time came when I fancied I was standing too much. He took to me altogether too conspicuously. I could never go into the smoking-room but he would come wallowing towards me, and sometimes he came and gormandised round and about me while I had my lunch. He seemed at times almost to be clinging to me. He was a bore, but not so fearful a bore as to be limited to me; and from the first there was something in his manner – almost as though he knew, almost as though he penetrated to the fact that I *might* – that there was a remote, exceptional chance in me that no one else presented.

'I'd give anything to get it down,' he would say – 'anything,' and peer at me over his vast cheeks and pant. Poor old Pyecraft! He has just gonged,[340] no doubt to order another buttered teacake!

He came to the actual thing one day. 'Our Pharmacopoeia,'[341] he said, 'our Western Pharmacopoeia, is anything but the last word of medical science. In the East, I've been told – '

He stopped and stared at me. It was like being at an aquarium.

I was quite suddenly angry with him. 'Look here,' I said, 'who told you about my great-grandmother's recipes?'

'Well – ' he fenced.

'Every time we've met for a week,' I said – 'and we've met pretty often – you've given me a broad hint or so about that little secret of mine.'

'Well,' he said, 'now the cat's out of the bag, I'll admit, yes, it is so. I had it – '

'From Pattison?'

'Indirectly,' he said, which I believe was lying, 'yes.'

'Pattison,' I said, 'took that stuff at his own risk.'

He pursed his mouth and bowed.

'My great-grandmother's recipes,' I said, 'are queer things to handle. My father was near making me promise – '

'He didn't?'

'No. But he warned me. He himself used one – once.'

'Ah! . . . But do you think – ? Suppose – suppose there did happen to be one – '

'The things are curious documents,' I said. 'Even the smell of 'em . . . No!'

But after going so far Pyecraft was resolved I should go farther. I was always a little afraid if I tried his patience too much he would fall on me suddenly and smother me. I own I was weak. But I was also annoyed with Pyecraft. I had got to that state of feeling for him that disposed me to say, 'Well, *take* the risk!' The little affair of Pattison to which I have alluded was a different matter altogether. What it was doesn't concern us now, but I knew, anyhow, that the particular recipe I used then was safe. The rest I didn't know so much about, and, on the whole, I was inclined to doubt their safety pretty completely.

Yet even if Pyecraft got poisoned –

I must confess the poisoning of Pyecraft struck me as an immense undertaking.

That evening I took that queer, odd-scented sandalwood box out of my safe and turned the rustling skins over. The gentleman who wrote the recipes for my great-grandmother evidently had a weakness for skins of a miscellaneous origin, and his handwriting was cramped to the last degree. Some of the things are quite unreadable to me – though my family, with its Indian Civil Service associations, has kept up a knowledge of Hindustani from generation to generation – and none are absolutely plain sailing. But I found the one that I knew was there, soon enough, and sat on the floor by my safe for some time looking at it.

'Look here,' said I to Pyecraft next day, and snatched the slip away from his eager grasp.

'So far as I can make it out, this is a recipe for Loss of Weight.' ('Ah!' said Pyecraft.) 'I'm not absolutely sure, but I think it's that. And if you take my advice you'll leave it alone. Because, you know – I blacken my blood in your interest, Pyecraft – my ancestors on that side were, so far as I can gather, a jolly queer lot. See?'

'Let me try it,' said Pyecraft.

I leant back in my chair. My imagination made one mighty effort and fell flat within me. 'What in heaven's name, Pyecraft,' I asked, 'do you think you'll look like when you get thin?'

He was impervious to reason. I made him promise never to say a word to me about his disgusting fatness again whatever happened – never, and then I handed him that little piece of skin.

'It's nasty stuff,' I said.

'No matter,' he said, and took it.

He goggled at it. 'But – but – ' he said.

He had just discovered that it wasn't English.

'To the best of my ability,' I said, 'I will do you a translation.'

I did my best. After that we didn't speak for a fortnight. Whenever he approached me I frowned and motioned him away, and he respected our compact, but at the end of a fortnight he was as fat as ever. And then he got a word in.

'I must speak,' he said. 'It isn't fair. There's something wrong. It's done me no good. You're not doing your great-grandmother justice.'

'Where's the recipe?'

He produced it gingerly from his pocketbook.

I ran my eye over the items. 'Was the egg addled?'[342] I asked.

'No, ought it to have been?'

'That,' I said, 'goes without saying in all my poor dear great-grandmother's recipes. When condition or quality is not specified you must get the worst. She was drastic or nothing . . . And there's one or two possible alternatives to some of these other things. You got *fresh* rattlesnake venom.'

'I got a rattlesnake from Jamrach's.[343] It cost – it cost – '

'That's your affair, anyhow. This last item – '

'I know a man who – '

'Yes. H'm. Well, I'll write the alternatives down. So far as I know the language, the spelling of this recipe is particularly atrocious. By the by, dog here probably means pariah dog.'[344]

For a month after that I saw Pyecraft constantly at the club and as fat and anxious as ever. He kept our treaty, but at times he broke the spirit of it by shaking his head despondently. Then one day in the cloakroom he said, 'Your great-grandmother – '

'Not a word against her,' I said; and he held his peace.

I could have fancied he had desisted, and I saw him one day talking to three new members about his fatness as though he was in search of other recipes. And then, quite unexpectedly, his telegram came.

'Mr Formalyn!'[345] bawled a pageboy under my nose, and I took the telegram and opened it at once.

'*For heaven's sake come – Pyecraft.*'

'H'm,' said I, and to tell the truth I was so pleased at the rehabilitation of my great-grandmother's reputation this evidently promised that I made a most excellent lunch.

I got Pyecraft's address from the hall porter. Pyecraft inhabited the upper half of a house in Bloomsbury, and I went there so soon as I had done my coffee and Trappistine.[346] I did not wait to finish my cigar.

'Mr Pyecraft?' said I, at the front door.

They believed he was ill; he hadn't been out for two days.

'He expects me,' said I, and they sent me up.

I rang the bell at the lattice-door upon the landing.

'He shouldn't have tried it, anyhow,' I said to myself. 'A man who eats like a pig ought to look like a pig.'

An obviously worthy woman, with an anxious face and a carelessly placed cap, came and surveyed me through the lattice.

I gave my name and she let me in a dubious fashion.

'Well?' said I, as we stood together inside Pyecraft's piece of the landing.

' 'E said you was to come in if you came,' she said, and regarded me, making no motion to show me anywhere. And then, confidentially, ' 'E's locked in, sir.'

'Locked in?'

'Locked himself in yesterday morning and 'asn't let anyone in since, sir. And ever and again *swearing*. Oh, my!'

I stared at the door she indicated by her glances.

'In there?' I said.

'Yes, sir.'

'What's up?'

She shook her head sadly, ' 'E keeps on calling for vittles,[347] sir. 'Eavy vittles 'e wants. I get 'im what I can. Pork 'e's 'ad, sooit puddin', sossiges, noo bread. Everythink like that. Left outside, if you please, and me go away. 'E's eatin', sir, somethink *awful*.'

There came a piping bawl from inside the door: 'That Formalyn?'

'That you, Pyecraft?' I shouted, and went and banged the door.

'Tell her to go away.'

I did.

Then I could hear a curious pattering upon the door, almost like someone feeling for the handle in the dark, and Pyecraft's familiar grunts.

'It's all right,' I said, 'she's gone.'

But for a long time the door didn't open.

I heard the key turn. Then Pyecraft's voice said, 'Come in.'

I turned the handle and opened the door. Naturally I expected to see Pyecraft.

Well, you know, he wasn't there!

I never had such a shock in my life. There was his sitting-room in a state of untidy disorder, plates and dishes among the books and writing things, and several chairs overturned, but Pyecraft –

'It's all right, o' man; shut the door,' he said, and then I discovered him.

There he was right up close to the cornice in the corner by the door, as though someone had glued him to the ceiling. His face was anxious and angry. He panted and gesticulated. 'Shut the door,' he said. 'If that woman gets hold of it – '

I shut the door, and went and stood away from him and stared.

'If anything gives way and you tumble down,' I said, 'you'll break your neck, Pyecraft.'

'I wish I could,' he wheezed.

'A man of your age and weight getting up to kiddish gymnastics – '

'Don't,' he said, and looked agonised. 'Your damned great-grand-mother – '

'Be careful,' I warned him.

'I'll tell you,' he said, and gesticulated.

'How the deuce,' said I, 'are you holding on up there?'

And then abruptly I realised that he was not holding on at all, that he was floating up there – just as a gas-filled bladder might have floated in the same position. He began a struggle to thrust himself away from the ceiling and to clamber down the wall to me. 'It's that prescription,' he panted, as he did so. 'Your great-gran – '

'*No!*' I cried.

He took hold of a framed engraving rather carelessly as he spoke and it gave way, and he flew back to the ceiling again, while the picture smashed on to the sofa. Bump he went against the ceiling, and I knew then why he was all over white on the more salient curves and angles of his person. He tried again more carefully, coming down by way of the mantel.

It was really a most extraordinary spectacle, that great, fat, apoplectic-looking man upside down and trying to get from the ceiling to the floor. 'That prescription,' he said. 'Too successful.'

'How?'

'Loss of weight – almost complete.'

And then, of course, I understood.

'By Jove, Pyecraft,' said I, 'what you wanted was a cure for fatness! But you always called it weight. You would call it weight.'

Somehow I was extremely delighted. I quite liked Pyecraft for the time. 'Let me help you!' I said, and took his hand and pulled him down. He kicked about, trying to get a foothold somewhere. It was very like holding a flag on a windy day.

'That table,' he said, pointing, 'is solid mahogany and very heavy. If you can put me under that – '

I did, and there he wallowed about like a captive balloon, while I stood on his hearthrug and talked to him.

I lit a cigar. 'Tell me,' I said, 'what happened?'

'I took it,' he said.

'How did it taste?'

'Oh, *beastly*!'

I should fancy they all did. Whether one regards the ingredients or the probable compound or the possible results, almost all of my great-grandmother's remedies appear to me at least to be extraordinarily uninviting. For my own part –

'I took a little sip first.'

'Yes?'

'And as I felt lighter and better after an hour, I decided to take the draught.'

'My dear Pyecraft!'

'I held my nose,' he explained. 'And then I kept on getting lighter and lighter – and helpless, you know.'

He gave way to a sudden burst of passion. 'What the goodness am I to do?' he said.

'There's one thing pretty evident,' I said, 'that you mustn't do. If you go out of doors, you'll go up and up.' I waved an arm upward. 'They'd have to send Santos-Dumont[348] after you to bring you down again.'

'I suppose it will wear off?'

I shook my head. 'I don't think you can count on that,' I said.

And then there was another burst of passion, and he kicked out at adjacent chairs and banged the floor. He behaved just as I should have expected a great, fat, self-indulgent man to behave under trying circum-stances – that is to say, very badly. He spoke of me and my great-grandmother with an utter want of discretion.

'I never asked you to take the stuff,' I said.

And, generously disregarding the insults he was putting upon me, I sat down in his armchair and began to talk to him in a sober, friendly fashion.

I pointed out to him that this was a trouble he had brought upon himself, and that it had almost an air of poetical justice. He had eaten too much. This he disputed, and for a time we argued the point.

He became noisy and violent, so I desisted from this aspect of his lesson. 'And then,' said I, 'you committed the sin of euphuism. You called it, not Fat, which is just and inglorious, but Weight. You – '

He interrupted to say he recognised all that. What was he to *do*?

I suggested he should adapt himself to his new conditions. So we came to the really sensible part of the business. I suggested that it would not be difficult for him to learn to walk about on the ceiling with his hands –

'I can't sleep,' he said.

But that was no great difficulty. It was quite possible, I pointed out, to make a shake-up under a wire mattress, fasten the under things on with tapes, and have a blanket, sheet and coverlet to button at the side. He would have to confide in his housekeeper, I said; and after some squabbling he agreed to that. (Afterwards it was quite delightful to see the beautifully matter-of-fact way with which the good lady took all these amazing inversions.) He could have a library ladder in his room, and all his meals could be laid on the top of his bookcase. We also hit on an ingenious device by which he could get to the floor whenever he wanted, which was simply to put the *British Encyclopaedia* (tenth edition)[349] on the top of his open shelves. He just pulled out a couple of volumes and held on, and down he came. And we agreed there must be iron staples along the skirting, so that he could cling to those whenever he wanted to get about the room on the lower level.

As we got on with the thing I found myself almost keenly interested. It was I who called in the housekeeper and broke matters to her, and it was I chiefly who fixed up the inverted bed. In fact, I spent two whole days at his flat. I am a handy, interfering sort of man with a screwdriver, and I made all sorts of ingenious adaptations for him – ran a wire to bring his bells within reach, turned all his electric lights up instead of down, and so on. The whole affair was extremely curious and interesting to me, and it was delightful to think of Pyecraft like some great, fat blowfly, crawling about on his ceiling and clambering round the lintels of his doors from one room to another, and never, never, never coming to the club any more . . .

Then, you know, my fatal ingenuity got the better of me. I was sitting by his fire drinking his whisky, and he was up in his favourite corner by the cornice, tacking a Turkey carpet to the ceiling, when the idea struck me. 'By Jove, Pyecraft!' I said, 'all this is totally unnecessary.'

And before I could calculate the complete consequences of my notion I blurted it out. 'Lead underclothing,' said I, and the mischief was done.

Pyecraft received the thing almost in tears. 'To be right ways up again – ' he said.

I gave him the whole secret before I saw where it would take me. 'Buy sheet lead,' I said, 'stamp it into discs. Sew 'em all over your under-clothes until you have enough. Have lead-soled boots, carry a bag of solid lead, and the thing is done! Instead of being a prisoner here you may go abroad again, Pyecraft; you may travel – '

A still happier idea came to me. 'You need never fear a shipwreck. All you need do is just slip off some or all of your clothes, take the necessary amount of luggage in your hand, and float up in the air – '

In his emotion he dropped the tack-hammer within an ace of my head. 'By Jove!' he said, 'I shall be able to come back to the club again.'

The thing pulled me up short. 'By Jove!' I said faintly. 'Yes. Of course – you will.'

He did. He does. There he sits behind me now, stuffing – as I live – ! A third go of buttered teacake. And no one in the whole world knows – except his housekeeper and me – that he weighs practically nothing; that he is a mere boring mass of assimilatory matter, mere clouds in clothing, *niente*, *nefas*,[350] the most inconsiderable of men. There he sits watching until I have done this writing. Then, if he can, he will waylay me. He will come billowing up to me . . .

He will tell me over again all about it, how it feels, how it doesn't feel, how he sometimes hopes it is passing off a little. And always somewhere in that fat, abundant discourse he will say, 'The secret's keeping, eh? If anyone knew of it – I should be so ashamed . . . Makes a fellow look such a fool, you know. Crawling about on a ceiling and all that . . . '

And now to elude Pyecraft, occupying, as he does, an admirable strategic position between me and the door.

Jimmy Goggles the God [351]

'It isn't everyone who's been a god,' said the sunburnt man. 'But it's happened to me. Among other things.'

I intimated my sense of his condescension.

'It don't leave much for ambition, does it?' said the sunburnt man. 'I was one of those men who were saved from the *Ocean Pioneer*. Gummy![352] How time flies! It's twenty years ago. I doubt if you'll remember anything of the *Ocean Pioneer*?'

The name was familiar, and I tried to recall when and where I had read it. The *Ocean Pioneer*? 'Something about gold dust,' I said vaguely, 'but the precise – '

'That's it,' he said. 'In a beastly little channel she hadn't no business in – dodging pirates. It was before they'd put the kybosh on[353] that business. And there'd been volcanoes or something and all the rocks was wrong. There's places about by Soona[354] where you fair have to follow the rocks about to see where they're going next. Down she went in twenty fathoms before you could have dealt for whist, with fifty thousand pounds' worth of gold aboard, it was said, in one form or another.'

'Survivors?'

'Three.'

'I remember the case now,' I said. 'There was something about salvage – '

But at the word salvage the sunburnt man exploded into language so extraordinarily horrible that I stopped aghast. He came down to more ordinary swearing, and pulled himself up abruptly. 'Excuse me,' he said, 'but – salvage!'

He leant over towards me. 'I was in that job,' he said. 'Tried to make myself a rich man, and got made a god instead. I've got my feelings –

'It ain't all jam being a god,' said the sunburnt man, and for some time conversed by means of such pithy but unprogressive axioms. At last he took up his tale again.

'There was me,' said the sunburnt man, 'and a seaman named Jacobs, and Always, the mate of the *Ocean Pioneer*. And him it was that set the whole thing going. I remember him now, when we was in the jolly boat,[355] suggesting it all to our minds just by one sentence. He was a wonderful hand at suggesting things. 'There was forty thousand pounds,' he said, 'on that ship, and it's for me to say just where she went down.' It didn't need much brains to tumble to that. And he was the leader from the first to the last. He got hold of the Sanderses and their brig; they were brothers, and the brig was the *Pride of Banya*, and he it was bought the diving dress – a second-hand one with a compressed air apparatus instead of pumping. He'd have done the diving too, if it hadn't made him sick going down. And the salvage people were mucking about with a chart he'd cooked up, as solemn as could be, at Starr Race, a hundred and twenty miles away.

'I can tell you we was a happy lot aboard that brig, jokes and drink and bright hopes all the time. It all seemed so neat and clean and straightforward, and what rough chaps call a 'cert'. And we used to speculate how the other blessed lot, the proper salvagers, who'd started two days before us, were getting on, until our sides fairly ached. We all messed together[356] in the Sanderses' cabin – it was a curious crew, all officers and no men – and there stood the diving-dress waiting its turn. Young Sanders was a humorous sort of chap, and there certainly was something funny in the confounded thing's great fat head and its stare, and he made us see it too. 'Jimmie Goggles', he used to call it, and talk to it like a Christian. Asked if he was married, and how Mrs Goggles was, and all the little Goggleses. Fit to make you split. And every blessed day all of us used to drink the health of Jimmy Goggles in rum, and unscrew his eye and pour a glass of rum in him, until, instead of that nasty mackintosheriness, he smelt as nice in his inside as a cask of rum. It was jolly times we had in those days, I can tell you – little suspecting, poor chaps! what was a-coming.

'We weren't going to throw away our chances by any blessed hurry, you know, and we spent a whole day sounding our way towards where the *Ocean Pioneer* had gone down, right between two chunks of ropy grey rock – lava rocks that rose nearly out of the water. We had to lay off about half a mile to get a safe anchorage, and there was a thundering row, over who should stop on board. And there she lay just as she had gone down, so that you could see the top of the masts that was still standing perfectly distinctly. The row ended in all coming in the boat. I went down in the diving-dress on Friday morning directly it was light.

'What a surprise it was! I can see it all now quite distinctly. It was a queer-looking place, and the light was just coming. People over here think every blessed place in the tropics is a flat shore and palm trees and surf, bless 'em! This place, for instance, wasn't a bit that way. Not common rocks they were, undermined by waves; but great curved banks like ironwork cinder heaps, with green slime below, and thorny shrubs and things just waving upon them here and there, and the water glassy calm and clear, and showing you a kind of dirty grey-black shine, with huge flaring red-brown weeds spreading motionless, and crawling and darting things going through it. And far away beyond the ditches and pools and the heaps was a forest on the mountain flank, growing again after the fires and cinder showers of the last eruption. And the other way forest, too, and a kind of broken – what is it – ? amby-theatre[357] of black and rusty cinders rising out of it all, and the sea in a kind of bay in the middle.

'The dawn, I say, was just coming, and there wasn't much colour about things, and not a human being but ourselves anywhere in sight up or down the channel. Except the *Pride of Banya*, lying out beyond a lump of rocks towards the line of the sea.

'Not a human being in sight,' he repeated, and paused.

'I don't know where they came from, not a bit. And we were feeling so safe that we were all alone that poor young Sanders was a-singing. I was in Jimmy Goggles, all except the helmet. 'Easy,' says Always, 'there's her mast.' And after I'd had just one squint over the gunwhale,[358] I caught up the bogey[359] and almost tipped out as old Sanders brought the boat round. When the windows were screwed and everything was all right, I shut the valve from the air belt in order to help my sinking, and jumped overboard, feet foremost – for we hadn't a ladder. I left the boat pitching, and all of them staring down into the water after me as my head sank down into the weeds and blackness that lay about the mast. I suppose nobody, not the most cautious chap in the world, would have bothered about a lookout at such a desolate place. It stunk of solitude.

'Of course, you must understand that I was a greenhorn at diving. None of us were divers. We'd had to muck about with the thing to get the way of it, and this was the first time I'd been deep. It feels damnable. Your ears hurt beastly. I don't know if you've ever hurt yourself yawning or sneezing, but it takes you like that, only ten times worse. And a pain over the eyebrows here – splitting – and a feeling like influenza in the head. And it isn't all heaven in your lungs and things. And going down feels like the beginning of a lift, only it keeps on. And you can't turn your head to see what's above you, and you can't get a fair squint at what's happening to your feet without bending down something painful. And being deep it was dark, let alone the blackness of the ashes and mud that formed the bottom. It was like going down out of the dawn back into the night, so to speak.

'The mast came up like a ghost out of the black, and then a lot of fishes, and then a lot of flapping red seaweed, and then whack I came with a kind of dull bang on the deck of the *Ocean Pioneer*, and the fishes that had been feeding on the dead rose about me like a swarm of flies from road stuff[360] in summer time. I turned on the compressed air again – for the suit was a bit thick and mackintoshery after all, in spite of the rum – and stood recovering myself. It struck coolish down there, and that helped take off the stuffiness a bit.

'When I began to feel easier, I started looking about me. It was an extraordinary sight. Even the light was extraordinary, a kind of reddy-coloured twilight, on account of the streamers of seaweed that floated up on either side of the ship. And far overhead just a moony, deep green-blue. The deck of the ship, except for a slight list to starboard, was level, and lay all dark and long between the weeds, clear except where the masts had snapped when she rolled, and vanishing into black night towards the forecastle.[361] There wasn't any dead on the decks, most were in the weeds alongside, I suppose; but afterwards I found two skeletons lying in the passengers' cabins, where death had come to them. It was curious to stand on that deck and recognise it all, bit by bit: a place against the rail where I'd been fond of smoking by starlight, and the corner where an old chap from Sydney used to flirt with a widow we had aboard. A comfortable couple they'd been, only a month ago, and now you couldn't have got a meal for a baby crab off either of them.

'I've always had a bit of a philosophical turn, and I dare say I spent the best part of five minutes in such thoughts before I went below to find where the blessed dust was stored. It was slow work hunting, feeling it was for the most part, pitchy dark, with confusing blue gleams down the companion.[362] And there were things moving about, a dab at my glass once, and once a pinch at my leg. Crabs, I expect. I kicked a lot of loose stuff that puzzled me, and stooped and picked up something all knobs and spikes. What do you think? Backbone! But I never had any particular feeling for bones. We had talked the affair over pretty thoroughly, and Always knew just where the stuff was stowed. I found it that trip. I lifted a box one end an inch or more.'

He broke off in his story. 'I've lifted it,' he said, 'as near as that! Forty thousand pounds' worth of pure gold! Gold! I shouted inside my helmet as a kind of cheer and hurt my ears. I was getting confounded stuffy and tired by this time – I must have been down twenty-five minutes or more – and I thought this was good enough. I went up the companion again, and as my eyes came up flush with the deck, a thundering great crab gave a kind of hysterical jump and went scuttling off sideways.

Quite a start it gave me. I stood up clear on deck and shut the valve behind the helmet to let the air accumulate to carry me up again – I noticed a kind of whacking from above, as though they were hitting the water with an oar, but I didn't look up. I fancied they were signalling me to come up.

'And then something shot down by me – something heavy, and stood a-quiver in the planks. I looked, and there was a long knife I'd seen young Sanders handling. Thinks I, he's dropped it, and I was still calling him this kind of fool and that – for it might have hurt me serious – when I began to lift and drive up towards the daylight. Just about the level of the top spars of the *Ocean Pioneer*, whack! I came against something sinking down, and a boot knocked in front of my helmet. Then something else, struggling frightful. It was a big weight atop of me, whatever it was, and moving and twisting about. I'd have thought it a big octopus, or some such thing, if it hadn't been for the boot. But octopuses don't wear boots. It was all in a moment, of course. I felt myself sinking down again, and I threw my arms about to keep steady, and the whole lot rolled free of me and shot down as I went up – '

He paused.

'I saw young Sanders's face, over a naked black shoulder, and a spear driven clean through his neck, and out of his mouth and neck what looked like spirts of pink smoke in the water. And down they went clutching one another, and turning over, and both too far gone to leave go. And in another second my helmet came a whack, fit to split, against the niggers'[363] canoe. It was niggers! Two canoes full.

'It was lively times, I tell you! Overboard came Always with three spears in him. There was the legs of three or four black chaps kicking about me in the water. I couldn't see much, but I saw the game was up at a glance, gave my valve a tremendous twist, and went bubbling down again after poor Always, in as awful a state of scare and astonishment as you can well imagine. I passed young Sanders and the nigger going up again and struggling still a bit, and in another moment I was standing in the dim again on the deck of the *Ocean Pioneer*.

' 'Gummy,' thinks I, 'here's a fix! Niggers?' At first I couldn't see anything for it but Stifle below or Stabs above. I didn't properly understand how much air there was to last me, but I didn't feel like standing very much more of it down below. I was hot and frightfully heady quite apart from the blue funk[364] I was in. We'd never reckoned with these beastly natives, filthy Papuan beasts. It wasn't any good coming up where I was, but I had to do something. On the spur of the moment, I clambered over the side of the brig and landed among the weeds, and set off through the darkness as fast as I could. I just stopped once and knelt and twisted back my head in the helmet and had a look up. It was a most extraordinary bright green-blue above, and the two canoes and the boat floating there very small and distant like a kind of twisted H. And it made me feel sick to squint up at it, and think what the pitching and swaying of the three meant.

'It was just about the most horrible ten minutes I ever had, blundering about in that darkness – pressure something awful, like being buried in sand, pain across the chest, sick with funk, and breathing nothing as it seemed but the smell of rum and mackintosh. Gummy! After a bit, I found myself going up a steepish sort of slope. I had another squint to see if anything was visible of the canoes and boats, and then kept on. I stopped with my head a foot from the surface, and tried to see where I was going, but of course, nothing was to be seen but the reflection of the bottom. Then out I dashed like knocking my head through a mirror. Directly I got my eyes out of the water, I saw I'd come up a kind of beach near the forest. I had a look round, but the natives and the brig were both hidden by a big, hummucky heap of twisted lava. The born fool in me suggested a run for the woods. I didn't take the helmet off, but eased open one of the windows, and after a bit of a pant, went on out of the water. You'd hardly imagine how clean and light the air tasted.

'Of course, with four inches of lead in your boot soles, and your head in a copper knob the size of a football, and having been thirty-five minutes under water, you don't break any records running. I ran like a plough-boy going to work. And halfway to the trees I saw a dozen niggers or more coming out in a gaping, astonished sort of way to meet me.

'I just stopped dead, and cursed myself for all the fools out of London. I had about as much chance of cutting back to the water as a turned turtle. I just screwed up my window again to leave my hands free, and waited for them. There wasn't anything else for me to do.

'But they didn't come on very much. I began to suspect why. "Jimmy Goggles," I says, "it's your beauty does it." I was inclined to be a little light-headed, I think, with all these dangers about and the change in the pressure of the blessed air. "Who're ye staring at?" I said, as if the savages could hear me. "What d'ye take me for? I'm hanged if I don't give you something to stare at," I said, and with that I screwed up the escape valve and turned on the compressed air from the belt, until I was swelled out like a blown frog. Regular imposing it must have been. I'm blessed if they'd come on a step; and presently one and then another went down on their hands and knees. They didn't know what to make of me, and they was doing the extra polite, which was very wise and reasonable of them. I had half a mind to edge back seaward and cut and run, but it seemed too hopeless. A step back and they'd have been after me. And out of sheer desperation I began to march towards them up the beach, with slow, heavy steps, and waving my blown-out arms about in a dignified manner. And inside of me I was singing as small as a tomtit.[365]

'But there's nothing like a striking appearance to help a man over a difficulty – I've found that before and since. People like ourselves, who're up to diving-dresses by the time we're seven, can scarcely imagine the effect of one on a simple-minded savage. One or two of these niggers cut and run, the others started in a great hurry trying to knock their brains out on the ground. And on I went as slow and solemn and silly-looking and artful as a jobbing plumber. It was evident they took me for something immense.

'Then up jumped one and began pointing, making extraordinary gestures to me as he did so, and all the others began sharing their attention between me and something out at sea. 'What's the matter now?' I said. I turned slowly on account of my dignity, and there I saw, coming round a point, the poor old *Pride of Banya* towed by a couple of canoes. The sight fairly made me sick. But they evidently expected some recognition, so I waved my arms in a striking sort of non-committal manner. And then I turned and stalked on towards the trees again. At that time I was praying like mad, I remember, over and over again: "Lord help me through with it! Lord help me through with it!" It's only fools who know nothing of dangers can afford to laugh at praying.

'But these niggers weren't going to let me walk through and away like that. They started a kind of bowing dance about me, and sort of pressed me to take a pathway that lay through the trees. It was clear to me they didn't take me for a British citizen, whatever else they thought of me, and for my own part I was never less anxious to own up to the old country.

'You'd hardly believe it, perhaps, unless you're familiar with savages, but these poor misguided, ignorant creatures took me straight to their kind of joss place[366] to present me to the blessed old black stone there. By this time I was beginning to sort of realise the depth of their ignorance, and directly I set eyes on this deity I took my cue. I started a baritone howl, "Wow-wow," very long on one note, and began waving my arms about a lot, and then very slowly and ceremoniously turned their image over on its side and sat down on it. I wanted to sit down badly, for diving-dresses ain't much wear in the tropics. Or, to put it different like, they're a sight too much. It took away their breath, I could see, my sitting on their joss, but in less time than a minute they made up their minds and were hard at work worshipping me. And I can tell you I felt a bit relieved to see things turning out so well, in spite of the weight on my shoulders and feet.

'But what made me anxious was what the chaps in the canoes might think when they came back. If they'd seen me in the boat before I went down, and without the helmet on – for they might have been spying and hiding overnight – they would very likely take a different view from the others. I was in a deuce of a stew about that for hours, as it seemed, until the shindy of the arrival began.

'But they took it down – the whole blessed village took it down. At the cost of sitting up stiff and stern, as much like those sitting Egyptian images[367] one sees as I could manage, for pretty nearly twelve hours, I should guess at least, on end, I got over it. You'd hardly think what it meant in that heat and stink. I don't think any of them dreamt of the man inside. I was just a wonderful leathery great joss that had come up with luck out of the water. But the fatigue! The heat! The beastly closeness! The mackintosheriness and the rum! And the fuss! They lit a stinking fire on a kind of lava slab there was before me, and brought in a lot of gory muck – the worst parts of what they were feasting on outside, the beasts – and burnt it all in my honour. I was getting a bit hungry, but I understand now how gods manage to do without eating, what with the smell of burnt offerings about them. And they brought in a lot of the stuff they'd got off the brig and, among other stuff, what I was a bit relieved to see, the kind of pneumatic pump that was used for the compressed air affair, and then a lot of chaps and girls came in and danced about me something disgraceful. It's extraordinary the different ways different people have of showing respect. If I'd had a hatchet handy I'd have gone for the lot of them – they made me feel that wild. All this time I sat as stiff as company, not knowing anything better to do. And at last, when nightfall came, and the wattle joss-house place got a bit too shadowy for their taste – all these here savages are afraid of the dark, you know – and I started a sort of "Moo" noise, they built big bonfires outside and left me alone in peace in the darkness of my hut, free to unscrew my windows a bit and think things over, and feel just as bad as I liked. And, Lord! I was sick.

'I was weak and hungry, and my mind kept on behaving like a beetle on a pin, tremendous activity and nothing done at the end of it. Come round just where it was before. There was sorrowing for the other chaps, beastly drunkards certainly, but not deserving such a fate, and young Sanders with the spear through his neck wouldn't go out of my mind. There was the treasure down there in the *Ocean Pioneer*, and how one might get it and hide it somewhere safer, and get away and come back for it. And there was the puzzle where to get anything to eat. I tell you I was fair rambling. I was afraid to ask by signs for food, for fear of behaving too human, and so there I sat and hungered until very near the dawn. Then the village got a bit quiet, and I couldn't stand it any longer, and I went out and got some stuff like artichokes in a bowl and some sour milk. What was left of these I put away among the other offerings, just to give them a hint of my tastes. And in the morning they came to worship, and found me sitting up stiff and respectable on their previous god, just as they'd left me overnight. I'd got my back against the central pillar of the hut, and, practically, I was asleep. And that's how I became a god among the heathen – a false god no doubt, and blasphemous, but one can't always pick and choose.

'Now, I don't want to crack myself up as a god beyond my merits, but I must confess that while I was god to these people they was extraordinary successful. I don't say there's anything in it, mind you. They won a battle with another tribe – I got a lot of offerings I didn't want through it – they had wonderful fishing, and their crop of pourra[368] was exceptional fine. And they counted the capture of the brig among the benefits I brought 'em. I must say I don't think that was a poor record for a perfectly new hand. And, though perhaps you'd scarcely credit it, I was the tribal god of those beastly savages for pretty nearly four months . . .

'What else could I do, man? But I didn't wear that diving-dress all the time. I made 'em rig me up a sort of holy of holies, and a deuce of a time I had too, making them understand what it was I wanted them to do. That indeed was the great difficulty – making them understand my wishes. I couldn't let myself down by talking their lingo badly – even if I'd been able to speak at all – and I couldn't go flapping a lot of gestures at them. So I drew pictures in sand and sat down beside them and hooted like one o'clock.[369] Sometimes they did the things I wanted all right, and sometimes they did them all wrong. They was always very willing, certainly. All the while I was puzzling how I was to get the confounded business settled. Every night before the dawn I used to march out in full rig and go off to a place where I could see the channel in which the *Ocean Pioneer* lay sunk, and once even, one moonlight night, I tried to walk out to her, but the weeds and rocks and the dark clean beat me. I didn't get back till full day, and then I found all those silly niggers out on the beach praying their sea-god to return to them.

I was that vexed and tired, messing and tumbling about, and coming up and going down again, I could have punched their silly heads all round when they started rejoicing. I'm hanged if I like so much ceremony.

'And then came the missionary. That missionary! It was in the afternoon, and I was sitting in state in my outer temple place, sitting on that old black stone of theirs when he came. I heard a row outside and jabbering, and then his voice speaking to an interpreter. "They worship stocks and stones," he said, and I knew what was up, in a flash. I had one of my windows out for comfort, and I sang out straight away on the spur of the moment. "Stocks and stones!" I says. "You come inside," I says, "and I'll punch your blooming head." There was a kind of silence and more jabbering, and in he came, Bible in hand, after the manner of them – a little sandy chap in specks and a pith helmet. I flatter myself that me sitting there in the shadows, with my copper head and my big goggles, struck him a bit of a heap at first. "Well," I says, "how's the trade in calico?"[370] For I don't hold with missionaries.

'I had a lark with that missionary. He was a raw hand, and quite outclassed with a man like me. He gasped out who was I, and I told him to read the inscription at my feet if he wanted to know. Down he goes to read, and his interpreter, being of course as superstitious as any of them, took it as an act of worship and plumped down like a shot. All my people gave a howl of triumph, and there wasn't any more business to be done in my village after that journey, not by the likes of him.

'But, of course, I was a fool to choke him off like that. If I'd had any sense I should have told him straight away of the treasure and taken him into Co.[371] I've no doubt he'd have come into Co. A child, with a few hours to think it over, could have seen the connection between my diving-dress and the loss of the *Ocean Pioneer*. A week after he left I went out one morning and saw the *Motherhood*, the salver's ship[372] from Starr Race, towing up the channel and sounding. The whole blessed game was up, and all my trouble thrown away. Gummy! How wild I felt! And guying it in that stinking silly dress! Four months!'

The sunburnt man's story degenerated again. 'Think of it,' he said, when he emerged to linguistic purity once more. 'Forty thousand pounds' worth of gold.'

'Did the little missionary come back?' I asked.

'Oh, yes! Bless him! And he pledged his reputation there was a man inside the god, and started out to see as much with tremendous ceremony. But there wasn't – he got sold again. I always did hate scenes and explanations, and long before he came I was out of it all – going home to Banya along the coast, hiding in bushes by day and thieving food from the villages by night. Only weapon, a spear. No clothes, no money. Nothing. My face was my fortune, as the saying is. And just a squeak off [373] eight thousand pounds of gold – fifth share. But the natives cut up rusty,[374] thank goodness, because they thought it was him had driven their luck away.'

The Flowering of the Strange Orchid

The buying of orchids always has in it a certain speculative flavour. You have before you the brown shrivelled lump of tissue, and for the rest you must trust your judgement, or the auctioneer, or your good luck – as your taste may incline. The plant may be moribund or dead, or it may be just a respectable purchase, fair value for your money, or perhaps – for the thing has happened again and again – there slowly unfolds before the delighted eyes of the happy purchaser, day after day, some new variety, some novel richness, a strange twist of the labellum,[376] or some subtler coloration or unexpected mimicry. Pride, beauty and profit blossom together on one delicate green spike, and, it may be, even immortality. For the new miracle of nature may stand in need of a new specific name, and what so convenient as that of its discoverer? 'Johnsmithia'! There have been worse names.

It was perhaps the hope of some such happy discovery that made Winter-Wedderburn such a frequent attendant at these sales – that hope, and also, maybe, the fact that he had nothing else of the slightest interest to do in the world. He was a shy, lonely, rather ineffectual man, provided with just enough income to keep off the spur of necessity, and not enough nervous energy to make him seek any exacting employments. He might have collected stamps or coins, or translated Horace, or bound books, or invented new species of diatoms.[377] But, as it happened, he grew orchids, and had one ambitious little hothouse.

'I have a fancy,' he said over his coffee, 'that something is going to happen to me today.' He spoke – as he moved and thought – slowly.

'Oh, don't say *that*!' said his housekeeper – who was also his remote cousin. For 'something happening' was a euphemism that meant only one thing[378] to her.

'You misunderstand me. I mean nothing unpleasant, though what I do mean I scarcely know.

'Today,' he continued, after a pause, 'Peters are going to sell a batch of plants from the Andamans and the Indies.[379] I shall go up and see what they have. It may be I shall buy something good, unawares. That may be it.'

He passed his cup for his second cupful of coffee.

'Are these the things collected by that poor young fellow you told me of the other day?' asked his cousin as she filled his cup.

'Yes,' he said, and became meditative over a piece of toast.

'Nothing ever does happen to me,' he remarked presently, beginning to think aloud. 'I wonder why? Things enough happen to other people. There is Harvey. Only the other week – on Monday he picked up sixpence, on Wednesday his chicks all had the staggers,[380] on Friday his cousin came home from Australia and on Saturday he broke his ankle. What a whirl of excitement! – Compared to me.'

'I think I would rather be without so much excitement,' said his housekeeper. 'It can't be good for you.'

'I suppose it's troublesome. Still . . . you see, nothing *ever* happens to me. When I was a little boy I never had accidents. I never fell in love as I grew up. Never married . . . I wonder how it feels to have something happen to you, something really remarkable.

'That orchid-collector was only thirty-six – twenty years younger than myself – when he died. And he had been married twice, and divorced once; he had had malarial fever four times, and once he broke his thigh. He killed a Malay once, and once he was wounded by a poisoned dart. And in the end he was killed by jungle-leeches. It must have all been very troublesome, but then it must have been very interesting, you know – except, perhaps, the leeches.'

'I am sure it was not good for him,' said the lady, with conviction.

'Perhaps not.' And then Wedderburn looked at his watch. 'Twenty-three minutes past eight. I am going up by the quarter to twelve train, so that there is plenty of time. I think I shall wear my alpaca jacket[381] – it is quite warm enough – and my grey felt hat and brown shoes. I suppose – '

He glanced out of the window at the serene sky and sunlit garden, and then nervously at his cousin's face.

'I think you had better take an umbrella if you are going to London,' she said, in a voice that admitted of no denial. 'There's all between here and the station coming back.'

When he returned he was in a state of mild excitement. He had made a purchase. It was rare that he could make up his mind quickly enough to buy, but this time he had done so.

'These are Vandas,' he said, 'and a Dendrobe and some Palaeo-nopsis.'[382] He surveyed his purchases lovingly as he consumed his soup. They were laid out on the spotless tablecloth before him, and he was telling his cousin all about them as he slowly meandered through his dinner. It was his custom to live all his visits to London over again in the evening, for her and his own entertainment.

'I knew something would happen today. And I have bought all these. Some of them – some of them – I feel sure, do you know, that some of them will be remarkable. I don't know how it is, but I feel just as sure as if someone had told me that some of these will turn out remarkable.'

'That one – ' he pointed to a shrivelled rhizome – 'was not identified. It may be a Palaeonopsis or it may not. It may be a new species, or even a new genus. And it was the last that poor Batten ever collected.'

'I don't like the look of it,' said his housekeeper. 'It's such an ugly shape.'

'To me it scarcely seems to have a shape.'

'I don't like those things that stick out,' said his housekeeper.

'It shall be put away in a pot tomorrow.'

'It looks,' said the housekeeper, 'like a spider shamming dead.'

Wedderburn smiled and surveyed the root with his head on one side. 'It is certainly not a pretty lump of stuff. But you can never judge of these things from their dry appearance. It may turn out to be a very beautiful orchid indeed. How busy I shall be tomorrow! I must see tonight just exactly what to do with these things, and tomorrow I shall set to work.

'They found poor Batten lying dead, or dying, in a mangrove swamp – I forget which,' he began again presently, 'with one of these very orchids crushed up under his body. He had been unwell for some days with some kind of native fever, and I suppose he fainted. These mangrove swamps are very unwholesome. Every drop of blood, they say, was taken out of him by the jungle-leeches. It may be that that very plant cost him his life to obtain.'

'I think none the better of it for that.'

'Men must work, though women may weep,' said Wedderburn, with profound gravity.[383]

'Fancy dying away from every comfort in a nasty swamp! Fancy being ill of fever with nothing to take but chlorodyne and quinine[384] – if men were left to themselves they would live on chlorodyne and quinine – and no one round you but horrible natives! They say the Andaman islanders[385] are most disgusting wretches – and, anyhow, they can scarcely make good nurses, not having the necessary training. And just for people in England to have orchids!'

'I don't suppose it was comfortable, but some men seem to enjoy that kind of thing,' said Wedderburn. 'Anyhow, the natives of his party were sufficiently civilised to take care of all his collection until his colleague, who was an ornithologist, came back again from the interior; though they could not tell the species of the orchid and had let it wither. And it makes these things more interesting.'

'It makes them disgusting. I should be afraid of some of the malaria clinging to them. And just think, there has been a dead body lying across that ugly thing! I never thought of that before. There! I declare I cannot eat another mouthful of dinner!'

'I will take them off the table if you like, and put them in the window-seat. I can see them just as well there.'

The next few days he was indeed singularly busy in his steamy little hothouse, fussing about with charcoal, lumps of teak, moss, and all the other mysteries of the orchid cultivator. He considered he was having a wonderfully eventful time. In the evening he would talk about these new orchids to his friends, and over and over again he reverted to his expectation of something strange.

Several of the Vandas and the Dendrobium died under his care, but presently the strange orchid began to show signs of life. He was delighted and took his housekeeper right away from jam-making to see it at once, directly he made the discovery.

'That is a bud,' he said, 'and presently there will be a lot of leaves there, and those little things coming out here are aerial rootlets.'

'They look to me like little white fingers poking out of the brown,' said his housekeeper. 'I don't like them.

'Why not?'

'I don't know. They look like fingers trying to get at you. I can't help my likes and dislikes.'

'I don't know for certain, but I don't *think* there are any orchids I know that have aerial rootlets quite like that. It may be my fancy, of course. You see they are a little flattened at the ends.'

'I don't like 'em,' said his housekeeper, suddenly shivering and turning away. 'I know it's very silly of me – and I'm very sorry, particularly as you like the thing so much. But I can't help thinking of that corpse.'

'But it may not be that particular plant. That was merely a guess of mine.'

His housekeeper shrugged her shoulders. 'Anyhow, I don't like it,' she said.

Wedderburn felt a little hurt at her dislike of the plant. But that did not prevent his talking to her about orchids generally, and this orchid in particular, whenever he felt inclined.

'There are such queer things about orchids,' he said one day; 'such possibilities of surprises. You know, Darwin studied their fertilisation, and showed that the whole structure of an ordinary orchid-flower was contrived in order that moths might carry the pollen from plant to plant.[386] Well, it seems that there are lots of orchids known the flower of which cannot possibly be used for fertilisation in that way. Some of the Cypripediums,[387] for instance; there are no insects known that can possibly fertilise them, and some of them have never been found with seed.'

'But how do they form new plants?'

'By runners and tubers, and that kind of outgrowth. That is easily explained. The puzzle is, what are the flowers for?

'Very likely,' he added, '*my* orchid may be something extraordinary in that way. If so, I shall study it. I have often thought of making researches as Darwin did. But hitherto I have not found the time, or something else has happened to prevent it. The leaves are beginning to unfold now. I do wish you would come and see them!'

But she said that the orchid-house was so hot it gave her a headache. She had seen the plant once again, and the aerial rootlets, which were now some of them more than a foot long, had unfortunately reminded her of tentacles reaching out after something; and they got into her dreams, growing after her with incredible rapidity. So that she had settled to her entire satisfaction that she would not see that plant again, and Wedderburn had to admire its leaves alone. They were of the ordinary broad form, and a deep glossy green, with splashes and dots of deep red towards the base. He knew of no other leaves quite like them. The plant was placed on a low bench near the thermometer, and close by was a simple arrangement by which a tap dripped on the hot-water pipes and kept the air steamy. And he spent his afternoons now with some regularity meditating on the approaching flowering of this strange plant.

And at last the great thing happened. Directly he entered the little glass house he knew that the spike had burst out, although his great *Palaeonopsis Lowii* [388] hid the corner where his new darling stood. There was a new odour in the air, a rich, intensely sweet scent that over-powered every other in that crowded, steaming little greenhouse.

Directly he noticed this he hurried down to the strange orchid. And, behold! The trailing green spikes bore now three great splashes of blossom, from which this overpowering sweetness proceeded. He stopped before them in an ecstasy of admiration.

The flowers were white, with streaks of golden orange upon the petals; the heavy labellum was coiled into an intricate projection, and a wonderful bluish purple mingled there with the gold. He could see at once that the genus was altogether a new one. And the insufferable scent! How hot the place was! The blossoms swam before his eyes.

He would see if the temperature was right. He made a step towards the thermometer. Suddenly everything appeared unsteady. The bricks on the floor were dancing up and down. Then the white blossoms, the green leaves behind them, the whole greenhouse, seemed to sweep sideways and then in a curve upwards.

At half-past four his cousin made the tea, according to their invariable custom. But Wedderburn did not come in for his tea. 'He is worshipping that horrid orchid,' she told herself, and waited ten minutes. 'His watch must have stopped. I will go and call him.'

She went straight to the hothouse, and, opening the door, called his name. There was no reply. She noticed that the air was very close, and loaded with an intense perfume. Then she saw something lying on the bricks between the hot-water pipes.

For a minute, perhaps, she stood motionless.

He was lying, face upward, at the foot of the strange orchid. The tentacle-like aerial rootlets no longer swayed freely in the air but were crowded together, a tangle of grey ropes, and stretched tight, with their ends closely applied to his chin and neck and hands.

She did not understand. Then she saw from one of the exultant tentacles upon his cheek there trickled a little thread of blood.

With an inarticulate cry she ran towards him, and tried to pull him away from the leechlike suckers. She snapped two of these tentacles, and their sap dripped red.

Then the overpowering scent of the blossom began to make her head reel. How they clung to him! She tore at the tough ropes, and he and the white inflorescence[389] swam about her. She felt she was fainting, knew she must not. She left him and hastily opened the nearest door, and after she had panted for a moment in the fresh air, she had a brilliant inspiration. She caught up a flowerpot and smashed in the windows at the end of the greenhouse. Then she re-entered. She tugged now with renewed strength at Wedderburn's motionless body and brought the strange orchid crashing to the floor. It still clung with the grimmest tenacity to its victim. In a frenzy, she lugged it and him into the open air.

Then she thought of tearing through the sucker rootlets one by one, and in another minute she had released him, and was dragging him away from the horror.

He was white and bleeding from a dozen circular patches.

The odd-job man was coming up the garden, amazed at the smashing of glass, and saw her emerge, hauling the inanimate body with red-stained hands. For a moment he thought impossible things.

'Bring some water!' she cried, and her voice dispelled his fancies. When, with unnatural alacrity, he returned with the water, he found her weeping with excitement, and, with Wedderburn's head upon her knee, wiping the blood from his face.

'What's the matter?' said Wedderburn, opening his eyes feebly, and closing them again at once.

'Go and tell Annie to come out here to me, and then go for Dr Haddon at once,' she said to the odd-job man so soon as he had brought the water; and added, seeing he hesitated, 'I will tell you all about it when you come back.'

Presently, Wedderburn opened his eyes again, and seeing that he was troubled by the puzzle of his position, she explained to him, 'You fainted in the hothouse.'

'And the orchid?'

'I will see to that,' she said.

Wedderburn had lost a good deal of blood, but beyond that he had suffered no very great injury. They gave him brandy mixed with some pink extract of meat, and carried him upstairs to bed. His housekeeper told her incredible story in fragments to Dr Haddon. 'Come to the orchid-house and see,' she said.

The cold outer air was blowing in through the open door, and the sickly perfume was almost dispelled. Most of the torn aerial rootlets lay already withered amidst a number of dark stains upon the bricks. The stem of the inflorescence was broken by the fall of the plant, and the flowers were growing limp and brown at the edges of the petals. The doctor stooped towards it, then saw that one of the aerial rootlets still stirred feebly, and hesitated.

The next morning the strange orchid still lay there, black now and putrescent. The door banged intermittently in the morning breeze, and all the array of Wedderburn's orchids was shrivelled and prostrate. But Wedderburn himself was bright and garrulous upstairs in the glory of his strange adventure.

The Argonauts of the Air 390

One saw Monson's Flying Machine from the windows of the trains passing either along the South-Western main line or along the line between Wimbledon and Worcester Park[391] – to be more exact, one saw the huge scaffoldings which limited the flight of the apparatus.[392] They rose over the tree-tops, a massive alley of interlacing iron and timber, and an enormous web of ropes and tackle, extending the best part of two miles. From the Leatherhead branch this alley was fore-shortened and in part hidden by a hill with villas; but from the main line one had it in profile, a complex tangle of girders and curving bars, very impressive to the excursionists from Portsmouth and Southampton and the West. Monson had taken up the work where Maxim had left it, had gone on at first with an utter contempt for the journalistic wit and ignorance that had irritated and hampered his predecessor, and had spent (it was said) rather more than half his immense fortune upon his experiments. The results, to an impatient generation, seemed inconsiderable. When some five years had passed after the growth of the colossal iron groves at Worcester Park, and Monson still failed to put in a fluttering appearance over Trafalgar Square, even the Isle of Wight trippers felt their liberty to smile. And such intelligent people as did not consider Monson a fool stricken with the mania for invention denounced him as being (for no particular reason) a self-advertising quack.

Yet now and again a morning trainload of season-ticket holders would see a white monster rush headlong through the airy tracery of guides and bars, and hear the farther stays, nettings and buffers snap, creak and groan with the impact of the blow. Then there would be an efflorescence of black-set white-rimmed faces along the sides of the train, and the morning papers would be neglected for a vigorous discussion of the possibility of flying (in which nothing new was ever said by any chance), until the train reached Waterloo, and its cargo of season-ticket holders dispersed themselves over London. Or the fathers and mothers in some multitudinous train of weary excursionists returning exhausted from a day of rest by the sea, would find the dark fabric, standing out against the evening sky, useful in diverting some bilious child from its introspection, and be suddenly startled by the swift transit of a huge black flapping shape that strained upwards against the guides. It was a great and forcible thing beyond dispute, and excellent for conversation; yet all the same, it was but flying in leading-strings, and most of those who witnessed it scarcely counted its flight as flying. More of a switchback it seemed to the run of the folk.

Monson, I say, did not trouble himself very keenly about the opinions of the press at first. But possibly he, even, had formed but a poor idea of the time it would take before the tactics of flying were mastered, the swift assured adjustment of the big soaring shape to every gust and chance movement of the air; nor had he clearly reckoned the money this prolonged struggle against gravitation would cost him. And he was not so pachydermatous[393] as he seemed. Secretly he had his periodical bundles of cuttings sent him by Romeike,[394] he had his periodical reminders from his banker; and if he did not mind the initial ridicule and scepticism, he felt the growing neglect as the months went by and the money dribbled away. Time was when Monson had sent the enterprising journalist, keen after readable matter, empty from his gates. But when the enterprising journalist ceased from troubling,[395] Monson was anything but satisfied in his heart of hearts. Still day by day the work went on, and the multitudinous subtle difficulties of the steering diminished in number. Day by day, too the money trickled away, until his balance was no longer a matter of hundreds of thousands, but of tens. And at last came an anniversary.

Monson, sitting in the little drawing-shed, suddenly noticed the date on Woodhouse's calendar.

'It is five years ago today that we began,' he said to Woodhouse suddenly.

'Is it?' said Woodhouse.

'It's the alterations play the devil with us,' said Monson, biting a paper-fastener.

The drawings for the new vans[396] to the hinder screw lay on the table before him as he spoke. He pitched the mutilated brass paper-fastener into the wastepaper basket and drummed with his fingers. 'These alterations! Will the mathematicians ever be clever enough to save us all this patching and experimenting? Five years – learning by rule of thumb, when one might think that it was possible to calculate the whole thing out beforehand. The cost of it! I might have hired three senior wranglers[397] for life. But they'd only have developed some beautifully useless theorems in pneumatics.[398] What a time it has been, Woodhouse!'

'These mouldings will take three weeks,' said Woodhouse. 'At special prices.'

'Three weeks!' said Monson, and sat drumming.

'Three weeks certain,' said Woodhouse, an excellent engineer, but no good as a comforter. He drew the sheets towards him and began shading a bar.

Monson stopped drumming, and began to bite his fingernails, staring the while at Woodhouse's head.

'How long have they been calling this Monson's Folly?' he said suddenly.[399]

'Oh! Year or so,' said Woodhouse carelessly, without looking up.

Monson sucked the air in between his teeth, and went to the window. The stout iron columns carrying the elevated rails upon which the start of the machine was made rose up close by, and the machine was hidden by the upper edge of the window. Through the grove of iron pillars, red painted and ornate with rows of bolts, one had a glimpse of the pretty scenery towards Esher.[400] A train went gliding noiselessly across the middle distance, its rattle drowned by the hammering of the workmen overhead. Monson could imagine the grinning faces at the windows of the carriages. He swore savagely under his breath, and dabbed viciously at a blowfly that suddenly became noisy on the window-pane.

'What's up?' said Woodhouse, staring in surprise at his employer.

'I'm about sick of this.'

Woodhouse scratched his cheek. 'Oh!' he said, after an assimilating pause. He pushed the drawing away from him.

'Here these fools . . . I'm trying to conquer a new element – trying to do a thing that will revolutionise life. And instead of taking an intelligent interest, they grin and make their stupid jokes, and call me and my appliances names.'

'Asses!' said Woodhouse, letting his eye fall again on the drawing.

The epithet, curiously enough, made Monson wince. 'I'm about sick of it, Woodhouse, anyhow,' he said, after a pause.

Woodhouse shrugged his shoulders.

'There's nothing for it but patience, I suppose,' said Monson, sticking his hands in his pockets. 'I've started. I've made my bed, and I've got to lie on it. I can't go back. I'll see it through, and spend every penny I have and every penny I can borrow. But I tell you, Woodhouse, I'm infernally sick of it, all the same. If I'd paid a tenth part of the money towards some political greaser's expenses[401] – I'd have been a baronet before this.'

Monson paused. Woodhouse stared in front of him with a blank expression he always employed to indicate sympathy, and tapped his pencil-case on the table. Monson stared at him for a minute.

'Oh, *damn*!' said Monson suddenly, and abruptly rushed out of the room.

Woodhouse continued his sympathetic rigour for perhaps half a minute. Then he sighed and resumed the shading of the drawings. Something had evidently upset Monson. Nice chap, and generous, but difficult to get on with. It was the way with every amateur who had anything to do with engineering – wanted everything finished at once. But Monson had usually the patience of the expert. Odd he was so irritable. Nice and round that aluminium rod did look now! Woodhouse threw back his head, and put it first this side and then that to appreciate his bit of shading better.

'Mr Woodhouse,' said Hooper, the foreman of the labourers, putting his head in at the door.

'Hello!' said Woodhouse, without turning round.

'Nothing happened, sir?' said Hooper.

'Happened?' said Woodhouse.

'The governor just been up the rails swearing like a tornader.'[402]

'*Oh!*' said Woodhouse.

'It ain't like him, sir.'

'No?'

'And I was thinking perhaps – '

'Don't think,' said Woodhouse, still admiring the drawings.

Hooper knew Woodhouse, and shut the door suddenly with a vicious slam. Woodhouse stared stonily before him for some further minutes, and then made an ineffectual effort to pick his teeth with his pencil. Abruptly he desisted, pitched that old, tried and stumpy servitor across the room, got up, stretched himself, and followed Hooper.

He looked ruffled – it was visible to every workman he met. When a millionaire who has been spending thousands on experiments that employ quite a little army of people suddenly indicates that he is sick of the undertaking, there is almost invariably a certain amount of mental friction in the ranks of the little army he employs. And even before he indicates his intentions there are speculations and murmurs, a watching of faces and a study of straws.[403] Hundreds of people knew before the day was out that Monson was ruffled, Woodhouse ruffled, Hooper ruffled. A workman's wife, for instance (whom Monson had never seen), decided to keep her money in the savings-bank instead of buying a velveteen dress. So far-reaching are even the casual curses of a millionaire.

Monson found a certain satisfaction in going on the works and behaving disagreeably to as many people as possible. After a time even that palled upon him, and he rode off the grounds, to everyone's relief there, and through the lanes south-eastward, to the infinite tribulation of his house steward at Cheam.[404]

And the immediate cause of it all, the little grain of annoyance that had suddenly precipitated all this discontent with his life-work was – these trivial things that direct all our great decisions! – half a dozen ill-considered remarks made by a pretty girl, prettily dressed, with a beautiful voice and something more than prettiness in her soft grey eyes. And of these half-dozen remarks, two words especially – 'Monson's Folly'. She had felt she was behaving charmingly to Monson; she reflected the next day how exceptionally effective she had been, and no one would have been more amazed than she had she learned the effect she had left on Monson's mind. I hope, considering everything, that she never knew.

'How are you getting on with your flying-machine?' she asked. ('I wonder if I shall ever meet anyone with the sense not to ask that,' thought Monson.) 'It will be very dangerous at first, will it not?' ('Thinks I'm afraid.') 'Jorgon is going to play presently; have you heard him before?' ('My mania being attended to, we turn to rational conversation.') Gush about Jorgon; gradual decline of conversation, ending with – 'You must let me know when your flying-machine is finished, Mr Monson, and then I will consider the advisability of taking a ticket.' ('One would think I was still playing inventions in the nursery.') But the bitterest thing she said was not meant for Monson's ears. To Phlox, the novelist, she was always conscientiously brilliant. 'I have been talking to Mr Monson, and he can think of nothing, positively nothing, but that flying-machine of his. Do you know, all his workmen call that place of his "Monson's Folly"? He is quite impossible. It is really very, very sad. I always regard him myself in the light of sunken treasure – the Lost Millionaire, you know.'

She was pretty and well educated – indeed, she had written an epigrammatic novelette; but the bitterness was that she was typical. She summarised what the world thought of the man who was working sanely, steadily and surely towards a more tremendous revolution in the appliances of civilisation, a more far-reaching alteration in the ways of humanity than has ever been effected since history began. They did not even take him seriously. In a little while he would be proverbial. 'I *must* fly now,' he said on his way home, smarting with a sense of absolute social failure. 'I must fly soon. If it doesn't come off soon, by God! I shall run amuck.'[405]

He said that before he had gone through his pass-book and his litter of papers. Inadequate as the cause seems, it was that girl's voice and the expression of her eyes that precipitated his discontent. But certainly the discovery that he had no longer even one hundred thousand pounds' worth of realisable property behind him was the poison that made the wound deadly.

It was the next day after this that he exploded upon Woodhouse and his workmen, and thereafter his bearing was consistently grim for three weeks, and anxiety dwelt in Cheam and Ewell, Maldon, Morden and Worcester Park, places that had thriven mightily on his experiments.

Four weeks after that first swearing of his, he stood with Woodhouse by the reconstructed machine as it lay across the elevated railway, by means of which it gained its initial impetus. The new propeller glittered a brighter white than the rest of the machine, and a gilder, obedient to a whim of Monson's, was picking out the aluminium bars with gold. And looking down the long avenue between the ropes (gilded now with the sunset), one saw red signals, and two miles away an ant-hill of workmen busy altering the last falls of the run into a rising slope.

'I'll *come*,' said Woodhouse. 'I'll come right enough. But I tell you it's infernally foolhardy. If only you would give another year – '.

'I tell you I won't. I tell you the thing works. I've given years enough – '

'It's not that,' said Woodhouse. 'We're all right with the machine. But it's the steering – '

'Haven't I been rushing, night and morning, backwards and forwards, through the squirrel's cage? If the thing steers true here, it will steer true all across England. It's just funk,[406] I tell you, Woodhouse. We could have gone a year ago. And besides – '

'Well?' said Woodhouse.

'The money!' snapped Monson over his shoulder.

'Hang it! I never thought of the money,' said Woodhouse, and then, speaking now in a very different tone to that with which he said the words before, he repeated, 'I'll come. Trust me.'

Monson turned suddenly, and saw all that Woodhouse had not the dexterity to say shining on his sunset-lit face. He looked for a moment, then impulsively extended his hand. 'Thanks,' he said.

'All right,' said Woodhouse, gripping the hand, and with a queer softening of his features. 'Trust me.'

Then both men turned to the big apparatus that lay with its flat wings extended upon the carrier, and stared at it meditatively. Monson, guided perhaps by a photographic study of the flight of birds, and by Lilienthal's methods, had gradually drifted from Maxim's shapes towards the bird form again.[407] The thing, however, was driven by a huge screw behind in the place of the tail; and so hovering, which needs an almost vertical adjustment of a flat tail, was rendered impossible. The body of the machine was small, almost cylindrical, and pointed. Forward and aft on the pointed ends were two small petroleum engines for the screw, and the navigators sat deep in a canoe-like recess, the foremost one steering, and being protected by a low screen, with two plate-glass windows, from the blinding rush of air. On either side a monstrous flat framework with a curved front border could be adjusted so as either to lie horizontally or to be tilted upward or down. These wings worked rigidly together, or, by releasing a pin, one could be tilted through a small angle independently of its fellow. The front edge of either wing could also be shifted back so as to diminish the wing-area about one-sixth. The machine was not only not designed to hover, but it was also incapable of fluttering. Monson's idea was to get into the air with the initial rush of the apparatus, and then to skim, much as a playing-card may be skimmed, keeping up the rush by means of the screw at the stern. Rooks and gulls fly enormous distances in that way with scarcely a perceptible movement of the wings. The bird really drives along on an aerial switchback. It glides slanting downward for a space, until it has gained considerable momentum, and then altering the inclination of its wings, glides up again almost to its original altitude. Even a Londoner who has watched the birds in the aviary in Regent's Park knows that.

But the bird is practising this art from the moment it leaves its nest. It has not only the perfect apparatus, but the perfect instinct to use it. A man off his feet has the poorest skill in balancing. Even the simple trick of the bicycle costs him some hours of labour. The instantaneous adjustments of the wings, the quick response to a passing breeze, the swift recovery of equilibrium, the giddy, eddying movements that require such absolute precision – all that he must learn, learn with infinite labour and infinite danger, if ever he is to conquer flying. The flying-machine that will start off some fine day, driven by neat 'little levers', with a nice open deck like a liner, and all loaded up with bombshells and guns, is the easy dreaming of a literary man.[408] In lives and in treasure the cost of the conquest of the empire of the air may even exceed all that has been spent in man's great conquest of the sea. Certainly it will be costlier than the greatest war that has ever devastated the world.

No one knew these things better than these two practical men. And they knew they were in the front rank of the coming army. Yet there is hope even in a forlorn hope. Men are killed outright in the reserves sometimes, while others who have been left for dead in the thickest corner crawl out and survive.

'If we miss these meadows – ' said Woodhouse presently in his slow way.

'My dear chap,' said Monson, whose spirits had been rising fitfully during the last few days, 'we mustn't miss these meadows. There's a quarter of a square mile for us to hit, fences removed, ditches levelled. We shall come down all right – rest assured. And if we don't – '

'Ah!' said Woodhouse. 'If we don't!'

Before the day of the start, the newspaper people got wind of the alterations at the northward end of the framework, and Monson was cheered by a decided change in the comments Romeike forwarded him. 'He will be off some day,' said the papers. 'He will be off some day,' said the South-Western season-ticket holders one to another; the seaside excursionists, the Saturday-to-Monday trippers from Sussex and Hampshire and Dorset and Devon, the eminent literary people from Haslemere,[409] all remarked eagerly one to another, 'He will be off some day,' as the familiar scaffolding came in sight. And, actually, one bright morning, in full view of the ten-past-ten train from Basingstoke, Monson's flying-machine started on its journey.

They saw the carrier running swiftly along its rail, and the white and gold screw spinning in the air. They heard the rapid rumble of wheels, and a thud as the carrier reached the buffers at the end of its run. Then a whirr as the Flying-Machine was shot forward into the networks. All that the majority of them had seen and heard before. The thing went with a dropping flight through the framework and rose again, and then every beholder shouted, or screamed, or yelled, or shrieked after his kind. For instead of the customary concussion and stoppage, the Flying-Machine flew out of its five years' cage like a bolt from a crossbow, and drove slantingly upwards into the air, curved round a little, so as to cross the line, and soared in the direction of Wimbledon Common.

It seemed to hang momentarily in the air and grow smaller, then it ducked and vanished over the clustering blue treetops to the east of Coombe Hill, and no one stopped staring and gasping until long after it had disappeared.

That was what the people in the train from Basingstoke saw. If you had drawn a line down the middle of that train, from engine to guard's van, you would not have found a living soul on the opposite side to the flying-machine. It was a mad rush from window to window as the thing crossed the line. And the engine-driver and stoker never took their eyes off the low hills about Wimbledon, and never noticed that they had run clean through Coombe and Malden and Raynes Park, until, with returning animation, they found themselves pelting, at the most indecent pace, into Wimbledon station.

From the moment when Monson had started the carrier with a 'Now!' neither he nor Woodhouse said a word. Both men sat with clenched teeth. Monson had crossed the line with a curve that was too sharp, and Woodhouse had opened and shut his white lips; but neither spoke. Woodhouse simply gripped his seat, and breathed sharply through his teeth, watching the blue country to the west rushing past, and down, and away from him. Monson knelt at his post forward, and his hands trembled on the spoked wheel that moved the wings. He could see nothing before him but a mass of white clouds in the sky.

The machine went slanting upwards, travelling with an enormous speed still, but losing momentum every moment. The land ran away underneath with diminishing speed.

'Now!' said Woodhouse at last, and with a violent effort Monson wrenched over the wheel and altered the angle of the wings. The machine seemed to hang for half a minute motionless in mid-air, and then he saw the hazy blue house-covered hills of Kilburn and Hampstead jump up before his eyes and rise steadily, until the little sunlit dome of the Albert Hall appeared through his windows. For a moment he scarcely understood the meaning of this upward rush of the horizon, but as the nearer and nearer houses came into view, he realised what he had done. He had turned the wings over too far, and they were swooping steeply downward towards the Thames.

The thought, the question, the realisation were all the business of a second of time. 'Too much!' gasped Woodhouse. Monson brought the wheel halfway back with a jerk, and forthwith the Kilburn and Hampstead ridge dropped again to the lower edge of his windows. They had been a thousand feet above Coombe and Malden station; fifty seconds after they whizzed, at a frightful pace, not eighty feet above the East Putney station, on the Metropolitan District line, to the screaming astonishment of a platformful of people. Monson flung up the vans[410] against the air, and over Fulham they rushed up their atmospheric switchback again, steeply – too steeply. The buses went floundering across the Fulham Road, the people yelled.

Then down again, too steeply still, and the distant trees and houses about Primrose Hill leapt up across Monson's window, and then suddenly he saw straight before him the greenery of Kensington Gardens and the towers of the Imperial Institute. They were driving straight down upon South Kensington. The pinnacles of the Natural History Museum rushed up into view. There came one fatal second of swift thought, a moment of hesitation. Should he try and clear the towers, or swerve eastward?

He made a hesitating attempt to release the right wing, left the catch half released, and gave a frantic clutch at the wheel.

The nose of the machine seemed to leap up before him. The wheel pressed his hand with irresistible force, and jerked itself out of his control.

Woodhouse, sitting crouched together, gave a hoarse cry, and sprang up towards Monson. 'Too far!' he cried, and then he was clinging to the gunwale[411] for dear life, and Monson had been jerked clean overhead, and was falling backwards upon him.

So swiftly had the thing happened that barely a quarter of the people going to and fro in Hyde Park and Brompton Road and the Exhibition Road saw anything of the aerial catastrophe. A distant winged shape had appeared above the clustering houses to the south, had fallen and risen, growing larger as it did so; had swooped swiftly down towards the Imperial Institute, a broad spread of flying wings, had swept round in a quarter circle, dashed eastward, and then suddenly sprung vertically into the air. A black object shot out of it, and came spinning downward. A man! Two men clutching each other! They came whirling down, separated as they struck the roof of the Students' Club, and bounded off into the green bushes on its southward side.

For perhaps half a minute, the pointed stem of the big machine still pierced vertically upward, the screw spinning desperately. For one brief instant, that yet seemed an age to all who watched, it had hung motionless in mid-air. Then a spout of yellow flame licked up its length from the stern engine, and swift, swifter, swifter, and flaring like a rocket, it rushed down upon the solid mass of masonry which was formerly the Royal College of Science.[412] The big screw of white and gold touched the parapet, and crumpled up like wet linen. Then the blazing spindle-shaped body smashed and splintered, smashing and splintering in its fall upon the north-westward angle of the building.

But the crash, the flame of blazing paraffin that shot heavenward from the shattered engines of the machine, the crushed horrors that were found in the garden beyond the Students' Club, the masses of yellow parapet and red brick that fell headlong into the roadway, the running to and fro of people like ants in a broken ant-hill, the galloping of fire-engines, the gathering of crowds – all these things do not belong to this story, which was written only to tell how the first of all successful flying-machines was launched and flew. Though he failed, and failed disastrously, the record of Monson's work remains a sufficient monument – to guide the next of that band of gallant experimentalists who will sooner or later master this great problem of flying. And between Worcester Park and Malden there still stands that portentous avenue of iron-work, rusting now, and dangerous here and there, to witness to the first desperate struggle for man's right of way through the air.

Miss Winchelsea's Heart [413]

Miss Winchelsea was going to Rome. The matter had filled her mind for a month or more, and had overflowed so abundantly into her conversation that quite a number of people who were not going to Rome, and who were not likely to go to Rome, had made it a personal grievance against her. Some indeed had attempted quite unavailingly to convince her that Rome was not nearly such a desirable place as it was reported to be, and others had gone so far as to suggest behind her back that she was dreadfully 'stuck up' about 'that Rome of hers'. And little Lily Hardhurst had told her friend Mr Binns that so far as she was concerned Miss Winchelsea might 'go to her old Rome and stop there; *she* [Miss Lily Hardhurst] wouldn't grieve'. And the way in which Miss Winchelsea put herself upon terms of personal tenderness with Horace and Benvenuto Cellini and Raphael and Shelley and Keats [414] – if she had been Shelley's widow she could not have professed a keener interest in his grave – was a matter of universal astonishment. Her dress was a triumph of tactful discretion, sensible, but not too 'touristy' – Miss Winchelsea, had a great dread of being 'touristy' – and her *Baedeker* was carried in a cover of grey to hide its glaring red. [415] She made a prim and pleasant little figure on the Charing Cross platform, in spite of her swelling pride, when at last the great day dawned and she could start for Rome. The day was bright, the Channel passage would be pleasant, and all the omens promised well. There was the gayest sense of adventure in this unprecedented departure.

She was going with two friends who had been fellow-students with her at the training college, nice honest girls both, though not so good at history and literature as Miss Winchelsea. They both looked up to her immensely, though physically they had to look down, and she anticipated some pleasant times to be spent in 'stirring them up' to her own pitch of aesthetic and historical enthusiasm. They had secured seats already, and welcomed her effusively at the carriage door. In the instant criticism of the encounter she noted that Fanny had a slightly 'touristy' leather strap, and that Helen had succumbed to a serge jacket with side pockets, into which her hands were thrust. But they were much too happy with themselves and the expedition for their friend to attempt any hint at the moment about these things. As soon as the first ecstasies were over – Fanny's enthusiasm was a little noisy and crude, and consisted mainly in emphatic repetitions of, 'Just *fancy*! We're going to Rome, my dear! – Rome! – ' they gave their attention to their fellow-travellers. Helen was anxious to secure a compartment to themselves, and, in order to discourage intruders, got out and planted herself firmly on the step. Miss Winchelsea peeped out over her shoulder, and made sly little remarks about the accumulating people on the platform, at which Fanny laughed gleefully.

They were travelling with one of Mr Thomas Gunn's parties[416] – fourteen days in Rome for fourteen pounds. They did not belong to the personally conducted party of course – Miss Winchelsea had seen to that – but they travelled with it because of the convenience of that arrangement. The people were the oddest mixture, and wonderfully amusing. There was a vociferous red-faced polyglot personal conductor in a pepper-and-salt suit,[417] very long in the arms and legs and very active. He shouted proclamations. When he wanted to speak to people he stretched out an arm and held them until his purpose was accomplished. One hand was full of papers, tickets, counterfoils of tourists. The people of the personally conducted party were, it seemed, of two sorts: people the conductor wanted and could not find, and people he did not want and who followed him in a steadily growing tail up and down the platform. These people seemed, indeed, to think that their one chance of reaching Rome lay in keeping close to him. Three little old ladies were particularly energetic in his pursuit, and at last maddened him to the pitch of clapping them into a carriage and daring them to emerge again. For the rest of the time, one, two or three of their heads protruded from the window wailing enquiries about 'a little wickerwork box' whenever he drew near. There was a very stout man with a very stout wife in shiny black; there was a little old man like an aged hostler.[418]

'What can such people want in Rome?' asked Miss Winchelsea. 'What can it mean to them?' There was a very tall curate in a very small straw hat, and a very short curate encumbered by a long camera stand. The contrast amused Fanny very much. Once they heard someone calling for 'Snooks'. 'I always thought that name was invented by novelists,' said Miss Winchelsea. 'Fancy! Snooks. I wonder which is Mr Snooks.' Finally they picked out a very stout and resolute little man in a large check suit. 'If he isn't Snooks, he ought to be,' said Miss Winchelsea.

Presently the conductor discovered Helen's attempt at a corner in carriages. 'Room for five,' he bawled, with a parallel translation on his fingers. A party of four together – mother, father and two daughters –

blundered in, all greatly excited. 'It's all right, Ma – you let me,' said one of the daughters, hitting her mother's bonnet with a handbag she struggled to put in the rack. Miss Winchelsea detested people who banged about and called their mother 'Ma'. A young man travelling alone followed. He was not at all 'touristy' in his costume, Miss Winchelsea observed; his Gladstone bag[419] was of good pleasant leather with labels reminiscent of Luxembourg and Ostend, and his boots, though brown, were not vulgar. He carried an overcoat on his arm. Before these people had properly settled in their places came an inspection of tickets and a slamming of doors, and behold! they were gliding out of Charing Cross station on their way to Rome.

'Fancy!' cried Fanny, 'we are going to Rome, my dear! Rome! I don't seem to believe it, even now.'

Miss Winchelsea suppressed Fanny's emotions with a little smile, and the lady who was called 'Ma' explained to people in general why they had 'cut it so close' at the station. The two daughters called her 'Ma' several times, toned her down in a tactless effective way, and drove her at last to the muttered inventory of a basket of travelling requisites. Presently she looked up. 'Lor'!' she said, 'I didn't bring them!' Both the daughters said, 'Oh, Ma!' but what 'them' was did not appear. Presently Fanny produced Hare's *Walks in Rome*,[420] a sort of mitigated guidebook very popular among Roman visitors; and the father of the two daughters began to examine his books of tickets minutely, apparently in a search after English words. When he had looked at the tickets for a long time right way up, he turned them upside down. Then he produced a fountain pen and dated them with considerable care. The young man, having completed an unostentatious survey of his fellow travellers, produced a book and fell to reading. When Helen and Fanny were looking out of the window at Chislehurst – the place interested Fanny because the poor dear Empress of the French[421] used to live there – Miss Winchelsea took the opportunity to observe the book the young man held. It was not a guidebook, but a little thin volume of poetry – *bound*.[422] She glanced at his face – it seemed a refined pleasant face to her hasty glance. He wore a little gilt *pince-nez*.[423] 'Do you think she lives there now?' said Fanny, and Miss Winchelsea's inspection came to an end.

For the rest of the journey Miss Winchelsea talked little, and what she said was as pleasant and as stamped with refinement as she could make it. Her voice was always low and clear and pleasant, and she took care that on this occasion it was particularly low and clear and pleasant. As they came under the white cliffs the young man put his book of poetry away, and when at last the train stopped beside the boat, he displayed a graceful alacrity with the impedimenta[424] of Miss Winchelsea and her friends. Miss Winchelsea hated nonsense, but she was pleased to see the young man perceived at once that they were ladies, and helped them without any violent geniality; and how nicely he showed that his civilities were to be no excuse for further intrusions. None of her little party had been out of England before, and they were all excited and a little nervous at the Channel passage. They stood in a little group in a good place near the middle of the boat – the young man had taken Miss Winchelsea's hold-all there and had told her it was a good place – and they watched the white shores of Albion[425] recede and quoted Shakespeare and made quiet fun of their fellow travellers in the English way.

They were particularly amused at the precautions the bigger-sized people had taken against the waves – cut lemons and flasks prevailed, one lady lay full length in a deck chair with a handkerchief over her face, and a very broad resolute man in a bright brown 'touristy' suit walked all the way from England to France along the deck, with his legs as widely apart as Providence permitted. These were all excellent precautions, and nobody was ill. The personally conducted party pursued the conductor about the deck with enquiries in a manner that suggested to Helen's mind the rather vulgar image of hens with a piece of bacon rind, until at last he went into hiding below. And the young man with the thin volume of poetry stood at the stern watching England receding, looking rather lonely and sad to Miss Winchelsea's eye.

And then came Calais and tumultuous novelties, and the young man had not forgotten Miss Winchelsea's hold-all and the other little things. All three girls, though they had passed government examinations in French to any extent, were stricken with a dumb shame of their accents, and the young man was very useful. And he did not intrude. He put them in a comfortable carriage and raised his hat and went away. Miss Winchelsea thanked him in her best manner – a pleasing, cultivated manner – and Fanny said he was 'nice' almost before he was out of earshot. 'I wonder what he can be,' said Helen. 'He's going to Italy, because I noticed green tickets in his book.' Miss Winchelsea almost told them of the poetry, and decided not to do so. And presently the carriage windows seized hold upon them and the young man was forgotten. It made them feel that they were doing an educated sort of thing to travel through a country whose commonest advertisements were in idiomatic French, and Miss Winchelsea made unpatriotic comparisons because there were weedy little signboard advertisements by the rail side instead of the broad hoardings that deface the landscape in our land. But the north of France is really uninteresting country, and after a time Fanny reverted to Hare's *Walks* and Helen initiated lunch. Miss Winchelsea awoke out of a happy reverie; she had been trying to realise, she said, that she was actually going to Rome, but she perceived at Helen's suggestion that she was hungry, and they lunched out of their baskets very cheerfully. In the afternoon they were tired and silent until Helen made tea. Miss Winchelsea might have dozed, only she knew Fanny slept with her mouth open; and as their fellow passengers were two rather nice critical-looking ladies of uncertain age – who knew French well enough to talk it – she employed herself in keeping Fanny awake. The rhythm of the train became insistent, and the streaming landscape outside became at last quite painful to the eye. They were already dreadfully tired of travelling before their night's stoppage came.

The stoppage for the night was brightened by the appearance of the young man, and his manners were all that could be desired and his French quite serviceable. His coupons availed for the same hotel as theirs, and by chance as it seemed he sat next Miss Winchelsea at the *table d'hôte*.[426] In spite of her enthusiasm for Rome, she had thought out some such possibility very thoroughly, and when he ventured to make a remark upon the tediousness of travelling – he let the soup and fish go by before he did this – she did not simply assent to his proposition, but responded with another. They were soon comparing their journeys, and Helen and Fanny were cruelly overlooked in the conversation. It was to be the same journey, they found; one day for the galleries at Florence – 'from what I hear,' said the young man, 'it is barely enough – ' and the rest at Rome. He talked of Rome very pleasantly; he was evidently quite well read, and he quoted Horace about Soracte.[427] Miss Winchelsea had 'done' that book of Horace for her matriculation, and was delighted to cap his quotation. It gave a sort of tone to things, this incident – a touch of refinement to mere chatting. Fanny expressed a few emotions, and Helen interpolated a few sensible remarks, but the bulk of the talk on the girls' side naturally fell to Miss Winchelsea.

Before they reached Rome this young man was tacitly of their party. They did not know his name nor what he was, but it seemed he taught, and Miss Winchelsea had a shrewd idea he was an extension lecturer.[428] At any rate he was something of that sort, something gentlemanly and refined without being opulent and impossible. She tried once or twice to ascertain whether he came from Oxford or Cambridge, but he missed her timid importunities. She tried to get him to make remarks about those places to see if he would say 'come up' to them instead of 'go down' – she knew that was how you told a 'Varsity man. He used the word ' 'Varsity' – not university – in quite the proper way.

They saw as much of Mr Ruskin's Florence[429] as the brief time permitted; he met them in the Pitti Gallery and went round with them, chatting brightly, and evidently very grateful for their recognition. He knew a great deal about art, and all four enjoyed the morning immensely. It was fine to go round recognising old favourites and finding new beauties, especially while so many people fumbled helplessly with Baedeker. Nor was he a bit of a prig,[430] Miss Winchelsea said, and indeed she detested prigs. He had a distinct undertone of humour, and was funny, for example, without being vulgar, at the expense of the quaint work of Beato Angelico.[431] He had a grave seriousness beneath it all, and was quick to seize the moral lessons of the pictures. Fanny went softly among these masterpieces; she admitted 'she knew so little about them', and she confessed that to her they were 'all beautiful'. Fanny's 'beautiful' inclined to be a little monotonous, Miss Winchelsea thought. She had been quite glad when the last sunny Alp had vanished, because of the staccato of Fanny's admiration. Helen said little, but Miss Winchelsea had found her a little wanting on the aesthetic side in the old days and was not surprised; sometimes she laughed at the young man's hesitating delicate little jests and sometimes she didn't, and sometimes she seemed quite lost to the art about them in the contemplation of the dresses of the other visitors.

At Rome the young man was with them intermittently. A rather 'touristy' friend of his took him away at times. He complained comically to Miss Winchelsea. 'I have only two short weeks in Rome,' he said, 'and my friend Leonard wants to spend a whole day at Tivoli looking at a waterfall.'[432]

'What is your friend Leonard?' asked Miss Winchelsea abruptly.

'He's the most enthusiastic pedestrian I ever met,' the young man replied – amusingly, but a little unsatisfactorily, Miss Winchelsea thought.

They had some glorious times, and Fanny could not think what they would have done without him. Miss Winchelsea's interest and Fanny's enormous capacity for admiration were insatiable. They never flagged – through pictures and sculpture galleries, immense crowded churches, ruins and museums, Judas trees and prickly pears, wine carts and palaces, they admired their way unflinchingly. They never saw a stone pine or a eucalyptus but they named and admired it; they never glimpsed Soracte but they exclaimed. Their common ways were made wonderful by imaginative play. 'Here Caesar may have walked,' they would say. 'Raphael may have seen Soracte from this very point.' They happened on the tomb of Bibulus.[433]

'Old Bibulus,' said the young man.

'The oldest monument of Republican Rome!' said Miss Winchelsea.

'I'm dreadfully stupid,' said Fanny, 'but who *was* Bibulus?'

There was a curious little pause.

'Wasn't he the person who built the wall?' said Helen.

The young man glanced quickly at her and laughed. 'That was Balbus,' he said.[434] Helen reddened, but neither he nor Miss Winchelsea threw any light upon Fanny's ignorance about Bibulus.

Helen was more taciturn than the other three, but then she was always taciturn, and usually she took care of the tram tickets and things like that, or kept her eye on them if the young man took them, and told him where they were when he wanted them. Glorious times they had, these young people, in that pale brown cleanly city of memories that was once the world. Their only sorrow was the shortness of the time. They said indeed that the electric trams and the '70 buildings[435], and that criminal advertisement that glares upon the Forum,[436] outraged their aesthetic feelings unspeakably; but that was only part of the fun. And indeed Rome is such a wonderful place that it made Miss Winchelsea forget some of her most carefully prepared enthusiasms at times, and Helen, taken unawares, would suddenly admit the beauty of unexpected things. Yet Fanny and Helen would have liked a shop window or so in the English quarter if Miss Winchelsea's uncompromising hostility to all other English visitors had not rendered that district impossible.

The intellectual and aesthetic fellowship of Miss Winchelsea and the scholarly young man passed insensibly towards a deeper feeling. The exuberant Fanny did her best to keep pace with their recondite admiration by playing her 'beautiful' with vigour, and saying, 'Oh! *let's* go,' with enormous appetite whenever a new place of interest was mentioned. But Helen developed a certain want of sympathy towards the end that disappointed Miss Winchelsea a little. She refused to 'see anything' in the face of Beatrice Cenci – Shelley's Beatrice Cenci![437] – in the Barberini Gallery; and one day, when they were deploring the electric trams, she said rather snappishly that 'people must get about somehow, and it's better than torturing horses up these horrid little hills'. She spoke of the Seven Hills of Rome[438] as 'horrid little hills'!

And the day they went on the Palatine[439] – though Miss Winchelsea did not know of this – she remarked suddenly to Fanny, 'Don't hurry like that, my dear; *they* don't want us to overtake them. And we don't say the right things for them when we *do* get near.'

'I wasn't trying to overtake them,' said Fanny, slackening her excessive pace; 'I wasn't indeed.' And for a minute she was short of breath.

But Miss Winchelsea had come upon happiness. It was only when she came to look back across an intervening tragedy that she quite realised how happy she had been, pacing among the cypress-shadowed ruins, and exchanging the very highest class of information the human mind can possess, the most refined impressions it is possible to convey. Insensibly emotion crept into their intercourse, sunning itself openly and pleasantly at last when Helen's modernity was not too near. Insensibly their interest drifted from the wonderful associations about them to their more intimate and personal feelings. In a tentative way information was supplied; she spoke allusively of her school, of her examination successes, of her gladness that the days of 'Cram' were over. He made it quite clear that he also was a teacher. They spoke of the greatness of their calling, of the necessity of sympathy to face its irksome details, of a certain loneliness they sometimes felt.

That was in the Colosseum, and it was as far as they got that day, because Helen returned with Fanny – she had taken her into the upper galleries. Yet the private dreams of Miss Winchelsea, already vivid and concrete enough, became now realistic in the highest degree. She figured that pleasant young man, lecturing in the most edifying way to his students, herself modestly prominent as his intellectual mate and helper; she figured a refined little home, with two bureaus, with white shelves of high-class books, and autotypes of the pictures of Rossetti and Burne-Jones, with Morris's wallpapers[440] and flowers in pots of beaten copper. Indeed she figured many things. On the Pincio[441] the two had a few precious moments together, while Helen marched Fanny off to see the *muro Torto*,[442] and he spoke at once plainly. He said he hoped their friendship was only beginning, that he already found her company very precious to him, that indeed it was more than that.

He became nervous, thrusting at his glasses with trembling fingers as though he fancied his emotions made them unstable. 'I should of course,' he said, 'tell you things about myself. I know it is rather unusual my speaking to you like this. Only our meeting has been so accidental – or providential – and I am snatching at things. I came to Rome expecting a lonely tour . . . and I have been so very happy, so very happy. Quite recently I found myself in a position – I have dared to think . . . And – '

He glanced over his shoulder and stopped. He said, 'Demn!'[443] quite distinctly – and she did not condemn him for that manly lapse into profanity. She looked and saw his friend Leonard advancing. He drew nearer; he raised his hat to Miss Winchelsea, and his smile was almost a grin. 'I've been looking for you everywhere, Snooks,' he said. 'You promised to be on the Piazza steps[444] half an hour ago.'

Snooks! The name struck Miss Winchelsea like a blow in the face. She did not hear his reply. She thought afterwards that Leonard must have considered her the vaguest-minded person. To this day she is not sure whether she was introduced to Leonard or not, nor what she said to him. A sort of mental paralysis was upon her. Of all offensive surnames – Snooks!

Helen and Fanny were returning, there were civilities, and the young men were receding. By a great effort she controlled herself to face the enquiring eyes of her friends. All that afternoon she lived the life of a heroine under the indescribable outrage of that name, chatting, observing, with 'Snooks' gnawing at her heart. From the moment that it first rang upon her ears, the dream of her happiness was prostrate in the dust. All the refinement she had figured was ruined and defaced by that cognomen's unavoidable vulgarity.

What was that refined little home to her now, spite of autotypes, Morris papers, and bureaus? Athwart it in letters of fire ran an incredible inscription: 'Mrs Snooks.' That may seem a little thing to the reader, but consider the delicate refinement of Miss Winchelsea's mind. Be as refined as you can and then think of writing yourself down: 'Snooks'. She conceived herself being addressed as Mrs Snooks by all the people she liked least, conceived the patronymic touched with a vague quality of insult. She figured a card of grey and silver bearing 'Winchelsea' triumphantly effaced by an arrow, Cupid's arrow, in favour of 'Snooks'. Degrading confession of feminine weakness! She imagined the terrible rejoicings of certain girl friends, of certain grocer cousins from whom her growing refinement had long since estranged her. How they would make it sprawl across the envelope that would bring their sarcastic congratulations. Would even his pleasant company compensate her for that? 'It is impossible,' she muttered; 'impossible! Snooks!'

She was sorry for him, but not so sorry as she was for herself. For him she had a touch of indignation. To be so nice, so refined, while all the time he was 'Snooks'; to hide under a pretentious gentility of demeanour the badge sinister[445] of his surname seemed a sort of treachery. To put it in the language of sentimental science she felt he had 'led her on'.

There were of course moments of terrible vacillation, a period even when something almost like passion bid her throw refinement to the winds. And there was something in her, an unexpurgated vestige of vulgarity, that made a strenuous attempt at proving that Snooks was not so very bad a name after all. Any hovering hesitation flew before Fanny's manner, when Fanny came with an air of catastrophe to tell that she also knew the horror. Fanny's voice fell to a whisper when she said Snooks. Miss Winchelsea would not give him any answer when at last, in the Borghese,[446] she could have a minute with him; but she promised him a note.

She handed him that note in the little book of poetry he had lent her, the little book that had first drawn them together. Her refusal was ambiguous, allusive. She could no more tell him why she rejected him than she could have told a cripple of his hump. He too must feel something of the unspeakable quality of his name. Indeed he had avoided a dozen chances of telling it, she now perceived. So she spoke of 'obstacles she could not reveal' – 'reasons why the thing he spoke of was impossible'. She addressed the note with a shiver, 'E. K. Snooks'.

Things were worse than she had dreaded; he asked her to explain. How *could* she explain? Those last two days in Rome were dreadful. She was haunted by his air of astonished perplexity. She knew she had given him intimate hopes, she had not the courage to examine her mind thoroughly for the extent of her encouragement. She knew he must think her the most changeable of beings. Now that she was in full retreat, she would not even perceive his hints of a possible correspondence. But in that matter he did a thing that seemed to her at once delicate and romantic. He made a go-between of Fanny. Fanny could not keep the secret, and came and told her that night under a transparent pretext of needing advice. 'Mr Snooks,' said Fanny, 'wants to write to me. Fancy! I had no idea. But should I let him?' They talked it over long and earnestly, and Miss Winchelsea was careful to keep the veil over her heart. She was already repenting his disregarded hints. Why should she not hear of him sometimes – painful though his name must be to her? Miss Winchelsea decided it might be permitted, and Fanny kissed her good-night with unusual emotion. After she had gone Miss Winchelsea sat for a long time at the window of her little room. It was moonlight, and down the street a man sang 'Santa Lucia' with almost heart-dissolving tenderness . . . She sat very still.

She breathed a word very softly to herself. The word was '*Snooks*'. Then she got up with a profound sigh, and went to bed. The next morning he said to her meaningly, 'I shall hear of you through your friend.'

Mr Snooks saw them off from Rome with that pathetic interrogative perplexity still on his face, and if it had not been for Helen he would have retained Miss Winchelsea's hold-all in his hand as a sort of encyclopaedic keepsake. On their way back to England, Miss Winchelsea on six separate occasions made Fanny promise to write to her the longest of long letters. Fanny, it seemed, would be quite near Mr Snooks. Her new school – she was always going to new schools – would be only five miles from Steely Bank, and it was in the Steely Bank Polytechnic, and one or two first-class schools, that Mr Snooks did his teaching. He might even see her at times. They could not talk much of him – she and Fanny always spoke of 'him', never of Mr Snooks – because Helen was apt to say unsympathetic things about him. Her nature had coarsened very much, Miss Winchelsea perceived, since the old training-college days; she had become hard and cynical. She thought he had a weak face, mistaking refinement for weakness as people of her stamp are apt to do, and when she heard his name was Snooks, she said she had expected something of the sort. Miss Winchelsea was careful to spare her own feelings after that, but Fanny was less circumspect.

The girls parted in London, and Miss Winchelsea returned, with a new interest in life, to the Girls' High School in which she had been an increasingly valuable assistant for the last three years. Her new interest in life was Fanny as a correspondent, and to give her a lead she wrote her a lengthy descriptive letter within a fortnight of her return. Fanny answered, very disappointingly. Fanny indeed had no literary gift, but it was new to Miss Winchelsea to find herself deploring the want of gifts in a friend. That letter was even criticised aloud in the safe solitude of Miss Winchelsea's study, and her criticism, spoken with great bitterness, was 'Twaddle!' It was full of just the things Miss Winchelsea's letter had been full of, particulars of the school. And of Mr Snooks, only this much: 'I have had a letter from Mr Snooks, and he has been over to see me on two Saturday afternoons running. He talked about Rome and you; we both talked about you. Your ears must have burnt, my dear . . .'

Miss Winchelsea repressed a desire to demand more explicit information, and wrote the sweetest long letter again. 'Tell me all about yourself, dear. That journey has quite refreshed our ancient friendship, and I do so want to keep in touch with you.' About Mr Snooks she simply wrote on the fifth page that she was glad Fanny had seen him, and that if he *should* ask after her, she was to be remembered to him very kindly (underlined). And Fanny replied most obtusely in the key of that 'ancient friendship', reminding Miss Winchelsea of a dozen foolish things of those old schoolgirl days at the training college, and saying not a word about Mr Snooks!

For nearly a week Miss Winchelsea was so angry at the failure of Fanny as a go-between that she could not write to her. And then she wrote less effusively, and in her letter she asked point blank, 'Have you seen Mr Snooks?' Fanny's letter was unexpectedly satisfactory. 'I have seen Mr Snooks,' she wrote, and having once named him she kept on about him; it was all Snooks – Snooks this and Snooks that. He was to give a public lecture, said Fanny, among other things. Yet Miss Winchelsea, after the first glow of gratification, still found this letter a little unsatisfactory. Fanny did not report Mr Snooks as saying anything about Miss Winchelsea, nor as looking a little white and worn, as he ought to have been doing. And behold! before she had replied, came a second letter from Fanny on the same theme, quite a gushing letter, and covering six sheets with her loose feminine hand.

And about this second letter was a rather odd little thing that Miss Winchelsea only noticed as she re-read it the third time. Fanny's natural femininity had prevailed even against the round and clear traditions of the training college; she was one of those she-creatures born to make all her m's and n's and u's and r's and e's alike, and to leave her o's and a's open and her i's undotted. So that it was only after an elaborate comparison of word with word that Miss Winchelsea felt assured Mr Snooks was not really 'Mr Snooks' at all! In Fanny's first letter of gush he was Mr 'Snooks', in her second the spelling was changed to Mr 'Senoks'. Miss Winchelsea's hand positively trembled as she turned the sheet over – it meant so much to her. For it had already begun to seem to her that the name of Mrs Snooks might be avoided at too great a price, and suddenly – this possibility! She turned over the six sheets, all dappled with that critical name, and everywhere the first letter[447] had the form of an e! For a time she walked the room with a hand pressed upon her heart.

She spent a whole day pondering this change, weighing a letter of enquiry that should be at once discreet and effectual, weighing too what action she should take after the answer came. She was resolved that if this altered spelling was anything more than a quaint fancy of Fanny's, she would write forthwith to Mr Snooks. She had now reached a stage when the minor refinements of behaviour disappear. Her excuse remained uninvented, but she had the subject of her letter clear in her mind, even to the hint that 'circumstances in my life have changed very greatly since we talked together'. But she never gave that hint. There came a third letter from that fitful correspondent Fanny. The first line proclaimed her 'the happiest girl alive'.

Miss Winchelsea crushed the letter in her hand – the rest unread –

and sat with her face suddenly very still. She had received it just before morning school, and had opened it when the junior mathematicians were well under way. Presently she resumed reading with an appearance of great calm. But after the first sheet she went on to the third without discovering the error: 'told him frankly I did not like his name' the third sheet began. 'He told me he did not like it himself – you know that sort of sudden frank way he has' – Miss Winchelsea did know. 'So I said, "Couldn't you change it?" He didn't see it at first. Well, you know dear, he had told me what it really meant; it means Sevenoaks,[448] only it has got down to Snooks – both Snooks and Noaks, dreadfully vulgar surnames though they be, are really worn forms of Sevenoaks. So I said – even I have my bright ideas at times – 'if it got down from Sevenoaks to Snooks, why not get it back from Snooks to Sevenoaks?' And the long and the short of it is dear, he couldn't refuse me, and he changed his spelling there and then to Senoks for the bills of the new lecture. And afterwards, when we are married, we shall put in the apostrophe and make it Se'noks. Wasn't it kind of him to mind that fancy of mine, when many men would have taken offence? But it is just like him all over; he is as kind as he is clever. Because he knew as well as I did that I would have had him in spite of it, had he been ten times Snooks. But he did it all the same.'

The class was startled by the sound of paper being viciously torn, and looked up to see Miss Winchelsea white in the face, and with some very small pieces of paper clenched in one hand. For a few seconds they stared at her stare, and then her expression changed back to a more familiar one. 'Has anyone finished number three?' she asked in an even tone. She remained calm after that. But impositions ruled high[449] that day. And she spent two laborious evenings writing letters of various sorts to Fanny, before she found a decent congratulatory vein. Her reason struggled hopelessly against the persuasion that Fanny had behaved in an exceedingly treacherous manner.

One may be extremely refined and still capable of a very sore heart. Certainly Miss Winchelsea's heart was very sore. She had moods of sexual hostility, in which she generalised uncharitably about mankind. 'He forgot himself with me,' she said. 'But Fanny is pink and pretty and soft and a fool – a very excellent match for a Man.' And by way of a wedding present she sent Fanny a gracefully bound volume of poetry by George Meredith, and Fanny wrote back a grossly happy letter to say that it was '*all* beautiful'. Miss Winchelsea hoped that some day Mr Senoks might take up that slim book and think for a moment of the donor. Fanny wrote several times before and about her marriage, pursuing that fond legend of their 'ancient friendship', and giving her happiness in the fullest detail. And Miss Winchelsea wrote to Helen for the first time after the Roman journey, saying nothing about the marriage, but expressing very cordial feelings.

They had been in Rome at Easter, and Fanny was married in the August vacation. She wrote a garrulous letter to Miss Winchelsea, describing her homecoming, and the astonishing arrangements of their 'teeny weeny' little house. Mr Se'noks was now beginning to assume a refinement in Miss Winchelsea's memory out of all proportion to the facts of the case, and she tried in vain to imagine his cultured greatness in a 'teeny weeny' little house. 'Am busy enamelling a cosy corner,' said Fanny, sprawling to the end of her third sheet, 'so excuse more.' Miss Winchelsea answered in her best style, gently poking fun at Fanny's arrangements and hoping intensely that Mr Se'noks might see the letter. Only this hope enabled her to write at all, answering not only that letter but one in November and one at Christmas.

The two latter communications contained urgent invitations for her to come to Steely Bank on a visit during the Christmas holidays. She tried to think that *he* had told her to ask that, but it was too much like Fanny's opulent good-nature. She could not but believe that he must be sick of his blunder by this time; and she had more than a hope that he would presently write her a letter beginning 'Dear Friend'. Something subtly tragic in the separation was a great support to her, a sad misunderstanding. To have been jilted would have been intolerable. But he never wrote that letter beginning 'Dear Friend'.

For two years Miss Winchelsea could not go to see her friends, in spite of the reiterated invitations of Mrs Sevenoaks – it became full Sevenoaks in the second year. Then one day near the Easter rest she felt lonely and without a soul to understand her in the world, and her mind ran once more on what is called Platonic friendship. Fanny was clearly happy and busy in her new sphere of domesticity, but no doubt *he* had his lonely hours. Did he ever think of those days in Rome – gone now beyond recalling? No one had understood her as he had done; no one in all the world. It would be a sort of melancholy pleasure to talk to him again, and what harm could it do? Why should she deny herself? That night she wrote a sonnet, all but the last two lines of the octave – which would not come, and the next day she composed a graceful little note to tell Fanny she was coming down.

And so she saw him again.

Even at the first encounter it was evident he had changed; he seemed stouter and less nervous, and it speedily appeared that his conversation had already lost much of its old delicacy. There even seemed a justification for Helen's description of weakness in his face – in certain lights it *was* weak. He seemed busy and preoccupied about his affairs, and almost under the impression that Miss Winchelsea had come for the sake of Fanny. He discussed his dinner with Fanny in an intelligent way. They only had one good long talk together, and that came to nothing. He did not refer to Rome, and spent some time abusing a man who had stolen an idea he had had for a textbook. It did not seem a very wonderful idea to Miss Winchelsea. She discovered he had forgotten the names of more than half the painters whose work they had rejoiced over in Florence.

It was a sadly disappointing week, and Miss Winchelsea was glad when it came to an end. Under various excuses she avoided visiting them again. After a time the visitor's room was occupied by their two little boys, and Fanny's invitations ceased. The intimacy of her letters had long since faded away.

A Vision of Judgement [450]

1

Bru-a-a-a.

I listened, not understanding.

Wa-ra-ra-ra.

'Good Lord!' said I, still only half awake. 'What an infernal shindy!'

Ra-ra-ra-ra-ra-ra-ra-ra-ra. Ta-ra-rra-ra.

'It's enough,' said I, 'to wake – ' and stopped short. Where was I?

Ta-rra-rara – louder and louder.

'It's either some new invention – '

Toora-toora-toora! Deafening!

'No,' said I, speaking loud in order to hear myself. 'That's the Last Trump.'

Tooo-rraa!

2

The last note jerked me out of my grave like a hooked minnow.

I saw my monument (rather a mean little affair, and I wished I knew who'd done it), and the old elm tree and the sea view vanished like a puff of steam, and then all about me – a multitude no man could number, nations, tongues, kingdoms, peoples – children of all ages, in an amphitheatral space as vast as the sky. And over against us, seated on a throne of dazzling white cloud, the Lord God and all the host of his angels. I recognised Azreal [451] by his darkness and Michael [452] by his sword, and the great angel who had blown the trumpet stood with the trumpet still half raised.

3

'Prompt,' said the little man beside me. 'Very prompt. Do you see the angel with the book?'

He was ducking and craning his head about to see over and under and between the souls that crowded round us. 'Everybody's here,' he said. 'Everybody. And now we shall know –

'There's Darwin,' he said, going off at a tangent. '*He'll* catch it!'[453] And there – you see? – That tall, important-looking man trying to catch the eye of the Lord God, that's the Duke. But there's a lot of people one doesn't know.

'Oh! There's Priggles, the publisher. I have always wondered about printers' overs.[454] Priggles was a clever man . . . But we shall know now – even about him.

'I shall hear all that. I shall get most of the fun before . . . *My* letter's S.'

He drew the air in between his teeth.

'Historical characters, too. See? That's Henry the Eighth. There'll be a good bit of evidence. Oh, damn! He's Tudor.'[455]

He lowered his voice. 'Notice this chap, just in front of us, all covered with hair. Paleolithic, you know. And there again – '

But I did not heed him, because I was looking at the Lord God.

4

'Is this *all*?' asked the Lord God.

The angel at the book – it was one of countless volumes, like the British Museum Reading-Room Catalogue[456] – glanced at us and seemed to count us in the instant.

'That's all,' he said, and added: 'It was, O God, a very little planet.'

The eyes of God surveyed us.

'Let us begin,' said the Lord God.

5

The angel opened the book and read a name. It was a name full of A's, and the echoes of it came back out of the uttermost parts of space. I did not catch it clearly, because the little man beside me said, in a sharp jerk, '*What's* that?' It sounded like 'Ahab' to me; but it could not have been the Ahab of Scripture.

Instantly a small black figure was lifted up to a puffy cloud at the very feet of God. It was a stiff little figure, dressed in rich outlandish robes and crowned, and it folded its arms and scowled.

'Well?' said God, looking down at him.

We were privileged to hear the reply, and indeed the acoustic properties of the place were marvellous.

'I plead guilty,' said the little figure.

'Tell them what you have done,' said the Lord God.

'I was a king,' said the little figure, 'a great king, and I was lustful and proud and cruel. I made wars, I devastated countries, I built palaces, and the mortar was the blood of men. Hear, O God, the witnesses against me, calling to you for vengeance. Hundreds and thousands of witnesses.' He waved his hands towards us. 'And worse! I took a prophet – one of your prophets – '

'One of my prophets,' said the Lord God.

'And because he would not bow to me, I tortured him for four days and nights, and in the end he died. I did more, O God, I blasphemed. I robbed you of your honours – '

'Robbed me of my honours,' said the Lord God.

'And caused myself to be worshipped in your stead. No evil was there, but I practised it; no cruelty wherewith I did not stain my soul. And at last you smote me, O God!'

God raised his eyebrows slightly.

'And I was slain in battle. And so I stand before you, meet for your nethermost Hell! Out of your greatness daring no lies, daring no pleas, but telling the truth of my iniquities before all mankind.'

He ceased. His face I saw distinctly, and it seemed to me white and terrible and proud and strangely noble. I thought of Milton's Satan.[457]

'Most of that is from the Obelisk,'[458] said the Recording Angel, finger on page.

'It is,' said the Tyrannous Man, with a faint touch of surprise.

Then suddenly God bent forward and took this man in his hand, and held him up on his palm as if to see him better. He was just a little dark stroke in the middle of God's palm.

'*Did* he do all this?' said the Lord God.

The Recording Angel flattened his book with his hand.

'In a way,' said the Recording Angel, carelessly.

Now when I looked again at the little man his face had changed in a very curious manner. He was looking at the Recording Angel with strange apprehension in his eyes, and one hand fluttered to his mouth. Just the movement of a muscle or so, and all that dignity of defiance was gone.

'Read,' said the Lord God.

And the angel read, explaining very carefully and fully all the wickedness of the Wicked Man. It was quite an intellectual treat. – A little 'daring' in places, I thought, but of course Heaven has its privileges . . .

6

Everybody was laughing. Even the prophet of the Lord whom the Wicked Man had tortured had a smile on his face. The Wicked Man was really such a preposterous little fellow.

'And then,' reading the Recording Angel, with a smile that set us all agog, 'one day, when he was a little irascible from over-eating, he – '

'Oh, not *that*,' cried the Wicked Man, 'nobody knew of *that*.

'It didn't happen,' screamed the Wicked Man. 'I was bad – I was really bad. Frequently bad, but there was nothing so silly – so absolutely silly – '

The angel went on reading.

'O God!' cried the Wicked Man. 'Don't let them know that! I'll repent! I'll apologise . . . '

The Wicked Man on God's hand began to dance and weep. Suddenly shame overcame him. He made a wild rush to jump off the ball of God's little finger, but God stopped him by a dexterous turn of the wrist. Then he made a rush for a gap between hand and thumb, but the thumb closed. And all the while the angel went on reading – reading. The Wicked Man rushed to and fro across God's palm, and then suddenly turned about and fled up the sleeve of God.

I expected God would turn him out, but the mercy of God is infinite.

The Recording Angel paused.

'Eh?' said the Recording Angel.

'Next,' said God, and before the Recording Angel could call upon the name, a hairy creature in filthy rags stood upon God's palm.

7

'Has God got Hell up his sleeve then?' said the little man beside me.

'Is there a Hell?' I asked.

'If you notice,' he said – he peered between the feet of the great angels – 'there's no particular indication of the Celestial City.'

'Ssh!' said a little woman near us, scowling. 'Hear this blessed Saint!'

8

'He was Lord of the Earth, but I was the prophet of the God of Heaven,' cried the Saint, 'and all the people marvelled at the sign. For I, O God, knew of the glories of thy Paradise. No pain, no hardship, gashing with knives, splinters thrust under my nails, strips of flesh flayed off, all for the glory and honour of God.'

God smiled.

'And at last I went, I in my rags and sores, smelling of my holy discomforts – '

Gabriel laughed abruptly.

'And lay outside his gates, as a sign, as a wonder – '

'As a perfect nuisance,' said the Recording Angel, and began to read, heedless of the fact that the Saint was still speaking of gloriously unpleasant things he had done that Paradise might be his.

And behold, in that book the record of the Saint also was a revelation, a marvel.

It seemed not ten seconds before the Saint also was rushing to and fro over the great palm of God. Not ten seconds! And at last he also shrieked beneath that pitiless and cynical exposition, and fled also, even as the Wicked Man had fled, into the shadow of the sleeve. And it was permitted us to see into the shadow of the sleeve. And the two sat side by side, stark of all delusions, in the shadow of the robe of God's charity, like brothers.

And thither also I fled in my turn.

9

'And now,' said God, as he shook us out of his sleeve upon the planet he had given us to live upon, the planet that whirled about green Sirius[459] for a sun, 'now that you understand me and each other a little better . . . try again.'

Then he and his great angels turned themselves about and suddenly had vanished.

The Throne had vanished.

All about me was a beautiful land, more beautiful than any I had ever seen before – waste, austere and wonderful; and all about me were the enlightened souls of men in new clean bodies . . .

The Land Ironclads[460]

The young lieutenant lay beside the war correspondent and admired the idyllic calm of the enemy's lines through his field-glass.[461]

'So far as I can see,' he said at last, 'one man.'

'What's he doing?' asked the war correspondent.

'Field-glass at us,' said the young lieutenant.

'And this is war!'

'No,' said the young lieutenant; 'it's Bloch.'[462]

'The game's a draw.'

'No! They've got to win or else they lose. A draw's a win for our side.'

They had discussed the political situation fifty times or so, and the war correspondent was weary of it. He stretched out his limbs. 'Aaai s'pose it *is*!' he yawned.

Flut!

'What was that?'

'Shot at us.'

The war correspondent shifted to a slightly lower position. 'No one shot at him,' he complained.

'I wonder if they think we shall get so bored we shall go home?'

The war correspondent made no reply.

'There's the harvest, of course . . .'

They had been there a month. Since the first brisk movements after the declaration of war things had gone slower and slower, until it seemed as though the whole machine of events must have run down. To begin with, they had had almost a scampering time; the invader had come across the frontier at the very dawn of the war in half a dozen parallel columns behind a cloud of cyclists and cavalry, with a general air of coming straight on the capital, and the defender horsemen had held him up, and peppered him and forced him to open out to outflank, and had then bolted to the next position, in the most approved style, for a couple of days, until in the afternoon, bump! They had the invader against their prepared lines of defence. He did not suffer so much as had been hoped and expected; he was coming on, it seemed, with his eyes open; his scouts winded[463] the guns, and down he sat at once without the shadow of an attack and began grubbing trenches for himself, as though he meant to sit down there to the very end of time. He was slow, but much more wary than the world had been led to expect, and he kept convoys tucked in and shielded his slow-marching infantry sufficiently well to prevent any heavy adverse scoring.

'But he ought to attack,' the young lieutenant had insisted.

'He'll attack us at dawn, somewhere along the lines. You'll get the bayonets coming into the trenches just about when you see,' the war correspondent had held until a week ago.

The young lieutenant winked when he said that.

When one early morning the men the defenders sent to lie out five hundred yards before the trenches, with a view to the unexpected emptying of magazines into any night attack, gave way to causeless panic and blazed away at nothing for ten minutes, the war correspondent understood the meaning of that wink.

'What would you do if you were the enemy?' said the war correspondent, suddenly.

'If I had men like I've got now?'

'Yes.'

'Take those trenches.'

'How?'

'Oh – dodges! Crawl out halfway at night before moonrise and get into touch with the chaps we send out. Blaze at 'em if they tried to shift, and so bag some of 'em in the daylight. Learn that patch of ground by heart, lie all day in squatty holes, and come on nearer next night. There's a bit over there, lumpy ground, where they could get across to rushing distance – easy. In a night or so. It would be a mere game for our fellows; it's what they're made for . . . Guns? Shrapnel and stuff wouldn't stop good men who meant business.'

'Why don't they do that?

'Their men aren't brutes enough; that's the trouble. They're a crowd of devitalised townsmen, and that's the truth of the matter. They're clerks, they're factory hands, they're students, they're civilised men. They can write, they can talk, they can make and do all sorts of things, but they're poor amateurs at war. They've got no physical staying power, and that's the whole thing.[464] They've never slept in the open one night in their lives; they've never drunk anything but the purest water-company water; they've never gone short of three meals a day since they left their feeding-bottles. Half their cavalry never cocked leg over horse till it enlisted six months ago. They ride their horses as though they were bicycles – you watch 'em! They're fools at the game, and they know it. Our boys of fourteen can give their grown men points . . . Very well – '

The war correspondent mused on his face with his nose between his knuckles.

'If a decent civilisation,' he said, 'cannot produce better men for war than – '

He stopped with belated politeness. 'I mean – '

'Than our open-air life,' said the young lieutenant.

'Exactly,' said the war correspondent. 'Then civilisation has to stop.'

'It looks like it,' the young lieutenant admitted.

'Civilisation has science, you know,' said the war correspondent. 'It invented and it makes the rifles and guns and things you use.'

'Which our nice healthy hunters and stockmen and so on, rowdy-dowdy cow-punchers and nigger-whackers,[465] can use ten times better than – *What's that?*'

'What?' said the war correspondent, and then seeing his companion busy with his field-glass he produced his own: 'Where?' said the war correspondent, sweeping the enemy's lines.

'It's nothing,' said the young lieutenant, still looking.

'What's nothing?'

The young lieutenant put down his glass and pointed. 'I thought I saw something there, behind the stems of those trees. Something black. What it was I don't know.'

The war correspondent tried to get even by intense scrutiny.

'It wasn't anything,' said the young lieutenant, rolling over to regard the darkling evening sky, and generalised: 'There never will be anything any more for ever. Unless – '

The war correspondent looked enquiry.

'They may get their stomachs wrong, or something – living without proper drains.'

A sound of bugles came from the tents behind. The war correspondent slid backwards down the sand and stood up. 'Boom!' came from somewhere far away to the left. 'Halloa!' he said, hesitated, and crawled back to peer again. 'Firing at this time is jolly bad manners.'

The young lieutenant was uncommunicative for a space.

Then he pointed to the distant clump of trees again. 'One of our big guns. They were firing at that,' he said.

'The thing that wasn't anything?'

'Something over there, anyhow.'

Both men were silent, peering through their glasses for a space. 'Just when it's twilight,' the lieutenant complained. He stood up.

'I might stay here a bit,' said the war correspondent.

The lieutenant shook his head. 'There's nothing to see,' he apologised, and then went down to where his little squad of sun-browned, loose-limbed men had been yarning in the trench. The war correspondent stood up also, glanced for a moment at the businesslike bustle below him, gave perhaps twenty seconds to those enigmatical trees again, then turned his face towards the camp.

He found himself wondering whether his editor would consider the story of how somebody thought he saw something black behind a clump of trees, and how a gun was fired at this illusion by somebody else, too trivial for public consumption.

'It's the only gleam of a shadow of interest,' said the war correspondent, 'for ten whole days.

'No,' he said presently; 'I'll write that other article, "Is War Played Out?" '

He surveyed the darkling lines in perspective, the tangle of trenches one behind another, one commanding another, which the defender had made ready. The shadows and mists swallowed up their receding contours, and here and there a lantern gleamed, and here and there knots of men were busy about small fires. 'No troops on earth could do it,' he said . . .

He was depressed. He believed that there were other things in life better worth having than proficiency in war; he believed that in the heart of civilisation, for all its stresses, its crushing concentrations of forces, its injustice and suffering, there lay something that might be the hope of the world; and the idea that any people, by living in the open air, hunting perpetually, losing touch with books and art and all the things that intensify life, might hope to resist and break that great development to the end of time, jarred on his civilised soul.

Apt to his thought came a file of the defender soldiers, and passed him in the gleam of a swinging lamp that marked the way.

He glanced at their red-lit faces, and one shone out for a moment, a common type of face in the defender's ranks: ill-shaped nose, sensuous lips, bright clear eyes full of alert cunning, slouch hat[466] cocked on one side and adorned with the peacock's plume of the rustic Don Juan turned soldier, a hard brown skin, a sinewy frame, an open, tireless stride, and a master's grip on his rifle.

The war correspondent returned their salutations and went on his way.

'Louts,' he whispered. 'Cunning, elementary louts. And they are going to beat the townsmen at the game of war!'

From the red glow among the nearer tents came first one and then half a dozen hearty voices, bawling in a drawling unison the words of a particularly slab[467] and sentimental patriotic song.

'Oh, go it!'[468] muttered the war correspondent, bitterly.

It was opposite the trenches called after Hackbone's Hut that the battle began. There the ground stretched broad and level between the lines, with scarcely shelter for a lizard, and it seemed to the startled, just-awakened men who came crowding into the trenches that this was one more proof of that inexperience of the enemy of which they had heard so much. The war correspondent would not believe his ears at first, and swore that he and the war artist, who, still imperfectly roused, was trying to put on his boots by the light of a match held in his hand, were the victims of a common illusion. Then, after putting his head in a bucket of cold water, his intelligence came back as he towelled. He listened. 'Gollys!'[469] he said; 'that's something more than scare firing this time. It's like ten thousand carts on a bridge of tin.'

There came a sort of enrichment to that steady uproar. 'Machine-guns!'

Then, 'Guns!'

The artist, with one boot on, thought to look at his watch, and went to it hopping.

'Half an hour from dawn,' he said. 'You were right about their attacking, after all . . . '

The war correspondent came out of the tent, verifying the presence of chocolate in his pocket as he did so. He had to halt for a moment or so until his eyes were toned down to the night a little. 'Pitch!' he said. He stood for a space to season his eyes before he felt justified in striking out for a black gap among the adjacent tents. The artist coming out behind him fell over a tent-rope. It was half-past two o'clock in the morning of the darkest night in time, and against a sky of dull black silk the enemy was talking searchlights, a wild jabber of searchlights. 'He's trying to blind our riflemen,' said the war correspondent with a flash, and waited for the artist and then set off with a sort of discreet haste again. 'Whoa!' he said, presently. 'Ditches!'

They stopped.

'It's the confounded searchlights,' said the war correspondent.

They saw lanterns going to and fro, near by, and men falling in to march down to the trenches. They were for following them, and then the artist began to get his night eyes. 'If we scramble this,' he said, 'and it's only a drain, there's a clear run up to the ridge.' And that way they took. Lights came and went in the tents behind, as the men turned out, and ever and again they came to broken ground and staggered and stumbled. But in a little while they drew near the crest. Something that sounded like the impact of a tremendous railway accident happened in the air above them, and the shrapnel bullets seethed about them like a sudden handful of hail. 'Right-ho!' said the war correspondent, and soon they judged they had come to the crest and stood in the midst of a world of great darkness and frantic glares, whose principal fact was sound.

Right and left of them and all about them was the uproar, an army-full of magazine fire, at first chaotic and monstrous, and then, eked out by little flashes and gleams and suggestions, taking the beginnings of a shape. It looked to the war correspondent as though the enemy must have attacked in line and with his whole force – in which case he was either being or was already annihilated.

'Dawn and the dead,' he said, with his instinct for headlines. He said this to himself, but afterwards by means of shouting he conveyed an idea to the artist, 'They must have meant it for a surprise,' he said.

It was remarkable how the firing kept on. After a time he began to perceive a sort of rhythm in this inferno of noise. It would decline – decline perceptibly, droop towards something that was comparatively a pause – a pause of enquiry. 'Aren't you all dead yet?' this pause seemed to say. The flickering fringe of rifle-flashes would become attenuated and broken, and the whack-bang of the enemy's big guns two miles away there would come up out of the deeps. Then suddenly, east or west of them, something would startle the rifles to a frantic outbreak again.

The war correspondent taxed his brain for some theory of conflict that would account for this, and was suddenly aware that the artist and he were vividly illuminated. He could see the ridge on which they stood, and before them in black outline a file of riflemen hurrying down towards the nearer trenches. It became visible that a light rain was falling, and farther away towards the enemy was a clear space with men – 'our men?' – running across it in disorder. He saw one of those men throw up his hands and drop. And something else black and shining loomed up on the edge of the beam-coruscating flashes; and behind it and far away a calm, white eye regarded the world. 'Whit, whit, whit,' sang something in the air, and then the artist was running for cover, with the war correspondent behind him. Bang came shrapnel, bursting close at hand as it seemed, and our two men were lying flat in a dip in the ground, and the light and everything had gone again, leaving a vast note of interrogation upon the night.

The war correspondent came within bawling range. 'What the deuce was it?[470] Shooting our men down!'

'Black,' said the artist, 'and like a fort. Not two hundred yards from the first trench.'

He sought for comparison in his mind. 'Something between a big blockhouse and a giant's dish-cover,' he said.

'And they were running!' said the war correspondent.

'You'd run if a thing like that, with a searchlight to help it, turned up like a prowling nightmare in the middle of the night.'

They crawled to what they judged the edge of the dip and lay regarding the unfathomable dark. For a space they could distinguish nothing, and then a sudden convergence of the searchlights of both sides brought the strange thing out again.

In that flickering pallor it had the effect of a large and clumsy black insect, an insect the size of an ironclad cruiser, crawling obliquely to the first line of trenches and firing shots out of port-holes in its side. And on its carcass the bullets must have been battering with more than the passionate violence of hail on a roof of tin.

Then in the twinkling of an eye the curtain of the dark had fallen again and the monster had vanished, but the crescendo of musketry marked its approach to the trenches.

They were beginning to talk about the thing to each other, when a flying bullet kicked dirt into the artist's face, and they decided abruptly to crawl down into the cover of the trenches. They had got down with an unobtrusive persistence into the second line, before the dawn had grown clear enough for anything to be seen. They found themselves in a crowd of expectant riflemen, all noisily arguing about what would happen next. The enemy's contrivance had done execution upon the outlying men, it seemed, but they did not believe it would do any more. 'Come the day and we'll capture the lot of them,' said a burly soldier.

'Them?' said the war correspondent.

'They say there's a regular string of 'em, crawling along the front of our lines . . . Who cares?'

The darkness filtered away so imperceptibly that at no moment could one declare decisively that one could see. The searchlights ceased to sweep hither and thither. The enemy's monsters were dubious patches of darkness upon the dark, and then no longer dubious, and so they crept out into distinctness. The war correspondent, munching chocolate absent-mindedly, beheld at last a spacious picture of battle under the cheerless sky, whose central focus was an array of fourteen or fifteen huge clumsy shapes lying in perspective on the very edge of the first line of trenches, at intervals of perhaps three hundred yards, and evidently firing down upon the crowded riflemen. They were so close in that the defender's guns had ceased, and only the first line of trenches was in action.

The second line commanded the first, and as the light grew, the war correspondent could make out the riflemen who were fighting these monsters, crouched in knots and crowds behind the transverse banks that crossed the trenches against the eventuality of an enfilade.[471] The trenches close to the big machines were empty save for the crumpled suggestions of dead and wounded men; the defenders had been driven right and left as soon as the prow of a land ironclad had loomed up over the front of the trench. The war correspondent produced his field-glass, and was immediately a centre of enquiry from the soldiers about him.

They wanted to look, they asked questions, and after he had announced that the men across the traverses seemed unable to advance or retreat, and were crouching under cover rather than fighting, he found it advisable to loan his glasses to a burly and incredulous corporal. He heard a strident voice, and found a lean and sallow soldier at his back talking to the artist.

'There's chaps down there caught,' the man was saying. 'If they retreat they got to expose themselves, and the fire's too straight . . . '

'They aren't firing much, but every shot's a hit.'

'Who?'

'The chaps in that thing. The men who're coming up – '

'Coming up where?'

'We're evacuating them trenches where we can. Our chaps are coming back up the zigzags . . . No end of 'em hit . . . But when we get clear our turn'll come. Rather! Those things won't be able to cross a trench or get into it; and before they can get back our guns'll smash 'em up. Smash 'em right up. See?' A brightness came into his eyes. 'Then we'll have a go at the beggars inside,' he said.

The war correspondent thought for a moment, trying to realise the idea. Then he set himself to recover his field-glasses from the burly corporal.

The daylight was getting clearer now. The clouds were lifting, and a gleam of lemon-yellow amidst the level masses to the east portended sunrise. He looked again at the land ironclad. As he saw it in the bleak, grey dawn, lying obliquely upon the slope and on the very lip of the foremost trench, the suggestion of a stranded vessel was very strong indeed. It might have been from eighty to a hundred feet long – it was about two hundred and fifty yards away – its vertical side was ten feet high or so, smooth for that height, and then with a complex patterning under the eaves of its flattish turtle cover. This patterning was a close interlacing of port-holes, rifle barrels and telescope tubes – sham and real – indistinguishable one from the other. The thing had come into such a position as to enfilade the trench, which was empty now, so far as he could see, except for two or three crouching knots of men and the tumbled dead. Behind it, across the plain, it had scored the grass with a train of linked impressions, like the dotted tracings sea-things leave in sand. Left and right of that track dead men and wounded men were scattered – men it had picked off as they fled back from their advanced positions in the searchlight glare from the invader's lines. And now it lay with its head projecting a little over the trench it had won, as if it were a single sentient thing planning the next phase of its attack . . .

He lowered his glasses and took a more comprehensive view of the situation. These creatures of night had evidently won the first line of trenches and the fight had come to a pause. In the increasing light he could make out by a stray shot or a chance exposure that the defender's marksmen were lying thick in the second and third line of trenches up towards the low crest of the position, and in such of the zigzags as gave them a chance of a converging fire. The men about him were talking of guns. 'We're in the line of big guns at the crest, but they'll soon shift one to pepper them,' the lean man said, reassuringly.

'Whup,' said the corporal.[472]

'Bang! Bang! Bang! Whir-r-r-r!' It was a sort of nervous jump, and all the rifles were going off by themselves. The war correspondent found himself and the artist, two idle men crouching behind a line of preoccupied backs, of industrious men discharging magazines. The monster had moved. It continued to move regardless of the hail that splashed its skin with bright new specks of lead. It was singing a mechanical little ditty to itself, 'Tuf-tuf, tuf-tuf, tuf-tuf,' and squirting out little jets of steam behind. It had humped itself up, as a limpet does before it crawls; it had lifted its skirt and displayed along the length of it – *feet*![473] They were thick, stumpy feet, between knobs and buttons in shape – flat, broad things, reminding one of the feet of elephants or the legs of caterpillars; and then, as the skirt rose higher, the war correspondent, scrutinising the thing through his glasses again, saw that these feet hung, as it were, on the rims of wheels. His thoughts whirled back to Victoria Street, Westminster, and he saw himself in the piping times of peace, seeking matter for an interview.

'Mr – Mr Diplock,' he said; 'and he called them Pedrails . . . Fancy meeting them here!'

The marksman beside him raised his head and shoulders in a speculative mood to fire more certainly – it seemed so natural to assume the attention of the monster must be distracted by this trench before it – and was suddenly knocked backwards by a bullet through his neck. His feet flew up, and he vanished out of the margin of the watcher's field of vision. The war correspondent grovelled tighter, but after a glance behind him at a painful little confusion, he resumed his field-glass, for the thing was putting down its feet one after the other, and hoisting itself farther and farther over the trench. Only a bullet in the head could have stopped him looking just then.

The lean man with the strident voice ceased firing to turn and reiterate his point. 'They can't possibly cross,' he bawled. 'They – '

'Bang! Bang! Bang! Bang – !' drowned everything.

The lean man continued speaking for a word or so, then gave it up, shook his head to enforce the impossibility of anything crossing a trench like the one below, and resumed business once more.

And all the while that great bulk was crossing. When the war correspondent turned his glass on it again it had bridged the trench, and its queer feet were rasping away at the farther bank in the attempt to get a hold there. It got its hold. It continued to crawl until the greater bulk of it was over the trench – until it was all over. Then it paused for a moment, adjusted its skirt a little nearer the ground, gave an unnerving 'toot, toot', and came on abruptly at a pace of, perhaps, six miles an hour straight up the gentle slope towards our observer.

The war correspondent raised himself on his elbow and looked a natural enquiry at the artist.

For a moment the men about him stuck to their position and fired furiously. Then the lean man in a mood of precipitancy slid backwards, and the war correspondent said, 'Come along,' to the artist, and led the movement along the trench.

As they dropped down, the vision of a hillside of trench being rushed by a dozen vast cockroaches disappeared for a space, and instead was one of a narrow passage, crowded with men, for the most part receding, though one or two turned or halted. He never turned back to see the nose of the monster creep over the brow of the trench; he never even troubled to keep in touch with the artist. He heard the 'whit' of bullets about him soon enough, and saw a man before him stumble and drop, and then he was one of a furious crowd fighting to get into a transverse zigzag ditch that enabled the defenders to get under cover up and down the hill. It was like a theatre panic. He gathered from signs and fragmentary words that on ahead another of these monsters had also won to the second trench.

He lost his interest in the general course of the battle for a space altogether; he became simply a modest egotist, in a mood of hasty circumspection, seeking the farthest rear, amidst a dispersed multitude of disconcerted riflemen similarly employed. He scrambled down through trenches, he took his courage in both hands and sprinted across the open, he had moments of panic when it seemed madness not to be quadrupedal, and moments of shame when he stood up and faced about to see how the fight was going. And he was one of many thousand very similar men that morning. On the ridge he halted in a knot of scrub, and was for a few minutes almost minded to stop and see things out.

The day was now fully come. The grey sky had changed to blue, and of all the cloudy masses of dawn there remained only a few patches of dissolving fleeciness. The world below was bright and singularly clear. The ridge was not, perhaps, more than a hundred feet or so above the general plain, but in this flat region it sufficed to give the effect of an extensive view. Away on the north side of the ridge, little and far, were the camps, the ordered wagons, all the gear of a big army; with officers galloping about and men doing aimless things. Here and there men were falling in, however, and the cavalry was forming up on the plain beyond the tents. The bulk of men who had been in the trenches were still on the move to the rear, scattered like sheep without a shepherd over the farther slopes. Here and there were little rallies and attempts to wait and do – something vague; but the general drift was away from any concentration. There on the southern side was the elaborate lace-work of trenches and defences, across which these iron turtles, four-teen of them spread out over a line of perhaps three miles, were now advancing as fast as a man could trot, and methodically shooting down and breaking up any persistent knots of resistance. Here and there stood little clumps of men, outflanked and unable to get away, showing the white flag, and the invader's cyclist infantry was advancing now across the open, in open order, but unmolested, to complete the work of the machines. Surveyed at large, the defenders already looked a beaten army. A mechanism that was effectually ironclad against bullets, that could at a pinch cross a thirty-foot trench, and that seemed able to shoot out rifle-bullets with unerring precision, was clearly an inevitable victor against anything but rivers, precipices and guns.

He looked at his watch. 'Half-past four! Lord! What things can happen in two hours. Here's the whole blessed army being walked over, and at half-past two –

'And even now our blessed louts haven't done a thing with their guns!'

He scanned the ridge right and left of him with his glasses. He turned again to the nearest land ironclad, advancing now obliquely to him and not three hundred yards away, and then scanned the ground over which he must retreat if he was not to be captured.

'They'll do nothing,' he said, and glanced again at the enemy.

And then from far away to the left came the thud of a gun, followed very rapidly by a rolling gunfire.

He hesitated and decided to stay.

3

The defender had relied chiefly upon his rifles in the event of an assault. His guns he kept concealed at various points upon and behind the ridge ready to bring them into action against any artillery preparations for an attack on the part of his antagonist. The situation had rushed upon him with the dawn, and by the time the gunners had their guns ready for motion, the land ironclads were already in among the foremost trenches. There is a natural reluctance to fire into one's own broken men, and many of the guns, being intended simply to fight an advance of the enemy's artillery, were not in positions to hit anything in the second line of trenches. After that the advance of the land ironclads was swift. The defender-general found himself suddenly called upon to invent a new sort of warfare, in which guns were to fight alone amidst broken and retreating infantry. He had scarcely thirty minutes in which to think it out. He did not respond to the call, and what happened that morning was that the advance of the land ironclads forced the fight, and each gun and battery made what play its circumstance dictated. For the most part it was poor play.

Some of the guns got in two or three shots, some one or two, and the percentage of misses was unusually high. The howitzers, of course, did nothing.[474] The land ironclads in each case followed much the same tactics. As soon as a gun came into play the monster turned itself almost end-on, so as to minimise the chances of a square hit, and made not for the gun, but for the nearest point on its flank from which the gunners could be shot down. Few of the hits scored were very effectual; only one of the things was disabled, and that was the one that fought the three batteries attached to the brigade on the left wing. Three that were hit when close upon the guns were clean shot through without being put out of action. Our war correspondent did not see that one momentary arrest of the tide of victory on the left; he saw only the very ineffectual fight of half-battery 96B close at hand upon his right. This he watched some time beyond the margin of safety.

Just after he heard the three batteries opening up upon his left he became aware of the thud of horses' hoofs from the sheltered side of the slope, and presently saw first one and then two other guns galloping into position along the north side of the ridge, well out of sight of the great bulk that was now creeping obliquely towards the crest and cutting up the lingering infantry beside it and below as it came.

The half-battery swung round into line – each gun describing its curve – halted, unlimbered and prepared for action . . .

'Bang!'

The land ironclad had become visible over the brow of the hill, and just visible as a long black back to the gunners. It halted, as though it hesitated.

The two remaining guns fired, and then their big antagonist had swung round and was in full view, end-on, against the sky, coming at a rush.

The gunners became frantic in their haste to fire again. They were so near, the war correspondent could see the expression of their excited faces through his field-glass. As he looked he saw a man drop, and realised for the first time that the ironclad was shooting.

For a moment the big black monster crawled with an accelerated pace towards the furiously active gunners. Then, as if moved by a generous impulse, it turned its full broadside to their attack, and scarcely forty yards away from them. The war correspondent turned his field-glass back to the gunners and perceived it was now shooting down the men about the guns with the most deadly rapidity.

Just for a moment it seemed splendid, and then it seemed horrible. The gunners were dropping in heaps about their guns. To lay a hand on a gun was death. 'Bang!' went the gun on the left, a hopeless miss, and that was the only second shot the half-battery fired. In another moment half a dozen surviving artillerymen were holding up their hands amidst a scattered muddle of dead and wounded men, and the fight was done.

The war correspondent hesitated between stopping in his scrub and waiting for an opportunity to surrender decently, or taking to an adjacent gully he had discovered. If he surrendered it was certain he would get no copy off; while, if he escaped, there were all sorts of chances. He decided to follow the gully, and take the first offer in the confusion beyond the camp of picking up a horse.

4

Subsequent authorities have found fault with the first land ironclads in many particulars, but assuredly they served their purpose on the day of their appearance. They were essentially long, narrow, and very strong steel frameworks carrying the engines, and borne upon eight pairs of big pedrail wheels, each about ten feet in diameter, each a driving wheel and set upon long axles free to swivel round a common axis. This arrangement gave them the maximum of adaptability to the contours of the ground. They crawled level along the ground with one foot high upon a hillock and another deep in a depression, and they could hold themselves erect and steady sideways upon even a steep hillside. The engineers directed the engines under the command of the captain, who had lookout points at small ports all round the upper edge of the adjustable skirt of twelve-inch iron-plating which protected the whole affair, and who could also raise or depress a conning-tower set above the port-holes through the centre of the iron top cover. The riflemen each occupied a small cabin of peculiar construction, and these cabins were slung along the sides of and before and behind the great main framework, in a manner suggestive of the slinging of the seats of an Irish jaunting-car.[475] Their rifles, however, were very different pieces of apparatus from the simple mechanisms in the hands of their adversaries.

These were in the first place automatic, ejected their cartridges and loaded again from a magazine each time they fired, until the ammunition store was at an end, and they had the most remarkable sights imaginable, sights which threw a bright little camera-obscura[476] picture into the light-tight box in which the riflemen sat below. This camera-obscura picture was marked with two crossed lines, and whatever was covered by the intersection of these two lines, that the rifle hit. The sighting was ingeniously contrived. The rifleman stood at the table with a thing like an elaboration of a draughtsman's dividers in his hand, and he opened and closed these dividers, so that they were always at the apparent height – if it was an ordinary-sized man – of the man he wanted to kill. A little twisted strand of wire like an electric-light wire ran from this implement up to the gun, and as the dividers opened and shut the sights went up or down. Changes in the clearness of the atmosphere, due to changes of moisture, were met by an ingenious use of that meteorologically sensitive substance catgut, and when the land ironclad moved forward the sights got a compensatory deflection in the direction of its motion. The rifleman stood up in his pitch-dark chamber and watched the little picture before him. One hand held the dividers for judging distance, and the other grasped a big knob like a door-handle. As he pushed this knob about the rifle above swung to correspond, and the picture passed to and fro like an agitated panorama. When he saw a man he wanted to shoot he brought him up to the cross-lines, and then pressed a finger upon a little push like an electric bell-push, conveniently placed in the centre of the knob. Then the man was shot. If by any chance the rifleman missed his target he moved the knob a trifle, or readjusted his dividers, pressed the push, and got him the second time.

This rifle and its sights protruded from a port-hole, exactly like a great number of other port-holes that ran in a triple row under the eaves of the cover of the land ironclad. Each port-hole displayed a rifle and sight in dummy, so that the real ones could only be hit by a chance shot, and if one was, then the young man below said 'Pshaw!'[477] turned on an electric light, lowered the injured instrument into his camera, replaced the injured part, or put up a new rifle if the injury was considerable.

You must conceive these cabins as hung clear above the swing of the axles, and inside the big wheels upon which the great elephant-like feet were hung, and behind these cabins along the centre of the monster ran a central gallery into which they opened, and along which worked the big compact engines. It was like a long passage into which this throbbing machinery had been packed, and the captain stood about the middle, close to the ladder that led to his conning-tower, and directed the silent, alert engineers – for the most part by signs. The throb and noise of the engines mingled with the reports of the rifles and the intermittent clangour of the bullet hail upon the armour. Ever and again he would touch the wheel that raised his conning-tower, step up his ladder until his engineers could see nothing of him above the waist, and then come down again with orders. Two small electric lights were all the illumination of this space – they were placed to make him most clearly visible to his subordinates; the air was thick with the smell of oil and petrol, and had the war correspondent been suddenly transferred from the spacious dawn outside to the bowels of this apparatus he would have thought himself fallen into another world.

The captain, of course, saw both sides of the battle. When he raised his head into his conning-tower there were the dewy sunrise, the amazed and disordered trenches, the flying and falling soldiers, the depressed-looking groups of prisoners, the beaten guns; when he bent down again to signal 'half speed', 'quarter speed', 'half circle, round towards the right', or what not, he was in the oil-smelling twilight of the ill-lit engine-room. Close beside him on either side was the mouthpiece of a speaking-tube,[478] and ever and again he would direct one side or other of his strange craft to 'concentrate fire forward on gunners', or to 'clear out trench about a hundred yards on our right front'.

He was a young man, healthy enough but by no means suntanned, and of a type of feature and expression that prevails in His Majesty's Navy: alert, intelligent, quiet. He and his engineers and riflemen all went about their work, calm and reasonable men. They had none of that flapping strenuousness of the half-wit in a hurry, that excessive strain upon the blood-vessels, that hysteria of effort which is so frequently regarded as the proper state of mind for heroic deeds.

For the enemy these young engineers were defeating they felt a certain qualified pity and a quite unqualified contempt. They regarded these big, healthy men they were shooting down precisely as these same big, healthy men might regard some inferior kind of nigger.[479] They despised them for making war; despised their brawling patriotisms and their emotionality profoundly; despised them, above all, for the petty cunning and the almost brutish want of imagination their method of fighting displayed. 'If they must make war,' these young men thought, 'Why in thunder don't they do it like sensible men?' They resented the assumption that their own side was too stupid to do anything more than play their enemy's game, that they were going to play this costly folly according to the rules of unimaginative men. They resented being forced to the trouble of making man-killing machinery; resented the alternative of having to massacre these people or endure their truculent yappings; resented the whole unfathomable imbecility of war.

Meanwhile, with something of the mechanical precision of a good clerk posting a ledger, the rifleman moved their knobs and pressed their buttons . . .

The captain of Land Ironclad Number Three had halted on the crest close to his captured half-battery. His lined up prisoners stood hard by and waited for the cyclists behind to come for them. He surveyed the victorious morning through his conning-tower.

He read the general's signals. 'Five and Four are to keep among the guns to the left and prevent any attempt to recover them. Seven and Eleven and Twelve, stick to the guns you have got; Seven, got into position to command the guns taken by Three. Then we're to do something else, are we? Six and One, quicken up to about ten miles an hour and walk round behind that camp to the levels near the river – we shall bag the whole crowd of them,' interjected the young man. 'Ah, here we are! Two and Three, Eight and Nine, Thirteen and Fourteen, space out to a thousand yards, wait for the word, and then go slowly to cover the advance of the cyclist infantry against any charge of mounted troops. That's all right. But where's Ten? Halloa! Ten to repair and get movable as soon as possible. They've broken up Ten!'

The discipline of the new war machines was businesslike rather than pedantic, and the head of the captain came down out of the conning-tower to tell his men: 'I say, you chaps there. They've broken up Ten. Not badly, I think; but anyhow, he's stuck.'

But that still left thirteen of the monsters in action to finish up the broken army.

The war correspondent stealing down his gully looked back and saw them all lying along the crest and talking fluttering congratulatory flags to one another. Their iron sides were shining golden in the light of the rising sun.

5

The private adventures of the war correspondent terminated in surrender about one o'clock in the afternoon, and by that time he had stolen a horse, pitched off it, and narrowly escaped being rolled upon; found the brute had broken its leg, and shot it with his revolver. He had spent some hours in the company of a squad of dispirited riflemen, had quarrelled with them about topography at last, and gone off by himself in a direction that should have brought him to the banks of the river and didn't. Moreover, he had eaten all his chocolate and found nothing in the whole world to drink. Also, it had become extremely hot. From behind a broken, but attractive, stone wall he had seen far away in the distance the defender-horsemen trying to charge cyclists in open order, with land ironclads outflanking them on either side. He had discovered that cyclists could retreat over open turf before horsemen with a sufficient margin of speed to allow of frequent dismounts and much terribly effective sharpshooting, and he had a sufficient persuasion that those horsemen, having charged their hearts out, had halted just beyond his range of vision and surrendered. He had been urged to sudden activity by a forward movement of one of those machines that had threatened to enfilade his wall. He had discovered a fearful blister on his heel.

He was now in a scrubby gravelly place, sitting down and meditating on his pocket-handkerchief, which had in some extraordinary way become in the last twenty-four hours extremely ambiguous in hue. 'It's the whitest thing I've got,' he said.

He had known all along that the enemy was east, west and south of him, but when he heard land ironclads Number One and Six talking in their measured, deadly way not half a mile to the north he decided to make his own little unconditional peace without any further risks. He was for hoisting his white flag to a bush and taking up a position of modest obscurity near it until someone came along. He became aware of voices, clatter, and the distinctive noises of a body of horses, quite near, and he put his handkerchief in his pocket again and went to see what was going forward.

The sound of firing ceased, and then as he drew near he heard the deep sounds of many simple, coarse, but hearty and noble-hearted soldiers of the old school swearing with vigour.

He emerged from his scrub upon a big level plain, and far away a fringe of trees marked the banks of the river.

In the centre of the picture was a still intact road bridge, and a big railway bridge a little to the right. Two land ironclads rested, with a general air of being long, harmless sheds, in a pose of anticipatory peacefulness right and left of the picture, completely commanding two miles and more of the river levels. Emerged and halted a few yards from the scrub was the remainder of the defender's cavalry, dusty, a little disordered and obviously annoyed, but still a very fine show of men. In the middle distance three or four men and horses were receiving medical attendance, and nearer a knot of officers regarded the distant novelties in mechanism with profound distaste. Everyone was very distinctly aware of the twelve other ironclads, and of the multitude of townsmen soldiers, on bicycles or afoot, encumbered now by prisoners and captured war-gear, but otherwise thoroughly effective, who were sweeping like a great net in their rear.

'Checkmate,' said the war correspondent, walking out into the open. 'But I surrender in the best of company. Twenty-four hours ago I thought war was impossible – and these beggars have captured the whole blessed army! Well! Well!' He thought of his talk with the young lieutenant. 'If there's no end to the surprises of science, the civilised people have it, of course. As long as their science keeps going they will necessarily be ahead of open-country men. Still . . . ' He wondered for a space what might have happened to the young lieutenant.

The war correspondent was one of those inconsistent people who always want the beaten side to win. When he saw all these burly, suntanned horsemen, disarmed and dismounted and lined up; when he saw their horses unskilfully led away by the singularly not equestrian cyclists to whom they had surrendered; when he saw these truncated Paladins[480] watching this scandalous sight, he forgot altogether that he had called these men 'cunning louts' and wished them beaten not four-and-twenty hours ago. A month ago he had seen that regiment in its pride going forth to war, and had told of its terrible prowess, how it could charge in open order with each man firing from his saddle, and sweep before it anything else that ever came out to battle in any sort of order, foot or horse. And it had had to fight a few score of young men in atrociously unfair machines!

'Manhood versus Machinery' occurred to him as a suitable headline. Journalism curdles all one's mind to phrases.

He strolled as near the lined-up prisoners as the sentinels seemed disposed to permit, and surveyed them and compared their sturdy proportions with those of their lightly built captors.

'Smart degenerates,' he muttered. 'Anaemic cockneydom.'[481]

The surrendered officers came quite close to him presently, and he could hear the colonel's high-pitched tenor. The poor gentleman had spent three years of arduous toil upon the best material in the world perfecting that shooting from the saddle charge, and he was enquiring with phrases of blasphemy, natural in the circumstances, what one could be expected to do against this suitably consigned ironmongery.

'Guns,' said someone.

'Big guns they can walk around. You can't shift big guns to keep pace with them, and little guns in the open they rush. I saw 'em rushed. You might do a surprise now and then – assassinate the brutes, perhaps – '

'You might make things like 'em.'

'What? More ironmongery? Us . . . ?'

'I'll call my article,' meditated the war correspondent, ' "Mankind versus Ironmongery", and quote the old boy at the beginning.'

And he was much too good a journalist to spoil his contrast by remarking that the half-dozen comparatively slender young men in blue pyjamas who were standing about their victorious land ironclad, drinking coffee and eating biscuits, had also in their eyes and carriage something not altogether degraded below the level of a man.

The Flying Man [482]

The ethnologist looked at the *bhimraj* feather [483] thoughtfully. 'They seemed loth to part with it,' he said.

'It is sacred to the chiefs,' said the lieutenant; 'just as yellow silk, [484] you know, is sacred to the Chinese emperor.'

The ethnologist did not answer. He hesitated. Then opening the topic abruptly, 'What on earth is this cock-and-bull story they have of a flying man?'

The lieutenant smiled faintly. 'What did they tell you?'

'I see,' said the ethnologist, 'that you know of your fame.'

The lieutenant rolled himself a cigarette. 'I don't mind hearing about it once more. How does it stand at present?'

'It's so confoundedly childish,' said the ethnologist, becoming irritated. 'How did you play it off upon them?'

The lieutenant made no answer, but lounged back in his folding-chair, still smiling.

'Here am I, come four hundred miles out of my way to get what is left of the folklore of these people, before they are utterly demoralised by missionaries and the military, and all I find are a lot of impossible legends about a sandy-haired scrub of an infantry lieutenant. How he is invulnerable – how he can jump over elephants – how he can fly. That's the toughest nut. One old gentleman described your wings, said they had black plumage and were not quite as long as a mule. Said he often saw you by moonlight hovering over the crests out towards the Shendu country. [485] Confound it, man!'

The lieutenant laughed cheerfully. 'Go on,' he said. 'Go on.'

The ethnologist did. At last he wearied. 'To trade so,' he said, 'on these unsophisticated children of the mountains. How could you bring yourself to do it, man?'

'I'm sorry,' said the lieutenant, 'but truly the thing was forced upon me. I can assure you I was driven to it. And at the time I had not the faintest idea of how the Chin [486] imagination would take it. Or curiosity. I can only plead it was an indiscretion and not malice that made me replace the folklore by a new legend. But as you seem aggrieved, I will try and explain the business to you.

'It was in the time of the last Lushai expedition but one, [487] and

Walters thought these people you have been visiting were friendly. So, with an airy confidence in my capacity for taking care of myself, he sent me up the gorge – fourteen miles of it – with three of the Derbyshire men[488] and half a dozen sepoys,[489] two mules, and his blessing, to see what popular feeling was like at that village you visited. A force of ten – not counting the mules – fourteen miles, and during a war! You saw the road?'

'Road!' said the ethnologist.

'It's better now than it was. When we went up, we had to wade in the river for a mile, where the valley narrows, with a smart stream frothing round our knees and the stones as slippery as ice. There it was I dropped my rifle. Afterwards the sappers blasted the cliff with dynamite and made the convenient way you came by. Then below, where those very high cliffs come, we had to keep on dodging across the river – I should say we crossed it a dozen times in a couple of miles.

'We got in sight of the place early the next morning. You know how it lies, on a spur halfway between the big hills, and as we began to appreciate how wickedly quiet the village lay under the sunlight, we came to a stop to consider.

'At that they fired a lump of filed brass idol at us, just by way of a welcome. It came twanging down the slope to the right of us where the boulders are, missed my shoulder by an inch or so, and plugged the mule that carried all the provisions and utensils. I never heard such a death-rattle before or since. And at that we became aware of a number of gentlemen carrying matchlocks,[490] and dressed in things like plaid dusters, dodging about along the neck between the village and the crest to the east.

' "Right about face," I said. "Not too close together."

'And with that encouragement my expedition of ten men came round and set off at a smart trot down the valley again hitherward. We did not wait to save anything our dead had carried, but we kept the second mule with us – he carried my tent and some other rubbish – out of a feeling of friendship.

'So ended the battle – ingloriously. Glancing back, I saw the valley dotted with the victors, shouting and firing at us. But no one was hit. These Chins and their guns are very little good except at a sitting shot. They will sit and finick over a boulder for hours taking aim, and when they fire running it is chiefly for stage effect. Hooker, one of the Derbyshire men, fancied himself rather with the rifle, and stopped behind for half a minute to try his luck as we turned the bend. But he got nothing.

'I'm not a Xenophon to spin much of a yarn about my retreating army.[491] We had to pull the enemy up twice in the next two miles when he became a bit pressing, by exchanging shots with him, but it was a fairly monotonous affair – hard breathing chiefly – until we got near the place where the hills run in towards the river and pinch the valley into a gorge. And there we very luckily caught a glimpse of half a dozen round black heads coming slanting-ways over the hill to the left of us – the east that is – and almost parallel with us.

'At that I called a halt. "Look here," says I to Hooker and the other Englishmen; "what are we to do now?" and I pointed to the heads.

' "Headed orf, or I'm a nigger," said one of the men.

' "We shall be," said another. "You know the Chin way, George?"

' "They can pot every one of us at fifty yards," says Hooker, "in the place where the river is narrow. It's just suicide to go on down."

'I looked at the hill to the right of us. It grew steeper lower down the valley, but it still seemed climbable. And all the Chins we had seen hitherto had been on the other side of the stream.

' "It's that or stopping," says one of the sepoys.

'So we started slanting up the hill. There was something faintly suggestive of a road running obliquely up the face of it, and that we followed. Some Chins presently came into view up the valley, and I heard some shots. Then I saw one of the sepoys was sitting down about thirty yards below us. He had simply sat down without a word, apparently not wishing to give trouble. At that I called a halt again; I told Hooker to try another shot, and went back and found the man was hit in the leg. I took him up, carried him along to put him on the mule – already pretty well laden with the tent and other things which we had no time to take off. When I got up to the rest with him, Hooker had his empty Martini[492] in his hand, and was grinning and pointing to a motionless black spot up the valley. All the rest of the Chins were behind boulders or back round the bend. "Five hundred yards," says Hooker, "if an inch. And I'll swear I hit him in the head."

'I told him to go and do it again, and with that we went on again.

'Now the hillside kept getting steeper as we pushed on, and the road we were following more and more of a shelf. At last it was mere cliff above and below us. "It's the best road I have seen yet in Chin Lushai land," said I to encourage the men, though I had a fear of what was coming.

'And in a few minutes the way bent round a corner of the cliff. Then, finis![493] The ledge came to an end.

'As soon as he grasped the position one of the Derbyshire men fell a-swearing at the trap we had fallen into. The sepoys halted quietly. Hooker grunted and reloaded, and went back to the bend.

'Then two of the sepoy chaps helped their comrade down and began to unload the mule.

'Now, when I came to look about me, I began to think we had not been so very unfortunate after all. We were on a shelf perhaps ten yards across it at widest. Above it the cliff projected so that we could not be shot down upon, and below was an almost sheer precipice of perhaps two or three hundred feet. Lying down we were invisible to anyone across the ravine. The only approach was along the ledge, and on that one man was as good as a host. We were in a natural stronghold, with only one disadvantage, our sole provision against hunger and thirst was one live mule. Still we were at most eight or nine miles from the main expedition, and no doubt, after a day or so, they would send up after us if we did not return.

'After a day or so . . . '

The lieutenant paused. 'Ever been thirsty, Graham?'

'Not that kind,' said the ethnologist.

'H'm. We had the whole of that day, the night, and the next day of it, and only a trifle of dew we wrung out of our clothes and the tent. And below us was the river going giggle, giggle, round a rock in mid stream. I never knew such a barrenness of incident, or such a quantity of sensation. The sun might have had Joshua's command still upon it [494] for all the motion one could see; and it blazed like a near furnace. Towards the evening of the first day one of the Derbyshire men said something – nobody heard what – and went off round the bend of the cliff. We heard shots, and when Hooker looked round the corner he was gone. And in the morning the sepoy whose leg was shot was in delirium, and jumped or fell over the cliff. Then we took the mule and shot it, and that must needs go over the cliff too in its last struggles, leaving eight of us.

'We could see the body of the sepoy down below, with the head in the water. He was lying face downwards, and so far as I could make out was scarcely smashed at all. Badly as the Chins might covet his head, they had the sense to leave it alone until the darkness came.

'At first we talked of all the chances there were of the main body hearing the firing, and reckoned whether they would begin to miss us, and all that kind of thing, but we dried up as the evening came on. The sepoys played games with bits of stone among themselves, and afterwards told stories. The night was rather chilly. The second day nobody spoke. Our lips were black and our throats afire, and we lay about on the ledge and glared at one another. Perhaps it's as well we kept our thoughts to ourselves. One of the British soldiers began writing some blasphemous rot on the rock with a bit of pipeclay, about his last dying will, until I stopped it. As I looked over the edge down into the valley and saw the river rippling I was nearly tempted to go after the sepoy. It seemed a pleasant and desirable thing to go rushing down through the air with something to drink – or no more thirst at any rate – at the bottom. I remembered in time, though, that I was the officer in command, and my duty was to set a good example, and that kept me from any such foolishness.

'Yet, thinking of that, put an idea into my head. I got up and looked at the tent and tent ropes, and wondered why I had not thought of it before. Then I came and peered over the cliff again. This time the height seemed greater and the pose of the sepoy rather more painful. But it was that or nothing. And to cut it short, I parachuted.[495]

'I got a big circle of canvas out of the tent, about three times the size of that table-cover, and plugged the hole in the centre, and I tied eight ropes round it to meet in the middle and make a parachute. The other chaps lay about and watched me as though they thought it was a new kind of delirium. Then I explained my notion to the two British soldiers and how I meant to do it, and as soon as the short dusk had darkened into night, I risked it. They held the thing high up, and I took a run the whole length of the ledge. The thing filled with air like a sail, but at the edge I will confess I funked and pulled up.

'As soon as I stopped I was ashamed of myself – as well I might be in front of privates – and went back and started again. Off I jumped this time – with a kind of sob, I remember – clean into the air, with the big white sail bellying out above me.

'I must have thought at a frightful pace. It seemed a long time before I was sure that the thing meant to keep steady. At first it heeled sideways. Then I noticed the face of the rock, which seemed to be streaming up past me and me motionless. Then I looked down and saw in the darkness the river and the dead sepoy rushing up towards me. But in the indistinct light I also saw three Chins, seemingly aghast at the sight of me, and that the sepoy was decapitated. At that I wanted to go back again.

'Then my boot was in the mouth of one, and in a moment he and I were in a heap with the canvas fluttering down on the top of us. I fancy I dashed out his brains with my foot. I expected nothing more than to be brained myself by the other two, but the poor heathen had never heard of Baldwin, and incontinently bolted.[496]

'I struggled out of the tangle of dead Chin and canvas, and looked round. About ten paces off lay the head of the sepoy staring in the moonlight. Then I saw the water and went and drank. There wasn't a sound in the world but the footsteps of the departing Chins, a faint shout from above, and the gluck of the water. So soon as I had drunk my fill I started off down the river.

'That about ends the explanation of the flying man story. I never met a soul the whole eight miles of the way. I got to Walters's camp by ten o'clock, and a born idiot of a sentinel had the cheek to fire at me as I came trotting out of the darkness. So soon as I had hammered my story into Walters's thick skull, about fifty men started up the valley to clear the Chins out and get our men down. But for my own part I had too good a thirst to provoke it by going with them.

'You have heard what kind of a yarn the Chins made of it. Wings as long as a mule, eh – ? And black feathers! The gay lieutenant bird! Well, well.'

The lieutenant meditated cheerfully for a moment. Then he added, 'You would scarcely credit it, but when they got to the ridge at last, they found two more of the sepoys had jumped over.'

'The rest were all right?' asked the ethnologist.

'Yes,' said the lieutenant; 'the rest were all right, barring a certain thirst, you know.'

And at the memory he helped himself to soda and whisky again.

In the Avu Observatory[497]

The observatory at Avu, in Borneo, stands on the spur of the mountain. To the north rises the old crater, black at night against the unfathomable blue of the sky. From the little circular building, with its mushroom dome, the slopes plunge steeply downward into the black mysteries of the tropical forest beneath. The little house in which the observer and his assistant live is about fifty yards from the observatory, and beyond this are the huts of their native attendants.

Thaddy, the chief observer, was down with a slight fever. His assistant, Woodhouse, paused for a moment in silent contemplation of the tropical night before commencing his solitary vigil. The night was very still. Now and then voices and laughter came from the native huts, or the cry of some strange animal was heard from the midst of the mystery of the forest. Nocturnal insects appeared in ghostly fashion out of the darkness, and fluttered round his light. He thought, perhaps, of all thc possibilities of discovery that still lay in the black tangle beneath him; for to the naturalist the virgin forests of Borneo are still a wonderland full of strange questions and half-suspected discoveries. Woodhouse carried a small lantern in his hand, and its yellow glow contrasted vividly with the infinite series of tints between lavender-blue and black in which the landscape was painted. His hands and face were smeared with ointment against the attacks of the mosquitoes.

Even in these days of celestial photography, work done in a purely temporary erection, and with only the most primitive appliances, in addition to the telescope, still involves a very large amount of cramped and motionless watching. He sighed as he thought of the physical fatigues before him, stretched himself and entered the observatory.

The reader is probably familiar with the structure of an ordinary astronomical observatory. The building is usually cylindrical in shape, with a very light hemispherical roof capable of being turned round from the interior. The telescope is supported upon a stone pillar in the centre, and a clockwork arrangement compensates for the earth's rotation, and allows a star once found to be continuously observed. Besides this, there is a compact tracery of wheels and screws about its point of support, by which the astronomer adjusts it. There is, of course, a slit in the movable roof which follows the eye of the telescope in its survey of the heavens. The observer sits or lies on a sloping wooden arrangement, which he can wheel to any part of the observatory as the position of the telescope may require. Within it is advisable to have things as dark as possible, in order to enhance the brilliance of the stars observed.

The lantern flared as Woodhouse entered his circular den, and the general darkness fled into black shadows behind the big machine, from which it presently seemed to creep back over the whole place again as the light waned. The slit was a profound transparent blue, in which six stars shone with tropical brilliance, and their light lay, a pallid gleam, along the black tube of the instrument. Woodhouse shifted the roof, and then proceeding to the telescope, turned first one wheel and then another, the great cylinder slowly swinging into a new position. Then he glanced through the finder, the little companion telescope, moved the roof a little more, made some further adjustments, and set the clockwork in motion. He took off his jacket, for the night was very hot, and pushed into position the uncomfortable seat to which he was condemned for the next four hours. Then with a sigh, he resigned himself to his watch upon the mysteries of space.

There was no sound now in the observatory, and the lantern waned steadily. Outside there was the occasional cry of some animal in alarm or pain, or calling to its mate, and the intermittent sounds of the Malay and Dyak[498] servants. Presently one of the men began a queer chanting song, in which the others joined at intervals. After this it would seem that they turned in for the night, for no further sound came from their direction, and the whispering stillness became more and more profound.

The clockwork ticked steadily. The shrill hum of a mosquito explored the place, and grew shriller in indignation at Woodhouse's ointment. Then the lantern went out and all the observatory was black.

Woodhouse shifted his position presently, when the slow movement of the telescope had carried it beyond the limits of his comfort.

He was watching a little group of stars in the Milky Way, in one of which his chief had seen or fancied a remarkable colour variability. It was not a part of the regular work for which the establishment existed, and for that reason perhaps Woodhouse was deeply interested. He must have forgotten things terrestrial. All his attention was concentrated upon the great blue circle of the telescope field – a circle powdered, so it seemed, with an innumerable multitude of stars, and all luminous against the blackness of its setting. As he watched he seemed to himself to become incorporeal, as if he too were floating in the ether of space. Infinitely remote was the faint red spot he was observing.

Suddenly the stars were blotted out. A flash of blackness passed, and they were visible again.

'Queer,' said Woodhouse. 'Must have been a bird.'

The thing happened again, and immediately after the great tube shivered as though it had been struck. Then the dome of the observatory resounded with a series of thundering blows. The stars seemed to sweep aside as the telescope – which had been unclamped – swung round and away from the slit in the roof.

'Great Scott!' cried Woodhouse. 'What's this?'

Some huge vague black shape, with a flapping something like a wing, seemed to be struggling in the aperture of the roof. In another moment the slit was clear again, and the luminous haze of the Milky Way shone warm and bright.

The interior of the roof was perfectly black, and only a scraping sound marked the whereabouts of the unknown creature.

Woodhouse had scrambled from the seat to his feet. He was trembling violently and in a perspiration with the suddenness of the occurrence. Was the thing, whatever it was, inside or out? It was big, whatever else it might be. Something shot across the skylight, and the telescope swayed. He started violently and put his arm up. It was in the observatory then, with him. It was clinging to the roof apparently. What the devil was it? Could it see him?

He stood for perhaps a minute in a state of stupefaction. The beast, whatever it was, clawed at the interior of the dome, and then something flapped almost into his face, and he saw the momentary gleam of star-light on a skin like oiled leather. His water-bottle was knocked off his little table with a smash.

The sense of some strange bird-creature hovering a few yards from his face in the darkness was indescribably unpleasant to Woodhouse. As his thought returned he concluded that it must be some night-bird or large bat. At any risk he would see what it was, and pulling a match from his pocket, he tried to strike it on the telescope seat. There was a smoking streak of phosphorescent light, the match flared for a moment, and he saw a vast wing sweeping towards him, a gleam of grey-brown fur, and then he was struck in the face and the match knocked out of his hand. The blow was aimed at his temple, and a claw tore sideways down to his cheek. He reeled and fell, and he heard the extinguished lantern smash. Another blow followed as he fell. He was partly stunned, he felt his own warm blood stream out upon his face. Instinctively he felt his eyes had been struck at, and turning over on his face to save them, tried to crawl under the protection of the telescope.

He was struck again upon the back, and he heard his jacket rip, and then the thing hit the roof of the observatory. He edged as far as he could between the wooden seat and the eyepiece of the instrument, and turned his body round so that it was chiefly his feet that were exposed. With these he could at least kick. He was still in a mystified state. The strange beast banged about in the darkness, and presently clung to the telescope, making it sway and the gear rattle. Once it flapped near him, and he kicked out madly and felt a soft body with his feet. He was horribly scared now. It must be a big thing to swing the telescope like that. He saw for a moment the outline of a head black against the starlight, with sharply pointed upstanding ears and a crest between them. It seemed to him to be as big as a mastiff's. Then he began to bawl out as loudly as he could for help.

At that the thing came down upon him again. As it did so his hand touched something beside him on the floor. He kicked out, and the next moment his ankle was gripped and held by a row of keen teeth. He yelled again, and tried to free his leg by kicking with the other. Then he realised he had the broken water-bottle at his hand, and, snatching it, he struggled into a sitting posture, and feeling in the darkness towards his foot, gripped a velvety ear, like the ear of a big cat. He had seized the water-bottle by its neck and brought it down, with a shivering crash upon the head of the strange beast. He repeated the blow, and then stabbed and jabbed with the jagged end of it, in the darkness, where he judged the face might be.

The small teeth relaxed their hold, and at once Woodhouse pulled his leg free and kicked hard. He felt the sickening feel of fur and bone giving under his boot. There was a tearing bite at his arm, and he struck over it at the face, as he judged, and hit damp fur.

There was a pause; then he heard the sound of claws; and the dragging of a heavy body away from him over the observatory floor. Then there was silence, broken only by his own sobbing breathing, and a sound like licking. Everything was black except the parallelogram of the blue skylight with the luminous dust of stars, against which the end of the telescope now appeared in silhouette. He waited, as it seemed, an interminable time.

Was the thing coming on again? He felt in his trouser-pocket for some matches, and found one remaining. He tried to strike this, but the floor was wet, and it spat and went out. He cursed. He could not see where the door was situated. In his struggle he had quite lost his bearings. The strange beast, disturbed by the splutter of the match, began to move again. 'Time!' called Woodhouse, with a sudden gleam of mirth,[499] but the thing was not coming at him again. He must have hurt it, he thought, with the broken bottle. He felt a dull pain in his ankle. Probably he was bleeding there. He wondered if it would support him if he tried to stand up. The night outside was very still. There was no sound of anyone moving. The sleepy fools had not heard those wings battering upon the dome, nor his shouts. It was no good wasting strength in shouting. The monster flapped its wings and startled him into a defensive attitude. He hit his elbow against the seat, and it fell over with a crash. He cursed this, and then he cursed the darkness.

Suddenly the oblong patch of starlight seemed to sway to and fro. Was he going to faint? It would never do to faint. He clenched his fists and set his teeth to hold himself together. Where had the door got to? It occurred to him he could get his bearings by the stars visible through the skylight. The patch of stars he saw was in Sagittarius and south-eastward; the door was north – or was it north by west? He tried to think. If he could get the door open he might retreat. It might be the thing was wounded. The suspense was beastly. 'Look here!' he said, 'If you don't come on, I shall come at you.'

Then the thing began clambering up the side of the observatory, and he saw its black outline gradually blot out the skylight. Was it in retreat? He forgot about the door, and watched as the dome shifted and creaked. Somehow he did not feel very frightened or excited now. He felt a curious sinking sensation inside him. The sharply defined patch of light, with the black form moving across it, seemed to be growing smaller and smaller. That was curious. He began to feel very thirsty, and yet he did not feel inclined to get anything to drink. He seemed to be sliding down a long funnel.

He felt a burning sensation in his throat, and then he perceived it was broad daylight, and that one of the Dyak servants was looking at him with a curious expression. Then there was the top of Thaddy's face upside down. Funny fellow, Thaddy, to go about like that! Then he grasped the situation better, and perceived that his head was on Thaddy's knee, and Thaddy was giving him brandy. And then he saw the eyepiece of the telescope with a lot of red smears on it. He began to remember.

'You've made this observatory in a pretty mess,' said Thaddy.

The Dyak boy was beating up an egg in brandy. Woodhouse took this and sat up. He felt a sharp twinge of pain. His ankle was tied up, so were his arm and the side of his face. The smashed glass, red-stained, lay about the floor, the telescope seat was overturned, and by the opposite wall was a dark pool. The door was open, and he saw the grey summit of the mountain against a brilliant background of blue sky.

'Pah!' said Woodhouse. 'Who's been killing calves here? Take me out of it.'

Then he remembered the Thing, and the fight he had had with it.

'What was it?' he said to Thaddy – 'The Thing I fought with?'

'You know that best,' said Thaddy. 'But, anyhow, don't worry yourself now about it. Have some more to drink.'

Thaddy, however, was curious enough, and it was a hard struggle between duty and inclination to keep Woodhouse quiet until he was decently put away in bed, and had slept upon the copious dose of meat extract Thaddy considered advisable. They then talked it over together.

'It was,' said Woodhouse, 'more like a big bat than anything else in the world. It had sharp, short ears, and soft fur, and its wings were leathery. Its teeth were little but devilish sharp, and its jaw could not have been very strong or else it would have bitten through my ankle.'

'It has pretty nearly,' said Thaddy.

'It seemed to me to hit out with its claws pretty freely. That is about as much as I know about the beast. Our conversation was intimate, so to speak, and yet not confidential.'

'The Dyak chaps talk about a Big Colugo, a Klangutang [500] – whatever that may be. It does not often attack man, but I suppose you made it nervous. They say there is a Big Colugo and a Little Colugo, and a something else that sounds like gobble. They all fly about at night. For my own part, I know there are flying foxes and flying lemurs about here, but they are none of them very big beasts.'

'There are more things in heaven and earth,' said Woodhouse – and Thaddy groaned at the quotation – 'and more particularly in the forests of Borneo, than are dreamt of in our philosophies. [501] On the whole, if the Borneo fauna [502] is going to disgorge any more of its novelties upon me, I should prefer that it did so when I was not occupied in the observatory at night and alone.'

The Triumphs of a Taxidermist [503]

Here are some of the secrets of taxidermy. They were told me by the taxidermist in a mood of elation. He told me them in the time between the first glass of whisky and the fourth, when a man is no longer cautious and yet not drunk. We sat in his den together: his library it was, his sitting and his eating-room – separated by a bead curtain, so far as the sense of sight went, from the noisome den where he plied his trade.

He sat on a deck chair, and when he was not tapping refractory bits of coal with them, he kept his feet – on which he wore, after the manner of sandals, the holey relics of a pair of carpet slippers – out of the way upon the mantelpiece, among the glass eyes. And his trousers, by the by – though they have nothing to do with his triumphs – were a most horrible yellow plaid, such as they made when our fathers wore side-whiskers and there were crinolines in the land. Further, his hair was black, his face rosy, and his eye a fiery brown; and his coat was chiefly of grease upon a basis of velveteen. And his pipe had a bowl of china showing the Graces,[504] and his spectacles were always askew, the left eye glaring nakedly at you, small and penetrating; the right, seen through a glass darkly, magnified and mild. Thus his discourse ran: 'There never was a man who could stuff like me, Bellows, never. I have stuffed elephants and I have stuffed moths, and the things have looked all the livelier and better for it. And I have stuffed human beings – chiefly amateur ornithologists.[505] But I stuffed a nigger once.

'No, there is no law against it. I made him with all his fingers out and used him as a hat-rack, but that fool Homersby got up a quarrel with him late one night and spoilt him. That was before your time. It is hard to get skins, or I would have another.

'Unpleasant? I don't see it. Seems to me taxidermy is a promising third course to burial or cremation. You could keep all your dear ones by you. Bric-à-brac[506] of that sort stuck about the house would be as good as most company, and much less expensive. You might have them fitted up with clockwork to do things.

'Of course they would have to be varnished, but they need not shine more than lots of people do naturally. Old Manningtree's bald head . . . Anyhow, you could talk to them without interruption. Even aunts.

There is a great future before taxidermy, depend upon it. There is fossils again . . . '

He suddenly became silent.

'No, I don't think I ought to tell you that.' He sucked at his pipe thoughtfully. 'Thanks, yes. Not too much water.

'Of course, what I tell you now will go no further. You know I have made some dodos and a great auk?[507] No! Evidently you are an amateur at taxidermy. My dear fellow, half the great auks in the world are about as genuine as the handkerchief of St Veronica, as the Holy Coat of Trèves.[508] We make 'em of grebes' feathers[509] and the like. And the great auk's eggs too!'

'Good heavens!'

'Yes, we make them out of fine porcelain. I tell you it is worth while. They fetch – one fetched three hundred pounds only the other day. That one was really genuine, I believe, but of course one is never certain. It is very fine work, and afterwards you have to get them dusty, for no one who owns one of these precious eggs has ever the temerity to clean the thing. That's the beauty of the business. Even if they suspect an egg they do not like to examine it too closely. It's such brittle capital at the best.

'You did not know that taxidermy rose to heights like that. My boy, it has risen higher. I have rivalled the hands of Nature herself. One of the *genuine* great auks – ' his voice fell to a whisper – 'one of the *genuine* great auks *was made by me*.

'No. You must study ornithology, and find out which it is yourself. And what is more, I have been approached by a syndicate of dealers to stock one of the unexplored skerries[510] to the north of Iceland with specimens. I may – some day. But I have another little thing in hand just now. Ever heard of the dinornis?

'It is one of those big birds recently extinct in New Zealand. "Moa" is its common name, so called because extinct: there is no moa now.[511] See? Well, they have got bones of it, and from some of the marshes even feathers and dried bits of skin. Now, I am going to – well, there is no need to make any bones about it – going to *forge* a complete stuffed moa. I know a chap out there who will pretend to make the find in a kind of antiseptic swamp, and say he stuffed it at once, as it threatened to fall to pieces. The feathers are peculiar, but I have got a simply lovely way of dodging up[512] singed bits of ostrich plume. Yes, that is the new smell you noticed. They can only discover the fraud with a microscope, and they will hardly care to pull a nice specimen to bits for that.

'In this way, you see, I give my little push in the advancement of science.

'But all this is merely imitating Nature. I have done more than that in my time. I have – beaten her.'

He took his feet down from the mantel-board, and leant over confidentially towards me. 'I have *created* birds,' he said in a low voice. '*New* birds. Improvements. Like no birds that was ever seen before.'

He resumed his attitude during an impressive silence.

'Enrich the universe; *rath*-er. Some of the birds I made were new kinds of humming birds, and very beautiful little things, but some of them were simply rum. The rummest, I think, was the *Anomalopteryx Jejuna*.[513] *Jejunus-a-um* – empty – so called because there was really nothing in it: a thoroughly empty bird – except for stuffing. Old Javvers has the thing now, and I suppose he is almost as proud of it as I am. It is a masterpiece, Bellows. It has all the silly clumsiness of your pelican, all the solemn want of dignity of your parrot, all the gaunt ungainliness of a flamingo, with all the extravagant chromatic conflict of a mandarin duck.[514] *Such* a bird. I made it out of the skeletons of a stork and a toucan and a job lot of feathers. Taxidermy of that kind is just pure joy, Bellows, to a real artist in the art.

'How did I come to make it? Simple enough, as all great inventions are. One of those young genii who write us Science Notes in the papers got hold of a German pamphlet about the birds of New Zealand, and translated some of it by means of a dictionary and his mother-wit – he must have been one of a very large family with a small mother – and he got mixed between the living apteryx and the extinct anomalopteryx;[515] talked about a bird five feet high, living in the jungles of the North Island, rare, shy, specimens difficult to obtain, and so on. Javvers, who, even for a collector, is a miraculously ignorant man, read these paragraphs, and swore he would have the thing at any price. Raided the dealers with enquiries. It shows what a man can do by persistence – will-power. Here was a bird-collector swearing he would have a specimen of a bird that did not exist, that never had existed, and which, for very shame of its own profane ungainliness, probably would not exist now if it could help itself. And he got it. *He got it.*

'Have some more whisky, Bellows?' said the taxidermist, rousing himself from a transient contemplation of the mysteries of will-power and the collecting turn of mind. And, replenished, he proceeded to tell me of how he concocted a most attractive mermaid, and how an itinerant preacher, who could not get an audience because of it, smashed it because it was idolatry, or worse, at Burslem Wakes.[516] But as the conversation of all the parties to this transaction, creator, would-be preserver and destroyer, was uniformly unfit for publication, this cheerful incident must still remain unprinted.

The reader unacquainted with the dark ways of the collector may perhaps be inclined to doubt my taxidermist, but so far as great auks' eggs, and the bogus stuffed birds are concerned, I find that he has the confirmation of distinguished ornithological writers. And the note about the New Zealand bird certainly appeared in a morning paper of unblemished reputation, for the taxidermist keeps a copy and has shown it to me.

A Deal in Ostriches [517]

'Talking of the prices of birds, I've seen an ostrich that cost three hundred pounds,' said the taxidermist, recalling his youth of travel. 'Three hundred pounds!'

He looked at me over his spectacles. 'I've seen another that was refused at four.'

'No,' he said, 'it wasn't any fancy points. They was just plain ostriches. A little off colour, too – owing to dietary. And there wasn't any particular restriction of the demand either. You'd have thought five ostriches would have ruled cheap on an East Indiaman. [518] But the point was, one of 'em had swallowed a diamond.

'The chap it got it off was Sir Mohini Padishah, a tremendous swell, a Piccadilly swell you might say up to the neck of him, and then an ugly black head and a whopping turban, with this diamond in it. The blessed bird pecked suddenly and had it, and when the chap made a fuss, it realised it had done wrong, I suppose, and went and mixed itself with the others to preserve its *incog*. [519] It all happened in a minute. I was among the first to arrive, and there was this heathen going over his gods, and two sailors and the man who had charge of the birds laughing, fit to split. It was a rummy [520] way of losing a jewel, come to think of it. The man in charge hadn't been about just at the moment, so that he didn't know which bird it was. Clean lost, you see. I didn't feel half sorry, to tell you the truth. The beggar had been swaggering over his blessed diamond ever since he came aboard.

'A thing like that goes from stem to stern of a ship in no time. Everyone was talking about it. Padishah went below to hide his feelings. At dinner – he pigged at a table by himself, him and two other Hindus – the captain kind of jeered at him about it, and he got very excited. He turned round and talked into my ear. He would not buy the birds; he would have his diamond. He demanded his rights as a British subject. His diamond must be found. He was firm upon that. He would appeal to the House of Lords. The man in charge of the birds was one of those wooden-headed chaps you can't get a new idea into anyhow. He refused any proposal to interfere with the birds by way of medicine. His instructions were to feed them so-and-so and treat them so-and-so, and it was as much as his place was worth not to feed them so-and-

so and treat them so-and-so. Padishah had wanted a stomach-pump –
though you can't do that to a bird, you know. This Padishah was full of
bad law, like most of these blessed Bengalis, and talked of having a
lien[521] on the birds, and so forth. But an old boy, who said his son was a
London barrister, argued that what a bird swallowed became *ipso facto*[522]
part of the bird, and that Padishah's only remedy lay in an action for
damages, and even then it might be possible to show contributory
negligence.[523] He hadn't any right of way about an ostrich that didn't
belong to him. That upset Padishah extremely, the more so as most of
us expressed an opinion that that was the reasonable view. There wasn't
any lawyer aboard to settle the matter, so we all talked pretty free. At
last, after Aden, it appears that he came round to the general opinion,
and went privately to the man in charge and made an offer for all five
ostriches.

'The next morning there was a fine shindy at breakfast. The man
hadn't any authority to deal with the birds, and nothing on earth would
induce him to sell; but it seems he told Padishah that a Eurasian named
Potter had already made him an offer, and on that Padishah denounced
Potter before us all. But I think the most of us thought it rather smart of
Potter, and I know that when Potter said that he'd wired[524] at Aden to
London to buy the birds, and would have an answer at Suez, I cursed
pretty richly at a lost opportunity.

'At Suez, Padishah gave way to tears – actual wet tears – when Potter
became the owner of the birds, and offered him two hundred and fifty
right off for the five, being more than two hundred per cent. on what
Potter had given. Potter said he'd be hanged if he parted with a feather
of them – that he meant to kill them off one by one and find the
diamond; but afterwards, thinking it over, he relented a little. He was
a gambling hound, was this Potter, a little queer[525] at cards, and this
kind of prize-packet business must have suited him down to the ground.
Anyhow, he offered, for a lark, to sell the birds separately to separate
people by auction at a starting price of eighty pounds for a bird. But
one of them, he said, he meant to keep for luck.

'You must understand this diamond was a valuable one – a little Jew
chap, a diamond merchant, who was with us, had put it at three or four
thousand when Padishah had shown it to him – and this idea of an
ostrich gamble caught on. Now it happened that I'd been having a few
talks on general subjects with the man who looked after these ostriches,
and quite incidentally he'd said one of the birds was ailing, and he
fancied it had indigestion. It had one feather in its tail almost all white,
by which I knew it, and so when, next day, the auction started with it, I

capped Padishah's eighty-five by ninety. I fancy I was a bit too sure and eager with my bid, and some of the others spotted the fact that I was in the know. And Padishah went for that particular bird like an irresponsible lunatic. At last the Jew diamond merchant got it for a hundred and seventy-five, and Padishah said a hundred and eighty just after the hammer came down – so Potter declared. At any rate the Jew merchant secured it, and there and then he got a gun and shot it. Potter made a Hades of a fuss because he said it would injure the sale of the other three, and Padishah, of course, behaved like an idiot; but all of us were very much excited. I can tell you I was precious glad when that dissection was over, and no diamond had turned up – precious glad. I'd gone to one-forty on that particular bird myself.

'The little Jew was like most Jews – he didn't make any great fuss over bad luck; but Potter declined to go on with the auction until it was understood that the goods could not be delivered until the sale was over. The little Jew wanted to argue that the case was exceptional, and as the discussion ran pretty even, the thing was postponed until the next morning. We had a lively dinner-table that evening, I can tell you, but in the end Potter got his way, since it would stand to reason he would be safer if he stuck to all the birds, and we owed him some consideration for his sportsmanlike behaviour. And the old gentleman whose son was a lawyer said he'd been thinking the thing over and that it was very doubtful if, when a bird had been opened and the diamond recovered, it ought not to be handed back to the proper owner. I remember I suggested it came under the laws of treasure-trove – which was really the truth of the matter. There was a hot argument, and we settled it was certainly foolish to kill the bird on board the ship. Then the old gentleman, going at large through his legal talk, tried to make out the sale was a lottery and illegal, and appealed to the captain; but Potter said he sold the birds as ostriches. He didn't want to sell any diamonds, he said, and didn't offer that as an inducement. The three birds he put up, to the best of his knowledge and belief, did not contain a diamond. It was in the one he kept – so he hoped.

'Prices ruled high next day all the same. The fact that now there were four chances instead of five of course caused a rise. The blessed birds averaged two hundred and twenty-seven pounds, and, oddly enough, this Padishah didn't secure one of 'em – not one. He made too much shindy, and when he ought to have been bidding he was talking about liens, and besides, Potter was a bit down on him. One fell to a quiet little officer chap, another to the little Jew, and the third was syndicated by the engineers. And then Potter seemed suddenly sorry for having sold them, and said he'd flung away a clear thousand pounds, and that very likely he'd draw a blank and that he always had been a fool, but when I went and had a bit of a talk to him, with the idea of getting him to hedge on his last chance, I found he'd already sold the bird he'd reserved to a political chap that was on board, a chap who'd been studying Indian morals and social questions in his vacation. That last was the three-hundred-pound bird. Well, they landed three of the blessed creatures at Brindisi – though the old gentleman said it was a breach of the Customs regulations – and Potter and Padishah landed too. The Hindu seemed half mad as he saw his blessed diamond going this way and that, so to speak. He kept on saying he'd get an injunction – he had injunction on the brain – and giving his name and address to the chaps who'd bought the birds, so that they'd know where to send the diamond. None of them wanted his name and address, and none of them would give their own. It was a fine row I can tell you – on the platform. They all went off by different trains. I came on to Southampton, and there I saw the last of the birds, as I came ashore; it was the one the engineers bought, and it was standing up near the bridge, in a kind of crate, and looking as leggy and silly a setting for a valuable diamond as ever you saw – if it was a setting for a valuable diamond.

'*How did it end?* Oh! Like that. Well – perhaps. Yes, there's one more thing that may throw light on it. A week or so after landing I was down Regent Street doing a bit of shopping, and who should I see arm in arm and having a purple [526] time of it but Padishah and Potter. If you come to think of it –

'Yes. *I've* thought that. Only, you see, there's no doubt the diamond was real. And Padishah was an eminent Hindu. I've seen his name in the papers – often. But whether the bird swallowed the diamond certainly is another matter, as you say.'

Through a Window[527]

After his legs were set, they carried Bailey into the study and put him on a couch before the open window. There he lay, a live – even a feverish man down to the loins, and below that a double-barrelled mummy swathed in white wrappings. He tried to read, even tried to write a little, but most of the time he looked out of the window.

He had thought the window cheerful to begin with, but now he thanked God for it many times a day. Within, the room was dim and grey, and in the reflected light, the wear of the furniture showed plainly. His medicine and drink stood on the little table, with such litter as the bare branches of a bunch of grapes, or the ashes of a cigar upon a green plate, or a day-old evening paper. The view outside was flooded with light, and across the corner of it came the head of the acacia, and at the foot, the top of the balcony-railing of hammered iron. In the foreground was the weltering[528] silver of the river, never quiet and yet never tiresome. Beyond was the reedy bank, a broad stretch of meadow land, and then a dark line of trees ending in a group of poplars at the distant bend of the river, and upstanding behind them, a square church tower.

Up and down the river, all day long, things were passing. Now a string of barges drifting down to London, piled with lime or barrels of beer; then a steam-launch, disengaging heavy masses of black smoke, and disturbing the whole width of the river with long rolling waves; then an impetuous electric launch, and then a boatload of pleasure-seekers, a solitary sculler,[529] or a four from some rowing club. Perhaps the river was quietest of a morning or late at night. One moonlight night some people drifted down singing, and with a zither playing – it sounded very pleasantly across the water.

In a few days Bailey began to recognise some of the craft; in a week he knew the intimate history of half a dozen. The launch *Luzon*, from Fitzgibbon's,[530] two miles up, would go fretting by, sometimes three or four times a day, conspicuous with its colouring of Indian-red and yellow, and its two Oriental attendants; and one day, to Bailey's vast amusement, the houseboat *Purple Emperor* came to a stop outside, and breakfasted in the most shameless domesticity. Then one afternoon, the captain of a slow-moving barge began a quarrel with his wife as

they came into sight from the left, and had carried it to personal
violence before he vanished behind the window-frame to the right.
Bailey regarded all this as an entertainment got up to while away his
illness, and applauded all the more these moving incidents. Mrs Green,
coming in at rare intervals with his meals, would catch him clapping
his hands or softly crying, 'Encore!' But the river players had other
engagements, and his encore went unheeded.

'I should never have thought I could take such an interest in things
that did not concern me,' said Bailey to Wilderspin, who used to come
in in his nervous, friendly way and try to comfort the sufferer by being
talked to. 'I thought this idle capacity was distinctive of little children
and old maids. But it's just circumstances. I simply can't work, and
things have to drift; it's no good to fret and struggle. And so I lie here
and am as amused as a baby with a rattle at this river and its affairs.

'Sometimes, of course, it gets a bit dull, but not often.

'I would give anything, Wilderspin, for a swamp[531] – just one swamp –
once. Heads swimming and a steam launch to the rescue, and a chap or
so hauled out with a boat-hook[532] . . . There goes Fitzgibbon's launch!
They have a new boathook, I see, and the little blackie is still in the
dumps. I don't think he's very well, Wilderspin. He's been like that for
two or three days, squatting sulky-fashion and meditating over the
churning of the water. Unwholesome for him to be always staring at the
frothy water running away from the stern.'

They watched the little steamer fuss across the patch of sunlit river,
suffer momentary occultation from the acacia, and glide out of sight
behind the dark window-frame.

'I'm getting a wonderful eye for details,' said Bailey: 'I spotted that
new boathook at once. The other nigger is a funny little chap. He never
used to swagger with the old boathook like that.'

'Malays, aren't they?' said Wilderspin.

'Don't know,' said Bailey. 'I thought one called all that sort of mariner
Lascar.'[533]

Then he began to tell Wilderspin what he knew of the private affairs
of the houseboat *Purple Emperor*. 'Funny,' he said, 'how these people
come from all points of the compass – from Oxford and Windsor,
from Asia and Africa – and gather and pass opposite the window just
to entertain me. One man floated out of the infinite the day before
yesterday, caught one perfect crab[534] opposite, lost and recovered a
scull, and passed on again. Probably he will never come into my life
again. So far as I am concerned, he has lived and had his little troubles
perhaps thirty – perhaps forty – years on the earth, merely to make an

ass of himself for three minutes in front of my window. Wonderful thing, Wilderspin, if you come to think of it.'

'Yes,' said Wilderspin; 'isn't it?'

A day or two after this Bailey had a brilliant morning. Indeed, towards the end of the affair, it became almost as exciting as any window show very well could be. We will, however, begin at the beginning.

Bailey was all alone in the house, for his housekeeper had gone into the town three miles away to pay bills, and the servant had her holiday. The morning began dull. A canoe went up about half-past nine, and later a boat-load of camping men came down. But this was mere margin. Things became cheerful about ten o'clock.

It began with something white fluttering in the remote distance where the three poplars marked the river bend. 'Pocket-handkerchief,' said Bailey, when he saw it. 'No. Too big! Flag perhaps.'

However, it was not a flag, for it jumped about. 'Man in whites running fast, and this way,' said Bailey. 'That's luck! But his whites are precious loose!'

Then a singular thing happened. There was a minute pink gleam among the dark trees in the distance, and a little puff of pale grey that began to drift and vanish eastward. The man in white jumped and continued running. Presently the report of the shot arrived.

'What the devil!' said Bailey. 'Looks as if someone was shooting at him.'

He sat up stiffly and stared hard. The white figure was coming along the pathway through the corn. 'It's one of those niggers from the Fitzgibbon's,' said Bailey; 'or may I be hanged! I wonder why he keeps sawing with his arm.'

Then three other figures became indistinctly visible against the dark background of the trees.

Abruptly on the opposite bank a man walked into the picture. He was black-bearded, dressed in flannels, had a red belt, and a vast, grey felt hat. He walked, leaning very much forward and with his hands swinging before him. Behind him one could see the grass swept by the towing-rope of the boat he was dragging. He was steadfastly regarding the white figure that was hurrying through the corn. Suddenly he stopped. Then, with a peculiar gesture, Bailey could see that he began pulling in the tow-rope hand over hand. Over the water could be heard the voices of the people in the still invisible boat.

'What are you after, Hagshot?' said someone.

The individual with the red belt shouted something that was in-audible, and went on lugging in the rope, looking over his shoulder at the advancing white figure as he did so. He came down the bank, and the rope bent a lane among the reeds and lashed the water between his pulls.

Then just the bows of the boat came into view, with the towing-mast and a tall, fair-haired man standing up and trying to see over the bank. The boat bumped unexpectedly among the reeds, and the tall, fair-haired man disappeared suddenly, having apparently fallen back into the invisible part of the boat. There was a curse and some indistinct laughter. Hagshot did not laugh, but hastily clambered into the boat and pushed off. Abruptly the boat passed out of Bailey's sight.

But it was still audible. The melody of voices suggested that its occupants were busy telling each other what to do.

The running figure was drawing near the bank. Bailey could now see clearly that it was one of Fitzgibbon's Orientals, and began to realise what the sinuous thing the man carried in his hand might be. Three other men followed one another through the corn, and the foremost carried what was probably the gun. They were perhaps two hundred yards or more behind the Malay.

'It's a man hunt, by all that's holy!' said Bailey.

The Malay stopped for a moment and surveyed the bank to the right. Then he left the path, and breaking through the corn, vanished in that direction. The three pursuers followed suit, and their heads and gesticulating arms above the corn, after a brief interval, also went out of Bailey's field of vision.

Bailey so far forgot himself as to swear. 'Just as things were getting lively!' he said. Something like a woman's shriek came through the air. Then shouts, a howl, a dull whack upon the balcony outside that made Bailey jump, and then the report of a gun.

'This is precious hard on an invalid,' said Bailey.

But more was to happen yet in his picture. In fact, a great deal more. The Malay appeared again, running now along the bank upstream. His stride had more swing and less pace in it than before. He was threatening someone ahead with the ugly krees[535] he carried. The blade, Bailey noticed, was dull – it did not shine as steel should.

Then came the tall, fair man, brandishing a boathook, and after him three other men in boating costume, running clumsily with oars. The man with the grey hat and red belt was not with them. After an interval the three men with the gun reappeared, still in the corn, but now near the river bank. They emerged upon the towing-path, and hurried after the others. The opposite bank was left blank and desolate again.

The sick-room was disgraced by more profanity. 'I would give my life to see the end of this,' said Bailey. There were indistinct shouts upstream. Once they seemed to be coming nearer, but they disappointed him.

Bailey sat and grumbled. He was still grumbling when his eye caught something black and round among the waves. 'Hello!' he said. He looked narrowly and saw two triangular black bodies frothing every now and then about a yard in front of this.

He was still doubtful when the little band of pursuers came into sight again, and began to point to this floating object. They were talking eagerly. Then the man with the gun took aim.

'He's swimming the river, by George!' said Bailey.

The Malay looked round, saw the gun, and went under. He came up so close to Bailey's bank of the river that one of the bars of the balcony hid him for a moment. As he emerged the man with the gun fired. The Malay kept steadily onward – Bailey could see the wet hair on his forehead now and the krees between his teeth – and was presently hidden by the balcony.

This seemed to Bailey an unendurable wrong. The man was lost to him for ever now, so he thought. Why couldn't the brute have got himself decently caught on the opposite bank, or shot in the water?

'It's worse than *Edwin Drood*,'[536] said Bailey.

Over the river, too, things had become an absolute blank. All seven men had gone downstream again, probably to get the boat and follow across. Bailey listened and waited. There was silence. 'Surely it's not over like this,' said Bailey.

Five minutes passed – ten minutes. Then a tug with two barges went upstream. The attitudes of the men upon these were the attitudes of those who see nothing remarkable in earth, water or sky. Clearly the whole affair had passed out of sight of the river. Probably the hunt had gone into the beech woods behind the house.

'Confound it!' said Bailey. 'To be continued again, and no chance this time of the sequel. But this is hard on a sick man.'

He heard a step on the staircase behind him and looking round saw the door open. Mrs Green came in and sat down, panting. She still had her bonnet on, her purse in her hand, and her little brown basket upon her arm. 'Oh, there!' she said, and left Bailey to imagine the rest.

'Have a little whisky and water, Mrs Green, and tell me about it,' said Bailey.

Sipping a little, the lady began to recover her powers of explanation.

One of those black creatures at the Fitzgibbon's had gone mad, and was running about with a big knife, stabbing people. He had killed a groom, and stabbed the under-butler, and almost cut the arm off a boating gentleman.

'Running amuck[537] with a krees,' said Bailey. 'I thought that was it.'

And he was hiding in the wood when she came through it from the town.

'What! Did he run after you?' asked Bailey, with a certain touch of glee in his voice.

'No, that was the horrible part of it.' Mrs Green explained. She had been right through the wood and had *never known he was there*. It was only when she met young Mr Fitzgibbon carrying his gun in the shrubbery that she heard anything about it. Apparently, what upset Mrs Green was the lost opportunity for emotion. She was determined, however, to make the most of what was left her.

'To think he was there all the time!' she said, over and over again.

Bailey endured this patiently enough for perhaps ten minutes. At last he thought it advisable to assert himself. 'It's twenty past one, Mrs Green,' he said. 'Don't you think it time you got me something to eat?'

This brought Mrs Green suddenly to her feet.

'Oh Lord, sir!' she said. 'Oh! Don't go making me go out of this room, sir, till I know he's caught. He might have got into the house, sir. He might be creeping, creeping, with that knife of his, along the passage this very – '

She broke off suddenly and glared over him at the window. Her lower jaw dropped. Bailey turned his head sharply.

For the space of half a second things seemed just as they were. There was the tree, the balcony, the shining river, the distant church tower. Then he noticed that the acacia was displaced about a foot to the right, and that it was quivering, and the leaves were rustling. The tree was shaken violently, and a heavy panting was audible.

In another moment a hairy brown hand had appeared and clutched the balcony railings, and in another the face of the Malay was peering through these at the man on the couch. His expression was an unpleasant grin, by reason of the krees he held between his teeth, and he was bleeding from an ugly wound in his cheek. His hair wet to drying stuck out like horns from his head. His body was bare save for the wet trousers that clung to him. Bailey's first impulse was to spring from the couch, but his legs reminded him that this was impossible.

By means of the balcony and tree, the man slowly raised himself until he was visible to Mrs Green. With a choking cry she made for the door and fumbled with the handle.

Bailey thought swiftly and clutched a medicine bottle in either hand.

One he flung, and it smashed against the acacia. Silently and deliberately, and keeping his bright eyes fixed on Bailey, the Malay clambered into the balcony. Bailey, still clutching his second bottle, but with a sickening, sinking feeling about his heart, watched first one leg come over the railing and then the other.

It was Bailey's impression that the Malay took about an hour to get his second leg over the rail. The period that elapsed before the sitting position was changed to a standing one seemed enormous – days, weeks, possibly a year or so. Yet Bailey had no clear impression of anything going on in his mind during that vast period, except a vague wonder at his inability to throw the second medicine bottle. Suddenly the Malay glanced over his shoulder. There was the crack of a rifle. He flung up his arms and came down upon the couch. Mrs Green began a dismal shriek that seemed likely to last until Doomsday. Bailey stared at the brown body with its shoulder blade driven in that writhed painfully across his legs, rapidly staining and soaking the spotless bandages. Then he looked at the long krees, with the reddish streaks upon its blade, that lay an inch beyond the trembling brown fingers upon the floor. Then at Mrs Green, who had backed hard against the door and was staring at the body and shrieking in gusty outbursts as if she would wake the dead. And then the body was shaken by one last convulsive effort.

The Malay gripped the krees, tried to raise himself with his left hand, and collapsed. Then he raised his head, stared for a moment at Mrs Green, and twisting his face round looked at Bailey. With a gasping groan the dying man succeeded in clutching the bedclothes with his disabled hand, and by a violent effort, which hurt Bailey's legs exceedingly, writhed sideways towards what must be his last victim. Then something seemed released in Bailey's mind and he brought down the second bottle with all his strength on to the Malay's face. The krees fell heavily upon the floor.

'Easy with those legs,' said Bailey, as young Fitzgibbon and one of the boating party lifted the body off him.

Young Fitzgibbon was very white in the face. 'I didn't mean to kill him,' he said.

'It's just as well,' said Bailey.

The Temptation of Harringay [538]

It is quite impossible to say whether this thing really happened. It depends entirely on the word of R. M. Harringay, who is an artist.

Following his version of the affair, the narrative deposes that Harringay went into his studio about ten o'clock to see what he could make of the head that he had been working at the day before. The head in question was that of an Italian organ-grinder, and Harringay thought – but was not quite sure – that the title would be 'The Vigil'. So far he is frank, and his narrative bears the stamp of truth. He had seen the man expectant for pennies, and, with a promptness that suggested genius, had had him in at once.

'Kneel. Look up at that bracket,' said Harringay. 'As if you expected pennies.

'Don't *grin*!' said Harringay. 'I don't want to paint your gums. Look as though you were unhappy.'

Now, after a night's rest, the picture proved decidedly unsatisfactory. 'It's good work,' said Harringay. 'That little bit in the neck . . . But – '

He walked about the studio and looked at the thing from this point and from that. Then he said a wicked word. In the original the word is given.

'Painting,' he says he said. 'Just a painting of an organ-grinder – a mere portrait. If it was a live organ-grinder I wouldn't mind. But somehow I never make things alive. I wonder if my imagination is wrong.' This, too, has a truthful air. His imagination *is* wrong.

'That creative touch! To take canvas and pigment and make a man – as Adam was made of red ochre! [539] But this thing! If you met it walking about the streets you would know it was only a studio production. The little boys would tell it to "Garnome and git frimed." [540] Some little touch . . . Well – it won't do as it is.'

He went to the blinds and began to pull them down. They were made of blue holland [541] with the rollers at the bottom of the window, so that you pull them down to get more light. He gathered his palette, brushes and mahl stick [542] from his table. Then he turned to the picture and put a speck of brown in the corner of the mouth; and shifted his attention thence to the pupil of the eye. Then he decided that the chin was a trifle too impassive for a vigil.

Presently he put down his impedimenta,[543] and lighting a pipe surveyed the progress of his work. 'I'm hanged if the thing isn't sneering at me,' said Harringay, and he still believes it sneered.

The animation of the figure had certainly increased, but scarcely in the direction he wished. There was no mistake about the sneer. ' "Vigil of the Unbeliever",' said Harringay. 'Rather subtle and clever that! But the left eyebrow isn't cynical enough.'

He went and dabbed at the eyebrow, and added a little to the lobe of the ear to suggest materialism. Further consideration ensued. ' "Vigil" is off, I'm afraid,' said Harringay. 'Why not "Mephistopheles"? But that's a bit *too* common. "A Friend of the Doge" – not so seedy. The armour won't do, though. Too Camelot.[544] How about a scarlet robe and call him "One of the Sacred College"? [545] Humour in that, and an appreciation of Middle Italian history.[546]

'There's always Benvenuto Cellini,'[547] said Harringay; 'with a clever suggestion of a gold cup in one corner. But that would scarcely suit the complexion.'

He describes himself as babbling in this way in order to keep down an unaccountably unpleasant sensation of fear. The thing was certainly acquiring anything but a pleasing expression. Yet it was as certainly becoming far more of a living thing than it had been – if a sinister one – far more alive than anything he had ever painted before. 'Call it "Portrait of a Gentleman",' said Harringay; ' "A Certain Gentleman".[548]

'Won't do,' said Harringay, still keeping up his courage. 'Kind of thing they call Bad Taste. That sneer will have to come out. That gone, and a little more fire in the eye – never noticed how warm his eye was before – and he might do for – ? What price "Passionate Pilgrim"? But that devilish face won't do – this side of the Channel.

'Some little inaccuracy does it,' he said; 'eyebrows probably too oblique – ' therewith pulling the blind lower to get a better light, and resuming palette and brushes.

The face on the canvas seemed animated by a spirit of its own. Where the expression of diablerie[549] came in he found impossible to discover. Experiment was necessary. The eyebrows – it could scarcely be the eyebrows? But he altered them. No, that was no better; in fact, if anything, a trifle more satanic. The corner of the mouth? Pah! More than ever a leer – and now, retouched, it was ominously grim. The eye, then? Catastrophe! He had filled his brush with vermilion instead of brown, and yet he had felt sure it was brown! The eye seemed now to have rolled in its socket, and was glaring at him an eye of fire. In a flash of passion, possibly with something of the courage of panic, he struck the brush full of bright red athwart the picture; and then a very curious thing, a very strange thing indeed, occurred – if it *did* occur.

The diabolified Italian before him shut both his eyes, pursed his mouth, and wiped the colour off his face with his hand.

Then the *red eye* opened again, with a sound like the opening of lips, and the face smiled. 'That was rather hasty of you,' said the picture.

Harringay states that, now that the worst had happened, his self-possession returned. He had a saving persuasion that devils were reasonable creatures.

'Why do you keep moving about then,' he said, 'making faces and all that – sneering and squinting, while I am painting you?'

'I don't,' said the picture.

'You *do*,' said Harringay.

'It's yourself,' said the picture.

'It's *not* myself,' said Harringay.

'It *is* yourself,' said the picture. 'No! Don't go hitting me with paint again, because it's true. You have been trying to fluke[550] an expression on my face all the morning. Really, you haven't an idea what your picture ought to look like.'

'I have,' said Harringay.

'You have *not*,' said the picture: 'You *never* have with your pictures. You always start with the vaguest presentiment of what you are going to do; it is to be something beautiful – you are sure of that – and devout, perhaps, or tragic; but beyond that it is all experiment and chance. My dear fellow! you don't think you can paint a picture like that?'

Now it must be remembered that for what follows we have only Harringay's word.

'I shall paint a picture exactly as I like,' said Harringay, calmly.

This seemed to disconcert the picture a little. 'You can't paint a picture without an inspiration,' it remarked.

'But I *had* an inspiration – for this.'

'Inspiration!' sneered the sardonic figure; 'A fancy that came from your seeing an organ-grinder looking up at a window! Vigil! Ha, ha! You just started painting on the chance of something coming – that's what you did. And when I saw you at it I came. I want a talk with you!

'Art, with you,' said the picture – 'it's a poor business. You potter. I don't know how it is, but you don't seem able to throw your soul into it. You know too much. It hampers you. In the midst of your enthusiasms you ask yourself whether something like this has not been done before. And . . .'

'Look here,' said Harringay, who had expected something better than criticism from the devil. 'Are you going to talk studio to me?' He filled his number-twelve hoghair with red paint.

'The true artist,' said the picture, 'is always an ignorant man. An artist who theorises about his work is no longer artist but critic. Wagner[551] . . . I say! – What's that red paint for?'

'I'm going to paint you out,' said Harringay. 'I don't want to hear all that tommy-rot.[552] If you think just because I'm an artist by trade I'm going to talk studio to you, you make a precious mistake.'

'One minute,' said the picture, evidently alarmed. 'I want to make you an offer – a genuine offer. It's right what I'm saying. You lack inspirations. Well. No doubt you've heard of the Cathedral of Cologne, and the Devil's Bridge,[553] and – '

'Rubbish,' said Harringay. 'Do you think I want to go to perdition simply for the pleasure of painting a good picture, and getting it slated.[554] Take that.'

His blood was up. His danger only nerved him to action, so he says. So he planted a dab of vermilion in his creature's mouth. The Italian spluttered and tried to wipe it off – evidently horribly surprised. And then – according to Harringay – there began a very remarkable struggle, Harringay splashing away with the red paint, and the picture wriggling about and wiping it off as fast as he put it on.

'*Two* masterpieces,' said the demon. 'Two indubitable masterpieces for a Chelsea artist's soul.[555] It's a bargain?'

Harringay replied with the paint brush.

For a few minutes nothing could be heard but the brush going and the spluttering and ejaculations of the Italian. A lot of the strokes he caught on his arm and hand, though Harringay got over his guard often enough. Presently the paint on the palette gave out and the two antagonists stood breathless, regarding each other. The picture was so smeared with red that it looked as if it had been rolling about a slaughterhouse, and it was painfully out of breath and very uncomfortable with the wet paint trickling down its neck. Still, the first round was in its favour on the whole. 'Think,' it said, sticking pluckily to its point, 'two supreme masterpieces – in different styles. Each equivalent to the Cathedral . . . '

'*I* know,' said Harringay, and rushed out of the studio and along the passage towards his wife's boudoir.

In another minute he was back with a large tin of enamel – Hedge Sparrow's Egg Tint,[556] it was, and a brush. At the sight of that the artistic devil with the red eye began to scream. '*Three* masterpieces – culminating masterpieces.'

Harringay delivered cut two across the demon, and followed with a thrust in the eye. There was an indistinct rumbling. '*Four* masterpieces,' and a spitting sound.

But Harringay had the upper hand now and meant to keep it. With rapid, bold strokes he continued to paint over the writhing canvas until at last it was a uniform field of shining Hedge Sparrow Tint. Once the mouth reappeared and got as far as '*Five* master – ' before he filled it with enamel; and near the end the red eye opened and glared at him indignantly. But at last nothing remained save a gleaming panel of drying enamel. For a little while a faint stirring beneath the surface puckered it slightly here and there, but presently even that died away and the thing was perfectly still.

Then Harringay – according to Harringay's account – lit his pipe and sat down and stared at the enamelled canvas, and tried to make out clearly what had happened. Then he walked round behind it, to see if the back of it was at all remarkable. Then it was he began to regret he had not photographed the Devil before he painted him out.

This is Harringay's story – not mine. He supports it by a small canvas (24" x 20") enamelled a pale green, and by violent asseverations. It is also true that he never has produced a masterpiece, and in the opinion of his intimate friends probably never will.

The Beautiful Suit 557

There was once a little man whose mother made him a beautiful suit of clothes. It was green and gold, and woven so that I cannot describe how delicate and fine it was, and there was a tie of orange fluffiness that tied up under his chin. And the buttons in their newness shone like stars. He was proud and pleased by his suit beyond measure, and stood before the long looking-glass when first he put it on, so astonished and delighted with it that he could hardly turn himself away.

He wanted to wear it everywhere, and show it to all sorts of people. He thought over all the places he had ever visited, and all the scenes he had ever heard described, and tried to imagine what the feel of it would be if he were to go now to those scenes and places wearing his shining suit, and he wanted to go out forthwith into the long grass and hot sunshine of the meadow wearing it. Just to wear it! But his mother told him, 'No.' She told him he must take great care of his suit, for never would he have another nearly so fine; he must save it and save it, and only wear it on rare great occasions. It was his wedding-suit, she said. And she took the buttons and twisted them up with tissue paper for fear their bright newness should be tarnished, and she tacked little guards over the cuffs and elbows, and wherever the suit was most likely to come to harm. He hated and resisted these things, but what could he do? And at last her warnings and persuasions had effect, and he consented to take off his beautiful suit and fold it into its proper creases, and put it away. It was almost as though he gave it up again. But he was always thinking of wearing it, and of the supreme occasions when some day it might be worn without the guards, without the tissue paper on the buttons, utterly and delightfully, never caring, beautiful beyond measure.

One night, when he was dreaming of it after his habit, he dreamt he took the tissue paper from one of the buttons, and found its brightness a little faded, and that distressed him mightily in his dream. He polished the poor faded button and polished it, and if anything, it grew duller. He woke up and lay awake, thinking of the brightness slightly dulled, and wondering how he would feel if perhaps when the great occasion (whatever it might be) should arrive, one button should chance to be ever so little short of its first glittering freshness, and for days and days that thought remained with him distressingly. And when next his mother let him wear his suit, he was tempted and nearly gave way to the temptation just to fumble off a bit of tissue paper and see if indeed the buttons were keeping as bright as ever.

He went trimly along on his way to church, full of this wild desire. For you must know his mother did, with repeated and careful warnings, let him wear his suit at times, on Sundays, for example, to and from church, when there was no threatening of rain, no dust blowing, nor anything to injure it, with its buttons covered and its protections tacked upon it, and a sunshade in his hand to shadow it if there seemed too strong a sunlight for its colours. And always, after such occasions, he brushed it over and folded it exquisitely as she had taught him, and put it away again.

Now all these restrictions his mother set to the wearing of his suit he obeyed, always he obeyed them, until one strange night he woke up and saw the moonlight shining outside his window. It seemed to him the moonlight was not common moonlight, nor the night a common night, and for a while he lay quite drowsily, with this odd persuasion in his mind. Thought joined on to thought like things that whisper warmly in the shadows. Then he sat up in his little bed suddenly very alert, with his heart beating very fast, and a quiver in his body from top to toe. He had made up his mind. He knew that now he was going to wear his suit as it should be worn. He had no doubt in the matter. He was afraid, terribly afraid, but glad, glad.

He got out of his bed and stood for a moment by the window looking at the moonshine-flooded garden, and trembling at the thing he meant to do. The air was full of a minute clamour of crickets and murmurings, of the infinitesimal shoutings of little living things. He went very gently across the creaking boards, for fear that he might wake the sleeping house, to the big dark clothes-press wherein his beautiful suit lay folded, and he took it out garment by garment, and softly and very eagerly tore off its tissue-paper covering and its tacked protections until there it was, perfect and delightful as he had seen it when first his mother had given it to him – a long time it seemed ago. Not a button had tarnished, not a thread had faded on this dear suit of his; he was glad enough for weeping as in a noiseless hurry he put it on. And then back he went, soft and quick, to the window that looked out upon the garden, and stood there for a minute, shining in the moonlight, with his buttons twinkling like stars, before he got out on the sill, and, making as little of a rustling as he could, clambered down to the garden path below. He stood before his mother's house, and it was white and nearly as plain as by day, with every window-blind but his own shut like an eye that sleeps. The trees cast still shadows like intricate black lace upon the wall.

The garden in the moonlight was very different from the garden by day; moonshine was tangled in the hedges and stretched in phantom cobwebs from spray to spray. Every flower was gleaming white or crimson black, and the air was a-quiver with the thridding[558] of small crickets and nightingales singing unseen in the depths of the trees.

There was no darkness in the world, but only warm, mysterious shadows, and all the leaves and spikes were edged and lined with iridescent jewels of dew. The night was warmer than any other night had ever been; the heavens by some miracle at once vaster and nearer, and, in spite of the great ivory-tinted moon that ruled the world, the sky was full of stars.

The little man did not shout or sing for all his infinite gladness. He stood for a time like one awe-stricken, and then, with a queer small cry and holding out his arms, he ran out as if he would embrace at once the whole round immensity of the world. He did not follow the neat set paths that cut the garden squarely, but thrust across the beds and through the wet, tall, scented herbs, through the night-stock[559] and the nicotine[560] and the clusters of phantom[561] white mallow flowers and through the thickets of southernwood[562] and lavender, and knee-deep across a wide space of mignonette.[563] He came to the great hedge, and he thrust his way through it; and though the thorns of the brambles scored him deeply and tore threads from his wonderful suit, and though burrs[564] and goose-grass[565] and havers[566] caught and clung to him, he did not care. He did not care, for he knew it was all part of the wearing for which he had longed. 'I am glad I put on my suit,' he said; 'I am glad I wore my suit.'

Beyond the hedge he came to the duck-pond, or at least to what was the duck-pond by day. But by night it was a great bowl of silver moonshine all noisy with singing frogs, of wonderful silver moonshine twisted and clotted with strange patternings, and the little man ran down into its waters between the thin black rushes, knee-deep and waist-deep and to his shoulders, smiting the water to black and shining wavelets with either hand, swaying and shivering wavelets, amidst which the stars were netted in the tangled reflections of the brooding trees upon the bank. He waded until he swam, and so he crossed the pond and came out upon the other side, trailing, as it seemed to him, not duckweed but very silver, in long, clinging, dripping masses. And up he went through the transfigured tangles of the willow-herb[567] and the uncut seeding grasses of the farther bank. He came glad and breathless into the high-road. 'I am glad,' he said, 'beyond measure, that I had clothes that fitted this occasion.'

The high-road ran straight as an arrow flies, straight into the deep-blue pit of the sky beneath the moon, a white and shining road between the singing nightingales, and along it he went, running now and leaping, and now walking and rejoicing, in the clothes his mother had made for him with tireless, loving hands. The road was deep in dust, but that for him was only soft whiteness; and as he went a great dim moth[568] came fluttering round his wet and shimmering and hastening figure. At first he did not heed the moth, and then he waved his hands at it, and made a sort of dance with it, as it circled round his head. 'Soft moth!' he cried, 'dear moth! And wonderful night, wonderful night of the world! Do you think my clothes are beautiful, dear moth? As beautiful as your scales and all this silver vesture of the earth and sky?'

And the moth circled closer and closer until at last its velvet wings just brushed his lips . . .

And next morning they found him dead, with his neck broken, in the bottom of the stone pit, with his beautiful clothes a little bloody, and foul and stained with the duckweed from the pond. But his face was a face of such happiness that, had you seen it, you would have understood indeed how that he had died happy, never knowing that cool and streaming silver for the duckweed in the pond.

ENDNOTES

Abbreviations, explanations and acknowledgements:

BC = before Christ (I eschew the 'politically correct' and illogical 'BCE'.)

c. = *circa* (Latin): approximately

cf. = *confer* (Latin): compare

EA = H. G. Wells, *Experiment in Autobiography* (2 volumes; Victor Gollancz and Cresset Press, London, 1934)

e.g. = *exempli gratia* (Latin): for example

ibid. = *ibidem* (Latin): in the same place.

i.e. = *id est* (Latin): that is

op. cit. = *opera citato* (Latin): in the work cited.

Biblical references are to the King James Bible. Shakespeare references are to the Wordsworth Shakespeare Series, edited by Cedric Watts. For readers who use these notes selectively, I have duplicated some glosses. I was helped by H. G. Wells, *The Country of the Blind and Other Stories*, edited by Patrick Parrinder, with notes by Andy Sawyer (Penguin, London, 2007); and I am grateful to Professor Parrinder and to Professor Laurence Davies for advice on particular notes.

THE CRYSTAL EGG

1 (Title, p. 1) 'The Crystal Egg' was first published in the *New Review* (edited by W. E. Henley) in May 1897. In the same year, Wells serialised *The War of the Worlds* in *Pearson's Magazine*. 'The Crystal Egg' postulates round-headed Martians 'with prehensile organs, like long tentacles, under the mouth'; they make mobile mechanisms 'of shining metals'. In *The War of the Worlds*, the Martians have 'round bodies, or rather heads' with 'almost whip-like tentacles' round the mouth; they make mobile metal fighting-machines. Of course, tentacles round the mouth characterise the monstrous squid of 'In the Abyss'.

2 (p. 1) *Seven Dials* a location in the West End of London where seven streets converge. In the nineteenth century, part of the area became a slum.

3 (p. 1) *five pounds* a very high price, given that, at that time, a London clerk could earn one pound and five shillings per week.

4 (p. 2) *thirty shillings* one pound and ten shillings, the decimal translation being one pound and fifty pence.

5 (p. 3) *ten guineas* equivalent to ten pounds and ten shillings. A shilling nominally equals five decimal pence.

6 (p. 4) *bedabbled affidavit* statement under oath, the oath here probably being 'bloody'.

7 (p. 4) *amuck* (also 'amok') running violently wild.

8 (p. 7) *Pasteur Institute* The Institut Pasteur, a medical institution located in Paris, was founded in 1887 and named after Louis Pasteur, chemist and microbiologist (1822–95).

9 (p. 8) *canal* In 1887, the Italian astronomer Giovanni Schiaparelli (1835–1910) had observed *canali* (channels) on Mars. Percival Lowell (1855–1916) claimed in his book *Mars* (1895) that they were probably actual canals, built by Martians 'who are in advance of us'.

10 (p. 9) *red weeds* Camille Flammarion (1842–1925), in *La Planète Mars et ses conditions d'habitabilité* (1892), postulated red vegetation on Mars.

11 (p. 9) *methyl* used in methylated spirits, a preservative (e.g. of the frogs that Cave supplies).

12 (p. 11) *en rapport* (French:) in harmony.

13 (p. 12) *two small moons* the two Martian moons, Phobos (Fear) and Deimos (Terror), discovered in 1877.

14 (p. 12) *St Martin's Church* The church of St Martin-in-the-Fields stands at the north-eastern corner of Trafalgar Square near the centre of London. It has a lofty steeple.

15 (p. 14) The Daily Chronicle *and* Nature The *Daily Chronicle* was a Liberal newspaper established in 1872; it merged in 1930 with the *Daily News*. *Nature*, a scientific journal, was founded in 1869 and continued into the twenty-first century.

THE CONE

16 (Title, p. 17) 'The Cone' was first published in the *Unicorn* magazine on 18 September 1895. In 1888, the young Wells visited Basford, above the Etruria Valley. There he was fascinated by 'the strange landscape of the Five Towns, with its blazing iron foundries, its steaming canals, its clay-whitened pot-banks . . .' (*EA*, I, p. 306).

17 (p. 17) *Gehenna*   Greek name for a valley outside ancient Jerusalem known as 'The Valley of the Son of Hinnom', where fires burnt to destroy rubbish, and where apostate Jews and others allegedly sacrificed children. It became a synonym for Hell. (See Jeremiah 7:30–32, 19:2–6.)

18 (p. 18) *penthouse brows*   jutting eyebrows. 'A penthouse' originally meant an overhanging roof. In *Macbeth*, 1.3.22, a 'penthouse lid' is an eyelid.

19 (p. 20) *Hanley and Etruria*   industrial districts of Stoke-on-Trent, the location of the Shelton Iron, Steel and Coal Company and the Etruria Potteries.

20 (p. 20) *reeking*   smoking.

21 (p. 21) *Burslem*   then an important pottery-producing district of Stoke-on-Trent.

22 (p. 22) *puddlers*   The puddlers stir oxidised iron into the heated pig iron in the furnace so as to refine it..

23 (p. 22) *Pillars . . . night*   Exodus 13:21   'And the LORD went before them by day in a pillar of cloud, to lead them the way; and by night in a pillar of fire, to give them light . . .'

24 (p. 23) *tuyères*   French (often anglicised variously): nozzles for blasts of air.

25 (p. 24) *Newcastle*   Newcastle-under-Lyme, in Staffordshire, west of the 'Potteries' towns.

THE COUNTRY OF THE BLIND

26 (Title, p. 27)   'The Country of the Blind' was first published in the *Strand* magazine in April 1904. An expanded version was published by the Golden Cockerel Press in 1939. In that version, the sighted man returns to the community of blind people. The name Nunez anglicises Núñez.

27 (p. 27) *Chimborazo . . . Cotopaxi*   Chimborazo is an inactive volcano in the Andes of Ecuador, more than 20,000 feet high, with an ice-cap; Cotopaxi is an active volcano in those Andes, more than 19,000 feet high, with an ice-cap.

28 (p. 27) *Mindobamba*   a fictional volcano; but Riobamba, which perhaps suggested the name, is the capital of the Chimborazo province of central Ecuador. It is located in the 'Avenue of Volcanoes', and was devastated by an earthquake in 1797.

29 (p. 27) *Quito . . . Yaguachi . . . Guayaquil*   Quito is the capital of

Ecuador and the second largest city in the land; Yaguachi is a river-side town in western Ecuador; and Guayaquil city is the capital of the Ecuadorian province of Guayas and the country's main port.

30 (p. 27) *Arauca* This is the name of the capital city of the Arauca district of north-east Colombia: the region is flat and subject to flooding from the river Arauca. It does not fit the geography of the tale.

31 (p. 27) *Cordilleras* mountain ranges.

32 (p. 28) *old Peru* The Mochica people of Peru were renowned for their irrigation system, architecture, ceramic pottery and metalwork. Later, in the fifteenth century, the Incas of Peru ruled an extensive empire in which the sun was worshipped. In the sixteenth century, that empire was conquered by the Spaniards.

33 (p. 29) *Parascotopetl . . . Andes* Parascotopetl is an imaginary mountain in the Andes chain; the name may have been suggested by Popocatapetl, an active volcano in Mexico. The Matterhorn is a dramatically steep mountain on the Swiss-Italian border which has attracted (sometimes fatally) many teams of mountaineers. It was first climbed in 1865.

34 (p. 31) *talus* slope.

35 (p. 33) *'In the Country . . . King.'* This translates the Latin maxim in the *Collecteana Adagiorum* (1500, later augmented) by Desiderius Erasmus (1466–1536): 'In regione caecorum rex est luscus.'

36 (p. 33) *Bogota* Bogotá is the capital of Colombia, located on a high plateau in the Andes mountains.

37 (p. 37) *coup d'état* sudden political take-over of the state.

THE MAN WHO COULD WORK MIRACLES

38 (Title and subtitle, p. 49) 'The Man Who Could Work Miracles' was first published in the *Illustrated London News* in July 1898. In 1936 it was greatly expanded and adapted as a film, starring Ralph Richardson, for which the script was written by Wells. In the sub-title 'A Pantoum in Prose', a pantoum, properly *pantun* (pronounced 'pan-*toon*') is a verse-form (originally Malay) with quatrains rhyming abab, bcbc, etc., but returning to rhyme 'a' at the end. The tale has a kindred structure, for it ends where it started.

39 (p. 49) *Torres Vedras tactics* At Torres Vedras in Spain, the Duke of Wellington established between 1810 and 1811 a system of

fortifications which, coupled with a 'scorched earth' policy, defeated the prolonged attacks of the Napoleonic forces. Mr Beamish's tactics are as impregnable as the Duke's defences.

40 (p. 51) *safety-match* Whereas an ordinary match can be ignited by rubbing its head against a rough surface, the safety-match's head must be rubbed against a chemically-prepared surface.

41 (p. 53) *Moses' rod* Exodus 4:2–5: God commanded Moses to cast his rod down, and it turned into a snake before becoming a rod again.

42 (p. 53) Tannhäuser . . . *programme* Near the end of Richard Wagner's opera *Tannhäuser und der Sängerkrieg auf Wartburg* (1845), pilgrims arrive bearing a priest's staff which miraculously sprouts leaves, to symbolise Tannhäuser's salvation. In 1869, the Philharmonic Society of London introduced annotated programmes.

43 (p. 53) *Poona-Penang lawyer* a walking stick with a bulbous head, made from the stem of an East Asian palm. The phrase 'Penang Lawyer' may derive from the Malay phrase *pinang liyar*, identifying a wild areca palm. Poona (or Pune, pronounced '*Poo*-na') is a city where such sticks were made.

44 (p. 54) *Hades* euphemism for Hell, Hades being the region of the dead in the classical underworld, named after Hades who was its stern ruler.

45 (p. 54) *Rhodian arch* an arch recalling that made by the legs of the ancient statue of Helios at Rhodes.

46 (p. 55) *thaumaturgist* a worker of miracles.

47 (p. 56) *Mahomet . . . Yogis' miracles . . . Blavatsky.* The miracles said to have been performed by Allah (by the hand of the prophet Muhammad) include the splitting of the moon and the transportation of Muhammad in one night from Mecca to Jerusalem. Indian yogis purport to work miracles: for instance, Trailanga Swami (supposedly 1607–1887) claimed to have lived for centuries and was said to have drunk poisons with no ill effects. Helena Blavatsky (1831–91), leader of the Theosophical Society, purported to be the agent of various miracles, e.g. the depositing of 'astral letters' and the replacement of damaged crockery by sound crockery. A report by Richard Hodgson in 1885 denounced her as an impostor. Wells depicted spiritualist charlatanry in *Love and Mr Lewisham* (1900).

48 (p. 56) *Duke of Argyll* George Douglas Campbell, the eighth Duke

of Argyll (1823–1900), defended the principle of the efficacy of prayer. In *The Reign of Law* (1867) he argued that the laws of nature are subject to the divine will.

49 (p. 56) *mijitly* Fotheringay's pronunciation of 'immediately'.

50 (p. 57) *scorched . . . be* He is thinking of the Hell defined by Christianity, which (according to Revelation 21:8) has a lake 'which burneth with fire and brimstone'.

51 (p. 59) *post-prandial* after the meal.

52 (p. 60) *moon . . . 'Joshua!'* Joshua 10:12–14 says that the sun and moon stood still at Joshua's command, so that his people would have more time for killing their enemies.

53 (p. 61) *nine miles per second* If the village rotates at more than five hundred miles per hour, as the narrator claims, the approximate distance per second would be little more than a seventh of a mile.

A STORY OF THE STONE AGE

54 (Title, p. 65) 'A Story of the Stone Age' was serialised between May and September 1897 in the *Idler* magazine.

55 (p. 65) *Leith Hill, and Pitch Hill, and Hindhead* part of a line of hills running through what is now Surrey.

56 (p. 65) *Wey* The River Wey is a tributary of the Thames which meets the Thames at Weybridge, nine miles west of Epsom.

57 (p. 65) *Fifty thousand years ago* In *The Outline of History* (1920), Wells says that Neanderthal Man, long extinct, flourished fifty thousand years ago.

58 (p. 65) *ranunculus . . . lady's-smock* The ranunculus is a family of flowering plants including the buttercup and lesser celandine; the lady's-smock is the cuckoo-flower, a meadow plant with whitish and bluish flowers.

59 (p. 66) *Royal Fern* *Osmunda regalis*, which has huge spreading fronds.

60 (p. 66) *char* fuel reduced to carbon.

61 (p. 66) *tines* spikes of antlers.

62 (p. 66) *prognathous* with projecting jaw.

63 (p. 67) *a squirrel . . . scold her* The talking animals in this tale recall those in Rudyard Kipling's *The Jungle Book* (1894).

64 (p. 67) *scandalising* malicious buzzing.

65 (p. 68) *started* driven from its hiding-place.

66 (p. 70) *lady (. . . upbringing)* The narrator purports to assume that the *Idler*'s reader is female. The cover of the magazine depicted a man lazing in a hammock.

67 (p. 74) *Wealden mountains* The Wealden region of south-eastern England is bordered by the high chalk escarpments of the North and South Downs.

68 (p. 78) *haft* fix to a handle.

69 (p. 79) *Cockney beanfeasters* A cockney is a Londoner, particularly one born within hearing of Bow Bells. A beanfeast was an annual dinner given by employers to their workers.

70 (p. 80) *St John's wort* *Hypericum*, a plant with a yellow flower.

71 (p. 88) *winded them* 'got wind of them': smelt them.

72 (p. 90) *winding* encircling.

73 (p. 92) *the Epsom Stand* the grandstand of Epsom Downs Race-course on the North Downs.

74 (p. 93) *jury-mast* simple temporary mast replacing the customary mast (here, short and stubby).

THE STAR

75 (Title, p. 113) 'The Star' was first published in the *Graphic* in December 1897. Camille Flammarion's *La Fin du monde* had appeared in 1893: it recorded that, on 9 November 1572, a brilliant star appeared in the constellation of Cassiopeia, and astrologers deemed it a portent of the Final Judgement; but that star diminished and departed harmlessly. Wells's novel *In the Days of the Comet* (1906) tells how the world's population experiences a benign transformation as a comet disintegrates in the earth's atmosphere.

76 (p. 113) *Ogilvy* This fictional astronomer is a transtextual character: he also appears at the beginning of *The War of the Worlds*.

77 (p. 113) *intelligence* news.

78 (p. 114) *Boers . . . Hottentots* Boers were people of Dutch descent who settled in South Africa. The Gold Coast was later called Ghana. The name 'Hottentots' (now deemed derogatory) refers to the Khoikhois, indigenous people of south-western Africa.

79 (p. 115) *spectroscope* device for analysing light.

80 (p. 115) *throbbing tape* Ticker-tape machines printed on paper strips the messages transmitted by telegraph.

81 (p. 115) *frost flowers* Before central heating was in common use,

moisture on the inside of windows would often, in cold weather, be frozen into patterns, sometimes resembling flowers or (more usually) ferns.

82 (p. 116) '*You . . . now*'   The mathematician echoes a famous paragraph from the *Pensées* of Blaise Pascal (1623–62), first published in 1670. In translation, it is:

> Man is only a reed, the weakest in nature, but he is a *thinking* reed. There is no need for the whole universe to take up arms to crush him: a vapour, a drop of water suffices to kill him. But even if the universe were to destroy him, man would still be nobler than his slayer, because he *knows* that he is dying; he *knows* the advantage the universe has over him. The universe knows nothing of this.

83 (p. 117) *pointer of the Bear*   In the constellation Ursa Major (the Great Bear), the stars Merak and Dubhe point to the Pole Star.

84 (p. 117) *belling of bees*   loud buzzing of bees.

85 (p. 117) *bellying*   bulging.

86 (p. 118) *1000 . . . end*   The French monk Rodulfus Glaber (985–1047) alleged that towards the end of the tenth century, many people fearfully anticipated the end of the world.

87 (p. 118) *Greenwich time*   the time specified at Greenwich Observatory in London. In 1884, an international conference had established Greenwich as the co-ordinator of the world's time-zones.

88 (p. 119) *the St Lawrence valley . . . reek*   The valley of the St Lawrence River, which begins at the outflow of Lake Ontario, flows through Canada and the United States, and eventually reaches the Atlantic at the Gulf of St Lawrence. The noun 'reek' means here 'dense vapour'.

89 (p. 119) *Cotopaxi*   an active volcano of the Andes Mountains in Ecuador, about 120 miles from the Pacific Ocean.

90 (p. 120) *Burmah and Hindostan*   'Burmah' (Burma) is now often called Myanmar; and 'Hindostan' referred to north-west India.

91 (p. 121) *titanic*   gigantic, as were the Titans of Greek mythology.

92 (p. 121) *Baffin's Bay*   a marginal sea of the North Atlantic Ocean, located between Baffin Island and the south-west coast of Greenland.

THE RED ROOM

93 (Title, p. 123)   'The Red Room' was first published in the *Idler* in March 1896.

94 (p. 125) *sent . . . to the right-about*   dismissed. (In military drill, a 'right-about turn' of 180 degrees often precedes the order 'Dismiss!')

95 (p. 125) *sconces*   candlesticks on wall-brackets.

96 (p. 125) *Ganymede and Eagle*   In a familiar version of the ancient legend, Zeus took the form of an eagle in order to carry away the beautiful youth Ganymede to be the cup-bearer to the gods.

97 (p. 125) *Chinaman . . . startled me*   Even today, porcelain Chinamen with nodding heads can be purchased. A 'buhl table' is a table decorated with an intricate form of inlay, and named after André Charles Boulle (1642–1732), cabinet-maker to Louis XIV.

98 (p. 126) *valances*   hanging borders of drapery.

99 (p. 127) *rhymes . . . Ingoldsby fashion*   *The Ingoldsby Legends* was a collection of poetry, myths, legends and ghost-stories by 'Thomas Ingoldsby' (actually Richard Harris Burnham), first published in 1837 in *Bentley's Magazine* and the *New Monthly Magazine*.

100 (p. 128) *penumbra*   half-shadow; fainter shadow.

101 (p. 128) *snuffing them*   removing with a snuffer the burnt residue from the wicks to make candles burn brighter.

102 (p. 128) *volley*   number of simultaneous actions.

103 (p. 130) *Fear!*   He echoes Roderick Usher in Edgar Allan Poe's tale, 'The Fall of the House of Usher'.

104 (p. 130) *black Fear*   *atra cura* (Latin: black care or fear) in classical phrasing.

IN THE ABYSS

105 (Title, p. 131)   'In the Abyss' was first published in *Pearson's Magazine*, 1 August 1896.

106 (p. 131) *Steevens*   George Warrington Steevens, the *Daily Mail*'s leading war correspondent, was (like Wells) a member of the 'Henley Regatta' (the group of writers closely associated with W. E. Henley) and was fascinated by new technology.

107 (p. 131) *Pool of London*   the stretch of the River Thames from London Bridge to Limekiln Creek; at that time, a very busy part of the Port of London.

108 (p. 131) *Myers apparatus*   A device to absorb carbon dioxide and release stored oxygen was invented by Henry Fleuss in 1879. 'Myers' may be fictional but perhaps recalls the German chemist

Julius Lothar Meyer, who devised an apparatus for measuring the gas content of blood.

109 (p. 131) *a man . . . safety*   In Jules Verne's *De la Terre à la lune* (*From the Earth to the Moon*, 1865), the space-craft is fired from a gun, and is elaborately designed (with ample padding) to save the occupants from injury. Both that novel and *Vingt mille lieues sous les mers* (*Twenty Thousand Leagues under the Sea*, 1870) raise the problem of providing oxygen while controlling carbon dioxide.

110 (p. 132) *Daubrée*   Gabriel-Auguste Daubrée (1854–96), Professor of Mineralogy and Geology at the University of Strasbourg, subsequently held the Chair of Geology at the Muséum d'Histoire Naturelle at Paris. He synthesised a variety of minerals under conditions of high pressure and high temperature.

111 (p. 132) *jigger*   crane.

112 (p. 134) *stern chains*   small platforms on either side of the hull of a ship at the stern.

113 (p. 134) *middy*   midshipman.

114 (p. 134) *crickled . . . A.B.*   'Crickled' means 'rippled'; and an 'A.B.' is an able-bodied seaman, having a higher rating than an ordinary sailor.

115 (p. 135) *eight bells*   A bell is struck eight times at noon to conclude the forenoon watch.

116 (p. 136) *since . . . together*   Genesis 1: 9–10.

117 (p. 141) *trees of crinoid*   A crinoid is a marine feather-star or sea-lily with cup-shaped body and branching arms.

118 (p. 142) *placoid scales*   tough scales that cover the skin of sharks and rays.

119 (p. 142) *Adams*   possibly Henry Brooks Adams (1838–1918), historian, novelist, geologist and travel writer.

120 (p. 142) *Theriomorpha . . . age*   'Theriomorpha' was a Victorian classification of an extinct order of reptiles (which flourished in the Early Mesozoic Age) with affinities to certain amphibians and to mammals. The New Red Sandstone Age was established between 280 million and 200 million years ago.

121 (p. 143) Ptarmigan   a grouse-like northern game-bird.

122 (p. 144) *He never returned*   like the time-traveller in *The Time Machine*.

THE PLATTNER STORY

123 (Title, p. 145) 'The Plattner Story' was first published in the *New Review* in April 1896.

124 (p. 145) *Eusapia's patrons!* Eusapia Palladino or Paladino (1854–1918) was an Italian spiritualist medium whose credulous patrons included such celebrities as Pierre Curie, Cesare Lombroso and Oliver Lodge. She was exposed as fraudulent.

125 (p. 145) *Alsatian* from the currently French province of Alsace, on the German border, many of the inhabitants being of German ancestry. It was long ruled by France, but between 1871 and 1918 it was under German rule.

126 (p. 146) *cyclist* Cycling became very popular in the 1890s, and Wells was an enthusiast. The 'rule of the road'; keep to the left.

127 (p. 146) *'Gem' photographs* These were 'tintypes', each photograph being made by creating a direct positive on a thin sheet of metal coated with a dark lacquer or enamel. Popular in the 1860s and 1870s, the process was still used in the early twentieth century. The image is usually a mirror image, so that the right side in the original appears to be the left side in the photograph. The young Wells found a shop in Maidenhead 'where one could be photographed and get a dozen tintypes for a shilling or a shilling and sixpence' (*EA*, I, 129–30).

128 (p. 146) *Nordau* Max Nordau (1849–1923) was a Zionist and cultural critic, who, in *Degeneration* (1892; English translation, 1895), denounced many current artistic trends (e.g. Wagnerism, Pre-Raphaelitism and Symbolism) as degenerate and verging on madness.

129 (p. 147) *Fourth Dimension* The fourth dimension is commonly regarded as time (the other dimensions being spatial: length, breadth, depth); but it is sometimes, as here, treated as a further temporal or spatial dimension. In *The Chronic Argonauts* and *The Time Machine*, time becomes a dimension to be explored; in 'The Strange Case of Davidson's Eyes' and 'The Plattner Story', a further dimension of space is described.

130 (p. 147) *Board or elementary schools* established in 1870 to provide free education for working-class children.

131 (p. 147) *Three Gases* hydrogen, oxygen and nitrogen.

132 (p. 148) *temerarious* reckless.

133   (p. 149) *mumchancer*   stupidly silent person.

134   (p. 149) *not a wrack behind*   Prospero in Shakespeare's *The Tempest* (4.1.153–6) says that eventually 'The great globe . . . shall leave . . . not a wrack behind' ('a wrack' being a piece of wreckage).

135   (p. 149) *proverbial*   For example, *The Twelve Tissue Remedies of Schüssler* (1888) refers to administering as much *Ferrum phos.* 'as would cover a sixpenny piece'.

136   (p. 150) *colourable*   false but plausible.

137   (p. 150) *coruscating iridescence*   glittering play of rainbow colours.

138 (p. 151) *exoteric*   public.

139   (p. 151) *the Society . . . Phenomena*   Wells knew of the Society for Psychical Research, founded in 1882, which sought to investigate scientifically various unusual psychical occurrences.

140   (p. 151) *ostended*   displayed.

141   (p. 151) *Journal of Anatomy*   The *Journal of Anatomy*, the periodical of the Anatomical Society, founded in 1887, continues into the twenty-first century.

142   (p. 152) *Chislehurst*   suburban district of south-east London.

143   (p. 154) *Euclid riders*   an exercise in geometry to deduce pro–positions from previous propositions (a 'rider' being a logical supplement to prior information). The exercise is named after Euclid of Alexandria, who flourished in the fourth century BC. (The young Wells solved Euclidian riders easily.)

144   (p. 155) *human heads . . . tadpole-like body*   The Martians in *The War of the Worlds* (1898) and the evolved human being of 'The Man of the Year Million' (1893) appear similar.

145   (p. 157) *devil's dyke*   Various locations in England are called 'Devil's Dyke', but the most famous is probably the 300-feet-deep valley on the South Downs near Brighton, its overlooking summit being then a popular resort for tourists. (According to legend, that dyke was dug by the devil but left incomplete, part of its earth forming the Isle of Wight.)

146   (p. 160) *Allbeeding*   Upper and Lower Beeding are villages in western Sussex.

THE NEW ACCELERATOR

147 (Title, p. 163) 'The New Accelerator' was first published in *Strand Magazine* in December 1901.

148 (p. 163) *Folkestone* a harbour town in south-east Kent. Wells was living there when he wrote this tale.

149 (p. 163) Strand Magazine The *Strand Magazine* (with offices near the Strand in London) lasted from 1891 to 1950, publishing fiction and articles of general interest. (A magazine with the same title was launched in the USA in 1998.)

150 (p. 163) *Mephistophelian* wicked. Mephistopheles is an emissary of Satan in the legend of Doctor Faustus.

151 (p. 163) *Upper Sandgate Road* The Upper, or main, Sandgate Road is not far from the Leas and the sea-front at Folkestone (the Lower Sandgate Road being much closer to the sea). The coastal village of Sandgate is now a western district of Folkestone.

152 (p. 163) *hospital* University College Hospital, part of University College, London, was then located in Gower Street.

153 (p. 164) *ganglion . . . axis fibre* The ganglion cell is a type of nerve-cell located near the inner surface of the retina of the eye. An axis fibre is a cell through which impulses are transmitted.

154 (p. 164) *Gibberne's B Syrup* Patent medicines then abounded and were extensively advertised. William Radam's 'Microbe Killer' promised to 'cure all diseases', and Ebenezer Sibly's 'Solar Tincture' claimed to 'restore life in the event of sudden death'. In *Tono-Bungay* (1909), Wells satirised such patent medicines, which were widely advertised in the nineteenth and early twentieth centuries.

155 (p. 164) *viscera . . . plexus* viscera: organs within the chest and the abdomen; solar plexus: network of nerves behind the stomach.

156 (p. 164) *hypophosphites* James Fellows's 'Compound Syrup of Hypo-phosphites' sold widely in the nineteenth century as a 'recuperative tonic' which was supposedly a remedy for pulmonary tuberculosis and other ailments. It contained strychnine, a potent poison.

157 (p. 165) *'Worth . . . drop'* 'Worth a guinea a box' was an advertising slogan for Beecham's Pills, a laxative popular in the nineteenth and twentieth centuries.

158 (p. 166) *what nature . . . Orientals* These 'racial' generalisations are invalid but reflect prejudicial beliefs of the time.

159 (p. 167) *Harley Street specialist*   Harley Street in London was and
     is the distinguished location of medical experts.

160 (p. 168) *'gas'*   Nitrous oxide (colloquially 'laughing gas') was
     widely used then as an anaesthetic.

161 (p. 169) *charabancs*   A charabanc was a long open vehicle with
     transverse seats. (French: *char à banc*: carriage with benches).

162 (p. 169) *Leas*   a promenade with flower-gardens, 1.5 miles long,
     providing a view of Folkestone and the English Channel. In 1900
     the Leas and the under-cliff area had three bandstands.

163 (p. 170) *capelline*   light woollen hood.

164 (p. 170) *Panama hat*   lightweight brimmed straw hat, suitable for
     sunny locations.

165 (p. 170) *Bath-chairs*   wheeled chairs for invalids, then often seen
     in Bath.

166 (p. 172) *these absurd days*   Mysticism and psychic interests enjoyed
     a vogue around 1900. W. B. Yeats, George Russell, Conan Doyle
     and Rider Haggard were writers who pursued mystical researches.
     The Society for Psychical Research (founded in 1882) publicised
     apparently mystical phenomena.

167 (p. 173) *Metropole*   then a large and impressive hotel; subsequently
     converted into a block of flats.

168 (p. 174) *Time . . . Carlyle speaks*   In book 3, Chapter 8, of *Sartor
     Resartus* (serialised 1833–4, book 1835), Thomas Carlyle claims
     that the 'Time-vesture' conceals eternity from us: 'Your grand
     anti-magician, and universal wonder-hider, is this same lying
     Time. Had we but the Time-annihilating Hat, . . . we should see
     ourselves in a World of Miracles . . . '

A SLIP UNDER THE MICROSCOPE

169 (Title, p. 175)   'A Slip under the Microscope' was first published
     in the *Yellow Book* in January 1896. It recalls Wells's time at the
     Normal School of Science, as does the novel *Love and Mr Lewisham*
     (1899). The term 'slip' is aptly ambiguous: it refers to the glass slip
     bearing a sample, and also to the lapse or blunder made by Hill.

170 (p. 175) *rocker microtome*   The Cambridge Rocker microtome,
     first marketed in 1885, was a device to cut very thin sections of
     tissue (half the width of a hair) which could then be examined
     under a microscope.

171 (p. 175) News . . . Nowhere   *News from Nowhere* was a Utopian novel (1890) by William Morris, advocating libertarian anarchism and depicting a future England which eschews money and where people collaborate freely. 'Holy wedlock' has been abolished, and couples cohabit as they wish.

172 (p. 175) *Oratory clock*   This was located at the Brompton Oratory on the Brompton Road, not far from the then Royal College of Science.

173 (p. 176) *College . . . America*   In 1881 the Normal School of Science was established in South Kensington. It was renamed the Royal College of Science in 1890; and in 1907 it became part of Imperial College in London University. The college accepted female students alongside males, at a time when neither Oxford nor Cambridge did so: at those universities, women were segregated in separate colleges. London University admitted women for degrees in 1878, Oxford in 1920, Cambridge in 1948.

174 (p. 176) *scholarships*   The Normal School of Science accepted students from impecunious backgrounds by means of government scholarships or 'studentships': Wells, like Hill, was a beneficiary.

175 (p. 176) *holland*   smooth, hard-wearing linen fabric, first made in Holland.

176 (p. 176) *From ovum . . . .said*   In *Life and Habit* (1878), Samuel Butler says: 'It has, I believe, been often remarked that a hen is only an egg's way of making another egg.'

177 (p. 179) *Landport*   then a residential part of the city of Portsmouth in Hampshire.

178 (p. 179) *blue paper*   This bore the offer of a scholarship to candidates who fared well in school examinations.

179 (p. 179) *a guinea a week*   A guinea was the sum of one pound and one shilling. At that time, the average earnings of an adult male in Britain approximated £56 per year. Wells, in London, found his guinea insufficient: 'Pay day was Wednesday and not infrequently my money had run out before Monday or Tuesday . . . ' (*EA*, I, 205).

180 (p. 179) *island of Portsea*   flat island which bears the city of Portsmouth.

181 (p. 179) *seventh standard*   the highest class in the Board Schools, which were established in 1870 for the education of working-class children.

182 (p. 179) *Carlyle*   Thomas Carlyle (1795–1881), influential and controversial Victorian philosopher and historian.

183 (p. 180) *mesoblastic somites*   middle layers of the body segments of embryos. They develop into the skeleton and the muscular and connective tissues.

184 (p. 180) *blastopore*   opening in an embryo which may develop into a mouth or anus.

185 (p. 180) *alisphenoid*   bone at the base of the skull.

186 (p. 180) *Browning*   Robert Browning (1812–89): prolific poet, some of whose works were (by Victorian standards) sexually bold.

187 (p. 180) *Harvey . . . Medal*   William Harvey (1578–1657), pioneer in investigating the circulation of the blood.

188 (p. 181) *fluent . . . Hemans*   The 'fluent numbers' are flowing metrical lines. Henry Wadsworth Longfellow (1807–82, American), Alfred, Lord Tennyson (1809–92), William Shakespeare (1564–1616), Alexander Pope (1688–1744) and Percy Bysshe Shelley (1792–1822) were 'canonical' poets, unlike the popular but relatively sentimental Eliza Cook (1818–89), author of 'The Old Arm-Chair', and Mrs Felicia Hemans (1793–1835), author of 'Casablanca' ('The boy stood on the burning deck').

189 (p. 182) *'mugger'*   a 'crammer' who memorises facts for examination purposes without fully understanding them.

190 (p. 182) *Kew*   district of London which is the location of the Royal Botanical Gardens.

191 (p. 183) *righteousness*   Psalm 106:30–1 says that Phinehas by executing judgement ended the plague sent by God: 'And that was counted unto him for righteousness unto all generations for evermore.'

192 (p. 183) *Hill . . . hated Wedderburn*   Wedderburn's point is that George Bernard Shaw (1856–1950), though a Fabian socialist, is ostentatiously egoistic; that William Morris (1834–96), though a libertarian anarchist, produces first editions and wallpapers which only the rich can afford; and that Walter Crane (1845–1915), the socialist artist, depicts blatantly idealised working people.

193 (p. 184) *finger-bowl shibboleths . . . asylum*   Only the wealthy and sophisticated used finger-bowls to wash their hands during meals. Judges 12:5–6 said that Ephraimites were unable to pronounce correctly the word Shibboleth (meaning 'ear of grain': they said Sibboleth), and the Gileadites, having thus identified them, slew

them. So a shibboleth is a criterion to separate members of a privileged group from outsiders. The 'cities of refuge' were six towns in the kingdoms of Israel and Judah in which perpetrators of manslaughter could claim the right of asylum.

194   (p. 184) *Ruskin . . . attitudes*   Actually, John Ruskin (1819–1900), the influential writer on art and social issues, said in *Sesame and Lilies* (1865) that the wife's role is 'a *guiding*, not a determining function', adding: 'the man's work for his own home is . . . to secure its maintenance, progress, and defence; the woman's to secure its order, comfort, and loveliness.' Miss Haysman is probably familiar with the 'New Woman' fiction of the time: for example, Shaw's *Mrs Warren's Profession* (1894) and *Keynotes* (1893) by 'George Egerton' (Mary Clairmonte). Thomas Hardy's *Jude the Obscure* (1895) might give the impression that 'men's activities are determined by women's attitudes'.

195   (p. 184) *Aerated Bread Shop*   The Aerated Bread Company pumped carbon dioxide into dough to accelerate the rising of the bread. In 1864 it converted its shops into restaurants, and the 'ABC' outlets endured for over a century.

196   (p. 185) *Bradlaugh . . . Burns*   Charles Bradlaugh (1833–91) was an advocate of birth control and an atheist who, by refusing to take a religious oath, was denied his place in Parliament for five years, being eventually admitted in 1866. The son of a clerk, he left school at the age of eleven and became an errand-boy. John Burns (1858–1943), son of a washerwoman, left school at the age of ten and worked as an apprentice engineer. He became an orator for the left-wing Social-Democratic Federation, was sentenced to jail for 'unlawful assembly' in 1887, and in 1905 became a member of the Liberal Cabinet as President of the Local Government Board: the first working-class man to gain Cabinet office.

197   (p. 187) Q. Jour. Mi. Sci . . . *lenticels*   *The Quarterly Journal of Mining Science*; a lenticel is a breathing spore in the stem of a woody plant.

198   (p. 187) *Brompton Road*   in Knightsbridge, not far from Imperial College.

199   (p. 187) *threepenny . . . classics*   cheap editions of classic works. 'Threepenny' was then pronounced '*threp*-nee'.

200   (p. 189) Meistersingers   *Die Meistersinger von Nürnberg*, an opera by Richard Wagner (1813–83) first performed in 1868.

201   (p. 190) *suddenly hot*   revealing that Wedderburn had cheated.

THE STOLEN BACILLUS

202 (Title, p. 191) 'The Stolen Bacillus' was first published in the *Pall Mall Budget*, 21 June 1894. A 'bacillus' is a rod-shaped bacterium.

203 (p. 192) '*Go forth . . . cisterns*' Genesis 1:28: 'God said unto them [i.e., Adam and Eve], Be fruitful, and multiply, and replenish the earth . . . '

204 (p. 192) *Anarchist . . . bombs* In the early 1890s, before the publication of this tale, French anarchists, among them Émile Henry, Théodore Meunier, François Koenigstein (known as Ravachol) and Auguste Vaillant, had bombed restaurants, a barracks, and the Chamber of Deputies.

205 (p. 193) *apron* A cabriolet ('cab') had a large rigid hinged apron to protect the passenger from the waist down.

206 (p. 193) *Haverstock Hill* in Hampstead, London NW3, extending north-west from Chalk Farm.

207 (p. 193) *screw of a horse* an old or worn-out horse.

208 (p. 194) '. . . *to rights*,' . . . *ostler boy* The idiom 'to rights' means 'without question; caught in the act'. An ostler is a person who tends horses at an inn.

209 (p. 194) *fieldmale* mispronunciation of 'female'.

210 (p. 194) *Camden Town High Street* in London NW1.

211 (p. 194) *Ravachol, Vaillant* François Claudius Koenigstein, known as Ravachol (1859–92), was a French anarchist who planted bombs at the living quarters of the Advocate General and of Édouard Benoit (who had presided over an Assizes Court), and he bombed the Restaurant Véry. Sentenced to death for three murders, he was publicly guillotined. Auguste Vaillant (1861–94) was another French anarchist: he hurled a bomb at the French Chamber of Deputies on 9 December 1893, in revenge for the death of Ravachol. He was sentenced to death and executed.

212 (p. 194) *Great St Andrew's Street* at Seven Dials (between Covent Garden and Soho), and now part of Monmouth Street.

213 (p. 195) *Wellington Street* in London WC2, near Waterloo Bridge over the Thames.

214 (p. 195) *Vive l'Anarchie!* 'Long live anarchy!': a slogan of anarchists and the last words of Auguste Vaillant.

THE REMARKABLE CASE OF DAVIDSON'S EYES

215 (Title, p. 197) 'The Remarkable Case of Davidson's Eyes' was first published in the *Pall Mall Budget*, 28 March 1895.

216 (p. 197) *intercalary*   inserted within normal time.

217 (p. 197) *Harlow Technical College*   a college in Harlow, Essex; originally St Mary's College, which opened in 1862; but that is more than fifteen miles from Highgate Archway.

218 (p. 197) *Highgate Archway*   bridge built in 1812, carrying Hornsey Lane over what is now Archway Road.

219 (p. 197) *'Great Scott!' he said*   The interjection (probably a euphemistic alteration of 'Great God') dates from 1857 and became out of date in the 1950s. The Scott in question has sometimes been identified as General Winfield Scott of the US Army and sometimes as Sir Walter Scott, the novelist.

220 (p. 198) *electrometers*   An electrometer is a device for measuring electrical potential.

221 (p. 199) *cryohydrates*   A cryohydrate is a mixture of ice and another substance, calculated to find the minimum melting or freezing point.

222 (p. 199) *davits*   A davit is a crane-like device for raising and lowering some object, e.g. a ship's boat.

223 (p. 199) *hull down*   As the ship is distant, the hull is almost out of sight, being mainly below the horizon.

224 (p. 200) *'Bishop Berkeley,' said Davidson*   Bishop George Berkeley (1685–1753) held that entities exist only when they are perceived; fortunately (he explained) God perceives all.

225 (p. 201) *Dogs' . . . Cross*   The Dogs' Home was founded in Holloway in 1860; it moved to its present location in Battersea in 1871. King's Cross Railway Station is to the south of Camden Town.

226 (p. 202) *special* Pall Mall   The *Pall Mall Budget* (in which this story first appeared) was a weekly supplement to the *Pall Mall Magazine*, a British monthly magazine issued between 1893 and 1914.

227 (p. 203) *group . . . cross*   the Southern Cross constellation, visible only in the Southern Hemisphere of the earth.

228 (p. 203) *changing . . . lantern*   images projected from a 'magic lantern' which might 'dissolve' from one to another.

229 (p. 204) *Antipodes Island*   an outlying island south of New Zealand, approximately three miles from north to south and three miles from west to east, so called because it is opposite to Britain on the globe.

230 (p. 204) *Fourth Dimension*   See note 129.

231 (p. 205) *St Pancras installation*   St Pancras Railway Station on the Euston Road opened in 1868.

THE LORD OF THE DYNAMOS

232 (Title, p. 207)   'The Lord of the Dynamos' was first published in the *Pall Mall Budget* on 6 September 1894.

233 (p. 207) *Camberwell*   a district of south London, most of which forms part of the Borough of Southwark. London's first deep underground railway opened in 1890. Its generators were located not in Camberwell but in nearby Stockwell.

234 (p. 207) *Carnot's cycle*   a theoretical thermodynamic cycle specified by the French physicist Nicolas Carnot (1796–1832) in 1824. He defined the process of expansion and contraction in an engine powered by heat.

235 (p. 207) *Pooh-bah*   'The Lord High Everything Else' in the comic opera *The Mikado* (1885) by William Gilbert and Arthur Sullivan.

236 (p. 207) *Lord Clive . . . Settlements*   Robert Clive (1725–74) was a British general whose military victories in India ensured British rule. The Straits Settlements were territories along the Straits of Malacca formerly controlled by the East India Company: Penang, Malacca and Singapore.

237 (p. 207) *the delights of Shadwell*   The district of Shadwell is in the East End of London on the north bank of the Thames between Wapping and Ratcliff. In Victorian times, the area was partly a slum and was notorious for prostitution and opium-dens. Many eastern seamen ('Lascars') stayed there.

238 (p. 208) *blackleg*   pejorative term for someone who works while his colleagues are on strike.

239 (p. 208) *Twelve per cent.*   the dividend paid to shareholders in the railway. 'Per cent.' abbreviates the Latin *per centum*: 'for a hundred'.

240 (p. 209) *captive . . . Solomon*   The biblical King Solomon (*c.* 1000 BC–928 BC), wise king of Israel, was said to have subjugated devils.

I Kings 9:26 says: 'And King Solomon made a navy of ships.' So the 'British Solomon' is the British fleet-building counterpart to Solomon, in Azuma-zi's imagination.

241 (p. 209) *the Buddhas . . . Rangoon* Of the numerous statues of Buddha in Rangoon (Yangon), the biggest is the huge reclining Buddha at the Ngahtatgyi Pagoda.

242 (p. 209) *meteoric . . . Juggernaut* Muslims have long venerated a black stone located in the eastern corner of the Kaaba (cubic building) at Mecca. A Juggernaut was a huge wagon bearing the image of a Hindu god. It was believed that some devout Hindus would throw themselves beneath its wheels.

243 (p. 210) *anointing . . . oil* Holy anointing oil is used in the rituals of various religions. (At the British coronation service, the monarch is anointed.)

244 (p. 211) *Fetich* usually 'fetish'. In *The Outline of History*, I, p. 67, Wells says that primordial man 'did things we should now think unreasonable to produce desired ends – for that is all fetishism amounts to'.

245 (p. 211) *ball governors* rotating metal balls which regulate the speed of a steam engine by increasing or reducing the flow of steam.

THE GRISLY FOLK

246 (Title, p. 215) 'The Grisly Folk' was first published (as 'The Grisly Folk and Their War with Men') in *Storyteller Magazine*, April 1921. The adjective 'grisly' usually means 'horrifying', but Wells uses it to mean 'bristly': later a 'Neandertaler male' will have 'his mane and beard bristling horribly', and, in 'A Story of the Stone Age', 'grisly' swine have 'bristling' backs.

247 (p. 215) *Chellean, Mousterian, Solutrian* Louis Laurent Gabriel de Mortillet (1821–98), who taught Prehistoric Anthropology at l'École d'Anthropologie in Paris, published in 1882 *Le Préhistoire, Origine et Antiquité de l'Homme*, in which he characterised periods by the name of a site, e.g. Chelléan (Chellean), after the town of Chelles, a suburb of Paris, where bones had been found. Moustérien (Mousterian) derived its name from Le Moustier, a rock shelter in the Dordogne region of France; and Solutréan (Solutrian) derived from La Roche de Solutré, a limestone escarpment five miles west of Mâcon in France.

248 (p. 216) *Neandertalers* Neandertalers or Neanderthalers are named after the Neander Valley (about seven miles east of Düsseldorf), where fossils were found in the nineteenth century.

249 (p. 216) *impossible . . . ours* The DNA of a Neanderthaler is now deemed to be 99.5% the same as that of a modern human, and it is believed that Neanderthalers interbred with members of *Homo sapiens*. The Neanderthaler had shorter legs and a larger body than did *Homo sapiens*, but had a larger brain.

250 (p. 217) *thirty . . . years ago* Neanderthalers are now thought to have become extinct between 40,000 and 28,000 years ago.

251 (p. 217) *Australoid savage* In 1870, Thomas Huxley (who later taught Wells) proposed that human beings comprised four races, one being the Australioid (a name which became shortened to Australoid), characterised by dark skin, black hair and large jutting jaw.

252 (p. 221) *woldy hills* hills with open upland slopes

253 (p. 224) *Paladins* heroic warriors, e.g. the knights of Charlemagne who fought for Christendom against the Saracens

254 (p. 225) *says Atkinson* In *Primal Law* (1903), James Jasper Atkinson, the anthropologist, discussed the origins of the incest taboos. In his *Outline of History*, I, p. 68, Wells cites *Primal Law* as 'an ingenious analysis of those primitive taboos which are found among savage peoples all over the world . . . ' Atkinson claims that 'pure maternal love' eventually reconciled 'father and son, who . . . had been the most deadly of enemies'.

255 (p. 225) *savants* One of the *savants* (wise men) was Boucher de Perthes (1788–1868), who for many years excavated gravel deposits in the Somme valley and, in 1863, found a human jawbone, apparently a relic of the Quaternary period. Other *savants* (Verne uses the same term as Wells), including Henri Milne-Edwards and Armand de Quatrefages, hailed this discovery. The jawbone proved to be a hoax. De Perthes did, however, find stone hatchets and flint arrowheads: these were later deemed to be the work of Neanderthalers or of *Homo erectus*. These findings of de Perthes are discussed in Verne's *Voyage to the Centre of the Earth*, Chapter 38. The same chapter notes the discovery of fossilised bones 'sculptured and carved'. Palaeolithic art included paintings on bone.

256 (p. 225) *modern minds* In his *Outline of History*, I, pp. 68–9, Wells says:

The psycho-analysis of Freud and Jung has done much to help us to realise how great a part Father fear and Mother love still play in the adaptation of the human mind to social needs. Their exhaustive study of childish and youthful dreams and imaginations has done much to help in the reconstruction of the soul of primitive man.

THE DOOR IN THE WALL

257 (Title, p. 226) 'The Door in the Wall' was first published in the *Daily Chronicle*, 14 July 1906.

258 (p. 229) *old-fashioned* precocious, behaving like a grown-up

259 (p. 234) *North-West Passage* Nineteenth-century explorers attempted to find a maritime route from the north Atlantic via the Arctic to the Pacific Ocean. In 1845 Sir John Franklin led a British two-ship expedition, but none of the men survived. The boy's game is clearly one of finding a new and shorter route to school.

260 (p. 234) *Campden Hill* an area of high ground in west London between Notting Hill, Kensington and Holland Park

261 (p. 235) *Crawshaw major* If two brothers attended a public school, it was customary for the elder to be termed 'major' (Latin for 'greater') and the younger to be termed 'minor' (Latin for 'lesser').

262 (p. 236) *Paddington* the London station from which one would take trains to Oxford and the West Country.

263 (p. 236) *apron* the protective leg-screen of a hansom carriage (a carriage for hire)

264 (p. 237) *Earl's Court* a densely-populated district in the Borough of Kensington and Chelsea, Kensington being to the west, north and east, and Chelsea being to the south

265 (p. 237) *counting Stonehenge* A superstition associated with Stonehenge was that a person who counts the stones twice never attains the same number.

266 (p. 238) *snatch division* an unexpected vote in Parliament, obliging the government to muster its supporters hastily

267 (p. 238) *unpaired* When Members of Parliament know that they will be absent from a vote, they seek to be 'paired' (nominally linked) with absent members who would have voted in the opposite way, so that the result is unaffected by their absence.

268 (p. 240) Gazette   The *Westminster Gazette* was a Liberal news-paper published from 1893 to 1928, when it merged with the *Daily News*.

269 (p. 240) *East Kensington Station*   Wells's account brings to mind the South Kensington Underground Station, where the deep level platform opened in 1906, the year in which this tale was published.

THE DIAMOND MAKER

270 (Title, p. 243)   'The Diamond Maker' was first published in the *Pall Mall Budget* on 16 August 1894.

271 (p. 243) *Chancery Lane*   This street in London connects Fleet Street with High Holborn; it is not far from the Victoria Embank-ment, which was completed in 1870.

272 (p. 243) *towers of Westminster*   particularly the Houses of Parliament and their clock tower.

273 (p. 244) *octahedron*   a solid bounded by eight plane faces.

274 (p. 245) *Behemoth*   In Job 40:15–24, God, as evidence of his power, describes behemoth, a huge powerful creature with bones like bars of iron; it can drink a river. So, the phrase 'a Behemoth' may denote any huge or imposing entity.

275 (p. 245) *corundum*   a crystalline form of aluminium oxide, extremely hard, and therefore often used as an abrasive.

276 (p. 245) *Kaffirs at the Cape*   The term 'Kaffir' (originally meaning 'person without religion') was used in the nineteenth century by whites to refer to South African blacks. The term is now regarded as racist. So 'light-fingered Kaffirs at the Cape' would be black employees in diamond mines in Cape Colony who were guilty of stealing diamonds.

277 (p. 245) *Moissan*   James Ballantyne Hannay in 1878 and Ferdinand Frédéric Henri Moissan in 1893 claimed that they had made artificial diamonds. Moissan's method was to heat charcoal and iron in a furnace to convert the charcoal into diamonds; but they were indeed very small. The commercially viable production of artificial diamonds did not begin until the 1950s.

278 (p. 246) *Kentish Town*   in north-west London. It was a poor area in Victorian times.

279 (p. 246) *Daubrée: . . . Salpêtres*   Gabriel Auguste Daubrée (1814–1896) was an eminent French geologist, director of the École des Mines, and famed for his often dangerous experiments to produce

minerals artificially. The Laboratoire Central des Poudres et Salpêtres at Paris was the main laboratory for research into explosives.

280 (p. 247) " *'Nerchist,'* " i.e. Anarchist.

281 (p. 247) *Father of Lies* Satan. See John 8:44: Jesus told his Jewish critics, 'Ye are of your father the devil . . . When he speaketh a lie, he speaketh of his own: for he is a liar, and the father of it.'

282 (p. 247) " *'siffiiwas a ge 'm'* " as if I was a gentleman.

283 (p. 248) *half-crown* coin worth one-eighth of a pound.

284 (p. 248) *archway leading into Essex Street* Even now, pedestrians gain access to Essex Street, north of the Victoria Embankment, by a steep narrow flight of steps beneath a high archway.

UNDER THE KNIFE

285 (Title, p. 251) 'Under the Knife' was first published in the *New Review* for January 1896.

286 (p. 251) *Primrose Hill* north of Regent's Park, affording wide views over London.

287 (p. 251) *youth . . . blood . . . self-pity* In *EA*, I, pp. 297–304, Wells describes his experience, as a young man, of coughing blood and being diagnosed with tuberculosis of the lungs: 'I had . . . some beautiful moments of exquisite self-pity.'

288 (p. 251) *the higher . . . animal* In *Parerga and Paralipomena* (1851), Arthur Schopenhauer says: 'Man is at base a dreadful wild animal. We know this wild animal only in the tamed state called civilisation and we are therefore shocked by occasional outbreaks of its true nature . . . ' Darwin's *On the Origin of Species* (1859) gave further impetus to the view that 'the simple animal' underlies human complexities. Émile Zola and the Naturalist writers made this point; so does Joseph Conrad's tale 'Falk'.

289 (p. 252) *Regent's Park Canal . . . Gardens* The canal curves round the northern edge of Regent's Park: it was designed to link the Grand Union Canal to the River Thames and the London Docks. The Zoological Gardens opened to the public in 1847, and were subsequently known as London Zoo.

290 (p. 252) *Broad Walk* This wide tree-lined pathway is in the eastern section of the park. Its 'green seats' are now free of charge.

291 (p. 253) *that crescent* Park Crescent, between Marylebone Road and Portland Place.

292 (p. 253) *Minton* possibly Minton's Ltd, celebrated makers of fine ceramics, originally based at Stoke-on-Trent.

293 (p. 254) *I was puzzled . . . condition* The term 'out-of-the-body experience' was coined in 1942 by George Tyrrell in his book *Apparitions* (published by the Society for Psychical Research), and it superseded such terms as 'astral projection', 'soul travel' and 'spirit walking'.

294 (p. 255) *portal vein* This vein conducts blood from the gastro-intestinal tract and the spleen to the liver.

295 (p. 255) *galvanometer* A galvanometer detects and measures electrical current. Some galvanometers used a miniature mirror and a beam of light to amplify the effect of small currents.

296 (p. 256) *Ealing* west London suburb.

297 (p. 257) *Egyptian sculpture* Ancient Egyptian temples bear depictions of a globe with wings extending on each side of it, to symbolise the power and apparent mobility of the sun.

298 (p. 257) *solar corona* Produced by the diffraction of light, a solar corona resembles a coloured disc of light, whitish at the centre and red at the outside.

299 (p. 257) *flocculent* woolly.

300 (p. 260) *gibbous* unequally convex on two sides, as when the moon is between half and full.

301 (p. 260) *jack-o'-lantern* i.e. Will-o'-the-wisp, fool's fire, or *ignis fatuus*: the flickering light caused by the combustion of marsh gas (methane).

302 (p. 261) *the hour . . . noise . . . 'There will be no more pain'* Revelation 3:3, 19:6 and 21:4: 'Thou shalt not know what hour I will come upon thee'; 'as the voice of many waters'; 'neither shall there be any more pain'. (As the shining circle becomes the face of the clock, and the rod becomes the bed-rail, the words 'There will be no more pain' may be those of Haddon: the patient indeed finds that the feeling in his side 'could scarce be spoken of as pain'.)

THE SEA-RAIDERS

303 (Title, p. 263) 'The Sea-Raiders' was first published in the *Weekly Sun Literary Supplement* for 6 December 1896. In some subsequent publications, the hyphen was deleted from the title.

304 (p. 263) *Sidmouth*   port in Devon on the south coast of England.

305 (p. 263) *Haploteuthis ferox*   'singular ferocious squid'. In recent times, documentary films have shown people being attacked by squid: e.g. the 'YouTube' item, 'Diver Mauled in Squid Attack'. In 2015, a gigantic squid was found on a beach at Punakaiki, New Zealand.

306 (p. 263) *Azores*   In 1888 and 1895, remains of large squid were found in the Azores Islands.

307 (p. 263) *Land's End*   the most westerly tip of mainland Cornwall

308 (p. 263) *cephalopod*   literally, 'head-foot': marine mollusc of the class Cephalopoda, having a distinct head with large eyes and a ring of tentacles around a beaked mouth. This class includes the octopus, the squid and the cuttlefish. A mollusc is an invertebrate with a soft body and often a hard shell. The octopus has eight arms; the squid and cuttlefish have eight arms and two tentacles; and the cuttlefish has a hard internal shell.

309 (p. 263) *Prince of Monaco's discovery*   In 1895, Prince Albert I of Monaco (1848–1922) reported having found remains of cephalopods in the regurgitation and the stomach of a sperm whale. The report was 'Notes sur un Cachalot' in the *Bulletin du Muséum d'histoire naturelle*, 1895, number 8, pp. 305–10. Wells's account follows closely the Prince's report.

310 (p. 263) *Cachalot . . . Terceira*   A cachalot is a sperm whale. Terceira Island is in the Azores archipelago.

311 (p. 263) *screws*   A screw is a form of propeller with twisted blades which repel water.

312 (p. 264) *Ladram Bay*   secluded bay just under two miles southwest of Sidmouth.

313 (p. 264) *skerry*   reef of rock.

314 (p. 266) *laminaria*   brown seaweeds with large leathery fronds.

315 (p. 266) *spiring*   entwining.

316 (p. 270) *Preventive Service boats*   The Preventive Waterguard (also known as the Preventative Boat Service) was founded in 1809 to combat smuggling. In 1909 it became part of the Customs and Excise service; and in 1972 it was abolished.

317 (p. 271) *Sark*   a small island of the Channel Islands, off the coast of Normandy, France.

THE PURPLE PILEUS

318 (Title, p. 273) 'The Purple Pileus' was first published in *Black and White Magazine* in December 1896. A pileus is the cap of a mushroom-type fungus.

319 (p. 273) *astrachan* usually 'astrakhan', a luxurious fur deriving from lambs.

320 (p. 273) *banjo tunes* Travelling minstrel shows had popularised the banjo in Victorian England. Banjo tunes could be lively and raucous. (In Jerome K. Jerome's *Three Men in a Boat*, 1889, George endeavours to play the banjo but is 'bound over to keep the peace for six months'.)

321 (p. 274) *bright drab* This is an apparent oxymoron; but 'drab' is a thick strong grey cloth, and, when combined with the white cravat and the pearl-and-silver pin, the effect might be 'bright', compared with the traditional black suits worn by respectable gentlemen on Sundays.

322 (p. 274) *juice* cockney pronunciation of 'deuce', here a euphemism for 'devil'.

323 (p. 275) Self-Help *Self-Help* (1859) by Samuel Smiles (1812–1904) was a best-selling book recommending thrift and self-discipline as the means to success in life.

324 (p. 275) *Mephistopheles* the wicked tempter, an agent of Satan in the legend of Faust.

325 (p. 276) *the luxuries of divorce . . . altogether* Lawrence Stone's *The Road to Divorce* (1990) says that in England and Wales at that period 'the more affluent could obtain divorce and judicial separation . . . ; the poor . . . could get separation orders from local magistrates' courts'. In 1891, the number of divorce decrees was 369; by 1911 it was 580; but, between 1897 and 1906, 87,000 separation and maintenance orders were issued by magistrates' courts.

326 (p. 277) 'E – lomore ye'.' He means, 'I'll eat a lot more yet.'

327 (p. 277) *He felt . . . cheerful* Psilocybin mushrooms contain the psychedelic compounds psilocybin and psilocin. They can give the consumer feelings of euphoria and an altered sense of time. Such 'magic mushrooms' became popular during the psychedelic era of the 1960s. The first recorded use in England was noted in the *London Medical and Physical Journal* for 1799: a man gave his family for breakfast some mushrooms that he had gathered in Green Park, London: his son had 'fits of immoderate laughter'.

328 (p. 277) *red ones . . . yellow*   The hallucinogenic 'fly agaric' mushroom has a cap which is red with white spots; the red fades to an orange-yellow with age or in wet weather.

329 (p. 278) *shilling*   coin to the value of one-twentieth of a pound.

330 (p. 278) *Dorset butter*   In *Human Nature in Politics* (1908), Graham Wallas says that in 1902 a soldier in the audience wept when, in a play, two men had to eat 'inferior Dorset' butter. *Mrs Beeton's Book of Household Management* (1871) says, '*Epping butter* is the kind most esteemed in London.'

331 (p. 279) *Went . . . lamb . . . lay*   Proverbially, *either* the month of March comes in like a lion and goes out like a lamb, *or*, *if* it comes in like a lion, it goes out like a lamb. 'I'll lay' means 'I'll bet'.

332 (p. 279) *'Tose-stools, too. Brosher.'*   'Toadstools, too. Brother.'

333 (p. 280) joie de vivre   (French) joy of living.

334 (p. 280) *Good Templar*   The International Order of Good Templars (first established in America in the 1850s) advocated temperance, i.e. abstinence from alcohol.

335 (p. 281) *caravanserai*   an unfurnished inn or enclosed area along a desert trade route where travellers and their camels could rest.

THE TRUTH ABOUT PYECRAFT

336 (Title, p. 283)   'The Truth about Pyecraft' was first published in the *Strand* magazine in April 1903.

337 (p. 283) *Truth . . . truth!*   People presenting evidence in English courts of law have said: 'I swear by Almighty God that the evidence I shall give shall be the truth, the whole truth and nothing but the truth.'

338 (p. 284) *'You . . . cricketer,' he said*   In that period, a famous cricketer was an Indian prince, Ramjitsinhji Vibhaji ('Ramji', 1872–1933): he played for Sussex and England, and became captain of Sussex's team in 1899. His nephew also played for England.

339 (p. 284) a priori   logically, reasoning from cause to effect.

340 (p. 284) *gonged*   struck a gong to summon a waiter.

341 (p. 284) *Pharmacopoeia*   array of drugs and medicaments.

342 (p. 286) *addled*   rotten.

343 (p. 286) *Jamrach's*   Charles Jamrach (1815–91) was a dealer in wild creatures for zoos.

344 (p. 286) *pariah dog*   ownerless outcast cur.

345 (p. 287) *Formalyn*   Formalin is a compound used as an antiseptic or preservative. By ancestry and by surname, the narrator is linked to the medical world.

346 (p. 287) *coffee and Trappistine*   coffee fortified by a liqueur made by the Trappist religious order.

347 (p. 287) *vittles*   (pronunciation of) victuals: food.

348 (p. 289) *Santos-Dumont*   Alberto Santos-Dumont (1873–1932), Brazilian pioneering aviator.

349 (p. 290) *British . . . (tenth edition)*   The tenth edition of the *Encyclopaedia Britannica* had just been issued (1902–3) in thirty-six volumes.

350 (p. 291) *Niente, nefas*   *Niente* is Italian for 'nothing'; *nefas* is Latin for 'horrible object'.

JIMMY GOGGLES THE GOD

351 (Title, p. 293)   'Jimmy Goggles the God' was first published in the *Graphic*, December 1898. 'Goggles' here probably means 'with prominent eyeglass'.

352 (p. 293) *Gummy!*   an exclamation deriving from 'By gum', euphemism for 'By God'.

353 (p. 293) *put the kybosh on*   (slang) end completely.

354 (p. 293) *Soona*   perhaps Sunahoara, a district of Bougainville Island, east of Papua.

355 (p. 293) *jolly boat*   small rowing-boat carried on ships.

356 (p. 294) *messed together*   took meals together.

357 (p. 295) *amby-theatre*   He means 'amphitheatre'.

358 (p. 295) *gunwhale*   usually 'gunwale', pronounced '*gunnel*': the upper edge of a ship's side.

359 (p. 295) *bogey*   here slang for helmet.

360 (p. 296) *road stuff*   mainly horses' dung.

361 (p. 296) *forecastle*   (pronounced '*foke*-sull') enclosed area at the foremost part of a ship.

362 (p. 296) *companion*   ship's stairway.

363 (p. 297) *niggers*   They are Papuans. 'Nigger' was then a mildly derogatory term for a dark-skinned person, a term criticised by

R. B. Cunninghame Graham in his essay ' "Bloody Niggers" ' (1897). In Joseph Conrad's *The Nigger of the 'Narcissus'* (1897), James Wait says: 'You wouldn't call me nigger if I wasn't half dead . . . '

364 (p. 297) *blue funk*   great fear.

365 (p. 299) *tomtit*   very small bird, e.g. titmouse or blue-tit.

366 (p. 299) *joss place*   place where an idol is worshipped.

367 (p. 300) *Egyptian images*   e.g. the funerary statue of the Pharaoh Khafre, now at Cairo.

368 (p. 301) *pourra*   edible root.

369 (p. 301) *like one o'clock*   (slang) vigorously.

370 (p. 302) *calico*   Western missionaries introduced calico cotton to the Pacific islands.

371 (p. 302) *into Co.*   into the company.

372 (p. 302) *salver's ship*   salvaging ship.

373 (p. 303) *just a squeak off*   extremely close to.

374 (p. 303) *cut up rusty*   became hostile.

THE FLOWERING OF THE STRANGE ORCHID

375 (Title, p. 305)   'The Flowering of the Strange Orchid' was first published in the *Pall Mall Budget* on 2 August 1894.

376 (p. 305) *labellum*   central petal at the base of an orchid flower.

377 (p. 305) *diatom*   a microscopic unicellular alga found as plankton and forming fossil deposits.

378 (p. 305) *only one thing*   perhaps menstruation.

379 (p. 305) *Andamans and the Indies*   The Andaman Islands form an archipelago in the Bay of Bengal between India and Burma (Myanmar). The 'Indies' are the East Indies, lands of south and south-east Asia.

380 (p. 306) *staggers*   a disease of animals, marked by staggering or loss of balance.

381 (p. 306) *alpaca jacket*   light jacket, its cloth made from the long silken wool of the alpaca animal.

382 (p. 306) *Vandas, . . . Dendrobe . . . Palaeonopsis*   The vanda and dendrobium orchids are cultivated for their beauty. The palaeonopsis is also known as the 'moth orchid', a popular species.

383 (p. 307) *Men . . . gravity*   'For men must work, and women must weep' is a line in the poem 'Three Fishers' (1851) by Charles Kingsley (1819–75).

384 (p. 307) *chlorodyne and quinine*   Chlorodyne was a patent medicine intended to treat cholera. (As it contained laudanum, cannabis and chloroform, it could become addictive.) Quinine was a medicine used to prevent and treat malaria.

385 (p. 307) *Andaman islanders*   The population of the Andaman Islands, reputedly cannibalistic in the nineteenth century, included the hunter-gatherer Sentinelese.

386 (p. 308) *Darwin . . . plant*   In 1862, Charles Darwin published *On the Various Contrivances by which British and Foreign Orchids are Fertilised by Insects: and on the Good Effects of Intercrossing*. It told how orchids attract the insects which fertilise them.

387 (p. 309) *Cypripediums*   The *Cypripedium* is a genus of hardy orchid, widespread across the northern hemisphere. Some species grow in the tundras of Alaska and Siberia.

388 (p. 309) Palaeonopsis Lowii   a species of orchid named after Hugh Low, a Victorian collector of plants who was the colonial administrator of Labuan, Borneo.

389 (p. 310) *inflorescence*   the complete flower-head of a plant.

THE ARGONAUTS OF THE AIR

390 (Title, p. 313)   'The Argonauts of the Air' was first published in *Phil May's Annual*, December 1895. In ancient Greek mythology, the Argonauts ('*Argo*-sailors') were warriors who accompanied Jason on the ship *Argo* to Colchis to find the Golden Fleece.

391 (p. 313) *passing . . . Worcester Park*   The London and South-Western Railway system, constructed in the 1830s, extended from London's Vauxhall through Wimbledon, Surbiton and Woking in Surrey to Southampton in Hampshire. A branch line ran from Worcester Park to Leatherhead and Guildford.

392 (p. 313) *huge . . . apparatus*   In England in the late 1880s and the 1890s, Hiram S. Maxim (1840–1916), inventor of the Maxim machine-gun, experimented with a flying craft. Maxim (mentioned later in the paragraph) is a source of Wells's Monson. Maxim invented an aeroplane with twin propellers powered by two steam engines delivering together 362 horse-power. At Baldwyn Park in

Bexley, it ran on an 1800-foot track with outriggers and restraining rails to prevent it from lifting off, rather like a roller coaster. On 31 August 1894 the machine briefly took off after breaking through its restraints: Maxim shut off the steam and aborted its journey. Later, Maxim built tethered craft as fairground amusements. He was knighted in 1902. In 1903, in the USA, the Wright brothers made successful flights in an engine-driven heavier-than-air machine: Orville Wright flew it for 120 feet (in 12 seconds), and Wilbur flew it 852 feet (in 89 seconds).

393 (p. 314) *pachydermatous*   thick-skinned.

394 (p. 314) *Romeike*   In 1881, Henry Romeike (1855–1903) founded a press-cuttings agency in London; later in the 1880s, he opened another agency in New York.

395 (p. 314) *troubling*   Job 3:17: 'There the wicked cease from troubling; and there the weary be at rest.'

396 (p. 314) *vans*   blades.

397 (p. 314) *senior wranglers*   The senior wrangler is the person who gains the highest mark among the wranglers, the students at Cambridge who take first-class honours degrees in mathematics.

398 (p. 314) *pneumatics*   the science of the properties of gases.

399 (p. 315) *Folly . . . suddenly*   A folly is (1) a construction which is ornamental rather than functional (e.g. a tower to adorn a landscape), or (2) a foolish enterprise.

400 (p. 315) *Esher*   a suburban town in Surrey bisected by the road from London to Portsmouth, described as 'the pretty Surrey village of Esher' by Dr Watson in Conan Doyle's 'The Adventure of Wisteria Lodge' (1908).

401 {p. 315) *greaser's expenses*   A political greaser is a fixer, a person who bribes or 'greases palms' to secure advantages.

402 (p. 316) *tornader*   tornado.

403 (p. 316) *study of straws*   'A straw shows which way the wind blows' is proverbial.

404 (p. 317) *Cheam*   suburban township in the London Borough of Sutton, bordered at the north-west by Worcester Park.

405 (p. 317) *run amuck*   (or 'run amok':) go on a rampage, assaulting anyone encountered.

406 (p. 318) *funk*   fear.

407 (p. 318) *Lilienthal's . . . Maxim's . . . again* Otto Lilienthal (1848–96), known as 'the Glider King', was a German pioneer experimenter with gliders. He wrote *Der Vogelflug als Grundlage der Fliegekunst* (*Bird-flight as the Basis of Aviation*), 1889. On 9 August 1896 a glider that he was piloting stalled and crashed, and he subsequently died from his injuries. Hiram S. Maxim concentrated on engine-powered flight. Monson tries to combine the two methods, using adjustable wings and petroleum engines.

408 (p. 319) *The flying-machine . . . bombshells and guns . . . man* 'easy dreaming', but all too prophetic of the military use of aircraft in the Great War and subsequently.

409 (p. 320) *Haslemere* Haslemere in Surrey is near Hindhead, where Wells's literary friends Grant Allen and Richard Le Gallienne lived.

410 (p. 321) *vans* here, 'wings'.

411 (p. 322) *gunwale* upper edge of the side.

412 (p. 322) *formerly . . . Science* The 'formerly' implies the irony that the Royal College of Science (which continued until it was absorbed by Imperial College, London, in 2002) was destroyed by this scientific aeronautical experiment.

MISS WINCHELSEA'S HEART

413 (Title, p. 325) 'Miss Winchelsea's Heart' was conceived in March 1898, when Wells and his wife were in Rome on holiday. Wells said: ' "Miss Winchelsea's Heart" came into my head to tell my friend George Gissing on the Pincio [the Pincian Hill] one spring morning in 1898.' (Gissing greatly enjoyed it.) It was first published in the *Queen*, October 1898. The surname 'Winchelsea' is apt. (Winchelsea is a picturesque, historic old town in Sussex. It was once a harbour, but the harbour silted up, and the town is now inland.) The tale's leading figure is named after a town, so she should perceive the irony that Mr Snooks's name, too, derives from that of a town.

414 (p. 325) *Horace . . . Keats* Quintus Horatius Flaccus (65 BC–8 BC), known as Horace, was a celebrated Roman poet who lived in the reign of Augustus. Benvenuto Cellini (1500–1571), the Italian sculptor, goldsmith and author, did much of his work in Rome. Percy Bysshe Shelley (1792–1822), the Romantic poet, drowned while sailing off Viareggio; and his ashes were buried in the Protestant Cemetery at Rome. John Keats (1795–1821), his fellow

Romantic poet, died of tuberculosis while staying in Rome at a villa on the Spanish Steps; and he, too, was buried in the Protestant Cemetery.

415 (p. 325) *Baedeker . . . red* Karl Baedeker (1827–59), the German publisher, established the highly successful red-bound series of travel guides. The business was continued by his three sons. The Baedeker guide, in English, to Central Italy and Rome was published in 1867.

416 (p. 326) *Thomas Gunn's parties* Wells is thinking of Thomas Cook (1808–92), who founded the travel agency Thomas Cook and Son, which organised travel abroad, initially for British people.

417 (p. 326) *pepper-and-salt suit* suit of mingled black and white material.

418 (p. 326) *hostler* person who tends horses at an inn.

419 (p. 327) *Gladstone bag* travelling suitcase that opens out into two equal sections; named after W. E. Gladstone, a Liberal Prime Minister.

420 (p. 327) *Hare's . . . Rome* Augustus J. C. Hare (1834–1903) was a British author of biographies and travel books. His *Walks in Rome* was published in 1871.

421 (p. 327) *Chislehurst . . . French* Chislehurst: a suburban district of south-east London. The French Emperor's wife, the Empress Eugénie, came to live there in 1870, being joined by the exiled Emperor, Napoléon III, in 1871. She left Chislehurst for Farnborough in 1881. He died in 1873, she in 1920.

422 (p. 327) bound Poetry was sometimes sold in paperback form, to be bound if and as the purchaser wished.

423 (p. 327) *pince-nez* a pair of spectacles held on the face by a spring that grips the bridge of the nose.

424 (p. 328) *impedimenta* baggage.

425 (p. 328) *Albion* poetic name for England, from Latin *albus*, white, referring to the white cliffs of south-east England.

426 (p. 329) table d'hôte here, a communal table for all the guests at a hotel.

427 (p. 329) *Horace . . . Soracte* Horace's ode 1:9 is called the 'Soracte Ode', as it begins with an image of Mount Soracte deep in snow; it ends with a lovers' tryst. It is a '*carpe diem*' poem, urging the readers to enjoy life and love while they can, so it reflects ironically on this

tale of Miss Winchelsea. Monte Soratte (Soracte in ancient times) is a limestone ridge 28 miles north of Rome.

428 (p. 329) *extension lecturer* An extension lecturer addressed audiences not eligible for university entrance (particularly women at that time).

429 (p. 330) *Ruskin's Florence* John Ruskin (1819–1900), influential art critic and cultural pundit, published *Mornings in Florence* in 1881. (Ruskin viewed paintings in the Palatine Gallery of Florence's Pitti Palace.)

430 (p. 330) *prigs* A prig is a self-righteously correct or moralistic person (such as Miss Winchelsea).

431 (p. 330) *Beato Angelico* Fra Angelico (born Guido di Pietro), *c.*1395–1455, an Italian Renaissance artist, known to Italians as 'Il Beato Angelico' ('The Blessed Angelic Man'). In *Modern Painters*, Ruskin challenged the disparagement of Angelico which was then common. (Ruskin added that he was widely regarded as 'not an artist properly so-called but an inspired saint'.) Angelico's works include the frescos for the chapel of Pope Nicholas in the Vatican, among them scenes from the lives of Saint Stephen and Saint Lawrence.

432 (p. 330) *Tivoli . . . waterfall* Tivoli is a district set in hills nineteen miles to the east-north-east of Rome. The park known as Villa Georgiana is set in a gorge with a waterfall which has a 320-foot drop, the Grande Cascata (Great Cascade).

433 (p. 331) *Bibulus* Marcus Calpurnius Bibulus (*c.*102 BC–48 BC) fought against Julius Caesar in the civil war between Caesar and Pompey (49 BC). His tomb was erected at the foot of the Capitoline Hill.

434 (p. 331) *Balbus . . . said* Lucius Cornelius Balbus the Elder (born in the first century BC, exact dates unknown) served as Julius Caesar's chief engineer. *Gradatim: An Easy Latin Translation Book for Beginners* (1881, often reprinted), illustrates the relative noun thus: ' "Video murum, *quem* Balbus aedificavit": "*I see the wall*, which *Balbus built*." '

435 (p. 331) *the '70 buildings* In 1870, Rome became the capital of the new Kingdom of Italy, and numerous buildings in the neoclassical style were erected to house ministries and embassies.

436 (p. 331) *Forum* a rectangular plaza surrounded by the ruins of several important ancient buildings.

437 (p. 331) *Shelley's Beatrice Cenci!* Beatrice Cenci (1577–99) was an Italian noblewoman who joined a conspiracy to kill her father, Francesco Cenci, who had raped her. In the gallery of the Palazzo Barberini subsequently hung a painting by Guido Reni which was deemed to be a portrait of Beatrice; and this painting was said by Mary Shelley to have inspired P. B. Shelley's *The Cenci: A Tragedy in Five Acts* (1820). In Shelley's play, Beatrice kills her father to avenge his act of rape. Charles Dickens said that the Reni portrait expressed 'beautiful sorrow'. It is now deemed unlikely that the portrait is of Beatrice Cenci.

438 (p. 331) *The seven hills* These hills of Rome are the locations of historic buildings, monuments and parks.

439 (p. 331) *Palatine* This hill bears the ruins of the palaces of the emperors Augustus, Tiberius and Domitian.

440 (p. 332) *autotypes . . . Burne-Jones . . . papers* The 'autotypes' are photographs of paintings by the then-fashionable Pre-Raphaelite painters, D. G. Rossetti and Edward Burne-Jones. Wallpapers designed by William Morris and sold by Morris & Co. were also fashionable.

441 (p. 332) *the Pincio* 'Il Pincio', the Pincian Hill: the highest place in Rome, a beautiful and historic viewpoint.

442 (p. 332) *the* muro Torto 'distorted wall': an ancient Roman supporting wall located behind the Pincian Hill.

443 (p. 332) *Demn!* 'Damn!' uttered with an upper-class or upper-middle-class accent.

444 (p. 333) *Piazza steps* the Spanish Steps, between the Piazza di Spagna and the Piazza Trinità dei Monti.

445 (p. 333) *badge sinister* In heraldry, a 'bend sinister' (dividing line extending from the upper right to lower left) denotes illegitimacy. Here 'badge sinister' means 'indecent sign'.

446 (p. 334) *the Borghese* The Villa Borghese houses an art gallery and has large gardens.

447 (p. 336) *first letter* actually the second.

448 (p. 337) *Sevenoaks* name of a prosperous town in western Kent established by the thirteenth century. Distinguished people associated with Sevenoaks include John Donne, Edward Thomas, W. H. Davies and H. G. Wells. Alumni of Sevenoaks School are termed 'Old Senockians'.

449 (p. 338) *impositions . . . high* 'written punishments were frequent'.

A VISION OF JUDGEMENT

450 (Title, p. 341)   'A Vision of Judgment' was first published in the
Butterfly, September 1899. Later, in *Mr Britling Sees It Through*
(1916) and *God the Invisible King* (1917), Wells advocated belief in
God.

451 (p. 341) *Azreal*   often spelt 'Azrael': the archangel of death.

452 (p. 341) *Michael*   The Book of Revelation depicts him as leader of
the heavenly army that defeats Satan. Michael is often depicted as
wielding a sword.

453 (p. 341) He'll *catch it!* because Charles Darwin's theory of
evolution challenged the biblical account of creation.

454 (p. 342) *printers' overs*   If printing went well, a printer would sometimes produce more items than a customer had ordered and charge
the customer accordingly.

455 (p. 342) *Tudor*   beginning with a T, so the man 'whose letter is S'
will not hear the evidence.

456 (p. 342) *catalogue*   This consisted of many hefty leather-bound
volumes.

457 (p. 343) *Milton's Satan*   In *Paradise Lost* (1667) by John Milton
(1608–74), Satan is depicted as noble though damned.

458 (p. 343) *Obelisk*   Some ancient obelisks bear historical records.
The Assyrian White Obelisk of Ashurnasirpal I (erected between
1050 and 1031 BC) records that king's seizure of people and goods.

459 (p. 345) *Sirius*   the brightest of stellar objects in the night sky.
The star looks white, not green; but Thomas Hardy in *Tess of the
d'Urbervilles* (1891) associated it with greenness.

THE LAND IRONCLADS

460 (Title, p. 347)   'The Land Ironclads' was first published in the
Strand Magazine for December 1903. 'Ironclad' was a term coined
in the mid-nineteenthh century for a steam warship protected by
iron or steel plating.

461 (p. 347) *field-glass*   a spyglass or small telescope (also referred to
later as 'field-glasses' – binoculars).

462 (p. 347) *Bloch*   Jan Gotlib Bloch (1836–1902), also known as Jean
de Bloch, a Polish banker and expert on modern warfare, argued
in *Is War Now Impossible?* (1899) that future wars would be
characterised by the use of trenches, resulting in virtual stalemate;
armies would involve millions rather than thousands of troops; and
the war would be a battle of one state's economy versus another's,

with revolution as a possible consequence. His prophecies were vindicated in World War I.

463 (p. 347) *winded*   'took wind of': detected.

464 (p. 348) *They've got . . . thing*   In the First Boer War (1880–1) between Britain and the Transvaal Boers (farmers), the British troops were repeatedly out-manoeuvred by the mobile and accurate Boer marksmen. Eventually the British signed a truce which granted the Boers self-government. In the Second Boer War (1899–1902), which eventually, after many setbacks, was won by the British, the two independent Boer republics (the Orange Free State and the Transvaal Republic) were absorbed into the British Empire. In that war, 450,000 professional soldiers were needed to defeat an army of 35,000 farmers. Many of the volunteers for the British army were found to be physically unfit, raising national concern.

465 (p. 349) *rowdy-dowdy . . . nigger-whackers*   'turbulent cow-branders and beaters of black people': the lieutenant cites derogatory terms used to describe the fighters on his side.

466 (p. 350) *slouch hat*   a wide-brimmed cloth or felt hat tilted to one side. In the Boer War, such hats were popular with the Boers, but some fighters on the British side wore them; and they were sometimes indeed adorned with feathers: a detail which Wells associates with the serial lover, Don Juan. (When Molière's Don Juan was played by La Grange, he wore a feathered hat.)

467 (p. 350) *slab*   (slang) 'drivelling'.

468 (p. 350) *'go it!'*   (slang) 'go ahead vigorously!' – here sarcastic.

469 (p. 351) *Gollys!*   euphemistic exclamation modifying 'My God!'

470 (p. 352) *What the deuce was it?*   The phrase 'the deuce' is a euphemism for 'the devil'. Tanks were first used in warfare when British tanks were deployed on 15 September 1916 at the Battle of the Somme.

471 (p. 354) *an enfilade*   gunfire that goes from end to end.

472 (p. 355) *'Whup,' . . . corporal*   The exclamation 'Whup' probably means 'Watch out!'

473 (p. 355) feet!   The pedrail wheel was invented in 1903 by the Londoner, Bramah Joseph Diplock. Metal feet were fitted to wheels by ball-and-socket joints. The purpose of such feet was to ensure traction in uneven terrain. In 1910 Diplock abandoned work on the pedrail and developed designs in which wheels

rotated inside a moving belt, much like the eventual caterpillar track. In 1915 Winston Churchill ordered a number of 'landships' using pedrails, but eventually they were superseded by tanks using caterpillar tracks.

474 (p. 358) *The howitzers . . . nothing*   because the howitzer, unlike the longer-barrelled field gun, is designed to fire shells in relatively high trajectories.

475 (p. 360) *jaunting-car*   In an Irish horse-drawn 'jaunting-car', the passengers sat at the sides, at right-angles to the fore-and-aft axis, their seats being above and outside the wheels.

476 (p. 360) *camera-obscura*   dark chamber in which an image of outside objects is projected on to a screen.

477 (p. 361) *Pshaw!*   exclamation of impatience.

478 (p. 362) *speaking-tube*   an air-pipe, often ending in two cones, by which speech could be conveyed over an extended distance; in most cases superseded by the telephone.

479 (p. 362) *big . . . nigger*   again suggesting similarities between these foes and the Boers.

480 (p. 365) *truncated Paladins*   'humbled heroes'.

481 (p. 365) *cockneydom*   'vulgar Londoners'.

THE FLYING MAN

482 (Title, p. 367)   'The Flying Man' (originally 'The Advent of the Flying Man') was first published in the *Pall Mall Gazette* on 8 December 1893.

483 (p. 367) bhimraj *feather*   The bhimraj or racket-tailed drongo is a large jungle-haunting bird found in much of India, Burma and the Malay Peninsula. It has long tail-feathers.

484 (p. 367) *yellow silk*   Yellow was for a long time the symbolic colour of the Chinese royal court. Initially silk robes were worn only by the royal family; in public appearances, they wore robes of yellow silk.

485 (p. 367) *Shendu country*   On the north-east frontier of India, bordering on Burma (Myanmar), people living to the west of the Koladyne (or Kuladan) River were called the Lushais, while those living to the east were designated Shendus.

486 (p. 367) *Chin*   The Chin peoples are found mainly in western Myanmar (Burma), and in Victorian times were ruled by the British on a separate basis from the other Burmese.

487 (p. 367) *Lushai expedition but one*   In 1871–2, the British Indian Army conducted punitive incursions against the Lushais who had

carried out raids in Assam. In 1889–90, further punitive expeditions were made against the Lushai and Chin peoples; the army retrieved the heads of a surveying group slain in 1888.

488 (p. 368) *Derbyshire men*   Men of the Derbyshire Regiment served in the Lushai expeditions.

489 (p. 368) *sepoys*   A sepoy was an Indian soldier serving with the British army.

490 (p. 368) *matchlock*   an archaic form of gun in which a slow-burning match was held in place with a clip. When a lever or trigger was pulled, the match would ignite the priming powder, which in turn would ignite the main charge to propel a projectile.

491 (p. 369) *Xenophon . . . army*   Xenophon (*c.* 430–*c.* 354 BC) described in his *Anabasis* the retreat of Greek mercenaries known as 'the Ten Thousand'. Defeated at the Battle of Cunaxa in 401 BC, the Greeks returned homeward, harried by Persian soldiers, local forces and bad weather.

492 (p. 369) *Martini*   The Martini-Henry rifle was used by the British army from 1871 for about thirty years. The firing mechanism was modified by Friedrich von Martini, and the barrel rifling was designed by Alexander Henry.

493 (p. 369) *finis!*   (Latin) the end!

494 (p. 370) *Joshua . . . upon it*   Joshua 10:13: Joshua ordered the sun to stand still, and it obeyed him.

495 (p. 371) *I parachuted*   Although a viable parachute was designed by Leonardo da Vinci (1452–1519), the first recorded parachute jump was made on 26 December 1783 in Montpellier by the inventor Louis-Sébastien Lenormand (1757–1837). The first military use of the parachute was in World War I.

496 (p. 371) *Baldwin . . . bolted*   James Mark Baldwin (1861–1934), an American philosopher and psychologist, argued in his *Elements of Psychology* (1893) that human behavioural decisions made and sustained over generations as a set of cultural practices ought to be considered among the factors shaping the human character: this was known as the 'Baldwin Effect'. Contrary to Baldwin (but understandably, since they are surprised and frightened by the lieutenant's arrival) the Chins here abandon their practice of slaying enemies.

IN THE AVU OBSERVATORY

497 (Title, p. 373)   'In the Avu Observatory' was first published in the *Pall Mall Budget* on 9 August 1894.

498 (p. 374) *Dyak*   The Dyaks are the indigenous people of Borneo.

499 (p. 377) *'Time!' . . . mirth*   'Time': called for the start of a round in a boxing-match.

500 (p. 378) *a Big Colugo, a* Klangutang   Colugos ('flying lemurs') are arboreal gliding mammals found in south-east Asia; when fully grown, they are the size of a large squirrel. *Klangutang* (Malay): forest-dweller.

501 (p. 378) *There . . . earth . . . philosophies*   In Shakespeare's *Hamlet* (*c*. 1600), Hamlet says:

> There are more things in heaven and earth, Horatio,
> Than are dreamt of in your philosophy.   [1.5.165–6]

502 (p. 378) *fauna*   the assemblage of animals of a region.

THE TRIUMPHS OF A TAXIDERMIST

503 (Title, p. 379)   'The Triumphs of a Taxidermist' was first published anonymously in the *Pall Mall Gazette* on March 3 and 15, 1894. The taxidermist reappears in 'A Deal in Ostriches'.

504 (p. 379) *Graces*   In Greek mythology, the Three Graces are benign goddesses. In works of sculpture, they are traditionally depicted naked.

505 (p. 379) *I have stuffed . . . ornithologists*   Here 'stuffed' means (punningly) 'hoaxed': he has hoaxed amateur students of birds by selling them fakes.

506 (p. 379) *Bric-à-brac*   collectable curiosities; odds and ends.

507 (p. 380) *dodos . . . auk?*   The dodo was a flightless bird that lived on the island of Mauritius. It became extinct in the eighteenth century after being hunted by sailors. The great auk was another flightless bird which foraged in the North Atlantic. Its down was valued in Europe. It became extinct in the mid-nineteenth century.

508 (p. 380) *handkerchief . . . Trèves*   According to legend, Veronica was moved to pity when she saw Jesus carrying his cross to Golgotha. She gave him her veil to wipe the sweat from his brow. When he handed it back, an image of his face was imprinted on the material. The Cathedral at Trier (formerly Trèves) exhibits a robe said to be the seamless robe worn by Jesus shortly before his crucifixion.

509 (p. 380) *grebes' feathers*   Grebes are a widely-distributed order of diving birds, with unusual, dense and waterproof plumage.

510 (p. 380) *skerries*   small rocky islands.

511 (p. 380) *dinornis . . . moa now*   The great moa (*Dinornis*) was indeed an extinct species of bird that lived in New Zealand. The taxidermist likes puns: 'no moa [more] now'.

512 (p. 380) *dodging up*   using fraudulently.

513 (p. 381) Anomalopteryx Jejuna   empty odd-winged bird. The subsequent *Jejunus-a-um* conjugates the adjective, giving the nominative form and the vocative and accusative endings.

514 (p. 381) *extravagant . . . mandarin duck*   The mandarin duck is found in eastern Asia, and the adult male has a red bill, a white crescent above the eyes and an orange-red face; a blue, white and copper crest extends down his neck; and the flanks are ruddy, with two orange 'sails' rising from them.

515 (p. 381) *apteryx . . . anomalopteryx*   The kiwi genus, *Apteryx* (irregularly winged bird), lives in New Zealand. The *Anomalopteryx* (irregular wingless bird), an extinct bird genus known as the lesser moa or bush moa, inhabited much of the North Island and small parts of the South Island of New Zealand, and was more than 4 feet 4 inches (1.3 metres) in height.

516 (p. 381) *Burslem Wake*   This was the annual fair at Burslem, one of the six towns that amalgamated to form Stoke-on-Trent.

A DEAL IN OSTRICHES

517 (Title, p. 383)   'A Deal in Ostriches' was first published in the *Pall Mall Gazette* on 20 December 1894.

518 (p. 383) *East Indiaman*   usually the name for a sailing-ship operating under charter to any of the East India companies of European nations in the period extending from the seventeenth to the nineteenth centuries. The British East India Company was dissolved in 1874. So here, the name denotes a merchant sailing-ship operating between India and London in the late nineteenth century.

519 (p. 383) incog.   incognito, unidentifiability.

520 (p. 383) *rummy*   (slang) peculiar.

521 (p. 384) *lien*   a right to retain possession of another person's property until the owner pays a debt.

522 (p. 384) ipso facto   (Latin) by that very fact or deed.

523 (p. 384) *contributory negligence*   in failing to safeguard the jewel from theft.

524 (p. 384) *wired*   telegraphed.

525 (p. 384) *queer*   suspected of cheating.

526 (p. 386) *purple*   celebratory.

THROUGH A WINDOW

527 (Title, p. 387)   'Through a Window' (originally 'At a Window')
was first published in *Black and White* magazine on 25 August 1894.

528 (p. 387) *weltering*   agitated, undulating.

529 (p. 387) *sculler*   oarsman using a short, spoon-bladed oar.

530 (p. 387) *Fitzgibbon's*   evidently the boat-yard owned by Mr Fitzgibbon and his son.

531 (p. 388) *for a swamp*   for a boat to fill with water and sink.

532 (p. 388) *boat-hook*   (1) a pole with a hook at the end, for pulling or
pushing a boat; (2, later in the tale) the man who wields that
implement.

533 (p. 388) *Lascar*   oriental (originally Indian) sailor.

534 (p. 388) *caught one perfect crab*   sank the oar or scull far too deeply
into the water (*or* not deeply enough) and fell back in consequence.
As the man temporarily lost his scull, he evidently had let it go too
deep.

535 (p. 390) *krees*   (also 'kris' and 'crease') Malay dagger with a wavy
blade.

536 (p. 391) ' . . . *Edwin Drood*,' said Bailey   *The Mystery of Edwin
Drood* was the final novel by Charles Dickens (1812–70). It was
left unfinished at the time of Dickens's death, with the plot
unresolved.

537 (p. 392) *Running amuck*   (also 'running amok':) to run wildly,
assailing anyone in the way (as in 'The Lord of the Dynamos').

THE TEMPTATION OF HARRINGAY

538 (Title, p. 395)   'The Temptation of Harringay' was first published
on 9 February 1895 in the *St James's Gazette*.

539 (p. 395) *Adam . . . red ochre!*   Genesis 2:7 says that God made
Adam 'of the dust of the ground'. 'Adam' in Hebrew means 'man',
and the root of the word means 'red', while 'adamah' means 'earth'.
Red ochre is a natural earth pigment taking its colour from the
mineral hermatite, an iron oxide.

540 (p. 395) *Garnome and git frimed*   (cockney dialect) 'Go on home
and get framed.'

541 (p. 395) *holland*   coarse linen fabric.

542 (p. 395) *mahl stick*   (also 'maulstick') a stick used by painters to
rest the hand (German: *malen*, to paint) .

543 (p. 396) *impedimenta* equipment.

544 (p. 396) *Mephistopheles . . . Doge . . . Camelot* Mephistopheles is the emissary of Satan in the Faust legend. The Doge was the chief magistrate in republican Venice. 'Too Camelot' means 'too redolent of the castle and court of King Arthur', Camelot having been thoroughly exploited by nineteenth-century painters and poets.

545 (p. 396) *the Sacred College* The Sacred College of Cardinals (subsequently the College of Cardinals) is the assembly of all the cardinals of the Roman Catholic Church. They advise the Pope and elect a new Pope.

546 (p. 396) *appreciation of Middle Italian History* Reserving for the cardinals the power to elect the Pope meant a shift in power away from the Holy Roman Emperor.

547 (p. 397) *Cellini* Benvenuto Cellini (1500–1571), Italian artist, sculptor, goldsmith and autobiographer; guilty of homicides, fined for sodomy.

548 (p. 396) *A Certain Gentleman* 'The Prince of Darkness is a gentleman' (Shakespeare, *King Lear*, 3.4.136); 'sometimes / The Devil is a gentleman' (Shelley: *Peter Bell the Third*, lines 81–2).

549 (p. 396) *diablerie* devilry.

550 (p. 397) *fluke* have an accidental success in painting.

551 (p. 398) *Wagner* Richard Wagner (1813–83), composer of operas and musical dramas, cited here as an example of an artist who, wrongly, chose to theorise. Wagner's polemical writings on music, drama and politics were controversial.

552 (p. 398) *tommy-rot* total nonsense.

553 (p. 398) *Cathedral of Cologne . . . Devil's Bridge* There was a legend that Meister Gerhard, the architect of Cologne Cathedral, lost a wager with the Devil, and accordingly the architect perished, and for centuries the cathedral remained unfinished. The term 'Devil's Bridge' has been applied to numerous ancient bridges, each having a Devil-related legend. An example is Devil's Bridge, Ceredigion, Wales: the legend is that the Devil built the bridge in return for the soul of the first living thing to cross it, but an old woman tricked the Devil by sending her dog across.

554 (p. 398) *slated* criticised severely.

555 (p. 398) *Chelsea artist's soul* In the nineteenth century, Chelsea in London became home to an artists' colony: J. M. W. Turner, D. G. Rossetti, James McNeill Whistler, W. Holman Hunt and John Singer Sargent lived and worked there.

556 (p. 398) *Hedge Sparrow's Egg Tint . . . brush* The hedge sparrow's egg often has a turquoise colour. In the late Victorian period, women used enamel for cosmetic purposes.

THE BEAUTIFUL SUIT

557 (Title, p. 401) 'The Beautiful Suit' was first published as 'A Moonlight Fable' in *Collier's Weekly*, 10 April 1909.

558 (p. 403) *thridding* possibly from 'threading', and here meaning maintaining a repetitive pattern of sound, or a continuous chirruping.

559 (p. 403) *night-stock* the *Matthiola longipetala*, a plant that emits a pleasant odour in the evening and at night.

560 (p. 403) *nicotine* or *Nicotiana*, a genus of herbaceous plants and shrubs.

561 (p. 403) *phantom* transparent and hardly visible.

562 (p. 403) *southernwood* the *Artemisia abrotanum*, a plant with a strong camphor-like odour.

563 (p. 403) *mignonette* the *Reseda*, a genus of fragrant herbaceous plants.

564 (p. 403) *burrs* A burr is a prickly seedcase or flower-head that clings.

565 (p. 403) *goose-grass* the *Eleusine*, a genus of plants in the grass family. The name may derive from the eating or transmission of the plants by geese or from the fact that parts of some of the plants resemble a goose's foot.

566 (p. 403) *havers* A haver is a plant (*Avena sativa*) of the grass family.

567 (p. 403) *willow-herb* The willow herb (*Epilobium*) has leaves with a willow-like form.

568 (p. 404) *moth* The Greek word *psyche* means moth, butterfly and soul. The moth and the butterfly both have legendary associations with death and with the departure of the soul from the body.